MYSTERY

ALSO BY PETER STRAUB

Novels

Marriages

Under Venus

Julia

If You Could See Me Now

Ghost Story

Shadowland

Floating Dragon

The Talisman (with Stephen King)

Koko

Poetry

Open Air

Leeson Park & Belsize Square

Collection

Wild Animals

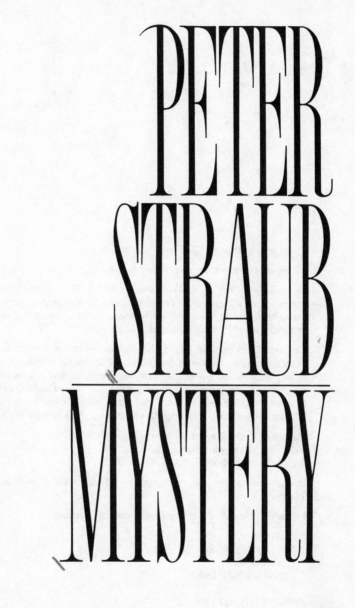

PETER STRAUB

MYSTERY

E. P. DUTTON / NEW YORK

Publisher's Note: This novel is a work of fiction. Names, characters, places, and incidents either are the product of the author's imagination or are used fictitiously, and any resemblance to actual persons, living or dead, events, or locales is entirely coincidental.

Published in the United States by E. P. Dutton,
a division of Penguin Books USA Inc.,
2 Park Avenue, New York, N.Y. 10016.

Published simultaneously in Canada by Fitzhenry and Whiteside, Limited, Toronto

Library of Congress Cataloging-in-Publication Data

Straub, Peter.
Mystery / Peter Straub.—1st ed.
p. cm.
ISBN: 0-525-24818-8
I. Title.
PS3569.T6914M97 1990
813′.54—dc20 89-7734
CIP

Designed by REM Studio

10 9 8 7 6 5 4 3 2 1

First Edition

For Lila Kalinich
and
For Ann Lauterbach

I need, therefore I imagine.

—CARLOS FUENTES

All human society is constructed on
complicity in a great crime.

—*FREUD*, PETER GAY

MYSTERY

Mill Walk does not exist on any map—let us acknowledge that at the beginning. Extending eastward off Puerto Rico like revisions to an incomplete sentence are the tiny Islas de Culebra and Vieques, in their turn followed by specks named St. Thomas, Tortola, St. John, Virgin Gorda, Anegada—the Virgin Islands—after which the little afterthoughts of Anguilla, St. Martin, St. Barthélemy, St. Eustatius, St. Kitts, Redondo, Montserrat, and Antigua begin to drip south; islands step along like rocks in a stream, Guadeloupe, Dominica, Martinique, St. Lucia, St. Vincent, Barbados, the almost infinitesimal Grenadines, and the little green bump of Grenada, an emerald the size of a doll's fingernail—from there on, only blue-green sea all the way to Tobago and Trinidad, and after that you are in South America, another world. No more revisions and afterthoughts, but another point of view altogether.

In fact, another continent of feeling, one layer beneath the known.

On the island of Mill Walk, a small boy is fleeing down the basement stairs, in so great a hurry to escape the sounds of his mother's screams that he has forgotten to close the door, and so the diminishing screams follow him, draining the air of oxygen. They make him feel hot and accused, though of an uncertain crime—perhaps only that he can do nothing to stop her screaming.

He hits the bottom stair and jumps down on the concrete floor, claps his hands over his ears, and runs between a shabby green couch and a wooden rocking chair to the heavy, scarred workbench which stands against the wall. Like the furniture, the workbench is his father's: despite all the tools—screwdrivers and hammers, rasps and files and tin cans full of nails, C-clamps and pliers, a jigsaw and a coping saw, a gimlet and a chisel and a plane, stacks of sandpaper—nothing is ever created or repaired at this bench. A thick layer of dust covers everything. The boy runs beneath the bench and puts his back to the wall. Experimentally, he takes his hands from his ears. One moment of quiet lengthens into another. He can breathe. The basement is cool and silent. He sits down on the concrete and leans against the grey block of the wall and closes his eyes.

The world remains cool, dark, and silent.

He opens his eyes again and sees a cardboard box, half-hidden in the gloom beneath the bench. This, too, is covered with a thick grey blanket of dust. All around the boy are the tracks of his passage—lines and erasures, commas and exclamation points, words written in an unknown language. He slides toward the box through the fuzz of dust, opens the lid, and sees that, although it is nearly empty, down at its bottom rests a small stack of old newspapers. He reaches in and lifts the topmost newspaper and squints at the banner of the headline. Though he is not yet in the first-grade, the boy can read, and the headline contains a half-familiar name. JEANINE THIELMAN FOUND IN LAKE.

One of their neighbors is named Thielman, but the first name, "Jeanine," is as mysterious as "found in lake." The next newspaper in the stack also has a banner headline. LOCAL MAN CHARGED WITH THIELMAN MURDER. *The next paper down, the last, announces* MYSTERY RESOLVED IN TRAGEDY. *Of these four words, the boy understands only "in." The boy unfolds this issue of the paper and spreads it out before him. He sees the word*

"Shadow," the words "wife," "children." None of the people in the photographs are people he knows.

Then he spreads out all the newspapers and sees a picture of a woman who looks something like his mother. She would like to see this picture, he thinks: he could give her the present of these interesting old newspapers he found beneath the workbench.

He clumsily gathers up the newspapers in his arms and walks out from beneath the bench and through the furniture. A section of pages slips away and splashes onto the floor, but he does not stoop to pick it up. The boy climbs the basement stairs into the warmer upper air, comes out into the kitchen, and walks through it to the hallway.

His mother stands in her blue nightgown, looking at him. Her hair is wild, and her eyes are somewhere else, like eyes that have rolled all the way over in her head and only seem to look out. Did you hear me?

He shakes his head.

You didn't hear your name?

He comes toward her, saying, I was in the basement—look at what I found—for you—

She floats toward him in her blue nightgown and wild hair. You don't have to hide from me.

His mother snatches away his present, already not a present but a terrible mistake, and more pages slither onto the floor. She holds up one of the sections of the newspaper. The boy sees her face go into itself the way her eyes had gone into themselves, as if she has been struck by some invisible but present demon, and she wobbles away toward the kitchen, the newspaper dripping from her hands. A laugh that is not a laugh but an inside-out scream flies out of her mouth. She lands in a chair and puts her face in her hands.

Part One

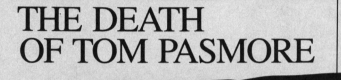

THE DEATH OF TOM PASMORE

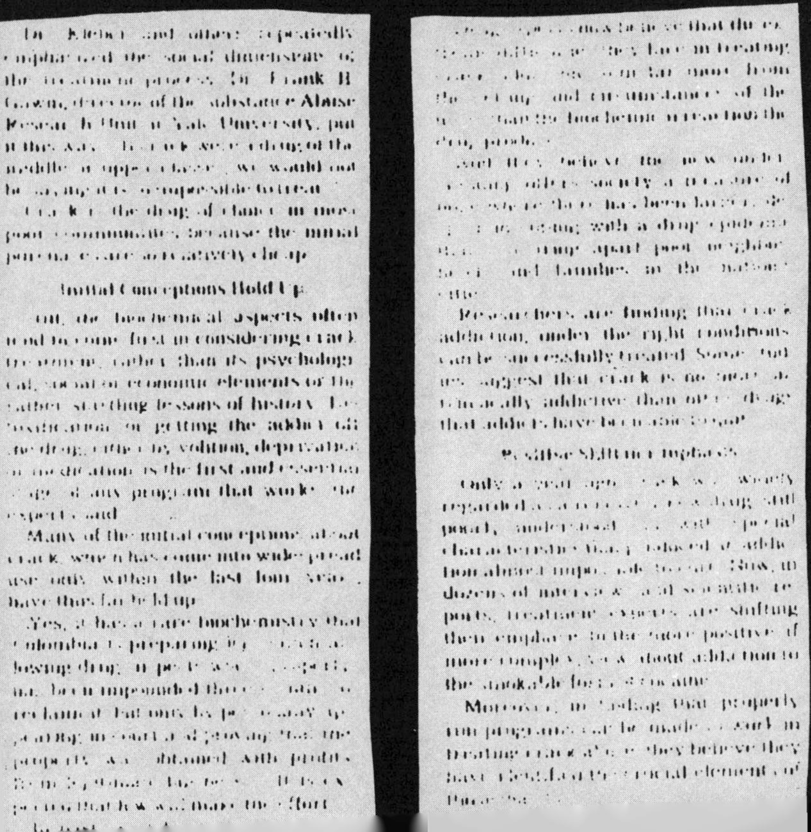

1

One June day in the mid-fifties Tom Pasmore, a ten-year-old boy with skin as golden as if he had been born with a good fourth-day suntan, jumped down from a milk cart and found himself in a part of Mill Walk he had never seen before. A sense of urgency, of *impendingness*, had awakened him with the screams that came from his mother's bedroom and clung to him during the whole anxious, jittery day, and when he waved his thanks to the driver, this feeling intensified like a bright light directed into his eyes. He thought of hopping back on the milk cart, but it was already jingling away down Calle Burleigh. Tom squinted into the bright dusty haze through which passed a steady double stream of bicycles, horse carts, and automobiles. It was late afternoon, and the light had a molten, faintly reddish cast that suddenly reminded him of panels from comic books: fires and explosions and men falling through the air.

In the next moment this busy scene seemed to suppress beneath it another, more essential scene, every particle of which overflowed with an intense, unbearable beauty. It was as if great engines had kicked into life beneath the surface of what he could see. For a moment Tom could not move. Nature itself seemed to have awakened, overflowing with being.

Tom stood transfixed in the heavy, slanting reddish light and the dust rising from the roadway.

He was used to the quieter, narrower streets of the island's far east end, and his glimpse of a mysterious glory might have been no more than a product of the change from Eastern Shore Road. What he was looking at *was* another world, one he had never seen before. He had no exact idea of how to get back to the far east end and the great houses of Eastern Shore Road, and less idea of why he was searching for a certain address. A bicycle bell gave a rasping cry like the chirp of a cricket, a horse's ironclad hoof struck the packed dirt of Calle Burleigh, and all the sounds of the wide avenue reached Tom once again. He realized that he had been holding his breath, and that his eyes were blurry with tears. Already far down the avenue, the milk driver tilted toward the sun and the sturdy brown cob that pulled his cart. The *ching-ching-ching* of the bottles had melted into the general hum. Tom wiped moisture from his face. He was not at all sure of what had just happened—another world? Beneath this world?

Tom continued to melt back into the scene before him, wondering if this experience, still present as a kind of weightlessness about his heart, was what had been impending all during the day. He had been *pushed*—pushed right out of his frame. For an elastically long second or two—for as long as the world had trembled and overflowed with being—he had been in the other world, the one beneath.

Now he smiled, distracted by this notion from Jules Verne or Robert Heinlein. He stepped back on the sidewalk and looked east. Both sides of the wide avenue were filled with horses and vehicles, at least half of which were bicycles. This varied crowd moved through the haze of light and dust and extended as far as Tom could see.

It seemed to Tom that he had never really known what the phrase "rush hour" meant. On Eastern Shore Road, rush hour consisted of a car or two honking at children to get out of the street. Once Tom had seen a servant ride a bicycle straight into the bicycle of another servant, spilling clean white laundry all over the warm red brick of the road—that was rush hour. Of course Tom had been in his father's office in the business district; he had seen the midday traffic on Calle Hoffmann; and he had gone to the harbor, Mill Key, with his parents and passed beneath rows of palms in the company of jitneys and cabs and broughams; and at Mill Key he had seen the conveyances drawn up to take the new arrivals downtown to their hotels, the Pforzheimer or the St. Alwyn. (Strictly speaking, Mill Walk had no tourist hotels. The Pforzheimer took in bankers and moneymen, and the St. Alwyn catered to drummers, traveling musicians like Glenroy Breakstone and the wondrous Targets, gamblers, that class of person.) He had never been in the business district at the close of a workday, and he had never seen anything like the sweep and the variety of the traffic moving east and west, primarily west, toward Shurz Bay and Elm Cove, on Calle Burleigh. It looked as though everyone on the island had simultaneously decided to dash off to the island's other side. For a moment of panic that seemed oddly connected to the wonderful experience he had just undergone, Tom wondered if he would ever be able to find his way back again.

But he did not want to go home, not until he had found a certain house, and he imagined that when the time came he would find someone as accommodating as the milk driver, who in spite of the NO PASSENGERS ALLOWED sign at the front of the cart had invited him to hop on board and then quizzed him about girlfriends all during the long trip west—Tom was big for his age, and with his blond hair and dark eyes and eyebrows he looked more like thirteen than ten. This *thing* had been nagging at him all day, making it impossible to read more than a page or two at a time, driving him from his bedroom to the living room to the white wicker furniture on the porch, until at last he had resorted to walking back and forth on the big front lawn, wondering vaguely if Mrs. Thielman's Sam might run into Mrs. Langenheim's Jenny again, or if a crazy drunk might wander into the street and start yelling and throwing rocks, as had happened two days before.

The funny thing was that though the feeling of glory, overflowing being, had passed, the other feeling did not fade with it but lingered, as powerful as ever.

He was being *pushed*, being *moved*.

Tom turned around to get a better fix on this strange area, and found himself looking between two sturdy wooden houses, each placed atop its own narrow slanting lawn like a nut on a cupcake, at another row of houses set behind them on the next street. Tall elms arched over this second street, which seemed as quiet as Eastern Shore Road. The houses beneath the elms were one notch less impressive than those on Calle Burleigh. Tom instantly understood that this second street was forbidden territory. This information was not ambiguous. The little street might as well have had a chain-link fence around it and a sign commanding him to KEEP OUT: a spear of lightning would sizzle right down out of the sky and impale him if he entered that street.

The imaginary light that shone on his face became stronger and hotter. He had been right to come all this way. He stepped sideways, and a little two-story wooden house painted a very dark brown on the top story and a bright buttery yellow on the bottom came into view on the forbidden street.

Two days earlier, Tom had been lying on the striped yellow chaise in the living room reading Jules Verne, inside the imaginary but total safety of words on a page organized into sentences and paragraphs—a world both fixed and flowing, always the same and always moving and always open to him. This was *escape*. It was *safety*. Then a loud noise, the sound of something striking the side of the house, had pulled him up on the yellow chaise as roughly as a hand shaking him from sleep. A moment later Tom heard a blurry voice shouting obscenities in the street. "Bastard! Shithead!" Another rock crashed against the side of the house. Tom had jumped from the chaise and moved to the front window, unconsciously keeping his place in the book with his index finger. A middle-aged man with a thick waist and short, thinning brown hair was weaving back and forth on the sidewalk beside a slumped canvas bag from which a few large stones had spilled. The man held a baseball-sized rock in each hand. "Do me like this!" he yelled. "Think you can treat Wendell Hasek like he's some kind of jerk!" He turned all the way around and nearly fell down. Then he rounded his shoulders like an ape and squinted furiously at the two houses—each with great columns, round turrets, and twin parapets—across the street. One of these, the Jacobs house, was empty because Mr. and Mrs. Jacobs had gone to the mainland for the summer; the other was inhabited by Lamont von Heilitz, a fantastic and sour old man who lived in the shadows and echoes of some vague ancient scandal. Mr. von Heilitz always wore gloves, pale grey or lemon yellow, changed clothes five or six times a day, had never worked *a single day in his whole life*, and darted out on his porch to yell at children who threatened to step on his lawn. The chaos-man hurled one of his rocks toward the von Heilitz house. The rock banged against the rough stone side of the house, missing a large leaded window by only a few inches. Tom had wondered if Mr. von Heilitz would materialize on his front porch shaking a fist in a smooth grey glove. Then the man twitched his head as if to dislodge a fly, staggered back a few steps, and bent down for another rock, either forgetting the spare in his left hand or feeling that one rock was simply not enough. He thrust his hand into the canvas sack and began rooting around, presumably for a rock of the proper dimensions. He wore wash pants and a khaki shirt unbuttoned half of the way down the bulge of his stomach. His suntan ended at an abrupt line just below his neck—the protruding stomach was a stark, unhealthy white. The chaos-man lost his balance as he leaned down deeper into the bag and toppled over on his face. When he got himself up on his knees again, blood covered the lower half of his face. He was squinting now at Tom's house, and Tom stepped back from the window.

Then Tom's grandfather, Glendenning Upshaw, the most imposing figure in his life, came heavily down the stairs in his black suit, passed his grandson without acknowledging him, and slammed the front door behind him. Tom instinctively knew that the chaos-man had come for his grandfather and no one else, and that only his grandfather could deal with him. Soon his grandfather appeared, making his way down the walkway toward the sidewalk, thumping the tip of his unfurled umbrella against the pavement. The intruder shouted at Tom's grandfather, but Tom's grandfather did not shout back. The intruder fired a rock into Gloria Pasmore's roses. He fell down again as soon as Tom's grandfather reached the sidewalk. To Tom's astonishment, his grandfather picked the man up, taking care not to bloody his suit, and shook him like a broken toy. Tom's mother began yelling incoherently from an upstairs window and then abruptly stopped, as if she had just taken in that the whole neighborhood could hear her. Tom's father, Victor Pasmore, came down and joined Tom at the window, staring out with a careful neutrality that excluded Tom. Tom slipped out of the living room, index finger still inserted between pages 153 and 154 of *Journey to the Center of the Earth*, moved through the empty hall, and continued on out through the open door. He feared that his grandfather had killed the chaos-man with the Uncle Henry knife he always carried in his trouser pocket. The heat was the muscular heat of the Caribbean in June, a steady downpouring ninety degrees. Tom went down the path to the sidewalk, and for a moment both the chaos-man and his grandfather stared at him. His grandfather waved him off and turned away, but the other man, Wendell Hasek, hunched his shoulders again and continued to stare fixedly at Tom. His grandfather pushed him backwards, and Hasek jerked away. "You know me," he said. "Are you gonna pretend you don't?" His grandfather marched the man to the end of the block and disappeared. Tom looked back at his house and saw his father shaking his head at him. His grandfather came trudging back around the corner of Eastern Shore Road and An Die Blumen, chewing his lip as he walked. The determination in his slow step suggested that he had pitched the chaos-man off the edge of the world. He glanced up and saw Tom, frowned, looked down at the sparkling sidewalk.

When he got back in the house he went wordlessly upstairs with Tom's father. Tom watched him go, and when both his father and grandfather had closed his mother's bedroom door behind them, he went into the study and pulled the Mill Walk telephone book onto his lap and turned the pages until he came to Wendell Hasek's name. Loud voices floated down the stairs. His grandfather said "*our*" or "*hour*."

2

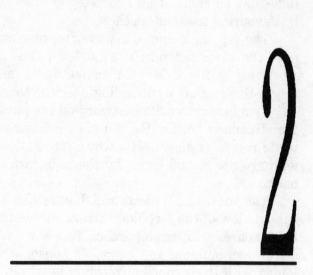

Tom became aware of a thin sound like the cry of an animal a moment after he had ceased to hear it: then he immediately wondered if he *had* heard it. The cry lingered in his inner ear, probably the only place it had ever existed. No sound as soft as that had a chance of being heard in the clopping and rattling from Calle Burleigh.

Tom longed to be home, not stranded in a foreign district. The traffic on both sides of the boulevard blocked his passage across Calle Burleigh as effectively as a wall. There were no traffic lights on Mill Walk in those days, and the rows of vehicles extended as far as he could see. He would have to wait for the end of rush hour to cross the street, and by then darkness would be very near.

Then he heard the actual sound, not its sudden absence. It surrounded all the other noises of Calle Burleigh like a membrane. The cry disappeared into itself and vanished by gradations, like an animal that begins by swallowing its tail and ends by devouring itself altogether.

The cry came again, a wavering rose-pink cloud rising up from the block behind Calle Burleigh. The cloud broke into a stuttering series of dots like smoke signals and coalesced into a bright thread that went sailing over the tops of the houses.

Tom began to drift eastward on the pavement, his back to the streaming traffic. He slid his hands into the pockets of his white cotton trousers. His white button-down shirt, streaked with grey here and there by the milk cartons, adhered to his back.

The houses on Calle Burleigh gave him a broken and interrupted view of the forbidden street. Between two massive red-brick houses with wide porches Tom saw the two-story yellow and brown building and a smaller house, of rough white stone joined with thick ropes of mortar, beside it. He found himself before a brown wooden house as ornately ornamented as a cuckoo clock. He kept moving and looked through to the backs of brick houses on the next street. Facing him was a taller, two-story building of dirty cream-colored brick in which a broken first-floor window had been replaced by grease paper. In a sudden cessation of noise as the traffic stopped, he heard chickens clucking in the yard.

The pink cloud rose above the houses and thickened and narrowed, thickened and narrowed.

The traffic started up with clanks and shouts, with heavy hooves striking the ground, with cracking whips and ringing bells.

Tom moved sideways to get to the other side of a gloomy Gothic structure with a turret and a widow's walk. A curtain shifted, and Tom had an impression of grey hair and a skull-like face peering out. The creature behind the window moved back just enough to become a grey blur.

The thin grey fingers disappeared, and the curtain dropped. Tom moved sideways, thinking in a way that was not quite verbal that he was not in his real life, but in some terrible dreamlike state from which he had to escape before it claimed him forever.

In the next instant the cry went up again, this time clearly from the little street Tom could see between the houses of Calle Burleigh.

At the end of the block he realized that he had been hearing the cries of an unhappy dog. It howled and whined at once, sending up another cloud of pink steam.

Funny, Tom thought—how much that dog managed to sound like a child.

3

Tom looked up at the street sign on the corner. TOWNSEND was the name of the side street. He knew nothing in this neighborhood; he had not even known of the long green open area with a bandshell, swings, a seesaw, luxuriant shade trees, and a few exhausted animals in tiny cages, which lay half a mile east on Calle Burleigh. The milk driver had been astonished that any resident of Mill Walk would not recognize Goethe Park.

Tom stepped around the corner. A dark green metal rectangle with the legend 44TH STREET stamped in relief and painted a shining, almost incandescent white faced him from the next corner. In the section of Mill Walk that Tom knew, streets had names like Beach Terrace and The Sevens, and this designation seemed eerily impersonal to him.

The creature sobbed and snarled and choked.

Tom saw a hairy half-human thing sprawled in the dust, a

thick chain lashed around its neck, its ragged fingernails digging into the dirt of its pen.

With the arrival of this image came a stomach pain so strong and sharp he nearly vomited. He clutched his stomach and sat down on the lawn of the corner house. It seemed to him that what he had seen was himself. His heart fluttered in his chest like a bird chained to its perch.

A door slammed behind him, and Tom turned to see a wide old woman assessing him from the front step of the corner house.

"Get off my lawn. Right now. That's trespassing, what you're doing. I won't have it." The woman spoke with a strong German accent that made each of her syllables strike Tom like a well-aimed brick. She was a nightmare version of Lamont von Heilitz.

Tom said, "I was feeling a little sick, and—"

The old woman's face darkened. "L-I-A-R! L-I-A-R! Get lost!"

She began grunting down the steps, and when she reached the bottom, waded toward him as if she intended to launch herself at him. "Talk back, hey? I won't have you tramping on my grass, you S-C-U-M, get back where you belong—"

Tom had already jumped up and was walking quickly backwards to the safety of the sidewalk.

"Back to your own place!" she shouted. Her blue housedress billowed around her as she advanced on Tom. He began backing up the sidewalk toward the next side street.

Now the woman stood on the very edge of her domain, with the toes of her flat slippers just overlapping the sidewalk. She had extended her arm and index finger very determinedly toward the alley and 44th Street. Her face was an amazing red-purple. "Sick and tired of you brats walking all over my property!"

Tom turned around and ran. He thought to cut up the alley between Calle Burleigh and 44th Street, but as soon as he swerved into the alley her voice exploded behind him: "Can't sneak into my yard that way! You want the police? Keep going!"

He looked over his shoulder and saw her surging down the sidewalk toward him. Tom swerved out of the entrance to the alley and ran toward 44th Street. The woman bawled out a phrase Tom did not understand, or which he misheard: "Cornerboy! Stupid cornerboy!"

On the corner of Townsend and 44th Street he turned around again. She was standing at the entrance to the alley, puffing hard, her hands on her hips. "S-C-U-M! That's what you are, you cornerboys!"

"Okay, okay," Tom said. His heart was still beating hard.

"I see you where you live!" she yelled.

He turned west into the next block, and after he had taken a few steps his view of her was cut off by the house on the corner.

The flawless enameled sky of the Caribbean had begun to show the first traces of the yellow that soon would flash over its entire surface and darken in a moment to purple, then into real night.

Tom wondered if the old woman had gone back into her house. She was probably waiting to make another run at him if he tried to sneak back around the corner.

He lifted his foot and forced his leg to thrust it forward. A forlorn wail immediately blossomed in the air before him. He froze. He glanced at the houses on either side of him—heavy curtains had been drawn over front windows in both houses, giving them a vacant, closed-up look. At this time of the year, nearly everybody in Mill Walk kept their windows open to catch the Atlantic breezes. Only Mr. von Heilitz kept his windows closed and his curtains drawn. Even the people who lived in the "native" houses, naturally cooler than the European or North American buildings, never closed their windows during the summer months.

Of course, Tom thought, they closed their windows so that they would not hear the creature.

Tom stepped forward again, and up ahead of him, off behind one of the houses across the street to his right, the creature uttered a protest that set the chickens flapping and clucking: He thought he was going to melt down into a stain on the sidewalk. He would have to take his chances on the old woman's having gone back inside her house. He turned around.

And then he was so startled he nearly jumped off the sidewalk, for no more than five or six feet behind him was a teenage boy his own height, frozen in place with one foot in advance of the other, his hands held out in a straight line from his elbows. The boy, who clearly had been trying to sneak up on Tom, looked as startled as his quarry. He stared at Tom's face as if he had been stuck with a pin.

"Okay," he said. "Hold it right there."

4

"What?" Tom said. He stepped backwards.

The teenage boy stared at Tom with a very careful absence of expression on his broad, sallow face. The only animation in his face was in his eyes. A scattering of pimples lay on his forehead beneath a fringe of black hair. A magnificent pimple reddened the entire area between the left corner of his mouth and his chin. He was wearing jeans and a dirty white T-shirt. Hard, stringy muscles stood out in his biceps, and premature lines of worry bracketed his mouth. At thirteen, he had the face he would carry with him through all of his adult life. What struck Tom most was the jumpiness in the boy's flat black eyes.

"Hey, calm down," the boy said. He licked his lips as he considered Tom's white button-down shirt and white trousers.

Tom retreated several steps. "Why were you sneaking up on me?"

"Tell me you don't know," the boy said. "Sure. You don't know anything about it, do you?" He licked his lips again, and this time really scrutinized Tom's clothes.

"I don't have any idea of what you're talking about," Tom said. "All I want to do is go home."

"Uh-huh." The boy disbelievingly moved his chin rightwards, then back to center, executing half of a head-shake. His gaze shifted from Tom to a point behind him and to his left, and the impatient expression softened with relief. "Okay," he said.

Tom looked back over his shoulder and saw a teenage girl marching toward him from what seemed to be the source of the creature's sounds. Her black hair hung straight to her collarbone and swung as she walked, and she wore tight black pedal pushers and a black halter top, very dark black sunglasses, and what looked like dance slippers. She was four or five years older than the boy. To Tom, she looked completely grown up. He saw that she did not care at all about her brother, and that she cared even less about him. She came toward them across the street on a diagonal line from the steps of the two-story brown and yellow house. A fat man with a stubbly brown crewcut leaned against one of the side windows in the little bay, his arms folded over the frame of the lower windowpane and his large fleshy face pressed against the upper pane.

The girl wore unusually dark lipstick, and had pushed her full, rounded lips together to form a pouty little nonsmiling smile. "Well, ho hum," she said. "And what are you gonna do now, Jerry Fairy?"

"Shut up," the boy said.

"Poor Jerry Fairy."

She was close enough now to examine Tom, and peered at him through the black sunglasses as if he were gunk on a laboratory slide. "Well, is that what Eastern Shore Road boys look like?"

"Shut up, Robyn."

Robyn slid the sunglasses down her nose and peered at Tom through amused dark eyes. For a second Tom thought she was going to stroke his cheek. Instead she pushed her glasses back up over her eyes. "What are you gonna do with him?"

"*I* don't know," said Jerry.

"Well, here comes the cavalry," said Robyn, smirking over her brother's shoulder. Jerry turned sideways, and Tom saw coming around the side of a native house a fat, angry-looking boy, with a striped T-shirt and stiff new jeans rolled up at least a foot, alongside another boy several inches shorter and almost skeletally thin. The second boy's shirt was so much too large for him that the shoulders fell halfway to his elbows and his neck swayed up out of the gaping collar. The smaller boy trotted beside the other, grinning widely. "They'll be a big help," Robyn said.

"More than you," said her brother.

"I wish you'd tell me what's going on," Tom said.

"You shut up too," Jerry fired at him. He blinked rapidly several times. "You want to know what's going *on*? Why don't you tell me, huh? What are you doing here?"

Tom opened his mouth and found that he had no answer to that question.

"Huh? Huh? All right, okay?" Jerry's tongue flicked over his lips again. "*You* tell *me*, okay?"

"I was just—"

Jerry's eyes flashed up at Tom, and the fury in his face killed the sentence.

Robyn made a gesture of distaste and stepped away.

"I'm going home," Tom said to the side of Jerry's outsized head. He moved backwards. Jerry's eyes flashed at him again, and then his arm flashed out, and before Tom knew what was happening the other boy had struck him in the chest. The blow almost knocked Tom off his feet. Before he had time to react or recover, Jerry shifted his feet and punched the side of his head.

Wholly instinctively, Tom pivoted on his left foot and with all his strength sent his right hand straight at the other's face. His fist landed squarely on Jerry's nose, and broke it. Blood began squirting down Jerry's face.

"Asshole!" screamed his sister.

Jerry dropped his hand from his face and began lumbering toward Tom. Blood jumped from his nose and spattered onto the T-shirt.

"Nappy! Robbie! Get him!" Jerry screamed in a high-pitched voice.

Tom stopped trotting backwards, suddenly angry enough to take on Jerry and his friends too. He lowered his hands and saw doubt move in Jerry's worried eyes. Again he threw out his right hand without actually aiming at anything, and this time struck Jerry's Adam's apple. Jerry went down on his knees. Fifteen yards away and gaining fast, the fat boy in the rolled jeans had taken a knife from his pocket and was waving it as he ran. The smaller boy also had a knife, one with a long narrow blade.

A red-gold gleam from the low sun bounced off the skinny knife. Tom skipped backwards, turned around virtually in mid-air, and ran.

The boys behind him began yelling. When Tom drew level with the brown and yellow house, the front door opened, and the man who had been leaning against the window came out on the front stoop. His face, as flat and impersonally unhappy as Jerry's, swiveled to track Tom's progress. He gestured to the running boys to hurry up, catch him, drag him down. All of this was communicated in a gloomy gestural shorthand.

The world beneath this one . . .

Tom managed to pick up speed, and the boys behind him yelled for him to stop, they would not hurt him. They just wanted to talk to him, they were putting away their knives. Look, the knives were gone, they could talk now.

What's the matter, was he too scared to talk?

Tom looked over his shoulder and saw with surprise that the smaller boy was standing in the middle of the street, canted on one hip and grinning. The pudgy boy in the new jeans was still charging after him. The chaos-man had left his front steps and was wobbling across the sidewalk toward his son, who was hidden behind the figure of the running boy. The fat boy still held his knife, and did not at all look as if he was interested in a friendly talk. His belly surged up and down with each step, his eyes were slits, and so much sweat came from his head that he was surrounded by an aureole of glistening drops. The skinny one pushed himself forward into a run a moment after Tom looked back, and began gaining at once on the fat boy and Tom.

The afternoon had passed into its last stage with tropical swiftness, and the air had turned a darkening purple. When Tom approached the next corner, the white of the cross street's name gleamed out with an unnatural clarity and spelled AUER, a word that seemed to reverberate with ominous lack of meaning.

Auer.

Our.

Hour.

5

Tom wheeled wide around the corner, and a block away saw the continuous stream of vehicles that filled Calle Burleigh. The haze of dust had vanished into the purple dark, and headlights, bicycle lamps, and shining lanterns moved along with the traffic like a swarm of attendant fireflies. An unhappy horse whinnied and stamped a foot.

One of the boys pounded around the corner, and, far sooner than Tom had expected, the other followed. Another glance over his shoulder showed him that the skeletal teenager had managed to run past the fat one and was now only some fifteen yards behind. He was lifting his arms and legs high in a natural runner's lope, the fish knife back in his hand, and he was still gaining on Tom. He had been so sure of being able to outrun Tom that he had pretended to get winded and drop out. The arrogance of this charade terrified Tom nearly as much as the knife: it was as if the boy could never be defeated. In a moment or two he would close in on Tom, and by then it would be so dark that the people leaning out of their windows, curious about all this running, would not be able to see what would happen next.

A stitch like a hot sword entered Tom's side.

At the corner of Auer and Calle Burleigh he could have turned right or left and tried to escape by running up or down Calle Burleigh. Either way, he thought, the skinny boy would get him. The clattering footsteps were so close to him now that he was afraid to look back. When he reached the corner, he simply kept running straight ahead.

Tom flew off the curb and held out his arms as he plunged into the traffic. Horns instantly blew all about him, and a man yelled something incomprehensible. Tom thought that his pursuer, already almost at the curb, shouted too. He dodged around the rear tire of a high black bicycle, and was aware of a horse rearing somewhere off to his left. Another bicycle, virtually at his elbow, tilted over to one side like a trick in the circus, but did not right itself and continued tilting until, with unnatural slowness, its rider was two feet from the ground, then a foot. The rider's grey hair flew back from his forehead, and his face expressed only the deep concentration of a man trying to think his way out of a particularly interesting puzzle, as his shoulder struck the ground. Then his bicycle slid straight out from beneath him. A horse the size of a mountain made of lather and hair appeared directly in front of Tom. He ducked to the left. The panicked horse bounded forward, and the wheels of its cab passed over the grey-haired man's body. Tom heard the thump of collisions and the screech of metal all around him; then an empty illuminated space magically opened before him, and he sprang forward into this empty space. A horn blatted twice. Tom looked sideways and saw a pair of headlights coming toward him with the same dreamy slowness as the falling bicycle. He was entirely incapable of moving. Between the headlights he could see the mesh of a tall metal grille, and beneath the grille was a wide steel band that looked burnished. Above the bumper and the grille a face, indistinct behind the windshield, pointed toward him as intently as the muzzle of a bird dog.

Tom knew that the car was going to hit him, but he could not move. He could not even breathe. The headlights grew larger, the distance between himself and the car halved and the headlights again doubled in size. An electrical coldness of which he was only barely conscious spread over and through Tom's body. He could do nothing but watch the car come closer and closer until it hit him.

Then at last it did hit him, and a series of irrevocable events began happening to Tom Pasmore. Searing pain enfolded and enveloped him as the impact snapped his right leg and crushed his pelvis and hip socket. His skull fractured against the grille, and blood began pouring from his eyes and nose. Almost instantly unconscious, Tom's body hugged the grille for a moment, then began to slide down the front of the car. A black rubber ornament shaped like a football held him up for the following two or three minutes as the car swerved through the confusion of felled bicycles and rearing horses. His right shoulder snapped, and the broken femur of his right leg sliced through muscle and skin like a jagged knife. Fifty feet down the road the car finally jerked to a stop as the nearest horses either settled down or galloped away. Tom flipped off the bumper ornament and slammed down on the roadbed.

His bladder and his bowels emptied into his clothing.

The driver of the car opened his door and jumped out. At some point during the next few moments, while the driver moved reluctantly toward the front of his car, another event, even more irrevocable than everything else that had occurred in the past sixty seconds, happened to Tom Pasmore. The accumulation of shock and pain stopped his heart, and he died.

Part Two

EARLY SORROWS

Dr. [illegible] and others repeatedly emphasized the social dimensions of the treatment process. Dr. Frank H. Gawin, director of the Substance Abuse Research Unit at Yale University, put it this way: "If crack were a drug of the middle or upper classes, we would not be saying it is so impossible to treat."

Crack is the drug of choice in most poor communities because the initial purchase price is relatively cheap.

Initial Conceptions Hold Up

But the biochemical aspects often tend to come first in considering crack treatment, rather than its psychological, social or economic elements or the rather startling lessons of history. Yet [illegible] on getting the addict off the drug [illegible] volition, deprivation [illegible] is the first and essential stage of any program that works, the experts [illegible].

Many of the initial conceptions about crack, which has come into wide-spread use only within the last four years, have thus far held up.

Yes, it has a rare biochemistry that [illegible] preparing [illegible] drug [illegible] been [illegible] at least [illegible] the property was obtained with profits from [illegible] It is expected that few will make the effort.

In past crackdowns on drug dealers, most seized properties were eventually returned to owners by [illegible] judges.

[illegible] on page 16.

[illegible] believe that the [illegible] they face in treating crack [illegible] far more from the [illegible] and circumstances of the [illegible] than its biochemical action the drug produces.

And they believe the new underclass [illegible] society a measure of [illegible] has been largely de[illegible] with a drug epidemic [illegible] apart poor neighborhoods and families in the nation's cities.

Researchers are finding that crack addiction, under the right conditions, can be successfully treated. Some studies suggest that crack is no more chemically addictive than other drugs that addicts have been able to quit.

Positive Shift in Emphasis

Only a year ago, crack was widely regarded as a [illegible] drug still poorly understood, with special characteristics that rendered its addiction almost impossible to cure. Now, in dozens of interviews and scientific reports, treatment experts are shifting their emphasis to the more positive if more complex views about addiction to the smokable form of cocaine.

Moreover, in finding that properly run programs can be made to work in treating crack addicts, they believe they have [illegible] the crucial element of [illegible]

6

Tom was aware of a feeling of great lightness and harmony, then that he no longer felt any pain. Some heavy force had held him down, and this force was desperately trying to haul him back into an enclosure too small for him. His sense of lightness, of freedom from gravity gently but relentlessly pulled him upward. The hooks and eyes and sticky fingers that wished to hold him back popped free one by one, until the last of these stretched out like a filament, wanting him back. The filament grew taut, and he nearly feared its snapping—he felt an uncomplicated wave of love for everything that wanted him back. The membrane released him with a final, soft, nearly impalpable *pop* and his love for all earthly things doubled and overflowed, and he knew, having lost the earth, that love was identical to grief and loss.

His tears washed his eyes, and he saw.

Down there beneath him was a man, then almost immediately another and another, bending over the body that had been his. Radiating out from the circle made by the leaning men and the prostrate boy was an expanding circle of chaos. Crumpled bicycles sprawled on the road like swatted insects, and overturned carts lay beside torn sacks of seed and cement. A horse struggled to right itself in front of an enormous white fan of spilled flour; another horse plunged through the stalled traffic and into an open stretch of road. Cars with running boards and cars with ornamental spare tire covers atop their trunks, cars with exhaust vents and ribbed chrome tubes and chrome latches, cars with statuettes of women stretching tiptoe like dancers on their hoods, stood in a disarranged confusion, pointing every which way as their headlights picked out the new arrivals working their way toward the damaged body he had just left and the other body, that of the man killed beneath the cart.

The world yearned toward invisibility, Tom saw, invisibility was the final condition toward which everything aspired.

He saw two teenage boys standing half-hidden in the crowd on the sidewalk. Running from them, he had felt mortal fear—how odd it was to remember that! They were not evil, not yet. Tom could not read their minds, but he *saw* that these two boys of fourteen, Nappy and Robbie, one so blubbery he had breasts and the other lean as a starved hound, lived at the periphery of a great cloud of error and confusion; and that they daily moved deeper into the cloud, and then he saw that they had made this cloud, produced it out of the choices they made, as a squid produces ink. . . .

If they had caught him, they would have pressed their knives against his chest, his throat; they would have enjoyed his terror but somewhere—even now—been shamed by it, and this shame would have formed another layer among a thousand layers that formed the inky cloud . . . and then Tom sensed or saw such ugliness that he turned away—

and saw that someone had covered him to the chest with an old green army blanket, and several of the men turned their heads to look out for the approach of an ambulance, which would be driven, Tom saw, by a chain-smoking elderly man named Esmond Walker. The ambulance was two-and-a-half miles away on Calle Bavaria, racing through the traffic with its siren whooping, and Tom heard the siren and knew that the sound would come to the waiting men in another eight minutes—

eight minutes

Tom looked down at the person he had been with some surprise, as well as with love and pity. His earthly self had been so new, so unformed and innocent. He had worked hard at his life with intent, innocent concentration, and his family would mourn him, his friends would miss him, there would for a time be a hole in the world that he had filled.

But the sense of lightness and harmony lifted him farther from the scene, and the patterns became clearer. At the epicenter of the confusion were two bodies, his own and that of the crushed man. Policemen in cars and policemen on bicycles had begun to arrive. Leading out from this crowded and unhappy scene with its flashing lights and calls for people to *Step back! Let him breathe!* was a gossamer trail only Tom could see.

This was the trail of what he would have done, where he would have gone, if he had lived. This trail of possibility was disappearing from the visible world, and what Tom saw was its disappearance.

He sees himself dodging through the traffic in a blare of horns and lights, sees himself running east, safe, on the other side of Calle Burleigh. Tom sees himself coming home to his enraged parents . . . and there his trail goes, glistening as it fades, from the steps of Miss Ellinghausen's Academy of Dance where an older Tom stands beside a pretty girl named Sarah Spence and looks up, his face transfixed by a fleeting apprehension—that older Tom Pasmore looks up, his face almost melting with feelings he cannot understand, moves down the hard white steps outside Miss Ellinghausen's Academy and vanishes long before he reaches the sidewalk. In a shabby room in the St. Alwyn Hotel, an even older Tom is reading a book called *The Temptations of Invisibility*, funny title, but he is not in the house on Eastern Shore Road, why is he in the St. Alwyn Hotel? Pain from an unlived future—what is that?

It had been three minutes since his death: the length of one of the songs on the radio to which his mother would listen with her head tilted, eyes half-closed, cigarette smoke curling up past her hair.

On Calle Burleigh a larger crowd packed the sidewalks, talking in a confused, ignorant way about what had caused all the trouble. *A bike flipped right over, I saw it happen right there—one a' them horses just got it into his head to go nuts, plain and simple—a boy ran out—somebody pushed a boy.*

No, Tom protested, none of that was exactly right, you're all wrong, it didn't happen like that.

Music had begun playing some time ago, but Tom became aware of it only now: some song, he didn't know what, saxophones and trumpets, and pretty soon the singer would rush on stage fiddling with his bow tie and plant himself before the mike and explain everything. . . .

In the end, music did explain everything.

The front doors of the houses on Calle Burleigh hung open, and the residents watched from their front stoops or their cement walkways or stood on the crowded sidewalk talking to each other. A big woman in a blue housedress caught his eye by jabbing her finger toward her side lawn as she said, *Cornerboy, always trouble, I sent him back scared, made him run, those boys over there, who knows about them*?

She pointed between the buildings toward 44th Street and carried Tom's eye with her. On 44th Street no front doors stood open, and the only visible human being was a drunken fat man who sat smoking on the stoop of a brown and yellow duplex, wondering what he was going to do next.

Esmond Walker's ambulance had turned off Calle Bavaria at the north end of Goethe Park and was beginning to move slowly through the stalled carts and leaning bicycles at the perimeter of the circle of disorder caused by Tom's accident. Mr. Walker edged past a wagon piled with tanned hides, gave a nudge to a delivery van from Ostend's Market that pulled up far enough to let him in, and changed the frequency of his siren from an ongoing whooping wail to a steady, more peremptory *bip-bip-bip*. He moved around two bicyclists who stared into the cab as if blaming him for the delay, tossed away his cigarette, and kept moving steadily through the crowd of vehicles slowly parting to let him through.

From his perch above the dissolving chaos, Tom heard the change in the siren's signal, and the change of tone seemed to nudge him as certainly as the Ostend's van, for the music began spreading out through the air around him, trumpets called, and the complicated scene beneath Tom darkened and fell away.

So that's how it happens, he thought, and then he was moving fast down a dark tunnel toward a warm bright light. He was not moving his arms and legs, but neither was he being carried in any way. He seemed almost to be flying, but upright, as though supported by an invisible walkway. The music he had heard surrounded him like the sound of humming, or bird song almost too soft to be audible, and the air carried him and the music toward the distant light.

The tunnel had imperceptibly widened, and he was moving through a gathering of shadowy figures who radiated welcome and protection—Tom knew that he had seen these people before, that every one of them had been known to him in his earthly life, and that even though he could not identify them right now, he was deeply relieved to see them again.

Tom's entire body felt full of light and the same feelings that had swept over him when he had jumped down from the milk cart. A delicious feeling of *absolute rightness*, of all worry having been thrown off, never again to be met, spread through him as he traveled through the protective crowd toward the light. Had he not always known these feelings? In some form? He thought they had been the deepest portion of his life, the most powerful but the least visible, the least known or understood, at once the most trusted and least dependable. They were the feelings caused by the sense of a real radiance existing at the center of life—now he knew that the radiance *was* real, for he was traveling toward it amidst people who loved him and wished him comfort and peace in his new condition, a condition he hungered for and needed more intensely with every inch of ground he flew over on his way to the light. For every inch meant an increase in clarity and certainty of understanding, and he felt like a starving man rushing toward a banquet.

Then a long filament attaching him to his old life caught him like a thrown hook, and he abruptly ceased to move forward. Another filament caught him. The people attending and welcoming him began to recede. Tom felt himself slipping away from the banquet of sense and understanding that had awaited him. He was being pulled back down the tunnel like a resistant dog, and the light shrank as it sailed away from him.

Then, for one shocking moment as he fell past his former perch in the air, Tom saw a black man in a white uniform sliding a stretcher into the back of an ambulance. Most of the chaos on the road had cleared, and horses and bicycles swerved around the awkward length of the ambulance to continue west toward Elm Cove. A dense knot of people remained on the sidewalk.

The hooks and eyes and filaments wrenched Tom back into his body so forcefully he could not breathe. He felt as if he had been slammed down hard on a concrete surface. Everything that had happened to him since he jumped off a milk cart erased itself from his mind. For a moment he thought he heard humming music; a light in the roof of the ambulance shone cruelly into his eyes.

Tom lost consciousness against a wave of pain.

7

He woke up in a white room and looked through a confusion of wires and tubes at drawn faces. His parents gazed down at him as if they did not know him. A strange acrid smell hung over him; every bit of him seemed to hurt. He fled again into unconsciousness.

The next time he woke up, the pain in the middle of his body took a moment to arrive, then hit him like a blow. Everything at the joining of his upper and lower body felt destroyed. His right leg screamed, and his right arm and shoulder uttered a shrill but softer complaint. He was looking up at an unfamiliar ceiling through a confusion of tubes and cables, thinking vaguely that he had been *going* somewhere—hadn't he?—when another, deeper wave of pain struck the center of his body. He heard someone groan. He had nearly found *the place*, and all this pain could not be his. With a kind of passionate horror Tom realized how injured you would have to be to feel so much pain, and then with a sickening lurch of recognition knew that some horrible unknown thing had happened to him. He saw his body dismembered on the street, and blackness came rushing out at him from a deep inner cave. He tried to raise his head. Blackness surged over him for a moment; but his eyes opened to the same white ceiling and loops of plastic tubing. This time Tom lowered his eyes and looked down his body.

A long white object extended down the bed. Horror seized him again. His body had been cut away from him and replaced by this foreign object. At last he saw his own real left leg protruding from the object. Beside it lay a smooth white mound, a cast, that flowed up to the middle of his chest. He was in a hospital. A terrible premonition came to him, and he tried to touch his genitals with his right hand.

The motion caused by his panicky grab for his crotch scorched his shoulder and set the middle of his body aflame. His right hand, encased in another cast, was suspended above his chest. He began to cry. As if by itself, his left hand, which was miraculously not encased in plaster, slid up onto the cool white crust over his body and felt between his legs. He touched only a smooth hairless surface like a doll's groin. A tube ran from a hole in the plaster, which was otherwise featureless. He had been castrated. The comfort he had felt a moment before at being in a hospital disappeared into irony—he was in a hospital because that was the only place someone like him was acceptable; he would be in the hospital forever.

Beneath the flaring pain in his hips, groin, and right leg there moved another level of pain like a shark waiting to strike. This pain would obliterate the world. When he had experienced it he would never again be the person he had been. He would be set apart from himself and everything he had known. Tom expected this deep lurking pain to move upward and seize him, but it continued to circle inside his body, as lazily powerful as a threat.

Tom turned his head to look sideways, and caused only a minor flare from his right shoulder. As he did so, he unconsciously rubbed his left hand over the smooth rounded curve of his groin where his penis should have been—something down there was peeing, he could not imagine what, could not think about it or begin to picture it. Just past his head on the far end of the sheet stood three curved tubular guard rails that marked the edge of his bed, and past the bed was a white table with a glass holding water and a funny-looking straw. His mother's straw bag lay on a chair. A door stood open on a white corridor. Two doctors walked past. *I'm here*, he wanted to shout, *I'm alive*! His throat refused to make any sound at all. The doctors continued past the door, and Tom realized that he had seen a glass of water. His eyes came back to the glass on the bedside table. Water! He reached for the glass with his left hand. In the instant his hand touched the table Tom heard his mother's voice coming in through the open door.

"STOP IT!" she yelled. "I CAN'T TAKE IT ANYMORE!"

His hand jerked by itself and knocked the glass into a stack of books. Water sheeted out over the table and fell to the floor like a solid pane of silver.

"I TOOK IT ALL MY LIFE!" his father yelled back.

The secret pain deep in his body opened its mouth to devour him, and far too quietly to be heard Tom cried out and fainted again.

The next time he opened his eyes a jowly face peered down at him with quizzical seriousness.

"Well, young man," said Dr. Bonaventure Milton. "I thought you were coming up for air. Some people have been waiting to talk to you."

His great head swung back and away, and the faces of Tom's parents crowded into the empty space.

"Hiya, kid," his father said, and his mother said "Oh, Tommy."

Victor Pasmore glared at his wife for a second, then turned back to his son. "How do you feel?"

"You don't have to talk," his mother said. "You're going to get better now." Her face flushed, and tears filled her eyes. "Oh, Tommy, we were so—you didn't come home, and then we heard—but the doctors say you're going to heal—"

"Of course he's going to heal," said his father. "What kind of guff is that?"

"Water," Tom managed to say.

"You knocked that glass right off your table," his father said. "Sounded like you threw a baseball through the window. You sure got our attention."

"He wants a drink," said Gloria.

"I'm the doctor, I'll get a new glass," the doctor said. Tom heard him walk out of the toom.

For a moment the Pasmores were silent.

"Keep breaking those glasses, you'll cost us a fortune in glassware," his father said.

His mother burst into outright tears.

Victor Pasmore leaned down closer to his son, bringing a dizzying mix of aftershave, tobacco, and alcohol. "You got pretty banged up, Tommy, but everything's under control now, isn't it?" He managed to shrug while leaning over the bed.

Tom forced words out through his throat. "Is my . . . am I . . . ?"

"You got hit by a car, kiddo," his father said.

And then he remembered the grille and the bumper advancing toward him.

"I had to go through hell and back to get a new glass," complained Dr. Milton, coming back into the room. He stepped up alongside his father and looked down. "I think our patient could use some rest, don't you?" He held the glass in front of Tom's face and gently inserted the curved plastic straw between his lips.

The water, liquid silk, invaded him with the tastes of strawberries, milk, honey, air, sunshine. He drew another mouthful up from the glass, parted his lips to breathe, and the doctor slid the straw from his mouth.

"Enough for now, son," he said.

His mother brushed his left hand with her fingers before stepping back.

Sometime after that, an hour or a day, Tom opened his eyes to a vision that seemed as unreal as a dream—at first he thought he *had* to be dreaming, for what he saw was the slim, fantastic figure of his cranky old neighbor on Eastern Shore Road, Lamont von Heilitz, gliding toward him from a dark corner of the room. Mr. von Heilitz was wearing one of his splendid suits, a pin-striped light grey, with a pale yellow vest that had wide lapels; in his left hand he held gloves of the same shade. Yes, it was a nightmare, for the darkness seemed to follow the old man as he approached the bed and blinking Tom, who feared that his strange neighbor would begin shaking his fist and screaming at him.

But he did not. With webs of shadowy darkness dripping from his shoulders, Mr. von Heilitz quietly patted his left arm and looked down with far more compassion than Dr. Bonaventure Milton. "I want you to get better, Tom Pasmore," he whispered. Mr. von Heilitz leaned down over Tom's body, and Tom saw the shadows that accompanied him spread across the fine network of lines in his white forehead. The wings of his grey hair shone. "Remember this," he whispered, stepped back into darkness that seemed to await him, and was gone.

The small window opposite Tom's bed was no more than a hole punched into a dingy whiteness, smudged here and there with ancient stains. Dirty-looking spiderwebs darkened the walls near the ceiling. Periodically these would mysteriously disappear, and some few days later as mysteriously reappear. Next to his bed was a table that held a glass of water and his books. A tray beneath the table swung out toward him at mealtimes. Near the door were two green plastic chairs. Behind his bedside table stood the pole to which were attached the various bags and bottles that nourished him. Through the door he could see the hospital corridor with its black and white tile floor over which moved a constant traffic of doctors, nurses, cleaners, orderlies, visitors, and his fellow patients. Even with the door closed, Tom was unaware of this traffic only when his pain was at its most ambitious.

For the hospital was as noisy as a foundry. The cleaners roamed the corridors at all hours, talking to themselves and playing their radios as they mopped with bored, angry movements of their arms. Their carts rattled and squealed, and the metal clamps of their ammoniac mops rang against their pails. Someone was always hauling laundry through the corridors, someone was always greeting a visitor with loud outcries, most often someone was groaning or screaming. During visiting hours the halls were crowded with mobs of people talking in falsely cheerful voices, and children pounded from one end of the corridor to another, clutching the strings of balloons.

His world was dominated by physical pain and the necessity of controlling that pain. Every three hours a nurse holding a small square tray marched quickly across his room and lifted a tiny white paper cup from among the other similar cups on the tray even before she reached his bedside, so that by the time she reached him she was in position to extend the cup to his waiting lips. Then there was an agonizing period in which the sweet, oily stuff in the cup temporarily failed to work. Sometimes during this period, the nurse, if she were Nancy Vetiver or Hattie Bascombe, would hold his hand or stroke his hair.

These small coins of affection soothed him.

In a minute or two the pain that had come up out of his body's deepest places began to settle like a large animal going to sleep, and all the sharp smaller pains would turn fuzzy and slow.

One day during Tom's third week in the hospital Dr. Milton entered his room while he was having a conversation with Nancy Vetiver, one of his two favorite nurses. She was a slim young blond woman of twenty-six with close-set brown eyes and harsh lines at the sides of her mouth. Nancy had his hand in hers and was telling him a story about her first year at Shady Mount—the raucous dormitory she had lived in, the food that had made her feel half-sick. Tom was hoping to get her to tell him something about the night nurse, Hattie Bascombe, whom he considered a wondrous and slightly fearsome character, but Nancy glanced over her shoulder as the doctor came in, squeezed his hand, and looked impassively at the doctor.

Tom saw Dr. Milton frown at their joined hands as he approached the bed. Nancy gently took her hand from his, and then stood up.

Dr. Milton tucked in his ample chin and frowned at her a moment before turning to Tom.

"Nurse Vetiver, isn't it?" he asked.

Nancy was wearing a name tag, and Tom knew that the doctor must have encountered her many times before.

"It is," she said.

"Aren't there some essential aspects of your job that you ought to be seeing to?"

"This is an essential aspect of my job, Dr. Milton," Nancy said.

"You feel—let me be sure I state this correctly—it medically beneficial to complain to this boy, who is of a good family, in fact a very good family"—here he glanced over at Tom with what was supposed to be a look of reassurance—"about the mutton served in the nurses' residence?"

"That's exactly what I feel, Doctor."

For a moment the nurse and the doctor merely stared at each other. Tom saw Dr. Milton decide that it was not worth his while to debate hospital etiquette with this underling. He sighed. "I'll want you to think about what you owe to this institution," he said in a weary voice that suggested that he had said similar things many times before. "But we do have a patient, and an important one"—another curdled smile for Tom—"to deal with at the moment, Nurse Vetiver. This young man's grandfather, my good friend Glen Upshaw, is still on the board of this hospital. Perhaps you might be good enough to let me conduct an examination?"

Nancy stepped back, and Dr. Milton leaned down to peer at Tom's face.

"Feeling better, are we?"

"I guess," Tom said.

"How's the pain?"

"Pretty bad at times."

"You'll be back on your feet in no time," the doctor said. "Nature is a great healer. I suppose we could increase your medication . . . ?" He straightened up and turned his head to glance at Nancy. "Suppose we think about increasing his medication, shall we?"

"We'll think about it," she said. "Yes, sir."

"Very good, then." He vaguely patted Tom's cast. "I thought it might be useful for me to pop in and have a chat with the boy, and now I see that it was. Yes, very useful. Everything going all right, nurse?"

Nancy smiled at the doctor with a face subtly changed, older, tougher, more cynical. She looked less beautiful to Tom, but more impressive. "Of course," she said. She glanced at Tom, and when Tom met her eyes he understood: nothing said by Dr. Milton was of any importance at all.

"I'll just add a note on his chart, then," the doctor said, and busied himself with his pen for a moment.

He hooked the chart back on the bottom of his bed, gave Nancy a glance full of meaning Tom did not know how to interpret, and said, "I'll tell your grandfather you're doing splendidly, good mental attitude, all that sort of thing. He'll be pleased." He looked at his watch. "Well. You're eating well, I assume? No mutton here, is there, Nurse? You must eat, you know—that's nature's way. Sometimes good solid food is the best medicine you can have." Another glance at his watch. "Important appointment, I'm afraid. Glad we could get that little matter straightened out, Nurse Vetiver."

"It's a great relief to us all," Nancy said.

Dr. Bonaventure Milton cast Nancy a lazy glance, nearly smiled with the same indifferent laziness, and after nodding to Tom, wandered out of the room. "Yes, *sir*," Nancy said, as if to herself. So Tom understood everything he would ever have to understand about his doctor.

Later there was a "complication" with his leg, which had begun to feel as if helium were being pumped into it, making it so light that it threatened to shatter its cast and sail away into the air. Tom had ignored this feeling for as long as he could, but within a week it became a part of the pain that threatened to devour the whole of the world, and he had to confess it to someone. Nancy Vetiver said to tell Dr. Milton, really *tell* him; Hattie Bascombe, speaking from the darkness in the middle of the night, said, "You save up your knife from your supper, and when old Boney starts pattin' your cast and tellin' you that you just imaginin' that feeling, you take that knife and stick it in his old fat fish-colored hand." Tom thought that Hattie Bascombe was the other side of Nancy Vetiver, and then thought that every object and person must have its other, opposite side—the side that belonged to night.

As Hattie predicted, Dr. Milton scoffed at his story of a "light" pain, an "airy" pain, and even his parents did not believe in it. They did not want to believe that their doctor, the distinguished Bonaventure Milton, could be in error (nor did the surgeon, a Dr. Bostwick, an otherwise blameless man), and above all they did not want to believe that Tom would need yet another operation. Nor did Tom—he just wanted them to cut open the cast and let the air out. Of course that was no solution, the doctors would not do that. And so the abscess within his leg grew and grew, and by the time Nancy and Hattie got Dr. Bostwick to examine this "imaginary" complaint, Tom was found to need a new operation, which would not only remove the abscess but reset his leg. Which meant that first they would have to break it again—it was precisely as though he were to be propped up on Calle Burleigh and run over again.

Hattie Bascombe leaned toward him out of the night and said, "You're a scholar, and this here is your school. Your lessons are hard—*hard*—but you gotta learn 'em. Most people don't learn what you bein' taught until they a lot older. Nothing is safe, that's what you been learnin'. Nothing is whole, not for too damned long. The world is half night. Don't matter who your granddaddy is."

The world is half night—that was what he knew.

Tom spent the entire summer in Shady Mount Hospital. His parents visited him with the irregularity he came to expect of them, for he knew that they saw their visits as disruptive and upsetting, in some way harmful to his recovery: they sent books and toys, and while most of the toys came to pieces in his hands or were useless to one confined to bed, the books were always perfect, every one. When his parents appeared in his room, they seemed quieter and older than he remembered them, survivors of another life, and what they spoke of was the saga of what they had endured on the day of his accident.

The one time his grandfather came to the hospital, he stood beside the bed leaning on the umbrella he used as a cane, with something tight and hard in his face that doubted Tom, wondered about him. This, Tom suddenly remembered, was overwhelmingly familiar—the sensation that his grandfather disliked him.

Had he been running away?

No, of course not, why would he run away?

He didn't have any friends out there, did he? Had he maybe been going to Elm Cove? Two boys in his old class at Brooks-Lowood lived in Elm Cove, maybe he had taken it into his head to go all the way out there and see them?

His class was now his old class because he would miss a year of school.

Maybe, he said. I don't remember. I just don't remember. He could vaguely remember the day of his accident, could remember the milk cart and the NO PASSENGERS ALLOWED sign and the driver asking him about girlfriends.

Well, which one had he been going to see?

His memory turned to sludge, to pure resistance. His grandfather's insistent questions felt like blows.

Why had his accident happened on Calle Burleigh, eight miles east of Elm Cove? Had he been hitchhiking?

"Why are you asking me all these *questions?*" Tom blurted, and burst into tears.

There came a muted shocked exhalation from the door, and Tom knew that some of the hospital staff were lingering there to get a look at his grandfather.

"You'd better stick to your own part of town," his grandfather said, and the young doctors and lounging orderlies gave almost inaudible noises of approval.

At the end of August, during the last thirty minutes of visiting hours, a girl named Sarah Spence walked into his room. Tom put down his book and looked at her in astonishment. Sarah, too, seemed astonished to find herself in a hospital room, and looked around at everything in a wondering, wide-eyed way before she came across the room to his bed. For a moment Tom thought that yes, it was astonishing that he should be here, and that she should see him like this. In that moment he was the old Tom Pasmore, and when he saw how Sarah shyly inspected his massive cast with a smile of dismay, it seemed to him ridiculous that he should have been so unhappy.

Sarah Spence had been a friend of his since their earliest days at school, and when she met his eyes he felt restored to his life. He saw at once that her shyness had left her, and that unlike the boys from their class who had come to visit his room, she was not intimidated by the evidences of his injuries. By now his head wound had healed, and his right arm was out of its bandages and cast, so he looked far more like his old self than he had during most of July.

As they took each other in for a moment before speaking, Tom realized that Sarah's face was no longer that of a little girl, but almost a woman's, and her taller body was beginning to be a woman's too. He saw that Sarah was very much aware of the difference in her face and body.

"Oh, my God," she said. "Would you look at that cast?"

"I look at it a lot, actually," he said.

She smiled, and raised her eyes to meet his. "Oh, Tom," she said, and for a moment there hovered between them the possibility that Sarah Spence would hold his hand, or touch his cheek, or kiss him, or burst into tears and do all three—Tom almost went dizzy with his desire for her touch, and Sarah herself scarcely knew what she wished to do, or how to express the wave of tenderness and grief that had passed through her with his joke. She took a step nearer to him, and was on the verge of reaching out to touch him when she saw how pale his skin was, ashy just beneath the golden surface, and that his hair looked lank and matted. For just a moment her fifth-grade friend Tom Pasmore looked like a stranger. He seemed shrunken, and his bones were prominent, and even though this familiar stranger before her was a little boy—*a little boy*—he had ugly dark smudges under his eyes like an old man. Then Tom's face seemed to settle into well-known lines, and he was not a little boy with an old man's eyes but on the verge of adolescence again, the boy she liked best in her class, the friend who had spent hours every day talking and playing with her in summers and weekends past—but by then she had unconsciously taken a half-step backwards, and was folding her hands together at her waist.

They were suddenly awkward with each other.

To say something, anything at all, lest she run out of the room, Tom said, "Do you know how long I've been here?" And immediately regretted it, for it sounded to him as if he was accusing her of having ignored him.

And then it seemed to him that he was trying to tell Sarah Spence in one sentence about all the changes that had taken place in him. So he said, "I've been here forever."

"I heard yesterday," Sarah said. "We just got back from up north."

"*Up north,*" a phrase Tom understood as well as Sarah, did not refer to the northern end of the island, but to the northern tier of states in continental North America. Sarah's parents, like many far east end residents (though not the Pasmores), owned property in northern Wisconsin, and spent much of June, July, and August in a pine lodge beside a freshwater lake. At the end of June the Redwing clan, Mill Walk's most important family, moved virtually as a single organism to a separate compound on

Eagle Lake. "Mom found out from Mrs. Jacobs, when she was talking to her at Ostend's Market." She paused. "You got hit by a car?"

Tom nodded. She, too, he could see, had questions she could not ask: *How did it feel? Can you remember it? Did it hurt a lot?*

"How did that happen?" she asked. "You just walked in front of a car?"

"I guess I was way out on Calle Burleigh, and it was rush hour, and . . ." Unable to say any more, because all he could remember now of that day was how the car had looked just before it struck him, he shrugged.

"How dumb can you get?" she said. "What are you going to do next? Dive into an empty pool?"

"I think my next death-defying act is going to be trying to get out of this bed."

"And when do you do that? When do you get to go home?"

"I don't know."

Unsettlingly adult exasperation showed on her face. "Well, how are you going to go to school if you don't go home?" When he did not answer, the exasperation was replaced by a moment of pure confusion, and then by something like disbelief. "You're not coming back to school?"

"I can't," he said. "I'm going to be out a whole year. It's true," he added in the face of her growing incredulity. His depression had begun to return. "I can't even get out of bed for another eight weeks—that's what they told me anyhow. When I finally do get home, they're putting me in a hospital bed in the living room. How can I go to school, Sarah? I can't even get out of bed!" He was appalled to hear himself making terrible ragged noises as his pains began to announce themselves again. Tom thought that Sarah Spence looked as if she were sorry to have come to the hospital—and she was right, she did not belong here. In some way he had never quite realized, she had been his best and most important friend, and now a vast abyss lay between them.

Sarah did not run out of the room, but for Tom it was almost worse that she watched him dry his face and blow his nose as she uttered meaningless phrases about how everything would be all right. He saw her retreat into the world of ignorant daylight, backing away in polite horror from his fear and pain and anger. In any case, she did not know the worst thing—that he had been castrated and had nothing between his legs but a tube, a fact so terrible that Tom himself could not hold it clearly in his mind for more than a few seconds at a time. Now, without being aware of what he was doing, his left hand crept to the smooth groin of his body cast.

"You must itch a lot," Sarah said.

He pulled his hand away as if the cast were red hot. She remained until visiting hours were over, talking to him about a new puppy named Bingo and what she had done "up north," and how Fritz Redwing's cousin Buddy had taken one of his family's motorboats out into the middle of Eagle Lake and tried to dynamite the fish, and her voice went on and on, full of kindness and restraint and sympathy, as well as other feelings he could not or would not identify, until Nancy Vetiver came in to tell her that she had to leave.

"I didn't know you had such a pretty girlfriend," Nancy said. "I think I'm jealous."

Sarah's entire face turned pink, and she reached for her bag, promising to be back soon. When she left she sent no more than a glancing smile toward Tom, and did not speak or look at Nancy. She never came to the hospital again.

Two days later his door opened just before the end of visiting hours, and Tom looked up with his heart beating, expecting to see Sarah Spence. Lamont von Heilitz smiled flickeringly from the doorway, and somehow appeared to understand everything at once. "Ah, you've been waiting for someone else. But it's just your cranky old neighbor, I'm afraid. Shall I leave you alone?"

"Please don't, please come in," Tom said, more pleased than he would have thought possible at the sight of the old man. Mr. von Heilitz was wearing a dark blue suit with a double-breasted vest, a dark red rose in his buttonhole, and gloves of the same red as the rose. He looked silly and beautiful at once, Tom thought, and was visited by what seemed the odd desire that he might look a great deal like this when he was as old as Mr. von Heilitz. Then his mind snagged and caught on a buried memory, and he goggled at the old man, who smiled back at him, as if again he had understood everything before Tom had to say a word.

"You came to see me," Tom said. "A long time ago."

"Yes," the old man said.

"You said—you said to remember your visit."

"And so you did," said Mr. von Heilitz. "And now I have come again. I understand that you will be coming home soon, but thought that you might enjoy reading a few books I had around the place. It's all right if you don't. But you might give them a try, anyhow." And from nowhere, it seemed, he produced two slim books—*The Speckled Band* and *The Murders in the Rue Morgue*—and handed them over to Tom. "I hope you will be good enough to pay me a call sometime when you are out of the hospital and fully recovered."

Tom nodded, dumbfounded, and soon after Mr. von Heilitz glided out of the room.

"Who the hell was that?" Nancy asked him. "Dracula?"

Tom himself left the hospital on the last day of August, and was installed in the bed set up in the living room. The big cast had been replaced by one that encased him only from ankle to thigh. It seemed that he had not been castrated after all. Nancy Vetiver visited him after he had been home a few days, and at first seemed to bring into the house with her the whole noisy, well-regulated atmosphere of the hospital—for a moment it seemed that his lost world would be restored. She told him stories of the other nurses and the patients he had known, which involved him as Sarah Spence's tales of northern Wisconsin had not, and told him that Hattie Bascombe had said that she would put a hex on him if he didn't come visit her. But then his mother, who was having one of her good days and had left them alone to order groceries from Ostend's, came back in and was chillingly polite to the nurse, and Tom saw Nancy become increasingly uncomfortable under Gloria Pasmore's questions about her parents and her education. For the first time Tom noticed that Nancy's grammar was uncertain—she said "she don't" and "they was"—and that she sometimes laughed at things that weren't funny. A few minutes later, Tom's mother showed her to the door, thanking her with elaborate insincerity for all she had done.

When Gloria came back into the living room, she said, "I don't think nurses expect to be tipped, do you? I don't think they should."

"Oh, Mom," Tom said, knowing that this concealed a negative verdict.

"That young woman looked very hard to me," said his mother. "Very hard indeed. People as hard as that *frighten* me."

Part Three

HATRED AND SALVATION

[illegible] and others [illegible] the social dimension of the treatment process. Dr. Frank H. [illegible], director of the Substance Abuse Research [illegible] University, put it this way: [illegible] the middle or upper classes, we would not be saying it is so impossible to treat.

[illegible] the drug of choice in more poor communities because the initial purchases are relatively cheap.

Initial Conceptions Hold Up

[illegible] the biochemical aspects often tend to come first in considering crack treatment, rather than its psychological, social or economic elements or the rather [illegible] lessons of history. [illegible] on getting the addict off the drug, either by volition, deprivation or medication, is the first and essential stage of any program that works, the experts said.

Many of the initial conceptions about crack, which has come into widespread use only within the last four years, have thus far held up.

Yes, it has a rare biochemistry that [illegible] preparing [illegible] losing drug [illegible] been impounded [illegible] by [illegible] that the property was obtained with profits [illegible] the effort.

In past [illegible] on drug dealers, most seized properties were eventually returned to owners by [illegible].

[illegible] the differences they face in treating [illegible] far more from the [illegible] and circumstances of the [illegible] than the biochemical reaction the drug produces.

And they believe the new understanding offers society a measure of [illegible] has been largely de[illegible] with a drug epidemic [illegible] apart poor neighborhoods and families in the nation's cities.

Researchers are finding that crack addiction, under the right conditions, can be successfully treated. Some [illegible] suggest that crack is no more [illegible] addictive than other drugs that addicts have been able to quit.

Positive Shift in Emphasis

Only a year ago [illegible] widely regarded [illegible] drug still poorly understood [illegible] characteristics that [illegible] addiction almost impossible to treat. Now, in dozens of interviews and scientific reports, treatment experts are shifting their emphasis to the more positive if more complex [illegible] about addiction to the smokable form of cocaine.

Moreover, in finding that properly run programs can be made to work in treating crack addicts, they believe they have identified the crucial elements of [illegible].

[illegible] page [illegible]

8

Later in his life, when Tom Pasmore remembered the year he had spent alone at home, he could not summon up the faces of the practical nurses who came, were fired, and went away, nor of the tutors who tried to get him to stop reading for long enough for them to teach him something. Neither was he ever able to remember spending any length of time with his parents.

What he could remember without any difficulty at all was being alone and reading. His year at home divided itself into three sections—the eras of bed, wheelchair, and crutches—and during these, he read nearly every one of the books in his parents' house and virtually all of the books his father carried home, six at a time, from the public library. He read with nothing but appetite—without discrimination or judgment, sometimes without understanding. Tom reread all of his old children's books, read his father's Zane Grey, Eric Ambler, and Edgar Rice Burroughs, and his mother's S. S. Van Dine, E. Phillips Oppenheim, Michael Arlen, Edgar Wallace, and *The Search for Bridey Murphy*. He read Sax Rohmer, H. P. Lovecraft, and *Bulfinch's*

Mythology. He read the dog novels of Albert Payson Terhune, and the horse novels of Will James, and *Call of the Wild*, *Black Beauty*, and *Frog* by Colonel S. P. Meeker. He read a novel by a Hungarian about Galileo. He read hotrod novels by Henry Gregor Felsen, especially *Street Rod*, in which a boy was killed in an automobile accident. When his father began taking books from the library, he raced through everything they had by Agatha Christie, Ngaio Marsh, Dashiell Hammett, and Raymond Chandler. He read *Murder, Incorporated*, about the careers of Louis "Lepke" Buchalter and Abe "Kid Twist" Reles. Once an irritated Victor Pasmore came into the living room holding a bagful of hardback Nero Wolfe novels by Rex Stout that Lamont von Heilitz had pressed into his hands with instructions to give them to Tom, and Tom read them all in a row, one after the other. He read approximately one-third of the Bible and one-half of a collection of Shakespeare's plays that he found propping up a goldfish bowl. He went through Sherlock Holmes and Richard Hannay and Lord Peter Wimsey. He read *Jurgen* and *Topper* and *Slan*. He read novels in which young governesses went to ancient family estates in France and fell in love with young noblemen who might have been smugglers, but were not. He read *Dracula* and *Wuthering Heights* and *Bleak House*. After that he was launched into Dickens, and read *Great Expectations*, *The Pickwick Papers*, *Martin Chuzzlewit*, *Dombey and Son*, *The Mystery of Edwin Drood*, *Our Mutual Friend*, *A Tale of Two Cities*, and *David Copperfield*. On the recommendation of the puzzled librarian, he went from Dickens to Wilkie Collins, and lapped up *The Moonstone*, *No Name*, *Armadale*, and *The Woman in White*. He failed with Edith Wharton, another of the librarian's recommendations, but struck gold again with Mark Twain, Richard Henry Dana, and Edgar Allan Poe. Then he stumbled upon *The Castle of Otranto*, *The Monk*, and *Great Tales of Terror and the Supernatural*. Mr. von Heilitz once again intercepted his father on the street, and passed along *The House of the Arrow* and *Trent's Last Case* and *Brat Farrar*.

Before his accident, books had meant the safety of escape; for a long time afterwards, what they meant was life itself. Very rarely, a few of the boys who had been his friends would stop in and stay half an hour or more, and during these visits he learned that the world did not stop at his front door—Buddy

Redwing had been given a Corvette for his sixteenth birthday, and Jamie Thielman had been expelled from Brooks-Lowood for smoking behind the curtains on the school stage, the football team had won eight games in a row, and the basketball team, which played in a league with only four other teams, had an unbroken string of losses—but the boys seldom visited and soon left, and Tom, who really did hunger for information about what the big unknown world beyond his door, beyond Eastern Shore Road, beyond even Mill Walk was like, could forget while he read that he was crippled and alone. Through the transparent medium of books, he left behind his body and his useless anger and roamed through forests and cities in close company with men and women who plotted for money, love, and revenge, who murdered and stole and saved England from foreign conspiracies, who embarked on great journeys and followed their doubles like shadows through foggy nineteenth-century London. He hated his body and his wheelchair, though his arms and shoulders grew as muscular as a weightlifters's, and when he was put on his crutches, he loathed their awkwardness and the hobbled imitation of walking they represented: real life, his real life, was between the covers of several hundred novels. Everything else was horror and monstrosity—falling down, moving like an insect with his six limbs, screaming at his irritated tutors, dreaming at night of seas of blood, of a smashed and mutilated body.

A year after his accident, Tom set down his crutches and learned to walk again. By then he was in a great many ways a different person from the boy who had jumped down from the milk cart.

Both the elder Pasmores and their son would have pointed to Tom's immersion in books as the real cause of the changes in him. To Tom's parents, it seemed that the far more distant, now oddly unknowable boy holding on to tables and chairs as he tottered around the house on legs as unreliable as those of an eighteen-month-old child had taken a voluntary sidestep away from life—when not inexplicably enraged, he seemed to have chosen shadows, passivity, unreality.

Tom's own ideas were almost directly opposed to these. It seemed to him that he had stepped into the real stream of life: that all of his reading not only had saved him from the immediate insanity of rage and the slow insanity of boredom, but given him a rapid and seductive overview of adult life—he had been an invisible participant in hundreds of dramas, but even more important, had overheard thousands of conversations, witnessed as many acts of discrimination and judgment, and seen stupidity, cruelty, hyprocrisy, bad manners, and duplicity condemned in almost equal measure. The melody of the English language and a sense of its resources, an idea of eloquence as mysteriously good and moral in itself, had passed into his mind forever, as had the beginning of an understanding of human motives. Far more than anything provided by his tutors, the books Tom read were his education. At times, deep in a book, he felt his body begin to glow: an invisible but potent glory seemed to hover just behind the characters, and it seemed that they were on the verge of making some great discovery that would also be his—the discovery of a vast realm of radiant meaning that lay hidden just within the world of ordinary appearances.

By his junior year in Brooks-Lowood's Upper School, he could make half of his class convulse with laughter with a remark the other half would either resent or fail to understand; he jumped at loud noises and retreated into himself for long periods that were known as his "trances"; he had a reputation for being "nervous," for he had no physical repose and could not remain still longer than a few seconds without moving or twitching or rubbing his face or chattering to anybody who happened to be near. He was plagued with nightmares and he walked in his sleep. If he had been as good in school as his aptitude tests indicated he should, much of this behavior would have been put down to his being a "brain," a brilliant academic future would have been predicted for him, and the guidance counselor would have spoken to him about medical school—there was a perennial shortage of doctors on Mill Walk. As it was, his conduct merely made him odd, and the counselor handed him brochures for third-rate colleges in the southern states.

The nine months he had spent in a wheelchair had left him with large shoulders and well-developed biceps that remained even while the rest of his body lengthened to a height of six feet, four inches. The basketball coach, who was desperate after a long string of losing seasons, arranged a meeting of Tom and Victor Pasmore, himself, and the headmaster, who had long ago mentally convicted Tom Pasmore of malingering. Tom politely refused to have anything to do with the school's teams. "It's just an accident that I'm so tall," he said to the three stony-faced men in the headmaster's beautiful office. "Why don't you imagine me being a foot shorter?"

He meant that if they did so they would be closer to the truth, but the coach felt as though Tom were laughing at him, the headmaster felt insulted, and Victor Pasmore was enraged.

"Will you please talk to these people like a human being?" Victor bellowed. "You have to take part in things! You can't sit on your duff all day long anymore!"

"Sounds like basketball has just become a compulsory subject," Tom said, as if to himself.

"It just has—for you!" shouted his father.

And then Tom uttered a remark that turned the stomach of each of the three adult men in the room. "I don't know anything about basketball except for what I learned from John Updike. Have any of you ever read *Rabbit, Run?*"

Of course none of them had—the coach thought that Tom was talking about an animal book.

Tom went to basketball practice for a month. The coach discovered that his new acquisition could not dribble or pass, was completely incapable of hitting the basket with the ball, and did not even know the names of the positions. Tom did get his friend Fritz Redwing, one of the guards, interested in *Rabbit, Run* by describing an act of oral sex that took place in the book, and Fritz became so engrossed in the copy he filched from the An Die Blumen drugstore (no Redwing Tom ever knew would pay good money for anything as ridiculous as a book) that he excited the suspicions of his parents, who after three days plucked the paperback from his fingers and in horror, disbelief, and embarrassment found themselves staring at the very passage Tom Pasmore had described to their son.

The elder Redwings would very likely have been more comfortable with the thought of their son actually performing some of the acts depicted on the page before them than with the fact of his reading about them. In a boy, sexual experimentation could be put down to high spirits, but reading about such things smacked of perversion. They were shocked, and though they did not quite perceive this, they felt their values betrayed. Fritz quickly confessed that Tom Pasmore had told him about the dreadful book. And because the Redwings were the richest, most powerful, and most respected family on Mill Walk, Tom's reputation underwent a subtle darkening. He was perhaps not—perhaps not entirely *reliable.*

Tom's response was that he preferred being not perhaps entirely reliable. Certainly he had no interest in being an imitation Redwing, though that was the goal of most of what passed for society on Mill Walk. Redwing reliability consisted of thoughtless, comfortable adherence to a set of habits and traits that were generally accepted more as the only possible manners than as simple good manners.

One arrived at business appointments five minutes late, and half an hour late for social functions. One played tennis, polo, and golf as well as possible. One drank whiskey, gin, beer, and champagne—one did not really know much about other wines—and wore wool in the winter, cotton in summer. (Only certain brands and labels were acceptable, all others being either comically inappropriate or more or less invisible.) One smiled and told the latest jokes; one never publicly disapproved of anything, ever, nor too enthusiastically gave public approval, ever. One made money (or in the Redwings' case, conserved it) but did not vulgarly discuss it. One owned art, but did not attach an unseemly importance to it: paintings, chiefly landscapes or portraits, were intended to decorate walls, increase in value, and testify to the splendor of their owners. (When the Redwings and members of their circle decided to donate their "art" to Mill Walk's Museo del Kunst, they generally stipulated that the Museo construct facsimiles of their living rooms, so that the paintings could be seen in their proper context.) Similarly, novels told stories designed to be the summer entertainment of women; poetry was either prettily rhymed stuff for children or absurdly obscure and self-important; and "classical" music obligingly provided a set of familiar melodies as a background for being seen in public in one's best clothes. One ignored as far as was possible any distasteful, uncomfortable, or irritating realities. One spent the summers in Europe, buying things, at South American resorts, buying other things, or "up north," ideally at Eagle Lake, drinking, fishing, organizing lavish parties, and committing adultery. One spoke no foreign language, the idea was ridiculous, but a faulty and rudimentary knowledge of German, if assimilated at the knee of a grandparent who had once owned a great deal of eastern shore property and made a very good thing of it, was acceptable. One attended Brooks-Lowood and played in as many sports as possible, ignored and ridiculed the unattractive and unpopular, despised the poor and the natives, thought of any other part of the Western Hemisphere except Eagle Lake and its environs as unfortunate in exact relation to its dissimilarity to Mill Walk, went away to college to be polished but not corrupted by exposure to interesting but irrelevant points of view, and returned to marry and propagate oneself, to consolidate or create wealth. One never really looked worried, and one never said anything that had not been heard being said before. One belonged to the Mill Walk Founders Club, the Beach & Yacht Club, one or both of two country clubs, the alumni club of one's college, the Episcopal Church, and in the case of young businessmen, the Kiwanis Club, so as not to appear snobbish.

Generally, one was taller than average, blond, blue-eyed. Generally one had perfect teeth. (The Redwings themselves, however, tended to be short, dark, and rather heavyset, and to have wide spaces between their teeth.)

One branch of the Redwing family attempted to install fox hunting—"riding to hounds"—as a regular part of island life, but due to the absence of native foxes and the unfailing ability of the native cats and ferrets to evade the panting, heat-stricken imported hounds, the custom swiftly degenerated to regular annual participation at the Hunt Ball, with the local males dressed in black boots and pink hacking jackets. As the nature of this attempt at an instant tradition might indicate, Mill Walk society was reflexively Anglophile in its tastes, drawn to chintz and floral patterns, conservative clothing, leather furniture, wood paneling, small dogs, formal dinners, the consumption of game birds, "eloquent" portraits of family pets, indifference to intellectual matters, cheerful philistinism, habitual assumption of moral superiority, and the like. Also Anglophile, perhaps, was the assumption that the civilized world—the world that mattered—by no means included all of Mill Walk, but only the far east end where the Redwings, their relatives, friends, acquaintances, and hangers-on lived, and, though this was debatable, Elm Cove, which lay to the western end of Glen Hollow

Golf Club. Other outposts of the civilized world were: Bermuda, Mustique, Charleston, particular sections of Brazil and Venezuela—especially "Tranquility," the Redwing hideaway there—certain areas of Richmond, Boston, Philadelphia, New York, and London, Eagle Lake, the Scottish highlands, and the Redwing hunting lodge in Alaska. One might go anywhere in the world, certainly, but there was surely no real need to go anywhere but to these places, which between them made up the map of all that was desirable to a right-minded person.

To a *reliable* person, one could say.

9

Tom became interested in Mill Walk's few murders, and kept a scrapbook of clippings from the *Eyewitness* that concerned them. He did not know why he was interested in these murders, but every one of them left behind, on a hillside or in a room, a prematurely dispossessed body, a body that would otherwise be filled with life.

Gloria was distressed when she discovered this scrapbook, which was of ordinary, even mundane appearance, with its dark board covers that resembled leather and large stiff yellow pages—part of her distress was the contrast between the homely scrapbook, suggestive of matchbook collections and photographs from summer camp, and the headlines that jumped from its pages: BODY DISCOVERED IN TRUNK. SISTER OF FINANCE MINISTER MURDERED IN ROBBERY ATTEMPT. She considered removing the scrapbook from his room and confronting him with it, but almost immediately decided to pretend that she had not seen it. The scrapbook was merely one of a thousand things that distressed, alarmed, or upset Gloria.

Most of Mill Walk's murders were as ordinary as the scrapbook into which Tom glued their newspaper renderings. A pig farmer was hit in the head with a brick and dumped, to be trampled and half-devoured by his livestock, into a pen beside his barn. BRUTAL MURDER OF CENTRAL PLAINS FARMER, said the *Eyewitness*. Two days later, the newspaper reported SISTER OF FARMER CONFESSES: *Says He Told Me He Would Marry, I Had To Leave Family Farm.* A bartender in the old slave quarter was killed during a robbery. One brother killed another on Christmas Eve: SANTA CLAUS DISPUTE LEADS TO DEATH. After a native woman was found stabbed to death in a Mogrom Street hovel, SON MURDERED MOTHER FOR MONEY IN MATTRESS—MORE THAN $300,000!

Gloria eventually decided to seek reassurance from a sympathetic source.

Tom's English teacher at Brooks-Lowood, Dennis Handley, Mr. Handley, or "Handles" to the boys, had come to Mill Walk from Brown University, looking for sun, enough money to live reasonably well, a picturesque apartment overlooking the water, and a life reasonably free of stress. Since he enjoyed teaching, had spent the happiest years of his life at a draconian prep school in New Hampshire, was of an even-tempered, friendly nature, and had virtually no sexual desires whatsoever, Dennis Handley had enjoyed his life on Mill Walk from the first. He had found that apartments on the water were beyond his price range, but almost everything else about his life in the tropics suited him.

When Gloria Pasmore told him about the scrapbook, he agreed to have a talk with the boy. He did not know exactly why, but the scrapbook sounded *wrong*. He thought it might be a sourcebook for future stories, but the whole tone of the thing disturbed him—too morbid, too twisted and obsessive. Surely Tom Pasmore was not thinking of writing crime novels? Detective novels? Not good enough, he said to himself, and told Gloria, who seemed to have gone perhaps two drinks over her limit, that he would find out what he could.

Some time ago Dennis Handley had mentioned to Tom that he had begun collecting rare editions of certain authors while at Brown—Graham Greene, Henry James, and F. Scott Fitzgerald, primarily—and that Tom might come to look at these books any time he liked. On the Friday after his conversation with Gloria Pasmore, Dennis asked Tom if he would be free after school to look over his books and see if he'd like to borrow anything. He offered to drive him to his apartment and bring him back home afterward. Tom happily agreed.

They met outside Dennis's classroom after the end of school and in a crowd of rushing boys walked down the wide wooden stairs past a window with a stained glass replica of the school's circular seal. Because he was a popular teacher, many of the boys stopped to speak to Dennis or to wish him a good weekend, but few even said as much as hello to Tom. They scarcely looked at him. Except for the healthy glow of his skin, Tom was not a particularly handsome boy, but he was six-four. His hair was the same rough silky-looking blond as his mother's, and his shoulders stuck out impressively, a real rack of muscle and bone under his rumpled tweed jacket. (At this stage of his life, Tom Pasmore never gave the impression of caring about, or even much noticing, what clothes he had happened to put on that morning.) At first glance, he looked like an unusually youthful college professor. The other boys acted as though he were invisible, a neutral space. They stood suspended on the stairs for a moment as the departing boys swirled about them, and as Dennis Handley talked to Will Thielman about the weekend's homework, he glanced at Tom, slouched in the murky green-and-red light streaming through the colored glass. The teacher saw how thoroughly Tom allowed himself to be effaced, as if he had learned how to melt away into the crowd—all the students poured downstairs through the dim light and the shadows, but Tom Pasmore alone seemed on the verge of disappearance. This notion gave Dennis Handley, above all a creature of sociability, of good humor and gossip, an unpleasant twinge.

Soon they were outside in the faculty parking lot, where the English teacher's black Corvette convertible looked superbly out of place among the battered Ford station wagons, ancient bicycles, and boatlike sedans that were the conventional faculty vehicles. Tom opened the passenger door, folded himself in half to get in, and sat with his knees floating up near the vicinity of his nose. He was smiling at his discomfort, and the smile dispelled the odd atmosphere of secrecy and shadows, which Handley had surely only imagined about the boy. He was the tallest person who had ever been in the Corvette, and Dennis told him this as they left the lot.

It was like sitting next to a large, amiable sheep dog, Dennis thought, as he picked up speed on School Road and the wind ruffled the boy's hair and fluttered his tie. "Sorry the space is so tight," he said. "But you can push the seat back."

"I already did push the seat back," Tom said, grinning through the uprights of his thighs. He looked like a circus contortionist.

"Well, it won't be long," Dennis said, piloting the sleek little car south on School Road to Calle Berghofstrasse, then west past rows of shops selling expensive soaps and perfumes to the four lanes of Calle Drosselmeyer, where they drove south again for a long time, past the new Dos de Mayo shopping center and the statue of David Redwing, Mill Walk's first Prime Minister, past rows of blacksmiths and the impromptu booths of sidewalk fortune-tellers, past auto repair shops and shops dealing in pythons and rattlesnakes. They moved along in the usual bustle of cars and bikes and horse carts. Past the tin can factory and the sugarcane refinery, and further south through the little area of hovels, shops, and native houses called Weasel Hollow, where the woman who slept on "a king's ransom" (the *Eyewitness*) had been murdered by her son. Dennis swerved expertly onto Market Street, weaved through and around a series of vans delivering produce to Ostend's Market, and zipped through the last seconds of a yellow light onto Calle Burleigh, where at last he turned west for good.

Tom spoke for the first time since they had left the school. "Where do you live?"

"Out near the park."

Tom nodded, thinking that he meant Shore Park, and that he must be planning on doing some shopping before he went home. Then he said, "I bet my mother asked you to talk to me."

Dennis snapped his head sideways.

"Why do you think she'd want me to talk to you?"

"You know why."

Dennis found himself in a predicament. Either he confessed that Gloria Pasmore had described Tom's scrapbook to him, thereby admitting to the boy that his mother had looked through it, or he denied any knowledge of Gloria's concern. If he denied everything, he could hardly bring up the matter of the scrapbook. He also realized that denial would chiefly serve to make him look stupid, which went against his instincts. It would also set him subtly against Tom and "on the side of" his parents, also counter to all his instincts.

Tom's next statement increased his discomfort. "I'm sorry you're worried about my scrapbook. You're concerned, and you really shouldn't be."

"Well, I—" Handley stopped, not knowing how to proceed. He realized that he felt guilty, and that Tom was perceptive enough to see that too.

"Tell me about your books," Tom said. "I like the whole idea of rare books and first editions, and things like that."

So with evident relief, Dennis began describing his greatest bookfinding coup, the discovery of a typed manuscript of *The Spoils of Poynton* in an antiques shop in Bloomsbury. "As soon as I walked into that shop I had a feeling, a real *feeling*, stronger than anything I'd ever known," he said, and Tom's attention was once again completely focused on him. "I'm no mystic, and I do not believe in psychic phenomena, not even a little bit, but when I walked into that shop it was like something *took possession* of me. I was thinking about Henry James anyhow, because of the scene in the little antiques shop in *The Golden Bowl*, where Charlotte and the Prince buy Maggie's wedding present—do you know the book?"

Tom nodded, extraordinary boy, and listened intently to the catalogue of goods in the antiques shop, the slightly enhanced depiction of the shop's proprietor, the grip of the mysterious "feeling" that increased as Handley wandered through the shabby goods, the excitement with which he had come across a case of worn books at the very back of the shop, and at last the discovery of a box of typed papers wedged between an atlas and a dictionary on the bottom shelf. Dennis had opened the box, almost knowing what he would find within it. At last he had dared to look. "They began in the middle of a scene. I recognized that it was *The Spoils of Poynton* after a few sentences—that's how keyed up I was. Now. That book was the first one James ever dictated—and he didn't dictate the whole thing. He had begun to have wrist trouble, and he hired a typist named William

McAlpine after he began work on it. I knew I'd found McAlpine's dictation copy of the book, which he had later retyped, including James's handwritten chapters, to prepare a correct copy to send to James's publisher. I could never prove it, probably, but I didn't have to prove it. I knew what I had. I took it up to the little man, trembling like a leaf, and he sold it to me for five pounds, clearly thinking that I was a lunatic who'd buy anything at all. He thought I was buying it for the box, actually."

Dennis paused, in part because his listeners usually laughed at this point and in part because he had not described this moment for several years and his retelling had brought back to him its sensations of triumph and nearly uncontainable jubilation.

Tom's response brought him thumping to earth.

"Have you been reading about the murder of Marita Hasselgard, the sister of the Finance Minister?"

They were back to the scrapbook—Tom had whipsawed him. "Of course I have. I haven't had my head in a bag during the past month." He looked across at the passenger seat with real irritation. Tom had propped his legs on the dashboard, and was rolling a ballpoint pen in his mouth as if it were a cigar. "I thought you were interested in what I was saying."

"I'm very interested in what you were saying. What do you think happened to her?"

Dennis sighed. "What do I think happened to Marita Hasselgard? She was killed by mistake. An assassin mistook her for her brother because she was in his car. It was late at night. When he discovered his mistake, he pushed her body into the trunk and left the island in a hurry."

"So you think that the newspaper is right?"

The theory that Dennis Handley had just expressed, held by most citizens of Mill Walk, had first been outlined in the editorial columns of the *Eyewitness*.

"Basically, yes. I suppose I do. I hadn't quite remembered that the paper put it like that, but if they did, then I think they are right, yes. Would you mind telling me how this relates to *The Spoils of Poynton?*"

"Where do you think the assassin came from?"

"I think he was hired by some political enemy of Hasselgard—by someone who opposed his policies."

"Any policy in particular?"

"It could have been anything."

"Don't you think Hasselgard ought to be careful now? Shouldn't he be heavily guarded?"

"Well, the attempt failed. The assassin took off. The police are looking for him, and when they find him, he'll tell them who hired him. If anybody ought to be afraid, it's the man who hired the killer."

All this, too, was conventional wisdom.

"Why do you think he put the sister's body in the trunk?"

"Oh, I don't really care where he put Marita," Dennis said. "I don't see what bearing that can possibly have on anything. The man looked into the car. He saw that he'd killed his intended victim's sister. He hid the body in the trunk. Why are we talking about this sordid business, anyway?"

"Do you remember what sort of car it was?"

"Of course. It was a Corvette. Identical to this one, in fact. I hope this is the end of these questions."

Tom leaned sideways toward him. He took the pen out of his mouth. "Just about. Marita was a big woman, wasn't she?"

"I can't see any possible point in going on—"

"I only have two more questions."

"Promise?"

"Here's the first one. Where do you suppose that woman in Weasel Hollow got the money she put under her mattress?"

"What's the second question?"

"Where do you think that feeling in the antiques shop came from, that feeling of knowing you were going to find something?"

"Is this still a conversation, or are we just free associating?"

"You mean you have no idea where the feeling came from?"

Dennis just shook his head.

For the first time since they had turned onto Calle Burleigh, Tom paid some attention to the landscape of sturdy houses surrounding them. "We're nowhere near Shore Park."

"I don't live anywhere near Shore Park. Why would you think—oh." He smiled over at Tom. "I live near Goethe Park, not Shore Park. Just next to the old slave quarter. Ninety percent of the houses were built in the twenties and thirties, I think, and they're good, solid, middle-class houses, with porches and arches and some interesting details. This area is tremendously underrated." He had by now recovered his habitual good humor.

"I don't see why Brooks-Lowood shouldn't widen its net, so to speak."

Tom slowly turned his head to face the teacher. "Hasselgard didn't attend Brooks-Lowood."

"Well, after all," the teacher said, "I can't see that where Hasselgard went to secondary school has any bearing on his sister's murder." Tom's expression had begun to alarm him. Within a few seconds, his face had taken on an almost sunken look, and his skin seemed very pale beneath the thin golden surface. "Would you like to rest for a bit? We could stop off in the park and look at the ziggurats."

"I can't go any farther," Tom said.

"What?"

"Pull over to the side of the road. You can drop me off here. I feel a little queasy. Don't worry about me. Please."

Dennis had already pulled up to the curb and stopped his car. Tom had bent over to rest his head on the dashboard.

"You don't really think I'm going to drop you off on the side of the road, do you?"

Tom rolled his head from side to side on the dashboard. The gesture seemed so childlike that Dennis stroked Tom's thick hair.

"Good, because of course I'm not. I think I'll just take you back to my place and let you lie down for a bit."

He gently helped Tom lean back to rest his head against the seat. The boy's eyes glittered and seemed without depth, like shiny painted stones.

"Let me get you home," Dennis said.

Tom very slowly shook his head, then wiped his hands over his face. "Would you take me somewhere else?"

Dennis raised his eyebrows.

"Weasel Hollow."

Tom turned his head toward Dennis, and the English teacher felt as if he were looking not at a seventeen-year-old boy overcome by a sudden illness, but a powerful adult. He reached for the ignition key and started his car again.

"Anywhere in particular in Weasel Hollow?"

"Mogrom Street."

"Mogrom Street," Dennis repeated. "Well, that makes sense. Anywhere in particular on Mogrom Street?"

Tom had closed his eyes, and appeared to be asleep.

The original native civilization and culture on Mill Walk had completely disappeared by the beginning of the eighteenth century. Its only real remains, apart from the gap-toothed natives themselves, were the two little pyramidal ziggurats in the open field that had become Goethe Park. At the base of one was inscribed the word MOGROM; at the base of the other, RAMBICHURE. Though no one now knew the meaning of these enigmatic words, they had been wholeheartedly adapted by the surviving native population. At the bottom of the narrow valley that was Weasel Hollow, Mogrom Street intersected Calle Rambichure. On opposing corners were the Mogrom Diner and Rambichure Pizza. Rambichure Hardware and Mogrom Stables and Smithy flanked Rambi-Mog Pawnbrokers. On Calle Rambichure stood the Ziggurat School for Children of Indigenous Background, the Zig-Ram Drugstore, Rambi's Hosiery, the Mogrom Adult Bookstore, and M-R Artificial Limbs.

Dennis silently drove up Calle Burleigh, turned north on Market Street and zipped past Ostend's. He came to the rise called Pforzheimer Point. Across the narrow valley the long grey shapes of the Redwing Impervious Can Company and Thielman's Sugarcane Refinery defined the opposite horizon. Weasel Hollow lay below. Tom still seemed to be drowsing. Dennis drove over the lip of the hill and down toward Mogrom.

"Well, then," Tom said. He was sitting up straight, as if a puppeteer had pulled a string attached to the top of his head. He looked impatient, even slightly feverish. Dennis felt that if he drove downhill too slowly Tom would jump out of the car.

At the foot of the hill, Mogrom Street went east to Calle Rambichure and the center of Weasel Hollow. The western half of the street led directly into a maze of tarpaper shacks, tents made of blankets suspended on poles, native houses of pink and white stone, and huts that appeared to be made of propped-up boards. Two blocks down, a large black dog lay panting in the middle of the street. Goats and chickens wandered through the yellow grass between wrecked cars and ruined pony traps. Dennis dimly heard rock and roll coming from a radio.

Tom leaned forward to examine the numbers beside the porch of a native house. "Turn right."

"You do realize, don't you, that I have no idea what's going on?"

"Just drive slowly."

Handley drove. Tom inspected the houses and hovels on his side of the street. A goat swung his head, and chickens moved jerkily through the grass. They came up an intersection with a hand-painted sign reading CALLE FRIEDRICH HASSELGARD. Two small native children with dirty faces, one of them in brown military-style shorts and carrying a toy gun, the other entirely naked, had materialized beside the sign and gazed at Dennis with a grave sober impertinence.

"Next block," Tom said.

Dennis moved slowly past the staring children. The dog lifted his head from the dust and watched them draw near. Dennis steered around it. The dog lowered its muzzle and sighed.

"Stop," Tom said. "This is it."

Dennis stopped. Tom had twisted sideways to look at a wooden shack. Waves of heat radiated up from the corrugated tin roof. It was obviously empty.

Tom opened the door and went through the tall yellow grass toward the house. Dennis expected him to look into the window beside the front door, but the boy disappeared around the side of the house. Behind the wheel of the Corvette, Dennis felt fat and hot and conspicuous. He imagined that he heard someone creeping up behind his car, but when he stuck his head through the window, it was only the dog thrashing its legs in its sleep. Dennis looked at his watch, and saw that four minutes had passed. He closed his eyes and moaned. Then he heard footsteps crackling through the brittle grass and opened his eyes to the sight of Tom Pasmore walking back toward the car.

Tom was walking very quickly, his face as closed as a fist. He folded himself in half and dropped into the other seat without looking at Dennis. "Go around the corner."

Dennis twisted the key in the ignition, lifted his foot from the clutch, and the car jerked forward.

"La Bamba" came from one of the shuttered native houses, and for a moment Dennis thought of how like paradise it would be to stretch out his legs on a couch and take a long swallow of a gin and tonic.

"Into the alley," Tom said. "Slow."

Dennis turned into the narrow walled alley; the Corvette shuddered down the narrow space between crumbling walls.

"Stop." Tom said. They had drawn up to a collapsed portion of the wall, and Tom leaned his head through the passenger window to peer into a thicket of waist-high yellow grass. "Farther," Tom said. Dennis let the car roll forward.

After a moment they came to the green doors of a one-horse stable converted into a garage. Two dusty windows covered with spiderwebs faced the narrow alley. "Here," Tom said, and jumped out of the car. He shielded his eyes to look through one of the windows. He immediately moved to the other, then back again. He straightened himself up to his full height and then covered his face with his hands.

"Is this over now?" Dennis asked.

Tom folded himself back into the car.

"I'm going to take you home," Dennis said.

"Mr. Handley, you are going to drive me around the block. We are going to go up and down every street and every alley in this part of Weasel Hollow, if that is what we have to do."

No, I'm going to take you home, Dennis said very clearly in his mind, but his mouth said, "If that's what you want," and he rolled forward to the end of the narrow alley, and turned deeper into Weasel Hollow.

At the next corner he turned right onto a street lined with shacks, rusting cars up on their rims, and a few native houses set far back on dead yellow lawns. Goats nibbled weeds in front of dwellings that were blankets slung tepee-style around leaning poles. Tom uttered a noise that sounded amazingly like a purr. Twenty yards ahead and across the street, partially obscured by a mound of garbage—tin cans, empty bottles, rotting onion peels, and slimy bits of fly-encrusted meat—was a car identical to his, so highly polished that it sparkled.

"Let me off here," Tom said. He was opening the door before Dennis came to a stop.

Tom ran toward the sleek black car and laid his hands on the hood.

For a moment—a long moment, but no more than that—Tom experienced a sensation something like déjà vu, an echo of a sensation more than the sensation itself, that he had become invisible to the ordinary physical world and had entered a realm in which every detail spoke of its true essence: as if he had slipped beneath the skin of the world. A sweet, dangerous familiarity filled him. Sweat seemed to have risen up out of every pore of his body. Tom slowly moved around to the driver's side. He bent down. A neat bullet hole half an inch wide perforated the driver's window. The driver's seat was spattered with blood. A thick film of blood covered the passenger seat.

Tom moved to the back of the car and fiddled with the trunk for a moment, then succeeded in opening it. Here, too, was a quantity of blood, though much less than on the seats. For a hallucinatory second he saw the pudgy corpse wadded into this small space. Finally he went to the passenger door, opened it, and knelt down. He ran his hands over the smooth black leather. Flakes of dried blood shredded onto the ground. Again he gently passed his fingers over the leather and near the bottom of the door touched a clump of dried fuzz stained black with blood. He delicately prodded. Beneath the shredded leather he felt a hard round nugget of metal.

Tom exhaled and stood up. His body seemed oddly light, as if it might continue to rise and leave the ground entirely. A vanishing glow momentarily touched the mound of bald tires in the front yard of the pink house across the street, also an old green sedan down the street. Tom looked toward Dennis Handley, who was wiping his forehead with a large white pocket handkerchief, and felt a goofy smile spread across his face. He began to walk toward Handley on legs that seemed immensely long. A movement where there should have been none caught his eye like a waving flag, and Tom swiveled his head to look at the green sedan parked by the opposite curb. Lamont von Heilitz leaned toward the window of its back seat. A moment of total recognition passed between them, and then the old man raised a gloved finger to his lips.

Dennis Handley drove his best and most puzzling student home in a silence that was broken only by his increasingly hesitant questions and the boy's monosyllabic answers. Tom seemed pale and exhausted during the drive, and Dennis had the odd feeling that he was saving himself for one further effort. When Dennis tried to picture the nature of this effort, he could do no better than to picture Tom Pasmore seated before an old Underwood upright—a typewriter very like the one on which he typed out his end-of-term comments—and typing with one finger upon the middle of a page of good bond the cornball motto THE CASE OF THE BLOODY CAR SEAT. In ten minutes he was turning off An Die Blumen into Eastern Shore Road, and thirty seconds after that he sat in his car and watched Tom's tall, wide-shouldered figure move up the path toward the front door of his house.

Dennis was halfway home before he realized that he was driving twenty miles an hour over the speed limit. He realized he was angry only after he had nearly run down a bicyclist.

Two weeks later Dennis met a definitely tipsy Gloria Pasmore at a dinner party at the Thielmans' and said that he didn't think there was anything to worry about. The boy was just going through some sort of adolescent phase. And, in answer to a question from Katinka Redwing, no, he had not been following any of the stories in the *Eyewitness* about Finance Minister Hasselgard—that sort of thing did not interest him at all, not at all.

10

Tom did spend the evening of that day typing on a small green Olivetti portable his parents had been persuaded to give him the year before, but what he wrote was a letter, not the awkward beginning of a detective novel. This letter was addressed to Captain Fulton Bishop, the detective named in the *Eyewitness*. He rewrote it before dinner, then rewrote it again at night. He signed the letter "A Friend."

It was nine o'clock at night when he folded the letter and sealed it inside the envelope. The telephone had rung twice while he wrote, but he had not been interrupted at his work. He had heard the back door close and the noises of a car starting up and driving away, so only one of his parents was still in the house. He thought he had a good chance of getting out without having to answer any questions, but just in case, he slid the letter into a copy of *The Lady in the Lake* and anchored the book under his arm before he left his room.

From the top of the stairs Tom saw that the lights were burning in the living room, and the doors of the room on the other side of the staircase were closed. The sound of amplified voices drifted toward him.

Tom moved quietly down the stairs. Only a few yards from the bottom, he heard the rattle of the library doorknob and unconsciously straightened up as the door opened on a wave of shouts and gunshots. His father stood outlined against a smoky, flickering pale blue background, like a figure at the mouth of a cave.

"You think I'm deaf?" his father asked. "Think I can't hear you creeping downstairs like a priest in a brothel?"

"I was just going out for a little bit."

"What the hell is there to do outside, this time of night?"

Victor Pasmore had crossed over the line between a little bit drunk and a little bit drunker, which meant moving from a sort of benevolent elation to surliness.

"I'm supposed to take this book over to Sarah Spence." He held it out toward his father, who glanced at the cover and squinted up at his son. "She asked me to bring it over once I was through with homework."

"Sarah *Spence*," his father said. "You two used to be pretty good friends."

"That was a long time ago, Dad."

"Hey—have it your way. What do I know?" He glanced back into the library, where the noises coming from the television had just increased dramatically—squealing tires and more gunshots. "I suppose you did finish your homework, huh?"

"Yes."

He chewed on some unspoken thought for a second, and looked back into the flickering blue cave. "Step in here for a second, will you? I wasn't going to say anything about this, but—"

Tom followed his father into the television room. Victor moved to the table beside his chair and picked up a half empty glass. A grinning woman holding up a container of dishwashing liquid filled the screen, and the music suddenly became much louder. Victor took several big swallows, backed into his chair, and sat down without taking his eyes off the television.

"Got a funny call a little earlier. From Lamont von Heilitz. That make any sense to you?"

Tom said nothing.

"I'm waiting, but I'm not hearing anything."

"I don't know anything about it."

"What do you suppose that old coot wanted? He hasn't called since Gloria's mother died and we moved in."

Tom shrugged. "He wanted to invite you for dinner."

"Lamont von Heilitz never invited anyone for dinner, as far as I know. He sits in that big house all day long, he changes suits to come outside and pull a dandelion out of his lawn—I know because I've seen it—and the only time I've ever known him to act like a human being was when you had that accident and he gave me books for you to read. Which did you more harm than good, in my opinion." Victor Pasmore raised his glass to his mouth and gulped, glaring at Tom over the rim as if to challenge him.

Tom was silent.

His father lowered the glass and licked his lips. "You know what they used to call him? The Shadow. Because he doesn't exist. There's something wrong with him. Some people have a bad smell that follows them around—you ought to know this, you're getting out in the world. Some day you'll have a business, kid, I know it's a shock, but you're gonna work for a living, and you'll have to know that some people it's better to avoid. Lamont von Heilitz *never worked a day in his whole life.*"

"Why did he call?"

Victor turned back to the television set. "He called to invite *you* to dinner. I told him you could make that decision for yourself. I didn't wanna tell him no straight to his face. Let a couple weeks go by, let him forget about it."

"I'll think about it," Tom said, and began moving toward the door.

"I guess you haven't been listening to me," Victor Pasmore said. "I don't want you to have anything to do with that freak. He's bad news. Your grandfather would tell you the same thing."

"I guess I better get going," Tom said.

"Keep it in your pants."

Outside in the warm humid darkness, a fat black cat named Corazon, a pet of the Langenheims', materialized beside him. "Cory, Cory, Cory," Tom crooned, and bent down to stroke the animal's silky back. The big cat pushed its heavy body against his shins. Tom scratched its wedge-shaped head, and Corazon looked up at him with uncanny yellow eyes and trotted ahead of him down the path to the sidewalk, her thick tail raised like a flag. When they reached the sidewalk the cat stood beside him for a moment in a round circle of light. Tom took a step left toward An Die Blumen, which led to The Sevens, the street on which the Spences inhabited a thirty-room Spanish extravaganza with an interior courtyard, a fountain, and a chapel that had been converted into a screening room. Corazon tilted her head, and light from the street lamp turned her eyes to transparent mystery. She began moving across the street with a gliding muscular step and disappeared into the darkness between the Jacobs's house and Mr. von Heilitz's.

Tom swallowed. He looked at the letter protruding from the book in his hand, then across the street to Mr. von Heilitz's heavily curtained windows. All evening he had seen the image of Mr. von Heilitz's pale face, swimming out at him from the back seat of a wrecked green sedan with a look of pure recognition.

Tom walked toward An Die Blumen through pools of light alternating with hour-glass shaped areas of darkness. He came to the red pillar postbox on the corner of An Die Blumen and withdrew the long white envelope from the pages of the novel. The typing on the envelope, *Captain Fulton Bishop, Central Police Headquarters, Homicide Division, Armory Place, Mill Walk, District One*, looked disturbingly adult and authoritative. Tom pushed the long envelope into the open mouth of the pillar box, pulled it part of the way out again, then pushed it into the box until his fingers touched the warm metal. Then he released the envelope, and a second later heard it fall softly on the mound of mail at the bottom of the pillar box.

In a sudden depression Tom turned around and looked down An Die Blumen to the corner of The Sevens, where an enclosed wooden telephone booth stood half-engulfed by an enormous stand of bougainvillaea. He began to walk slowly down the block.

The inside of the booth was permeated with the thick, heavy perfume of bougainvillaea. Tom hesitated only a moment, wishing that he really had been able to turn into The Sevens and ring Sarah Spence's doorbell, and then dialed the number for directory inquiries. The operator told him that there were four listings for Lamont von Heilitz. Did he want the listing on Calle Ranelagh, Eastern Shore Road, or—

"That one," he said. "Eastern Shore Road."

When he had the number, he dialed again. The phone rang twice, and a surprisingly youthful voice answered.

"Maybe I have the wrong number," Tom said. "I was trying to reach a Mr. von Heilitz."

"Is this you, Tom Pasmore?" the voice asked.

"Yes," Tom said, so softly he could scarcely hear his own voice.

"Your father seems not to want you to accept my invitation to dinner. Are you at home?"

"I'm out on the street," Tom said. "In a call box."

"The one around the corner?"

"Yes," Tom virtually whispered.

"Then I'll see you in a few seconds," said the old man's vibrant voice. He hung up.

Tom replaced the receiver on the hook. He felt intensely afraid and intensely alive.

Scent leaked from the closed-up parchment of the bougainvillaea blossoms. Geckos and salamanders scurried through the grass and flew along dark plaster walls.

Tom came to Eastern Shore Road and turned left. Down behind the houses the water washed rhythmically up on the shoreline. An enclosed horse-drawn carriage came rattling down Eastern Shore Road. The coachman wore a neat grey uniform almost invisible in the night, and the horses were matched bays with sleek muscles and arching necks. The equipage moved smoothly past Tom Pasmore, making surprisingly little sound, like an image from a dream but so secure in its reality that it made Tom feel as if he were the dream. The elegant apparition continued past the corner and rolled north down the drive toward the Redwing compound.

Light escaped in chinks and beams from the curtained windows of Lamont von Heilitz's house.

When he got to the front door of the von Heilitz house, Tom hesitated as he had before dropping the letter into the pillar box. He wanted to flee across the street and escape upstairs into his room. For a moment Tom regretted everything that had made him commandeer poor Dennis Handley and his car. At that moment, he could have given up and gone home, chosen what he already knew instead of the mystery of what he did not. At a turning point such as this, many people do turn away from what they do not know—their fear, not only of the risk, is too great. They say no. Tom Pasmore wanted to say no, but he raised his hand and knocked on the door.

Of course when he did this, he had no idea at all of what he was doing.

It opened almost immediately, as if the old man had been standing behind it, waiting for Tom to decide.

"Good," Lamont von Heilitz said. Until this moment, when his eyes met a pair of very pale blue eyes, Tom had never quite realized that the old man was nearly his own height. "Very good, in fact. Please come into my house, Tom Pasmore."

He moved out of the way, and Tom stepped inside.

For a moment he was too surprised to speak. He had expected what Eastern Shore Road defined as a domestic interior. The entry hall might have been enclosed or not, but it should have opened into a sitting room with couches, tables, and chairs, perhaps a grand piano; beyond that, there might be a less formal living room, similarly furnished. Somewhere a door would open into a grand dining room, generally lined with ancestral portraits (not necessarily of actual ancestors). Off to the side would be a door, perhaps a pocket door, into a billiard room paneled in walnut or rosewood. Another door would lead to a large modern kitchen. There might be a library with glass-enclosed books or an art gallery or even an orangery. A prominent staircase would lead up to the dressing rooms and bedrooms, and a separate, narrow staircase would go up to the servants' rooms. There would be a general impression, given by Oriental carpets, sculptures, paintings in massive ornate frames with their own indirect lighting, cushions, the right magazines, of luxury either frank or understated, of money consciously spent to attain comfort and splendor.

Lamont von Heilitz's house was nothing like this.

Tom's first impression was that he had walked into a warehouse; his second, that he was in a strange combination of furniture store, office, and library. The entry hall and most of the downstairs walls had been removed, so that the front door opened directly into a single vast room. This enormous room was filled with file cabinets, stacks of newspapers, ordinary office desks, some heaped with books, some littered with scissors and glue and cut-up newspapers. Couches and chairs stood seemingly at random in the maze of papers and cabinets and, throughout the room, old-fashioned upright lamps and low library lamps on the desks shone tiny and bright as stars, or glowed with a wide mellow illumination like the street lamps outside. At the back of the amazing room, pushed up against dark mahogany paneling, was a Sheraton dining table with a linen tablecloth and an open bottle of red Bordeaux beside a pile of books. Then Tom noticed the wall of books beside the table, and took in that at least three-fourths of the enormous room was walled with books in ceiling-high dark wooden cases. Before these walls stood high-backed library chairs or leather couches and coffee tables with green-shaded brass library lamps. Interspersed through the long sections of wall given over to bookshelves were sections of the same dark paneling as behind the dining table. Paintings glowed from these dark walls, and Tom correctly thought he identified a Monet landscape and a Degas ballet dancer. (He looked at, but did not recognize, paintings by Bonnard, Vuillard, Paul Ranson, Maurice Denis, and a drawing of flowers by Joe Brainard that in no way seemed out of place.)

Wherever he looked, he saw something new. A huge globe stood on a stand on one of the desks. An intricate bicycle leaned against a file cabinet, and a hammock had been slung between two other cabinets. To one side of it was a rowing machine. The most impressive hi-fi system Tom had ever seen in his life took up most of a huge table at the back of the room; tall speakers stood in each of the room's corners.

In something like wonder, he turned to Mr. von Heilitz, who had his arms crossed over his chest and was smiling at him. Mr. von Heilitz was wearing a pale blue linen suit with a double-breasted vest, a pale pink shirt and a dark blue silk tie, and very pale blue gloves that buttoned at his wrists. His grey hair still swept back in perfect wings at the sides of his head, but a thousand wrinkles as fine as horsehair had printed themselves into the old man's face since Tom had seen it in the hospital. Tom thought he looked wonderful and silly at the same time. Then he thought—*no, he's dignified, he doesn't look silly at all.*

He could not be other than this. This was what he was. He was—

Tom opened his mouth but found that he did not know what he wanted to say, and the fine horse-hair wrinkles around the old man's mouth and eyes etched themselves more deeply into his face. It was a smile.

"What are you?" Tom finally said.

The old man raised his chin—it was as if he had expected something better from him. "I thought you might have known, after this morning," he said. "I am an amateur of crime."

Part Four

THE SHADOW

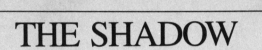

Dr. Kleber and others repeatedly emphasized the social dimensions of the treatment process. Dr. Frank H. Gawin, director of the Substance Abuse Research Unit at Yale University, put it this way: "If crack were a drug of the middle or upper classes, we would not be saying it is so impossible to treat."

Crack is the drug of choice in most poor communities, because the initial purchases are relatively cheap.

Initial Conceptions Hold Up

Still, the biochemical aspects often tend to come first in considering crack treatment, rather than its psychological, social or economic elements or the rather startling lessons of history. Detoxification, or getting the addict off the drug, either by volition, deprivation or medication, is the first and essential stage of any program that works, the experts said.

Many of the initial conceptions about crack, which has come into widespread use only within the last four years, have thus far held up:

Yes, it has a rare biochemistry that [illegible] preparing [illegible] losing drug [illegible] has been impounded [illegible] mechanical [illegible] properly [illegible] obtained with profits [illegible] It is expected that few will make the effort [illegible]

[illegible] believe that the [illegible] difference they face in treating [illegible] far more [illegible] the [illegible] and circumstances of [illegible] than the biochemic[al] [illegible] drug produces.

And they believe the new crack [illegible] society a measure [illegible] has been largely [illegible] with a drug epidemic [illegible] tearing apart poor neighborhoods and families in the nation's cities.

Researchers are finding that crack addiction, under the right conditions, can be successfully treated. Some studies suggest that crack is no more chemically addictive than other drugs that addicts have been able to beat.

Positive Shift in Emphasis

Only a year ago, crack was widely regarded as a [illegible] drug, still poorly understood, with special characteristics that rendered addiction almost impossible to treat. Now, in dozens of interviews and scientific reports, treatment experts are shifting their emphasis to the more positive, if more complex, view that addiction to the drug is treatable [illegible].

Moreover, in finding that properly run programs can be made to work in treating crack addicts, they believe they have isolated the crucial elements of those [illegible]

11

"An absurd phrase, of course," Lamont von Heilitz said to him a few minutes later. "It might be more accurate to call myself an amateur homicide detective, but I have certain objections to that phrase. I certainly cannot call myself a private detective, because I no longer accept money from clients. The only sort of crime that interests me is murder. I can't deny that my interest is quite intense—a passion, in fact—but it is a private passion—"

Tom sipped from a Coca-Cola the old man had poured into a crystal glass, so exquisite it was nearly weightless, etched with gauzy images of women in flowing robes.

Mr. von Heilitz was leaning forward slightly in one of the chairs around the massive table. His back was very straight, and he was twirling in the gloved fingers of his right hand the stem of a wine glass etched like Tom's goblet. "You're something like me, you know," he said in his incongruously vibrant voice. His eyes seemed very kind. "Do you remember seeing me, when you were a child? I don't mean the times I chased you and the other ruffians off my lawn, though I ought to tell you, I suppose, that I couldn't afford—"

"To have us look in your windows," Tom said, suddenly understanding.

"Exactly."

"Because we would talk about—well, about all this after we got home." Tom paused. "And you probably thought that you . . ."

Von Heilitz waited for him to finish. When Tom did not complete his sentence, he said, "That my reputation was already peculiar enough?"

"Something like that," Tom said.

Mr. von Heilitz smiled back at him. "Doesn't it seem to you that much of what people call intelligence is really sympathetic imagination? And that sympathetic imagination virtually . . . ? Well, in any case, you know why I became the neighborhood grouch." He lifted his wine glass, glanced at Tom, and sipped. "I am still curious as to whether you remember the first time I saw you—really saw you. It took place on a significant day for you."

Tom nodded. "You came to the English hospital. And you brought books." Now Tom grinned. "Sherlock Holmes. And the Poe novel, *Murders in the Rue Morgue*."

"There was an earlier time, but that's not important now." Before Tom could question him about this statement, he said, "And of course we saw each other this morning. You know who shot Miss Hasselgard?"

"Her brother."

Mr. von Heilitz nodded. "And of course she was sitting in the passenger seat of his Corvette when he killed her."

"And he put her body in the trunk because he had to drive to Weasel Hollow, and she was so big that otherwise everybody who looked at the car would have seen her," Tom said. "He was born in Weasel Hollow, wasn't he?"

"How did you work that out?"

"The *Eyewitness*," Tom said. "I really knew it all along, but this afternoon, I remembered that one of the articles said that he had gone to—"

"The Ziggurat School. Very good."

"Who was the woman who hid the money for him?"

"She was his aunt."

"I suppose Hasselgard stole—what do you call it, embezzled the money, or took it as a bribe—"

"We don't know yet. But my feeling is that it was a bribe."

"—and Marita learned about it—"

"She must have actually *seen* him take the money, because she felt she had a claim on it."

"—and she demanded half of it or something, and he told her to get into his car—"

"Or she got into it, demanding that he take her to the money."

"And he leaned in the driver's window and shot her in the head. He rolled up the driver's window and shot through it to make it look as if Marita had been behind the wheel. Then he put her body in the trunk and drove to the native district. He abandoned his car and made his way home. And a week later, the old lady was killed for the money."

"And the same money is confiscated by the government of Mill Walk, which turns it over to Friedrich Hasselgard, the Minister of Finance."

"What were you waiting for, this morning?" Tom asked.

"To see who would come. In the best of all worlds, Finance Minister Hasselgard would have appeared, and dug the first bullet out of the door with a pocket knife."

"What would you have done, if he had?"

"Watched him."

"I mean, would you have gone to the police then?"

"No."

"You wouldn't even have written the police about what you knew?"

Mr. von Heilitz tilted his head and looked at Tom in a way that made him uncomfortable—it had too many shades and meanings, and it went straight through him to his deepest secrets. "You wrote to Fulton Bishop, didn't you?"

Tom was surprised to see Mr. von Heilitz now looking at him with undisguised impatience.

"What? What's wrong?"

"What did your father tell you about me? When he said that I'd called? He must have warned you off."

"Well . . . he did, yes. He said that it might be better to

avoid you. He said you were bad luck. And he said that you used to be called the Shadow."

"Because of my first name, of course."

Tom, who was trying to figure out why the old man was irritated, looked blank.

"Lamont Cranston?"

Tom raised his eyebrows.

"My God." Mr. von Heilitz sighed. "Back in pre-history, a fictional character named Lamont Cranston was the hero of a radio series called 'The Shadow.' *That* was my bad luck, if you like. But what your father was talking about is something else."

The old man sipped his wine, and again regarded Tom with what looked like irritated impatience. "When I was twelve years old, both of my parents were murdered. Butchered, really. I came home from school and found their bodies. My father was lying dead in this room. He had been shot several times, and there was a tremendous amount of blood. As well as what is still probably called 'gore.' I found my mother near the back door, in the kitchen. She had obviously been trying to escape. I thought she might still be alive, and I rolled her body over. Suddenly my hands were red with blood. She had been shot in the chest and the stomach. Until I rolled her over and saw what they had done to her, I hadn't even noticed all the blood on the floor."

"Did they ever find who did it?"

"*I* found out who did it, years later. When this house was closed, I went to live with an aunt and uncle while the police investigated my parents' murders. I don't suppose you knew that my father was David Redwing's Minister of Internal Affairs after Mill Walk became independent? He was an important man. Not as important as David Redwing, but important all the same. So a vigorous investigation took place. It went nowhere, and its failure was an ongoing sorrow. As if in recompense for the inability of the police to solve his murder, my father was posthumously awarded the Mill Walk Medal of Merit. I have it in a desk drawer somewhere over there—I could show it to you." He was staring off into some internal space now, not looking at Tom at all.

"I waited nearly ten years," he finally continued. "I inherited this house and everything in it. After I graduated from

Harvard, I came back here to live. I had enough money not to have to worry about it for the rest of my life. I wondered what I was going to do. I could have gone into business. If I had been a different sort of person, I could have gone into local politics. My father was a local martyr, after all. But I had another purpose, and I set about it. Almost immediately I discovered that the police had learned very little. So I turned to the only sources I had, the public record. I obtained a complete file of the *Eyewitness*. I examined *everything*—property transfers, land deals, steamship arrivals, court records, death notices. I had so much material that I had to alter the house in order to be able to store it all. I was looking for patterns that no one else had seen. And, after three years, I began to find them. It was the most tedious and frustrating work I had ever done, but also the most satisfying. I felt that I was *saving my own life*. Eventually I was concentrating on a single man—a man who had come and gone from Mill Walk many times, a former member of our secret police who went into retirement when the secret police were disbanded. He had houses here and in Charleston. I went to Charleston and followed him. The man who had murdered my father and mother seemed ordinary—he might have been a property developer who had made enough money to devote all his time to golf. I had thought I might kill him, but found that I was no murderer. I came back to Mill Walk and presented my research to the Secretary of Internal Defense, Gonzalo Redwing, who had been a friend of my father's. A week later, the murderer returned to Mill Walk to attend a charity function, and the militia arrested him on the dock at Mill Key. He was jailed, tried, convicted, and eventually executed on the gallows at the Long Bay prison compound."

Mr. von Heilitz turned to Tom with an expression the boy could not read at all. "It should have been a moment of triumph for me. I had found out who I was. I had discovered my life's work. I was an amateur detective—an amateur of crime. But my triumph almost immediately did worse than go sour. It turned into disgrace. During the months between his arrest and execution, the man I had found never stopped talking. He implicated my father in his own murder."

"How could he do that?" Tom asked.

"I don't mean he said that my father wanted to be killed,

but that he was executed. According to this man, my father had participated in certain arrangements that were set up just around the time of Mill Walk's independence. He was an active partner in these arrangements. The arrangements had to do with the sugar revenues, with the way tax revenues were handled, with the bidding on road construction and garbage disposal, with water allocations, the banks, with certain fundamental structures that were set up at that time. There were irregularities, and my father was deeply involved in them. According to the murderer, my father had ceased to be cooperative. He wanted a disproportionate share of all these fundamental arrangements. And so this man had been hired to kill him. It was supposed to look like a robbery."

"But who was supposed to have hired him?"

"He never knew. He was given instructions through a Personals ad in the *Eyewitness*, and money was paid into his Swiss bank account. Of course the implication was that the highest officials in Mill Walk were involved, and the more he said, the more the public was outraged—he was obviously clouding the issue, trying to take the spotlight off himself and blame everybody else. The secret police were suspect anyhow, and had been disbanded shortly after independence. When this man's record was made public, even those who had thought there might be something to his charges turned against him. His own stories counted against him, in the end. I myself had a certain amount of fame, as the one who had led to his arrest."

"Then why . . . ?"

"Why did I end up living like this? Why do I object to your writing to Captain Bishop?"

"Yes," Tom said.

"First of all, I'd like to know if you signed the letter."

Tom shook his head.

"It was an anonymous letter? Good boy. Don't be surprised if nothing is done. You know what you know, and that is enough."

"But after the police read the letter, they at least have to look at the car more carefully, instead of just taking Hasselgard's story as fact. And when they find the bullet, they'll know that Hasselgard's story wasn't the truth."

"Captain Bishop already knows it wasn't," said the old man.

"I don't believe that."

"I discovered, soon after the execution of my father's murderer, that except for one detail the man had been telling the truth all along. My father's death had been ordered by the highest levels of our government. Corruption was a fact of life on Mill Walk."

"Well, that was a long time ago," Tom said.

"Nearly fifty years ago. There have been many, many changes on Mill Walk since then. But the Redwings still exert a large influence."

"They're not even in government anymore," Tom protested. "They just do business. They're social. Half of them are too wild to do anything but race cars and throw parties, and the other half is so respectable they don't do anything but go to church and clip coupons."

"Such are our leaders," the old man said, smiling. "We will see what happens."

A few minutes later Lamont von Heilitz stood up from the table, and walked into the maze of files. Tom heard the opening of a metal drawer. "Have you ever been to Eagle Lake, in Wisconsin?" he called to Tom, who could just see the top of his silvery head over a stack of papers atop an iron-grey cabinet.

"No, I haven't," Tom called back.

"You may be interested in this." He reappeared with a large leather-bound book under his arm. "I own a lodge in Eagle Lake—it was my parents', of course. We spent our summers 'up north,' as Mill Walk says, all during my boyhood, and after I had returned from Harvard I used the lodge for a number of years." He put the thick book down on the table before Tom and leaned over his shoulder. His index finger rested on the book's wide brown cover, and when Tom looked he saw that the old man was smiling. "The way you've been talking—the way I can see that you feel—all of that, even though you haven't said half of what's been going through your head—reminded me of this case. It must have been the third or fourth time I used my methods to discover the identity of a murderer, and it was one of the first times I made the results of my investigations public. As you will see."

"How many cases have you investigated?" Tom suddenly wanted to know.

Von Heilitz lifted his hand from the book and put it on Tom's shoulder. "I've lost count now. Something over two hundred, I think."

"Two hundred! How many of those did you solve?"

The old detective did not answer the question directly. "I once spent a very interesting year in New Orleans, looking into the poisoning deaths of a series of prominent businessmen. I was poisoned myself, in fact, but had taken the precaution of supplying myself with a good supply of the antidote." He nearly laughed out loud at the expression on Tom's face. "I regret to say that the antidote did not save me from an extremely uncomfortable week in the hospital."

"Was that the only time you were injured?"

"I was shot once—in the shoulder—and shot at four times. A bear of a man in Norway, Maine, broke my right arm when he found me photographing a Mercedes-Benz that was up on blocks in a shed out behind his house. Two men have cut or stabbed me with knives, one in a native house a block from where we saw each other in Weasel Hollow and the other in a motel called The Crossed Keys in Bakersfield, California. I was beaten up seriously only once, by a man who jumped me from behind in an alley off Armory Place, near police headquarters. But in Fort Worth, Texas, a state senator who had killed nearly a dozen prostitutes nearly killed me too, by hitting me in the back of my head with a hammer. He fractured my skull, but I was out of the hospital in time to see him hanged."

He patted Tom's shoulder. "It's a sorry calling at times, I fear."

"Have you ever killed anyone?"

"The only man I ever had to kill was the one who broke my arm. That was in 1941. The end of every investigation brings a depression, but that one was my worst. I came back to Mill Walk with my arm in a cast, and I refused to answer my phone or go out of this house for two months. I scarcely ate. I suppose it was a kind of breakdown. In the end I checked myself into a clinic, and stayed there another two months. 'Why do you always wear gloves?' the doctors asked me. 'Is the world so dirty?' 'I'm at least as dirty as the world,' I remember saying; 'maybe I want to keep from contaminating it, instead of the other way around.' I can remember catching sight of my face in the mirror one day and being shocked by what I saw—I saw an adult, the person I had become. Soon my depression began to lift. I came back here. I found that I was refusing many more cases on the mainland than I accepted. After a while, my reputation wasn't even a dim memory, and I was free to live as I wished." He took his hand from Tom's shoulder and pulled back his chair. "And some years ago, I saw you in an unexpected place. And I knew that we would meet some day and have this conversation."

He sat down, with an old man's briskness, on his chair. "I wanted to show you the first pages in this book, and instead I talked your ear off. Let's take a look at this before you fall asleep."

Tom had never felt less sleepy. He looked at Lamont von Heilitz sitting a yard away from him with his eyebrows raised and his gloved fingers just opening the big leather journal. The old man looked drawn and noble, the refinement of his face starker than ever in the soft light, the grey wing of hair on the side of his head glowing silver. Tom realized that he was looking at *the real thing*. Seated a yard away from him, slightly imperious and slightly ravaged, more than slightly diminished by age, was a great detective, the actuality behind literally thousands of novels, movies, and stage plays. He did not raise orchids, inject a seven percent solution of cocaine, or say things like "Archons of Athens!" He was an old man who seldom left his father's house. All Tom's life, he had lived across the street.

The book, a more elegant version of his scrapbook, lay open on the table. Tom read the huge headline on the left-hand page. MILLIONAIRE SUMMER RESIDENT DISAPPEARS FROM HOME. Beneath the headline ran the subhead: *Jeanine Thielman, Mill Walk Figure, Last Seen Friday.* Beneath this was a grainy picture of a blond woman in a fur coat stepping down from a coach-and-four. A diamond necklace glittered at her throat, and her hair was swept back from her forehead. She looked sleek, rich, and powerful, stepping down from the platform with a long, outstretched leg. Her smile for the camera was a grimace of willed artifice. Tom understood immediately that the woman had been photographed arriving at a charity ball. She reminded him of his mother, in old photographs taken when she had been Gloria Upshaw, a member of Mill Walk's Junior League.

Tom looked at the name and date of the newspaper—the *Eagle Lake Gazette* of June 17, 1925.

"The seventeenth of June was the day after I arrived in Eagle Lake that year. Jeanine Thielman, who was the first wife of our neighbor's father, Arthur Thielman, had disappeared during the night of the fifteenth. Arthur found her missing when he looked into her bedroom in the morning, sent a messenger around to the other lodges, including the Redwing compound, to see if she had been visiting one of her friends, found that no one had seen her since a dinner party at the senior Langenheims' the night before, and waited through all of the sixteenth before riding over to the police station in the town of Eagle Lake. See? It looks like nothing more than newspaper hysteria over a rich woman. People gossiped about this young couple sleeping in separate bedrooms."

Mr. von Heilitz pointed to the page on the left-hand side of the big journal. "This is the day I arrived. I found Arthur Thielman sitting on my porch furniture with a big setter bitch lying beside him. He'd heard I was due, and told his servants he was going to take his dog out for a walk. Arthur was a rude man, and he started telling me I had to help find his wife even before I got out of my carriage." MYSTERY DEEPENS, the big headline read. "Told me I had to stop off in Miami, where they had an apartment, before going back to Mill Walk. I was not to tell anyone what I was doing. He thought the Eagle Lake police were incompetent, but he didn't want anyone to know he'd hired me. *'You're the Shadow, aren't you?'* Arthur said—he was trying not to yell. *'I want you to behave like a goddamned shadow. Just find her and report back to me. I want this thing to die down quickly.'* He'd pay me anything I wanted. Then he astonished me—he apologized for ruining my vacation. I told him I wasn't interested in his money, but that I would see what I could do from Eagle Lake. He wasn't very satisfied with that, but in the end he was grateful—so I got the feeling that he thought that she might be somewhere in the area, after all. At any rate, by that point he regretted having panicked and gone to the police. Because of these headlines, he was a prisoner in his lodge—he couldn't show his face at the club, and he was sick of talking only to his servants and the local constable."

Tom looked at a photograph of Arthur Thielman standing

beside his lodge, a rustic building with porches on two levels. Arthur Thielman was a corpulent, aggressive-looking man in a tweed jacket and high muddy boots. His rigid, Victorian face bore only the smallest resemblance to that of his son, now the Pasmores' middle-aged neighbor.

"Two days later, Kathleen Duffield, a girl from Atlanta who was being groomed to marry Ralph Redwing's cousin Jonathan, caught her hook on something in the marshy, north end of the lake. Jonathan wanted to cut the line and move to more promising territory—nobody ever fished the north end. Kate just thought it looked pretty up there, I gather. Anyhow, the girl kept on pulling, and eventually Jonathan jumped over the side to prove to his fiancée that all she'd hooked was a sunken rowboat. He followed the line underwater and found that she had snagged her hook on a clump of weeds. Not far away, halfway down a drop-off, he saw a rolled up length of old curtain fabric. He swam over to look at it. When he lifted the fabric, Jeanine Thielman's body rolled out of it. She had been shot in the back of the head."

Von Heilitz flipped over the page, and two new headlines blared out at Tom: JEANINE THIELMAN FOUND IN LAKE and LOCAL MAN CHARGED WITH THIELMAN MURDER. Pictures showed three policemen in lace-up boots and Sam Browne belts standing on a pier beneath a rear view of the Thielman lodge; a long slack thing beneath a sheet; an owl-eyed man moving down a corridor surrounded by policemen.

Tom thought: That's what Eagle Lake looks like. He had a flash of Sarah Spence breaking the surface of the grey water, her hair streaming down her shoulders and her eyes gleeful. Then he felt that he had seen all of this before, in some dreamtime before his accident: the very shape of the letters was familiar to him.

"The man they arrested, Minor Truehart, was a half-Winnebago guide who baited hooks and found bass for half a dozen families on the lake, including the Thielmans. He lived in a cabin near the lake with his wife and kids. He stayed sober until about noon, and after that the summer residents found him either annoying or amusing, but hiring him was a kind of tradition. Apparently he had some kind of disagreement with Jeanine Thielman the day before she disappeared—he turned up smelling of whiskey, she ordered him off, he claimed to be able to work just fine, and she blew her top. They were on the Thielman pier, and lots of people heard her screaming at him. Truehart eventually gave up and loped off. He claimed that he couldn't remember what happened during the rest of the day, and that he woke up in the woods about five o'clock the next morning, with a godalmighty hangover. The police searched his cabin and found a long-barreled Colt revolver under the bed, which they sent off to the state lab for examination."

"Was it his gun?" Tom asked.

"He said he had a gun, but that wasn't it. He recognized it, though—he had sold it, he said, to old Judge Backer, a widower who came up to Eagle Lake for two weeks every summer and enjoyed target shooting. His wife said that a lot of guns came in and out of the house. Her husband made a little money dealing in them, looking out for special items for the gun collectors among the summer people. She didn't recognize that one."

Tom considered for a moment. "Did she remember the names of any of his gun customers?"

Lamont von Heilitz leaned back in his chair and gave Tom an almost paternal smile. "I'm afraid that Minor Truehart was the sort of husband who never tells his wife anything. But of course I thought about what might have happened to Judge Backer's gun, all the more so when the Judge denied the entire story. He had never illegally purchased a weapon from anyone, of course. If it could be proved that he had, he could have lost his seat on the bench. I found myself wondering how likely it was that a drunken guide, enraged by the behavior of a customer's wife, would shoot her in the back of the head."

"What did you do?" Tom asked.

"I spoke to Judge Backer and his valet, Wendell Hasek, a boy from the west side of the island. I talked to people at the club. I went to the offices of the *Eagle River Gazette* and looked very closely at issues from earlier in the summer. I spoke to the local sheriff, who knew my name from the publicity about the few cases I had worked on. I had a long talk with Arthur Thielman."

"He did it," Tom said. "He stole the gun from the Judge's lodge, shot his wife, rowed her body out to the end of the lake nobody ever used, and dropped her in. Then he framed the guide by sneaking into his cabin and hiding the gun. He probably tore down one of his own curtains and used it to wrap up the body."

"Think about my situation," the old man said, ignoring this. "It was a year after I had seen my parents' murderer executed. I had almost inadvertently solved a very minor case several months before—I had noticed a detail, nothing more, a question of the shoes a certain man had worn on the day of the murder—which added to my reputation, but left me feeling flat and dull. I had gone to Eagle Lake to forget the world, and to try to plan what I might do for the rest of my life. And here this murder is thrust in my face from the moment I reached my lodge, in the person of the unpleasant Arthur Thielman, sitting on my porch with his huge dog, seething with impatience, all willing to buy my time and attention, to buy me, in fact. . . ." *'You're the Shadow, aren't you?'* I wished I *were* a shadow, so I could slip by him and lock him out of my house! I was so exhausted I said I'd help him just so he'd leave me alone. I thought it was very likely that she had simply run away from him. As soon as I had had a good night's rest, I determined to have nothing to do with either of the Thielmans. I would ignore the entire matter."

"But then the body was discovered," Tom said.

"And the guide was arrested. And Arthur Thielman told me that he did not want my services anymore. I was to stop going around talking to all these people. He seemed particularly distressed that I'd spoken to Wendell Hasek, the Judge's valet."

"I told you," Tom said. "He wanted to get rid of you. He was afraid of what you'd discover."

"In a way. Remember my saying that I had a feeling he thought she might be somewhere in the Eagle Lake area, after all?"

"Of course. He knew she was deep in the lake, rolled up in an old curtain."

The old man smiled and coughed into his fist. "Perhaps. It's an intelligent supposition, in any case."

Tom felt enormously complimented.

"Remember that he saw me as a kind of private detective, one unaccountably of his own class. He would not want to admit to any stranger that his wife had probably run away from him.

And when she was found murdered, that put an end to that embarrassment—he didn't need me to save him from it anymore. And he certainly wished no deeper embarrassment."

"Wait a second," Tom said. "What deeper embarrassment? He killed her."

"I said that I wanted you to think about my situation, and I want you now to consider my state of mind. Once the body had been discovered, I noticed a change in everything about me. I could say that I had become more alert, more involved in things, or that Eagle Lake had become more interesting. But it was much more than that. Eagle Lake had become more *beautiful.*"

Tom wanted to shake him. "How did you get him to confess?"

"Listen to me. The solution is not what I am talking about here. I am describing a sudden change in my most basic feelings. When I walked beside my lodge and looked at the lake and the lodges scattered around it, at the docks, at the pilings outside the Redwing compound, the tall Norway pines and enormous oaks, it all seemed—charged. Every bit of it *spoke* to me. Every leaf, every pine needle, every path through the woods, every bird call, had come alive, was vibrant, full of meaning. Everything *promised.* Everything *chimed.* I knew more than I knew. There was a secret beating away beneath the surface of everything I saw."

"Yes," Tom said, not knowing why this raised goose bumps on his arms.

"Yes," the old man said. "You have it too. I don't know what it is—a capability? A calling?"

Tom suddenly realized why Lamont von Heilitz always wore gloves, and nearly blurted it out.

Von Heilitz saw Tom looking at his hands, and folded his hands before him on the table. "I rode over to Judge Backer's lodge, and saw Wendell Hasek tinkering with the Judge's coupe. Hasek was no more than eighteen, and he began to look guilty the second he saw me—he didn't want to lose his job, and he was afraid of what I might get out of him."

"What did you do?" Tom asked, unable not to look at the old man's hands in their neat blue gloves, unable not to see blood on the hands of the boy the old man had been.

"I told him that I already knew that Truehart had sold the long-barreled Colt to his boss, and that the Judge had given it to Arthur Thielman for some reason. I just wanted to know the reason. I promised him—not entirely forthrightly—that the Judge's ownership of the gun would never become public knowledge.

" 'No one will know about the Judge?' he asked me. 'No one will know I told you?' 'No one,' I said. 'Judge Backer wanted to get rid of that gun,' Hasek said. 'Fired off to the left. Made him madder than a hornet that a halfbreed got good money for a bad gun. So he sold it to Mr. Thielman, who's such a bad shot he doesn't know enough to blame the gun.' "

"Okay!" Tom said. "You had him!" He began to laugh. "Arthur Thielman was such a bad shot he had to sneak up behind his wife and put the barrel two inches from her head to be sure of hitting her at all!"

The old man smiled. "Arthur Thielman wasn't his wife's murderer, but the real killer would not have been at all unhappy to have me think he was. The murderer knew that he had furnished Arthur with one of the most traditional motives for murder." His smile deepened at the expression on Tom's face. "Jeanine had not only been unfaithful to her husband, but her lover thought that she was going to leave Arthur for him. And Arthur thought she had left him—he thought she had run off with the other man."

For the second time that night, Tom was too surprised to speak. At length he said, "That was the deeper embarrassment you were talking about?"

Von Heilitz nodded. "So all I had to do was learn which of the men visiting Eagle Lake that summer had been away from the lake on the day of Jeanine's disappearance. I went back to the Truehart cabin to see if anyone had canceled a date with the guide. If that didn't work, I intended to question the other two or three men who worked as guides for the summer people, but I didn't have to go any further. Minor's wife worked as a cleaning woman for most of the same people her husband guided. On the sixteenth of June, she had two cleaning jobs. She went to the first lodge at eight in the morning, but the man who lived there didn't get up to answer the door. She thought he must have been sleeping off a heavy night, and went through the woods to the second job, where she cleaned house until about two in the afternoon. Then she returned to the first house. Again, no one answered her knock—no one came even when she called out. She decided that he had left for town, or some other destination, without bothering to tell her that he wouldn't be home. She scribbled a note that she would be back the next day, and walked back through the woods to her cabin. When she came back on the seventeenth, he opened the door to her, saying that he was very sorry but that he'd had to take a sudden business trip to Hurley, a larger town about twenty miles south. He'd taken the six-thirty train, and hadn't returned until after nightfall. He paid her double for the day, and asked her not to mention his absence to any of her other customers—his business involved a real estate matter that he wanted kept secret."

"But if he was going to run away with her and killed her instead, why did he leave by himself?"

"He hadn't gone anywhere. Arthur Thielman just thought he had. Mrs. Truehart found two empty whiskey bottles in his trash, another half-empty on the kitchen counter, and the remains of several packs of Lucky Strikes in the wastebaskets. He'd holed up in his lodge, drinking himself into a stupor. She was told to stay out of the guest room, and she thought he must have had some woman's belongings in there that he didn't want her to see. He was a sentimental man. He shot his lover in the back of the head when she refused to leave with him, and then spent the rest of the night and the next day mourning her. Sentimentality is a mask for violence."

"Who was he? What was his name?"

"Anton Goetz."

Tom felt a decided letdown. "I've never heard of him."

"I know you haven't, but he was an interesting figure—a German who had come to Mill Walk some fifteen years earlier and made a lot of money. He bought into the St. Alwyn Hotel, and then developed some tracts of land on the west side of the island. He never married. Excellent manners. Good stories—most of them entirely invented, I think. He built that huge Spanish house around the corner, on The Sevens. The Spence house. I've always thought that it revealed the man very exactly—all that grandiosity, the sort of overreaching quality of the house." He took in Tom's expression again, and quickly added, "Perhaps you think it's beautiful. It is rather beautiful, in its way. And of course we're all used to it now."

"Did you have any proof against Goetz?"

"Well, I had the curtain, of course. He would have been caught sooner or later, because he'd had his lodge decorated that spring, just after he began his affair with Jeanine Thielman. The old curtains were stored in one of the outbuildings next to his lodge. Until she refused to leave with him, Goetz had imagined that she would get divorced and marry him, and that they would return to Mill Walk and live as a couple. Jeanine may have gone along with this fantasy, but she never took it seriously."

"But how did you know they were having an affair? Just because the cleaning woman didn't get into his house?"

"Aha! One night the previous summer, I went into the club late, and met Jeanine rushing down the stairs from the bar in the dining room. She didn't say anything to me, just went past me with an embarrassed smile. When I got upstairs, I saw Goetz at the bar by himself, in front of two glasses and an ashtray full of cigarettes. He told me a story about having met her there by accident, which I took at face value. But for the rest of that summer, I never saw the two of them saying anything at all to each other in public. They even went out of their way to avoid being seen together in public, and I wouldn't have suspected anything at all if it hadn't been for that one time when they had clearly spent an hour or two together. So it seemed to me that they were doing everything they could not to attract suspicion, and of course it had the opposite effect on me."

He stood up and began pacing with slow strides back and forth alongside the table. "There was a party scheduled at the Eagle Lake Club the night after I spoke to Mrs. Truehart. Of course it had been canceled, but a lot of people were planning to stop in there anyhow to talk things over, have a few drinks, that sort of thing. More from the lack of anything better to do than anything else. I walked over to the club about six in the evening, and I was still in the grip of that feeling I described—of a kind of radiance of significance shining through everything I saw. But when I went to the upstairs bar and saw Anton Goetz on the terrace, what I mainly felt was sorrow. Goetz had been taking his meals home for a few days, staying out of sight. He was sitting at a table with Maxwell Redwing, David's son, and some of the younger Redwing cousins. Maxwell was the Redwing patriarch of those days—the one who really took the family out of public life. He was something like your grandfather, in fact.

"To tell the truth, I don't know if my sorrow was for poor Goetz, who looked flushed and hectic and was obviously struggling to resemble his old self in the midst of this attractive crowd, or for myself, because it was all coming to an end. I went to the end of the bar and ordered a drink. I stared at Goetz until he looked up and noticed me. I nodded, and he looked away. I kept on staring at him—it seemed to me that I could see his entire life. Everything, all the emotions and excitement that had swirled around me in the past few days, had come down to this one wretched human being, who was trying to ingratiate himself with Maxwell Redwing. He kept looking up, seeing me, and turning away to gulp his drink.

"At last Goetz excused himself and stood up. He walked across the terrace and stood beside me at the bar,, fidgeting. He was waiting for me to say something. When he pulled out one of his Luckies, I lit it for him. He exhaled and took a step backward. 'What's your game, sport?' he finally asked me.

" 'You are,' I said. 'You don't have a chance. Even if I hadn't figured it out, sooner or later someone would start to think about that length of curtain. They'd check to see if you ever took that train to Hurley. There'll be someone who saw you and Jeanine together. They'll examine your boat, and they'll find threads from the carpet, or a bloodstain, or one of Jeanine's hairs . . .'

"His face had gone bright red. He looked back out at the veranda, toward that group of chattering Redwing cousins. He literally straightened his back. Then he asked me what I intended to do. I said that I wanted to take him into town, and get Minor Truehart out of jail as soon as possible. 'You really are the Shadow, aren't you?' he asked me. Then he turned toward me so his back would be to the veranda. He leaned forward to whisper, and his face was already pleading. 'Give me one more night,' he said. 'I won't try to get away. I just want to have one last night here at Eagle Lake.' He was a sentimentalist, you see. I told him I'd give him until nightfall."

"Why until nightfall? Why give him any time at all?"

"Well, it might sound funny, but I wanted to give him some

time to think about things while he was still a free man. Only he and I knew what he had done, and that changed everything for both of us. If I gave him only the hour or two until nightfall, I could make sure that he didn't escape after it got dark. I intended to keep watch on his house, of course. So I agreed. I left the club and trotted home, ran down to my dock, untied my boat, and started across the lake. I thought my little outboard motor could get me to Goetz's dock before he got home. When I was in the middle of the lake, someone took a shot at me."

Tom opened his mouth in surprise, imagining himself out in the middle of a lake while Anton Goetz fired at him with a rifle.

"The shot hit the water about a foot from the dinghy. I cursed myself for letting him go and lay down in the bottom of the boat, soaking my clothes. A second later, there was another shot, and this one struck the side of the dinghy and went straight through to the bottom of the boat, about an inch from my head. I scrunched backwards, but I didn't dare lift my head for another minute or so. I was going around and around in a big circle. Finally I dared lift my head again and steered toward Goetz's dock, while still more or less lying down in the boat. At the dock I killed the motor and jumped out—the boat was about one-quarter full of water, and I just left it to fill up and sink. I ran up to the house, knowing that I'd made a terrible fool of myself—not only had he nearly killed me, but he had obviously managed to get away. I had to admit what I'd done and persuade the police to start looking for him. By the time I got to a telephone, Goetz could have been twenty miles away.

"But he hadn't gone anywhere. His door was wide open. I rushed in and threw myself on the floor, just in case he was waiting for me. Then I heard something dripping onto the wooden floor. I looked up and saw him. He was hanging from one of the crossbeams in his living room, with a length of high-test fishing line around his neck that had nearly taken his head off."

"He could have killed you!" Tom said.

"The funny thing was, he hadn't even stolen the Colt from Arthur Thielman. It was lying on a table outside near the Thielmans' dock the night Goetz thought he and Jeanine were going to run off. When she told him she had no intention of leaving her husband and turned away to go back inside, he picked it up and shot her in the back of the head. The next day, he thought that he could put the blame on Minor Truehart, and after Truehart's wife left his house to do her next job, he went out through the woods, dead drunk, to their cabin, and threw it under the bed. Arthur Thielman was careless with everything, including his wife and his weapons."

"Then who shot at you? It must have been Goetz."

Mr. von Heilitz smiled at Tom, then knitted his fingers behind the back of his head and yawned. "Your grandfather's lodge was about forty yards to the left of the Thielmans'. About the same distance to the right, in the direction of the club, was the boundary of the Redwing compound. This was only a year after I had exposed my parents' murderer, who had spoken at great length about corruption on Mill Walk. Of course, it might have been Goetz. He could have fired at me, tossed the rifle into the lake, and then hanged himself. But Goetz was a very good shot—from at least thirty feet away, he killed Jeanine with a pistol that pulled badly to the left."

He turned to the next page of the scrapbook. MYSTERY RESOLVED IN TRAGEDY read the banner across the top of the *Eagle Lake Gazette*. Two single-column articles on either side were headed GUIDE TRUEHART RELEASED TO SOBBING WIFE, CHILDREN and SHADOW STRIKES AGAIN! In the middle of the page was a two-column picture of a strikingly handsome man with wide-set clear eyes and a dark little gigolo's mustache above the caption *Killer Anton Goetz Confessed to Private Sleuth Minutes Before Grisly Suicide*. Beside this was another, smaller photograph, of a slim young man in a Norfolk jacket and a plaid shirt with an open collar. The young man looked as if he wished the photographer would point his camera at some more willing object. The caption beneath this photograph was *Twenty-five-Year-Old Amateur Detective von Heilitz, Known as "The Shadow," Seeks to Avoid Publicity*. Tom stared at the picture of the young man his neighbor had been, once again struck by the dreamlike familiarity of the page. MYSTERY. RESOLVED. TRAGEDY. Connected to these words, as to so much of his childhood, was the image of his mother locked into her encompassing misery.

The young Lamont von Heilitz had worn his hair shorter, though not as short as was the fashion at Brooks-Lowood School at the end of the 1950s, but the high cheekbones and intelligent, thin hawk's face was the same. What was different was the sense of taut nerves and tension that came from the young man's face and posture: he looked like a human seismograph, a person whose extreme sensitivity made much of ordinary daily life a nearly intolerable affair.

Tom looked up into the older face, affectionately regarding him from the other side of the big journal, and felt as if he had been given some enigmatic clue about his own life—some insight he had just failed to catch.

"I'll let you borrow that, if you like," von Heilitz said. "We've spent a lot of time together, and too much of it was spent with your being polite while I indulged myself with old memories. Next time, it's your turn to talk."

He slammed the old journal shut, picked it up with both hands and offered it to Tom, who took it gladly.

They moved toward the door through the aisles of the crowded room. Tom had one more question, which he asked as von Heilitz opened his front door.

Before him was the familiar world of Eastern Shore Road, almost a surprise: Tom had been so engrossed in the story of Jeanine Thielman and Anton Goetz that, without knowing it, he had half-expected to find a starry woods of Norway spruce and tall oak trees beyond the door, a wide blue lake and paths between big lodges with porches and balconies. "You know," Tom said, realizing that he was not after all asking a question, "I don't think 'The Shadow' was on the radio in 1925. I bet they named that program after you."

Lamont von Heilitz smiled and closed the door. Tom looked at his watch. It was nearly eleven o'clock. He walked back across the street in the darkness.

12

Without quite knowing that a new era of his life had begun, Tom lay on his bed until one o'clock, flipping through the thick leather-bound journal. Columns of newsprint from different newspapers covered each page. There were headlines from New Orleans, from California, from Chicago and Seattle. Sometimes the articles concerned the murders of prominent people, sometimes those of prostitutes, gamblers, homeless wanderers. Interspersed with the articles were telegrams sent to Lamont von Heilitz of Eastern Shore Road, Mill Walk.

WISH TO ENGAGE YOUR SERVICES ON MATTER OF GREAT DELICACY AND IMPORTANCE STOP

MY HUSBAND HAS UNJUSTLY BEEN PLACED UNDER SUSPICION STOP I PLEAD WITH YOU TO GIVE YOUR HELP STOP YOU ARE MY LAST RESORT STOP

IF YOU ARE AS GOOD AS PEOPLE SAY WE NEED YOU FAST STOP

Tom looked at pictures of his neighbor in clippings from newspapers in Louisiana, Texas, and Maine—in the latter, his left arm was encased in plaster and canvas, and his haggard face looked as white as the sling, completely out of key with the triumphant caption. *Famous Sleuth Unmasks, Kills Red Barn Murderer.*

The headlines from all these cities and towns celebrated his triumphs. THE SHADOW SUCCEEDS WHERE POLICE FAIL. VON HEILITZ UNCOVERS LONG HELD SECRET, REVEALS KILLER. TOWN CELEBRATES SHADOW'S VICTORY WITH BANQUET. And here was the young Lamont von Heilitz, impeccable and taut as ever, looking straight ahead with a ghostly smile as a hundred men at long tables washed down venison and roast boar with magnums of champagne. He had managed to avoid photographers on all but two other occasions, on each of which he faced the camera as if it were a firing squad. He had captured or revealed the identity of The Roadside Strangler, The Deep River Madman, The Rose of Sharon Killer, and The Terror of Route Eight. The Hudson Valley Poisoner had been proven to be a poetic-looking young pharmacist with complicated feelings about the six young women to whom he had proposed marriage. The Merry Widow, whose four wealthy husbands had suffered domestic accidents, turned out to be a doughy, uninspiring woman in her sixties, unremarkable in every way except for having both a brown and a blue eye. A Park Avenue gynecologist named Luther Nelson was the murderer who had written to *The New York Times* identifying himself as "Jack the Ripper's Grandson." The Parking Lot Monster, of Cleveland, Ohio, had been one Horace M. Fetherstone, the father of nine daughters and the regional manager of the Happy Hearts Greeting Card Company. In all these cases, Lamont von Heilitz, the "renowned amateur consulting detective and resident of the island of Mill Walk," had "offered invaluable assistance to the local police" or had "been helpful in providing evidence" or "by use of brilliant ratiocination, had advanced a coherent theory of the true nature and cause of the baffling crimes"—in other words, had done the work of the police for them.

Page after page, the cases went by. Mr. von Heilitz had worked ceaselessly during the late twenties and throughout the thirties. At a certain point in the late thirties, some of the news stories began referring to him as "the real-life counterpart of radio's most famous fictional detective, the Shadow." He camped in hotel rooms and the libraries and newspaper offices in which he did his research. The last of the detective's photographs contained in the book accompanied an article from the *St. Louis Post-Dispatch* entitled ECCENTRIC RENOWNED SLEUTH POUNDS BOOKS, NOT PAVEMENT and showed a man with greying hair seated at a desk buried under rifts of newspapers, notebooks, and boxes of papers. Except for the gloves on his hands, the excellence of his suit, and his habitual air of distinction, he looked like an overworked high school teacher.

The Shadow had abruptly left St. Louis after solving the murders of a brewer and his wife, refusing to grant any further interviews. (The *Post-Dispatch:* AFTER DEDUCTIVE TRIUMPH, ECCENTRIC SLEUTH GOES ON THE LAM.) After that, the flow of clippings continued, but contained far fewer references to the detective. In Boulder, Colorado, the murderer of a well-known novelist was found to be a local literary agent, incensed that his most lucrative client had intended to move to a New York firm; Boulder police credited the advice of a "self-styled amateur of crime" with helping them to identify the killer. Lamont von Heilitz was obviously concealed behind that phrase, and Tom saw his neighbor in the "anonymous source" who had assisted the police when a movie star was found shot to death in his Los Angeles bedroom; in the "concerned private citizen" who had appeared in Albany, Georgia, to give help to police when an entire family was found murdered in a city park.

In 1945, a letter from "an amateur expert in crime who wishes to preserve his anonymity" gave the police of Knoxville what they needed to arrest a local honor student for the murders of three of his classmates.

After 1945, all the clippings were of this kind. Von Heilitz had refused all invitations to assist individuals or police, and instead had followed only newspaper accounts of cases that interested him and solved them at long distance. Telegrams and letters begging for his aid—*Dear Mr. von Heilitz, I believe I am a detective too for I have tracked you down to your island lair. . .*—had been marked "No Reply" and pasted into the book. When he had become interested in a case, as with the Fox River Valley Menace, the Beast of Lover's Lane, and the Tattoo Killer, he had subscribed to community newspapers and written to the local police. "Somebody out there likes us," said Chief of Police

Austin Beer of Grand Forks, Nebraska, after arresting an elderly woman who had killed two children enrolled at a nursery school located across the street from her house. "One day we got this letter that just put things together in a new way. It wasn't from anywhere around here, but I'll tell you, this fellow knew all about us—he'd gone and followed property transfers from years back and worked out that Mrs. Ruppert had a grudge against the families of these children. That letter set us going in the right direction. I don't mind telling you, the whole thing makes you believe in the kindness of strangers." Chief Beers added that the letter had been signed only with the initials LVH, which had gone unrecognized. Twenty years after the detective's greatest fame, "The Shadow" was Lamont Cranston, not Lamont von Heilitz.

Then these cases, too, faded out of the big journal. The book's final pages confused Tom at first, for they contained nothing like the sequence of cases, of solutions flowing from carefully assembled evidence, that made up the rest of the journal. The entire journal seemed to mark a progress toward invisibility as the detective went from prominence to anonymity; in the final pages even the cases seemed to have disappeared. The focus was entirely on Mill Walk, and all the clippings came from the pages of the *Eyewitness*, but few of them concerned any obvious crime. Tom wondered if Mr. von Heilitz had merely clipped stories at random, searching for a pattern as invisible as he had become himself because none existed.

Tom's initial sense of dislocation was only partially explained by an odd distortion of the journal's chronology—the jumble of clippings from Mill Walk jumped back to the twenties. Among them were articles about the end of construction work on Shady Mount Hospital, "a medical facility," in the words of Maxwell Redwing, its first board chairman, "to rival any in the world." A row of Mill Walk citizens posed before Shady Mount's front door. These were the members of the hospital's first board of governors. Two familiar faces scowled toward him from the photograph. Dr. Bonaventure Milton, already showing the beginnings of his jowls and looking extremely satisfied with his accomplishments, had got himself up like a nineteenth-century prime minister in swallowtail coat, striped satin vest, and black bow tie. And between short, round Maxwell Redwing and pompous, inexplicably successful Dr. Milton, exuding power and rectitude, loomed Tom's grandfather.

Tom experienced the thrill of mingled respect, fear, and awe Glendenning Upshaw always inspired in him. His grandfather's wide commanding face stared out from the photograph, challenging all the world to deny that the hospital behind him was the finest it had to show. At thirty, he had recently founded Mill Walk Construction, and his broad bulllike body looked even stronger than it did in the old photographs that hung in the halls of Brooks-Lowood, taken in the days when Glen Upshaw had been the school's Head Boy and captain of the football team. "Designed to answer the medical needs of every citizen of our island," read the caption, though in practice Shady Mount had chosen to respond to the needs only of residents of the far east end. Shady Mount left Mill Walk's less advantaged citizens to the care of the less fashionable facility farther west, St. Mary Nieves. In the photograph above the optimistic caption, Glendenning Upshaw wore one of the heavy black suits he had adopted long before Tom's birth, after the death of Tom's grandmother. His large left hand clutched the lion's head handle of his unfurled, trademark umbrella. His right hand held his flat, wide-brimmed black hat.

Any other man, Tom thought, who invariably dressed in a black suit, worn always with a stiff white shirt, a black necktie, a black hat, and a loose black umbrella, would look so much like a priest that strangers on the street would call him "Father." Yet Glen Upshaw had never looked priestly. He looked like a bank vault or some forbidding public building, and the aura of the world, of money and luxurious rooms, of first-class suites on liners and large expensive appetites indulged behind closed doors, hung about him like a cloud. He made all of the other men in the photograph seem insignificant.

Tom turned the page.

Here was more chaos. Steamship arrivals and society parties, obituaries—Judge Morton Backer had died, and Tom stared at the name until he remembered that Judge Backer had been the man who had sold Arthur Thielman the long-barreled Colt pistol with which Jeanine Thielman had been murdered. Governmental appointments, long ago elections, business promotions, wedding announcements. Mill Walk Construction built a five-hundred-bed hospital in Miami. Here were his own parents, Victor Pasmore and Gloria Ross Upshaw, among a dozen other eastern shore residents of their age and station. Garden parties, lawn parties, Christmas parties, and New Year's parties, and country club balls.

Then his eye moved to yet another photograph he had seen before. His mother in her early twenties, splendidly dressed, stepping down from a carriage as she arrived at the Founders Club for a charity ball. It was of this picture that the photograph of Jeanine Thielman had reminded him. The pose was identical, a good-looking blond woman stepping down from a carriage with a long, elegant leg protruding from a whirl of clothing. Gloria Upshaw Pasmore, too, seemed to be grimacing instead of smiling, but she was fifteen years younger than Jeanine Thielman, less encrusted with jewelry, altogether less sleek. Because of the contrast with the photograph of the murdered woman, it struck Tom that his mother looked vulnerable even then. Just dimly visible behind her, bending forward to help her get out of the carriage, was her father, whose tuxedo made him seem to melt backwards into the darkness of the interior.

Lamont von Heilitz had tracked the most trivial events of Mill Walk life in the hope that some day a name here, a date there, would intersect to lead him to a conclusion. He had cast out his nets day after day, and hauled in these minnows. The last ten pages of the big journal were a fact collection, no more.

Various names caught his eye. Maxwell Redwing and family went to Africa on safari and returned intact. Maxwell's son, Ralph, announced that, like his father, he had no political ambitions and would devote his energies to "the private sphere, where so much remains to be done." He pledged "all my efforts to the improvement of the quality of life on our beloved island." The Redwing Holding Company put in a successful bid to purchase the Backer mansion, known as "The Palms," located in a section of Mill Key now too close to the growing downtown and business district to be fashionable, gutted and renovated it and then sold it to the Pforzheimer family for use as a luxury hotel.

Maxwell Redwing retired as president of the Redwing Holding Company and appointed his son, Ralph, as its new chief officer.

A man named Wendell Hasek, a night security guard at

Mill Walk Construction, was wounded in a payroll robbery and retired on full salary for the remainder of his life. Tom struggled to remember where he had heard the name before, and then did remember—Hasek had been Judge Backer's valet and driver, and had told Mr. von Heilitz about the sale of a pistol.

Two days later, the bank robbers were shot to death by police in a gun battle in the streets of the old slave quarter, but none of the stolen money, estimated to be in excess of thirty thousand dollars, was recovered.

Mill Walk Construction announced plans for an extensive housing development on the island's far west end, near Elm Cove.

Two days after selling his own construction company to Mill Walk Construction, Arthur Thielman died in his sleep, attended by his family and Dr. Bonaventure Milton.

Judge Backer, Wendell Hasek, Maxwell Redwing, and Arthur Thielman—Tom finally understood. Mr. von Heilitz was doing no more than following the careers of those who had been linked to the murder of Jeanine Thielman in Eagle Lake. That case, even more than the solution to the deaths of his parents, had determined the rest of his life. He had come into what became twenty years of prominence and activity because of it: in a way, Tom remembered, he had come fully to life at Eagle Lake. It was no surprise that he should never really let go of the case.

Tom undressed, turned off his lights, and got into bed, deciding to ask his grandfather about Lamont von Heilitz and the old days on Mill Walk. It was a strange thought—his grandfather and the Shadow must have grown up together.

Part Five

THE FOUNDERS CLUB

Dr. Kleber and others repeatedly emphasized the social dimension of the treatment process. Dr. Frank H. Gawin, director of the Substance Abuse Research Unit at Yale University, put it this way: [illegible] crack were a drug of the middle or upper classes, we would not be saying it is impossible to treat.

Crack is the drug of choice in many poor communities because the initial purchases are relatively cheap.

Initial Conceptions Hold Up

[illegible] the biochemical aspects often tend to come first in considering crack treatment, rather than its psychological, social or economic elements or the rather sobering lessons of history. Detoxification, or getting the addict off the drug, either by volition, deprivation or medication, is the first and essential stage of any program that works, the experts said.

Many of the initial conceptions about crack, which has come into widespread use only within the last four years, have thus far held up.

[illegible]

[illegible] believe that the [illegible] difficulties they face in treating crack [illegible] stem far more from the [illegible] and circumstances of the [illegible] than the biochemical reaction the drug produces.

And they believe the new [illegible] offers society a [illegible] of [illegible] where there has been [illegible] a drug epidemic [illegible] tearing apart poor neighborhoods and families in the nation's cities.

Researchers are finding that crack addiction, under the right conditions, can be successfully treated. Some studies suggest that crack is no more chemically addictive than other drugs that addicts have been able to quit.

Positive Shift in Emphasis

Only a year ago, crack was widely regarded as a [illegible] new drug still poorly understood [illegible] with special characteristics that [illegible] made addiction almost impossible to cure. Now, in dozens of interviews and scientific reports, treatment experts are shifting their emphasis to the more positive if more complex view about addiction to the smokable form of cocaine.

Moreover, in finding that properly run programs can be made to work in treating crack abuse, they believe they have [illegible] crucial element of [illegible]

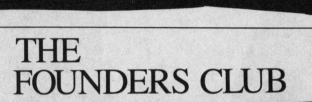

13

Letters mailed on Mill Walk usually arrived on the day they were posted, and mail put in the box at night always arrived the next day. Tom told himself that nothing would happen on the day Captain Bishop got his letter, that it could be a week or more before the police took action or released any information about the murder of Marita Hasselgard. And because this was a Saturday, it was always possible that his letter might not arrive on Fulton Bishop's desk until the following Monday. Everything went slower on the weekends. And if the letter arrived at headquarters on Monday, maybe it would sit half the day in the mail room before being rerouted to Bishop's office. And maybe Bishop took Saturdays off, or never looked at his mail until evening. . . .

"You know what I think?" his father said. "Wake up, I'm talking to you."

Tom's head snapped up. From the other side of the breakfast table, Victor Pasmore regarded him with an unusual intensity. Tom had not even heard his father come into the kitchen. Now he was leaning on the back of a chair, staring as Tom absent-mindedly used his fork to push around on his plate the eggs he had scrambled himself. Like many heavy drinkers, Victor was virtually immune to hangovers, and the way he now looked at Tom was heavily confidential, almost paternal in a way that was rare with him.

"You have a good time last night? With the Spence girl?"

"Pretty good."

Victor pulled the chair out and sat down. "The Spences are good people. Very good people."

Tom tried to remember if he had seen any clippings about Sarah's parents in the journal, and decided that he had not. He remembered something else, and on impulse asked his father about it.

"Do you know anything about the man who built their house?"

Victor's look was now of confused impatience. "The guy who built the Spence house? That's nothing but a waste of time."

"But do you remember anything about him?"

"Christ, what are you, an archeologist?" Victor visibly calmed himself, and went on in a softer voice. "I guess it was some German. Way before my time, he wanted to knock everybody's eyes out, and he pretty well succeeded. The guy was a real con man, I guess. He got into trouble up north, and nobody ever saw him again."

"Why is it a waste of time?"

Victor leaned forward, his impatience struggling with his desire to impart an insight. "Okay, you wanna know, I'll tell you. You look at that house, what do you see? You see dollars and cents. *Lots* of dollars and cents. Bill Spence started off as an accountant with your grandfather, he made some good investments, put himself where he is today. It doesn't matter anymore who built that place."

"You don't know anything about him?" Tom asked.

"No!" Victor yelled. "You're not listening to me! I'm making a point here. Look, it's all tied in with what I wanted to say to you. Have you thought about what you're going to do after Tulane?"

"Not really," Tom said, beginning to feel even more tense

than usual. It had been decided that he would attend Tulane, his grandfather's college, after graduation.

"Well, hear me out on this. My advice is, think about business opportunities—go out and start fresh, make your own life. Don't get stuck on this island the way I did." Victor paused after making this surprising remark, and looked down at the table for a moment before going on. His voice was much softer now. "Your grandfather is willing to help you get started."

"On the mainland," Tom said. When he looked into the future, he saw only a terrifying void. His father's advice seemed directed toward an entirely different sort of person, one who would understand what a business opportunity was.

"Your future isn't here," said Victor. "You can have a whole new life." He looked across the table as if he had much more to say.

"How did you get started?"

"Glen helped me out." The statement came out in a flat, grudging tone which meant that the conversation had essentially come to an end, and Victor Pasmore turned away from his son to look out the kitchen window. Outside in the flat hot sunlight, purple bougainvillaea blossoms, too heavy for their stalks, lolled on the white terrace wall. "Just like when you were sick, I mean after your accident, Glen paid for your nurses, the tutors, a lot of things like that. You have to be grateful to the old man."

It was not clear to Tom if Victor Pasmore were talking about himself or his son. The gratitude seemed heavy, an obligation endlessly paid for. His father turned from the window, unshaven, as was usual on weekends, dressed in an unconvincing sports shirt. "I'm just trying to talk sense to you," he said. "Save you from making mistakes. You think it's too early for a drink?" His father raised his thick eyebrows and pulled down the corners of his mouth in a comic grimace. The thought of having a drink had put him in a better mood.

"Think about what I said. Don't get—ah, you know." Victor stood up and moved toward the liquor cabinet. "Something *mild*, I think," he said, but he was no longer talking to Tom.

Tom spent the rest of the day walking around the house, unable to come to rest for longer than half an hour. He read a few pages of a novel, but kept losing his way in the sentences—the words jittered into a general blur as he pictured a uniformed policeman tossing his envelope onto Fulton Bishop's desk, Fulton Bishop glancing at it, either picking it up or ignoring it. . . .

Tom carried the book into the living room. From the other side of the staircase came the roars and yells of a Yankees game booming fuzzily from the television in the study, where his father had collapsed into his chair. The gladiatorial New York fans always made a lot of noise. The front windows framed Lamont von Heilitz's big grey house. Had von Heilitz's father ever advised him to start thinking about business opportunities? Tom jumped up and walked twice around the living room, wishing that the ball game would end so that he could switch the television to the Mill Walk station and wait for the news. Of course there would be nothing on the news. Church bake sales, the scores of the local Little League teams, the announcement of the construction of a new high rise parking lot . . . Tom wandered up the stairs and went into his room. He got to his knees and checked under his bed. The leather-bound journal was where he had left it. He heard his parents' bedroom door click open, and stood up in an almost guilty scramble. His mother's footsteps went down the front stairs. Tom left his bedroom and went down after her.

He found her in the kitchen, looking unhappily at the dishes in the sink and the empty beer cans his father had dropped on the table. She had brushed her hair and wore a long peach-colored satin nightgown and a matching bed jacket that looked like a compromise between underwear and clothing. "I'll wash the dishes, Mom," he said, realizing almost for the first time that, despite the uncertainty and puzzles of his life, his parents often made him feel as though they were his children.

For a moment Gloria seemed utterly confused about what to do next. She went uncertainly toward the table. "Are you all right?" he asked.

"I'm fine," she said, her voice as blurry as her face.

He went to the sink and turned on the hot water. Behind his back, Gloria moved around the kitchen turning on the kettle, rattling the cups, opening a box of tea. She seemed to be moving very slowly, and he thought that she was watching him busy himself with the pile of dirty dishes. He heard her pour hot water into the cup and sit down again with a sigh. Then he could not stand the silence any longer, and said, "Mr. Handley wanted me to come to his place after school yesterday, to show me some rare books. But I thought he really wanted to talk to me."

She uttered some indistinct sound.

"I thought that you asked him to talk to me. Because of my scrapbook." He turned from the sink. His mother was slumped over the cup of tea with her bright hair hanging like a screen before her face. "There isn't anything to worry about, Mom."

"Where does he live?" The question seemed to bore her, as if she had asked it only to fill a space in the conversation.

"Out near Goethe Park, but we didn't get to his place."

She brushed back her hair and looked heavily up at him.

"I got sick—dizzy. I couldn't go any farther. He drove me home."

"You were out on Calle Burleigh?"

He nodded.

"That's where you had your accident. I suppose . . . you know. Unpleasant memories."

She took in his start—Tom nearly dropped the dish he was drying—with an expression of grim confirmation. "Don't think that things like that go away. They don't, let me tell you." She sighed again, and seemed to tremble. She snatched up the cup of hot tea and bent over it so that again the bright curtain of her hair fell to hide her face. Tom still felt as if the insight she had casually tossed his way had knocked the breath out of his body. He had a quick, mysterious mental glimpse of a fat old woman yelling "Cornerboy!" at him and knew that he had actually seen her on the day of his accident. The world had cracked open to let him peek beneath its crust, then sealed itself shut again. Down below the surface was an angry old woman waving her fist, what else?

An instant before he realized that his mother was crying, he caught, like a sharp, distant odor, the urgent, driven feeling of that day. Then he noticed that his mother had curled down even further into herself, and that her shoulders were shaking.

He wiped his hands on his trousers and moved toward her. She was crying soundlessly, and when he reached her, she pressed her napkin to her eyes and forced herself to be still.

Tom's hand hovered over the nape of his mother's neck: he

could not tell if she would allow him to touch her. Finally he permitted his hand to come down softly on her neck.

"I'm so sorry that happened to you," she said. "Do you ever blame me?"

"Blame you?" He pulled a chair nearer and sat beside her. A tingle passed through his body with the realization that his mother was really talking to him.

"You couldn't say I was much of a mother." Gloria wiped her eyes with her napkin and sent him a look of such rueful self-awareness that she seemed momentarily like another person altogether: a person he seldom saw, the mother who really *was* present from time to time, who could see him because she could see out of herself. "I never wanted anything bad to happen to you, and I couldn't protect you, and you were nearly killed." She wadded the napkin in her lap.

"Nothing was your fault," Tom said. "And after all, it was a long time ago."

"You think that makes a difference?" Now she appeared slightly irritated with him. He felt her focus move away from him, and the person she might have been began to fade out of her face. Then he felt her make a conscious effort of concentration. "I remember when you were little," she said, and she actually smiled at him. Her hands were still. "You were so beautiful, looking at you sometimes made me cry—I couldn't stop looking at you—sometimes I thought I'd just melt, looking at you. You were perfect—you were *my child*." Gloria slowly reached for his hand and touched it almost shyly. Then she drew her hand back. "I felt so incredibly lucky to be your mother."

The look on his face caused her to turn away and buy a moment of self-possession by sipping her tea. He could not see her face.

"Oh, Mom," he said.

"Just don't forget I said this," she said. "It's the *truth*. I hate being the way I am."

What he needed, how much he needed it, made him lean toward her, hoping that she would hug him or at least touch him again. Her body seemed rigid, almost angry, but he did not think that she could be angry now.

"Mom?"

She turned her head sideways and showed him her ruined

face. Her hair dripped across her cheek, and a strand clung to her lip. She looked like an oracle, and Tom froze before the significance of whatever she was going to say.

Then she blinked. "You want to know something else?"

He could not move.

"I'm happy you're not a girl," she said. "If I had a daughter, I'd drown the little bitch."

Tom got to his feet so quickly he nearly overturned his chair, and in seconds was out of the room.

The day crawled by. Gloria Pasmore spent the afternoon in her bedroom listening to her old records—Benny Goodman, Count Basie, Duke Ellington, Glenroy Breakstone and the Targets—lying on the bed with her eyes closed and smoking one cigarette after another. Victor Pasmore left the television set only to go to the bathroom. By four-thirty he had passed out, and lay back in his recliner with his mouth open, snoring, in front of another baseball game. Tom took another chair, and for thirty minutes watched men whose names he did not know relentlessly score points against another team. He wondered what Sarah Spence was doing, what Mr. von Heilitz was doing behind his curtained windows.

At five o'clock he got out of the chair to change the channel to the local news. Victor stirred and blinked in his chair, and woke up enough to grope for the glass of watery yellow liquid beside the recliner. "What about the game?"

"Can we see the news?"

Victor swallowed warm whiskey and water, groaned at the taste, and closed his eyes again.

Loud theme music, an even louder commercial for Deepdale Estates on Lake Deepdale, which was "another Eagle Lake, only two miles away and twice as affordable!"

Tom's father snorted in genial contempt.

A man with short blond hair and thick-rimmed glasses smiled into the camera and said, "Things may be breaking on the island's most shocking murder in decades, the death of Marita Hasselgard, only sister of Finance Minister Friedrich Hasselgard, who also figures in today's news."

Tom said "Hey!" and sat up straight.

"Police Captain Fulton Bishop reported today that an

anonymous source has given police valuable information leading to the whereabouts of Miss Hasselgard's murderer. Captain Bishop has informed our reporters that the slayer of Marita Hasselgard, Foxhall Edwardes, is a recently released former inmate of the Long Bay Holding Facilities and a habitual offender. Mr. Edwardes was released from Long Bay the day before the slaying of Miss Hasselgard." The picture of a surly, wide-faced man with tight curling hair appeared on the screen.

"Hey," Tom said, in a different tone of voice.

"Whuzza big deal?" his father asked.

". . . many convictions for burglary, threatening behavior, petty larceny, and other crimes. Edwardes' last conviction was for armed robbery. He is thought to be in hiding in the Weasel Hollow district, which has been cordoned off by police until searches have been completed. Motorists and carriage traffic are advised to use the Bigham Road cutoff until further notice. I'm sure that all of you join us in hoping for a speedy resolution of this matter." He looked down at his desk, turned over a page, and looked up at the camera again. "In a related story, grief-stricken Finance Minister Friedrich Hasselgard is reported missing in heavy seas off the island's western coast. Minister Hasselgard apparently took out his vessel, the *Mogrom's Fortune*, for a solitary sail around the island at roughly three o'clock this afternoon, after hearing of the imminent capture of his sister's murderer. He is believed to have been overtaken by a sudden squall in the Devil's Pool area, and radio contact was lost soon after the squall began." The newscaster's eyes flicked down toward the desk again. "In a moment, traffic from our overhead observer, Ted Weatherhead's weather, and sports with Joe Ruddler."

"Okay," Victor Pasmore said. "They got him."

"They got who?"

He began to lever himself up out of the recliner. "The lowlife who bumped off Marita Hasselgard, who the hell do you think? I better start thinking about dinner. Your mother's a little under the weather today."

"What about Hasselgard?"

"What about him? Jumped-up natives like Hasselgard can sail anything, anywhere, through any storm that comes along.

I remember when Hasselgard was a kid in his twenties, he could thread needles with a sailboat."

"You knew him?"

"I sort of knew Fred Hasselgard. He was one of your granddad's discoveries. Glen took him out of Weasel Hollow, got him started. Back when they were developing the west side, Glen did that with a bunch of bright young native boys—saw to their education and put them on the right track."

Tom watched his father lumber toward the kitchen, then turned back to the television.

Joe Ruddler's violent red face filled the screen. "THAT'S IT, SPORTS FANS!" Ruddler shouted—aggressiveness was his trademark. "THAT'S ALL THE SPORTS FOR TODAY! THERE AIN'T NO MORE! YOU CAN BEG ALL YOU WANT TO, BUT IT WON'T DO ANY GOOD! RUDDLER'S CHECKIN' OUT UNTIL TEN O'CLOCK, SO PLAY IT COOL OR PLAY IT HARD—BUT YOU GOTTA KEEP PLAYIN' IT!" Tom switched off the television.

"You gotta keep playin' it," Victor chuckled from the kitchen. Tom's father loved Joe Ruddler. Joe Ruddler was a real man. "We got some steaks here we better eat before they go bad. You want a steak?"

Tom was not hungry, but he said, "Sure."

Victor walked out of the kitchen, wiping his hands on his trousers. "Look, would you cook them? Just put them on the grill. There's some lettuce and stuff, you could make a salad. I want to check on your mother, make her a drink or something."

Half an hour later Victor led Gloria down the stairs as Tom was setting the table in the dining room. In the peach satin outfit, her hair limp now, Tom's mother looked like a red-eyed ghost. She sat in front of her steak and sliced off a piece the thickness of a playing card and pushed it across the plate with her fork.

Tom asked her if she felt ill.

"We're going out for dinner tomorrow," Victor said. "You'll see, she'll be full of beans by tomorrow night. Won't you, Glor?"

"Leave me alone," she said. "Will everybody stop picking on me, please?" She sliced off another minuscule portion of steak, raised it part of the way to her mouth, then lowered her fork and scraped the tiny bit of meat back onto her plate.

“Maybe I should call Dr. Milton,” Victor said. “He could give you something.”

“I don’t need anything,” Gloria said, seething, “except to . . . be . . . left . . . alone. Why don’t you call my father, he’s the person who always fixes everything up for you.”

Victor ate the rest of his meal in silence.

Gloria turned her head to give Tom a look of real reproach. Her eyes seemed swollen. “He’ll help you get started too, anywhere you like. You can go anyplace.”

“Nobody wants me to stay on Mill Walk,” Tom said, understanding that his parents had virtually accepted his grandfather’s offer for him.

“Don’t you want to get off Mill Walk?” His mother’s voice was almost fierce. “Your father wishes he’d been able to get away from this place. Ask him!”

“I don’t think we’re very hungry tonight,” Victor said. “Let me take you upstairs, Glor. You want to be rested for tomorrow, dinner at the Langenheims’.”

“Whoopee. Dirty jokes and dirty looks.”

“I am going to call Dr. Milton,” Victor said.

Gloria slumped in her chair, letting her head loll alarmingly on her chest. Victor quickly stood up and moved behind her. He put his hands under her arms and pulled her up. She resisted for a second or two, then swatted away his hands and stood up by herself.

Victor took her arm and walked her out of the dining room. Tom heard them going up the stairs. The bedroom door closed, and his mother began screaming at a steady unhurried pulse. Tom walked twice around the dining room, then took the plates into the kitchen, wrapped the uneaten steaks in baggies and put them in the refrigerator. After Tom had washed the dishes, he walked out into the front hall and listened for a moment to his mother’s screams, which now sounded oddly *remembered*, disconnected from any real rage or pain. He went to the front door and leaned his head against it.

Less than half an hour later a carriage rolled up in front of the house. The doorbell rang. Tom left the television room, opened the front door, and let in Dr. Milton.

Victor stood on the lowest step of the staircase. A red wine stain shaped like the state of Florida covered the front of his shirt. Dr. Milton, who was dressed in the same outfit of cutaway and striped pants that he had worn for the picture in Lamont von Heilitz's journal, smiled at Tom and carried his black bag toward the stairs. "Is she better now?"

"I guess," Victor said.

Dr. Milton turned his ponderous face to Tom. "Your mother's a little high-strung, son. Nothing to worry about." He looked as if he wished to ruffle Tom's hair. "You'll see a big improvement in her tomorrow."

Tom said something noncommittal, and the doctor carried his bag upstairs after Victor Pasmore.

By ten o'clock Tom felt as if he were all alone in the house. The doctor had left hours before, and his parents had never come back downstairs. He turned on the television to watch the news and sat on the armrest of his father's recliner, tapping his foot.

"Dramatic conclusion to search for Marita Hasselgard's killer," said the reliable-looking man in the heavy glasses. "Finance Minister feared missing. Complete details after these messages."

Tom slid onto the seat and moved the recliner into its upright position. He waited through a string of commercials.

Then came color film of what looked like the entire police force of Mill Walk, equipped with automatic rifles and bulletproof vests, firing from behind cars and police vans at a familiar wooden house in Weasel Hollow. "The hunt for Foxhall Edwardes, suspected murderer of Marita Hasselgard, came to a dramatic conclusion late this afternoon after shots were fired inside a Mogrom Street bungalow early this evening. Two officers, Michael Mendenhall and Roman Klink, were injured in the early exchange of fire. Reinforcements quickly arrived on the scene, and Captain Fulton Bishop, who had been led to identify Edwardes as the murderer of Miss Hasselgard by an anonymous tip, spoke to the suspect through a bullhorn. Edwardes chose to shoot rather than surrender, and was killed in the resulting exchange of gunfire. The two injured policemen remain in critical condition."

On the screen, the windows and window frames of the little house splintered apart under the gunfire, and chips of stone flew away from the front of the house. Black holes like wounds appeared in the walls. Smoke boiled from the ruined door. Flames shot out onto the roof, and one side of the house collapsed in a roil of smoke and dust.

The announcer appeared again. "In a related story, Finance Minister Friedrich Hasselgard, reported earlier as lost in a squall in the Devil's Pool, was listed an hour ago as officially missing. His luxury sailing vessel is being towed back to Mill Walk harbor by members of Mill Walk's Maritime Patrol, who found the *Mogrom's Fortune* adrift at sea. It is presumed that Minister Hasselgard was swept overboard during the storm. Searches continue, but there is little hope for Minister Hasselgard's survival." The announcer looked down, as if in sorrow, then up again, upbeat and neutral at once. "After the break, the latest weather reports and Joe Ruddler's updated sports report. Stay with us."

Tom turned off the television, picked up the telephone, and dialed the number of the house across the street. He let it ring ten times before hanging up.

The next day, his mother floated down the stairs at noon, fully dressed, hair brushed so it shone, her face carefully and expertly made up, and came into the television room almost girlishly. The miracle had happened again. She was even wearing pearls and high heels, as if she planned to go out. "Goodness," she said, "I'm not used to sleeping so much, but I guess I needed the rest." She smiled at them both as she went across the room and sat on the arm of her husband's chair. "I think I just tried to do too much yesterday."

"That's right," Victor said, and patted her back.

Tried to do too much? Tom wondered. *Coming downstairs twice, listening to records, smoking about three packs of cigarettes?* She sat on the arm of the chair with her legs drawn up. "What are we all so engrossed in?"

"Ah, there's a big game on, but Tom wanted to watch the news."

Tom shushed them. Foxhall Edwardes' sister, a short, dark, overweight woman missing several teeth who spoke in the old native manner, was condemning the way the police had handled her brother's arrest. "Them had no need to kill he. Him-him was being deep scared, bad. Foxy would be talking with police, them no want talk, them want he dead. Foxy him be doing some badness, but him not being bad in himself. Him and him's da were close, and when him's da dies, him-him rob store. Tore he up inside, can you be feeling this? Time has been served. Out of jail three days only, him be seeing police with guns, him thinks they be go putting him-him back there. Fox him no be killing any bodies any time, but police be putting finger on him-him, be saying you our man. Him *convenient*. I am being protest this-this."

"I came down to see if I can make lunch for anybody." Gloria touched the pearls at her neck.

Victor stood up quickly. "I'll give you a hand."

He put his arm around her waist and walked her toward the door.

"Don't you love the way they talk?" Gloria said. " 'Him and him's da.' If it was a girl they'd say 'her and her's da.' " She giggled, and Tom heard one of the central sounds of his life, the hysteria capering beneath her brittle exterior.

Now Captain Fulton Bishop faced a press conference staged in the full congratulatory official manner, from behind a desk in a flag-filled reception room at Armory Place. Captain Bishop's smooth, suntanned head, as hard and expressionless as a knuckle, tilted toward the bank of microphones. "Of course his sister is distressed, but it would be unwise to take her allegations for anything more than the emotional outburst they are. We gave Mr. Edwardes ample opportunity to surrender. As you know, the suspect chose to respond with fire, and seriously injured the two brave men who were the first to see him."

"The two officers were injured inside the house?" asked a reporter.

"That is correct. The suspect admitted them to the house for the express purpose of killing them behind closed doors. He was not aware that backup teams had been ordered to the area."

"Backup teams were ordered before the first shots?"

"This was a dangerous criminal. I wanted my men to have all the protection they could have. No more questions."

Captain Bishop stood up and turned away from the table in a bubble of noise, but a shouted question reached him.

"What can you tell us about the disappearance of Minister Hasselgard?"

He turned back to the crowd of reporters and leaned over the microphones. Harsh white light bounced off the top of his smooth head. He paused a moment before speaking. "That matter is under full investigation. There will be a full disclosure of the results of that investigation in a matter of days." He paused again, and cleared his throat. "Let me say this. Certain matters in the Finance Ministry have recently come to light. If you ask me, Hasselgard wasn't washed off that boat—he jumped off it."

He straightened up into a roar of questions and smoothed his necktie over his shirt. "I would like to thank someone," he said, shouting to be heard over their questions. "Some good citizen wrote to me with information that led indirectly to the solution of Miss Hasselgard's murder. Whoever you are, I think you are watching me at this minute. I would like you to make yourself known to me or anyone here at Armory Place, so that we can demonstrate our gratitude for your assistance." He marched away from the table, ignoring the shouts of the reporters.

Setting out sandwiches and bowls of soup on the little breakfast table in the kitchen, Gloria reminded Tom of a glamorous mother in a television commercial. She smiled at him, her eyes bright with the effort to demonstrate how good she was being. "I'll leave some food in the refrigerator for you tonight, Tom, but here's something nice to tide you over. We're going out tonight, you know."

Then he understood—she had dressed for the dinner party as soon as she got out of bed. He sat down and ate. During lunch his father several times said how tasty the soup was, how much he enjoyed the sandwiches. It was a great lunch. Wasn't it a great lunch, Tom?

"Now they're claiming that Hasselgard drowned himself," Tom said. "They're going to announce that he was stealing from the treasury. If someone hadn't written to the police, none of this would have happened. If the police had never gotten that letter—"

"They would have nailed him anyway," his father broke in. "Hasselgard came too far too fast. Now drop the subject."

He was talking to Tom but watching Gloria, who had raised her sandwich halfway to her mouth, shuddered, and lowered it again to her plate. She looked up, but she did not see them.

" 'Her and her's da,' the servants used to say. Because there were just the two of us in this house."

"Let me help you upstairs." Victor shot Tom a dark look, and took his wife's arm to get her to her feet and lead her out of the room.

When his father came back down, Tom was in the little television room, eating the rest of his sandwich and watching one of the WMIL-TV reporters stand beside the hull of the *Mogrom's Fortune* at the police dock as he described how the Maritime Patrol had found the boat. "Here on the waterfront, they are scoffing at the theory that Hasselgard could have been washed overboard. Amid growing rumors—"

"Haven't you had enough of this?" Victor unceremoniously bent down and turned the channel indicator until a baseball game appeared on the screen. "Where's my sandwich?"

"On the table."

He left and returned almost immediately, the big sandwich dripping out of his hand. He lowered himself into his chair. "You're mother will be fine, no thanks to you."

Tom went up to his room.

At seven o'clock, his parents came downstairs together, and Tom turned off the television just before they came into the room. His mother looked exactly as she had at noon—dressed to go out in her pearls and high heels. He told them to have a good time, and called Lamont von Heilitz as soon as they walked out the door.

14

They sat on opposite sides of a leather-topped coffee table stacked with books. Lamont von Heilitz leaned against the high tufted back of a leather sofa and squinted at Tom through cigarette smoke.

"I feel restless, that's why I'm smoking," he said. "I never used to smoke when I worked. When I was a young man I used to smoke between cases, waiting to see who might appear on my doorstep. All in all I must be a weaker creature now than I was then. I didn't enjoy seeing the police in my house this afternoon."

"Bishop came to see you?" Tom asked. Everything about Mr. von Heilitz seemed different this night.

"He sent two detectives named Holman and Natchez home with me. The same two men invited me along to Armory Place last night to discuss the death of Finance Minister Hasselgard."

"They consulted you?"

Von Heilitz drew in smoke, then luxuriantly exhaled. "Not

quite. Captain Bishop thought I might have written them a certain letter."

"Oh, no," Tom said, remembering trying to call the old man after watching the previous night's news.

"Whatever they were doing down in Weasel Hollow kept interrupting the interrogation. I didn't get back here until nearly noon, and Detectives Holman and Natchez didn't leave until after three."

"They questioned you for another three hours?"

He shook his head. "They were looking for a typewriter that would match up with the letter. The search was slow and industrious. I'd forgotten how many typewriters I had accumulated. Holman and Natchez took it as particularly suspicious that one old upright was hidden away in the filing cabinets."

"Why did you hide one of your typewriters?"

"Just what Detective Natchez wanted to know. He seemed very distressed, this Detective Natchez. I gather that one of the young officers injured in Weasel Hollow—Mendenhall?—was important to him. In any case, the typewriter was a souvenir of the Jack the Ripper's Grandson business—did you read about it last night? It was the machine on which Dr. Nelson wrote his letters to the New York police." Von Heilitz smiled and smoked, sprawled out on his chesterfield, his feet up on the coffee table. He had spent a night at police headquarters, and a morning watching detectives paw through his files. He had showered, shaved, napped, and changed clothes, but he still looked exhausted to Tom.

"Nothing happened the way I thought it would," Tom said. "They keep you overnight—"

The old man shrugged.

"—and this man Edwardes is killed, and two policemen were shot, and Hasselgard killed himself—"

"He didn't kill himself," von Heilitz said, squinting at Tom through a cloud of smoke. "He was executed."

"But what did Foxhall Edwardes have to do with it?"

"He was just—what was the word his sister used? A convenience. He's the way they close the books."

"That means I killed him too. Hasselgard and Edwardes would still be alive if I hadn't written that letter."

"You didn't kill them. The system killed them to protect itself." He lowered his legs, sat up, and ground out the cigarette in an ashtray. "Do you remember my saying that the man who killed my parents told one lie? The lie, of course, was about my father's involvement in the corruption on Mill Walk—I think the truth was that he hated what had become of the island. And I think he must have gone to his friend David Redwing, and told him what he had discovered and what he planned to do about it. Let's say that David Redwing was as shocked as my father had been. He might have talked about my father's charges to the wrong person. Consider that for a second. If my father and mother were killed soon after David Redwing heard my father's tale, wouldn't he be suspicious of their deaths? The answer's obvious—of course he would. *Unless* someone he trusted absolutely had assured him that my father had been wrong in his allegations, and that an ordinary criminal had murdered my parents."

"Who do you think it was?"

"His own son. Maxwell Redwing. Until his resignation, Maxwell was his father's right-hand man."

Tom thought of Maxwell Redwing on the terrace of the club at Eagle Lake, entertaining young nieces and nephews who were old people now; he remembered the obituary in the *Eyewitness*.

"Tell me, what do you think I am working on these days?"

"I don't know," Tom said. "You were working on Hasselgard, but I suppose that's over now."

"Our late Finance Minister was only a little piece of it. It's my last case—I could even say *the* case. In fact, it goes all the way back to Jeanine Thielman."

He had done nothing but lead Tom back into the circle of his obsession with the Redwings. "Look," Tom began, "I don't want you to think—"

Von Heilitz stopped him by holding up a gloved hand. "Before you say anything, I want you to think about something. Do you imagine that anyone looking at you would guess what happened to you seven years ago?"

It took Tom a long time to realize that, like his mother that afternoon, von Heilitz was referring to his accident. It seemed utterly disconnected to him—buried within his recent life, as clay pipes and old bottles were now and then found buried in old back gardens.

"That is an essential part of who you are. Who you *are*."

Tom wanted to get out of the old man's house—it was as bad as being caught in a spiderweb.

"You nearly died. You had an experience most people have only once in their lives, and which very few live to remember or talk about. You're like a person who saw the dark side of the moon. Few people have been privileged to go there."

"Privileged," Tom said, thinking: *Jeanine Thielman, what makes her a part of this stuff?*

"Do you know what some people have reported of that experience?"

"I don't want to know," Tom said.

"They felt they were moving down a long tunnel in darkness. At the end of the tunnel was a white light. They report a sense of peace and happiness, even joy—"

Tom felt as though his heart might explode, as though everything in his body had misfired at once. He literally could not see for a moment. He tried to stand up, but none of his muscles obeyed him. He could not draw breath. As soon as he became aware that he was blind, he could see again, but panic still surged through his body. It was as if he had been blown apart into scattered atoms and then reassembled.

"Tom, you are a child of the night," von Heilitz said.

The words triggered something new in him. Above him Tom saw the vault of the night sky, as if the roof had been lifted off the house. Only a few widely scattered stars pierced the endless blackness. Tom remembered Hattie Bascombe saying, *"The world is half night."* Layer after layer of night, layer after layer of stars and darkness.

He said, "No more, I can't take any more of this—" He looked at his body, arranged loosely in Lamont von Heilitz's leather chair. It was the body of a stranger. His legs looked impossibly long.

"I just wanted you to know that you have all of that inside you," the old man said. "Whatever it is—pain, terror, wonder too."

Tom smelled gunpowder, then realized he was smelling himself. He felt that if he started, he would never stop crying.

The old man smiled at him. "What do you think you were doing on that day? Way out on the far west end?"

"I had a friend in Elm Cove. I guess I was going there." It sounded false the instant he said it.

For a moment neither spoke.

"I can remember this feeling—of having to get somewhere."

Von Heilitz said, "There."

"Yes. There."

"Have you ever been back to the Goethe Park area?"

"Once. I almost threw up. I couldn't stay there—anywhere around there. It was that day I saw you."

He was struck by the way the Shadow was looking at him—as if he were figuring out a thousand different things at once.

He fought to recover himself. "Could I ask you something about Jeanine Thielman?" he asked.

"You'd better."

"This sounds kind of stupid—probably I just forgot something."

"Ask me anyhow."

"You said that Arthur Thielman left the gun on a table near the dock, and that Anton Goetz picked it up and shot Jeanine in the back of the head from thirty feet away. How did Goetz know that the gun pulled to the left? You can't tell that just by looking at a gun, can you?"

Von Heilitz lowered his legs and leaned forward over the table, extending his hand. He gave Tom's hand a surprisingly firm grip, and laughed out loud.

"So I didn't miss anything?"

Von Heilitz was still pumping his hand. "Nothing at all. In fact, you saw what *was* missing." He released Tom's hand and leaned back, placing his hands on his knees. "Goetz knew that the gun pulled to the left because he took two shots. The first one hit the Thielman lodge. Goetz corrected instantly, and hit her with the second. I dug the first bullet out of the lodge myself."

"So you knew where Goetz had been standing. You figured out where the pistol had to be by backtracking from the bullet. Like with Hasselgard's car."

Von Heilitz smiled and shook his head.

"There were spent cartridges under the table."

"There were no spent cartridges."

"You saw it happen," Tom said. "No. You saw the gun on the table." He thought about this. "No. I can't figure it out."

"You were close. Another summer resident of Eagle Lake saw the gun on the table that evening. A single man in his mid-twenties, like myself. A widower with a young daughter, living alone in his family's lodge. He left Eagle Lake the morning after Jeanine was killed."

An unpleasant thrill went through Tom's body. "Who was it?"

"He was probably the only person to have heard the shots that night, because his was the next lodge in line. And there was a Redwing family party at the club that night, celebrating Jonathan Redwing's engagement to Kate Duffield. They had a band in from Chicago—Ben Pollack. Made a lot of noise."

In a quiet voice, Tom asked, "Was he building a hospital in Miami?"

"One of Mill Walk Construction's first big contracts. You saw the clipping in my book, did you? He had set up a separate office in Miami even then. I gather it still does a great deal of business."

"So my grandfather heard the shots. He must have thought . . ."

"That Arthur had killed Jeanine?" The Shadow crossed one leg over the other and interlaced his fingers over his nonexistent stomach. "I stopped off to see him in Miami after I made sure that Minor Truehart was out of jail. I wanted him to know what had happened up in Eagle Lake after he left. In fact, I brought him copies of all the Eagle Lake papers that covered the murder."

Some message was being passed to him, but Tom could not read it in either von Heilitz's words or his manner—it could not be that Glendenning Upshaw had witnessed a murder and calmly left the scene.

"The balcony of your grandfather's lodge overlooked the lake. He used to spend his evenings out there, thinking about how he could get a better discount on cement than Arthur Thielman, or whatever it was he thought about. From his balcony, Glen could see the Thielmans' dock as well as his own."

"He ran away the next morning?"

Von Heilitz snorted. "Glen Upshaw never ran away from anything in his life. I think he just never considered altering arrangements he had already made. In any case, that was the last summer he spent at Eagle Lake—the last time any member of your family was at the lake."

"No, no," Tom said. "It was grief. He stopped going to the lodge because of grief. My grandmother drowned that summer. He couldn't stand to see the place again."

"Your grandmother lost her life in 1924, the year before all this. It wasn't grief that made your grandfather leave Eagle Lake. It was business—the hospital was a lot more important to him than a marital dispute between a competitor and his wife."

"He would have let the guide be executed?"

"Well, all he told me was that he saw a long-barreled Colt lying on the table. The shots could have been anything—on a lake, it can be next to impossible to know where sounds are coming from. You do hear shots up there; people have guns. It's possible that he didn't know that Jeanine was dead."

"It's possible he did, you mean."

"How often do you see your grandfather?"

"Maybe once or twice a year."

"You're his only grandchild. He lives about fifteen miles from your house. Has he ever thrown a ball to you? Taken you riding or sailing? To a movie?"

Any such suggestion would have been ridiculous, and Tom's response must have shown in his face.

"No," said the old man. "I didn't think so. Glen is an aloof man—preposterously aloof. There's something missing in him, you know."

"Do you know how my grandmother happened to drown? Did she go out by herself at night? Was she drunk?"

The old man shrugged, and again looked as if he were thinking a thousand thoughts at once. "She went out at night," he finally said. "Everybody at Eagle Lake drank a lot in those days." He looked down at the hem of his suit jacket, lifted it, and crossed his left hand over his waist to flick away a blemish invisible to Tom. Then he looked up. "I'm worn out. You'd better be getting home."

The two of them stood up together. It seemed to Tom that Mr. von Heilitz communicated in two separate ways, and the way in which he said the important things was silently. If you didn't get it, you missed it.

Von Heilitz walked him through the files and past the lamps like stars and moons in the night sky. He opened his front door. "You're better than I was at your age."

Tom felt the old man's nearly weightless arm on his shoulders.

Across the street, one light burned in a downstairs window of his house. Down the block in the Langenheim house, every light blazed. Long cars and horse-drawn carriages stood at the curb. Uniformed drivers leaned and smoked against their cars, set apart from the carriage drivers who would not look at or speak to them.

"Ah, the night is so beautiful," the old man said. He stepped outside.

Tom said goodbye, and the Shadow waved a dark blue glove, nearly invisible in the crystalline moonlight.

15

For the next few weeks, the Friedrich Hasselgard scandal and a series of revelations about the Treasury filled the nightly broadcasts and the headlines of the *Eyewitness*. The Finance Minister had misappropriated funds, misdirected funds, buried funds, misplaced funds in transfers from one account to another and from ledger to ledger. Through a combination of criminality and incompetence he had lost or stolen an amount of money that multiplied with each new investigation until it appeared to add up to the almost unthinkable sum of ten million dollars. "Criminal associates," not terrorists, were now supposed to have shot the Minister's sister. By the time Dennis Handley told Katinka Redwing at a dinner party that he had not been following the stories about the scandal and was not at all interested in that kind of thing, few other adults on the island of Mill Walk would have been able to utter such a statement.

One day, Dennis Handley asked Tom to see him after the end of school.

As soon as Tom walked into his room, Dennis said, "I suppose I know the answer to this question, but I have to ask it anyway." He looked down at his desk, then out of the classroom window, which gave him a fine view of narrow, treelined School Road and the headmaster's house, opposite the school. Tom waited for the question.

"That car you wanted to find—the Corvette in Weasel Hollow. Did that car belong to the person I think it belonged to?"

Tom sighed. "It belonged to the person it obviously belonged to."

Dennis groaned and pressed his palms against his forehead.

"Why don't you want me to say his name? Do you think you might get in trouble?"

"A couple of weeks ago," Dennis said, "I wanted to have a friendly talk with you—your mother asked me to bring something up with you, a minor thing, but it was my idea to invite you to my apartment in order to see that manuscript, which I thought you might enjoy. Instead, you pretended to be sick and made me drive you all the way back across the island to a *crime scene*. The next day, the gentleman who owned that car disappears. Another man is gunned down. Blood is shed. *Two lives* are lost."

Dennis raised his hands in theatrical horror.

"Did you write that letter the policeman mentioned at his press conference?"

Tom frowned, but did not speak.

"I feel sick," Dennis said. "This whole situation is unhealthy, and my stomach knows it. Can't you see that you had no business meddling in that kind of thing?"

"A man got away with murder," Tom said. "Sooner or later they would have executed some innocent man and declared the whole thing solved."

"And what happened instead? Do you call that a tea party?" Dennis shook his head and gazed out the window again, rather than look at Tom. "I *am* sick. You were my hope—you have gift enough for two."

"For you and me both, you mean."

"I want you to concentrate on the things that matter," Dennis said in a slow, furious voice. "Don't throw yourself away on garbage. You have a treasure within you. Don't you see?" Dennis's broad, fleshy face, suited to jokes and confidences and ruminations about novelists, strained to express all he felt. "There is the real world and the false world. The real world is *internal.* If you're lucky, and you could be, you sustain it by the right work, by your responses to works of art, by loyalty to your friends, by a refusal to be caught up in public or private falsehoods. Think of E. M. Forster—*two* cheers for democracy."

"I'm not going to run for office, Mr. Handley," he said.

Dennis's face closed like a trap. He looked down at his thick, pale hands, locked together on top of his desk. "I know things are difficult for you at home, Tom. I want you to know that you can always come to me. I don't suppose I'll ever say this to another student, no matter how long I might teach, but you can call me any time."

A flash of perception that seemed to come from the adult he would be told Tom that Dennis would make a similar speech to a particularly favored student once every four or five years for the rest of his life.

"There's nothing wrong with my home life," he said, and heard his mother's almost unemotional screams.

"Just remember what I told you."

"Can I go now?"

Dennis sighed. "Listen, Tom—I just want you to know who you are. That's what I care about—who you are."

Tom could not stop himself from standing up. His breath had caught in a hot little pocket deep in his throat, and could not move up or down.

Dennis sent him a complicated look that combined resentment, surprise, and a desire to repeat everything he had just said. "Go on." Tom took a step backwards. "I won't keep you."

Tom left the room and found Fritz Redwing sitting in the hallway with his back against the plate glass window overlooking the school's courtyard. Fritz had been kept back at the start of what should have been his freshman year, and had been in Tom's class ever since.

"What'd he do?" Fritz scrambled to his feet.

Tom swallowed the burning air in his throat. "He didn't do anything."

"We can still make the cart to dancing class—the kids who had sports are still down in the locker room."

The two boys began moving down the corridor.

Fritz Redwing's hair was a thick blond thatch, but in most other ways he was a typical Redwing—short, broad-shouldered, with short thick legs and virtually no waist. Fritz was a kind and friendly boy, not very highly regarded by his family; he had been pleased to find his old friend Tom Pasmore back in the class into which failure had thrown him, almost as if he imagined that Tom kept him company in his disgrace. Tom knew that when people spoke of the stupidity of the younger Redwings, it was Fritz they had most in mind, but Fritz seemed merely slow to him, and for that reason not much inclined to thought. Thinking took time, and Fritz tended to be lazy. When he bothered to think, Fritz generally did all right. The top of his blond head came only to the middle of Tom's chest. Next to Tom, he resembled a small, shaggy blond bear.

Tom and Fritz came out of the school's side door and walked toward the parking lot in hot steady sunlight. The cart stood at the far end of the parking lot, and from it a hum of high-pitched voices, pierced now and then by a shriek, came to the two boys. Tom instantly saw Sarah Spence's blond head in the second of the four front rows, which had been filled with girls. The cart's fluttering cover cast a greenish shade over the rows of girls. For different reasons, both Tom and Fritz Redwing slowed their pace and turned off the path to stand in the darker shade at the side of the school building.

Tom thought that Sarah Spence, seated between Marion Hufstetter and Moonie Firestone on the second bench, flashed her eyes at him as she leaned over to whisper something in Marion's ear. He suspected that she was saying something about him, and his blood froze.

"You can pick your nose," Fritz said, turning to him with an upraised index finger, "and you can pick your friends. But you can't pick your friend's nose." He laughed; then because Tom remained silent, looked at him sideways with his queer light-filled eyes.

A lizard the size of a cat ran on pinwheeling legs across the asphalt parking lot and disappeared beneath the cart. Sarah Spence grinned at something said by Moonie Firestone. Tom thought she had forgotten he was there, but in the green shade her eyes moved toward him, and his blood froze again.

"I suppose Buddy's coming home soon," he said to Fritz.

"Buddy's so cool. Life is one big party to Buddy. You heard about how he wrecked his mom's car last summer. *Totaled* it. Just walked away. I can't wait till we get up to Eagle Lake this summer."

"But when is he coming home?"

"Who?"

"Buddy. Your cousin Buddy, the one-man demolition derby."

"Mr. Cool," Fritz said.

"When is Mr. Cool coming to Mill Walk?"

"He isn't," Fritz said. "He's going straight from Arizona to Wisconsin. Him and some other guys are going to drive straight through. *Par-ty.* All the way cross-country."

They watched a stream of third- and fourth-year boys pour from the Field House, slinging their jackets over their shoulders on their way up the hill to the parking lot. As soon as the other boys had passed them, Tom and Fritz began moving together toward the cart.

Miss Ellinghausen's Academy of Dance occupied a narrow four-story townhouse on a sidestreet off Calle Berghofstrasse. Only a small, gleaming brass plaque on the front door identified the dancing school. When the cart pulled up before the white stone steps, the Brooks-Lowood students climbed out and spread out along the sidewalk. The driver jingled the reins and drove around the block. While they waited on the sidewalk, the boys buttoned their collars, adjusted their neckties, and gave quick looks at their hands. The girls combed their hair and inspected their faces in hand mirrors. After a minute or two had passed, the door at the top of the stairs swung open, and Miss Ellinghausen, a tiny white-haired woman in a grey dress, pearls, and low-heeled black shoes, stepped out and said, "You may come in, my dears, and line up to be inspected."

Girls before boys, the students toiled up the steps. Inside the townhouse, they formed a long single line from the front door past the entrance to the parlor all the way to Miss Ellinghausen's kitchen, which smelled of disinfectant and ammonia. The little woman walked down the row of students, looking closely at their hands and faces. Fritz Redwing was sent upstairs to wash his hands, and all the rest filed into the larger of the two downstairs studios, a large bright room with a polished parquet floor and a bay window filled with an enormous arrangement of silk flowers. Miss Gonsalves, a woman as tiny and ancient as Miss Ellinghausen, but with glossy black hair and elaborate facial makeup, sat poised at an upright piano. Miss Ellinghausen and Miss Gonsalves lived on the upper floors of the Academy, and no one had ever seen either one of them anywhere but in this building.

When Fritz Redwing came back downstairs, grinning foolishly and wiping his hands on the back of his trousers, Miss Ellinghausen said, "We shall begin with a waltz, if you please, Miss Gonsalves. Partners, ladies and gentlemen, partners."

Since there were more girls than boys, two or three pairs of girls always partnered each other at these lessons. As Buddy Redwing's acknowledged girlfriend, Sarah Spence generally danced with Moonie Firestone, whose boyfriend was in a military school in Delaware.

On grounds of height rather than compatibility, Tom had long been partnered with a girl named Posy Tuttle, six feet tall exactly. She never spoke to Tom during the classes and avoided even looking him in the eye.

Miss Ellinghausen moved slowly through the laboriously waltzing couples, uttering brief remarks as she went, and gradually worked her way around to Tom and Posy. She stopped beside them, and Posy blushed.

"Try to *glide* a bit more, Posy," she said.

Posy bit her lip and tried to glide to the severe meter coming from the upright.

"Are your parents well?"

"Yes, Miss Ellinghausen," Posy said, blushing all the harder.

"And your mother, Thomas?"

"She's fine, Miss Ellinghausen."

"Such a . . . *delicate* child she was."

Tom pushed Posy around in a clumsy circle.

"Thomas, I'd like you to partner Sarah Spence for the rest of the lesson. Posy, I'm sure you will be of more assistance to Marybeth." This was Moonie's real name.

Posy dropped Tom's hand as if it were a hot brick, and Tom followed her across the polished floor to the corner where Sarah Spence and Moonie Firestone were executing bored, perfect waltz steps. "New partners, girls!" exclaimed the old woman, and Tom found himself inches away from Sarah Spence. She was almost instantly in his arms, smiling and looking gravely into his eyes. He heard Posy Tuttle begin rattling away in her flat, ironic voice to Moonie, saying everything she had been saving up.

For an instant Tom and Sarah were awkwardly out of rhythm with one another.

"Sorry," Tom said.

"Don't be," Sarah said. "I'm so used to dancing with Moonie, I forgot what it was like with a boy."

"You don't mind?"

"No, I'm glad."

That silenced Tom for a time.

"I haven't talked to you in so long," she said at last.

"I know."

"Are you nervous?"

"No," Tom said, though he knew that she could feel him trembling. "Maybe a little."

"I'm sorry I don't see you anymore."

"Are you?" said Tom, surprised.

"Sure. We were friends, and now I only see you in Miss Ellinghausen's cart."

The music ceased, and like the other couples Tom and Sarah broke apart and waited for instructions. He had not imagined that Sarah Spence actually paid any attention to him in the dancing school cart.

"Fox trot," the old woman said. Miss Gonsalves began thumping out "But Not For Me."

"Are you still doing Fritzie's homework for him?"

"Somebody has to do it," Tom said.

She laughed and hugged him in a manner that would have brought a reprimand if Miss Ellinghausen had seen it.

"Moonie and I were so bored with each other. You'd think we were being punished. I thought the only boy I'd ever dance with for the rest of my life was Buddy. And Buddy's sense of rhythm is a little *personal*."

"How is he?"

"Does Buddy Redwing seem to you like the kind of person

who would write letters? I'm sick of thinking about Buddy—I'm always sick of thinking about Buddy whenever he isn't around."

"And when he is around?"

"Oh, you know—Buddy's so active you can't think about anything."

This sentence left Tom feeling a little depressed. He looked down at her smiling up at him, and took in that she was smaller than he remembered, that her blue-grey eyes were very widely spaced, that she smiled easily and warmly and that her smile was surprisingly wide.

"It was so nice of Miss Ellinghausen to give you to me. Or would you rather dance with Posy Tuttle?"

"Posy and I didn't have much to say to each other."

"Posy was scared stiff of you, couldn't you tell?"

"What?"

"You're so *hulking*, for one thing, with those enormous shoulders. Posy is used to looking down at boys, that's why she has that terrible stoop. And I think she found your reputation forbidding. I mean your reputation as the school intellectual."

"Is that what I am?" This was a little disingenuous.

"But Not For Me" came to an end, and "Cocktails For Two" began.

"Do you remember when I visited you in the hospital?"

"You talked about Buddy then too."

"I was impressed with him, I will admit. It was interesting to—that he was a Redwing was interesting."

"Boys," Miss Ellinghausen said, "right hands on your partners' spines. Fritz, stop daydreaming."

When Tom said nothing, Sarah went on, "I mean, they're so *definite*. So set apart."

"What goes on at the compound?"

"They watch movies a lot. They talk about sports. The men get together and talk about business—I saw your grandfather a couple of times. He comes over to see Ralph Redwing. If it wasn't *them*, it'd be kind of boring. And Buddy isn't too boring." She looked up at him with a flickering smile. "I always think of you when I see your grandfather."

"I think of you too." Tom's depression had blown away as if it never existed.

"You're not shaking anymore," she said.

Miss Gonsalves began thumping out something that sounded like "Begin the Beguine."

"I was so stupid, that day I saw you in the hospital. You know how you go over certain conversations after you had them, and feel terrible about the dumb things you said? That's how I feel about that day."

"I was just happy you came."

"But you were—" She waited.

"You were so different. Grown up."

"Well, you've caught up with me! We're friends again, aren't we? We wouldn't have stopped being friends, if you hadn't walked in front of a car." She looked up at him with a face in which an idea was just being born. "Why don't you come up to Eagle Lake this summer? Fritz could invite you. I could see you every day. We could sit around and talk while Buddy is blowing up fish and wrecking cars."

Holding Sarah Spence in his arms, Tom felt himself claimed by the daily world, which had seemed so insubstantial in Lamont von Heilitz's house. This extraordinarily pretty and self-possessed girl seemed to imply, with her long warm smile and stream of sentences that went straight into him like a series of shapely arrows, that everything could always be as it was at this moment. He could dance, he could talk, he could hold Sarah Spence's surprisingly firm and solid body in his arms without shaking or stuttering. He was the school intellectual—the school something, anyhow. He was hulking, with his enormous shoulders.

"Aren't you glad they got that madman who killed Marita Hasselgard?" Sarah asked him, her voice bright and careless.

The music stopped. Miss Gonsalves began murdering "Lover." Miss Ellinghausen wandered past and nodded at him from behind Sarah Spence's back. She actually gave him a thin dusty smile.

"We should be friends," she said, and rested her head against his chest.

"Yes," he said, clearing his throat and separating from her as Miss Ellinghausen tapped Sarah's shoulder and tried to shrivel them with a betrayed, angry glance. "Yes, we really should."

16

At the end of the class, Miss Ellinghausen clapped her hands together, and Miss Gonsalves lowered the upright's polished lid. "Ladies and gentlemen, you are making excellent progress," Miss Ellinghausen said. "Next week I shall introduce the tango, a dance which comes to us from the land of Argentina. Basic knowledge of the tango has become essential in smart society, and, considered in itself, the tango is a refined vehicle in which the strongest emotions may find expression in a delicate and controlled fashion. Some of you will see what I mean. Please give my best wishes to your parents." She turned away to open the door to the hallway.

Sarah and Tom filed through the door and nodded to Miss Ellinghausen, who responded to each of the hasty nods given her by the students with an identical, machine-tooled dip of the head. For the first time since Tom had joined the class, the old lady interrupted her performance at the door long enough to ask a question. "Are the two of you satisfied with the new arrangement?"

"Yes," Tom said.

"Very," said Sarah.

"Fine," said Miss Ellinghausen, "there'll be no more nonsense, then," and dipped her head in her perfect nod.

Tom followed Sarah out on the broad top step of the townhouse. Fritz Redwing stood at the bottom of the steps, rolling his eyes and gesturing toward the waiting cart.

"Well," said Tom, wishing that he did not have to leave Sarah Spence, and wondering how she got home.

"Fritzie's waiting for you," Sarah said. "Next week we learn to express the strongest emotions in a delicate and controlled fashion."

"We could use more of that around here," he said.

Sarah smiled rather abstractly, looked down, then up over his shoulder. She moved sideways to make room for the students still coming through the door. To Tom, she seemed set apart from all of the others going up and down the stairs—she looked in some way like two people at once, and he thought that he had imagined the same thing once about someone else, but could not remember who it had been. She flicked her eyes at him, then went back to looking at empty space. Tom wished he could embrace or kiss or *capture* her. In the past fifty minutes he had held her, had spoken to her more than in the past five years, but now it seemed to him that he had missed everything and wasted every second of the time he had spent with her.

The last of the students who took the cart home stood in line on the sidewalk to jump up into the green shade of the cover. Fritz Redwing squirmed with impatience, looking as if he had to go to the bathroom.

"You'd better go," Sarah said.

"See you next week," he said, and started down the white stone steps.

She looked away, as if he had said something too obvious.

Tom moved down the white steps toward Fritz Redwing, and his contradictory feelings seemed to expand and declare war on him. He felt as if he had lost something of supreme value, and found himself overjoyed that the beautiful, necessary thing was gone forever. Some live object within him had broken free, and begun violently beating its wings.

Then for a moment the contradictory emotions coursing

through him obliterated all the rest of the world, and then seemed to obliterate *him*. He was dimly aware of Fritz Redwing staring at him in childish agitation, and of an ornate carriage turning from Calle Berghofstrasse into the shaded street. The carriage looked familiar. Everything about Tom seemed to sigh, and his hand on the railing grew suddenly pale and grainy, and then Tom realized that he could see right through his hand to the railing.

Somewhere directly behind him, invisible but hugely present, occurred a great explosion—a flash of red light and a sound of tearing metal and breaking glass. He was vanishing, becoming nothing. His body continued to disappear as he moved down the stairs. In seconds his hands and feet, his whole body, was only a shimmer in the air, then only an outline. When he reached the bottom step, he had disappeared altogether. He was dead, he was free. The fused but contradictory feelings within him burned on, and the catastrophe just behind him kept on happening. All of this was complete and whole. He stepped across the sidewalk. Fritz's mouth moved, but invisible words came out. On the side of the carriage rolling toward them, Tom saw a golden letter **R** so surrounded by scrolls and curls it resembled a golden snake in a golden nest. When he exhaled and moved toward the cart, he could hear Fritz Redwing complain about how slowly he was moving.

Tom stepped up into the cart and sat down in the last row beside Fritz, who had never noticed that for three or four endless seconds he had been completely invisible. The driver snapped his reins, and the cart pulled forward behind Miss Ellinghausen's slow-moving horses. Tom did not watch Sarah walk down the steps, but he heard the door of Ralph Redwing's carriage click massively open.

17

Once a year Gloria Pasmore drove Tom fifteen miles along the island's eastern shore, past the walls of the Redwing compound and empty canefields planted with rows of willows, to the guardhouse of the Mill Walk Founders Club. There a uniformed guard with a heavy pistol on his hip wrote down the number of their license plate and checked it against a sheet on a clipboard while another guard made a telephone call. When they were approved for entry, they took a narrow asphalt lane called Ben Hogan Way past sand dunes and broom grass down to the long flat ocean rolling in on their left. They continued past the enormous white and blue Moorish structure of the clubhouse toward the thirty acres of beachfront property on which the members of the Founders Club had built the big houses they called "the bungalows." When the road divided, they took the left fork, Suzanne Lenglen Lane, and wound through the dunes past the houses until they turned right on the branch nearest the ocean, Bobby Jones Trail, and pulled into the communal parking area just down the beach from the bungalow into which Glendenning Upshaw had moved when he left the house on Eastern Shore Road to his daughter and her husband.

Tom's mother got out of the car and looked almost warily at the two horse-drawn vehicles parked in the lot. Tom and Gloria knew them well. The small, slightly dusty trap hitched to a black mare belonged to Dr. Bonaventure Milton; the larger carriage from which a groom was just now leading a chestnut mare toward the stables belonged to Tom's grandfather.

It was the weekend after the dancing class, and Tom had felt drained and on edge all week. He had had the same nightmare several nights in a row, to the point where he nearly dreaded going to sleep. Gloria, too, seemed tired and anxious. She had said only one thing to him during the trip from Eastern Shore Road, in response to his comment that he and Sarah Spence were getting to be friends again. "Men and women can't be friends," she said.

Going to see Glendenning Upshaw was like going to Miss Ellinghausen's Academy in at least one respect, that Tom had to suffer an inspection before matters got underway. Gloria fretted over his fingernails, the knot in his tie, the condition of his shoes and hair. "I'm the one who has to pay for it, when he sees something he doesn't like. Did you bring a comb, at least?"

Tom pulled a pocket comb from his jacket and ran it through his hair.

"You have *bags* under your eyes! What have you been doing?"

"Playing cards, carousing, whoremongering, that kind of thing."

Gloria shook her head, looking very much as if she wanted to get back in the car and drive home. Behind them, a door closed across Bobby Jones Trail. "Uh-oh," she exhaled, and he could smell breath mints.

Tom turned around to see Kingsley, his grandfather's valet, proceeding slowly down the gleaming steps at the front of the bungalow. Kingsley was nearly as old as his employer. He always wore a long morning coat, a high collar, and striped pants. His bald head shone in the sunlight. Kingsley managed to get to the bottom step without injuring himself, and propped himself up on the railing. "We've been waiting for you, Miss Gloria," he called out in his reedy voice. "And Master Tom. You're looking to be a fine young man, Master Tom."

Tom rolled his eyes, and his mother shot him an agonized glance before leading him across Bobby Jones Trail toward Kingsley. The valet forced himself to stand upright as they approached, and bowed when Gloria greeted him. He led them slowly up to the terrace and beneath a white arch into a courtyard. A hummingbird zipped down the courtyard and over the top of the bungalow in one long fluid gesture. Kingsley opened the door and allowed them into the entry, tiled with small blue and white porcelain squares. Beside the door stood a Chinese umbrella stand into which had been jammed at least nine or ten unfurled black umbrellas. The year before, Glendenning Upshaw had told Tom that people who never thought about umbrellas until it rained stole them right out from under your eyes! Tom thought he had seen that the old man imagined that people stole his umbrellas because they were Glendenning Upshaw's umbrellas. Maybe they did.

"The parlor, Miss Gloria," Kingsley said, and tottered off to fetch his employer.

Gloria followed him out of the entry and turned in the opposite direction into a wide hallway. Long rugs woven with a mandala-like native design lay over red tiles, and a suit of Spanish armor the size and shape of a small potbellied boy stood guard over a refectory table. They went past the table and turned into a long narrow room with tall windows that looked down half a mile of perfect sand to the Founders Club beach. A few old men sat on beach chairs ogling girls in bikinis who ran in and out of the surf without ever getting their hair wet. A waiter dressed like Kingsley, but wearing a long white apron instead of the morning coat, passed among the men, offering drinks from a shining tray.

Tom turned from the windows and faced the room. His mother, already seated on a stiff brocaded couch, looked up at him as if she expected him to tip over a vase. Despite the high windows facing the scroll of beach and length of bright water, the parlor was dark as a cave. A dark green fern foamed over the top of a seven-foot grand piano no one played, and glass-fronted bookshelves covered the back wall with row upon row of unjacketed books that blurred into a brownish haze. These books had titles like *Proceedings of the Royal Geographic Society, Vol. LVI* and *Selected Sermons and Essays of Sydney Smith*. There was a little more furniture than the room could easily accommodate.

Gloria coughed into her fist, and when he looked at her she pointed fiercely at an overstuffed chair at right angles to the brocaded couch. She wanted him to sit so that he could stand up when her father walked into the room. He sat down on the overstuffed chair and looked at the hands folded in his lap. They were reassuringly solid.

His recurring dream had begun the night after the dancing class, and he supposed that the dream must be related to what had happened to him on the Academy steps. He could not see any connection, but . . . In the dream smoke and the smell of gunpowder filled the air. Off to his right, random small fires burned into the choking air, to his left was an ice-blue lake. The lake steamed or smoked, he could not tell which. It was a world of pure loss—loss and death. Some terrible thing had happened, and Tom wandered through its reverberating aftermath. The landscape looked like hell, but was not—the real hell was inside him. He experienced emptiness and despair so great that he realized it was *himself* he was looking at—this dead, ruined place was Tom Pasmore. He stumbled a few paces before noticing a corpse of a woman with tangled blond hair lying on the shore. Her blue dress had been shredded against the rocks, and lay about her in a shapeless puddle. In the dream Tom sank down and pulled the cold heavy body into his arms. The thought came to him that he knew who the dead woman was, but under another name, and this thought rocketed through his body and jolted him awake, groaning.

The world was half night, Hattie Bascombe said.

"What's wrong with you?" his mother whispered.

Tom shook his head.

"He's *coming*." They both straightened up and smiled as the door opened.

Kingsley entered and held the door. A moment later Tom's grandfather stumped into the room in his black suit. He brought with him, as always, the aura of secret decisions and secret powers, of Cuban cigars and midnight meetings. Tom and his mother stood up. "Gloria," he said, and, "Tom." He did not smile back at them. Dr. Milton came in just behind him, talking from the moment he came through the door as if to fill up the silence.

"What a treat, two of my favorite people." Dr. Milton beamed at Gloria as he advanced toward her, but Gloria kept her eyes on her father, who drifted ponderously around past the bookcases. Then the doctor was directly in front of her.

"Doctor." She leaned forward for a kiss.

"My dear." He looked at her professionally for a moment, then turned to shake Tom's hand. "Young man. I remember delivering you. Doesn't seem it could have been seventeen years ago."

Tom had heard variations of this speech many times and said nothing as he shook the doctor's plump hand.

"Hello, Daddy," Gloria said, and kissed her father, who had now come all the way around the room to bend down to kiss her.

Dr. Milton patted Tom's head and moved sideways. Glendenning Upshaw broke away from Gloria to stand before him. Tom leaned forward to kiss his grandfather's deeply lined, leathery cheek. It felt oddly cold to his lips, and his grandfather instantly broke away. "Boy," the old man said, and bothered to look directly at him. As always when this happened, Tom felt that his grandfather was looking straight into him and did not care for what he saw. This time, however, he noticed nearly with disbelief that he was looking down at the old man's broad, powerful face—he was an inch or two taller than his grandfather.

Dr. Milton noticed this too. "Glen, the boy's taller than you! An unaccustomed experience for you to look up to anyone, isn't it?"

"That's enough of that," said Tom's grandfather. "We all shrink with age, you included."

"Of course, no doubt about it," the doctor said.

"How does Gloria look to you?"

"Well, let's see." Smiling, the doctor moved once again up to Gloria.

"I didn't come here for a medical examination—I came for lunch!"

"Yes, yes," said her father. "Take a look at the girl, Boney."

Dr. Milton winked at Gloria. "All she needs is a little more rest than she's been getting."

"If she needs rest, give her something." Upshaw removed a fat cigar from a humidor on the drum table. He snapped off the end, rolled it in his fingers, and fired it up with a match.

Tom watched his grandfather going through the cigar ritual. His white hair was vigorous enough to be disorderly, like Tom's. He still looked strong enough to hoist the grand piano up on his back. He was as wide as two men, and part of the aura that had always surrounded him was crude physical power. It would be too much, Tom supposed, to expect someone like that to act like a normal grandfather.

Dr. Milton had written out a prescription, and snapped it off his pad. "That's the reason your father wanted me to wait until you came." He handed the sheet to Gloria. "Wanted a free consultation out of me."

The doctor looked at his watch. "Well, I have to be on my way back down-island. I wish I could stay for lunch, but a little something is going on at the hospital."

"Trouble?"

"Nothing serious. Not yet, anyhow."

"Anything I should know about?"

"Just something that needs looking into. A situation regarding one of the nurses." Dr. Milton turned to Tom with an expectant look. "Someone you might remember from your own stay there. You knew Nancy Vetiver, didn't you?"

Tom felt a small explosion deep in his chest, and remembered his nightmare. "Sure I do."

"Always a problem with that young woman's attitude, you may remember."

"She was *hard*," Gloria said. "I remember her. Very *hard*."

"And insubordinate," the doctor said. "I'll keep in touch, Glen."

Tom's grandfather blew out cigar smoke and nodded his head.

"Give me a call if you still have trouble sleeping, Gloria. Tom, you're a fine boy. Looking more like your grandfather every day."

"Nancy Vetiver was one of the best people at the hospital,"

Tom said. The doctor frowned, and Glen Upshaw tilted his massive head and squinted at Tom through cigar smoke.

"Well," the doctor said. "We shall see." He forced himself to smile at Tom, made another short round of goodbyes, and left the room.

They heard Kingsley walking the doctor to the entry and opening the door to the terrace. Tom's grandfather was still squinting at him, moving the cigar in and out of his mouth like a nipple.

"Boney'll straighten everything out. You liked the girl, eh?"

"She was a great nurse. She knew more about medicine than Dr. Milton."

"Ridiculous," his mother said.

"Boney is more of an administrator—could be," said his grandfather with dangerous mildness. "But he's always done well by me and my family."

Tom saw a thought move visibly through his mother's face like lightning, but all she said was, "That's right."

"Loyal man."

Gloria nodded grimly, then looked up at her father. "You're loyal to *him*, Daddy."

"Well, he takes care of my daughter, doesn't he?" The old man smiled, then looked speculatively at Tom. "Don't worry about your little nurse, boy. Boney will do the right thing, whatever it is. A little flap at the hospital is nothing to get excited about. Mrs. Kingsley is making us a nice lunch, and after I smoke some more of this cigar, we'll go out and enjoy it."

"I'm still worried about Nancy Vetiver," Tom said. "Dr. Milton doesn't like her. It would be awful if he let that influence his judgment, no matter what's going on—"

"Be hard *not* to let it influence your judgment," his grandfather said. "Girl ought to know better, in the first place. Boney's a doctor, no matter what you think of his medical skills, he did go to medical school and he does take care of us and most of our friends. He is also the top man at Shady Mount—been there from the beginning. And he's one of our people, after all."

And that was how it worked, Tom thought.

"I don't think he's one of my people," he said.

His mother shook her head vaguely, as if bothered by a fly.

His grandfather drew in a mouthful of smoke, exhaled, and cast a glance toward him that only appeared to be casual. He wandered over to the couch with the same false casualness and sat down near his mother. She waved smoke away.

"You seem to care about this nurse."

"Oh, Daddy, for Pete's sake," his mother said. "He's seventeen years old."

"That's what I mean."

"I haven't seen her since I was ten." Tom sat down on the piano bench. "She was a good nurse, that's all. She understood how to treat patients, and Dr. Milton just sort of came in and out. To have Dr. Milton decide whether or not Nancy Vetiver is in trouble just sort of seems upside-down, that's all."

"Upside-down." His grandfather uttered the words neutrally.

"I'm not trying to be rude. I don't dislike Dr. Milton."

"And of course you have no idea what is going on at Shady Mount. Which is serious enough to call Boney all the way back down-island."

Tom began feeling resentful and trapped. "Yes."

"Yet you unthinkingly take the side of this hospital employee over the doctor. And you assume that this same doctor, who delivered you and came out to help your mother a few nights ago, has no right to criticize her."

"I'm just going on what I saw," Tom said.

"When you were ten years old. And scarcely in a normal frame of mind."

"Well, I could be wrong—"

"I'm glad to hear you say it."

"—but I'm not." Part of him wondered what was making him say these things.

Tom looked up and saw that his grandfather was staring at him. "Let me remind you of certain facts. Bonaventure Milton grew up two blocks from where you now live. He attended Brooks-Lowood. He went to Barnable College and the University of St. Thomas Medical School. He belongs to the Founders Club. He is Chief of Staff at Shady Mount, and he is going to be Chief of Staff at the multimillion dollar facility we're going to build out here. Do you still think it would be upside-down, as you say, for Dr. Milton, with his background and qualifications, to criticize or judge this nurse, with hers?"

"She has no background," Gloria said in a faint voice. "She came to our house and expected a tip for nursing Tom."

"No, she didn't," Tom said. "And—"

"It was in her eyes," Gloria said.

"Grand-Dad, I just don't think Dr. Milton's background has anything to do with what kind of doctor he is. Cops and jitney drivers deliver babies. And all he does for Mom is give her shots and pills."

"I had no idea you were such a hot-blooded revolutionary."

"Is that what I am?"

He regarded Tom for a moment. "Would you like me to inform you of what this so-called situation at Shady Mount is all about? Since you are so interested in this nurse's career?"

"Oh, no," said Gloria.

"I'd like that. She was a great nurse, that's all."

"I will telephone you when I know what has happened. Then you can make your own determination."

"Thank you," Tom said.

"Well, I'm not sure I have any appetite left, but let's go through to lunch." He placed what was left of his cigar in an ashtray and stood up, holding out his hand to his daughter.

The dining room at the back of the bungalow opened out on a wide terrace. The table had been set for three, and Kingsley's wife stood beside it as they came out. She was wearing a black dress with a lace collar and white apron, and, like her husband, she visibly straightened when she saw them.

"Will you be having a drink today, sir?" she asked. Mrs. Kingsley was a thin old lady with sparse white hair skinned back into a tight bun.

"My daughter and myself will have gin and tonics," Upshaw said. "No. I want something stronger. Make that a martini. You too, Gloria?"

"Anything," Gloria said.

"And get Karl Marx here a beer."

Mrs. Kingsley disappeared through the arch into the dining room. Tom's grandfather pulled out Gloria's chair and then sat at the head of the table. Tom sat opposite his mother. It was cool and shady on the terrace. A breeze from the ocean stirred the bottom of the tablecloth and the leaves of the bougainvillaea growing along the divider at the end of the terrace. Gloria shivered.

Glendenning Upshaw glanced sourly at Tom, as if blaming him for his mother's discomfort, and said. "Shawl, Gloria?"

"No, Daddy."

"Food'll warm you up."

"Yes, Daddy." She sighed. Her eyes looked glassy to Tom, and he wondered if he had missed seeing Dr. Milton give her a pill. She sat waiting for her drink with parted lips. Tom wished he was sitting at the long table in the Shadow's house, having a conversation instead of whatever this was.

Then the memory of the leather-bound journal reminded him of something his father had said.

"Grand-Dad, didn't you give Friedrich Hasselgard his start?"

Upshaw grunted and frowned. He still looked sour. "What of it?"

"I'm just curious, that's all."

"That's nothing for you to be curious about."

"Do you think he killed himself?"

"Please," said Gloria.

"You heard your mother, do her the honor of obeying her," Upshaw said.

Mrs. Kingsley came back with a tray of drinks and passed them out. She did not seem to expect thanks. Glendenning Upshaw took in a mouthful of cold gin and settled back in his chair, tucking in his chin so that his face turned into a landscape of bumps and hollows. He had begun to look less unhappy as soon as he had tasted his drink. Friedrich Hasselgard had just disappeared, Tom thought: he had climaxed his career of government service by taking a three hundred thousand dollar bribe and killing his sister, and then he went out on his boat, and Glendenning Upshaw took a little swallow of a martini, and Friedrich Hasselgard watched himself disappear.

"Anyhow, I suppose he killed himself, yes. What else could have happened?"

"I'm not too sure," Tom said. "People don't just disappear, do they?"

"Upon occasion they do."

There was a silence, and Tom swallowed a mouthful of pale, slightly bitter Pforzheimer beer. "I've kind of been thinking about a neighbor of ours lately," he said. "Lamont von Heilitz."

Both his mother and his grandfather looked at him, Gloria in an unfocused way that made Tom wonder what kind of pills Dr. Milton gave her, his grandfather with a quick astounded irritation.

Gloria said, "Lamont? Did you say Lamont?"

His grandfather frowned and said, "Drop the subject."

"Did he say Lamont?"

Glendenning Upshaw cleared his throat and turned to his daughter. "How have you been, Gloria? Getting out much?"

She fell back into her chair. "Victor and I went to the Langenheims' last week."

"That's good. You enjoyed yourself?"

"Oh, yes. Yes, I enjoyed myself."

"Didn't you think it was interesting that Hasselgard disappeared from his boat on the same day the police killed that man in Weasel Hollow?" Tom asked. "What did you think about that, Grand-Dad?"

His grandfather lowered his glass and turned heavily toward Tom. "Are you asking me what I thought, or are you asking if I thought it was interesting?"

"What you really thought."

"I'm interested in what you thought, Tom. I wish you would tell me."

"It's pretty clear that he was stealing Treasury money, isn't it?" When Upshaw did not respond, Tom said, "At least, all the news stories make it sound that way. When he worked for you he must have been honest, but after he came into power he began stealing with both hands. When his sister wanted a cut, he murdered her and thought he could get away with it."

"That would be an odd assumption."

"It was just talk I heard. Um, from other students around school."

Upshaw was still staring at him. "What else did these students imagine?"

"That the police killed the Minister and framed that man."

"So the police department is corrupt too."

Tom did not answer.

"Which means that the government is corrupt too, I suppose."

"That's what it would mean," Tom said.

"How did these friends of yours account for the letter Fulton Bishop received?"

"Oh," Tom said.

"The letter from a private citizen that helped pinpoint this man Foxhall Edwardes as Miss Hasselgard's killer. I'd say that this letter pretty well negates most of your theory at one go. Because it means that Hasselgard did not murder his sister. Therefore, she did not demand a cut of the take, and therefore, the police did not cover up her murder—so the corruption seems to stop at Hasselgard. Do you believe that Captain Bishop got that letter, or do you think he invented the whole thing in order to corroborate the official version?"

"I think he got a letter," Tom said.

"Good. Paranoia has not completely destroyed your mind." He drained the rest of his martini, and, as if on cue, Mrs. Kingsley appeared with her tray clamped under her elbow and an ice bucket in her hands. From the top of the bucket protruded the neck of an open wine bottle. "You'll stick to beer?"

Tom nodded.

Mrs. Kingsley laboriously placed the heavy bucket beside Upshaw's plate and removed two glasses from the shaved ice around the bottle. She unclamped the tray and set Upshaw's martini glass on it, and then went around to place the second wineglass before Gloria. Gloria gripped her martini glass with both hands, like a child who fears the loss of a toy. Mrs. Kingsley faded back into the dining room. A minute later she returned with a larger tray containing three bowls of gazpacho, which she placed atop their plates.

She went back inside the house. Glendenning Upshaw sampled the cold soup and looked at Tom again. He was no longer angry. "In a way, I'm almost happy that you have spoken as you have this morning. It means that I've come to the right decision."

Gloria froze with her spoon halfway to her mouth.

"I think your horizons need widening."

"My father said something about your being willing to set me up in business after I get out of college. That's very generous. I don't quite know what to say, except thanks. So thank you."

His grandfather waved this away. "You're applying to Tulane?"

Tom nodded.

"Louisiana is full of opportunities. I know a lot of good men there. Some of them would be happy to take you on once you have your engineering degree."

"I haven't really decided what I'll take in college," Tom said.

"Stick with engineering."

"Oh, yes, Tom," his mother said.

"It's a foundation. It'll give you everything you need. If you want to study poetry and the collected works of V.I. Lenin, you can do it in your spare time."

"I don't know if I'd be a good engineer," Tom said.

"Well, just what do you think you'd be good at? Biting the hand that feeds you? Insulting your family? I don't think Tulane offers degrees in those subjects yet." He simmered for a while. Tom and Gloria occupied themselves with their soup. After a moment he remembered the wine, and angrily snatched the bottle from the bucket. He poured wine into his glass, then into Gloria's. "Let me tell you something. Engineering is the only real subject. Everything else is just an academic exercise."

"It's going to take time to work things out," Tom said.

"It's a wonderful idea, Daddy," Gloria said.

"Let's hear Tom say that." He pushed his bowl away.

"Go *on*," Gloria said.

"It's a wonderful idea." Tom could feel his face getting hot. He thought: *This is how people become invisible.*

"Your tuition will be taken care of, of course. Ah, Mrs. Kingsley, what are we having, lobster salad? Excellent. We are celebrating my grandson's decision to major in engineering at Tulane."

"That's beautiful," the old woman said, placing another tray on the table.

Almost as soon as they had begun eating, Tom's grandfather said, "Have you ever seen Eagle Lake?"

Tom looked up in surprise.

"You haven't, have you? Gloria, when was the last time you saw Eagle Lake?"

"I don't remember." Gloria had a guarded, suspicious expression on her face.

"You were just a little girl, anyhow." He turned to Tom again. "Eagle Lake has an unhappier meaning for us than it does for our friends." Tom thought he was referring to Jeanine Thielman, then realized that he meant the death of his wife. "We suffered a great loss there. I've found reasons to stay away ever since." *Except for the summer after your loss*, Tom thought. "I was a busy man, of course, my work just ran me off my feet—but was I as busy as all that? I can't be sure."

"You were working hard," Gloria said, and shivered.

Upshaw glanced impatiently at his daughter. "At any rate, the lodge has been there all these years, under the care of various housekeepers. You remember Miss Deane, don't you, Gloria? Barbara Deane?"

She looked down at her plate. "Of course."

"Barbara Deane has taken care of the lodge for something like twenty years—local people named Truehart did the job before that."

Tom wondered at his mother's sulkiness, and thought that Barbara Deane must have been another of Glendenning Upshaw's old mistresses.

"Anyhow," the old man said, with the air of wheeling some heavy object into view, "the old place hasn't seen any real company for decades. Ordinarily, a young man of your situation would have spent every summer of the past ten years up north. Most of your friends must spend their summers there, and I've been thinking that our tragedy has kept you from it for too long."

Gloria said something soft but vehement to herself.

"Glor?"

She shook her head.

He went back to Tom. "I've been thinking of showing our old lodge a bit of life. How do you think you'd like to spend a month or so at the lake?"

"I'd love to. It would be great."

His mother uttered an almost inaudible sigh, and patted her lips with a pink napkin.

"A carefree summer before your hard work begins."

And then Tom understood—Eagle Lake was a reward for having agreed to major in engineering. His grandfather was not a subtle man.

"I can't go to Eagle Lake," his mother said. "Or aren't I included in this invitation?"

"We want to keep you here, Gloria. I'll feel easier, having you around."

"You want to keep me here. You'd feel easier, having me around. What you mean is, you want to take everything away from me all over again—don't pretend you don't know what I mean, because you do."

Upshaw set down his knife and fork and assumed a bland, innocent look. "Are you implying that you do want to go? Or that I wouldn't worry about you, all the way up there?"

"You *know* I can't go there. You know I couldn't stand it. Why not just say it?"

"Don't upset yourself, Gloria. And you won't be all alone. Victor will be with you. His main job, as far as I am concerned, has always been to look after your welfare."

"Thank you," she said. "Thank you so much. Thank you above all for saying that in front of Tom."

"Tom is a young man."

"You mean he's old enough to think—"

"I mean he is of an age when he may go off and enjoy himself with other people of his own age. In the proper surroundings. Right, Tom?"

"I guess," Tom said, but the expression of gathering misery on his mother's face made him wish to retract the lukewarm agreement. He tingled with shame. As soon as his grandfather had spoken, Tom had known that he was hearing the truth—his father's real job was taking care of his mother. Tom felt slightly sickened.

"I'll stay home, Mom," he said.

She gave him a black look. "Don't say that to please me, because it doesn't please me. It just makes me angry."

"Are you sure?" Tom asked across the table.

His mother did not look up. “I don’t need you to take care of me.”

“Six weeks would be good,” said Upshaw. “Long enough to have a real experience. And when you’re out on your own, those times when business leaves you free, it’ll be there for you.”

“Say thank you,” his mother said in a flat voice.

“Thank you,” Tom said.

Part Six

HEAVEN

Dr. Kleber and others [illegible] emphasized the social dimensions of the treatment process. Dr. Frank H. [illegible], director of the Substance Abuse Research [illegible] at Yale University, put it this way: [illegible] were a drug of the middle or upper classes, we would not be saying it is impossible to treat.

[illegible] the drug of choice in more poor communities, because the initial purchases are relatively cheap.

Initial Conceptions Hold Up

[illegible] the biochemical aspects often tend to come first in considering crack treatment rather than its psychology [illegible] social or economic elements or the [illegible] lessons of history. [illegible] or getting the addict off the drug [illegible] volition, deprivation [illegible] is the first and essential [illegible] of any program that works [illegible] experts and [illegible].

Many of the initial conceptions about crack, which has come into widespread use only within the last four years, have thus far held up.

Yes, it has a rare biochemistry that [illegible] preparing [illegible] [illegible] properly [illegible] obtained with profits [illegible] that few will make the effort.

In past crackdowns on drug dealers, most seized properties were eventually returned to owners by [illegible].

[illegible] page 86.

[illegible] believe that the [illegible] they face in treating crack [illegible] far more from the [illegible] and circumstances of the [illegible] than its biochemical attraction the drug [illegible].

And they believe the new [illegible] society a measure of [illegible] there has been [illegible] with a drug epidemic [illegible] apart poor neighborhoods and families in the nation's cities.

Researchers are finding that crack addiction, under the right conditions, can be successfully treated. Some [illegible] suggest that crack is no more [illegible] addictive than other drugs that addicts have been able to [illegible].

[illegible] Still [illegible]

Only a year ago [illegible] widely regarded [illegible] drug still poorly understood [illegible] special characteristics [illegible] addiction almost impossible to treat. Now, in dozens of interviews and scientific reports, treatment experts are shifting their emphasis to the more positive [illegible] more complex [illegible] about addiction to the [illegible].

Moreover, in finding that properly run programs can be made to work in treating crack [illegible] they believe they have [illegible] crucial element of [illegible].

18

On the first day of his summer vacation, a troubled Tom Pasmore left his house and began moving aimlessly down Eastern Shore Road toward An Die Blumen.

The last days of school had been accompanied by a round of parties at which Tom had walked through one lavish room after another without seeing Sarah Spence in any of them. He had wondered why so many of these rooms had been painted varying shades of pink until he overheard Posy Tuttle's mother telling Moonie Firestone's mother that Katinka Redwing had found the *best* young decorator in New York, who was a genius with pink: "A genius—it's the only word! And of course Katinka found him first. Every evening at six I look out at the sea, you know, our beach, and it's the most beautiful thing—the sky is the same color as my walls!" In the next room, one of his classmates was throwing up into a champagne bucket in a room with walls the color of a pink sky, and several hours later another had passed out on the beach, the legs of his tuxedo trousers rolled up to his knees. But by then the sky was as black as Tom's mood.

He had danced clumsy tangos with Sarah at Miss Ellinghausen's last two classes of the year, but when he had asked her if Ralph Redwing picked her up after every class she had sulked and denied that he ever picked her up. "Sometimes he sends the carriage," she finally said. "They're possessive people, you know. Don't make a big deal out of it." She had smiled when he told her that he would be coming to Eagle Lake, but after that she had seemed nervous and quiet, not nearly as talkative as during their first day together; after class she had excused herself quickly and walked to Calle Berghofstrasse by herself—she still looked beautiful to Tom, but almost forlorn, a secret he would never know.

When Tom had come to the commencement exercises held behind Brooks-Lowood's main building in an atmosphere of striped tents and summery dresses, Sarah turned around to smile at him from her place in the front row with the other graduating seniors. Ralph Redwing, the speaker at one of every three Brooks-Lowood commencements, addressed the topic "Civic Responsibilities of Civic Leaders" by announcing that he was overseeing the publication of a book entitled *Historic Island Domiciles* which would feature full-page plates and floor plans of every house on Mill Walk in which members of the Redwing family had lived (gasps, rustles of anticipation from the Brooks-Lowood mothers). And after the diplomas had been handed out and the awards distributed, Tom had wandered out of the tea tent, stepped onto the soccer field, and looked across at the visitors' parking lot, where Sarah Spence and her parents were just climbing into Ralph Redwing's gleaming carriage.

Tom reached the corner of An Die Blumen and stood for a moment looking between the houses at the blue dazzle of the bay. The night before the commencement he had visited Lamont von Heilitz and felt as if he were returning to his true home—he loved both the vast eccentric crowded room and its extraordinary inhabitant—but the evening had felt tentative and inconclusive. The Shadow had seemed upset at the news of Tom's visit to Eagle Lake, and what had been more distressing to Tom was that for most of the evening the old man had denied his reluctance to have Tom make the trip.

"You don't think I should go to Eagle Lake," Tom had said. "I know you don't. Do you want me to stay here and work with you?"

"I suppose you'll do what you want to do," von Heilitz said. "It's a matter of timing, really."

"You mean you don't want me to go *now*?"

The Shadow answered him with another question. "Are you planning to go alone? Glen didn't include your mother in the invitation?"

Tom shook his head.

For the first time, the reclusive detective struck Tom as intensely lonely, in a way that illuminated Tom's own loneliness. If Tom spent six weeks away from Mill Walk, he would be depriving the old man of his only companionship. But Tom could not speak of this, and von Heilitz merely continued to look distressed and uncomfortable and as if he had things to do that Tom could not witness. So Tom felt excluded, as uncomfortable as his friend—it was the first real coolness between them. Tom had thought of asking von Heilitz if he knew of any trouble at Shady Mount Hospital, but the old man had moved across the room and put on a record. "Mahler," he said, and an instant later sounds like pistol shots and battlefield moans filled the room. The old man collapsed into a chair, put his feet up on his table, and closed his eyes. Tom let himself out. It was like his grandfather, he supposed—you couldn't expect a man like that to behave like an ordinary person.

Now he looked up from the sidewalk and saw the front door of an enormous Spanish mansion on The Sevens swing open. He immediately wished that he were invisible, then that he were right in front of the house. A small brown and white dog appeared first, tugging at a leash and bouncing on his forefeet. Tom gave in to his desire for invisibility, and moved to the side of the red booth. In a blue shirt with rolled sleeves, white shorts, and white tennis shoes, Sarah Spence appeared at the other end of the leash. Laughing, she said something to the dog and closed the door behind her.

Sarah followed the eager dog down the red brick steps, her hair swinging, and began moving down the wide stone walk to the sidewalk. Her free arm swung, her tanned slender legs swung, even her neat white feet swung. Her back was very straight, and her hair gathered and released with every step. The dog trotted out on the sidewalk and pulled Sarah down the block.

He stepped away from the telephone booth and watched her moving away from him. Then he crossed An Die Blumen and began walking down The Sevens, half a block behind her. The day, which he had hardly noticed earlier, now seemed astonishingly clean and fresh: limpid sunlight fell directly on Sarah's glowing hair and the straight line of her shoulders. He realized that he took pleasure simply in the eloquent way she walked, her golden legs almost striding and her feet skimming above the sidewalk as if they were winged.

Tom quickened his pace. He could not imagine why he had wanted to hide from Sarah Spence, nor what he would say to her when he finally caught up.

At that moment Sarah turned her head and saw him. "Tom!" she all but cried out, and stopped moving so abruptly that the dog's front legs rose up off the ground. She turned around to face him, transferred the leash to her other hand, and yielded one step to the dog, who began to sniff a tree. "Why are you grinning at me? Why didn't you say something?"

"I was going to catch up to you," he said, answering the second question.

"Good," she said. "You can help me walk Bingo. I don't think you ever met him, did you?"

He shook his head and looked down at the suddenly attentive dog, who looked back at him, pointed ears and thin rope of a tail perked up.

She bent down to pat the dog, who continued to look at Tom with very alert, intelligent eyes. "Tell Tom your name is Bingo, he's such a stranger he doesn't even know you."

"How old is he?"

"Seven. I *told* you about him—but I'm not surprised you didn't remember. It was that day I visited you in the hospital. When I covered myself with embarrassment."

Tom shook his head. His mouth open and tongue lolling, Bingo stopped looking at him and waited for his mistress to resume walking.

"It's okay—I got him the day I heard about your accident."

"So he's as old as I am," Tom said, not thinking at all about what he was saying. Then he took in Sarah's expression, and said, "Sorry, that must have sounded funny. I mean, ah, I guess I don't know what I meant." He took a step forward, and Sarah smiled at him, still with a trace of puzzled amusement clear in her face, and began walking beside him.

"I don't even know where you're going to college," he said after a few moments of silence.

"Oh, I was accepted at Hollins and Goucher, but I'm going to go to Mount Holyoke—it sounded interesting, and Moonie Firestone got accepted there too, so. . ." She glanced sideways up at him, and closed, then opened her mouth. She said, "Tom—" and then stopped. She looked down at the dog straining ahead, and then spoke again. "My parents really wanted me to go to a girls' school. I guess it's okay for a year or so, but I'm already thinking about transferring. Isn't that ridiculous? I'm not even there yet. Buddy thinks I ought to switch to Arizona. Do you know where you're going to go?"

"I guess I'll probably go to Tulane. If I get in."

"Maybe I'll transfer to Tulane, then." She looked up at him as she had before, and he suddenly remembered exactly how she had looked when she had come to the hospital—how the face she had now, which was the face of her young womanhood, had just formed itself out of her childhood, and how badly he had wanted her to touch him. He wanted to put his arm around her, but she spoke before he could decide to do it.

"Are you really going to come to Eagle Lake this summer?" He nodded. "Listen, I didn't even think when I was talking to you—at Miss Ellinghausen's. It's like, every time I talk to you I say something so dumb I want to curl up and die when I think about it later."

"What?"

"But if you're really coming, I guess it must be all right. It is, isn't it?"

"What must be all right?"

"Well, Eagle Lake isn't just an ordinary place for you, is it?"

He just looked down at her.

"And I understand that you couldn't think of it the way *we* do, so I just wondered . . ." When he still said nothing, Sarah stopped walking and lightly grasped his arm. "I know your mother drowned, um, died. . . ."

For a moment both of them looked utterly confused: Tom remembered headlines from Lamont von Heilitz's journal and saw a photograph of Jeanine Thielman extending a beautiful leg down from a carriage.

"Oh, my God," Sarah said. "I did it again. I don't know what's wrong with me. Please forgive me."

Sarah now looked distressed to the point of tears. "It wasn't my mother," he said. "That was my—"

"I know, I *know*," Sarah said. "I can't imagine what—I know it was your grandmother, but in my head it got—I guess because I never see your mother, and I started thinking that—" She threw out her hands, and Bingo growled. Both Tom and Sarah looked down at Bingo, then toward the empty corner at which Bingo fixedly stared. The dog was leaning forward against the leash, and kept up a low growl.

"It's easy to get mixed up," Tom said, feeling as if he were speaking from experience.

"I was so *sure*." She began to turn red. "How did I get into any college? How did I ever get out of grade school? I'm starting to sound like a *Redwing*!"

"It was just a mistake," Tom said. Bingo was still making angry, theatening noises and tugging at the leash.

"Bingo! He hates to be held up, he's so impatient. . . ." Stricken by what she had said, Sarah let the dog pull her forward. "I'm so sorry, I can't—" She shrugged, and made an elaborately apologetic gesture with her free hand.

Tom realized that he could walk down to the hospital and see for himself what had happened to Nancy Vetiver—then it seemed to him that he had been planning to go to Shady Mount ever since leaving his house.

"I have to go somewhere," Tom said, moving ahead of her and the straining dog, who cast him a wild-eyed, impatient look. "It's okay! I'll see you soon!"

She rolled her eyes and shook her head. "Please!" she shouted.

19

Tom looked back from the far corner of Sarah's street and saw her gazing toward him. The little terrier was still tugging at the leash, and she stepped forward and waved tentatively. He returned the wave, and crossed the intersection of Yorkminster Place. Houses he had seen and known all his life presented blank, lifeless façades; sprinklers whirred above grass that seemed to be made of spun sugar. Through windows left open to the breezes he saw immaculate empty rooms with grand pianos and looming portraits.

He walked past Salisbury Road, past Ely Place and Stonehenge Circle, past Victoria Terrace and Omdurman Road. Between Omdurman Road and Balaclava Lane the houses became slightly smaller and closer together, and by Waterloo Parade they were ordinary three-story frame and red brick houses. Here a few children rode tricycles up and down driveways, and thick low hedges were the only separation between the houses. A man reading a newspaper on his front porch looked up at him suspiciously but went back to the *Eyewitness* when he saw only a fairly ordinary Eastern Shore Road teenager.

Cars, bicycles, and pony traps streamed up and down Calle Berlinstrasse. An ambulance went by, then a second ambulance. After another step Tom realized that four police cars had pulled into a circular drive across the street. Lights whirled and flashed. Above the turmoil of ambulances and police cars before which a crowd had begun to gather stood the red brick building in which he had spent nearly three months of his tenth year.

When the light changed, he ran across the street and began to weave through the people peering over the tops of the police cars.

A policeman stood in front of the revolving door that led to the hospital's waiting room and front desk. He was in his mid-twenties, his uniform was pressed and spotless, and his face looked very white beneath his visor. His buttons, belt, and boots gleamed. He kept his eyes a careful foot or so above the heads of the crowd.

"What happened?" Tom asked a stout woman carrying a white plastic shopping bag.

She leaned over and looked up at him. "I'm just lucky, I was right here when all the cops pulled up—way it looks, somebody got killed in there."

Tom walked forward into the empty space between the spectators and the lone officer at the top of the hospital steps. The young cop gave him a hard glance, and then looked back out at nothing. When Tom started coming up the steps, he took his hand off his gun butt and crossed his arms over his chest.

"Officer, could you tell me what's happening?" He was half a foot taller than the policeman, who tilted his neck and glared at Tom.

"Are you going in or not? If not, get back down."

Tom pushed his way through the revolving door, took two steps toward the desk, and stopped short.

His past had been rewritten. The tiny waiting room with two or three rickety chairs and a low wooden partition before an equally tiny office with a switchboard and receptionist was now the size of a train station. Wooden benches and molded plastic chairs lined the walls on either side. Patients in bathrobes, most of them staring fixedly at their laps, occupied a few of these chairs. A whiskery old man in a wheelchair looked up sharply at Tom's entrance, and a strand of drool wobbled from his lower lip. At the far end of the great lobby a new partition of thick translucent glass or plastic divided the office from the lobby. Behind the partition women moved between file cases, sat at desks with telephones propped to their ears, and consulted papers at their desks.

On the wide marble floor between the revolving door and the partition stood two groups of policemen that reminded Tom of the huddles of opposing football teams. The lobby was much darker than the street.

"Natchez! What are you doing over there?" called an officer in the larger of the two groups. "We're here to do a job."

Tom had been trying to sidle past the old men in chairs. He looked up when he heard the name. A sturdy policeman in a business suit whispered a few words to his cohort and began moving toward the others. He looked like an athlete, muscular and self-contained. An angry flush covered his cheeks. In the way the other officers parted to admit him, then crowded a little too closely around him, Tom had an impression of barely concealed hostility. Then he remembered the name: Natchez was one of the two detectives who had searched the Shadow's house.

He backed away toward the wall and sat down to wait until the policemen left the lobby. Detective Natchez strode across the floor and punched an elevator button. Some of the other policemen continued to stare at him. The men to whom Natchez had been talking dispersed.

"My daughter is coming today," said the old man beside Tom.

"Do you know why all these policemen are here?" Tom asked him.

The old man's lower lip sagged, and his eyes were pink. "Do you know my daughter?"

"No," Tom said.

The old man gripped his upper arm and leaned very close. "Someone *died*," he uttered. "*Murdered*. It's my daughter's birthday."

Tom pulled his arm free of the old man's grip. A hole had opened in the surface of the earth, and he had just fallen through it.

"They want to shoot her full of lead," the man said, "but I won't let them."

Another old man a few chairs away hitched toward them, obviously wishing to join this interesting conversation, and Tom hastily stood up. One of the officers in the original group cast him a look of impersonal hostility. Tom looked down and turned away, and saw the bottoms of neatly pressed, dark blue trousers and polished black boots with buttons protruding from the bottom of the robe worn by the second old man. The first man, and nearly all of the other patients sitting in the lobby, wore limp pajamas and slippers. He looked at the man's face, and saw him looking back at him.

The second old man was at first indistinguishable from all the others—his grey hair fell about his face, his lip drooped, his head trembled. The man clutched his robe close about his neck, and bent forward to mumble something. Tom stepped away, but the man's eyes still held him. They were alert and intelligent, not at all the eyes of senility. A recognition jogged the boy. And then—with a shock that almost made him cry out—Tom realized that he was looking at Lamont von Heilitz.

Tom looked over his shoulder at the police. The hostile officer was sauntering up toward Natchez, the intention of saying something unpleasant clear upon his face. He slid onto the seat beside von Heilitz, glanced at him for a second, and looked away. The Shadow had whitened his face with makeup and pasted straggling thorny eyebrows over his own. His whole face looked gaunt and stupid and hopeless. "Look away." The words seemed to speak themselves.

Tom gazed across the vast emptying lobby. The officer in charge of the first group had begun moving toward a corridor to the right of the new desk. The others went toward the doors and the elevators: there was the same sense of inactivity Tom had felt when he first came in. "What are you doing here?" he whispered.

"My house, tonight," von Heilitz said in the same ventriloquial fashion.

"Somebody died?"

"Go," von Heilitz ordered, and Tom stood up as if he had been jabbed with a pin.

He wandered out into the great empty lobby. The elevator into which Detective Natchez had disappeared returned to the lobby, and when Tom reached the desk its doors opened. Detective Natchez and two uniformed policemen emerged on either side of a kind of wheeled sheet-covered cart, which obviously held a corpse. Tom again fell through the hole in the earth's surface. *I did that*, he thought. *I wrote a letter, and that man died.*

"May I help you?" The woman seated at the desk facing the partition had set down her telephone and was looking up at Tom with a crisp challenge that suggested she would much prefer not to do anything of the kind.

"Ah, I was visiting a friend of mine upstairs," Tom said, "and I saw all these policemen here, and—"

"No, you were not," she said.

"What?"

"You were not visiting a patient, not in this hospital," she said. Her perfectly black, lifeless-looking hair rolled back from her low forehead in a high crest, and half-glasses perched just beneath the bridge of her nose as if commanded to go no further. "I saw you enter the lobby no more than a minute or two ago, young man, and the only patients with whom you have had any contact are those two men seated against the wall. Are you going to leave this hospital by yourself, or will I have to have you escorted out?"

"I wonder if you could tell me what happened here," he said.

"That wouldn't be any business of yours now, would it?"

"Two people told me that someone was murdered."

Her eyes widened, and her chin tilted up another tiny portion of an inch.

"I'd like to see Nancy Vetiver," Tom said. "She's a nurse who used to—"

"Nurse Vetiver? Now it's Nurse Vetiver? And who would you like to see after that, King Louis the Fourteenth? Our people are too busy to be bothered by stray cats like you, most especially when they come babbling about— Officer! Officer! Will you come here, please?"

All the policemen in the lobby looked at them, and after a

momentary show of hesitation the officer who had sent Detective Natchez upstairs moved toward the desk. He said nothing, but looked first at Tom, then the receptionist, with a strained, impatient, wholly artificial smile.

"Officer . . . ?" the receptionist began.

"Get on with it," he said.

Suddenly the entire scene seemed wrong to Tom, essentially out of key. Even the receptionist had been nonplussed by the policeman's hostility. Some of the men in the lobby seemed angry, and some of them seemed almost triumphant beneath their mask of indifference.

"This young man," the receptionist began again, "has entered the hospital under false pretenses. He said something about a murder, he's asking about the nurses, he's disrupting—"

"*I* don't care, lady," the officer said. He walked away shaking his head.

"Is this how you do your job?" she called to him. Her voice was sharp enough to split wood. Then she saw a more likely source of aid. "Doctor, if you'll assist me—for a moment?"

Dr. Bonaventure Milton had just emerged from the corridor to the right of the desk, accompanied by a lean, brown, anonymous-looking man in a blue uniform with conspicuous braid. The fat little doctor in his pince-nez and black bow tie looked from the receptionist to him and smiled. "Of course, Miss Dragonette. You have a problem with my young friend here?"

"Friend?" Now she seemed startled. "This young man has been saying things about murder—trying to intrude himself into the hospital—asking for one of the nurses— I want him expelled."

Dr. Milton made soothing passes with his hands. "I'm sure we can straighten this out, Miss Dragonette. This young fellow is Glendenning Upshaw's grandson, Tom Pasmore. I saw him just a week or two ago at the Founders Club. Now what was it you wanted, Tom?"

Miss Dragonette had given up on the little doctor and was now trying to galvanize the officer beside him by drilling holes in his head with her eyes.

"I was just outside, and when I saw all the squad cars I wanted to come in—I realized that my grandfather had never called me back about Nancy Vetiver—" He looked at the face of the officer in the splendid uniform, and was disconcerted both by the coldness of the man's eyes and the sense that he had seen him somewhere before.

"I shouldn't wonder!" said Miss Dragonette.

"Is there some trouble?" the officer said, and this time Tom took in his bald head and the smooth knuckle of his face and recognized Captain Fulton Bishop. His stomach froze—for a moment all he wanted to do was turn and run. The Captain was shorter than he had appeared on television. There was no humor in the man at all. He looked like a torturer in a medieval drawing.

Dr. Milton looked quickly from Tom to Captain Bishop, then, questioningly, back again. "Oh, I don't think there is any trouble—do you? The boy was looking for Nurse Vetiver, an old favorite of his. By the way, Tom, this is Captain Bishop, who did all that excellent work bringing Miss Hasselgard's murderer to justice."

Neither Tom nor Captain Bishop offered to shake hands.

"An unhappy day for us all," the doctor went on. "One of the Captain's men, a patrolman named Mendenhall, died this morning. We did what we could, but the man had been quite severely wounded—died a hero's death, one of the first men into the killer's house, thought we could pull him through, did the best we could *despite* some interference"—here a meaningful glance at Tom—"but poor Mendenhall slipped away from us about half an hour ago. Tragic, of course."

"But why are there so many policemen here?" Tom asked. He was not quite aware of speaking, because he had just dropped through the earth's surface again.

"We came for the body," Bishop said flatly.

"Well, it didn't make any sense to *me*," said Miss Dragonette. "He did say something about a murder."

"An old man over there said something—he's senile, it didn't really make sense. . . ." Now both the doctor and Captain Bishop were staring at him.

"Which man over there?" the Captain said.

Tom looked again to the side of the room. Von Heilitz was gone. "The old man in the yellow bathrobe." He turned back to the doctor. "I really came in to see Nancy Vetiver."

"Mr. Williams doesn't know what day it is," said Miss Dragonette. "Sits there all day long, waiting for his daughter, but he wouldn't recognize her if she walked right in that door. Which isn't likely, since she lives in Bangor, Maine."

"Doctor, I'll speak to you later," the Captain said, and walked across the lobby and disappeared through the revolving door after the men wheeling the dead policeman's body.

Dr. Milton sighed and watched him go. "What are you trying to do? Do you have any notion . . . ?" He shook his head. "I'll take care of this, Miss Dragonette. Come with me, Tom."

The doctor led Tom into the corridor on the desk's right side. He slipped his arm through the boy's and said, "Let me make sure I understand all this. You came in here looking for Nurse Vetiver—because of the conversation you overheard at your grandfather's house. You wanted to be assured of her well-being, am I right? You saw the policemen in the lobby. You sat down next to that old fellow, who began babbling about a murder."

"That's right," Tom said.

"You understand—things get very sensitive when a police officer dies. Feelings run high."

Was that what he had seen? Tom wondered. A display of intense feeling? He remembered the two groups of policemen, the sense of hostility and some queer victory. His sense of guilt made him feel as though he were walking through thick fog, unable to see or think properly.

The doctor self-consciously looked into Tom's eyes. "You want to be careful, Tom. You don't want to upset people. Everyone is a little sensitive these days. The Hasselgard business, all of that—you know. You're an intelligent young man. You come from a good family, and you have a long life before you."

"That cop, Mendenhall, died because of 'the Hasselgard business.' "

"Indirectly, yes," the doctor said. He had begun to look annoyed.

"Because of the letter Captain Bishop got."

"What do you know about that letter? Who told you—"

"It was on the news. But nobody but Captain Bishop ever saw the letter, did they?"

"I don't quite see your point, if you have one."

"My point is—" Tom hesitated, then went on. "What if the letter actually said something else. What if it didn't say anything about a poor half-native ex-con named Foxhall Edwardes? What if it proved that someone else actually killed Marita Hasselgard, and that her death was directly related to what was going on at the Treasury?"

"This is ridiculous," the doctor said. "A man just died here."

"And a lot of other men in here didn't seem exactly unhappy about that," Tom said.

"Remember that there are both loyal and disloyal officers," Dr. Milton said. "What are you trying to do, Tom? Real letters and unreal letters, questions about murder . . . ?"

"How could that man Mendenhall be disloyal if he was killed in the line of duty? Disloyal to what?"

Dr. Milton visibly controlled himself. "Listen to me—loyal means sticking to your own people. You know who they are. Your neighbors, your friends, your family. They are *you*. Don't run away with yourself."

The doctor straightened his back and tugged at his vest. "You have to live in this world with the rest of us," the doctor said. He looked at his watch. "I want us both to forget this conversation. I still have a lot to do today. Please give my regards to your mother and your grandfather." He looked sharply up at Tom, still agitated, stepped around him, and began to walk back to the lobby. After a few steps, he stopped and faced Tom again. "By the way, Nurse Vetiver has been suspended. Let the whole matter drop, Tom."

"What about Hattie Bascombe?" Tom asked.

This time, the doctor laughed. "Hattie Bascombe! I imagine she's in the old slave quarter, if she's still alive. Retired years ago. Mumbling over a chicken bone and casting spells, I suppose. Quite a character, wasn't she?"

"Quite a character," Tom said to the doctor's retreating back.

20

"I wonder if you'd like to go on an excursion with me," Tom said. He was talking on the telephone to Sarah Spence, and it was just past four o'clock. His father was still at his office on Calle Hoffmann—or doing whatever he did when he was not at home—and Gloria Pasmore was upstairs in her room. When Tom returned from the hospital, he had opened her bedroom door on a wave of soft music and whiskey fumes and looked in to see her sprawled out asleep on her bed. It was her "afternoon nap."

"That sounds interesting, but I'm kind of busy," Sarah said. "Mom and I are getting ready to go up north. Dad suddenly announced that we're going early this year, so now we only have two days to pack. Well, what he said was that we're going up in the Redwings' private plane. And I can't find Bingo anywhere, but of course it's ridiculous to worry about *Bingo*." After a pause, she said, "What kind of excursion?"

"I thought we might walk somewhere."

"You won't suddenly gasp and turn pale and run away if I say something absolutely doltish?"

Tom laughed. "No, and I won't suddenly remember that I have to go somewhere else."

"So you want to begin all over again where we left off? I like that idea."

"I was thinking of going somewhere new," Tom said. "The old slave quarter."

"I've never even been there."

"Me neither. No one from the far east end has ever even thought of going there."

"Isn't it a long way away?"

"Not that far. We wouldn't spend more than half an hour there."

"Doing what? Investigating opium dens, or organizing a white slavery ring, or tracking down stolen Treasury money, or—"

"What kind of books do you read?"

"Mainly the trash I see you carrying through the halls. I just finished *Red Harvest*. What do you want to do?"

"I want to look up an old friend of mine," Tom said.

"Is this an excursion or an adventure? I wonder. And I wonder who the old friend could be."

"Someone I used to know. Someone from the hospital."

"That nurse who thought you were so cute? I remember *her*. Why would she be living in the old slave quarter? Maybe you want to set her free from a haunt of vice, and you need me to distract the Tuaregs and lascars."

"No, not that nurse, another one," Tom said, amused and disconcerted. "Named Hattie Bascombe. But she might be able to tell me something about the other one."

"Aha!" Sarah said. "I knew it. Okay, I'll come along, just to protect you. Are you bringing your gat, or should I pack mine?"

"Let's both pack our gats," Tom said.

"One more thing. I think this will be an automotive excursion, not a walking trip."

"I can't drive."

"But I can," Sarah said. "I'm an ace. I could barrel through a passel of gunsels as well as anybody in Dashiell Hammett. And this way I can look out for Bingo on the way."

"Should I come over there, or—"

"Be outside of your house in fifteen minutes," she said. "I'll be the doll in the shades and the snap-brim hat behind the wheel of the ostentatious car."

Twenty minutes later he was seated in the leather bucket seat of a little white Mercedes convertible with what seemed to him an abnormally loud engine, watching Sarah Spence downshift as she accelerated through a yellow light and turned on Calle Drosselmayer. "Bingo doesn't do things like this," she was saying. "He's not really a very adventurous dog. He seems to worry a lot about whether or not we're going to feed him."

"What happens to him when you go up north?"

"We put him in a kennel."

"Then he probably figured out that he was going back to the kennel in two days, and he wandered away to brood about it. I bet he'll be back by dinnertime."

"That's brilliant!" she said. "Even if it's not true, I feel better already." Then: "Bingo doesn't brood much, actually."

"He didn't strike me as a broody dog," Tom said. Sarah's driving delighted him—Sarah's company delighted him. He thought he had never been in a car with anyone who drove like Sarah, with as much control and exhilaration. His mother drove at an uncertain five miles under the limit, mumbling to herself most of the time, and his father drove wildly, in a rage at other drivers the second he pulled out of the driveway. Sarah laughed at what he had said. When she drew up at a stoplight, she leaned over and kissed him. "A broody dog," she said. "I think you're the broody dog, Tom Pasmore."

Then the light changed, and the little car flashed through the intersection, and sunlight fell all about them, and Tom felt that he had entered into a moment of almost inhuman perfection. His sense of guilty responsibility had suddenly disappeared. Sarah was still laughing, probably at the expression on his face. People on the sidewalk stared at them as they zipped past. The light streamed down, and the pretty shop fronts of Calle Drosselmayer, golden wood and sparkling glass, glowed and shone. Men and women sat beneath striped umbrellas at an outdoor café. Behind one great shining window, a model railway puffed through mountains and snowy passes, circling around again to a perfect scale model of Calle Drosselmayer—he saw their reflection in the window, and imagined himself and Sarah in a tiny white car on the model street. A great unconscious paradise lay all about him, the paradise of ordinary things.

Auer, Tom thought. *Our. Hour*. And remembered feeling this same way at least once before. Some buried subcontinent of his childhood broke the surface of his thoughts—he remembered a sense of *impendingness*, of some great thing about to happen, of imminent discovery in a forbidden place. . . .

Now they were in the lower end of Calle Drosselmayer, driving by the grey, prisonlike St. Alwyn Hotel. Years ago, someone had been murdered there—some scandal that had ended in a bigger scandal his parents had not let him read about, and which he had been too young to understand. . . .

"This isn't much like being with Buddy," she said. "He only ever wants to go to gun shops."

"Do you ever think about what you want to be?" she said when she drove them down the hill to Mogrom Street. "You must—I think about it a lot. My parents want me to get married to somebody nice with a lot of money and live about two blocks from them. They can't imagine why I'd want to do anything else."

"My parents want me to make a lot of money and live eight hundred miles away," Tom said. "But first they want me to get an engineering degree, so that I can set up a construction business. Mr. Handley wants me to write novels about Mill Walk. My grandfather wants me to keep my mouth shut and join the John Birch society. Brooks-Lowood School wants me to straighten up at last and learn how to play basketball—turn right here, go past the alley, and turn right again onto the next street—Miss Ellinghausen wants me to learn how to tango. Dr. Milton wants me to stop thinking altogether and be a loyal future member of the Founders Club."

"And what do you want?"

"I want—I want to be what I really am. Whatever that is. Here we are. Let's stop and get out."

Sarah gave him an uncertain, questioning look, but pulled over to the side and stopped nearly on the same few feet of roadway where Dennis Handley had parked his Corvette. Both of them got out. In the valley that was Weasel Hollow, the air steamed and stank.

The smell of boiled cabbage that came from the yellow house mingled with the stench of rotting garbage from the fly-encrusted, glistening heap some yards farther down the street. The pile of garbage had grown since Tom had been here with Dennis Handley: several broken chairs and a rolled-up carpet had been added to it, along with five or six stained paper bags. Tinny radios sent conflicting fragments of nearly inaudible music into the air. Far off, a child screeched.

"What was burning around here?" Sarah asked, sniffing.

"A house and a car. The house is a block away, but the car's just up ahead."

Sarah stepped out into the empty street and saw it. She turned to look at Tom. "You were here before?"

"The car hadn't been burned then. The owner abandoned it here because he thought it would be safe. He thought nobody would see it."

Tom walked into the dusty street and joined her. What was left of Hasselgard's Corvette looked like a crushed insect left in the sun. The seats, dashboard, and steering wheel had been burned away to metal skeletons; the tires were ashy black chips beneath the rims; the whole body was a blackened shell already turning orange with rust. Someone, probably a child, had hammered at it with a heavy stick and then tossed the stick through the empty windshield.

"Who was the owner?" Sarah said.

Tom did not answer this question. "I wanted to see if they'd really burn it. I was pretty sure they'd burn the house, because it was so destroyed by gunfire that it must have been in danger of collapsing. And they couldn't be sure of what might be inside it. But I wasn't really sure about the car. They must have come over on the same night—come right through the lots, carrying their gasoline cans." He looked up into Sarah's puzzled face. "It was Hasselgard's car."

She frowned, but said nothing.

"You see how they act? How they do things? They don't even sneak it away on the back of a truck—they just douse it with gasoline and burn the shit out of it. They solve everything with sledgehammers. The people around here certainly aren't going to say anything, are they? Because they know if they do, their own houses'll burn up. It wouldn't even be on the news."

"Are you saying that the police burned Hasselgard's car?"

"Didn't I make that clear?"

"But, Tom, why—"

It seemed, at last, that he had to tell her: the words nearly marched out of his mouth by themselves. "I wrote the letter the police got—the letter was supposed to be about that ex-con, Foxhall Edwardes. Fulton Bishop talked about it at his press conference. It was an anonymous letter, because I didn't want them to know a kid wrote it. I told them how and why Hasselgard killed his own sister. The next day, all hell broke loose. They killed Hasselgard, they killed this guy Edwardes, they killed a cop named Mendenhall, and injured his partner, Klink, they let loose this huge black cloud—"

He threw up his arms, stopped short by the incongruity of saying these terrible things to a beautiful girl in a blue shirt and white shorts who was thinking about a lost dog. "It's this whole place," he said. "Mill Walk! We're supposed to believe every word they say and keep on taking dancing lessons, we're supposed to keep on going to Boney Milton when we're sick, we're supposed to get excited about a picture book of every house the Redwings ever lived in!"

She took a step nearer to him. "I'm not saying I understand everything, but are you sorry you wrote the letter?"

"I don't know. Not exactly. I'm sorry those two men died. I'm sorry Hasselgard wasn't arrested. I didn't know enough."

Then she said something that surprised him. "Maybe you just wrote to the wrong person."

"You know," he said, "maybe I did. There's a detective named Natchez—I used to think he was one of the bad guys, but a friend of mine told me that he was close to Mendenhall. And this morning at the hospital I thought I saw that he and some of his friends . . ."

"Why don't you go to him?"

"I need more. I need to have something he doesn't already know."

"Who's this friend? The one who told you about Natchez and Mendenhall?"

"Somebody wonderful," he said. "A great man. I can't tell you his name, because you'd laugh at me if I did. But someday I'd like you to meet him. Really meet him."

"*Really* meet him? This isn't Dennis Handley, is it?"

Tom laughed. "No, not Handles. Handles has given up on me."

"Because he didn't get you into bed."

"What!"

She smiled at him. "Well, I'm glad it's not him anyhow. Are we still going to the old slave quarter?"

"Do you still want to?"

"Of course I do. In spite of what my parents want for me, I still haven't completely given up hoping I might have an interesting life." She moved nearer to him, and looked up with an expression that reminded him of the first time Miss Ellinghausen had brought them together. "I really do wonder where you're going. I wonder where you and I are going too."

She did not want him to kiss her, he saw—it was just that she saw more of him than he had ever expected her to see. She had not questioned or disbelieved him; he had not shocked her: she had taken every step with him. This girl he had just mentally accused of thinking of nothing more than a lost dog suddenly seemed surpassing, immense. "Me too," he said. "Maybe I shouldn't have told you all this stuff."

"You had to tell somebody, I suppose. Isn't that why you invited me on this excursion?"

And there she was again: in his very footsteps, this time before he had even made them.

"Are you going to introduce me to this Hattie Bascombe, or not?"

They smiled at each other and turned back to the car.

"I'm glad you're coming to Eagle Lake," she said, when they were both in their seats. "I have the feeling you might be safer there."

He thought of Fulton Bishop's face, and nodded. "I'm safe now, Sarah. Nothing's going to happen."

"Then if you're this great detective and all, find Bingo for me." She gunned the engine and shot forward.

21

Tom had been half-fearing, half-expecting that another spell of illness would overtake him as they approached Goethe Park; by now, he scarcely knew what he expected from a visit to Hattie Bascombe, but was certain at least that he did not want to get sick in front of Sarah Spence. He still had not told her that all he knew of the old nurse's whereabouts was that she lived in the old slave quarter, and that was embarrassment enough.

The street numbers marched from the twenties into the thirties as they drove down Calle Burleigh, and he was relieved to feel no symptoms of distress. Neither of them spoke much. When the row of houses and shops before them yielded to the great cream-colored façade of a church, and after that to trees and open ground, he told her to turn left at the next block, and Sarah went around the nose of a dray horse and through a cloud of bicycles into 35th Street.

To their right, children pulled their parents forward toward hot dog vendors and balloon men. Exhausted tigers and panthers lay flattened on the stone floors of their cages; some other animal howled in the maze of trails between cages. Tom closed his eyes.

For two blocks past the south end of Goethe Park, where young men in jeans and T-shirts played cricket before an audience of small children and wandering dogs, the houses continued neat and sober, with their porches and dormer windows and borders of bright flowers. Bicycles leaned against the palm trees on the sidewalks. Then Sarah drove up a tiny hill where a clump of cypress trees twisted toward the sun, and down into a different landscape.

Beside the grimy red brick and broken windows of an abandoned factory came a stretch of taverns and leaning edifices much added to at their back ends and connected by ramshackle passages and catwalks. On both sides of the street, handwritten signs in the windows advertised ROOMS TO LET and ALL SORTS OF JUNK PURCHASED AT GOOD PRICES. OLD CLOATHES CHEAP. HUMIN HAIR BOUGHT AND SOLD. The wooden buildings on both sides of the street blotted out the afternoon sun. At intervals, archways and passages cut into the tenements gave Tom glimpses of sunless courtyards in which lounging men passed bottles back and forth. From the windows a few faces stared out as blankly as the signs: BONES. WARES BOUGHT.

"I feel like a tourist here," Tom said.

"I do too. It's because we're never supposed to see this part of the island. We're not supposed to know about Elysian Courts, so it's kind of invisible."

Sarah drove around a hole in the middle of the narrow street.

"Is that what this is called?"

"Didn't you know about the Elysian Courts? They were built to get people out of the old slave quarter—because the quarter was built on a marsh, and it turned out to be unhealthy. Cholera, influenza, I don't know what. These tenements were put up in a hurry, and pretty soon they were even worse than the slave quarter."

"Where did you hear about them?"

"They were one of Maxwell Redwing's first projects, around 1920 or so. Not one of his most successful. Except financially, of course. I guess the people who live there call it Maxwell's Heaven."

Tom turned around on the seat to look back at the leaning tenements: their outer walls formed a kind of fortress, and through the arches and passages he could see dim figures moving within the mazelike interior.

They were out in the sun again, and the harsh light fell on the poor structures between the walls of Elysian Courts and the old slave quarter—tarpaper shacks and shanties jammed hip to hip on both sides of the narrow descending street. Hopeless-looking men lolled here and there in doorways, and a drunk swung back and forth on a lamppost with a shattered bulb, revolving south-east, east-south, like a broken compass.

The shanties came to an end at the bottom of the hill. Tiny wooden houses, each exactly alike with a minuscule roofed porch and a single window beside the door, stood on lots scarcely bigger than themselves. The whole of the small area, no more than four or five square blocks, seemed oppressively damp. At the far end of the old slave quarter, visible between the neat rows of houses, was an abandoned cane field that had evolved into a vast, crowded dump; beyond the chainlink fence enclosing the dump was the bright sea.

"So that's the old slave quarter," Sarah said. "After you've seen Maxwell's Heaven I suppose you're ready for anything. Where do we go? You have her address, don't you?"

"Turn right," Tom said, having seen something between the shacks.

"Aye-aye," Sarah said, and turned into the road that ran along the northern edge of the quarter. Before them was an isolated shack, two or three times the size of the others and in noticeably better condition, with a large handpainted sign propped on its roof.

"Go behind that store," Tom said. "Fast. He's coming out of her door."

She looked over to see if he were serious, and Tom pointed to the back of the store. Sarah jerked the car into low and stepped hard on the accelerator. The Mercedes flew over the mud and stones of the road, and skidded to a stop behind the store. It seemed to Tom that only a second had passed since he had spoken. His stomach was still back on the road.

"That fast enough for you?" Sarah said.

The face of a little girl with braids and an open mouth popped into a window at the back of the building.

"Yep."

"Now will you tell me what's going on?"

"Listen," he said.

In a few seconds they heard the clopping of hooves and the creaking of leather.

"Now watch the road," Tom said, and nodded back toward the way they had come. For a long time, the sound of the horse and its carriage came nearer the shop; then the sound subtly changed, and began going away from them. After a minute or two, a pony trap appeared retreating down the track, driven by a man in a black coat and black Homburg hat.

"That's Dr. Milton!" Sarah said. "What would he—"

A small scurrying shape hurtled around the side of the building and jumped into Sarah's arms. When it stopped whirling and began licking Sarah's face, Tom saw that it was Bingo.

She held the dog in both her arms and looked at Tom, amazed.

"I think Dr. Milton must have seen him somewhere near the hospital, recognized him, and decided to take him on his errand before bringing him back," he said.

"His errand? In the old slave quarter?" Sarah lifted her chin away from Bingo's tongue.

"He decided that he told me too much," Tom said. "But now I know where Hattie Bascombe lives."

Sarah deposited Bingo in the well behind the seats. "You mean, he came out here to tell her not to talk to you? To threaten her or something?"

"If I remember Hattie Bascombe right," Tom said, "it's not going to work."

Sarah parked behind a pile of fresh horse droppings, and Tom got out of the car. "What if he was just calling on a patient?" she said. "Isn't that at least a little bit possible?"

"Do you want to come with me and find out?"

Sarah gave him another long look, then patted Bingo on the head and said, "Stay here," and got out of the car. She looked around at the rows of shacks, at the chain-link fence and the long expanse of garbage. Gulls circled and dove; a faint but definite odor of human excrement and rot came to them.

"Maybe I should have brought my gat after all," Sarah said.

"I'm afraid the rats will come out to get Bingo." But she came around the front of the car to join him, and together they walked up on the porch. Tom knocked twice.

"Get away from here," said a voice from within the shack. "Git! Had enough—don't want any more of you."

Sarah backed down off the porch and looked toward her car.

"Hattie—"

"You *said* it all! Now you want to say it all again?" They heard her moving slowly toward the door. In a quieter voice: "I looked at you thirty years, Boney, I don't have to see you one day more."

"Hattie, it's not Boney," Tom said.

"No? Then I guess it must be Santa Claus."

"Open the door and find out."

She cracked the door and peered out. Alert black eyes in a suspicious face took in Tom's tall figure, then moved to Sarah. She opened the door a notch wider. Her white hair was skimmed back from her forehead, and the lines on her face that had seemed bitter now expressed a surprisingly youthful curiosity. "Well, you're a big one anyhow, aren't you? You people lost? How you know my name?" She looked hard at Tom, and her whole face softened. "Oh, my goodness."

"I was hoping you would recognize me," Tom said.

"If you hadn't turned into a giant, I would've recognized you right away."

Tom turned and introduced Sarah, who was lingering awkwardly in the little yard, her hands in the pockets of her shorts.

"Sarah Spence?" Hattie said. "Didn't I hear from Nancy Vetiver, all that time ago, that you visited our boy here in the hospital?"

Tom laughed at her perfect recall, and Sarah said, "I guess you did. But how could you remember . . . ?"

"I remember about everybody came to visit Tom Pasmore. I believe he was the most left-alone little boy I ever saw, all the time I worked at Shady Mount—you were, you know," she said directly to Tom. "I hope you two fine young people didn't plan on spending your whole visit here standing on my porch. You'll come in, won't you?"

Hattie smiled and stepped out to hold her door open, and Tom and Sarah went into the little interior.

"Oh, it's so pretty," Sarah said, a second before Tom could say the same thing. Threadbare but clean patterned rugs covered the floor, and every inch of the walls had been decorated with framed pictures of every kind—portraits and landscapes, photographs of children and animals and couples and houses. After a second, Tom saw that most of them had been clipped from magazines. Hattie had also framed postcards, newspaper articles, letters, hand-printed poems, and pages from books. She had brought the bent-back chairs and her table to a high shine which was increased by her brass lamps. Her bed was a burnished walnut platform softened by many pillows covered in fabrics; her table looked as though George Washington might have owned it. In one corner a huge birdcage held a stuffed hawk. The whole effect was of profusion and abundance. A dented kettle painted fire-engine red steamed on the gas hob beside the small white refrigerator against the back wall, covered like the others with photographs in frames. Tom saw Martin Luther King, John Kennedy, Malcolm X, Paul Robeson, Duke Ellington, and a self-portrait in a golden robe of Rembrandt that gazed out with the wisest and most disconcerting expression Tom had ever seen on any face.

"I do my best," Hattie said. "I live next to the biggest furniture store in all Mill Walk, and I'm a little bit handy, you know. Seems like rich people would rather throw things away than give 'em away, lots of times. I even know the houses a lot of my things came from."

"You got all this from the dump?" Sarah asked.

"You pick and choose, and you scrub and polish. People around here know I'm fond of pictures, and they bring me frames and such, when they find 'em." The kettle began to whistle. "I was making a cup of tea for Boney, but he wouldn't stay—just wanted to throw a scare into Hattie, was all *he* wanted. You two won't be in such a rush, will you?"

"We'd love some tea, Hattie," Tom said.

She poured the boiling water into a teapot and covered it. She brought three unmatched mugs from a little yellow cupboard to the table, a pint of milk, and sugar in a silver bowl. Then she sat beside them and began talking to Sarah about the original owners of some of her things while they waited for the tea to steep.

The big birdcage had been Arthur Thielman's—or rather, Mrs. Arthur Thielman's, the *first* Mrs. Arthur Thielman, and so had her brass lamps; some shoes and hats and other clothes had also been Mrs. Thielman's, for after her death her husband had thrown out everything that had been hers. Her little old-fashioned desk where she kept her papers and the old leather couch had come from a famous gentleman named Lamont von Heilitz, who had got rid of nearly half his furniture when he had done something—Hattie didn't know what—to his house. And the big gilded frame around that picture of Mr. Rembrandt—

"Mr. von Heilitz? Famous?" Sarah said, as if the name had just caught up with her. "He must be the most useless man ever born! He never even comes out of his house, he never sees anyone—how could he be famous?"

"You're too young to know about him," Hattie said. "I think our tea's ready by now." She began to pour for them. "And he comes out of his house now and again, I know—because he comes to see me."

"He comes to see you?" Tom asked, now as surprised as Sarah.

"Some old patients come around now and again," she said, smiling at him. "Mr. von Heilitz, he brought me some of his parents' things himself, instead of tossing them on the dump and making me drag them home. He might look like an old fool to you, but to me he looks like that picture of Mr. Rembrandt up on my wall." She sipped her tea. "Came to visit you too, didn't he? Back when you got hurt."

"But why was he famous?" Sarah asked.

"Everybody knew about the Shadow once," Hattie said. "Used to be the most famous man on Mill Walk. I think he was the greatest detective in the world—like someone you could read about in a book. He made a lot of people uncomfortable, he did—they had too many secrets, and they were afraid he'd know all about them. He still makes 'em uncomfortable. I think a lot of folks on this island would be happier if he passed real soon."

Sarah turned a reflective glance on Tom, and he said, "Hattie, did Dr. Milton come here to warn you off talking to me?"

"Let me ask you something. Are you making ready to sue

Shady Mount? And do you want Nancy Vetiver to help you do it?"

"Is that what he said?"

"Because you had to have that second operation—they made a mess of the first one, you know. Tom ain't that stupid, I said. If you could be sued on this island, it would have happened a long time ago. But if you want to, Tom, you go ahead—you might not be able to win, but you could smear him a little."

"Dr. Milton?" asked Sarah.

"Hattie once told me I ought to take my fork and stab him in his fat fish-colored hand."

"Should have too. Anyhow, you want Nancy's address, I got it. I see Nancy once a week or so—she drops in to talk to me. Boney can try to get me thrown out of my house here, it might be harder than he thinks."

"He said he'd get you evicted? Don't you own this place?"

"Tossed out on my old black ass, was the way he said it. Every month but June, July, and August, I pay rent to a man who comes collecting for the Redwing Holding Company. Jerry Hasek is his name, and he's just the man you'd send if you wanted to scare the rent out of seventy-seven-year-old ladies. He wouldn't be good for much else. In September, he takes four months' money all at once. Summers, he goes up north with all the Redwings, and a couple other no-goods Ralph Redwing keeps on the payroll."

"I know him," Sarah said. "Well, I know who he is. Acne scars, always looks worried about something?"

"That's him, that's my rent collector."

"*You* know him?" Tom asked.

"Sure—he drives Ralph, when Ralph uses a car. And he's a kind of bodyguard."

"So," Hattie said. "You gonna take on Boney? It don't look that way to me."

"No," Tom said. "I just saw him at the hospital this morning—I asked him about Nancy, and he told me she was suspended, but he wouldn't say why. I don't think he wants you to tell me why, either."

Hattie scowled down into her mug of tea, and all the lines in her face deepened alarmingly. An almost ferocious sadness had claimed her, and Tom saw that it had always been there, underlying everything she had said. "This tea's gone cold," she said. Hattie pushed herself up and went to the sink, where she rinsed out the mug. "I guess that man died. That policeman who got shot. Reminds me of the old days, with Barbara Deane."

"Mendenhall," Tom said. "Yes, he died this morning. I saw them taking his body out of the hospital."

Hattie leaned back against her sink. "You think Nancy Vetiver was a bad nurse?"

"I think she was the only one as good as you," Tom said.

"That girl was a *nurse*, same as me," Hattie said. "She could have been a doctor but nobody would let her, so she did the next best thing. Didn't have the money to be a doctor, anyhow, so she went to the nursing school at St. Mary Nieves, same as me, and when they saw how good she was, they hired her for Shady Mount." She looked at each of them with the fierce sadness Tom had seen earlier. "You can't tell someone like that not to do her job—you can't say, do bad now, we don't want you to be good today." Hattie lowered her head and wrapped her arms around her chest. "This island, this is some place. This can be some damn place, Mill Walk." She turned from them, and seemed to look at her wall of framed photographs.

"Nancy came here a couple times, the last few weeks. Seemed like it was getting worse. See, if she got suspended, that meant she couldn't keep her place anymore, because the hospital owned her apartment. They told her. *Told* her."

Hattie turned around again. "You know what? Boney's scared of something. Tells you Nancy got suspended, and doesn't have sense enough to make up a good lie about why." She crossed her arms over her chest again, and looked amazingly like the stuffed hawk in the birdcage. "Makes me mad—*damn* mad. Because I halfway believed the man."

She looked up at Tom. "Everything about this thing makes me mad. Two kinds of law—two kinds of medicine. Boney coming out here, all sweet and nice, then telling me that if I talk to you he might have to—to 'respond to my disloyalty,' that's how he said it—hard as that would be for him, he says, when he already *got* Nancy out of the hospital. See, he went too far then too!" She seemed to blaze as she came across the floor to Tom:

it was as if the hawk had come to life and swooped toward him. She put her thin old hand on his shoulder, and he felt her talons clamp down. "He doesn't know who you are, Tom. He *thinks* he knows, he thinks he knows all about you. Thinks you'll be just like all the rest—except *one*. You know who I mean, don't you?"

"The Shadow." He looked at Sarah, who sipped her tea and looked calmly back across the top of the cup. "You said something about a woman named Barbara Deane? She was a nurse?"

"For a time. Barbara Deane was your midwife." She dug her fingers into his skin. "You want to see Nancy Vetiver? If you do, I'll take you to her."

"I want to come too," Sarah said.

"You don't know where she is." Hattie turned sharply to face her.

"I bet I do. Dr. Milton or whoever it was wanted to scare her into doing what they wanted, right? So who owns the hospital? And what else do they own?"

Hattie nodded. "Dressed like that? Looking like you look? You can't."

"Can't what?" Tom asked.

"Go with you to the Elysian Courts."

Tom looked up at Hattie, and Hattie raised her eyebrows, amused and impressed.

"Give me something else to wear, then. I don't care what it is, I just need something to cover me up."

"I got something here might work," Hattie said. She moved across the room, knelt by the bed, and pulled a trunk from beneath it. She opened the trunk, swept aside layers of bright fabrics, and drew out a long black shapeless thing. "Nobody's touched this since the first Mrs. Arthur Thielman."

"What's that?" Tom asked. "A parachute?"

"It's a cape," Sarah said, springing up to try it on. "It's perfect."

The red lining flashed against the black silk as Sarah twirled the cape over her shoulders, and then the whole thing gathered and swung and fell back into its natural folds, covering Sarah from her neck to her feet. She instantly looked ten years older and more sophisticated, another kind of person altogether.

For a second, Tom thought he was seeing Jeanine Thielman.

Then Sarah said, "Wow! I love it!" and she was Sarah Spence again, and in the next second, swept to the window and bent down to see if her dog was still where she had left him. Evidently he was, for she straightened up and made another twirl that exposed her tennis shoes. "Jamie's grandmother used to wear this? What do you think she was like?"

Hattie gave Tom a sly look, and said, "Tuck your hair in, turn up the collar, keep the front closed, and we'll be ready to visit Nancy, I reckon. Nobody'll mess with you now, as long as I'm with you."

Hattie ushered both of them back outside into the hot sun, the sweet, sickening odor drifting from the dump, the wheeling gulls, and the rows of identical houses.

Bingo barked once, then recognized Sarah.

"How do you get three people and one dog into that car?" Hattie asked.

"Do you mind sitting on Tom's lap?" Sarah asked.

"Not if he doesn't," Hattie said. "We can put the car across the street from Maxwell's Heaven. Friend of mine will keep it safe—the dog too."

Hattie climbed in after Tom, and seemed to weigh no more than Bingo. As if she were a child, he could see over the top of her head.

"Tuaregs and lascars, here we come," Sarah said, and turned around on the narrow road.

"God help us," said Hattie.

Soon they were driving in the darkness between the listing tenements. Hattie told Sarah to turn down into a nearly invisible cobblestone path beneath a shadowy archway, and around various corners past curtained windows and peeling walls until they came to a small cobbled court with a blue scrap of sky at its top, as if they were deep in a well. Barred windows and heavy doors stood on every side, and the air smelled of must. One of the heavy doors creaked open, and a large bearded man with a leather cap and apron peered out at them. He frowned at the car before recognizing Hattie, but immediately agreed to keep watch on the car and look after the dog for half an hour. Hattie introduced him as Percy, and Percy took the willing dog under his arm and led them into the building and up stairs and through vast empty rooms and small rooms crowded with bags and barrels. Bingo stared at everything with intent interest. "Who is Percy?" Tom whispered, and Hattie said, "Bone merchant. Human hair." The man took them through a dusty parlor and back out into the slanting street. They were across the street from Maxwell's Heaven.

22

"Just follow me now, and don't talk to anyone or stop to stare at anything," Hattie said.

Tom crossed the narrow street a step behind her. Sarah gripped his arm through the cape. The series of linked tenements built by Maxwell Redwing seemed to grow taller with every step.

"Are you sure you want to come with us?" he whispered.

"Are you kidding?" she whispered back. "I'm not going to let you go in there alone!"

Hattie walked unhesitatingly into an arched passageway and disappeared. Tom and Sarah followed. The light died. Hattie was visible only as a small dark outline before them. The air instantly became colder, and the odors of must and dry rot—along with a thousand others—seeped from the walls. They hurried forward, and seconds later followed Hattie out of the passageway.

"This is the First Court," Hattie said, looking around them. "There are three, altogether. Nancy's in the second. I've only been as far as her place, and I suppose I'd get lost if I tried to go any farther."

In the jumble of first impressions, Tom had taken in only that the space around him looked vaguely like a prison, vaguely like a European slum, and more than either of these like an illustration from a sinister comic book—tilting little streets connected by wooden passages like freight cars suspended in the air.

Three or four ragged men had begun shambling toward them from a doorway next to a lighted window across the court. Hattie turned to face them. The men shuffled and whispered to each other. One of them gave Hattie a wave that flapped the entire sleeve of his coat. They shambled back toward their doorway, and sat down, puddled in their coats, before Bobcat's Place.

"Don't mind those old boys," Hattie said. "They know me. . . . Tom! Read this writing."

He moved beside her and looked down. At his feet was a square brass plaque on which the raised lettering had been rubbed away to near illegibility, like the letters on an old headstone:

ELYSIAN COURTS
DESIGNED BY THE PHILANTHROPIST MAXWELL REDWING
BUILT BY GLENDENNING UPSHAW
AND MILL WALK CONSTRUCTION CO.
FOR THE GREATER GOOD
OF THE PEOPLE OF THIS ISLAND
1922
"LET EACH MAN HAVE A HOME
TO CALL HIS OWN"

"See that?" Hattie said. "That's what they said—'Let each man have a home to call his own.' Philanthropists, that's what they called themselves."

1922: two years before the death of his wife, three years before the murder of Jeanine Thielman and the construction of the hospital in Miami. Elysian Courts had been Mill Walk Construction's first big project, built with Maxwell Redwing's money.

Maxwell's Heaven looked like a small city. Crooked little streets twisted off the court, which was lined with a jumble of bars, liquor stores, and lodging houses, connected overhead by the wooden passages that reminded Tom of freight cars. Through the lanes and mazelike passages, he saw an endlessly proliferating warren of cramped streets, leaning buildings, walls with narrow doors and wooden stiles. Neon signs glowed red and blue. FREDO'S. 2 GIRLS. BOBCAT'S PLACE. Laundry hung on drooping lines strung between windows.

"Look out below!" a woman yelled from above them. She was leaning out of a narrow window in a building across the court. She overturned a black metal bowl, and liquid streamed down, seeming to dissolve into the air before it struck the ground. A barefoot man in torn clothes led an exhausted donkey and a ragged child through one of the passages into the maze.

Hattie took them toward the passage from which the man with the donkey had come. White letters in the brick gave its name as Edgewater Trail. It led beneath one of the suspended wooden freight cars.

Hattie said, "Old Maxwell and your grandfather thought that street names from your part of town would be a good influence on the people in here—over there's Yorkminster Place, and where we're going there's Ely Place and Stonehenge Circle." Her black eyes flashed at him as she led them into the passage.

"Doesn't the mail ever get mixed up?" Tom asked.

"There's no mail here," Hattie said from in front of him. "No police, either, and no firemen, no doctors, no schools, except for what they teach themselves, no stores but liquor stores, no nothin' but what you see."

They had emerged into a wide cobbled lane lined with high blackened wooden walls inset here and there with slanted windows. The same white inset letters, some of which had fallen off or been removed, gave its name as Vic or a Terrace. A crowd of dirty children ran past the front of the lane, splashing in a stream that ran down the middle of the street. Now the odor was almost visible in the air, and Sarah held an edge of the cape over her nose and mouth.

Hattie jumped over the stream and led them up a flight of wooden steps. Another crooked flight, marked Waterloo Lane, led upward toward darkness. Hattie scurried down a murky corridor, and began to move quickly toward the next set of stairs.

"What do they do here?" Tom asked. "How do they live?"

"They sell things to Percy—their own hair, or their own rags. Some get out, like Nancy. These days, most young ones manage to get out, soon as they can. Some of 'em like it here."

They had come to a wide space where wooden walkways spanned the fronts of the buildings on all sides. Rows of doors stood on the far sides of the walks. A man leaned against the railing of the second walkway, gazing down at them and smoking a pipe.

"You see," Hattie said, "this here is a world, and we're in the center of it now. Nobody sees this world, but here it is." She looked up at the man leaning on the railing. "Is Nancy home, Bill?"

The man pointed with his pipe at a door farther along the walkway.

Hattie led them up the wooden steps to the second walkway. "How is she, Bill?" she asked when they had come near to him.

The man turned his head and looked at each of them from beneath the brim of his soft cap. His face was very dirty, full of hard lines, and in the grey light of the Courts, his cap, face, and pipe all seemed the same muddy color. He took a long time to speak. "Busy."

"And you, Bill?"

He was staring at Sarah's hair, and again took a long time to respond. "Good. Helped a man move a piano, two days ago."

"We'll go along and see her, then," Hattie said, and Bill turned back to the railing.

The three of them walked down the creaking boards until they had nearly reached the end of the walkway. Tom looked over the railing, and Sarah asked Hattie, "Is Bill a friend of yours?"

"He's Nancy's brother," Hattie said.

Tom would have turned around to make sure he had heard her correctly, but just then a man in a grey suit and a grey turtleneck appeared, moving soundlessly and easily down the steps of the wooden structure over the drainage ditch. Bill took his pipe from his mouth and stepped back from the railing. The man in grey stepped into the Second Court and began walking in a straight line that would bring him directly beneath Tom. Bill gestured for Tom to move back, and Tom hesitated before pushing back from the railing. The man was bald, and his face was a smooth anonymous mask. Tom did not realize that he was Captain Fulton Bishop until he had begun to move back into the protection of the walkway. Hattie knocked on the last door, and knocked again. Captain Bishop glanced up without breaking stride as Tom moved back, and the boy saw his eyes through the gaps in the railing, as alive and alert as two match flames.

Then the door opened, and Captain Bishop passed out of the Second Court and went deeper into Maxwell's Heaven. His footsteps clicked against the stone. Tom heard Nancy Vetiver saying, "Who'd you bring me, Hattie?"

She smiled from Hattie to Sarah, and then included him in the same smile. She did not recognize him, but he would have known her instantly if he had seen her on any street in Mill Walk. Her hair, a darker blond than Sarah's, had been cut to a rough shag, and the lines bracketing her mouth seemed deeper, but she was otherwise the same woman who had helped him endure the worst months of his life. He realized that he had loved her absolutely then, and that part of him still did love her.

"An old patient of ours came calling," Hattie said.

Nancy looked from Sarah to Tom and back to Sarah, trying to work out which was the old patient. "Well, you'd better come on in and find something to sit on, and I'll be able to spend some time with you in a minute." She smiled, looking a little baffled but not at all irritated, and stepped back to let them in.

Hattie went in first, then Sarah. Tom moved into the room. Several children, some of them bandaged, sat in chairs pushed against the wall. All of them were gaping at Sarah, who had pulled her hair out of the collar of the cape. "Oh, my God," Nancy said as he went past her. "It's Tom Pasmore." She laughed out loud—a real ringing laugh that sounded out of place in Elysian Courts—and then put her arms around him and squeezed him. Her head came to the middle of his chest. "How'd you get so *big*?" Nancy pulled away and crowed to Hattie, "He's a *giant*!"

"That's what I told him," Hattie said, "but it didn't shrink him any."

Now all the children in the chairs gaped at Tom instead of Sarah. His face grew hot and red.

"And I know you too," Nancy said to Sarah, after giving Tom a final squeeze. "I remember seeing you with Tom, way back then—Sarah."

"How can you remember me?" Sarah said, looking pleased and embarrassed. "I was only there once!"

"Well, I remember most of the things that happen to my good patients." Smiling broadly, Nancy put her hands on her hips and looked them both over. "Why don't you sit down wherever you can find space, and I'll take care of the rest of these desperate characters, and then we'll have a long talk, and I'll find out why Hattie dragged you into this godforsaken place."

Sarah twirled the cape off her shoulders and folded it over the back of a chair. The children gaped. She and Tom sat on a padded bench, and Hattie plunked herself down on the edge of the little low bed beside them.

Nancy went from child to child, changing bandages and dispensing vitamins, listening to whispered complaints, stroking heads and holding hands, now and then leading some bedraggled boy or girl to a sink at the back of the room and making them wash. She looked down throats and into ears, and when one sticklike little boy burst into tears, she took him into her lap and comforted him until he stopped.

Two old quilts, washed almost to colorlessness, hung on the walls. An ornate lamp with most of its bulbs and fixtures intact stood on a drum table like the one in his grandfather's living room. An empty gilt frame, clearly salvaged from the dump, hung on the far wall near the sink.

Hattie saw him looking at it, and said, "I brought that for Nancy—looks almost as pretty empty as filled, but I'm looking for another picture of Mr. Rembrandt, like the one I got. You saw it."

"Oh, Hattie, I don't need a picture of *Rembrandt*," Nancy said, bandaging a splint onto a boy's finger. "I'd rather have a picture of you any day. Anyhow, I'll be back in my own place before long."

"Could be," Hattie said. "When you are, I'll come in here,

couple times a week, to bandage up these little ruffians. If your brother won't mind."

When the last child had been sent off, Nancy washed her hands, dried them on a dish towel, and sat down on one of the chairs against the wall and at last looked at Tom hard and long. "I am so glad to see you, even here," she said.

"And I'm so glad to see you," he said. "Even here. Nancy, I heard that—"

She held up a hand to stop him. "Before we get serious, does anybody want a beer?"

Hattie shook her head, and Tom and Sarah said they would split one.

"You'll split one, all right," Nancy said. She went to a small refrigerator next to the sink and removed three bottles; took two glasses from a shelf; popped off the caps, and came back carrying the bottles by their necks in one hand and the glasses in the other. She gave a glass and a bottle each to Tom and Sarah, sat down and raised her own bottle. "Cheers." Tom laughed, and raised his own bottle to Nancy and drank from it. Sarah poured some into her glass and thanked Nancy.

"If you're not going to use that glass, maybe I will have a little bit, after all," Hattie said. Tom poured some from his bottle into the empty glass and Sarah did the same, and then they all sat smiling at each other for a moment.

"I wondered about you, you know," Nancy said to Tom.

"I know you did," Hattie said.

"Wondered what?" Sarah asked.

"Well, Tom had this special thing inside him. He *saw* things. He saw how I felt about Boney right away. But I don't mean just that." She pointed her beer bottle at Tom and squinted, trying to get the right words. "I don't really know how to say this, I guess—but when I looked at you in the bed sometimes, I used to think you'd be something like a really good painter when you got older. Because you had this way of looking at things, like you could see parts of them nobody else could. Sometimes, it looked like the world could just make you glow. Or tear you apart inside, when you saw the bad."

"I told him that," Hattie said.

Tom had the strangest desire to cry.

"It was like you had some kind of destiny," Nancy said. "And the reason I'm saying all this is, I can still see it."

"Sure you can," Hattie said. "It's clear as day. Sarah can see it."

"Leave me out of this," Sarah said. "He's conceited enough already. And anyhow, it isn't what I can see, or what you can see, or even Tom can see, it's—" She gave Tom an embarrassed look, and threw up her hands.

"It's what he does," Hattie said. "That's right. Well, he must of done something, because Boney rode all the way out to see me today and gave me a cock and bull story about Tom Pasmore getting ready to sue him and the hospital, and how if the boy or his lawyers showed up, I was to turn 'em all away. And a minute later, here comes this tall fellow, and I thought he was a young lawyer, until I took a good look at him."

"Boney did what?" Nancy asked, and Hattie had to repeat the whole story.

"I asked why you were suspended," Tom said. "And he got flustered. The place was full of police."

"*Flustered*," Nancy said. "This was today? At the hospital?"

Tom nodded.

"Oh, dear," Nancy said. "Oh, damn. Oh, shit." She jumped up and went to the back of the room and opened a cupboard and banged it shut.

"That's right," Hattie said. "That boy died."

"Oh, hell," Nancy said.

Sarah reached for Tom's hand, and held it tightly. "Does this have anything to do with that letter? Because Tom told me—"

He pressed her hand, and she fell silent.

Nancy turned around, angrier than Tom had ever seen her.

"Why were you suspended?" Tom asked.

"I wasn't going to let him die alone. He needed someone to talk to. You remember how I used to come in and spend time with you?"

"They ordered you to stay away from him?"

"Mike Mendenhall was getting weaker and weaker—in a coma most of the time—I wasn't going to let him be all alone those times when he was awake. And it wasn't an order—nobody ordered us to stay out of that room. After the first time Boney learned I was giving time to him, he reminded me that he asked the nursing staff to do no more than change his linens and attend to strictly medical functions. And I said, if that's an order, I'd like to see it posted on the board, and he said he was sure I understood that he could not do that."

"Did Mendenhall talk to you, when he was conscious?"

"Of course he talked to me."

"Would you tell me what he said?"

Nancy looked troubled and shook her head. Tom turned to Hattie. "Two kinds of law, two kinds of medicine. Isn't that what you said at your house, Hattie?"

"You know I did," Hattie said. She had her hawk look again. "I didn't say, *quote* me, though."

Tom said, "I'll tell you why I'm asking about this." And he told her about his realization that Hasselgard had killed his sister, about his letter to the police captain, and everything that followed. Nancy Vetiver leaned forward with her elbows on her knees and listened. "That letter is the real reason you're here instead of your apartment."

"I said you must of done something, and I guess you did," Hattie said. "Tell him, Nancy. You can't get him in any deeper than he already got himself."

"Are you sure you want to hear this, Sarah?" Nancy asked.

"I'm leaving the island in two days, anyway."

"Well, after everything Tom said, maybe it's not such a big deal, after all." She took a deep swallow of her beer. "Mike Mendenhall was a bitter man. He went to Weasel Hollow to arrest a man named Edwardes for murder, and he knew it was dangerous—a lot of things had been going on at Armory Place that upset him."

"What kind of things?" Tom asked.

"He said there was this one honest detective, Natchez, David Natchez, who had the backing of all the honest officers, and the rest of them would do anything they were told. Before they learned he was honest, some of the older cops used to say anything in front of him, you know, they'd brag about Mill Walk always being the same. As long as they arrested ordinary criminals and kept down street crime, they could do anything they liked, because they were protected. Honestly, Tom, this is terrible, but it's hardly news to people from Maxwell's Heaven and the old slave quarter. We know what they are."

"Why don't we, then?" Tom asked.

"Everything looks just dandy from Eastern Shore Road. When people over there get too near something that sounds too rough for them, they turn their heads away. It's too scary, and they wait for it to go away. From where they sit, everything works."

Tom remembered Dennis Handley, and knew she was telling him the truth.

"It's always been that way," Nancy said. "If somebody gets caught, they make a big public fuss about it, and then everybody's reassured. Everything's hunky-dory all over again, and it's business as usual."

"But Hasselgard was bigger trouble than they were used to," Tom said. "They had to do something drastic, and do it fast. Did Mendenhall talk about what happened on the day he got shot?"

"A little," Nancy said. "He didn't even know who Edwardes was supposed to have murdered. He knew he would be safe, because his partner would be with him. Roman Klink had been on the force for fifteen years. I got the feeling he thought Klink was too lazy to be really crooked, and too much one of the guys to be absolutely straight."

"How did they know where Edwardes was?"

"They had an address. Mike went up to the door first. He yelled 'Police!' and then pushed in the door. *He* didn't think anybody was there—he thought Edwardes had probably taken the boat to Antigua. I guess he went in—"

"Alone?" Tom asked.

"Ahead of Klink, anyhow. He didn't see anybody in the living room, so he went toward the kitchen. Edwardes jumped out of the kitchen and shot him in the stomach, and he went down. Klink came in shooting. Mike saw Klink dodging toward the bedroom, and that's when all hell broke loose. The whole police force came screaming up to the house. Captain Bishop started shouting through a bullhorn. Someone in the house fired a shot, and then the police shot hell out of the house. Mike was hit four more times. He was so *angry*—he knew they wanted to kill him. They wanted to kill all three of them. Klink was expendable too."

Nancy looked down at her lap. She drank more beer, but Tom didn't think she tasted it.

"He managed to tell you a lot," he said.

She looked up without changing position in any way, and seemed as forlorn as one of her small patients. "I'm smoothing it all out a lot. He wasn't talking to me, half the time. Sometimes he thought I was Roman Klink. Twice he thought I was Captain Bishop. He was out a lot of the time, and he had two long operations. Captain Bishop went into his room once, but he was in a coma most of that day."

"What about Klink?"

"Basically, all we had to do was take out a bullet and sew him up. Last week, Bill saw him tending bar at Mulroney's. Said he was talking like a hero. The man who got Marita Hasselgard's killer. He was drinking a lot, Bill said."

"Said a lot, for Bill," Hattie put in.

"Took him most of the night to get that much out. My brother doesn't talk much," Nancy said to Tom, smiling at him. "He has a good heart, Bill. He lets me see the kids here in the afternoons, even though it must turn his whole life upside down."

"On the balcony, Bill and I saw Captain Bishop walking through the court," Tom said. Hattie and Nancy glanced at each other. "If it weren't for Bill, I think Bishop would have seen me—he motioned me back from the railing."

"Are you sure he didn't see you?"

"I don't think so," Tom said. "I didn't recognize him at first, because he wasn't wearing his uniform."

Hattie snorted, and Nancy still looked uneasy. "Well, he just slides through. He might as well be invisible." She laughed, but not happily. "You look at him, your eye just slips off his face. He's not a person you want to have anything to do with."

"He might have been visiting," Hattie said.

"Visiting?" Tom asked.

"That devil was born in the Third Court," Hattie said.

"His sister Carmen lives back in there," Nancy said, as if she were talking about a deep jungle. "On Eastern Shore Road—the Third Court. Peers through her curtains, day in and day out."

"Looks so meek and mild until you look at her eyes—"

"And then you see she'd be happy to slit a child's throat for the sake of the pennies out of its pockets."

Nancy stretched her arms sideways and yawned with her

whole face, somehow managing not to look ugly as she did so. Then she put her hands at the base of her spine, and arched her back. She looked like a cat, with her small supple body and short shaggy hair. Tom realized that he had been looking at her face nearly the whole time they had been in her room—he had not even noticed what she was wearing. Now he noticed: a lightweight white turtleneck and tight wheat-colored jeans and white tennis shoes like Sarah's, but scuffed and dirty.

"We should let Bill back into his room," she said. "It's been so good to see you again, Tom. And you too, Sarah. I shouldn't have let you get me talking, though."

She stood up and ruffled her hands through her hair.

"You'll be back at work soon?" Tom asked.

She glanced at Hattie. "Oh, I reckon Boney'll get word to me in a couple of days. Damn him anyhow."

"You got that right," Hattie said.

They began to move toward the door. Nancy suddenly hugged Tom again, so hard that he couldn't breathe. "I hope—oh, I don't know what I hope. But be careful, Tom."

They were out on the ramshackle wooden walkway in the dismal air before he was entirely aware of having let go of her. Bill straightened up from the railing and drew on his pipe.

"She look okay to you, Hat?" he said in a low growl that cut through the hum of noise from all about them.

"That girl's *strong*," Hattie said.

"Always was," Bill said. "Folks."

Tom put his hand in his pocket and pulled out the first note he found. In the gloom, it took a moment to see that it was a ten dollar bill. He put it in Bill's hand and whispered, "For whatever she needs."

The bill disappeared into the shabby clothes. Nancy's brother winked at Tom, and began to make his way toward the door at the end of the walkway. "Oh," he said, and turned around. The three of them stopped at the top of the stairs. "You got by." He must have seen that Tom did not understand. "Didn't spot you."

Sarah clamped herself on Tom's arm, and together they followed Hattie beneath the overhanging passages, through the narrow streets with mocking names, along the tilting walls. The air stank of sewage. Children jeered at them, and hard-faced men moved toward Sarah until they noticed Hattie, and then backed away. Finally they hurried across the crazed concrete of the First Court, through the darkness of the arch, and back out into the shadowy street, which seemed impossibly sweet and bright.

Even Percy's dusty emporium, with its dim parlors and endless stairs, seemed sweet and light after Maxwell's Heaven. Down in the small cobbled court, Percy and Bingo sat companionably on a bus seat from which horsehair foamed through slashes and split seams. Bingo's nose was deep in the folds of Percy's leather apron, and his tail moved frantically from side to side. "The girl okay?" Percy asked.

"Nothin' can get that girl down," Hattie said.

"That's what *I* said." Percy handed the whining, wriggling Bingo back over to Sarah, and Bingo continued to give longing, ardent glances to the leather apron until they had turned into the narrow uphill drive, and even then whined and looked back at it. "Fickle animal," Sarah said, sounding genuinely grumpy.

When they came to the top of the drive and out on the street, a police car sped past them and squealed around the corner down the south end of Elysian Courts, its siren screaming. Another screaming police car followed it.

Sarah drove, more slowly than before, downhill toward the sea, the dump, and the old slave quarter.

"I have a high opinion of you, young lady," Hattie said from her perch on Tom's lap. "And so did Nancy Vetiver."

"You do?" Sarah seemed startled. "She did?"

"Otherwise, why did she say so much? Ask yourself that. Nancy Vetiver's not a loquacious fool, you know."

"Not any kind of fool," Sarah said.

At her shack, Hattie took the cape and kissed them both before saying good-bye.

Sarah leaned over and rested her head on the steering wheel. After a moment, she sighed and started the car.

"I'm sorry," Tom said.

She gave him a smoky look. "Are you? For what?"

"For dragging you into that place. For mixing you up in everything."

"Oh," she said. "That's what you're sorry about." She rocketed away from the curb, and Bingo flattened out in his well behind the seats.

She did not speak until they were past Goethe Park and maneuvering through the eastbound traffic on Calle Burleigh. Finally she asked him what time it was.

"Ten past six."

"Is that all? I thought it was a lot later." Another lengthy silence. Then: "I guess because it seemed like night inside there."

"If I'd known how bad it was going to be, I would have gone alone."

"I'm not sorry I went there, Tom. I'm happy I saw the inside of that place. I'm happy I met Hattie. I'm happy about everything."

"Okay," he said. She passed three cars in a row, causing temporary pandemonium in the westbound lanes.

"I meant everything I said to you today," she said. "I'm not Moonie Firestone or Posy Tuttle. My idea of paradise isn't a rich husband and a lodge at Eagle Lake and a trip to Europe every other year. We really did see the Tuaregs and the lascars, and I saw places I'd never seen before in my life, and I really *found out* some things, and I met two amazing women who haven't seen you in seven years and *still* think you're wonderful." She floored the Mercedes to pass a carriage on the right. "Every time Hattie Bascombe said 'Mr. Rembrandt' I wanted to hug her."

She cut in front of the carriage, and its driver shouted a string of four-letter words. Sarah flipped her hand up in a mocking wave and tore off through the traffic again.

"Oh, well," she said when they skirted Weasel Hollow, and when they passed the St. Alwyn Hotel on Calle Drosselmayer, "She *is* really beautiful, isn't she?"

"Every now and then I thought she looked sort of like her stuffed hawk," Tom said.

"Her stuffed hawk?" Sarah turned to him with her mouth open and an expression in her eyes that convicted him of a profoundly irritating idiocy.

"Inside that big cage."

She snapped her head forward. "I don't mean Hattie. I mean that Nancy Vetiver is really beautiful. She is, isn't she?"

"Well, maybe. I was sort of surprised by her. She turned

out to be another kind of person than I thought she was. My mother used to say she was hard, and she certainly isn't, but I can see what she meant. Nancy's tough."

"And she's beautiful besides."

"I think you're beautiful," Tom said. "You should have seen yourself in that cape."

"I'm pretty," Sarah said. "I own a mirror, I know that much. People have been telling me I was pretty all my life. I was just lucky enough to be born with good hair and good teeth and visible cheekbones. If you want to know the truth, my mouth is too big and my eyes are too far apart. I look at my face and I see my baby pictures. I see a perfect Brooks-Lowood girl. I hate prettiness. It means you're supposed to spend half your time thinking about how you look, and most other people think you're a sort of toy who will do whatever they want. I bet Nancy Vetiver hardly ever looks in the mirror, I bet she cut her hair short because she could wash it in the shower and dry it with a towel, I bet it's a big deal for her to buy a new lipstick—and she's beautiful. Every good thing in her, every feeling she ever had, is in her face. When I was in that little room, I even envied her those little lines on her face—you can tell she doesn't let other people make her do things. In fact the whole idea of being like me would strike her as ridiculous!"

"I think you ought to marry her," Tom said. "We could all live together in Maxwell's Heaven, Nancy and you and me. And Bill."

She punched him in the shoulder, hard. "You forgot Bingo."

"Actually, Bingo and Percy seemed made for each other."

She smiled at last.

"What's all that stuff about being a toy, and doing what other people want?"

"Oh, never mind," she said. "I got carried away."

"I don't think your eyes are too far apart. Posy Tuttle's eyes are actually on opposite sides of her head, and she sees different things out of each of them, like a lizard."

Sarah had turned from Calle Berlinstrasse into Edgewater Trail, and coming toward them from the opposite direction, smiling and raising his homburg from the seat of his trap, was Dr. Bonaventure Milton. "Sarah! Tom!" he called out. "A word, please!"

She pulled up alongside the pony trap, and the doctor looked earnestly down at them, removed his homburg, and wiped his sweaty head with a handkerchief. "I have an apology for you, Sarah. I saw your little dog running loose around the hospital earlier this afternoon, and took him up here with me—thought I'd drop him off at your place when I was through with my calls. The little fellow got away from me somehow, I'm sorry to say, but I'm sure he'll come back as soon as he gets hungry."

"No problem," she said. "In fact, Bingo's been with us all afternoon."

Hearing his name, Bingo popped his head out of the well. He barked at the doctor, whose horse twitched sideways in his traces.

"Well," said the doctor. "Well, well, well. Hah! Seems I was in error. Hah!"

"But you're so sweet to worry about him, Dr. Milton. You're the nicest doctor on the whole island."

"And you're looking remarkably pretty today, my dear," the doctor said, smiling and bowing in a ghastly attempt at gallantry.

"You're so *complimentary*, Doctor."

"Not at all." He raised his hat again, and shook his reins. His trap rolled away toward the hospital.

"I'm going home," Sarah declared. "The Redwings are coming over in a little while, to discuss airplane etiquette or something, and I have to take a bath. I want to look *just* like my baby pictures."

23

"You're pretty quiet," Victor Pasmore said. "Excuse me, did somebody say something? Did I say 'you're pretty quiet' just now? Nobody said anything back, so maybe I was just dreaming." They were eating a dinner Victor had prepared with many grumbles and complaints, and though Tom's mother had not emerged from her bedroom since he had returned home, a plate of unidentifiable meat and overcooked vegetables had been set for her. Booming noises from the television mingled with the dim sound of music that drifted down the stairs.

"What the hell, you're always quiet," Victor said. "This is nothing new. I oughta be used to this act by now. You say something, and your kid plays with his food."

"I'm sorry," Tom said.

"Jesus Christ, a sign of life!" Victor shook his head sourly. "I must be dreaming. You think next your mother will come downstairs and eat this food? Or will she just stay up there listening to *Blue Rose* over and over?"

"Blue Rose?"

"Yeah, you mean you never heard of it? Your old lady plays the damn thing over and over, I don't think she hears it anymore, she just—"

"*Blue Rose* is the name of a record?"

" '*Blue Rose* is the name of a record?' " His father's voice was a mincing drawl. "Yeah, it's the name of a record. Glenroy Breakstone's famous all-ballad record, which your mother would rather listen to than come down here and eat the dinner I made. Which is par for the course, I suppose, like you sitting there looking goofy when I ask you what you did all day."

"I went for a ride with Sarah Spence."

"Big man, aren't you?"

Tom looked across the table at his father. A smear of grease shone on his chin. Sweat stains darkened the armpits of the shirt he had worn to the office. Broken veins and black pores covered his nose. Dark, wet-looking hair stuck to his forehead. His father was hunched over his plate, holding on to a glass of bourbon and water with both hands. His black eyes glittered. Hostility seemed to come from him in an icy stream. He was much drunker than Tom had realized.

"What did you do all day?" he asked.

Tom saw his father considering saying something he thought astounding—he really wanted to say this astounding thing, alcohol and anger pushed it up into his throat, and he lifted the glass and swallowed whiskey to keep it down. He grinned like an evil dwarf. His eyes had absolutely no depth at all, and the pupils were invisible—light bounced right off them.

"Ralph Redwing came to my office today. The big man himself. To talk to me."

His father could not reveal what to him was surpassingly good news without gloating—his news was an insuperable advantage over the person to whom he presented it. He took another swallow of his drink, and grinned absolutely mirthlessly. "The Redwing building is a block away from my building—but do you think Ralph Redwing walks anywhere? Like hell he does. His driver brought him over in his Bentley—that's serious business, when Ralph uses a car. He bought two five-dollar cigars at the stand in the lobby. 'What floor is Pasmore Trading on?' he asks—like he doesn't know, see? He just wants 'em to know that Ralph Redwing respects Vic Pasmore."

"That's great," Tom said. "What did he want?"

"What's the only reason Ralph Redwing pays a call on Vic Pasmore? You don't know me, Tom—you think you know me, but you're fooling yourself. You don't. Nobody knows Vic Pasmore." He leaned over his plate and showed two rows of small peglike teeth in what was less a smile than the gesture of a disagreeable dog guarding some nasty treasure. Then he straightened up, looked at Tom as if from far above him, and cut a bit of meat. He began chewing. "You still don't get it, do you? You don't have the faintest idea what I'm talking about, do you? Who do you think Ralph Redwing visits? Who do you think he gives five-dollar cigars to?"

Whoever he wants to bamboozle, Tom thought, but said, "Not too many people, I guess."

"NOBODY! You know what your problem is? You don't have the faintest idea what's going on. The older you get, the more I think you're one of those guys who never gets anywhere. There's too much of your mother in you, kid."

"Did he offer you a job?" Tom said. His father had no awareness that what he was saying might be insulting; he had the air of offering great impartial truths.

"You think a man like that comes waltzing into an office and says, hey, how about a new job, Vic? If that's what you think, you got another think coming."

This was what his father was like when he was really happy.

"He says he's been noticing how well I run my little business—maybe not the past few years, when things haven't been so good, but right up to that. He *hints*. Maybe he needs what he calls a good general businessman—someone who isn't wearing blinders, like most of the assholes on Mill Walk. Maybe he was thinking of buying my business and letting someone else run it, so I can handle bigger things for him."

"Is that what he said?"

"He *hints*, I said." More chewing; more swallowing; more bourbon. "But you know what I think? I think I'm gonna finally get out from under the thumb of Glendenning Upshaw. And there isn't a good goddamned thing I'd rather do than that."

"How are you under his thumb?"

"Oh, Jesus." His father shook his head. The triumph had left his face, leaving only the sour temper. "Let's just pretend it takes a lot of money to live on Eastern Shore Road, okay? And let's say *this*—when I first came here, Glen sort of got me started—but how did he do it? Did he make me vice-president of Mill Walk Construction, which is what I thought he'd do? Is that how he takes care of people? Hell, no. I kept my nose clean for seventeen years, now it's time for me to get some of the gravy. I goddamn deserve it."

"I hope it works out," Tom said.

"Ralph Redwing has this island in his hip pocket, don't you kid yourself about that. Glen Upshaw is an old man, and he's on the way out. Ralph has things worked out."

"What kind of things?"

"I don't know, kid, I just know that. Ralph Redwing sets things up way in advance. You think he's gonna let Buddy go on being wild? Buddy's on a shorter leash than you think, kid, and pretty soon he's gonna find himself with responsibilities—gonna wander into the honey trap. The man doesn't take any risks."

The look of malignant triumph was back in full force now.

"What do you mean, the honey trap?"

"Finish your dinner and get out of my sight."

"I'm finished now," Tom said. He stood up.

"You get one more year in this house," his father said. "That's it. Then you go to the mainland, and Glen Upshaw pays a quarter every time you take a piss." He smiled, and looked as if he were going to take a bite out of something. "Believe me, it'll be better for you. I told you that already. Take what you can get, as long as you can get it. Because you don't exist."

"I DO!" Tom yelled, pushed too far now. "Of course I exist!"

"Not to me, you don't. You always made me sick."

Tom felt as if he had been bludgeoned. For a second all he wanted to do was to pick up a knife and stab his father in the heart.

"What do you want?" he shouted. "You want me to be just like you? I wouldn't be like you for a million dollars! You lived off your father-in-law all your life, and now you're happier than a pig in shit because you think you got a better offer!"

Victor overturned his chair standing up, and had to catch himself on the table to keep from falling down. His face had turned red, and his eyes and mouth seemed to have grown smaller—he did look like a pig, Tom thought, a red-faced pig staggering away from the trough. For a second he thought his father was going to rush at him. "You keep your trap shut!" Victor bellowed. "You hear me?"

So he was just going to yell. Tom was shaking uncontrollably, and his hands were in fists.

"You don't know anything about me," Victor said, still loudly but not quite yelling.

"I know enough," Tom said, louder.

"You don't know anything about yourself, either!"

"I know more than you think," Tom shouted at him. His mother began to wail upstairs, and the ugliness of this scene made him want to cry. He was still shaking.

His father's whole manner changed—he was still red-faced but suddenly much more sober. "What do you know?"

"Never mind," Tom said, disgusted.

Upstairs, Gloria settled into a pattern of steady, rhythmical wails, like a desolate child banging its head against the crib.

"On top of everything else," Victor said. "Now we got that."

"Go up and calm her down," Tom said. "Or does that stop too, now that your buddy Ralph bought you a cigar?"

"I'm going to take care of you, smartass." Victor grabbed a napkin from the table and wiped his face. Remembering the cigar and Ralph Redwing's visit had restored him.

The telephone began ringing in the study. His father said, "You get that, and if it's for me say I'll call back in five minutes," and pushed through the door.

Tom went into the study and picked up the phone.

"What's that, the television?" came his grandfather's voice. "Turn it down so I can tell you something."

Tom turned off the television.

"We have to talk about Eagle Lake," said his grandfather. "And what were you doing at the hospital this morning?"

"I wanted to find out what happened to Nancy Vetiver."

"Didn't I call you back about that?"

"I guess you forgot," Tom said.

"She'll be back on duty in a day or two. Seems she called in sick four or five days in a row. Dr. Milton scouted around, found out she was staying out too late, probably drinking too much, and bawled her out. She gave him a runaround, and he suspended her for a couple of weeks. Had to make an example of her, or they'd all be doing it. None of those girls have any background, of course. That's the whole story." He coughed loudly, and Tom pictured him holding the receiver in one hand, his cigar in the other.

"She gave him a runaround?" Tom asked.

"Tried to lie her way out of it. But with the shortage of nurses, even Shady Mount has to take what it can get." He paused. "I trust that now this matter is closed."

"It's closed," Tom said. "Absolutely, completely, irrevocably closed."

"Glad you can listen to reason. Now, I have a suggestion for you concerning your trip to Eagle Lake."

Tom said nothing.

"You still there?" his grandfather shouted.

"Still here." He heard his mother screech something at his father. "Completely, entirely here, and no place else."

"What's wrong with you?"

"I'm not too sure. I just had a fight with Dad."

"Give him time to calm down, or apologize to him, or something." Tom's mother screamed again. "What was that?"

"The television."

His grandfather sighed. "Listen. To get to Eagle Lake in the old days, we had to get to Miami and take a train to Chicago, then change trains for Hurley. The whole thing took four days. I just worked out a way for you to do the whole thing in one haul, as long as you can leave the day after tomorrow. I think you should do it."

Tom nodded, but said nothing.

"Ralph Redwing uses a private plane to take himself and his friends back and forth to the lake. The plane is coming back here to pick up the Spences, and as a personal favor to me, Ralph has agreed to let you tag along. Get your things packed, and be at the field by eight Friday morning."

Tom said, "Okay. Thanks."

"Breathe some of that fresh air, take walks in the woods. Get in some swimming. You can use my membership at the club. Don't worry about getting back. We'll work that out when the time comes." Tom had never heard Glendenning Upshaw sound so friendly. "You'll love it up there. Gloria and I used to think of summers at Eagle Lake as the best time of the year. She loved that place. Used to spend hours sitting on the balcony, looking at the woods."

"And the lake, I suppose," Tom said.

"No, some of the lodges have raised verandas overlooking the lake, but ours is on the other side—looks right into the woods. You can sit on the dock, see the lake all you want."

"You can't see the other docks from the balcony?"

"Who wants to see other people's docks? Gloria and I went up there to get away from other people. In fact, until you came along—until Gloria got married and you came along—I used to think about retiring up there with her, when the time came. Didn't know I'd never want to retire."

"Wouldn't she like to come with me?"

"Gloria can't go back," his grandfather said. "We tried it once, the year after my wife died—didn't work. Didn't work at all. She couldn't handle it. Eventually I gave up and came back early, got on with my Miami business. Worked out for the best in the long run."

"Worked out for the best?" Tom asked, appalled.

"I got that hospital built in record time." Perhaps hearing that he and Tom had been talking about different things, he added, "I made a couple of appointments for Gloria with a doctor in Miami, the kind of fellow they called an alienist in those days. Turned out to be nothing but a quack. Most of those fellows are, you know. He wanted *me* to come in for appointments, and I told him that I was a lot saner than he was. Pulled the plug on that nonsense. Gloria was a child who had lost her mother the summer before, that was the whole of the trouble."

Tom remembered his mother gripping her martini glass at her father's table on the terrace.

"Can you think of anything else that could have upset her that summer?" Tom asked.

"Not at all. Apart from Glor's trouble, it was a perfect summer. One of the young Redwing boys, Jonathan, was getting married to a pretty girl from Atlanta. A Redwing wedding is always a real event, and it should have been a delightful summer, what with all the parties at the club."

"But it wasn't," Tom said.

"You'll have better luck. Just get to the airport on time."

Tom promised to do so, and his grandfather hung up without waiting to be thanked or saying good-bye.

Tom found himself in the hall at the foot of the staircase without any memory of leaving the study. Soft intermittent wails and wordless, high-pitched imprecations came from the floor above. He looked into the wide living room and saw that everything in it was dead. All the furniture, the chairs and tables and the long couch, was dead furniture. "So she gave him the runaround," he said. "So she tried to lie her way out of it." His father's voice rumbled. "It should have been a delightful summer," Tom said. Upstairs, something crashed and broke. His feet walked him back into the study. He sat on the arm of his father's recliner and looked at the smooth charcoal screen of the television for a time before realizing that it was switched off. His legs took him across the room, and his hand pushed the power button. In a row of men in sports jackets behind a long curved desk, Joe Ruddler grimaced violently toward the camera. Wide printing at the bottom of the screen announced ALL-ISLAND LIVE ACTION NEWS NEXT! A commercial for auto wax battered the air. Tom turned down the volume and moved to a wobbly rush-bottomed chair and waited.

"I hope you told 'em I'd call right back," his father said.

Tom turned his head and saw his father standing just outside the doors. "The call was for me. It was Grand-Dad."

A layer of cells died just below the surface of his father's face.

"We had a long talk. Probably the longest talk I've ever had with him. On a one-to-one basis, I mean."

Something happened to the dark pouches beneath his father's eyes.

"Ralph Redwing came up. I'm going up north on your buddy's plane the day after tomorrow. Grand-Dad sounded pleased with himself."

His father's eyes looked bruised—that was it. Not the pouches, the eyes themselves.

"I didn't say anything about the wonderful visit and the five-dollar cigar. I didn't tell him anything at all. How could I? I don't exist."

Victor placed his hands on the doorjamb and leaned the top

half of his body into the room. A black curl of hair plastered itself to his forehead. Victor's mouth opened, and the bruised look deepened in his eyes. "I'll take care of you later." He pushed himself back out of the room.

Brisk, bouncy theme music blared from the set, and a resonant voice announced: "It's time for your All-island live action news team!"

Bulging cheeks and flaring eyes flashed on the screen for a moment, declaring that Joe Ruddler was prepared to savage words, sentences, and paragraphs between his square white teeth.

Then a blond man with an almost clerical look of concern on his regular features looked at Tom and said, "Tragic death of a local hero. After this."

For thirty seconds, a shampoo commercial blew images of billowing hair at him.

The blond man looked at Tom again and said, "Today Mill Walk has lost a hero. Patrolman Roman Klink, one of two police officers wounded in the native quarter shootout that resulted in the death of suspected murderer Foxhall Edwardes, suffered fatal gunshot wounds in an armed robbery attempt at Mulroney's Taproom late this afternoon. When Patrolman Klink, working a temporary part-time job at the Taproom while awaiting full recovery from his wounds, pulled his service revolver and attempted to halt the robbery, his assailants gunned him down. Patrolman Klink died instantly of a head wound. Three men were observed fleeing the area, and though no identifications were obtained, arrests are considered imminent."

A fuzzy black and white Police Academy photograph of a wide-faced boy in a uniform cap appeared on the screen.

"A fifteen-year veteran of the Mill Walk police force, Patrolman Roman Klink was forty-two years old, and leaves a wife and one son."

The blond man glanced down at his desk, then back at the camera and Tom. "In a related story, Officer Klink's partner, Patrolman Michael Mendenhall, died today at Shady Mount Hospital of wounds suffered at the hands of Foxhall Edwardes in the Weasel Hollow shootout. Patrolman Mendenhall had been in a coma since the event, one of the most violent in Mill Walk's history.

"Both officers will be buried with full police honors at Christchurch Cemetery at two o'clock on Sunday following a memorial service at St. Hilda's Procathedral. Captain Fulton Bishop has announced that donations to the Police Welfare Fund will be gratefully accepted."

He turned his profile to the camera and said, "A sad commentary, Joe."

Joe Ruddler burst upwards out of a blue button-down shirt which had captured the tight knot of a yellow challis necktie. "TERRIBLE! OUTRAGEOUS! YOU KNOW WHAT I THINK? I'LL TELL YOU WHAT I THINK! SOME PEOPLE BELIEVE THAT PUBLIC HANGINGS—"

Tom stood up and switched off the television.

"Hey, that was Joe Ruddler," Victor said.

Tom turned around to see his father standing in the door frame. He had his hands in his pockets. "I like Joe Ruddler."

Tom's stomach clenched—his body from his lungs to his gut felt like a closed fist. He bent down and punched the power button. "—LILY-LIVERED, FAINT-HEARTED COWARDS WHO CAN'T ACCEPT—" Tom twisted the volume control and shut off the sound.

"A policeman got murdered today."

"Cops accept that risk. Believe me, they make up for it." Victor edged into the room, looking shamefaced. "Uh, Tom, I said some stuff. . . ." He shook his head. "It isn't . . . I don't want you to think. . . . "

"Nobody wants me to think," Tom said.

"Yeah, but, I mean it's good you didn't tell Glen anything about . . . you didn't, huh?"

"I noticed something about Grand-Dad," Tom said. "He likes to tell you interesting things, but he never wants to hear them himself."

"Okay. Okay. Good." Victor edged around Tom to get to his recliner. "You want to go up and see your mom now? Turn the sound up on that thing?"

Tom twisted the volume knob until Joe Ruddler was screaming. "SO SHOOT ME! THAT'S WHAT I THINK!" His father peeked at him. He left the room and went upstairs.

Gloria was lying on top of her bed in a wrinkled pair of men's pajamas, with a pillow bunched up behind her and the covers rumpled over a bunch of magazines. The shutters had been closed. A lamp covered by a scarf burned on top of her dressing table. The other lamp, which usually stood beside the bed, lay in two pieces, a thick stand and a long thin neck, on the floor beside the bed. Next to where the lamp should have been stood a brown plastic bottle with a typed prescription label. A few cloudy bits of glass glinted up from the blue carpet. Tom started picked pieces of broken glass out of the carpet. "You'll cut yourself," he said.

"I felt so tired all day I could hardly get out of bed, and then I thought I heard you and Victor shouting at each other, and . . ."

He looked up over the edge of the bed. She had covered her face with her hands. He snatched up as much of the broken glass as he could see, dropped it on the heap of white tissues in the wastebasket beside the bed, and sat down beside his mother. "We had a fight, but it's over now." He put his arms around his mother. She felt boneless and stiff at once. "It was just something that happened." For a moment she leaned her head against his shoulder, and then jerked away. "Don't touch me. I don't like that."

He instantly dropped his arms. She gave him a cloudy look and yanked at the pajama top and tugged it around until it satisfied her.

"Do you want me to leave?"

"Not really. But I hate fights—I get so scared when I hear people fighting."

"I hate hearing you scream," he said. "That makes me feel terrible. I don't think I can do anything for you—"

"Do you think I like it? It just happens. This little thing inside me goes *pop*, and then I hardly know where I am. I used to think—it was like the real me went away somewhere and I had to hide inside myself until she came back. Then later I realized that this was the real me—this thing like a dead person."

"You're not always like this," he said.

"Will you turn off the record player? Please?"

He had not noticed the record spinning on the turntable of

the portable record player atop a dresser. He turned around and pushed the reject button, and the tone arm lifted from the end grooves and returned to its post. Tom watched the label stop spinning until he could read the words on the label. *Blue Rose*, by Glenroy Breakstone and the Targets. He took the record from the turntable and searched for the sleeve in the row of records propped on the floor against the dresser, then saw it half-hidden under the bed. The split seams on its top and bottom had been repaired with yellowing transparent tape. Tom slid the record into the sleeve.

"What's he doing now? Watching television?"

Tom nodded.

"How does that make him so superior to me? I stay up here and listen to music, and he watches the stupid television downstairs and drinks."

"You're feeling better," Tom said.

"If I really felt better, I'd hardly know how to act." She moved sideways, and levered herself up so that she could pull down her covers and slide her legs beneath them. Some of the magazines slithered onto the floor. Gloria drew the covers up over her body and leaned against the pillows.

It was like being in the bedroom of a teenage girl, Tom suddenly thought: the little record player on the dresser, the men's pajamas, the mess of magazines, the darkness, the single bed. There should have been posters and pennants on the walls, but the walls were bare.

"Do you want me to go?" he asked.

"You can stay a little while." She closed her eyes. "He looked ashamed of himself, didn't he?"

"I guess."

Tom wandered from the side of the bed and sat down backwards on the chair before the dressing table. He was still holding the record in its sleeve. "Grand-Dad just called." Gloria opened her eyes and pushed herself up against the head of the bed. She reached for the bottle of pills and shook two out into her hand. "Did he?" She broke the pills in half and swallowed two of the small halves without water.

"He wants me to go to Eagle Lake the day after tomorrow. I can get a ride on the Redwing plane with the Spences."

"The Spences are flying up north on the Redwing plane?" After a second, she added, "And you're going with them?" She put the two small sections of the other pill in her mouth, made a face, and swallowed.

"Would you like me to stay here?" he asked. "I don't have to go."

"Maybe you should get out of the house for a while. Maybe it's nicer up north."

"You used to go there in the summers," he said.

"I used to go a lot of places. I used to have another kind of life, for a little while."

"Can you remember your place at the lake?"

"It was this big, big house. All made of wood. Everything was made of wood. All the lodges were. I knew where everybody lived. Even Lamont von Heilitz. Daddy didn't want me to talk about him at lunch—the day we went to the Founders Club, remember?"

Tom nodded.

"He was famous," his mother said. "He was a lot more famous than Daddy, and he did wonderful things. I always thought he was rather grand, Lamont von Heilitz."

Where does this come from? Tom wondered.

"And I knew a lady named Jeanine. She was a friend of mine too. That's another terrible story. One terrible story after another, that's what it adds up to."

"You knew Jeanine Thielman?"

"There's a lot I'm not supposed to talk about. So I don't."

"Why aren't you supposed to talk about Jeanine Thielman?" Tom asked.

"Oh, it doesn't matter anymore," Gloria said, and sounded more adult and awake. "But I could tell her things."

Tom asked, "How old were you when your mother died?"

"Four. I didn't really understand what happened for a long time—I thought she went away to make me feel bad. I thought she wanted to punish me."

"Mom, why would she want to do that?"

She cracked her eyes open, and her puffy face looked childish and sly. "Because I was bad. Because of my secrets." For a moment, Tom thought that the slyness was like a pat of butter in her mouth. "Sometimes Jeanine would come and talk to me. And hold me. And I talked to her. I hoped she would be my new Mommy. I really did!"

"I always wondered how my grandmother died," Tom said. "Nobody ever talked about it."

"To me either!" Gloria said. "You can't tell a little kid something like that."

"Something like what?"

"She killed herself." Gloria said this flatly, without any emotion at all. "I wasn't supposed to know. I don't think Daddy even wanted me to know she was dead, you know. You know Daddy. Pretty soon he was acting like there never was any Mommy. There was just the two of us. Her and her's Da." She pulled the covers around herself more tightly, and the magazines still on the bed moved up with them. "There was just her and her's Da, and that was all there ever was. Because he loved her, really, and she loved him. And she knew everything that happened."

She slid deeper into the bed. "But it was all a long time ago. Jeanine was angry, and then a man killed her and put her in the lake too. I heard him shooting—I heard the shots in my bedroom. *Pop! Pop! Pop!* And I went through the house and out on the veranda and saw a man running through the woods. I started to cry, and I couldn't find Daddy, and I guess I went to sleep, because when I woke up he was there. And I told him what I saw, and he took me to Barbara Deane's house. So I'd be safe."

"You mean he took you to Miami."

"No—first he took me to Barbara Deane's house, in the village, and I was there a little while. A few days. And he went back to the lake, to look for Jeanine, and then he came back, and *then* we went to Miami."

"I don't understand—"

She closed her eyes. "I didn't like Barbara Deane. She never talked to me. She wasn't nice."

She was silent for a long time, breathing deeply. "I'll be better tomorrow."

He stood up and went to the side of her bed. Her eyelids fluttered. He bent down to kiss her. When his lips touched her forehead, she shuddered and mumbled, "Don't."

In the study, Victor Pasmore lay tilted back in his recliner, asleep before the blaring television. A cigarette that was only a column of ash burned in the ashtray, sending up a thin line of smoke.

Tom went to the front door and let himself out into the cool night. Chinks of light showed through Lamont von Heilitz's curtains.

24

"You're upset," said Mr. von Heilitz as soon as he saw Tom on his doorstep. "Hurry on inside, and let me get a better look at you."

Tom moved through the door with what felt like the last of his energy and leaned against a file cabinet. The Shadow inserted a cigarette in his mouth, lit it, and squinted at Tom as he inhaled. "You look absolutely *ragged*, Tom. I'll pour you a cup of coffee, and then I want you to tell me all about it."

Tom straightened up and rubbed his face. "Being here makes me feel better," he said. "I heard so much today—listened to so much—and it's all sort of spinning around in my head. I can't figure it out—I can't get it straight."

"I'd better take care of you," von Heilitz said. "You sound a little overloaded." He led Tom back through the enormous room to his kitchen, took out two cups and saucers, and poured coffee from an old black pot that had been bubbling on a gas range, also black, that must have belonged to his parents. Tom liked the entire kitchen, with its wainscoting, hanging lamps, and old-fashioned sinks and high wooden shelves and mellow, clean wooden floorboards.

The old man said, "In honor of the occasion, I think we could add a little something to the coffee, don't you?"

He took a bottle of cognac from another shelf, and tipped a little into each cup.

"What occasion?" Tom asked.

"Your being here." He handed Tom one of the cups, and smiled at him.

Tom sipped the hot, delicious mixture, and felt the tension drain from him. "I didn't know that you knew Hattie Bascombe."

"Hattie Bascombe is one of the most extraordinary people on this island. That you know about our friendship means that you must have seen her today! But I'm not going to keep you in the kitchen. Let's go into the other room and hear about what has you so worked up."

Tom sprawled back on the old leather couch, and put his feet up on the coffee table covered with books. Von Heilitz said, "One minute," and put a record on his gleaming stereo equipment. Tom braced himself for more Mahler, but a warm, smoky tenor saxophone began playing one of Miss Ellinghausen's tunes, "But Not For Me," and Tom thought that it sounded just like the way the coffee and brandy tasted: and then he recognized it.

"That's *Blue Rose*," he said. "My mother has that record."

"Glenroy Breakstone's best record. It's what we ought to listen to, tonight." Tom looked at him with a mixture of pain and confusion, and von Heilitz said, "This state you're in—I know it's a terrible condition, but I think it means you're almost *there*. Events are almost moving by themselves now, and it's because of you." He sat down across from Tom, and drank from his cup. "Another man was murdered today—murdered because he talked too much, among other reasons."

"That policeman," Tom said.

"He was a loose end. They couldn't trust him, so they got rid of him. They'd do the same to me, and to you too, if they knew about us. We have to be very careful from now on, you know."

"Did you know that my grandmother committed suicide?" Tom asked. Von Heilitz paused with his cup halfway to his mouth. "It's like . . . it was a shock, but it *wasn't*. And you lied to me!" Tom burst out. "My grandfather couldn't have seen the Thielmans' dock from his balcony! It doesn't face the water, it faces the woods! So why did you say that? Why does everybody tell me so many lies? And why is my mother so *helpless*! How could my grandfather dump her at someone's house and go back to Eagle Lake by himself?" Tom let out a long sigh that was nearly a sob. He covered his face with his hands, then lowered them. "I'm sorry. I'm thinking about four or five things at once."

"I didn't lie to you. I just didn't tell you everything—there are a couple of things I didn't know then, and a few I still don't know." He waited a moment. "When do you go to Eagle Lake?"

"The day after tomorrow." When von Heilitz looked up sharply, he said, "It was just worked out. That's why my grandfather called. I'm going on the Redwing plane."

"Well, well." The old man crossed his legs and leaned back into his chair. "Tell me what happened to you today."

Tom looked across the table, and was met by a smile of pure understanding.

He told him everything. About the hospital and David Natchez and the dead man and Dr. Milton; about his "excursion" to the old slave quarter and Maxwell's Heaven; about seeing Fulton Bishop glide through the court like a hungry snake; about Nancy Vetiver and what Michael Mendenhall had said; Dr. Milton in the pony trap; his father's drunken hostility and the visit from Ralph Redwing; about the call from his grandfather; his mother in her bedroom, remembering Eagle Lake and her childhood.

"My God," the old man said when Tom had finished. "Now I know why you were in such a state when you arrived. I think all that calls for some more brandy, without the coffee this time. Will you have some?"

"I'd fall asleep if I had any more," Tom said. "I'm only half done with this." Putting it all into words had helped him. Despite what he said, he was tired but not at all sleepy, and he felt much calmer.

The Shadow smiled at him, patted his knee, and took his cup out into his kitchen. He returned with a snifter of brandy and set it on the table, then turned over the Glenroy Breakstone record and filled the room with the confidential, passionate sounds that Tom would associate with both this moment and his mother for the rest of his life.

He sat down again across from Tom and looked at him steadily—with what looked to the boy like steady unambiguous affection, as he swirled the brandy in his glass. "Just now, you told me two very useful bits of information, and confirmed something that I have always thought to be true—that you went out to the Goethe Park area seven years ago for the same reason that you made your English teacher drive you to Weasel Hollow. I saw you that day, and I knew that you saw me too. You didn't recognize me, but you saw me."

Mr. von Heilitz seemed very excited, and his excitement infected Tom. "You were there? You told me—that first time I came here, you asked if I remembered the first time—"

"And that was it, Tom! Think!"

And then Tom did remember a gloomy Gothic house, and a face that had looked skull-like peering through the curtains. His mouth dropped open. Von Heilitz was grinning at him. "You were in that house on Calle Burleigh!"

"I was in that house." His eyes glowed at Tom from over the top of the snifter as he drank. "I saw you coming down the block, looking between the houses to see 44th Street."

"What were you doing there?"

"I rent houses and apartments in various places on Mill Walk, and I use them when I have to keep an eye on things and stay out of sight. That place was as close as I could get to Wendell Hasek's house on 44th Street. From the top floor, I could see that whole block of 44th Street."

"Wendell Hasek," Tom said, and then *saw* him: a fat man with a crewcut leaning against a bay window in the brown and yellow house, and the same man appearing on its porch, signaling with his hand.

"He was there," he said. "He must have seen me. He sent out—" Tom stopped talking, seeing an older boy and a dark-haired girl in his memory. Jerry Fairy. *And what are you gonna do now, Jerry Fairy?* "He sent his children out to get me. Jerry and Robyn. They wanted to know—"

You want to know what's going on? Why don't you tell me, huh? What are you doing here?

"—what I was doing there. And then—"

He saw two other older boys, a fat boy who already looked angry and a boy as thin as a skeleton, rounding the corner of a native house. The whole crowded, frightening scene of those few minutes came back to him in a rush: he remembered Jerry hitting him, and the sudden flash of pain, and how he had lashed out and broken Jerry's nose—

Nappy! Robbie! Get him!

He remembered the knives. Running. Remembered seeing Wendell Hasek come out on his front steps and winding his hand in the air. The fear of it, and the sense of *uncanniness*: of being trapped in a movie, or a dream.

"Jerry must have sent for his friends," he said.

Tom began to shake. Now he could remember everything: the gleam bouncing off one of the knives, the insolent way the one called Robbie had lounged before he began running, the white street name in the purple air, AUER, the certainty that Robbie was going to shove his long knife into him, the traffic on Calle Burleigh suddenly dividing around him and a grey-haired man on a bicycle swooping toward the ground like a trick rider in a circus. He put his hands over his eyes. The mesh of a grille, and a face pointed toward him.

"Nappy and Robbie," he said.

"Nappy LaBarre and Robbie Wintergreen. That's right. The Cornerboys."

Tom's shaking had gradually subsided, and he stared at von Heilitz.

"That was what they called themselves," the detective said. "They all dropped out of school at fourteen, and they did a few things for Wendell Hasek. They stole. They kept a lookout for police. In general, they got up to no good until they reached their early twenties, when they suddenly turned respectable and started working for the Redwing Holding Company."

"What do they do for the Redwings?" He remembered something Sarah had said that afternoon. "Oh—they're bodyguards."

"I suppose that's what they're called."

"And what about Robyn?"

Von Heilitz smiled and shook his head. "Robyn got a job taking care of a sick old woman. When the old woman died while they were on a trip to the mainland, Robyn inherited her entire estate. The family took her to court on the mainland, but Robyn won the case. Now she's just spending her money."

"Hasek recognized me," Tom said. "That's why he sent for the Cornerboys. A few days before, he came to our house. He must have tracked down my grandfather—and he must have stopped at a couple of bars too, because he was smashed. Anyhow, he was shouting and throwing rocks, and my grandfather went outside to handle him. I followed him, and Hasek saw me. My grandfather ran him off, and I went back inside, and when Grand-Dad came back he went upstairs. They were all talking about it. I heard my mother screaming, *Where did that man come from? What did he want?* And my grandfather answered, *He came from the general vicinity of 44th and Auer, if you're interested. As for what he wants, what do you think he wants? He wants more money.*"

"And you overheard, and a few days later you went out there—across the island by yourself, at ten years of age. Because you'd heard enough to think that if you went to that place, you'd be able to understand everything. And instead you were almost killed, and wound up in the hospital."

"And that's why everybody kept asking me what I was doing out there," Tom said, and another level of confusion fell away from him. "Why were you at the hospital today?"

"I wanted to see for myself what you learned from Nancy Vetiver. I knew that poor Michael Mendenhall couldn't have much more time, and I spent a couple of hours a day in the lobby—in the disguise you saw—to see what would happen when he died. And I learned that my impression of David Natchez was correct—he's a real force for good. That he's stayed alive all this time means that he's also a resourceful character. Someday, Tom, we're going to need that man—and he is going to need us."

Von Heilitz stood up and pushed his hands into his pockets. He began pacing back and forth between his chair and the table.

"Now let me ask you another one. What do you know about Wendell Hasek?"

"He was wounded once," Tom said. "In a payroll robbery from my grandfather's company. The robbers were shot to death, but the money was never found."

Von Heilitz stopped pacing, and fixed his eyes on the Degas painting of a ballet dancer. He seemed to be listening very intently to the music. "And does that remind you of anything?"

Tom nodded. "It reminds me of lots of stuff. Hasselgard. The Treasury money. But what—"

Von Heilitz whipped around to face him. "Wendell Hasek, who was at Eagle Lake the summer Jeanine Thielman was murdered, came to your house looking for your grandfather. He wanted money, or so it seems. We can speculate that he felt he deserved more money for having been wounded in the payroll robbery, even though he had already been given enough to buy a house. When you turn up a short time later, he is anxious enough to send out his son, and to summon his son's friends, to see what you're doing there. Doesn't that suggest that he is concealing something?" He fixed Tom with his eyes.

"Maybe he organized the robbery," Tom said. "Maybe he was getting money from my grandfather for a deliberate injury."

"Maybe." Von Heilitz leaned against the back of his chair, and looked at Tom with the same excitement in his eyes. He was keeping something to himself, Tom understood: *Maybe* hid another possibility, one he wanted Tom to discover for himself. His next words seemed like a deliberate step away from the unspoken subject. "I want you to watch what is going on around you at Eagle Lake very carefully, and to write me whenever you see anything that strikes you. Don't just put your letters in your grandfather's mailbox. Give them to Joe Truehart—Minor's son. He works for the Eagle Lake post office, and he remembers what I did for his father. But don't let anybody see you talking to him. You can't take any unnecessary risks."

"All right," Tom said. "But what kind of risks could there be?"

"Well, things are reaching a certain pitch," von Heilitz said. "You may stir up something just by being there. At the very least, you have to expect that Jerry Hasek and his friends might recognize you. They'll certainly recognize your name—they must have thought they killed you. If they were helping Wendell

Hasek hide something seven years ago, it or its traces may still be hidden."

"The money?"

"When I watched his house from the top floor of my place on Calle Burleigh, twice I saw a car pull up in front of Hasek's. A man carrying a briefcase got out and was let into the house. The second time it was a different car, and a different man. Hasek went out his back door, unlocked a shed in his back garden, and came back with small packages in his hands. His visitors left, still carrying their briefcases."

"Why did he give the money away?"

"Payoffs." Von Heilitz raised his shoulders, as if to say: What else? "Certainly the police got some of that money, but who else did is a matter we can't answer yet."

"He was protecting stolen money," Tom said.

"The payroll money." And here again was the flavor of the unspoken subject. The old man lowered his head and seemed to examine his gloved hands, which rested on the curved back of the chair. "One thing you told me is very sinister, and another puts several crucial pieces into the whole puzzle of Eagle Lake. And do you know what I realized tonight? What only my vanity kept me from seeing before this?"

Too agitated to remain seated, von Heilitz had jumped to his feet in the middle of this surprising announcement, and was now pacing behind the chair again.

"What?" Tom said, alarmed.

"That I need you more than you need me!" He stopped, whirled to face Tom, and threw out his arms. His handsome old face blazed with so many contradictory feelings—astonishment, outrage, self-conscious despair, also a sort of goofy pleasure—that Tom smiled at this display. "It's true! It's absolutely true!" He lowered his arms theatrically. "All of this—this immense *case*, absolutely depends on you, Tom. It's probably the last, and certainly the most important, thing like it that I'll ever work on, it's the culmination of my life, and here it is the first real thing you've ever done, and without you I'd still be pasting clippings in my journals, wondering when I'd get what I needed to show my hand. I'm upstaged at my own final bow!" He laughed, and turned to the room, asking it to witness his comeuppance. He laughed again, with real happiness.

Von Heilitz put his hands in the small of his back and arched himself backwards. He sighed, and his hair dripped over his collar. "Ah, what's to become of us?"

He moved slowly around the chair and the table and sat beside Tom on the couch. He patted him on the back, twice. "Well, if we knew that, there'd be no sense in going on, would there?"

Von Heilitz propped his feet on the edge of the table, and Tom did the same. For a moment they sat in the identical posture, as relaxed as a pair of twins.

"Can I ask you something?" Tom finally said.

"Anything at all."

"What did I tell you that put another piece of the puzzle in place?"

"That your grandfather took your mother to a house owned by Barbara Deane for a few days, immediately after Jeanine Thielman's death. And that your mother saw a man running into the woods."

"She didn't recognize him."

"No. Or she did, but didn't want to, and told herself she didn't. There would have been few men up there that your mother didn't know."

"And what was the sinister thing I told you?"

"That Ralph Redwing paid a flattering call on your father." Von Heilitz lowered his legs and sat up straight. "I find that distressing, all things considered." He stood up decisively, and Tom did the same, wondering what was coming next. Von Heilitz looked at him in a way that was brimming with unspoken speech: but unlike Victor Pasmore, he did not utter the words that had come to him.

"You'd better be off," von Heilitz said instead. "It's getting late, and we don't want you to have to answer any awkward questions."

They began to move through the files and other clutter to the door. For a moment, two months seemed almost dangerously long, and Tom wondered if he would ever see this room again.

"What should I look for, up north?" he asked. "What should I do?"

"Ask around about Jeanine Thielman. See if anyone else

saw that man running into the woods." Von Heilitz opened the door. "I want you to stir things up a little. See if you can make things happen, without actually putting yourself in danger. Be careful, Tom. Please."

Tom held out his hand, but von Heilitz surprised him again, and hugged him.

Part Seven

EAGLE LAKE

Dr. Kleber and others repeatedly emphasized the social dimension of the treatment process. Dr. Frank H. Gawin, director of the Substance Abuse Research Unit at Yale University, put it this way: "If crack were a drug of the middle or upper classes, we would not be saying it is so impossible to treat."

Crack is the drug of choice in most poor communities because the initial purchases are relatively cheap.

Initial Conceptions Hold Up

Still, the biochemical aspects often tend to come first in considering crack treatment, rather than its psychological, social or economic elements or the rather startling lessons of history. Detoxification, or getting the addict off the drug, either by volition, deprivation or medication, is the first and essential stage of any program that works, the experts said.

Many of the initial conceptions about crack, which has come into widespread use only within the last four years, have thus far held up.

Yes, it has a rare biochemistry that Colombian [illegible] preparing [illegible] lowing drug [illegible] has been impounded [illegible] reclaimed [illegible] proving that the property was obtained with profits from [illegible]. It is expected that [illegible] will make the effort.

In past crackdowns on drug dealers, most seized properties were eventually returned to owners by [illegible].

[illegible] page 116.

[illegible] experts now believe that the real difficulties they face in treating crack addicts stem far more from the setting and circumstances of the user than the biochemical reaction the drug produces.

And they believe the new understanding offers society a measure of hope. [illegible] There has been largely despair in coping with a drug epidemic that is tearing apart poor neighborhoods and families in the nation's cities.

Researchers are finding that crack addiction, under the right conditions, can be successfully treated. Some studies suggest that crack is no more chemically addictive than other drugs that addicts have been able to quit.

Positive Shift in Emphasis

Only a year ago, crack was widely regarded as a [illegible] drug still poorly understood, with special characteristics that rendered its addiction almost impossible to cure. Now, in dozens of interviews and scientific reports, treatment experts are shifting their emphasis to the more positive, if more complex, view about addiction to the smokable form of cocaine.

Moreover, in finding that properly run programs can be made to work in treating crack addicts, they believe they have identified the crucial element of [illegible].

25

At seven-thirty in the morning, two days later, an unshaven Victor Pasmore set down one of Tom's suitcases just outside the main entrance of David Redwing Field. Victor's rumpled clothes smelled of perspiration, tobacco, and bourbon. Even his eyebrows were rumpled.

"Thanks for getting up to drive me here." Tom wished that he could hug his father, or say something affectionate to him, but Victor was irritated and hung over.

His father took a step away, and glanced anxiously at his car, parked across the sidewalk in a no-parking zone. Beyond the airport's access road, the nearly empty lot already radiated heat in the morning sun.

"You got everything you need? Everything okay?"

"Sure," Tom said.

"I, ah, I better get my car outa here. They move you along, at airports." Victor squinted at him. His eyes looked rumpled too. "Better not say anything to anybody about, you know, what I told you. It's still top secret. Details and that."

"Okay."

Victor nodded. A sour odor washed toward Tom. "So. Take it easy."

"Okay."

Victor got into his car and closed the door. He waved at Tom through the passenger window. Tom waved back, and his father jerked the car forward into the access road. Tom saw him peering from side to side, looking for other drivers to get angry with. When the car was out of sight, he picked up his bags and went into the terminal.

This was a long concrete block building with two airline counters, a car rental desk, a souvenir stand, and a magazine rack stocked with *The Lady*, *Harpers Queen*, *Vogue*, *Life*, and the American news magazines. At one end was the baggage area—a moving belt and twenty square yards of stained linoleum with a permanent pool of watery yellow liquid against the far wall—and at the other end, a bar called Hurricane Harry's with wicker stools, a thatched roof, and a vending machine that dispensed sandwiches.

Tom had tried to call Lamont von Heilitz three times on Saturday, but the Shadow had not answered his telephone. Curious about Barbara Deane, he had taken the grey metal box where his parents kept their important papers from its shelf in the study, and looked through the title to the house and the car, their marriage license, many legal documents and stock certificates, until he found his birth certificate. Dr. Bonaventure Milton had signed his birth certificate, Barbara Deane and Glendenning Upshaw had witnessed it, and a man named Winston Shaw, Registrar of the Island of Mill Walk, had testified to the correctness of the proceedings.

Tom flipped back to the marriage license and removed it from the box. This, too, had been witnessed by Glendenning Upshaw and Barbara Deane. Winston Shaw had again performed his office. Gloria Ross Upshaw of Mill Walk had married Victor Laurence Pasmore of Miami, Florida, United States of America, on February fifteenth, 1946.

First Tom noticed the oddity of his midwife having witnessed his parents' marriage; then something about the date made him wrinkle his forehead. His parents had been married in February: he had been born on October twentieth. He counted on his fingers, and saw that February and October were exactly nine months apart.

And that, Tom thought, was how an employee of Mill Walk Construction married the boss's daughter. There had been a romance: and when Glendenning Upshaw learned his daughter was pregnant, he flew her and her boyfriend back home to Mill Walk and ordered up a civil ceremony in the way he would order up room service in a hotel.

He had placed the metal box back on the shelf and gone into the kitchen, where his mother sat at the table in front of the lunch dishes, holding the brown plastic pill bottle in one hand and looking dully at the refrigerator. When she saw him she smiled like someone remembering how to do it, and slowly put his plate on top of hers. "I'll do it," he said, and took the plates from her and put them in the dishwasher. She handed him the glasses. "Are you all right?" he asked.

"I guess I'm a little weak," she said.

"Can I help you upstairs? Or do you want to go into another room?"

She shook her head. "Don't worry about me."

He sat down beside her. He knew that if he put his arm around her, she would push it off. "I was wondering about this Barbara Deane," he said.

Her eyes flicked toward him, then away, and a vertical line appeared between her eyebrows.

"She's taking care of your old lodge, or something like that. Do you know her?"

"She's a friend of Daddy's."

"Was she his girlfriend, or anything like that?"

The vertical line disappeared, and she smiled. "She was never anybody's girlfriend. Especially not Daddy's!" And added, "Barbara Deane worked at the hospital," as if that were all that had to be said. Then she looked straight at him. "Stay out of her way. She's *funny*."

"What makes her funny?"

"Oh, I don't know," Gloria sighed. "I don't want to talk about Barbara *Deane*."

But when he went up to pack, she came into his room and

made sure he was bringing a bathing suit, boat shoes, sweaters, ties, a jacket. He was taking his place in the world, and he had to be dressed for the cold nights.

At eight o'clock a big potbellied man in sunglasses and a cowboy hat carried an enormous suitcase through the revolving doors, followed by a blond woman with a Jackie Kennedy hairdo who wore huge sunglasses and a black miniskirt. She pulled a middle-sized suitcase behind her on rollers. The potbellied man squinted at the darkened bar, frowned at Tom, and shook his head at the women at the airline desks, who wilted back on their stools. Then Sarah Spence came through the electronic door, carrying a small suitcase like Baby Bear. She was dressed in a blue button-down shirt with rolled-up sleeves and khaki shorts. "Tom!" she cried. "Bingo was so unhappy! I think his heart broke! I wish we could give him Percy's—" Here she sketched a large apron before her with her free hand.

"Percy's what?" her mother said, lowering her sunglasses on her nose and giving Tom a clinical look.

Mr. Spence dropped his suitcase and examined Tom through his sunglasses. "So you're hitching a ride up north with us, are you?"

"Yes, sir," Tom said.

"Who's this Percy?" her mother said. "Give Bingo what?"

"Special dog food," Sarah said. "A friend of a friend of Tom's."

Mrs. Spence shoved her sunglasses back up her nose. She was a good-looking woman who obviously knew the names of every member of the Founders Club, and her legs were almost young enough for her miniskirt. "Are both those suitcases yours?"

Tom nodded, and Mrs. Spence looked at his suitcases through her dark glasses.

"Pilot ought to be here waiting," said Mr. Spence. "That was the deal. I guess I better go look for the guy." He cast another look at the bar, and set off toward the baggage area and the yellow puddle.

"Well, I don't see the reason for last-minute changes," said Mrs. Spence, speaking to the air. Then she fixed Tom with a smile that went all the way to the corners of her sunglasses. "And your mother is Gloria Upshaw, isn't she?"

"She was Gloria Upshaw," Tom said. "Before she got married."

"Such a dear," said Mrs. Spence.

"Okay, we got it straightened out," said Mr. Spence. "The pilot's waiting for us in the Redwing lounge."

"Of course he is," said Mrs. Spence.

Mr. Spence lifted his enormous suitcase and began moving toward a door next to the thatch of the bar, and Mrs. Spence muttered something and followed after with her medium-sized suitcase rolling after her handsome legs, and Sarah hugged him while their backs were turned and hit him in the back with her tiny suitcase and whispered, "Don't mind them too much, please, and *don't pay any attention to anything they say*."

On the other side of the door, black leather couches and chairs had been arranged around marble coffee tables on a thick grey carpet. A waiter in a white coat stood behind a bar on which stood a pitcher of orange juice, a silver coffeepot, and trays of breakfast rolls covered in Saran Wrap.

"Oh, my!" said Mrs. Spence. "Well, I *knew* it!"

A tall, well-tanned man in a dark blue uniform set down his coffee cup and stood up before one of the couches. "Spence family?"

"*And* a person named Tom Pasmore," said Mrs. Spence. "Did you know he was coming too?"

The pilot smiled. "There won't be any problem, Mrs. Spence." He opened a door beside the bar, and they stepped out into the heat. A sleek grey jet with a heraldic letter **R** sat on the tarmac a short distance away. "I am Captain Mornay, by the way, but Mr. Redwing's guests usually call me Ted," said the pilot.

"Oh, Ted, thank you so much," said Mrs. Spence, and swept across the tarmac toward the staircase leading up to the open door of the jet.

The interior of the plane matched the Redwing lounge. Grey carpeting covered the floor and bulkheads, and black leather chairs stood around black marble tables. A bar with a steward in a white jacket stood next to a curtained-off galley. On the other side of the bar and galley Tom saw two compartments separated by smoked glass. A door in the rear of the plane opened, and a porter began handing in their suitcases to the steward, who placed them on shelves at the rear end of the plane and secured them behind a carpeted door.

The steward asked them to choose their seats and fasten their seat belts, and slipped into the galley.

"Well, Tom, I think we'll sit in this nice little area right here," said Mrs. Spence, and smiled brightly. She took a seat in the second complement of chairs, looked at Sarah, and patted the chair beside hers. There were three chairs around the black table.

"Tom and I can sit here," Sarah said. "That way, we'll practically be at the same table." She sat in the chair of the first group nearest her mother's table, and swiveled it around to show how close they were.

Mr. Spence sat down, grunting, and put his cowboy hat on the table. Tom took the chair beside Sarah's. They all fastened their seat belts. Mrs. Spence pushed her sunglasses up into her hair, and smiled ferociously.

"Only twenty men in America have jets like this," said Mrs. Spence. "Frank Sinatra has one. And Liberace, I think. Some of the others are showier, but Ralph's is the most tasteful. I'm sure I'm happier in this jet than I would ever be in Frank Sinatra's. Or Liberace's."

"Oh, I'd like to be Liberace's private jet," said Sarah. "I'm sure I'd be happy in a jet where everything was piano-shaped and covered in ermine. Don't you think that private jets *shouldn't* be tasteful?"

"I suggest that you learn to like this one." Her mother's voice could have shaved a peach. "You'll be seeing a lot of it." She swiveled her chair, hitching her skirt even farther up her thighs, and looked back at the rest of the cabin. "Aren't those little booths cute? I adore those little booths. I can just see Buddy sitting in one of those little booths. Or in the cockpit. Buddy is sort of the pilot type, isn't he?"

"I can see Buddy piloting the bar," Sarah said.

"I don't understand you," her mother said. "You just say these things."

"Tom is very high-spirited, mother. He goes on wonderful excursions. He has interesting friends everywhere."

"Imagine that," said Mrs. Spence. "Do you think there is

any champagne on this flight? I think champagne would be just right, don't you?"

Mr. Spence pulled in his belly, stood up, and went to the curtained galley.

When a bottle of beer, two glasses of orange juice, and an ice bucket with a bottle of champagne sat on the table, Mrs. Spence raised her glass and said, "Here's to summer!" They all drank.

"Have you known Ralph Redwing long?" Tom asked.

"Of course," said Mrs. Spence, and "Not really," said Mr. Spence, more or less simultaneously. They looked at each other with differing degrees of irritation.

"Well, of course, we've moved in the same circles ever since Mr. Spence took over Corporate Accounting for Ralph," said Mrs. Spence. "But we've only really become close in the past two or three years. You'd have to say that Buddy and Sarah brought us together, and we're very happy about that. *Very* happy."

"You do all the accounting work for the Redwing Holding Company?" Tom asked.

"Not by a long shot," Mr. Spence said. "I handle the work for the can company, the real estate holdings, the brewery, a few other odds and ends. Keeps me hopping. Above me, there's the General Accountant, the man I report to, and then the Vice-President for Accounting, above him."

"So you do the accounting work relating to Elysian Courts and the old slave quarter?"

Mr. Spence nodded. "It's all revenue."

"I never saw any champagne that came in a clear bottle before," said Mrs. Spence, refilling her glass. "Doesn't it spoil that way, or something?"

"You might not know this," Mr. Spence said, "but your grandfather did me a big favor once. Your grandfather is the reason I work for Ralph now."

"Oh, yes?"

"I come from Iowa, orginally, and Mrs. Spence and I met in college there. When we got married, she wanted to live back on Mill Walk, where she was from. So I came down here and got a job with your grandfather. We had a nice little place out in Elm Cove. In ten years, I was doing about half his total accounting work—your grandfather does everything by the seat of his pants, you know—and we could get our house on The Sevens."

"One of the oldest houses in the far east end," said Mrs. Spence.

"Hadn't been lived in for better than twenty years. Like a museum in there when we moved in. Couple years later, he sold us our lodge—same deal. Sealed up since hell froze over. Anyhow, once we had the lodge, we came in contact a lot more with Ralph and his bunch. And when Ralph dropped into my office one day and said he'd like to give me a job, your grandfather gave me his blessings." He finished off his first beer while he spoke. "So everything worked out just right, you could say."

"Didn't a man named Anton Goetz own that house?"

"Nope. He worked for your grandfather—made a lot of money too! For an accountant, I mean. The actual ownership of the place was held by a shadow corporation that was part of Mill Walk Construction, if you looked hard enough. Same was true of our lodge. Saved a few pennies in taxes that way, I guess."

"I thought I heard once that Goetz owned the St. Alwyn Hotel," Tom said.

"He might have said he did, and he might have been listed here and there as the owner, but your grandfather still owns the St. Alwyn. In conjunction with Ralph, of course."

"Oh, of course," Tom said. "And I guess my grandfather owns part of Elysian Courts."

"And the old slave quarter. Sure. Way back when, Glendenning Upshaw and Maxwell Redwing pretty much divided up the island. All on the up and up, of course. So Glen and Ralph are pretty much partners in a lot of things these days. There's a lot of overlap in my work."

"That's enough talk about business," said Mrs. Spence. "I didn't come on this plane to hear about the slums of Mill Walk and who owns what. Sarah is going away to college in the fall . . . Tom"—it seemed difficult for her to utter his name—"we all thought that a year or two of college at a good school would help prepare her for the life we want her to have. I had two years of college myself, and that was all *I* needed. Of course"—she looked coyly at her daughter—"if she transfers out to Arizona, which is a wonderful school too, things might look different."

"Tom and I are going on an excursion together, Mother," Sarah said. "We are going to explore the back of this plane, and see if hidden recording devices have been placed in the ashtrays." She took Tom's hand and stood up.

"It's an interesting fact," said Mr. Spence, "that no Redwing I ever heard of ever married a woman who didn't come from his own crowd. They all marry people they've known most of their lives. That's how they keep that dynasty going. And I'll tell you another interesting fact"—he winked at Tom—"they all marry pretty women."

"And they find them at the pretty women discount outlet," Sarah said. She tugged Tom away from the table.

She stopped at the bar, and the steward leaned forward. "What do pretty women drink? What's a pretty drink?"

"Watch yourself, Sarah," her mother said.

The steward said that he knew a pretty drink, and poured a small amount of cassis into a flute glass, then filled the glass with champagne from a fresh bottle.

"This is certainly what pretty women drink," Sarah said. "Thank you. Tom, I'm sure there are some lascars hidden in the rear of this plane. Let's go consort with them."

She strode down the length of the jet and looked into each of the compartments until she came to the last, opposite the baggage compartment. "Here they are." She went inside and sat down on one of the long seats, sipped at her drink, and placed it on the table. Tom sat down opposite her. "The lascars are us," she said. "Drink half of this."

He sipped a little of the drink and put it back before her. Sarah's eyes burned toward him. She picked up the glass and gulped. "I'm going to chop off my hair. I'm going to wear turtlenecks and jeans and have a silent brother named Bill. I'll get my furniture from the dump. All the really tasteful stuff is there anyway."

Captain Ted Mornay's soothing voice came over a hidden speaker, advising them that they were flying at thirty thousand feet over South Carolina, that they were expected to land at Eagle Lake as scheduled, and that they should have a smooth flight.

Sarah took another swallow of the drink. "I could begin to see certain advantages in prettiness. Do you think it might be possible for you to go up to the bar and get another drink from that lovely man? I want to split these the way Nancy Vetiver splits beers."

Tom went back to the bar and got a second Kir Royale. Neither of the Spences looked at him.

When he got back to the compartment, Sarah said, "Good. Now you're a pretty woman too. Probably you'll marry very well."

He sat down beside her. The sweet, light drink fizzed on his tongue.

"Is it tacky to apologize for your parents even if they're really horrible?"

"You don't have to apologize. I liked talking to your father."

"Did you especially like the interesting facts?"

They both sipped from their drinks.

"At least now I understand what you were saying about other people making you do things."

"Well, that's something," Sarah said. "It's not just my parents, who are so thrilled they can't contain themselves, it's his parents too. Ralph Redwing sends his carriage to pick me up after dancing class! I'm escorted home! Katinka Redwing wants to give me golfing lessons! Why do you think we're in this plane?"

"They can't make you marry Buddy," Tom said.

"Ah, but it's like being the Dalai Lama. They pick you out in childhood, and plan the whole rest of your life. They surround you with thoughtfulness and gifts and their wonderful conviction that you're really special because you can be one of them, and then you *are* one of them. And your father gets a great new job, and your mother just assumes that —well, she just assumes, that's all. All of a sudden she's the Queen Mother."

"You still don't have to marry him," Tom said.

"Drink some more of that," she ordered.

He drank.

"More."

He took two swallows, and Sarah pointed at his glass. He drank again. Sarah's glass was empty.

Then her arms were around him, her face was a blur against his, and her mouth brushed his. Her tongue slid into his mouth. They kissed for a long time, and then she moved onto his lap, and they kissed even longer. Tom heard the Spences' voices come to him from a great distance away. "What do you think these compartments are for?" Sarah whispered. "We can barely hear them, and they can't hear us at all."

"Won't they come back here?"

"They wouldn't dare." Their faces were so close that Tom felt engulfed by Sarah Spence. "Do this," she said, and licked his upper lip. "And do this." She closed his right hand on her left breast.

It was as if a warm cloud had settled around him, infusing him with its warmth and softness. The Spences' voices receded. Sarah's face swam before him, ideally beautiful. Her shoulders, her small round breasts, her straight slim back and her round slender arms, all of these surrounded him. Sarah hitched herself up on her knees, straddling him, and quickly, smiling, undid his belt. "Get rid of those clothes," she whispered. "I want to see you."

"Here?"

"Why not? I can feel you."

Her hand slipped under the waistband of his underwear, and she ran her fingers along the length of his erection. Her fingers wrapped around him. "You feel beautiful," she breathed into his cheek.

"You *are* beautiful," he said, uttering the truest thing he knew.

She rubbed the tips of her breasts against his chest, and he levered himself up and pushed down his trousers. "Well, what shall we do with this thing?" Sarah said. "Here we are, aren't we? In this traveling Redwing love nest." In a flash she was naked, and all of her beautiful body had wrapped around him. She guided him between her legs, and they held to each other and moved as much as they could. Tom felt his entire body gather and gather itself, and she twisted back and forth upon him; and it felt as if he were exploding. Sarah bit his shoulder, and he stiffened again instantly. She tightened around him; her body quivered; and he felt all her warmth embracing him, and after some endless minutes it was as if he turned inside out, as if he were a tree turning into a river within her. Trembling and shaking with passion and what felt like a final, ultimate blessedness, he felt her trembling too. Finally she collapsed against him. Her face was wet against his cheek, and he saw that she had been crying.

"I love you," he whispered.

"I'm glad," she said, and he remembered her saying it at Miss Ellinghausen's.

She pulled away from him, and kissed him; and stepped into her shorts and hooked on her bra and pulled her shirt over her tender shoulders. He rearranged his clothing, feeling as though an aura clung to him. And then they were seventeen years old again, seated side by side and holding hands, but everything had changed forever.

"I can still feel you inside me," she said, "How can I marry Buddy Redwing, when Tom Pasmore is still inside me? I'm *branded.* There's this big TP on me somewhere."

They sat in silence, and the jet pushed its way through the air.

"How are you kids getting on?" Mr. Spence yelled from the bar.

"Fine, Daddy," Sarah called out in a clear, high-pitched voice that sounded like bells and made Tom's heart dissolve. "We have a lot to talk about."

"Enjoy yourselves," he yelled back. "Within reason, of course!"

"Reason had nothing to do with it," she whispered, and they leaned against one another and laughed.

Mrs. Spence shouted down the length of the plane: "Why don't you kids come up here and be sociable?"

"In a minute, mother," Sarah called back.

Again they sat in silence, looking at one another.

"I think it's going to be an interesting summer," Sarah said.

26

Grand Forks was a small town twenty miles from Eagle Lake, and because of travelers from Canada as well as Mill Walk, its little airport had a Customs and Immigration section, located in a concrete block shed adjacent to the terminal. Captain Mornay escorted his passengers and their bags to the Customs desk, where the inspector greeted him as Ted and chalked their bags without bothering to open them. Immigration stamped their crimson Mill Walk passports with tourist visas.

"I suppose Ralph sent a driver?" said Mrs. Spence, managing to sound offended by the necessity of asking the question.

"He generally does that, yes, ma'am," the pilot said. "If you'll take your bags through that glass door just ahead and take them into the main terminal, you should find the driver waiting for you."

The customs inspector and the Immigration official were staring raptly at Mrs. Spence's long legs, as was a young man in a brown leather jacket sprawled out in a chair against one of the grey walls of the shed.

Mrs. Spence covered most of her handsome face with the enormous sunglasses and swept toward the glass door, carrying nothing but a handbag.

"Enjoy your stay," the pilot said, and turned away to walk toward the grinning man in the leather jacket.

Mr. Spence picked up the Papa Bear suitcase and went after his wife.

One of Tom's cases had a long strap, which he put over a shoulder. He picked up his other, heavier suitcase by the handle, and with his left hand took the leash of the Mama Bear suitcase.

"Oh, let me do it," Sarah said. "After all, she's my awful mother, not yours." She took the thin strap from his hand, and Tom rearranged his own cases to balance the weight, and they went through the glass door.

Between the jet and the customs shed Tom had been too preoccupied with Sarah Spence to notice anything else except the freshness of the air and the unusual intensity of the sky; in the shorter distance between the customs shed and the terminal building, he felt the edge in the air, the hint of chill at the center of its warmth, and realized that he was thousands of miles farther north than he had ever been before. The sky here made the sky over Mill Walk seem to have been washed a thousand times. Sarah opened the door to the terminal with her hip, and he went in before her.

Mr. and Mrs. Spence stood at the opposite end of the terminal, talking with a stocky young man in his early twenties with a chauffeur's hat jammed low on his forehead and a dark blue sweatshirt that bulged over his belly. All three scowled at Tom and Sarah.

"Come on, kids," said Mr. Spence. "Let's get this show on the road."

"Give him my *bag*, Sarah," Mrs. Spence said.

The young man came forward and held out a thick hand for the strap of Mrs. Spence's suitcase. Mr. Spence coughed into his fist, and the young man picked up the big case with his other hand. He began moving toward the door.

A long black Lincoln sat at the curb. A policeman in a tight blue jacket and a Sam Browne belt jumped up from the fender. The chauffeur loaded the bags into the trunk and came around to open the back door. The Spences got into the back of the car, and Tom climbed into the passenger seat.

The Spences began talking to one another as the Lincoln rolled away from the curb. Tom leaned back and closed his eyes. Mrs. Spence was saying things she wanted the chauffeur to hear, and now and then some of the words blurred together. Tom opened his eyes, and caught the chauffeur glancing at him stonily.

They came out on a four-lane macadam highway. Thirty-foot pines crowded up to the gravel shoulder on both sides. Little tourist motels and fishing camps appeared at wide intervals, set deep down narrow gravel drives in the spreading trees as if far back in caves. Hand-painted signs shouted their names to the empty highway: MUSKIE LODGE and GILBERTSON'S HARMONY LAKE CAREFREE CABINS, LAKEVIEW RESORT, and BOB & SALLY RIDEOUT'S AAA FISHING CAMP & GUIDES. Little bars and bait shops sat back from the highway in sandy parking lots filled with old cars. LAKE DEEPDALE—DEEPDALE ESTATES, read a larger, professionally painted sign beside a glistening asphalt road on the right side of the highway. YOUR KEY TO THE NORTH COUNTRY! Dead raccoons lay flattened on the highway like overgrown cats.

"Jerry," said Mrs. Spence, who had fallen asleep for several minutes, "is Mr. Buddy at the compound yet?"

Tom turned his head to look at the scowling profile beside him. The chauffeur's right eye drifted toward him. He had small scars like tucks in his skin beneath the corner of his mouth.

"Yeah, Buddy's there. Got in two weeks ago with a bunch of friends."

"I thought you called him 'Mr. Buddy,' " said Sarah's mother, sounding a little put out by the chauffeur's tone.

"Some of the older help call him that," the man said. The shadowed eye drifted toward Tom again.

"Do you good to meet some of Buddy's friends, Sarah," her father told her. "You're liable to be seeing a lot of these people."

"Most of 'em left Friday," Jerry said. "Drove 'em to the airport myself. Had to spend about a hour cleaning out this car. One of those dopes drank about half a bottle of Southern Comfort in ten minutes, blew his guts apart right back where you're sitting."

"Oh!" said Mrs. Spence. "Where *who* is sitting?"

"I had to drive him back to the compound. Buddy threw him off the dock to clean him off."

"Oh, my." Tom heard the rustle of Mrs. Spence moving around to inspect the seat.

"You ever try to clean puke off cloth?" asked the driver. "The Cadillac's got fabric seats, I think that's why Ralph always sends the Lincoln for Buddy's pals."

"You must see a lot of Buddy," said Mr. Spence in a bright, hollow voice.

"Well, I do a lot of other stuff for Ralph most of the year. I hang out with Buddy when he's around." The eye shifted toward Tom again.

"Haven't we met?" Tom asked.

The eye seemed to widen and flare like the eye of a horse.

"I'm Tom Pasmore. I came to your house once."

"Never happened," Jerry said.

"Your friends Nappy and Robbie chased me around the corner and out into the traffic on Calle Burleigh, and I got hit by a car. They must have thought I was dead."

Shocked and outraged noises came from the back seat.

Jerry smiled at him, reminding Tom of the glassy eyes and needle teeth of the mounted fish in the Grand Forks airport. Was this how you stirred things up? Tom felt his face grow warm. It seemed to him that he was fading from view beneath the weight of Jerry's smile.

Jerry turned back to the road and drove into a tunnel of dark green. They had not passed or met another car since leaving the airport. A large white sign proclaimed the existence somewhere back in the woods of the WHITE BEAR NORTHERN INN & LODGINGS. A polar bear with a red napkin around its neck tipped a top hat.

"Oh, the White Bear!" said Mrs. Spence. "Is the food still so wonderful at the White Bear?"

"We generally eat in the compound," Jerry said.

"Lately, I've been wondering about what happened to the dog," Tom said.

The little scars beneath Jerry's mouth tightened as if the stitches had been pulled taut. His lips moved, and the eye drifted toward Tom.

“What?” Tom said.

“The dog died,” Jerry said in a barely audible voice.

“Oh, it can be a blessing when an old dog passes away,” said Mrs. Spence. “You hate to see them suffer.”

Eventually they passed a small brown sign with the words EAGLE LAKE—PRIVATE PROPERTY—NO TRESPASSING—NO SOLICITATIONS burned into the wood in ornate curving letters, and Jerry turned the car onto a bumpy narrow track between tall pines and oaks.

“Did I fall asleep?”

“Yes, Daddy,” Sarah said.

Boughs scraped the top of the car.

27

"Don't you love that it looks so secluded?" asked Mrs. Spence. The question was addressed to no one in particular, and no one answered it. "I love it, that it looks so secluded."

On either side of the car, the gaps between the pines and leafy oaks showed endless ranks of trees stretching upward and extending into endless, random, overgrown forest; sunlight slanted down to strike the trunks and make shimmering pools on the soft ground. Squirrels darted along branches and birds swooped beneath the canopy of green. The car went into shadow around a slight bend in the road, past a clearing with a long wooden bench strewn with dry grey leaves; then past a long row of mailboxes on a metal pipe. Tom glimpsed familiar names on the mailboxes: Thielman, R. Redwing, G. Redwing, D. Redwing, Spence, R. Deepdale, Jacobs, Langenheim, von Heilitz.

A crow cawed off in the woods, and leaves pattered down on the top of the car. Golden light flashed into the windshield, and the trees before them suddenly seemed spindly; then the trees parted and Tom saw a long expanse of deep blue beneath him, and a wake spreading out behind a motorboat just entering the path of the sun on the water. Tall solid buildings stood at wide intervals around the lake, each with a wide wooden dock protruding into the smooth glimmering water. On the broad terrace of a large multileveled structure with rows of high windows and several smaller terraces a waiter in a white coat carried a tray past a towel-sized pool toward a gentleman, a tiny pink pear supine on the bright yellow pad of a lounger. Next to that building, tall pilings like those around a stockade walled off the Redwing compound. A slim figure on a horse came into view from behind one of the lodges and passed out of sight behind a stand of fir trees.

"Buddy's out in his boat," Sarah said.

"And Neil Langenheim's getting pickled at the club," said her mother.

"Who's that with Buddy?" Sarah asked.

"His friend Kip," Jerry said. "Kip Carson. From Arizona. He's the one that stayed, when I took the other kids to Grand Forks."

"I wonder if Fritz is here," Tom said.

"Fritz Redwing?" Jerry shook his head. "He ain't here yet—him and his family come up in about two weeks. This is early. Lots of people ain't here yet. A bunch of the lodges are still empty. Even the compound's kinda empty."

The slim rider on the chestnut horse appeared between tall oaks on a trail extending past the rear of the lodges on the far side of the lake, then disappeared again behind a narrow lodge. Jerry steered the Lincoln slowly downhill toward the lake.

"Who is that on the horse?" Tom asked.

"Samantha Jacobs," said Mrs. Spence.

"Looked like Cissy Harbinger to me," said Mr. Spence.

"The Jacobses went to France. They won't be here at all this summer, the way I hear it. And Cissy Harbinger got married to some mechanic or something," Jerry said. "Her parents took her to Europe. They won't be here until maybe September."

"So who was that on the horse, since you know everything?" asked Mrs. Spence.

"Barbara Deane," Jerry said. "See, she'd come out now because almost nobody's around."

“Oh, Barbara Deane,” said Mrs. Spence, sounding a bit doubtful as to this name.

Tom had straightened up to look for her next appearance, but the straight slim figure on the chestnut horse did not show herself again.

Jerry drove the Lincoln down to the bottom of the track and came out into the open at a place where the road divided at the narrow, marshy north end of the lake. The car rolled to a stop facing the water. The Spences lowered their power windows, and the buzzing of the motorboat, executing a wide, sweeping turn down at the wide end of the kidney-shaped lake, came to them across half a mile of water like the racket of a motorcycle on a quiet night. “Where d'you want to go first?” Jerry asked.

“I want to get out of this car before we go another *inch*,” said Mrs. Spence. “I'm sure this seat is still *wet*.” She opened her door and climbed out and began twisting around to try to look at the seat of her miniskirt.

Tom got out on the loose mossy soil that led down to the marshy ground at the narrow end of the lake. The air smelled of pine needles and fresh water. For several yards, lathery green scum broken by reeds covered the lake's surface. He walked nearer the water, and the ground squelched beneath his feet. He could just see the tops of green-and-white striped umbrellas on the wide terrace of the clubhouse. The rest of the buildings stood around the long lake, their weathered grey wooden façades almost invisible behind the thick trees that surrounded them. A redwood lodge with clean modern lines at the far end of the lake perched on a treeless lawn like a green scoop out of the forest.

“So that's the club,” Tom said, pointing across twenty yards of reedy water to the structure with all the windows. “And that's the Redwing compound.” Over the tops of the tall stakes that enclosed the compound, the upper stories of several large wooden buildings could be seen.

“Next is our place,” Sarah said.

Smaller than the others, Anton Goetz's old lodge was dwarfed by the large oaks and firs that surrounded it. A weathered veranda faced the lake on its second floor. “Then comes Glen Upshaw's, where you'll be,” said Mrs. Spence. His grandfather's lodge was nearly twice the size of the Spences', and seemed to loom—like his grandfather—out of the surrounding trees while being concealed by them. Two bay windows and a massive dock protruded from the lake side of the lodge. Otherwise, only its grey roof was visible through the trees.

"Next is that abortion of Roddy Deepdale's," said Mrs. Spence. This was the redwood-and-glass building on the treeless expanse of lake front beside his grandfather's property. It looked even more aggressively contemporary from water level than from the hillside. "I don't know why he was allowed to put that up. He can do what he likes in Deepdale Estates, but here . . . well, you can certainly tell he was never a part of old Eagle Lake. Or old Mill Walk, either."

"Neither were we, Mother," Sarah said.

"On the other side of that eyesore, coming back this way on the south side of the lake, are the Thielmans, the Langenheims, the Harbingers, and the Jacobses." Ranging in size between the massiveness of his grandfather's lodge and the relative petiteness of Sarah's but of the same weathered wood, with proportionate docks and balconies on the lake, all but the Langenheim lodge were shuttered and empty.

On that side of the lake, just before the north end began to narrow and turn marshy, sited roughly opposite the wooded space between the clubhouse and the Redwing compound, stood a tall narrow building with a long front porch facing the hillside and a short, businesslike dock and stubby veranda barely wide enough for a couple of chairs and a round table. All of it seemed in need of fresh paint. This building, too, had been shuttered.

Tom asked about this lodge. "Oh, our other eyesore," said Mrs. Spence. "Really, I'd rather see that one torn down than Roddy's monstrosity."

"Who owns it?" Sarah said. "I've never seen anyone there."

Mr. Spence said, "I tried to buy that place, but the owner wouldn't even return my calls. Guy named—"

"Von Heilitz," Tom said, suddenly realizing. "Lamont von Heilitz. He lives across the street from us."

"Oh, look, Buddy sees us." Mrs. Spence jumped up and down and waved. The motorboat was noisily tearing up the length of the lake and, standing up behind the wheel, squat, black-haired Buddy Redwing made violent, meaningless gestures with his arms. He sounded a klaxon, and birds fled the trees. He gave a Nazi salute, sounded the klaxon again, then cut the wheel sharply and heeled the boat over, nearly shipping water, and pointed at the walls of the compound. His companion, whose shoulder-length blond hair streamed out behind him, did not move or respond to Buddy's antics in any way.

"Why, that's a girl in that boat with Buddy." Mrs. Spence put her hands on her hips, having undergone another sudden mood swing.

"Nah, that's Kip," Jerry said. "Good old Kip Carson, Buddy's buddy."

Buddy drew the speedboat up to the central Redwing dock, and Mrs. Spence avidly watched him jump out of the boat and lash a rope around a post. Buddy's soft belly hung out over his baggy black bathing trunks. His legs were short, thick, and bowed. Buddy leaned out over the rocking boat, extended a thick arm, and pulled his friend up on the dock. Kip Carson was naked and sunburned a bright red on his narrow shoulders. He tossed back his hair and reeled up the dock toward a stockade door. Buddy made drinking motions with his right hand, then trotted after his friend.

"Kip is a hippie, I guess they call it," Jerry said.

Mrs. Spence announced that Buddy had invited Sarah for a drink at the compound, so they would drop her off first. Jerry could leave the rest of them at the Spences' lodge, and Tom could carry his bags to his grandfather's place. She got back in the car, and pulled the short skirt firmly down as far as it would go. "I'm sure it doesn't matter what high-spirited boys do when they're alone together," Mrs. Spence said. " Buddy and his friend are practically stranded up here. That young man must be the only company the Redwings have in that big compound."

"Nah, there's an old lady," Jerry said. "But Buddy and Kip pretty much run by themselves. They shot a hole in the bar mirror at the White Bear two nights ago." He drove onto the road circling around the west side of the lake, and soon they were passing the empty parking lot of the clubhouse.

"I wonder who their other guest could be. We must know her."

"Ralph and Mrs. Redwing call her Aunt Kate," Jerry said. "She's a Redwing, but she lives in Atlanta."

“Oh, of course,” said Mrs. Spence. “We know her, dear.”

“I don’t,” said Mr. Spence.

The Lincoln drew up beside the front gates of the Redwing compound, and Mr. Spence labored out of the car to let Sarah out. “Come back to our place when you and Buddy have said your hellos,” Sarah’s mother called. “We’ll all have dinner with Ralph and Katinka tonight, I’m sure.”

“Tom, too,” Sarah said.

“Tom has things to do. We won’t impose invitations on him.”

Jerry pulled away as Sarah waved, and the car wound through the trees to the Spences’ lodge.

“Of course we know Aunt Kate,” Mrs. Spence said to her husband. “She’s the one who was married to Jonathan. They lived in Atlanta. She’s—she’d be—somewhere in her seventies now, and her maiden name—see, I even know *that*—her maiden name was—it was—”

“Duffield,” Tom said.

“See!” she cried. “Even he knows it was Duffield!”

Jerry dropped them in front of the porch of the Spence lodge and turned around on the seat to back down the narrow lake road to the compound. The Spences fumbled with bags and keys and moved up on their dusty porch with perfunctory good-byes to Tom, and he carried his two cases down through the trees to his grandfather’s lodge.

28

Four twenty-foot-long steps of big mortared fieldstones capped with a layer of concrete led up to Glendenning Upshaw's covered porch. Tom carried his heavy bags through wicker furniture and rapped on the screen door. To his right, he could see the point at which the trees abruptly stopped and gave way to Roddy Deepdale's shaved lawn. Light bounced off one of the windows in the long, angular Deepdale lodge.

The door opened to a vast dim space shot with cloudy streaks of light. "So you're here," said a tall young woman in black who stepped backwards immediately. "You're Glen's grandson? Tom Pasmore?"

Tom nodded. The woman shifted to look behind him, and the impression of her youthfulness vanished. There were grey streaks in her smooth hair and deep vertical lines in her cheeks. She was startlingly good-looking, despite her age. "I'm Barbara Deane," she said, and stood up straight to face him—for an instant, Tom felt that she was trying to see how he responded to her name. She wore a black silk blouse with a double strand of pearls and a close-fitting black skirt. These clothes neither called attention to nor disguised the natural curves of her body, which seemed to match some other, younger face. "Why don't you get your bags inside, and I'll show you your room. This is your first time here, isn't it?"

"Yes," Tom said, and carried his suitcases inside.

"We have two rooms on this level, this sitting room, and the study that leads out to the deck and the pier. The kitchen is back through the arch, and everything is in working order. Florrie Truehart came in to clean this morning, and it's all shipshape."

The walls and floor were of hardwood gone grey and dim with age. Antlers and mounted fish hung on the walls. Large colorless cushions softened the handmade furniture. A round walnut table and six round-back chairs took up a separate area near the kitchen. Big windows, streaky with dust, overlooking the lake admitted dim shafts of light. Two other windows looked out on the porch. Tom was sure that sheets had been taken off the furniture only that morning. "Well," said the woman beside him, "we did our best. The place will get to look a little livelier after you've been here a while."

"Mrs. Truehart is still the cleaning woman? I thought she'd be—"

"Miss Truehart. Florrie. Her brother is the mailman for this district." She began to move toward a wide wooden staircase covered with a dull red Indian carpet, and once again seemed like two people to Tom, a strong vital young woman and an autocratic older one.

"When does the mail come, by the way?" Tom had picked up his bags and followed her up the stairs.

She looked at him over her shoulder. "I think it's put in the boxes sometime around four o'clock. Why? Are you expecting something?"

"I thought I'd write some people while I was here."

She nodded as if she thought this point was worth remembering, and led him the rest of the way up the stairs. "The bedrooms are on this floor. I'm keeping some things in the front bedroom, so I've given you the larger of the other two. There's a bathroom right outside the door. Would you like help with those bags? I should have asked before."

Sweating, Tom set them both down and shook his head.

"Men," Barbara Deane said, and came near to him and lifted the larger of his two bags without any sign of effort.

His bedroom was at the back of the house and smelled like wax and lemon oil. The dark narrow planking of the walls and floor glistened. Barbara Deane lifted the big case onto the single bed covered with a faded Indian blanket, and Tom grimaced and put his beside it. He went to a windowed door in the exterior wall and looked out on a narrow wooden balcony nearly overgrown by a massive oak. "Your mother used this room," she said.

Forty years before, his mother had looked out this window and seen Anton Goetz running toward his lodge through the woods. Now he could not even see the ground.

He turned from the window. Barbara Deane was sitting on the bed beside his suitcases, looking at him. The black skirt came just to her knees, suggesting legs that would have looked better beneath a miniskirt than Mrs. Spence's. She pulled the edge of the skirt over the tops of her knees, and Tom blushed. "The lake's very quiet now. I prefer it like this, but it might be dull for you."

Tom sat on a spindly chair next to a small square table with an inlaid chessboard on its surface.

"Are you a friend of Buddy Redwing's?"

"I don't really know him. He's four or five years older than me."

"It's disconcerting—you look much older than you really are."

"Hard life," he said, but she did not answer his smile. "Do you live here all year-round?"

"I come to the lodge three or four days a week. The rest of the time I spend in a house I own in the town." She looked around the room as if she were inspecting it for dust. "What do you know about me?" She kept her eyes on the bare shining planks of the wall opposite the bed.

"Well, I know you were my midwife, or my mother's midwife, or however you say it."

She glanced sideways at him, and brushed an elegant strand of hair away from her eye.

"And I know you were one of the witnesses at my parents' wedding."

"And?"

"And I guess I knew that you took care of this place for my grandfather."

"And that's all?"

"Well, I know you ride," Tom said. "When we drove in this afternoon, we saw you riding between the lodges."

"I usually go riding early in the mornings," she said. "But there was a lot to be done in here, so I had to put it off. In fact, I just finished changing when you knocked on the door." She gave the ghostly sketch of a smile, and smoothed her skirt down over her thighs. "We will be here together at least part of every week, and I want you to know that my privacy is important to me. My room is out of bounds to you—"

"Of course," Tom said.

"I stay out of the way of people from Mill Walk, and I expect them to return the favor."

"Well, can we talk, at least?"

Her face softened for a moment. "Of course we can talk. We will talk. I didn't intend to be short with you, but . . ." She tossed her head, a gesture that looked feminine and petulant at once. She intended to tell him something she had thought to keep hidden. "My house was robbed last week. It upset me very much. I'm the kind of person—well, I don't even like most people to know where I *live*. And when I came back to the town from here and found my house ransacked . . ."

"I see," Tom said. It explained a great deal, he thought: but it did not explain why she was the kind of person who wanted to keep even her address a secret. "Did they find who did it?"

Barbara Deane shook her head. "Tim Truehart, the chief of police in Eagle Lake, thinks it was a gang from out of town—maybe as far away as Superior. There've been a number of burglaries around here in the past few summers. They hit the summer people's lodges, usually, and grab their stereo systems and TV sets. But you never think it's going to be you. Most people in Eagle Lake don't even lock their doors. I'll tell you the worst part."

She looked at him directly now, and twisted on the bed to

face him. "They killed my dog. I suppose I got him partly as a watchdog, but I didn't think of him that way anymore. He was just a big sweet animal—a Chow. They cut his throat and left his body in the kitchen like a—like a *calling card.*" She was struggling to control herself. "Anyhow, after that I moved some of my things over here, where they seemed safer. I'm still—jumpy. And angry. It's so *personal.*"

"I'm sorry," he said.

And that broke the spell. Barbara Deane jumped up from his bed and frowned. "I didn't mean to bore you with all of that. Don't mention this at the compound, will you? Eagle Lake people detest any kind of unpleasantness. I'm sure you'd like to get out and acquaint yourself with this place. They'll start serving dinner at the club at seven, unless you want me to cook something for you."

"I'll try the club," Tom said. "But could we talk later?"

"If you like," she said, and left him alone in the bedroom.

Tom listened to her footsteps moving down the hall. Her bedroom door clicked shut. He went to the bed and unzipped his suitcases, took out his books and clothes, and hung the clothes in a closet that looked like a coffin with a lightbulb. He pushed the bags under the narrow bed. When he stood up he looked around at the bare little room with its narrow planking. Without Barbara Deane in it, the whole room reminded him of a coffin. He picked up a book and went out into the hallway.

On the other side of the staircase, Barbara Deane's door remained closed. *What do you know about me?* He pictured her sitting in a chair, looking out at the lake.

A speedboat barked.

Tom went downstairs, imagining that Barbara Deane listened to every footfall and creak of the stairs. He walked through the big room, passed under the arch, and went into the kitchen. This was like Lamont von Heilitz's kitchen, with open shelves, broad counters, and a long black stove. The walls were of the same narrow board as his mother's old bedroom, once a pale brown and now a dim grey flaking with old varnish. Grey dust and ancient dirt had packed the gaps between the wide floorboards. The only modern appliance was a small white Kenmore refrigerator. A wrapped loaf of brown bread sat on the counter beside the refrigerator. Tom turned on the taps over the square brass sink and washed his hands and face with an old yellow bar of coal tar soap. He dried himself on a threadbare dishtowel. Barbara Deane had stocked the refrigerator with milk, eggs, cheese, bacon, bread, ground beef, and sandwich meat. He blew into a dusty glass and filled it with milk. Then he carried the glass through the other room and opened a handmade wooden door and let himself into the study.

Dim bookshelves filled with unjacketed books faced a long desk with a black Bakelite telephone and a green felt pad with a leather border and an empty penholder. An oval pink and green hooked rug lay on the floor, and a hooked rug in two shades of brown lay folded on a tan sofa with unfinished arms and metal-wrapped joints. An old standard lamp stood at the far end of the sofa, and another stood beside the desk. The room was almost hot. It evoked his grandfather more than any other part of the lodge: Tom understood instinctively that this little room overlooking the lake had been his grandfather's favorite part of the house. Streaky sunlight from two big windows partitioned into panes fell halfway into the room. The barking growl of the speedboat grew louder. Tom drank some of the milk and sat down behind the desk. He pulled open the drawers and found a few old paperclips, a stack of thick paper headed *Glendenning Upshaw, Eagle Lake, Wisconsin*, and a slim telephone book for the towns of Eagle Lake and Grand Forks. Tom turned to the pages for Eagle Lake and found the names beginning with D. Barbara Deane's telephone number was unlisted. He finished the milk, put the glass on top of the telephone book, and went outside.

Buddy Redwing was turning the boat in tight, repetitive figure eights in front of the compound and the clubhouse, at the top of the 8 ripping through the reeds. Two blond heads the size of ping-pong balls tilted from side to side as the boat heeled over. Kip Carson's hair was longer than Sarah's. Tom sat down at a scarred redwood picnic table on the broad deck and watched them go around and around. When the boat heeled over at the bottom of the 8, the two blond people threw up their hands like passengers on a roller coaster, and Buddy cawed. Sarah waved at him, and he waved back. Buddy bawled out something hoarse and unintelligible. Tom stood up, and Buddy wheeled the boat back up toward the reeds. Sarah raised her arms to him again.

Buddy cut the boat deeper into the marshy water, and the motor growled and whined and abruptly cut out, leaving a great silence spreading over the lake. A bird cried out, and another answered it. Buddy moved heavily to the back end of the boat and began yanking on the cord. Sarah pointed toward the clubhouse.

Tom stood up and walked out on the massive dock. A hundred feet away on their own dock, Mr. and Mrs. Spence took the air in new resort clothes. Mr. Spence's back was to Tom, and his hands rested on his fat hips. He was shaking his head over Buddy's mishandling of the boat. Mrs. Spence leaned self-consciously against a mooring, saw Tom, and turned away.

In the middle of the lake a fish broke the water and flashed blue-grey above the darker blue water before splashing back down. Ripples spread and melted back into the glassy surface.

To Tom's right, the Deepdale dock left the treeless shore and protruded into the water. Beyond it lay the Thielman dock. Tom walked out to the end of his own dock to be able to see the Thielman lodge, and found himself looking at a shoreline thickly covered with trees through which only a grey door, a shuttered window, and a scattered backdrop of grey wall was visible. The motor coughed twice, and fell silent. Tom turned to look past the Spences, and saw Kip Carson pushing on the front of the boat in waist-high water. His chest and arms were pale and skinny, and he looked weary. Buddy shouted "Jerry! Jerry!" again and again in the flat, demanding tone of a spoiled child. Finally Jerry Hasek appeared through the door in the compound fence. He had changed from his jeans and sweatshirt into a shiny grey suit. He looked at the boat and then disappeared back through the door into the compound.

Tom went back inside and took a handful of the stationery from the drawer. He crossed out his grandfather's name and printed his own beneath it. He thought for a moment, then began writing to Lamont von Heilitz. When he had covered a page, he heard Barbara Deane coming quickly down the stairs. Her footsteps crossed the larger sitting room. The door closed. Tom began on a second page. He heard a car starting up in the woods behind the house. About the time the car reached the wide stony path in front of the lodge, the motorboat started up again. Tom finished his long letter and looked at his watch. It was two-thirty. He folded the letter into thirds, and made another search of the desk drawers until he found a stack of envelopes. He scratched out his grandfather's name on the first one, wrote *Tom* above it and printed Lamont von Heilitz's address, and sealed the letter into the envelope. Then he left the lodge and began walking down the path.

Two cars were parked beside the gate into the compound, and five or six older, smaller cars had been pulled into spaces on the far side of the dusty parking lot in front of the clubhouse. "Who's that? Ahoy there!" called a voice from overhead, and Tom looked up to see Neil Langenheim leaning over a veranda railing and beaming down at him from beneath a green-and-white-striped canvas awning. His red forehead had begun to peel, and his jowls and double chin lapped over the collar of an unbuttoned peach-colored shirt. Neil Langenheim, the Pasmores' next-door neighbor, was a lawyer for the Redwings, and before this Tom had never seen him wearing anything but dark suits.

"It's Tom Pasmore, Mr. Langenheim."

"Tom *Pasmore?* Well! You staying at your grandfather's lodge?"

Tom said yes.

"Well, where are you going, boy? Come up here, and I'll buy you a beer. Hell, I'll buy you whatever you like."

"I'm going into Eagle Lake to mail a letter," Tom said. "I want to see the town too."

"Oh, nobody goes *there*," Mr. Langenheim protested. "Talk sense. And you can't write letters up here—nothing ever happens! And even if it did, all the people you'd write to are up here with you!"

Tom waved to him and set off again, and Mr. Langenheim shouted, "See you at dinner!"

29

Main Street was lined with gift shops, lunch counters, drugstores, liquor stores, cafés with names like The Red Tomahawk and The Wampum Belt, a shop that sold flyrods and hand-tied flies, a bijou little shop that sold Swiss watches and gold jewelry, an ice cream and candy store, shops that sold post cards and calendars with pictures of kittens in pine trees, a photographer's studio, an art gallery with paintings of ducks in formation and Indians around campfires, and two gun shops. Three small interconnected stores sold T-shirts with tourist slogans, wooden *I Pine Fir Yew* ashtrays, and kachina dolls. Cars parked on the bias. Jeeps and station wagons crowded with children rolled up and down the street, and families in short pants, fingernail polish, Indian headdresses, and Greek shepherd shirts carried plastic shopping bags printed with images of pine trees and leaping fish down plank sidewalks with hitching posts.

The two-story fieldstone building that housed the *Eagle Lake Gazette* stood between a wooden post office and the bow-fronted library at the top end of Main Street, where the tourists generally turned back to see if they had missed anything. A little fortresslike police station clung like a granite limpet to the side of the Victorian town hall across the street, and at the end of town hall was a large white sign reading EAGLE LAKE THANKS YOU FOR VISITING, and a smaller one that said MOOSE LAKE 6 MILES, LOST LOON LAKE 12 MILES, NORTH POLE 2,546 MILES. VISIT THE AUTHENTIC INDIAN SETTLEMENT.

Tom entered the newspaper office and went up to a wooden counter. A man with a bow tie and thinning brown hair fiddled with a pen and a stack of galleys at an overflowing desk; behind him, a tall skinny man in a plaid shirt and an eyeshade played a linotype machine like a pipe organ. The man in the bow tie crossed out a sentence on a length of galley, looked up and saw Tom. He pushed himself away from the desk and came up to the counter.

"Do you want to place an ad? You can write it out on one of these forms, if I can find them under here somewhere. . . ."

He bent to look under the counter, and Tom said, "I was hoping I could look through some old copies of your paper."

"How old? Last week's are on the rack beside the davenport there, but anything older gets put into binders and shelved in the morgue upstairs. You just want to see the paper, or are you looking for something in particular?" He looked back at his desk and the stack of galleys. "The morgue isn't really one of our tourist attractions."

"I wanted to see recent copies that would have stories about the local burglaries, especially the one at Barbara Deane's house, but as many of them as I could read about, and I also wanted to look at papers from the summer of 1925 that would deal with the Jeanine Thielman murder."

"What are you?" The man reared back from the counter, whipped a pair of round tortoiseshell glasses from his pocket, and peered up at Tom.

If I say I'm an amateur of crime, this guy is going to throw me out of here, Tom thought. *And he'd be right.*

"I'm a junior at Tulane," he said. "In sociology. I have to do a thesis next year, and since I'm spending the summer at Eagle Lake, I thought I'd do some of my research here."

"Crime in a resort area, that kind of thing?"

Tom said that was the general idea.

"Past and present, something like that?"

"Get any closer, you'll be writing it for me."

"All right," the man said. "In a couple of weeks, I'd have to say no, but things are still relatively calm around here. As crazy as things look out on the street now, by the middle of summer there are twice as many people around here. I'm Chet Hamilton, by the way. The proprietor and editor of this hole-in-the-wall operation."

The man at the linotype machine snickered.

Tom said his name, and they shook hands.

"I guess I can take you up there now and get you started, but I can't stick around and hold your hand. You'll have to put everything back and turn off the lights when you're done. Just tell me when you're through for the day."

"Great. Thanks."

Hamilton pushed up a hinged flap and came through to Tom's side of the counter. "I did a series on those burglaries, you might be able to use some of my stuff." He opened the front door and led Tom outside.

A man with knobby knees and a woman with frizzy hair and fat thighs were peering in the *Gazette*'s windows. "Hey, is this real or is it an exhibit?" the man asked Hamilton.

"I'm not too sure myself," the editor said.

"See?" the woman said. "I told you. But would you listen to me? No, every word I say is stupid."

Hamilton led Tom around the side of the building and pulled a crowded key ring from his pocket. "Consider this," he said, searching through the keys. "Back home, those two people are sensible, responsible individuals. They pay taxes and they hold down jobs. They come five hundred miles north to a resort, and suddenly they turn into drooling babies who can't see what's in front of their noses." He found the right key, and slotted it into the door. "Crime is different in a resort area, and that's the reason why. People change when they get away from home." He opened the door to a worn flight of stairs. "I'll go up and switch on the lights."

Tom followed him up the stairs.

"People who've never stolen anything in their lives turn into kleptomaniacs."

At the top of the stairs, he flicked a switch. Bound volumes of the *Gazette* stood in rows on metal shelves. At the far end of the room were a wooden desk and an office chair. "I suppose you're from Mill Walk?"

"Yes," Tom said.

"You'd have to be, you're up at Eagle Lake and that's been a hundred percent Mill Walk since before I was born. David Redwing bought all that land and parceled it out among his friends, and it stayed that way ever since." He took two volumes from a shelf and put them on the desk. "Besides that, you mentioned Jeanine Thielman. You'd have to be from Mill Walk to know that name. She was the first summer person to be killed up here, at least the first one that was ever proved." Hamilton strode back into the rows of metal shelves and put his hand on the two most recent volumes. "I think you'll find nearly everything on those break-ins in here." He slid them off the shelves and came back to the desk.

"It sounds like you think there was another murder of a summer resident before Mrs. Thielman," Tom said.

Hamilton grinned, and set down the new volumes on top of the old ones. "Well, my father certainly did. He was the editor of the *Gazette* in those days. A woman drowned in Eagle Lake the year before the Thielman murder. The coroner called it accidental death, and most people thought it was really suicide. My father was pretty sure that the coroner had been bought and paid for—see, in those days, we didn't have a real full-time coroner in Eagle Lake, we had three undertakers and they took the job in rotation, month by month."

Tom felt a chill in the hot, airless upstairs room. "Do you remember this woman's name?"

"I think it was Magda something."

Tom realized that he had never heard his grandmother's first name until this moment—so successfully had his grandfather erased her memory. "Magda Upshaw?"

"You got it." Hamilton leaned on the stack of bound newspapers and frowned down at Tom. "Are you sure you're as old as you say you are? You don't look like a junior in college to me."

"Magda Upshaw was my grandmother." He swallowed, and his Adam's apple felt as big as a baseball.

"Huh!" The editor straightened up. His hands flew to his

bow tie and tugged at its ends. "Well, I guess I'm *sorry*—I didn't mean—" He moved a step back from the table.

"Why did your father think she was murdered?"

"You can read about it, if you like. He had to be careful about the way he said things, but if you read between the lines you'll catch his drift." Hamilton dodged into the stacks again and came back with another old volume. "The Chief of Police in those days wasn't much—it was Prohibition, remember, and a lot of booze went through Eagle Lake. Some people made a lot of money out of it." He slid the bound volume on top of the others. "It could be the Chief didn't pay much attention to ordinary law enforcement, especially when it came to rich summer people who did a lot to keep the bootleggers in business."

"We have police like that in Mill Walk," Tom said.

"So I hear. You might notice that people here take a certain attitude toward folks from your island. Truth is, they don't even spend any money in Eagle Lake."

He slapped his hand on the stack of bound newspapers. "You'll probably be coming back tomorrow, so you can just leave these on the desk. But remember about the lights and the door, will you?"

Tom nodded.

Chet Hamilton removed his glasses and slid them back into his shirt pocket. He gave Tom a sober, questioning look: he was a decent man, and he was embarrassed and interested in about equal measure. "Even if I hadn't opened my big fat mouth, don't you think you would have realized that by going back a year from the Thielman case you could find out what we printed about your grandmother's death? It must have had a tremendous impact on your family."

"I think I had a lot of reasons for coming to Eagle Lake," Tom said.

"Well, maybe some of them are in this room." Hamilton thrust his hands into his pockets and shifted from side to side. "I'm kind of sorry I brought the whole thing up!" He backed toward the stairs. "I led you a long way from those break-ins you were interested in."

"Maybe not so far after all," Tom said.

"Seeing you up here reminds me of a kind of detective my father had to dinner a couple times, way back when. He was from Mill Walk too. People used to call him the Shadow—ever hear of him?"

"Did the Shadow read the files about my grandmother?" Tom asked.

"No—he was still interested in the Thielman case. I guess it meant a lot to him. It made him a hero around here, I can tell you that." Hamilton gave a half-hearted little wave, and went down the stairs. Tom heard the door close.

The linotype machine rattled beneath him. Traffic sounds came dimly through the windows at the front of the room. Tom opened the topmost volume, propped it on his lap, and began turning the pages.

S.L.H., Samuel Larabee Hamilton, the founder of the *Eagle Lake Gazette*, had seen his newspaper as an expression of his aggressively opinionated personality, and during the three hours he spent in the upstairs morgue, Tom learned as much about him as he did about Eagle Lake. Samuel Larabee Hamilton had considered Prohibition and income tax prime examples of governmental meddling. He had detested anti-vivisectionists, advocates of racial equality, female liberationists, Franklin Delano Roosevelt, social security, gun control, the University of Wisconsin, free trade laws, and Robert LaFollette. He loathed criminals and corrupt law-enforcement officials, and had not hesitated to give names.

Twice in the 1920s, some person or persons had fired bullets through the windows of the *Gazette* office, hoping to kill, wound, or scare off its editor. He had responded with 18-point headlines trumpeting THE COWARDS MISSED! and THEY MISSED AGAIN!

From the first, S.L.H. had opposed the Redwing interest in Eagle Lake as a "foreign invasion." Mill Walk was a "Caribbean police state" that depended on "every indecent practice known to those who rule by fear." One editorial was entitled THUGS IN OUR BACKYARD.

When a thirty-six-year-old woman was found dead in Eagle Lake with the pockets of her nightdress filled with rocks and was declared a victim of accidental death and cremated within two days, Hamilton had cried foul at the top of his lungs.

The first picture of his grandmother that Tom had ever seen showed a child's uncertain square face, hesitant eyes, and what looked like straw-gold hair tied back in a bun. Magda Upshaw was leaning against a railing at the Eagle Lake clubhouse, holding a fat little girl with sausage curls as if she were trying to shield her from something nobody else could see.

The *Gazette* told him that his grandmother was the daughter of Hungarian refugees who owned a small restaurant in Miami Beach. She had left school in the tenth grade, and had worked in her parents' restaurant until her marriage to a man eight years her junior.

Glendenning Upshaw had married an uneducated foreign woman much older than himself, pushed her into class-conscious, snobbish, Anglophile Mill Walk, and almost immediately began being unfaithful to her.

The whiff of a conviction came to Tom from the old newspapers: that his grandfather had been just as comfortable after his wife's death as before it. He had everything the way he wanted it: his business—his quasi-secret partnership with Maxwell Redwing, his first building contracts—his daughter, his privacy, the house on Eastern Shore Road.

Samuel Larabee Hamilton had turned up at Eagle Lake shortly after the discovery of Magda's body. The body had been pulled up with a drag after five days in the water, and the metal hooks of the drag, the rocks on the bottom of the lake, and the fish had all left their marks. The editor had thought that not all the wounds visible on the body had been due to these causes. What outraged him was that the body had been cremated after a perfunctory autopsy, and what looked at the least like a suicide had been whitewashed as an accidental death. Island justice; thugs in the backyard.

A week after Magda Upshaw's ashes had been returned to her parents, the management of the Eagle Lake clubhouse had replaced every waiter, busboy, cook, and bartender in the building with men from Chicago. No clubhouse employee would telephone the fractious local editor if another member should die under circumstances that might be misunderstood.

Not long after, Hamilton learned that gangsters were buying cabins and hunting lodges in the county, and he was off on another crusade.

In the next volume, Tom reread the accounts of Jeanine Thielman's death he had already seen at Lamont von Heilitz's house. MILLIONAIRE SUMMER RESIDENT DISAPPEARS FROM HOME. JEANINE THIELMAN FOUND IN LAKE. LOCAL MAN CHARGED WITH THIELMAN MURDER. MYSTERY RESOLVED IN TRAGEDY. Pictures of Mrs. Thielman, Minor Truehart, Lamont von Heilitz, Anton Goetz. What Tom had not understood, reading over his neighbor's shoulder, was how rapturously S.L.H. had greeted the appearance of Lamont von Heilitz. The Shadow was not only a celebrity, he was a hero. His investigation had saved an innocent local man, and rescued the reputation of the town of Eagle Lake in a way that might have been calculated to sell the maximum number of newspapers. He was the top: he was the Louvre Museum, the Coliseum, he was Mickey Mouse. He was just what S.L.H. had been waiting for.

Hamilton had sponsored a Lamont von Heilitz day; he had published the Shadow's opinions on great unsolved mysteries of the past; he had run a column that invited people to ask the famous detective whatever they most wanted to know about him; and the reclusive detective had submitted to both the lionization and the assault on his privacy. He had shaken hundreds of hands, had volunteered his favorite color (cobalt blue), music (a dead heat between Louis Armstrong's Hot Five and Haydn's *The Creation*), tailor (Huntsman's of Savile Row), novel (*The Golden Bowl*), and city (New York). He felt that good detectives were not born, like good artists, nor made, like good soldiers, but were produced by a combination of the two.

Tom searched the more recent volumes for articles about burglaries and break-ins around Eagle Lake. He learned which houses had been burgled and what had been stolen—a Harmon Karden amplifier and a Technics turntable here, a jade ring and Kerman rug there, television sets, musical instruments, paintings, antique furniture, prescription drugs, clothes, cash, anything that might have a resale value. The break-ins began three years before, in July, and took place between June and September; two dogs besides Barbara Deane's had been killed, both of them family pets. The burglars had begun with the houses of summer residents, but last year had struck several homes in Eagle Lake that belonged to full-time residents. Chet Hamilton's series elaborately restated the ideas he had described to Tom, and implied that wealthy college-age children of summer residents were committing the crimes.

Because he thought that Lamont von Heilitz would have done it, Tom scanned most of the articles and columns in the recent volumes, reading about property transfers, meetings of the town council, arrests for drunken driving and poaching and assault, new appointments to the Chamber of Commerce and the Epworth League, the 4-H Club trip to Madison, traffic accidents, hit and run accidents, bar brawls and knifings and gunshot wounds, applications for liquor licenses, and a squash of record size grown in the garden of Mr. and Mrs. Leonard Vale. He made a few notes on a sheet of his grandfather's old stationery he had folded into his shirt pocket, left the bound volumes on the desk, turned off the light, and went downstairs, thinking about Magda Upshaw, Barbara Deane's Chow dog, and the premises of an out-of-business machine shop on Summers Street that had been leased to the Redwing Holding Company.

On the other side of a thick hedge from the *Gazette* office, the post office looked like a frontier military post in an old John Ford Western. Tom stood on the sidewalk before it, wondering whether he should just put his letter to von Heilitz in the letterbox in front of the post office, or save it to give to the mailman the following day. It was a few minutes past five o'clock, and half of the tourists on Main Street had gone back to their resorts and fishing camps for the American Plan dinner. A powder blue Cadillac with pointed fins swung across the oncoming lanes to make a U-turn too narrow for its wheelbase. Stalled cars behind it honked, and drivers in the opposite lanes slammed on their brakes and skidded to stops. A man in a pink shirt and red shorts opened the door of the Cadillac and fell out into the street. He picked himself up, waved to the shouting people in the other cars, got uncertainly back behind the wheel and slowly backed up without closing his door. A blue mail van squirted around the front of the Cadillac, wove through the waiting cars, and rolled to a stop in front of the post office. A slim black-haired man in a blue postal service shirt and black jeans jumped out of the van and went around to the back to remove a half-filled mailbag.

Tom took a step nearer, and the mailman glanced at him. "A drunk in a Caddy. I hate to say it, but that's this town in the summer." He shook his head, shouldered the bag, and began going up the path to the post office.

"Excuse me," Tom said, "but do you know a man named Joe Truehart?"

The mailman stopped moving and stared at Tom. He looked neither friendly nor unfriendly. He did not even look expectant. After a beat, he lowered the bag from his shoulder. "Yeah, I know Joe Truehart. Pretty damn well. Who wants to know?"

"My name is Tom Pasmore. I just got here from Mill Walk, and a man named Lamont von Heilitz asked me to say hello to him."

The mailman grinned. "All right. Why didn't you say that in the first place? You found your man, Tom Pasmore. You tell him I said hello back." He stuck out a firm brown hand, and Tom shook it.

"Mr. von Heilitz asked me to write to him, and said that I should give my letters to you personally. He didn't want anybody to see me doing it, but I don't think anybody's looking at us."

Truehart looked over his shoulder, and grinned another brilliant grin. "They're all still gaping at the accident that didn't happen. Mr. von Heilitz told me to look out for you. You got a letter already?"

Tom handed it to him, and Truehart folded the letter into his back pocket. "I thought you'd show up near the mailboxes. I generally get out to Eagle Lake a little past four."

Tom explained that he had come into town before that, and said he would wait near the mailboxes whenever he had letters in the future.

"Don't wait out in the open," the mailman said. "Stick yourself back in the woods until you hear my van. If we're going to do this, let's do it right."

They shook hands again, and Tom began to walk down Main Street toward the crowd of people watching the traffic disentangle itself.

30

Inside the post office, Joe Truehart shouted hello to the postmaster, who was sorting mail at a long table out of sight behind the wall of boxes. He removed Tom's letter from his hip pocket and reached up to slide it on top of the parcel shelves, where the postmaster, a peppery grey-haired woman named Corky Malleson who was four-foot eleven and a half, would be unable to see it. Then he carried his bag back to the table and began transferring its contents into other bags for the five-thirty pickup. He helped Corky sort the third-class mail and put it into the boxes, and said good-bye to her when she went home to fix dinner for her husband.

Just before the truck arrived from the central district post office, he heard a knock at the side door marked EMPLOYEES ONLY which admitted himself and Corky into the back of the building. He jumped up from Corky's desk, where he had been adding up figures and filling out forms, and opened the door.

He exchanged a few words with the man on the threshold. Joe Truehart reached up for the letter on top of the parcel shelves and passed it to the man. He locked the door when the man left. Then he sat down again to wait for the arrival of the mail truck.

31

Grinding noises and the screech of metal against metal came up the street. Two blocks down from the post office, the back half of the powder blue Cadillac jutted out into the traffic. People in bright vacation clothes covered the plank sidewalks on both sides of the street, looking as if they were watching a parade.

Tom walked down the planks and saw that the Cadillac had ploughed into the back ends of several cars, crumpling in the first one so badly that it looked as if it had been hit by a truck. The driver had tried to get out of trouble by bulling through the obstructions, and when that had failed, had backed athwart the traffic halfway across the street, and killed his engine. Tom got to the edge of the growing crowd, and began working his way through. The man in the pink shirt got out of the Cadillac and looked around like a trapped bear. People began shouting. A policeman in a tight blue uniform ran down the middle of the street, yelling, "Break it up! Break it up!" He looked like a hero in a movie, with short blond hair and a square perfect jaw. A scrawny old party in a Hawaiian shirt popped out of the crowd around the wrecked cars and began yelling first at the drunk in the pink shirt, then at the policeman. The policeman strode toward him, put his hands on his hips, and spoke. The old man stopped yelling. The drunk drooped over the side of his car. "It's all over," the cop said in a loud voice that was not a shout. "Go back home."

The drunk in the pink shirt straightened up and tried to explain something to the cop. He pointed his finger at the cop's wide chest. The cop batted his hand away. He stepped to the side and pushed the drunk into the side of his car and grabbed his wrists and handcuffed him. He opened the Cadillac's rear door. Then he pulled the man backwards, put his right hand on the top of his head, and propelled him into the back of his car.

A few cheers and one or two scattered boos came from the sidewalks. The policeman straightened his hat, tugged on his Sam Browne belt, and swaggered around the car to get in behind the wheel. Gears ground, and the Cadillac drifted backwards. The cop spun the wheel and pulled forward. The battered Cadillac moved down the street at the head of a row of cars and turned left.

The crowd had turned cheerful and gossipy. It had no intention of leaving the scene. Tom stepped around a family of four that were chewing on sandwiches and staring at the cars beginning to pick up speed, and threaded his way between two couples who were arguing about whether to go into the Red Tomahawk for a beer or to buy a new shirt for someone named Teddy. He stepped into an empty space at the edge of the sidewalk and considered moving across the street, where the crowd looked thinner.

Someone whispered, "Watch it, kid," and before he could look around someone kicked him hard in his left ankle and someone else banged him in the back and shoved him into the traffic.

His arms flew out before him, and he staggered a few steps before his ankle began to melt. Screams and shouts came from the sidewalk. Horns blew. His heart stopped beating. A man and a woman with wide eyes and open mouths appeared behind the smeared windshield of a station wagon piled with suitcases lashed to its roof with bright green netting. Tom took in the expressions on their faces and the color of the netting with great clarity, and then saw only the massive hood and the bug-spattered grille of the station wagon. His ankle bent like a green twig. He struck the ground, and the air turned black and cacophonous.

A roaring noise filled his ears, and then a dim music replaced it, and the memory of a piercing harmony encased him, and his ten-year-old self bent toward him and said: *Music does explain everything*. Then dust and gravel sprang up in front of his eyes, and each speck of gravel threw a speck-sized shadow.

A high-pitched voice, the voice of a cartoon goose, called, "That boy's drunk!"

He pushed himself up. His ankle sang. In front of him, a startled man in a baseball cap stared out through the windshield of a Karmann Ghia. Tom looked over his shoulder and saw the rear end of a station wagon piled high with bags and cardboard boxes. Then a man with a crew cut and trembling arms was helping him stand. "That car just went right over you," he said. "You're one goddamned lucky son of a gun." The man's arms were trembling.

"Somebody pushed me," Tom said.

He heard the crowd repeating his words like an echo with different voices.

The man and woman got shakily out of the station wagon. Each of them took a step forward. The woman asked if he were all right.

"Somebody pushed me," Tom said.

The couple took another step forward, and Tom said, "I'm all right." They got back into the station wagon. The man in the crew cut helped Tom back to the sidewalk. The traffic began to whoosh past.

"Do you want to see a cop?" the man asked. "Do you want to sit down?"

"No, I'm okay," Tom said. "Did you see who pushed me?"

"All I saw was you, flyin' out into the street," said the man. He released Tom and stepped backwards. "If somebody pushed you, you oughta see a cop." He looked around as if trying to find one.

"Maybe it was an accident," Tom said, and the man nodded vigorously.

"You got dust all over your face," the man said.

Tom wiped his face and began brushing off his clothes, and

when he looked up again the man was gone. The other people on the sidewalk stared at him, but did not come near. His head felt as light as a balloon, his body as weightless as a thistle—a breeze could have knocked him over. Tom slapped the worst of the dust off his knees and limped down the sidewalk toward the highway.

32

Sarah Spence jumped up from the cast-iron bench near the mailboxes when Tom came limping down the track between the great pines and oaks. She had showered and changed into a sleeveless blue linen dress, and her hair glowed. "Where did you go?" And, a second later, after she had a better look at him: "What happened to you?"

"It's nothing serious. I went to Eagle Lake, and I fell down." He limped toward her.

"You fell down? Mr. Langenheim said you went into the town, but I thought he might have heard wrong. . . . Where did you fall down?"

She had come right up to him, and for a moment put her hands on his arms and looked up at him with her serious, wide-set eyes.

"Main Street," he said. "I was quite a spectacle."

"Are you okay?" She had not taken her eyes off his face, and her pupils darted crazily from side to side. He nodded, and she wrapped her arms around him and pushed her head against his chest like a cat. "How did you happen to fall down in the middle of Main Street?"

"Just lucky." He stroked her head, and felt something like ordinary feelings return to him. "I'll tell you about it later."

"Didn't you see me asking you to meet me at the club?"

"I wanted to mail a letter." She tilted her head and looked questioningly at him. "And I wanted to look up some old articles in the local paper."

They began moving down between the trees, their arms around each other. Tom forced himself not to limp.

"I've had at least three lifetimes today," she said. "The best one was on the plane. In our little compartment."

After a few more steps, she said, "Buddy's angry with me. I'm not so enchanted with him this summer. It's against the rules, not to be enchanted with Buddy Redwing."

"How angry is he?"

She looked up at him. "Why? Are you afraid of him?"

"Not exactly. But somebody pushed me off the sidewalk, right into the traffic. I fell down, and a car passed right over me."

"The next time you go on another excursion, I want you to bring me with you."

"You seemed pretty busy with Buddy and his friend."

"Oh sure, the great Kip Carson—you know what he does? You know why Buddy keeps him around? He carries this sack of pills around with him, and he gives them away like candy. Talking to him is like having a conversation with a druggist. Buddy loves these things called Baby Dollies. That's another reason he got mad at me. I wouldn't take any of them."

On the peak that descended to the lake, they looked down at the still blue water and the quiet lodges.

"I don't think Buddy is ever going to be a captain of industry, or whatever his father is," Sarah said. "But *he* couldn't have pushed you into the street. Around four he took two of those pills, and then he just sat on the dock with Kip and said Wow. Wow."

"How about Jerry Hasek?"

"The driver? Buddy made him get into the lake and push

our boat out. Kip tried, but Kip basically can't do anything but dole out pills."

"What about afterwards? Did you see Jerry or his two friends around the compound?"

The lodges looked deserted, and on a terrace of the clubhouse, a waiter in an unbuttoned white shirt leaned against a poolside bar and combed his hair with wide sweeping gestures.

"I guess they were in and out. Do you think it might just have been an accident?"

"Maybe. The whole town was a zoo."

Orange late afternoon light bounced off the water.

They walked down the hill in a silence that was loud with unspoken sentences. When they reached the marshy end of the lake, she dropped his hand.

"I thought you'd be safe up here," she said. "Nobody does anything around here but eat, drink, and gossip. But you're here one day, and somebody pushes you in front of a car!"

"It was probably an accident."

She smiled almost shyly at him. "You can eat dinner with us tonight, if you want. Just don't point your finger at somebody and accuse him of murder, like in the last chapter of a detective novel."

"I'll be good," Tom said.

Sarah put her arms around him. "Buddy and Kip invited me to come to the White Bear with them after dinner, but I said I wanted to stay home. So if *you're* going to stay home . . ."

Tom took a shower in the bathroom beside his mother's old room, wrapped a towel around himself, and went out into the hall. Barbara Deane slid something heavy off a shelf and put it down on a wooden surface. He hurried back into his room. He pulled back the soft old Indian blanket and stretched out beneath it. Beneath the odor of freshly laundered sheets, the bed smelled musty. Tom was asleep in seconds.

He awoke an hour and a half later. Nothing around him looked familiar. For a moment he was not even himself, merely a stranger in a bare but pleasant room. He sat up, saw the towel hanging over a chair, and remembered where he was. The entire fantastic day came back to him. He went to the closet and dressed in chinos, a wash-and-wear white button-down shirt, a tie, and the lightweight blue blazer his mother had made him pack. He pushed his feet into loafers and went downstairs. The house was empty.

Tom let himself out and walked quickly down the avenue of trees to the clubhouse.

33

A deeply tanned young man in a tight white dress shirt with ruffles, tight black trousers with a satin stripe, and highly polished black shoes but no black tie or jacket, appeared beside him on the ground floor of the club. "Yes?" He had a headful of oily-looking black curls tight enough to stretch his forehead. On both sides of the floating staircase which rose from the middle of the room to the second floor were padded wicker chairs and blond tables that shone with wax. Tiffany lamps stood by each circle of chairs, and though light still came in the long side windows, every lamp had been turned on. The room was completely empty except for Tom and the suntanned young man, and the young man looked as though he wanted to keep it that way.

Tom gave his name, and the young man lowered his chin a millimeter or two. "Oh, Mr. Pasmore. Mr. Upshaw informed us that you are to have full use of his membership and signing privileges for the length of your stay. Would you be dining alone tonight, and would you prefer to relax at the Mezzanine Bar before dining, or would you like to be shown directly to your table?" He looked straight at the middle of Tom's forehead as he spoke.

"Is Sarah Spence here yet?"

The man closed his eyes and opened them again. The movement was too calculated to be a blink. "Miss Spence is upstairs with her parents, sir. The Spences will be dining with a large party at the Redwing table this evening."

"I'll just go up," Tom said, and moved toward the low, gleaming first step of the staircase.

He came up on a wooden floor that extended fifty or sixty feet toward an open deck with three round white tables beneath green-and-white-striped sun umbrellas. Inside the dining room ten larger tables, one per lodge, stood on the gleaming floor. Three of these had been set with white tablecloths, candles, wineglasses, and flowers. A small bandshell and stage with a baby grand piano jutted out from the far left wall of the dining room. Neil Langenheim, seated opposite his wife at the only occupied table, looked up and waggled his glass at Tom. Tom smiled back.

Sarah's eyes flashed at him from the middle of a crowd of older people in sports clothes at the long bar on the right side of the room. She met him halfway between the stairs and the bar. "Why are you wearing that tie? Oh, never mind, I'm just glad you're here. Come and meet everybody."

She took him to the bar and introduced him to Ralph and Katinka Redwing. The head of the Redwing family smiled at Tom, showing the gap between his front teeth, and gave him a grinding, painful handshake. His small black eyes looked too lively for his pale, lacquered face. His wife, far more tanned and half a foot taller than he, flicked nearly colorless eyes at Tom. Her long blond hair had been frozen into place. "So you're Gloria's son," she said.

"Glen Upshaw's grandson," said her husband. "Your first time up here, isn't it? You'll love it. It's a great place. Sometimes I think about retiring here, just being alone with these wonderful woods, all that hunting and fishing. Peace and quiet. You'll love it."

Tom thanked him for letting him come up in the plane.

"Glad to do anything I can for old Glen—one of the old

island characters, you know. Solid man, *solid* man. You like the plane? They treat you all right?"

"I never had an experience like that before," Tom said.

Mrs. Spence edged up beside Ralph Redwing. She had changed out of the miniskirt, and wore a knee-length belted pink dress cut low in front. She looked like a big candy cane. "I think I'd rather be on your plane than Frank Sinatra's, really I would."

Redwing put a white, hairy arm around her waist. "There's no telling what Frank would do, if you showed up on his jet in that dress. Hah! Isn't that right!" He kept his arm around Mrs. Spence's waist another couple of beats, and his wife tilted a glass filled with transparent liquid and ice into her mouth.

"Have a good first day?" asked Mr. Spence. "Have any fun?"

"I didn't do much," Tom said. "I went to the village and met Chet Hamilton."

Redwing's face stopped moving, and his wife stepped back to the bar.

"Tom had a little excitement," Sarah said. "He thinks somebody pushed him off the sidewalk into the traffic. A car went right over him."

The lively black eyes had turned depthless. "Should have happened to Chet Hamilton. We don't talk about the Hamiltons, around here." He forced a smile. "We leave them alone, and they leave us alone. Word to the wise."

"What happened? What was that?" This came from a man on the outside of the Redwing group, who had been talking with two other people while glancing occasionally at Tom and had overheard Sarah's remark. He was about Redwing's age, and had crisp dark hair and a lightly suntanned, handsome face. In a striped shirt, with the arms of a blue cotton sweater loosely tied around his neck, he looked like every actor who had ever starred in a romantic comedy with Doris Day agreeably mixed together. "Somebody pushed you off the sidewalk into traffic? Were you injured at all?"

"Not really," Tom said.

Sarah said, "Tom, this is Roddy Deepdale. And Buzz."

A blond man in his mid-thirties with a blue scarf around his neck had moved up beside Roddy Deepdale to look at Tom with the same mixture of concern and fascination as the older man. He, too, was remarkably handsome. His bright yellow cotton sweater had been tied about his waist. Both men seemed more alarmed by what had happened to Tom than anyone in the Redwing party.

"Well, what happened, exactly?" Roddy said, and sipped a drink while Tom told the story. An old woman with a chinless, toadlike face peered at him between the broad, well-set-up figures of the two men. Except for Sarah, the others had turned back to the bar.

"My God, you could have been killed," Roddy Deepdale said. "You nearly were!"

Buzz asked if he had seen who pushed him.

"Well, that's just it. There were so many people on the sidewalk that it must have been an accident."

"Did you go to the police?"

"I didn't really have anything to tell them."

"You were probably right. Last summer, a week or two before we got here, someone broke every window in our lodge. Stole half of our things, even a double portrait by Don Bachardy which is sorely missed, let me tell you, but the physical damage was almost as bad. The squirrels got in, and a lot of birds, and the police couldn't do a thing."

"Everybody felt so bad about it, Roddy," Sarah said.

"Some people did," said Buzz.

"*I* did," interjected the old woman, who thrust her arm between Roddy and Buzz and laughed at the awkwardness of her position. Roddy and Buzz moved aside to admit her, and Roddy placed his hand on her hunched shoulder. "*I* felt terrible about it, I promise! And I'm distressed about what happened to you, Tom Pasmore, and I congratulate you on your survival!" Tom had taken her hand, which was surprisingly solid and long—longer than his own—in his. The impression of her ugliness had entirely disappeared. She had sagging dewlaps and prominent teeth and no chin, but now Tom saw the intelligence in her eyes, the soft wave of her white hair, and the calm width of her forehead. "I'm Kate Redwing," she said. "You've never heard of me, but I knew your mother when she was just a little girl."

"I was hoping I'd meet you," Tom said, "and now that I have, I'm delighted."

"And I'm delighted to meet you. Sit next to me at dinner, and we'll have a good long talk."

"Sarah said to give you this." Roddy Deepdale passed Tom a tall flute glass filled with a bubbling liquid tinged a pale pink. "I assume it's a reward for having survived your experience."

"If Sarah Spence is looking after you, you're going to be looked after very well," said Kate Redwing. "Do you suppose someone could look after *me*? I've had only one martini, and it was a very small one, and since my grand-nephew is still primping . . ."

Buzz smiled and went up to the empty half of the bar.

"You said a double portrait was stolen from your lodge. A double portrait of whom?"

"Of Buzz and me," Roddy Deepdale said. "It's still a terrible loss. I hated telling Don about it, but he was very civilized. He said that it would probably turn up one day, and he sent us a little drawing to compensate. Christopher said something very wicked and funny, but I'd better not repeat it."

Sarah, surrounded by her parents and Ralph and Katinka Redwing at the bar, winked at Tom and raised her glass.

"That Spence girl is really *something*, isn't she?" said Kate Redwing. "I'm not sure she's properly appreciated in these parts." She clinked her glass against his and gave him a sparkling, conspiratorial look over its brim as she drank.

A stir of movement took place at the bar, and Kate Redwing said, "The heir apparent."

Katinka Redwing swept toward the top of the stairs as Buddy came up beside the young man with oily hair. A tall, lanky young person with limp blond hair and a large nose trailed up behind them. Buddy wore a baggy polo shirt and large Bermuda shorts and boat shoes without socks; Kip Carson wore floppy jeans, sandals, and a cheesecloth Indian shirt. Buddy looked glazed and red, as if he had just come out of an oven.

"I think we could go to our table now, Marcello," said his mother.

"Who's the toad in the necktie?" Buddy asked. Baked eyes in the baked-apple face glared at Tom. "One of Roddy's playmates?"

The party at the bar broke up. Katinka Redwing bent whispering toward her son as they followed Marcello toward a long table near the terrace. Roddy and Buzz carried their drinks toward a table for two behind the Langenheims. The senior

Spences attached themselves to either side of Ralph Redwing, and Sarah rolled her eyes and fell in with Tom and Kate.

"Buddy enjoys being bad," the old woman said quietly as they followed the procession to the table. "But I must say, I've always rather liked toads myself. Useful little things. I've even sort of grown to resemble one, though a *nice* one, I trust. Do you suppose Buddy might have meant . . . no, I don't suppose he did." She grinned wickedly, but it might have been at the game of musical chairs going on at the head of the table. Mrs. Spence wished to sit between Ralph and Buddy Redwing, and Buddy wanted to sit beside Kip Carson; Katinka Redwing was determined to sit at the side of her husband and to banish Kip Carson to the table's other end. Mr. Spence and Mrs. Redwing urged Sarah into the chair opposite Buddy. Ralph Redwing took the chair at the head of the table. Everybody else sat down more or less where they wanted to. Tom sat opposite Kip and between Sarah and Kate Redwing, who was opposite Mr. Spence.

Marcello distributed handwritten menus the size of theater placards, and Kip passed two or three small objects to Buddy, and Buddy inserted them into his mouth. Both the host, and then Kip Carson, declared their willingness to live year-round in Eagle Lake. Mrs. Spence could be observed to grasp Ralph Redwing's knee, and Sarah slid her leg next to Tom's. Katinka Redwing stared into some private arctic space and alluded to the anticipation on Mill Walk of "Ralph's book." Buddy told a dirty joke, largely to Sarah, and an incomprehensible one about an elephant and a homosexual to the room at large. Everybody—everybody except Kip Carson, who ate nothing but drank six large glasses of water—ate hugely, drank hugely, and most talked without stopping or listening. Tom noticed that Sarah had been wrong about Buddy Redwing and Kate had been right: Buddy enjoyed being bad, he was acting up, but part of his awfulness was that he had no real talent for that kind of badness. He was too ordinary for it. In ten years, he would be talking with romantic nostalgia about how wild he used to be; in twenty, he would be an overweight tycoon who cheated at golf and thought that he had a divine right to steal whatever he could get his hands on.

"I'm glad you didn't take off your tie," Kate Redwing said to him.

"My mother told me to wear this tie," said Tom, smiling.

"She would have been thinking of the old Eagle Lake, when things were much more formal. She probably still has memories of eating at the club with her father. I can remember seeing her here, the summer I was engaged. How is she now?"

Tom hesitated for a moment, then said, "She could be better."

"Is your father a very sensitive man?"

Tom found himself unable to answer that question, and she patted his hand to tell him that she understood his silence. "Never mind. I'm sure that you make up for a lot. She must be very proud of you."

"I hope she can be," Tom said.

"I used to worry about your mother. She was a dear little thing, but absolutely forlorn. So very pretty, but so *unhappy*. This is none of my business, of course."

Up at the other end of the table, Ralph Redwing was explaining that he saw Eagle Lake as a world apart from his family's businesses, and that was why he had turned down many opportunities to invest in the area. He would not sully the place with money—he was content with their lake, their friends, their little piece of the woods.

"In spite of what we could do with this area," he said. This was a speech that required an audience, and all faces were turned to him, even those of Buddy and Kip. "We could turn this whole part of Wisconsin right around—we could wake it up—we could start putting money into people's pockets . . . "

"I daresay," Kate whispered to Tom.

". . . and there's another factor, which is the attitude of some of the locals. Some of these people resented anything new—anything successful. They made life pretty tough on us for a couple of years. We got back in a couple of ways, but it meant that we don't try to help them any, you can believe that."

"How did you try to get back?" Tom asked innocently.

"Yes, since you mention it," said Kate. "I've always wanted to know how to get back at someone."

"Remember, we're talking about a different time now," Redwing said. "We made our own perfect place up here, that we and our people enjoy, and they can beg us for help and advice, but we don't put a penny into the town of Eagle Lake. You see these fine young men who work here at the club? These are the finest waiters in the world, and my father hired their fathers from the best restaurants in Chicago in the twenties, they live right here in damn fine rooms they deserve, and they're loyal people."

A respectful silence followed all of this. Mrs. Spence said that she admired his . . . well, she admired everything, but something in particular, but she just couldn't find the word, but they all knew what she meant. Mrs. Redwing said she was sure they did, dear, and everybody went back to the same sort of conversations they had been having earlier.

"Do you come here a lot?" Tom asked Kate Redwing.

She grinned. "I'm just a peripheral Redwing from Atlanta, and I don't get up here more than once every two or three years. When my husband was alive, we used to come every summer. We had our own lodge in the compound, but when Jonathan died, they started putting me in a room in the main house."

"I want to talk to you about your first summer here," Tom said. "About my mother and my grandfather, and, if you don't mind, what happened to Jeanine Thielman."

"Oh, my goodness," she said. "You are a remarkable fellow." She turned to give him a long look full of intelligence and good humor. "Yes, you are. Do you happen to know a gentleman from your island named"—here she lowered her voice—"von Heilitz?"

Tom nodded.

"Well, he was remarkable too." She continued to look at him. "I think it would be better to have this conversation elsewhere—certainly *not* in the compound." She sipped at what was left of her watery martini. "I often drop in to see Roddy and Buzz for tea around four in the afternoon. Why don't you stop in there tomorrow?"

The meal ended a short time later. Ralph Redwing waved away Tom's thanks. Buddy waddled around the table toward Sarah, who whispered "Ten minutes" to Tom, and pushed herself away from the table. Tom said good-bye to Kate Redwing, who gave him a pert nod, to the Spences, who seemed not to hear him, and to Mrs. Redwing, who showed all her teeth and said, "Why, you're *wel*come!"

34

Sarah did not appear after ten minutes, nor after twenty. Tom read a page of Agatha Christie, then reread it when he realized that he had understood each individual word, but none of them in sequence. Noises on the porch made him jump up to open the door, but no one was there. The lodge made noises by itself. He looked down the long curved avenue of trees, lighted by his porch light and the Spences'.

After ten more minutes, he wandered out on the dock. Far down to his left, distinct areas of yellow light from the club lay on the black water like paint. The Spences' dock stood illuminated like a stage set. Moonlight silvered the tops of the trees surrounding the invisible lodges across the lake and laid a broad white path on the water. On the north end of the lake a bird called *Chk?*, and from past Roddy Deepdale's lodge a second bird answered it: *Chk! Chk!*

Male voices floated to him, and lights went on in the Deepdale lodge: another dock jumped into visibility. Tom walked back to the deck, found the switches for the outside lights, and turned them off. Light from Glendenning Upshaw's study fell out on the deck and the few camp chairs and a rough wooden table threw out long, decisive shadows. Now the dock was only a blur of darkness against the paler darkness of the lake. He sat down in one of the camp chairs and wondered how he would be able to stand the evenings at the club.

He went inside, sat down at the desk, opened the phone book and found the number for the Spence lodge.

Mrs. Spence said that Sarah had not come back from the club yet; and wasn't she going out to the White Bear with Buddy?

"I thought she changed her plans," Tom said.

"Oh, no, Sarah always goes out in the evening with Buddy. They have so much to talk about." She would tell Sarah he called. Her voice was blandly insincere.

Tom wrote *I'm on the deck—come around the side* on a sheet of his grandfather's paper, and folded it between the screen and the front door. Then he walked back around the side of the lodge and went up the steps to the deck. He turned on one of the lights and sat down to read Agatha Christie while he waited for Sarah.

Moths fluttered around the angled spotlights. The moon coasted through the sky. The light in Barbara Deane's bedroom switched off, and another degree of softness and wholeness appeared in the darkness beyond the circle of light on the deck. Hercule Poirot strolled onstage and began exercising his little grey cells. Tom sighed—he missed Lamont von Heilitz. On the other hand, maybe Monsieur Poirot would appear to explain what really had happened here at Eagle Lake forty years ago.

Tom wondered why the Shadow had not told him that Anton Goetz was an accountant for Mill Walk Construction; and how an accountant had been able to build the enormous house on The Sevens in the early twenties; and who had shot at Lamont von Heilitz; and why Anton Goetz had taken his meals home from the club, just at the time he should have tried most to act normal.

These were exactly the sort of questions to which Hercule Poirot and every other detective like him always had the answer. They were abstraction-machines, and you never had any idea at all of what it felt like to be like them, but by the last chapter they could certainly tell you who had left the footprint beneath the Colonel's window, and who had found the pistol on the bloody pillow and tossed it into the gorse bush. They were walking crossword puzzles, but at least they could do that.

Tom closed his book and looked across the lake. Featureless as ink blots, the empty lodges sat beneath the enormous trees. An off-duty waiter chorded on a guitar beside an open window on the third floor of the club building. Another person, probably another club waiter going home, carried a flashlight between the lodges across the lake.

But a club waiter only had to go upstairs to go home. The flashlight bobbed along, intermittently visible as it moved between the lodges and the trees. The only other light across the lake shone in an upstairs room in the Langenheim lodge, and the moving light disappeared behind a dark, barely visible corner of this structure. Neil Langenheim went out for a walk to sober up before he went to bed, Tom thought, and read another page of Agatha Christie while most of his mind listened for Sarah Spence's footsteps coming around the side of the lodge.

The next time he looked up, the flashlight was bobbing along between the Harbinger and Jacobs lodges. Tom watched it flicker until it disappeared. After a time the light emerged from behind the Jacobs lodge and began bobbing in and out of sight in the long stretch of wooded land between the Jacobs lodge and Lamont von Heilitz's. Tom set down his book and walked out on his dock. A big grey moth flew silently past his head and bumped against a window. From the end of his dock, Tom could see only the shadowy blackness of oaks and maples on von Heilitz's property and the front end of his stubby dock in the black water, tipped with yellow light from the clubhouse. The flashlight did not appear on the marshy end of the lake, working its way around to the club. When the light did not appear for another several minutes, Tom remembered that at least one empty Eagle Lake lodge had been broken into. He tilted the face of his watch toward the lighted window. It was ten-thirty, and nearly everyone around the lake would be asleep. Tom trotted back along the dock.

He stopped at the door to scribble *Wait for me—back soon* on the note for Sarah, and then moved down the steps into the dark track around the lake.

Tom ran past the Spences' lodge, where only the porch light burned, and then back into the darkness beneath the great trees until he came to the club. Tall lights burned in the parking lot, and in second and third-floor windows. The moon sailed through dark clouds and gave them silvery borders. Up at the narrow, treeless end of the lake, frogs croaked in the reeds. The guitarist in the club played the same chords over and over. No light shone among the trees around the Shadow's lodge. Tom ran around the top end of the lake, and his shoes slapped noisily on the beaten earth. Moonlight gave him the curve of the path back into the trees. The guitar grew fainter. Tom trotted past the narrow road coming down through the forest from the highway, and went back beneath the trees. Von Heilitz's lodge was only forty or fifty feet ahead, hidden by the darkness and the massive fir trees that grew down to the lake. Tom wondered what he would do if he saw someone carrying stereo equipment out of the lodge.

He moved off the track and walked quietly across von Heilitz's property until he came to within sight of the lodge. Moonlight streamed down between the trees. No light showed through the shuttered windows. He moved up on the porch, tried the door, and found that it was locked. Unless the burglar had left the house while Tom was rounding the top of the lake, he was still inside. There would be another door on the lake side of the lodge, and this was probably where he had entered. Tom stepped down from the porch and moved backwards toward the track to see if he could see any light moving behind the shutters in the upstairs rooms.

The house was completely dark. Tom stepped back on the track and looked west. Here the moonlight showed a white narrow trail, as clear as a path in a dream, leading westward. Far down this trail a spreading yellow beam bobbed from tree to tree, going away from Tom.

"Damn," he said. He had not been quick enough to catch the burglar inside the Shadow's lodge. Maybe the man had heard him coming and run off before getting inside. Tom began walking quickly after the figure with the flashlight.

He passed a big dark shape that had to be the Jacobs lodge, then the Harbinger lodge. The flashlight kept moving. Tom thought he would wind up following the man all the way to the compound.

By the time the track reached Neil Langenheim's lodge,

the trees on its right side blocked the moonlight. The beam of the flashlight bobbed and wandered, striking the grey bark of oaks, the dusty path, dense shrubbery between the trees. Tom managed to shorten the distance between himself and the man with the light. He could hear his heart beating.

Keeping his eye on the wandering beam of the flashlight, he slipped off his loafers, and started forward again with his shoes in his hand.

Somewhere between the Thielman lodge and Roddy Deepdale's place, the beam of light swung to the right, illuminating a cavern formed by leaves and branches, and disappeared into the cavern.

The cavern had to be a second path, beating deeper into the woods. He ran toward it. Small stones dug into his feet. Trees across from the Langenheim lodge closed in above his head and blocked the moonlight. The sense of open space before him disappeared. He stopped running and held his arms out before him. Then yellow light flashed between trees off to the right before him, disappeared, and flashed again. He made his way around the curve of the path before the Thielman lodge, and ran forward through an open patch of moonlight toward a gap like a dark narrow door between two maples that might have been a path. Yellow light danced like an ignis fatuus deep in the trees.

Tom turned into the gap between the maples, and the flashlight vanished again. He made his way forward in darkness. Animals whirred and scattered, and something scampered along a branch. He stepped forward. The light flashed again. In a sudden shaft of moonlight, he saw the path curving deep into the forest before him. He went ahead on complaining feet, his arms out before him.

A branch slapped the side of his head. His big toe struck something rough and scaly that might have been a root. Then he pushed away the branch, stepped over the obstruction, and inched forward. Another flash of light came from far ahead of him. The path kept melting away before him—spidery twigs scrabbled on his cheek, and his right foot landed on something cool and wet.

The traces of the flashlight disappeared completely into the forest. The side of his arm brushed the rough bark of an oak.

He had lost the path in the darkness. Tom turned around and began to inch his way back to the lodges.

Twigs snatched at his clothes, soft wet ground sucked at his feet. The path had disappeared from behind him as well as in front of him. Tom put his arms up before his face and pushed forward—he hoped it was forward.

A few panicky minutes later, he glimpsed light in front of him, and fought his way toward it. The light grew stronger and shone through gaps between the trees. Before him, the trees and underbrush came to an abrupt stop—he saw a tall spotlight and a wide plane of flat monochrome green like a golf course. It seemed entirely foreign, like nothing at Eagle Lake.

Tom wound through a dense stand of maples, walked over damp leaves, and came out into bright light and smooth short grass. Across the lawn stood a long straight redwood building with a high deck and curtained windows. He was standing on Roddy Deepdale's lawn.

He walked down to the water and made his way along the shore to Roddy's dock and padded across it in his wet socks. On the other side of the dock he walked along the shoreline, startling two birds into flight, until the trees on his grandfather's property began. Then the light on his own deck guided him through the oaks behind his grandfather's lodge.

A figure moved out of the shadows at the far side of the deck. "Tom?" Sarah Spence came into the light. "Where did you go?"

"How long have you been here?"

"About twenty minutes."

"I'm glad you didn't go home," he said. He climbed up on the deck and put his arms around her. "Did your mother tell you I called?"

She shook her head against his chest. "I didn't go home, I just came here as soon as Buddy let me go. He wasn't very happy with me. I had to promise I'd go out for a drive with him tomorrow afternoon." She pulled a broken twig off his jacket. "What have you been doing?"

"Do you know a path that leads up into the forest, near the Thielman lodge?"

"You tried to take a path through the woods in the middle of the night?"

"I saw someone prowling around the lodges on the other side of the lake. There have been a lot of burglaries up here in the past few years—"

"Besides the one at Roddy's?"

"You'd know about it, if Ralph Redwing let you read the local newspaper."

"So you followed him into the woods. Your whole life is one big *excursion*."

"So is yours," he said. He kissed her.

"Could we go inside?"

"Barbara Deane's upstairs."

"So what?" She took him to the door and led him inside. "Ah, a couch. That's what we need. Or is there something better in the next room?" She opened the door and peered into the big sitting room. "Ugh. It looks like a funeral parlor."

"Don't wake up Barbara Deane."

"What is she, anyhow? Your babysitter or your bodyguard?" Sarah closed the door and came back to Tom. "I hope she's not your bodyguard." She put her arms around him.

"Did you go back to the compound after dinner?"

She looked up at him. "Why?"

"Did you see Jerry and his friends there?"

"They leave Buddy and me alone, unless he wants them for something. He even sent Kip away—he wanted to make faces at me for paying too much attention to you. As far as I know, Jerry and the other guys were in their lodge. They have a whole big place all to themselves."

"Have you ever been inside it?"

"*No!*"

"Sometime when nobody's around, could you get me in there?"

She looked distinctly unhappy for a moment. "Maybe it wasn't such a good idea for you to come up here in the first place."

He sat down beside her. "Maybe we should have just stayed on the plane."

"Why don't we stop talking?" Sarah said.

35

The next morning Tom woke up in darkness, shocked out of sleep by a nightmare that blew apart into smoke as soon as he tried to remember it. He looked at his watch: six-thirty. He groaned and got out of bed. Millions of dots of water and a dozen trickling rivulets covered his window. The tree outside was a dark blur.

He brushed his teeth and splashed water on his face, and put on a bathing suit and a sweatshirt. Downstairs, he padded out on the deck.

For a moment only his shivers let him know that he was not still dreaming. Distinct, feathery curls of white-grey smoke rose up from every part of the lake and hung in place as if anchored to the hard blue surface of the water. A few of the curls of smoke moved very slightly, turned and leaned. Across the lake, a low fog hung in a gauzy white pane between the trunks of the trees, but this was not fog—the fog was not an endless series of frozen white dervishes held to the lake like balloons to the wrist of the balloon-man. The lake seemed to be smoldering deep within itself.

He pulled the sweatshirt over his head and tossed it on one of the chairs. Then he sat on the end of the dock and put his legs in silky, startlingly warm water. Tom lowered himself into the lake and pushed away from the dock. Instantly he was in another world. The ripple of his body cutting through the silken water was the loudest sound on earth.

White-grey feathers bent around him, slid through him, flattened against his eyes, swam through his skin and re-formed themselves when he was gone. He lifted his arm from the water, and saw the smoke drifting from his flesh. He swam into the shallow water near the dock and stood up. Curls of mist clung to his body like clouds. Dark air chilled his puckering skin. He climbed back up on the dock and the feathery little clouds dissipated against or into his body. A trace of red lay over the dark trees on the eastern horizon.

In jeans, a shirt, and a warm sweater, he got back to the deck in time to see the top of the red sun move up over the trees. The curls of mist on the lake vanished as the light touched them, and the surface of the water turned transparent, showing the dark blue beneath, like a second layer of skin. Separate rays of light struck the docks, and sparkled off the windows of the club and Sarah's lodge. At the north end of the lake, reeds glowed in the early sun. Tom moved down off the dock when the sun had cleared the tops of the trees on the horizon.

He walked around the side of the lodge and began moving north on the track, feeling as if he were seeing everything for the first time. The world looked impossibly clean, cleanly opened to reveal itself. Even the dust on the path sparkled with a secret freshness the day would gradually conceal. Past the compound, past the old cars against a whitewashed fence at the club; around the north end and the narrow marsh, where the reeds thrust up out of the ooze and a hundred silvery, nearly transparent fish the size of his little finger darted away in unison when his blunt shadow fell among them.

Tom walked through the trees to Lamont von Heilitz's lodge and looked for broken windows or scratches on the locks, any sign of actual or attempted break-in. The doors were locked, and every shutter was locked tight. The intruder must have heard him coming and fled up the path into the woods.

Tom walked past the shuttered lodges. Raccoons had tipped over a garbage can outside the Langenheims' place. Cigarette butts, beer cans, and vodka bottles lay strewn over pale wild grass at the foot of a forty-foot oak.

He cut toward the Thielman lodge, thinking about Arthur Thielman walking his dogs down to see the Shadow the day after his wife had been killed. He wished that he could *see* it—*see* what had happened on the dock in front of this lodge on that night. He went around to the front of the empty lodge, and saw the green space Roddy Deepdale had created around his own lodge. In those days only untouched land had stood between his grandfather's place and the Thielmans'. He jumped up on the deck and scuffed at dry leaves and a layer of grit. Across the lake, a stooped white-haired man in a white jacket moved across a window at the front of the club, setting up a table for breakfast.

Two deer, one of them a buck with lacy antlers, moved on delicate legs out of the trees on the far side of the compound and picked their way across soft ground between the docks to the edge of the water. The doe leaned forward, bent her front legs at the knees, and knelt to drink. The stag walked into the water and saw Tom standing on the dock across the lake. Tom did not move. Ankle-deep in the water, the stag watched him. Finally he lowered his head and drank. The fuzz on the tips of his antlers glowed a soft pinkish-brown. Tom saw the old waiter leaning against the window, watching the deer lap at the water. When they had finished they moved out of the water and drifted back into the trees. Tom left the dock and walked back around the side of the lodge.

A little way past the Thielman lodge, the trees on the right side of the track separated around a narrow path that led straight between the oaks and maples for something like twenty or thirty feet, then slanted west into deep forest. Leaf mulch and brown dry needles covered the surface of the path. Tom looked back along the track curving behind the lodges, and stepped on the path.

The lake disappeared behind him.

He came to the curve in the path, and went deeper into the

woods. Dense woodland stretched away on both sides. Pale, almost white light slanted down through the canopy and touched leaning trunks and brushy deadfalls. Here and there white fog still curled in the low places. The path led down a gorge, a basinlike valley in the forest, up through a stand of walnut trees with nuts like tough green baseballs, and back to level ground.

Far off to his right, so deep in the woods that it seemed a part of them, a grey-green shack materialized between the trunks of oak trees and disappeared into the background as soon as Tom took another step. On the other side of the path, a shack made of black boards, with a small black chimney pipe jutting from its roof, was half-hidden behind the thick trunks of walnut trees.

Something moved in the woods to his right. Tom snapped his head sideways. Light diffused through massive trunks, and trees felled by lightning or disease slanted grey through the brown and green. He moved forward, and again sensed movement on his right. This time he saw the head of a doe lifting toward him from beneath the diagonal line of a dead branch; then the rest of the doe came into focus, and she bounded off through a clear patch of sunlight. The doe disappeared behind a wall of fir trees. On the far side of the patch of sunlight, the white splash of a face appeared against a dark background of leaves, then disappeared like the doe.

Tom stopped moving.

The doe snapped branches as it ran deeper into the woods.

Tom stepped forward again, looked around, and saw only the patch of sunlight and the grey diagonal of the fallen branch.

The path widened before him. Pale morning light fell on the long grass of a clearing ahead and on the pine trees behind it. On the other side of the clearing, the path would wind through oaks and pines until it came to a road—maybe the highway between Grand Forks and Eagle Lake, maybe some deserted county trunk road. It was a long way to carry stolen goods, but nobody could say it wasn't secluded.

This theory collapsed halfway to the clearing, when the stone and glass side of a house appeared. He walked nearer. More of the house came into view. Additions of large mortared stone with windows in thick stone embrasures stood on either side of a small brown shack with a wooden stoop before its front door. A big stone chimney came out of the slanting roof of the right side. Bright pansies and geraniums grew around the front of the house.

Just as Tom decided to walk back to the lake, something stirred in the woods beside him. He looked over his shoulder. A burly, black-haired man in a red plaid shirt stood twenty yards away beside an oak. The oak was not larger around than the man. He crossed his arms over his chest and regarded Tom.

Tom's throat went dry.

A door slammed, and in an instant the man disappeared. He did not shift his body or move in any way, he just was not there anymore. A raspy voice screamed "Who are you?" Tom jumped. A little old man in jeans and an embroidered denim shirt stepped down on the grass in front of the wooden stoop. He had a hooked nose and a seamed face, and long white hair fell straight past his shoulders from a widow's peak. He was pointing a rifle at Tom. "What do you think you're doing around here?"

Tom moved backwards. "I went out for a walk, and the path took me here."

The old man moved nearer, holding the rifle on Tom's chest. "You get out of here, and don't come back." His eyes were flat and black. Tom stepped back and saw that the old man was a woman. "Too many thieving bastards around here," she said in her raspy shrieking voice.

Slowly, Tom turned around. Off to the side, the burly man in the plaid shirt emerged into visibility again.

"Get out!" shrieked the old woman.

Tom ran down the path.

Bitsy Langenheim was stooping over the ground near her garbage can in a tired grey sweatsuit, throwing the cans and bottles back in. She gave him a sour, hungover look. She tossed a vodka bottle at the can and missed. "What are you staring at?"

"Nothing."

"What were you doing back in those woods?"

"Taking a walk."

"Stay out of there. The Indians don't like it."

Tom wiped sweat off his forehead. "So I learned."

She grumbled at him and retrieved the bottle.

36

"Some men came to see you," Barbara Deane said. She stood up, gripping her purse in both hands. "About ten minutes ago. I told them I thought you were still in bed, but they wouldn't leave until I looked into your room. I hope you don't mind."

"Of course not," he said. "Who were they? Did you recognize them?"

"Ralph Redwing's bodyguards." She looked at the door, then back at him. "Is one of them named Hasek? He was the one who made me go up to your room."

"Did they say what they wanted?"

She took a step toward the door. "Only to see you. They didn't say any more." She looked back at him. "I don't have any idea what they wanted, but they looked awfully unpleasant."

"I think they want to warn me away from Buddy Redwing's girlfriend."

She surprised him with a smile. All at once, she looked less anxious and not at all autocratic. She relaxed her hold on the bag and tilted very slightly back to give him the full benefit of her smile. "Buddy Redwing, of course, being too important to do that by himself."

"I don't think Buddy does anything by himself," Tom said. "He likes to have at least one actual person around him."

"I think I know what you mean." She hesitated. "Did you have a decent sleep? The bed all right?"

"Fine," he said.

"I'm glad. I wanted things to be nice for you. You'll eat at the club tonight? I thought I might spend the night in my house."

He said he would eat at the club, and asked if she were going into town.

She raised her eyebrows.

"Would you mind giving me a lift?"

"Well, I guess it would be a pleasure," she said. "Yes, I don't see why it shouldn't be a pleasure."

They went outside together, and Tom followed her across the track to a rutted double path slanting into the trees. It had been deliberately obscured by a leafy branch she tugged out of the way. A little way down a dark green Volkswagen beetle stood beside a wild azalea bush. Barbara Deane asked him to wait while she moved the car, and he walked far enough down the path to see a weathered barn at the end of a small field bordered by forest. She turned to look at him through the rear window when she had pulled the car out, and he ran back and got into the seat beside her.

"I keep my horse in that barn," she said. "I ought to take him out and ride him every morning, but ever since the robbery, I get anxious whenever I'm away from home for too long. I guess I'll get up early tomorrow morning and take him out for a run." She pulled out on the track and moved slowly past the lodges.

Tom asked if she knew Jerry Hasek.

"I never actually met him until today." She drove past the club and onto the open stretch of land at the north end of the lake. "But he looks like his father."

"You knew Wendell Hasek?"

"I knew who he was." She turned up the hill. "He worked for Judge Backer, until the Judge fired him. I thought Wendell Hasek was a pretty unsavory character, but then I think his son seems unsavory too, and he works for the Redwings. So apparently I'm no judge."

"I think you're right on both counts," Tom said. "But why did Judge Backer hire this unsavory character? Was he unsavory too?"

She laughed. "Hardly. Wendell was really only a boy when he went to work for the Judge. In those days, there were some honest judges on Mill Walk. Some honest policemen too." She shook her head. "I shouldn't talk this way. I'm almost completely out of touch about what goes on on Mill Walk. And I suppose I'm a little bitter."

They did not speak again until she had turned off onto the highway. Then Tom said, "You must remember the summer of Jeanine Thielman's death very clearly."

"I certainly do!" She turned her head to look at him. "That was the summer after your grandmother died. You probably don't know anything about that."

"Why wouldn't I?"

"I know Glen Upshaw. He wouldn't even hear his wife's name after her death. Cut everything about her right out of his life. I guess he thought it would be better for Gloria that way."

"Do you think Magda was a good wife for him?"

She gave him a startled glance. "I don't think I can answer that. I'm not sure any woman could have been what people think of as a good wife to your grandfather."

"I learned some things about my grandmother not long ago. She seemed like a surprising woman for him to have married."

Her mouth twitched.

"Do you want to know what I really think?" She looked sideways at him, and he saw that this had been an important matter for her. "I don't know what you know about Magda, but she was like a child. She had no more independence than a kitten. When Glen met her, Magda was working as a waitress in her parents' restaurant—a pretty little blond thing who looked about nineteen even though she was in her thirties, and she was as quiet as a mouse. I think that's what Glen liked, having absolute control over her life. He told her what to wear, he told her what to say—he ran her life. He was like a god, as far as she was concerned."

"Did she have any friends?"

"Glen didn't encourage her to have a separate social life. After Gloria was born, she stopped going out. Glen fired their servants—in the days when all their friends had maids and laundresses and cooks and gardeners and God knows what else—and Magda did everything, and took care of the baby too. Like a shy little girl who wanted to please her father."

"So he had two children," Tom said.

"He had what he wanted. *Most* of what he wanted." She drove slowly down the empty highway.

"Why would Magda have killed herself? It seems to me that she must have had everything she wanted too. She was finally alone with her husband and her baby."

"Glen left her alone a good deal of the time. He'd take Gloria out with him when he went places, and leave Magda at home. And after Gloria's birth, Magda began to look her age. And that didn't do for Glen. Not at all. I suppose he just lost interest in her."

"So you don't think there was anything to the rumors about her death."

"You couldn't have heard about all this from Glen," she said.

"I read some old newspapers."

"Old Eagle Lake papers?" Tom said nothing, and after a moment, "Well, that editor was crazy. He was so against Mill Walk people that when one of them drowned, he saw stab wounds where there were none. Glen probably did pay off the coroner and arrange for Magda's cremation, but he wanted to hush up her suicide, not conceal a murder."

Tom nodded.

"Even people who disliked Glen didn't think he murdered Magda. That ridiculous editor should have been put out of business."

"You're very loyal to him," Tom said.

"I used to be loyal to him, I guess. I cleaned up after his messes, and I took in your mother when he asked me to. He stuck up for me once, when I was in trouble. Now I just work for him. I watch out for his property and I take his money for doing it. I don't talk about things he doesn't want me to talk about, so if that's what you—" She stopped talking and stared straight ahead. Her hands gripped the steering wheel, and she looked old and angry and confused.

"I'm sorry," she said. She swerved to the side of the road, put the car into the parking gear, and flattened her hands on her thighs. Her hands looked as though they belonged to someone else, rough and knotted with veins.

"He didn't ask me to check up on you," Tom said.

"I know." She slumped back in the seat.

"I don't suppose he even thought we'd ever talk, or get to know each other at all. That's not the way he thinks."

"No," she said. "It sure isn't." She looked over at him at last. "You're not very much like him, are you?"

"I don't know enough about him to know if I am or not," he said.

"Well, you're a lot more sympathetic. I suppose he just sent you up here the way he sent me up here."

"The way he sent my mother to your place after Jeanine Thielman disappeared."

"No, Gloria had formed some kind of attachment to Jeanine; Glen didn't want his daughter to know she'd suffered another terrible loss. I think he was trying to spare her some pain, and he did it in his usual way, by trying to wipe out the cause of the pain."

She was looking at him now, not angrily but as if waiting for him to challenge the picture of Glendenning Upshaw as a concerned father.

"My mother didn't say anything to you about seeing a man running through the woods on the night Mrs. Thielman disappeared?"

"No, but if she did, it's all the more reason for Glen to want to get her away from everybody. Don't you see? Gloria was a very disturbed little girl that summer. He certainly wouldn't have wanted to involve her with the police."

Gloria was a very disturbed little girl long before that summer, Tom thought, but said nothing.

"You're very interested in what happened back then, aren't you?" She put the car into gear again, and rolled back on the highway.

"It seems to me that what happened back then has a lot to do with what's still going on."

"But that was such a terrible time. There are things it might be better not to know."

"I don't believe that," he said.

She turned into Main Street. At eight o'clock in the morning, most of the shops were closed and only a few people were on the sidewalks. None of them looked like tourists. Barbara Deane pulled up to the sidewalk at the first intersection. A black and white sign said OAK STREET. "My house is right up the street. Is it all right if I drop you off here?"

She suddenly looked shy and uncertain. "I know you're busy, but would you think about coming to my house for dinner some night? It would be nice to cook for someone else, and I enjoy your company, Tom."

"I'd like that very much," he said.

"I might be able to tell you some things about the summer Jeanine died without being disloyal to your grandfather. After all, the important thing to remember is that whatever he did, he did it to protect your mother."

"Just name the day," Tom said.

She touched his arm to say one more thing.

"Your mother told you that she saw a man running through the woods on that night?"

"It must have been Anton Goetz. It couldn't have been anyone else."

"Well, it couldn't have been Anton Goetz, either. Goetz walked with a cane, and he limped. It was a very *romantic* limp. Anton Goetz couldn't move faster than a slow walk. Gloria might not have seen anything at all—she had a very active imagination, and she couldn't always tell the difference between it and reality."

"I know that," he said, and got out of the car.

37

As he walked back along the highway an hour later, the black Lincoln coasted past him, drew ahead, and pulled onto the shoulder of the road. The Lincoln's back doors opened, and two men in grey suits and sunglasses got out of the car. One of them was too fat to button his suit, and the other was as skinny as a hound. Both of them had long sideburns and swept-back Elvis hair. They looked at him with bored indifferent faces. The lean one put his hands in his pockets. Jerry Hasek, also in a grey suit but without the sunglasses, opened the driver's door and got out and looked unhappily at Tom across the top of the car. "We're going to give you a ride," he said. "Come on, get in the car."

"I'd rather walk." Tom looked sideways into the woods.

"Oh, don't do that," Jerry said. "What good is that? Just get in the car."

The other two began coming toward him.

"Nappy and Robbie," Tom said. "The Cornerboys."

Robbie took his hands out of his pockets and glanced at his

fat companion, who scowled at Tom. Nappy's sideburns almost reached his jaw.

"I remember you," Nappy said.

"Just get him in the car," Jerry said. "We already took too long doing this. Tom, get sensible. We don't want to hurt you, we're just supposed to bring you back."

"Why?"

"Somebody wants to talk to you."

"So get in the car," Nappy said in a thick, constricted voice that sounded as if someone had once stepped on his throat.

Tom walked past Nappy and Robbie and opened the front passenger door. All three bodyguards watched him get in, and then got in themselves.

"O*kay*," Nappy sighed. He looked like a bullfrog, seated in the back of the car.

"Okay," said Robbie. "Okay, okay, okay."

Jerry started the car and drove down the highway back toward the lake.

Nappy leaned forward from the back seat. "What's this Cornerboy stuff, huh? Where do you come off, with this Cornerboy stuff?"

"Just keep quiet, will you?" asked Jerry. "And you too, Pasmore. I want to talk about some stuff before we get back."

"Good," Tom said.

Jerry rubbed his face and glanced at him. "A long time ago, you came to my house. My sister and me came out to talk to you. When my friends turned up, you ran away and you got hurt. Nobody meant for that to happen."

"I don't think you were deliberately trying to kill me," Tom said. "I got scared when I saw these two guys waving knives."

"Everybody should have handled things in another way," Jerry said. "The main thing was, my father sent me out to see what you wanted."

"I realize that now," Tom said.

"I mean, there's already enough excitement," Jerry said.

"Right," Tom said.

"So what was that about the dog?" Jerry asked.

Robbie snickered.

"I heard something scream."

Nappy said, "I guess we all make mistakes, huh?"

"Nobody says another word about that," Jerry said. "You hear me?"

"Dog," Robbie said, and Nappy made a little *uh oh* sound that ended almost as soon as it had begun.

Jerry took his hands off the wheel and whirled around so fast that he seemed nearly not to have moved at all—Tom saw only a blur—and then Jerry was leaning over the back of the front seat, whacking Robbie with both hands.

"ASSHOLE! SHITHEAD! FUCKING RETARD!"

Robbie held his hands up before his face. "You hit my—you got my—"

"YOU THINK I CARE? GODDAMN YOU, I TOLD YOU—"

The Lincoln drifted slowly into the oncoming lane. Tom grabbed the wheel and steered it back. *The return of Vic Pasmore*, he thought. Jerry smacked Robbie once more and turned around and grabbed the wheel away from Tom. His face was a deep red.

"Okay? Okay? We got that straight?"

"We got it straight," Nappy said.

"We damn well better have that straight," Jerry said.

"You busted my shades," Robbie said.

Tom looked back over the seat. Nappy was staring straight ahead. He looked like a man on a bus. A smear of blood slid down Robbie's cheek. A cut on the bridge of his nose bled toward its tip. A bow had been snapped off his sunglasses. Robbie stared at the two broken pieces. He glowered at Tom, then rolled down his window and tossed the sunglasses into the road.

"All right," Jerry said. "Now we're all straight."

He swung the car into the bumpy track that led to the lake.

Tom expected them to pull up before the compound, but Jerry rolled past it without even a sideways glance. They continued past the Spence lodge and stopped in front of Glendenning Upshaw's. "Okay," he said. "Let's go in and finish this bullshit."

All four of them got out of the car.

"You first, sport," Jerry said. "This where you live, right?"

Tom rounded the car. Nappy and Robbie put their hands in their pockets and looked up at the big lodge as if they were thinking about buying it for a vacation home. Robbie had wiped the trickle of blood from the bridge of his nose, but two red stripes lay on the side of his face like warpaint. Tom went up the stone steps. Jerry crowded him from behind, and the other two sauntered toward the steps after them, looking up and down the path.

"Wipe the side of your face, for Chrissake," Jerry said.

Tom swung open the screen door, and Jerry held it while he opened the front door. They walked inside. Jerry still crowded him from behind.

Buddy Redwing stood up like a jack-in-the-box from the sofa that faced the door. He was wearing a stretched-out pale green polo shirt and wide khaki shorts. "You took enough time."

"We had to look all over the place for him." Jerry placed the tips of his fingers on Tom's shoulders and gently urged him forward.

Nappy and Robbie wandered to opposite sides of the big sitting room. Nappy sauntered to the door of the study, opened it, and peered in. Kip Carson, in only a faded pair of cut-off jeans and flip-flop sandals, walked through from the kitchen, holding a red can of Coca-Cola. He raised the can in a salute.

"What are you doing here?" Tom said.

"That's pretty good, coming from you," Buddy said. "As far as I know, you're a total charity case. You have no business being up here at all. You're nothing but a serious pain in the ass."

"Buddy, I wish you and your friends would get out of this lodge."

Buddy threw out his arms and turned from side to side, appealing to both sides of the room. "Oh my God, he wishes we would get out of this lodge. That's so . . . so fucking *decisive*, I hardly know what to say."

Nappy chuckled on cue, and Kip Carson took a slug of Coke and sat on the sofa behind Buddy to enjoy the show. Jerry and Robbie wandered around the room. When Buddy turned to them, they tried to look attentive. "I mean, this is really rare." He turned back to face Tom. "Let's get this straight. As far as I'm concerned, you're just this guy who all of a sudden appeared. You're a jerk. You don't understand anything—you don't know how things work."

"Are you finished?" Tom said. "Or is there more?"

Buddy pointed a thick index finger at Tom's chest. "You get a ride up here in our private plane with *my* guests. You sit at *my* table. You ride in *my* car." He took an angry, jittery step sideways, then moved in front of Tom again. "And the second you show up, my girlfriend suddenly decides she doesn't want to spend so much time with me. All of a sudden, everything's a little *different*. I get the feeling that you've been messing around where you don't belong, Pasmore."

"Where don't I belong?" Tom asked.

"You don't belong anywhere!" Buddy exploded. "Goddamn it! You know how long I've been going out with Sarah? Three years! We have a whole goddamned relationship!"

Tom smiled, and Buddy's eyes seemed to shrink within their sockets. "Don't you get it? Sarah belongs to me. Sarah is *mine*. You don't have anything to do with her."

"You can't own other people," Tom said. "People make up their minds by themselves."

Buddy reared back. "Is that what you think? You ought to know better, considering your family."

"Lay off my family, you spoiled, lazy, indifferent shithead," Tom said, stung.

Buddy pressed on into what he perceived as Tom's weakness. "We own old man Upshaw, Pasmore. You think he does anything we don't know about? Your grandfather belongs to us. There's no umbrella over you."

Tom blinked, but did not react in any other way.

"You want me to explain your problem to you?"

"Can you?"

Buddy waved his hand before his face as if scattering a cloud of gnats. "You problem is, you don't know the rules. Because you don't know the rules, you don't know the right way to act. I'm a Redwing. Let's start with that. Nothing happens up here unless it's okayed by us. The second thing is, you don't mess with another guy's girlfriend. That is an *error*. If you expect me to be civilized about this, you don't know me, because I don't *intend* to be civilized about it."

"It's funny," Tom said, "but I guess I never did expect you to be civilized, Buddy."

"You fucking twerp!" Buddy roared. "You see these guys here? They work for me! If I ask them to do something to you, they'll do it! But I don't need them to get rid of you—I can do that myself."

Tom stepped backwards, shaking with fear, anger, and distaste—an intense and unpleasant odor, of yeast and secret dirt, seemed to float out of Buddy's pores. "The dumbest thing you could have done was to try to send me home in a cast. Did you think that would make you irresistible?"

"Jesus, what bullshit," Buddy said. "Could somebody tell me what this guy is talking about?" He looked over his shoulder at Jerry.

"He's crazy," Jerry said.

"He's *all* fucked up," said Kip Carson, sounding faintly admiring.

"What bullshit," Buddy repeated in a wondering voice. "This guy can't say anything that isn't one hundred percent pure bullshit." He swayed back and forth, swinging his thick short arms. "Didn't I just say that I don't need anybody else to take care of you? Why do you think I brought you here? I'm telling you right now to stay away from Sarah Spence. Whatever you think about her is wrong. Do you understand that? Maybe she played with you a little bit—she could do that. But I understand her a lot better than you do, believe me."

"I don't think you understand her at all," Tom said.

"She's trying to make me jealous," Buddy said. "She knows I see a couple girls at Arizona, and she wanted to get back at me. And it worked! I'm jealous, okay? I'm pissed off—but you don't want me pissed off at you, Pasmore."

"Why, what are you going to do?" Tom asked.

Buddy shoved a forefinger into Tom's chest. "I'll leave you in pieces. Is that clear enough for you? You're so insignificant, I shouldn't have to take the trouble, but if you push me, I'll take you apart."

"I know what you should do," Tom said, pushed past self-control. "Tell yourself she isn't good enough for you. You're going to be saying that sooner or later, so why not start now? Tell yourself you're lucky you found out in time."

Nappy snickered. Buddy balled his fists and grimaced and swung a roundhouse punch at Tom's head. Tom ducked out of the way. Buddy swung with his other arm and missed again. Tom stepped back and took a quick look at Jerry and the others, who were doing nothing but looking on impassively. Buddy came flat-footed toward Tom and shot out his right hand. Instinctively, Tom stepped inside the blow, and hit him hard in the stomach. It was like ramming his fist into a bowl of oatmeal. Buddy clapped both hands to his stomach and sank to his knees.

"Oh, hell," Jerry said. He flapped his hand at Nappy, and the two of them got Buddy up on his feet and helped him toward the door. Kip Carson set down the can of Coke and followed them outside. Tom wiped his face with his hands and tried to stop trembling. He went through the open wooden door and pushed aside the screen. Jerry Hasek stood on the top step with his hands on his hips, and Kip was floating uncertainly alongside the car. Buddy struggled to breathe as Robbie and Nappy opened the Lincoln's passenger door and got him inside. Kip Carson climbed in the back and waited. "You talk too much," Jerry said from the top step.

"So does he," Tom said.

38

Tom spent the rest of the morning alone. He called Sarah, but no one answered in their lodge. He knocked on her door. No one responded, and he went down past the compound. The Lincoln and the Cadillac were both gone. He walked all the way around the lake, hearing nothing but birds and insects and an occasional fish slapping the water. Tom felt like the last person left on earth—the whole Redwing caravan had moved on. When he came back around Roddy Deepdale's lodge to his own, he changed into his bathing suit and swam until his muscles felt tired and relaxed.

At the club, Marcello sat beneath a lamp on a pale couch, reading a comic book. He stood when Tom entered, yawned, and strolled through a bleached wooden door marked OFFICE. Tom went upstairs to the empty dining room. The elderly waiter he had seen that morning got up from a bar stool and led him to a table near the bandshell.

"Where is everybody?" Tom asked.

"They don't tell me where they go," the waiter said, and placed the enormous menu in his hands.

After lunch, he took a novel out on the deck, and had just sat down on one of the hard wooden chairs when he heard the telephone ringing in his grandfather's study.

"So what happened?" Sarah asked him.

"Where were you?" he asked back. "I called your place, but nobody answered. There wasn't even anybody at the club."

"We all went to the White Bear. Ralph and Katinka were very disgruntled all through lunch, though they did their best not to show it, and Buddy told me that you said he was spoiled, lazy, and indifferent. Did you say that?"

"I couldn't help it," Tom said.

"You got two out of three. He's certainly spoiled and lazy, but I wouldn't call him indifferent."

"Did he yell at you?"

"He sort of yelled in whispers. He didn't want his parents to hear. I was at a table with him and Kip, and my parents were at another table with his parents and his aunt. Buddy usually watches himself around his parents, and I think he has to be on his good manners at the White Bear for a while."

"What did you tell him the other night?"

"Just that I wanted him to stop assuming that we were going to get married. I said that I liked you, too, and I said I wasn't sure I wanted to always live on Mill Walk. It was pretty uncomfortable."

"You didn't break off with him."

"I have to spend the whole summer here, Tom. I thought I was pretty good, actually. I told him that being a Redwing is a career, and I wasn't sure it was the one I wanted."

"I told him he should decide that you're not good enough for him."

"I like that," she said, meaning she did not. "Anyhow, will you *please* tell me what happened, please?"

He described as much as he could remember of the scene between himself and Buddy, except for the way it ended.

"Well, well. The compound is almost empty right now. So if you want to see where the bodyguards live, this is the time. The only person in the place should be Aunt Kate, and she takes a long nap every afternoon."

Tom said he'd meet her in front of her lodge.

"I suppose I must be crazy," she said, and hung up.

She stepped out from between the oaks as he walked toward her lodge. He went down the track to join her. She pulled him back between the big oaks and tilted her face toward his and gave him a long kiss. "I had to get out. My mother knows that something went wrong between Buddy and me, and I couldn't stand the interrogation anymore. I called you when she went upstairs to wash her hair."

They walked across the narrow parking area in front of the compound, and Sarah opened the door in the tall fence. "Here we go."

Gravel paths led to three highly ornamented wooden houses with long porches, gables, and dormer windows on the third floor. The houses were so perfectly maintained they looked artificial. Banks of flowers and bright green grass grew between the gravel paths. The whole thing looked like a toyland, like Disneyland. "Well, here you are," Sarah said. "This is it. The holy of holies. The one on Mill Walk looks just like it, except the houses are newer and they're not all alike."

Sarah led him up the steps of the lodge nearest the compound's lakeside wall. "I'd better stay out here in case they come home early," she said. "I'll bang on the door, or something."

"I won't be long," Tom said, and went inside.

The lodge smelled of cigarettes and grease. Discarded clothes and open magazines lay on the floor of the main downstairs room, and the kitchen was a mound of crusty dishes and empty beer bottles. Tom walked up the steps and peered into the bedrooms. Blue jeans, socks, and T-shirts covered the unmade beds and the bare floors. In the largest of the three bedrooms, a portable television and a tape deck stood on a low table. Tom opened the dresser drawers and found underwear, clean white shirts still in the dry cleaner's wrappings, and clean socks. On a shelf in the closet above two grey suits he saw a stack of pornographic magazines and, in a row of books about concentration camps, Hitler, Nazis, and famous criminals, four tattered paperback books called *The Torturer's Library.*

Pictures from muscle magazines decorated Nappy's room. Crumpled O Henry and Twinkies wrappers lay around the bed.

Robbie's room was a sty of beer bottles, dirty plates, and wadded-up tissues. A cheap portable record player like the one in Gloria Pasmore's room sat on the floor next to a stack of forty-fives and a full-length mirror where Robbie could watch himself pretend to play guitar.

Tom walked downstairs and went outside.

"I never realized that being lookout was such a tricky job," Sarah said. "I'm sure that several birds gave me very suspicious looks. My hands were clenched so tight I practically gave myself *bruises*. Did you find anything?"

"About what I expected," Tom said. "A lot of Vivaldi records and books by T.S. Eliot. Let's get out of here."

"Now would you mind telling me why you wanted to do this?"

"I was looking for—"

A car crunched onto the gravel of the little parking area beyond the fence. Car doors slammed shut. Voices floated toward them. Tom and Sarah were in the middle of the compound, halfway to the gate.

"Whoops," Sarah said.

The door in the fence opened, and Katinka Redwing came through, immediately followed by her husband. Both of them froze at the sight of Tom and Sarah.

"Oh, hi!" Sarah said. "I was just showing Tom what the compound looks like. It's so beautiful, isn't it?"

"Beautiful," Tom said. "So peaceful. I can really see why you love it."

Both Redwings stared at them with implacable faces.

"Well," Sarah said. "Tell Buddy I'm looking forward to our drive this afternoon."

They smiled and walked past the staring Redwings.

Outside the tall fence, Jerry Hasek leaned against the Cadillac, smoking. When Tom and Sarah appeared through the door, he took his cigarette out of his mouth and stared at them and bit his lower lip. His jaws worked as if he were chewing gum.

"See you later, Jerry," Sarah said. She and Tom walked across the gravel, and turned onto the path.

"Yeah," Jerry said. "I'll see you later."

At ten minutes to four Tom was standing back in the trees near the rank of mailboxes, and after a little while a blue and white mail van pulled up before the boxes. Joe Truehart jumped out and began sliding advertising circulars, catalogues, and magazines into the Redwings' boxes. Tom walked out of hiding and gave him another long letter to Lamont von Heilitz. The mailman said he would take care of it, and pushed it into his back pocket. Tom walked back down the long hill and went back to his lodge. He read for half an hour, and then walked over to the Deepdale lodge to see Kate Redwing.

39

Buzz opened the door and said, "Come on in!" His bathing suit was only a narrow strip of blue cloth, and his skin glistened with oil. A red polka dot bandanna was tied around his neck. His perfect teeth shone white. He stepped backwards, and Tom followed him into a long, loftlike room with oatmeal-colored couches and chairs, cut flowers in glass vases, a piano with framed photographs, and creamy yellow rectangular rugs on the polished wooden floor. A big stone fireplace stood against the back wall. Kate Redwing stood up and smiled from one end of the long couch facing him.

"Kate is having a cup of tea, would you care for one? I can give you a Coke or a 7-Up, or any kind of drink, if you'd prefer."

"Tea would be great," Tom said.

"Roddy and I are working on our tans out on the deck, and Kate says the two of you want to talk about graves and worms and epitaphs, so I'll just give you your tea and go back out, if that's all right." He put his hands on his narrow hips and gave

Tom a humorous inspection. "Have you completely recovered from your tumble the other day? You look as if you have."

"I think it's been one long tumble ever since," Tom said, and Buzz laughed and walked into the kitchen to boil up the water.

"Come sit next to me," Kate said. "Are you really all right?"

He walked around to her, nodding. Through the window wall on the far end of the room, Tom waved to Roddy Deepdale, who was lying back in a recliner. He wore the same nearly nonexistent kind of bathing suit as Buzz, and his chest and shoulders were turning a smooth, uniform gold. A brown plastic bottle of suntan lotion and a pile of books stood on the deck beside the recliner. Roddy propped himself up on one elbow and waved back. The kettle whistled in the kitchen.

"You've succeeded in stirring up my nephew and his wife, at any rate," Kate said. "There was some kind of unpleasantness between you and Buddy this morning, wasn't there? Of course everybody's terribly tactful, but I don't suppose you'll be able to keep me entertained at any more family dinners."

Tom said she probably wouldn't be able to entertain him, either.

"Maybe not at dinners, anyhow," she said, and he knew that this wonderful old woman was offering him her friendship. He said he supposed there were other times of the day.

"Well, exactly. Ralph doesn't think much of Roddy and Buzz either, but we never saw any reason for that to interfere with our enjoyment of each other. The world doesn't run according to the rules of a few Redwings." She patted his hand. "I gather that all this has to do with that beautiful young Spence girl. Of course I think it would be a shame for her to get engaged to my grand-nephew. On top of everything else, she's far too young. Ralph and Katinka will get over the shock sooner than you think, and before you know it Buddy will discover some other girl who will turn out to be much more appropriate. You should just be discreet and get as much out of this summer as you can."

"So that's what this talk is all about," Buzz said, returning with a steaming cup of tea. "Now I know I'd better get out of the way!" He set the tea down on the glass coffee table before them, and padded out through a side door. A minute later, he appeared on the deck, moving past the window toward a lounge chair.

"Does Buzz have a job?" Tom asked.

"He's a doctor." Kate Redwing smiled at him. "An excellent pediatrician, I hear. He had some trouble at the start of his career, when he worked with an important doctor, and he's had some rough patches, but he's doing very well now." She frowned into her cup, and then looked at him with bright lively eyes. "But that's not what you wanted to talk to me about. Weren't you interested in what happened during my first summer up here? When that poor woman was killed?"

"Didn't you and your fiancé find her body?" Tom asked.

"I suspect you know very well we did." She smiled at him again. "I wonder why you want to know about all this."

"Well," Tom said, "my mother got much worse during that summer, and I'm sure the murder had a lot to do with the trouble she had."

"Ah," said the old woman.

"And I've been talking about Mrs. Thielman's murder with Lamont von Heilitz ever since I met him."

"So he got you interested in it."

"I guess you could say that. I think there's a lot that's still unknown, or that was never explained, and the more I can find out . . . " He let the sentence go unfinished. "Maybe I'm not saying this right, but I'm interested in Mill Walk, and that murder involved a whole lot of important people who ran things on the island."

"I'm certainly glad not to be having this conversation at the compound. But I'll confess that it's fascinating. Do you really think that Lamont might have missed something?"

"Probably nothing important." He looked at the fireplace and saw the bare, slightly paler rectangle spot on the creamy wall above it where the portrait had hung.

"Well, I can tell you one thing. Everything about a murder is probably surprising, because all of a sudden you learn about other people's secrets, but it really was a surprise to me that Jeanine Thielman had been seeing Anton Goetz. And if it hadn't been for those curtains—the curtains that were wrapped around her when Jonathan found her underwater—I don't know if I would have believed that he had anything to do with it. That and the fact that he killed himself, of course. But the curtains were really damning, I thought."

"He never expected them to be found," Tom said.

"The lake is surprisingly deep up at that end, and there's a big drop-off where the reeds end. It was just his bad luck that my line snagged, and Jonathan dove underwater and saw something that looked funny to him."

"You didn't think Goetz was her type?"

"Anton Goetz! He seemed so *obvious*. He wanted to project a sort of terribly romantic masculine toughness, you know, always smoking and squinting his eyes, that sort of thing. That war injury helped. He was an excellent shot, by the way. A real marksman. Under the circumstances, that's a little ghoulish, isn't it? And he was supposed to own a rather unsavory hotel. Twenty years after all this happened, I thought of Anton Goetz when I saw *Casablanca*. Humphrey Bogart and Rick's Café Americain. Except that Goetz had one of those kind of buttery German accents."

"He doesn't sound much like an accountant," Tom said.

"Oh, he couldn't have been an accountant." She looked to see if he were teasing. "That's impossible. Do you remember when several people were killed in his hotel? The Alvin? The Albert?"

"The St. Alwyn," Tom said.

"That's it. There was a prostitute, and a musician, I think, and a group of other people? And there was something about the words 'blue rose'? And a detective on Mill Walk killed himself? Being here with Roddy and Buzz is what reminds me of all that, I guess. Anyhow, when I heard about it from my relatives on Mill Walk, I thought it was like Anton Goetz to own a hotel where something like that could happen. He couldn't have been an accountant. Could he?"

"According to Sarah's father, he was," Tom said. "He saw Goetz's name in the corporate ledgers. But it was actually my grandfather who owned the St. Alwyn."

She looked at him fixedly for a second, forgetting about the cup of tea she had lifted from its saucer. "Well now, that's very interesting. That explains something. On the night that it turned out that Jeanine Thielman disappeared, Jonathan and I had dinner with all the Redwings, as we did most of those nights. I was supposed to get to know his uncle Maxwell and the rest and, of course, they were supposed to give me a good looking over, which is certainly what they *did*. Those dinners got to be a little nerve-wracking, but I soldiered through, which is what we did in those days. Anyhow, on that night, Jon and I stayed after everyone else went back to the compound. We wanted to be by ourselves, and I asked him if we had to stay the entire summer. Jonathan thought we should, though he was very sympathetic. We didn't have an argument, but we went to and fro for a long time. At one point, I walked away from him and went to the balcony at the front of the club that overlooks the entrance. And I saw your grandfather talking with Anton Goetz."

She looked down and noticed the cup in her hand. She replaced it on the saucer and folded her hands on her lap. "Well, I was kind of startled, I suppose. I didn't know they knew each other that well—they weren't each other's sort at all. Of course I didn't think that Mr. Goetz and Mrs. Thielman were each other's sorts either, and it turned out they *were*. During the day, I'd never seen Glen and Anton Goetz do more than nod to each other. And there they were, having this intense conversation. They were each leaning on something—Anton Goetz on his cane and your grandfather on that umbrella he always carried. I guess so he could *hit* somebody with it if he got mad."

"Did it look like they were arguing?"

"I wouldn't say so, no. What struck me at the time was that Glen had left Gloria alone in their lodge. At night. And Glen never left Gloria alone, especially at night. He was a very thoughtful father."

Tom nodded. "Goetz always carried a cane?"

"He needed it to stand up. One of his legs was almost useless. He could walk, but only with a pronounced limp. The limp rather suited him—it went with his being such a good shot. It added to his *aura*."

"He couldn't run?"

Kate smiled. "Oh, my goodness, run? He would have fallen splat on his face. He wasn't the kind of man you could imagine running, anyhow." She looked at him with a new understanding clear in her intelligent face. "Did someone tell you that they saw him running? They're nothing but a liar, if they did."

"No, it wasn't that, exactly," Tom said. "My mother saw a

man running through the woods on the night Mrs. Thielman was killed, and I thought it had to be Goetz."

"It could have been almost anybody *but* him."

Out on the deck, Roddy Deepdale stood up and stretched. He picked up his books and disappeared from view for a moment before coming in the side door. Buzz followed him a moment later.

"Anybody for a drink before we get ready to go over to the club?" Roddy said. He smiled brilliantly, and went into his bedroom to put on a shirt.

"Don't you wish we had Lamont von Heilitz here, so we could ask him to sort of explain everything?" Kate said. "I'm sure he could do it."

"Did Roddy say something about a drink?" Buzz asked, coming in the side door.

"Maybe a little one," Kate said. "Everybody over there watches me so carefully, I think they're afraid I'm going to get maudlin."

"I'll get maudlin for you," Buzz said. "I have only another week of lying around on decks and getting tan before I have to go back to St. Mary Nieves."

Tom stayed another half hour. He learned that the Christopher who had said the wicked thing to Roddy Deepdale was Christopher Isherwood, and then had a surprisingly good time while they all talked about *Mr. Norris Changes Trains* and *Goodbye to Berlin* and their author, whom Roddy and Buzz considered a cherished friend. It was the first time in his life he had had such a conversation with any adults, and the first proof he'd ever had that literate conversation was a possibility at Eagle Lake, but he left bothered by the feeling that he had missed something crucial, or failed to ask some important question, during his talk with Kate Redwing.

When he got back inside his grandfather's lodge, he tried to write another letter to Lamont von Heilitz, but soon ran dry—he did not really have anything new to tell him, except that he wondered if he should not just go back to Mill Walk and start thinking seriously about becoming an engineer after all. He wondered how his mother was getting on, and if he could do anything to help her if he were at home. Home, just now, did not seem much more homelike than Glendenning Upshaw's lodge.

He took a shower, wrapped a towel around himself, and instead of going immediately back into his bedroom to get dressed, walked past the staircase to Barbara Deane's room. He opened her door and stepped inside the threshold.

It was a neat, almost stripped-down room, two or three times the size of his, with a double bed and a view of the lake through a large window. A half-open door revealed a tiled bathroom floor and the edge of a white tub with claw feet and a drawn shower curtain. The closet doors were shut. A bare desk stood against one wall, and a framed photograph hung above it like an icon. Tom took three steps closer and saw that it was an enlarged photograph of his grandfather, young, his hair slicked back, giving the camera a thousand-candlepower smile that the expression in his eyes made forced and unnatural. He was holding Gloria, four or five years old, in his arms—the chubby, ringleted Gloria Tom had seen in a newspaper photograph. She was smiling as if ordered to smile, and what Tom thought he saw in her face was fear. He stepped nearer and looked more closely, feeling his own vague sorrow tighten itself around him, and saw that it was not fear, but terror so habitual and familiar that even the photographer who had just shouted "Smile!" had not seen it.

40

Marcello led Tom to the table near the bandstand, dropped the menu in his lap as if he were radioactive, and spun around on his heel to inquire after the Redwings. Buddy scowled, Kip Carson blinked at him through a fog of Baby Dollies, and Ralph and Katinka never saw him at all. Aunt Kate's back was to him, and Sarah Spence sat a mile away, at one of the tables closest to the bar. Mrs. Spence gave him one obsidian glance, then ostentatiously ignored him and spoke in a high-pitched voice that was supposed to show what a good time she was having. Occasional words floated to Tom: *trout*, *waterskis*, *relaxed*. Sarah turned on her chair to send him a fellow-prisoner look, but her mother snapped her back with a sharp word. Neil Langenheim barely nodded at Tom—he sat upright on his chair, tucked in his chin, and despite the red raw skin on his nose and forehead, looked as rigid and contained as he did on Mill Walk. Only Roddy and Buzz were friendly, but they talked without a pause, in a way that suggested that this night's conversation was one segment of a lifelong dialogue that both of them found amusing and engrossing. They were the best couple in the room. Tom sat at his table and read, wondering how he would get through the rest of the summer.

The Langenheims left; the Spences bustled Sarah away; Roddy and Buzz left. Ralph Redwing glanced sideways at Tom, frozen-faced. Tom closed the Agatha Christie book, signed the check the elderly waiter slid on a corner of the table, and walked out of the dining room with the back of his neck tingling.

Huge clouds scudded across the moon.

He had forgotten to leave lights on in the lodge, and he groped around the big sitting room, walking into furniture that seemed to have moved and changed places while he was gone. Then his hand found a lampshade, his fingers met the cord, and the room came into being again, just as it had been before. He fell onto a couch. After a moment he got up and turned on another light. Then he stretched out on the couch again and read a few more pages of *The ABC Murders*. He remembered being dissatisfied with it yesterday, but could not remember why—it was a perfect book. It made you feel better, like a fuzzy blanket and a glass of warm milk. A kind of simple clarity shone through everything and everybody, and the obstacles to that clarity were only screens that could be rolled away by the famous little grey cells. You never got the feeling that a real darkness surrounded anyone, not even murderers.

Tom realized that Lamont von Heilitz had begun talking about Eagle Lake the first night they had met—almost as soon as Tom had walked in the door, von Heilitz had brought out his old book of clippings and turned the pages, saying *here* and *here* and *here*.

Tom swung his legs off the couch and stood up. He tossed the book down and went into his grandfather's study. Light from the big sitting room touched the hooked rug and the edge of the desk. Tom turned on the lamp beside the desk and sat behind it. He pulled the telephone closer to him. Then he lifted the receiver, dialed 0, and asked the operator if she could connect him to Lamont von Heilitz's number on Mill Walk.

She told him to hold the line. Tom turned to the window and saw his face and his dark blue sweater printed on the glass. "Your party does not answer at this time, sir," the operator told him. Tom placed the receiver back on the cradle.

He placed his hands on either side of the phone and stared at it. The telephone shrilled, and he knocked the receiver off the hook when he jumped. He fumbled for it, and finally put it to his ear.

"Hello," he said.

"What's going on up there?" his grandfather roared.

"Hello, Grand-Dad," he said.

"Hello, nothing. I sent you up there to enjoy yourself and get to know the right people, not so you could seduce Buddy Redwing's fiancée! And go around pumping people for information about some ancient business that doesn't concern you, not in the least!"

"Grand-Dad—" Tom said.

"And break into the Redwing compound and go snooping around with your popsy! Don't you know better than that?"

"I didn't break in anywhere. Sarah thought I might like to see—"

"Is her last name Redwing? If it isn't, she doesn't have any right to take you into that compound, because she doesn't have any right to go in there herself. You grew up on Eastern Shore Road, you went to the right school, you ought to know how to conduct yourself." He paused for breath. "And on top of everything else, on your first day there, you go into town and strike up a relationship with Sam Hamilton's son!"

"I was interested in—"

"I won't even mention your consorting with that nauseating queer, Roddy Deepdale, who ruined the lot next to mine, but I wonder what you thought you'd accomplish by physically assaulting a member of the Redwing family."

"I didn't assault him," Tom said.

"You hit him, didn't you? Frankly, once you got to Eagle Lake you set about destroying most of what I've been building up during my lifetime."

"So do you want me to come home?"

His grandfather did not speak.

Tom repeated the question. All he heard was his grandfather's breathing.

"Sarah Spence isn't going to marry Buddy Redwing," he said. "Nobody can make her do that—she isn't going to let herself be *bought*."

"I'm sure you're right," his grandfather said. His voice was surprisingly mild. "Tell me, what do you see when you look out the window, this time of night? I always liked nights up at Eagle Lake."

Tom leaned forward to try to see through his reflection. "It's pretty dark right now, and—"

The lamp beside the desk exploded, and something slammed into the wall or the floor with a sound like a brick falling on concrete. The chair shot out from beneath him, and he landed hard on the floor in the dark. His feet were tangled up in the legs of the chair, and small pieces of glass glinted up from the floor all around him. Other shreds of glass had fallen into his hair. His breath sounded as loud as a freight train chugging up a grade, and for a moment he could not move. He heard his grandfather's tinny voice coming through the phone, saying "Tom? Are you there? Are you there?"

He untangled his feet from the chair and raised his head above the top of the desk. One light burned in the Langenheim lodge. Cool air streamed through an empty hole that had once been an upper pane.

"Can you hear me?" came the shrunken, metallic sound of his grandfather's voice.

Tom snatched at the phone and pressed it to his face. A sliver of glass fell from his hair onto his wrist. "Hey," he said.

"Are you all right? Did something happen?"

"I guess I'm all right." He brushed the sparkling shred of glass off his wrist, then looked out at the still lake and the light in the Langenheims' lodge.

"Tell me what happened," his grandfather said.

"Somebody shot through the window," Tom said.

"Are you hit?"

"No. I don't think so. No. I'm just, ah, I'm just—I don't know."

"Did you see anybody?"

"No. There's nobody out there."

"Are you sure about what happened?"

"I'm not sure about anything," Tom said. "Somebody almost shot me. The lamp blew up. Part of the window's broken."

"I'll tell you what happened. Men from the town sometimes prowl through the woods, seeing if they can get an out of season deer. I remember hearing a lot of gunshots, up there. Hunters."

Tom remembered Lamont von Heilitz saying something similar, that first night in his house.

"Hunters," he said.

"One of them got off a wild shot. They'll be long gone by now. How do you feel now?"

"Kind of shaky."

"But you're okay."

"Yeah. Yes."

"I don't think there's any reason to call the police, unless you think you have to. After all, not much damage was done. The hunters will be halfway to the village by now. And the police up there never were much good."

"Somebody shot at me!" Tom said. "You don't think I should call the police?"

"I'm just trying to protect you. There's a whole history you don't know about, Tom." His grandfather was breathing heavily, and his voice was slow and heavy. "As you proved by going to see Sam Hamilton."

"Chet Hamilton," Tom said. "His son."

"*Chet* Hamilton! I don't care! You're not listening to me!" His grandfather's voice had turned ragged. "It's not like Mill Walk—the police are not on your side up there."

Tom almost laughed. Everything was upside down.

"Did you hear me?" his grandfather asked.

"I'm going to call the police now."

"Call me back when they leave," his grandfather said, and hung up.

Tom replaced the receiver and stood up by inches, looking out of the window as he did so. His bottom ached from the fall. He rubbed the sore place, and then righted the chair and sat on it. The head of the lamp lolled toward him, and a small ragged hole perforated the shade. He touched the hole, and then looked down sideways at the juncture of the floor and the wall. Without the light, he could see only shadows where the bullet must have stopped. He wanted to turn on the other lamp in the room, but his legs would not let him get out of the chair. His blood made a tidal sound in his ears. Tom tilted the chair and looked up into the lamp. The bulb had disappeared, and the twisted socket canted over like a broken neck.

His grandfather had saved his life.

Then he could stand again, and he pushed himself away from the desk and turned on the lamp across the room. One small windowpane was broken, and the top of the lamp beside the desk lolled like a broken flower. A glitter of broken glass lay across the desk. Tom turned on the deck lights with the switch inside the back door, and the window lit up and the lake disappeared. He went back to the desk and looked down—he thought he would find a smashed hole, broken boards, and shattered molding, but at first saw nothing at all, and then only something that looked like a shadow, and then at last a neat hole in the wooden wall, eight or nine inches above the molding.

In ten minutes someone knocked at the front door. Tom peered out and saw the blond policeman who had arrested the drunk on Main Street. "Mr. Pasmore?" he said. His police car had been pulled up in front of the lodge, and all its lights were turned off—Tom had expected a siren and flashing lights. "You're the person who called? I'm Officer Spychalla."

Tom stepped back and let him in.

"I understand you had some trouble. Show me where it happened, and then I'll take some information." Spychalla looked as if he were straining out of his uniform, stretching the dark blue cloth and the taut black leather. His belt creaked when he moved.

He gave the office a quick inspection, made some notes in a small ringbound notebook, and asked, "Where were you sitting at the time of the incident?"

"At the desk, talking on the telephone," Tom said.

Spychalla nodded, walked around the desk, looked at the lamp and the bullet hole, and then went out on the deck to see the window from the outside. He came back and made more notes. "There was only the single shot?"

"Isn't that enough?"

Spychalla raised his eyebrows and flipped to a new page in his notebook. "You're from Mill Walk? What are your age and occupation?"

"Officer, don't you think you should send some men up into the woods, and see if you can find who shot at me?"

"Your full-time residence is on the island of Mill Walk? What are your age and occupation?" His jaw was as square as a box, and the point of the pencil above the clean sheet of paper was perfectly sharp.

"I live on Mill Walk, I'm seventeen, I'm a student."

Spychalla raised his eyebrows again. "Date of birth?"

"Is that going to help you?" Spychalla waited with his pencil in his hand, and Tom gave his birth date.

"This lodge, are you staying here by yourself? What I know about this place is, it belongs to a man named Upshaw."

Tom explained that Mr. Upshaw was his grandfather.

"Sounds like a pretty good deal," Spychalla said. "You get to shack up here by yourself all summer, drink a lot of beer and chase girls, is that it?"

Tom began to think that his grandfather had been right about calling the police. Spychalla was giving him a hard little smile that was supposed to communicate a total understanding of the pleasures of being seventeen and alone for the summer. "Some of you kids get up to a pretty wild time, I guess."

"I guess you could say that being shot at is pretty wild."

Spychalla closed his notebook and put it back in his hip pocket. He still had the little smile on his face. "Shook you up a little."

Tom sat down behind the desk. "Aren't you going to do anything?"

"I'm going to explain something to you." Spychalla stepped nearer the desk. "You got a screwdriver or something like that? A long knife?"

Tom looked at him, trying to figure out what this request was about. Spychalla put his arms behind his back and did something with his arm and chest muscles that made his uniform creak.

Tom went into the kitchen and came back with a screwdriver. Spychalla went down on the toes of his boots and began to dig away the wood surrounding the shell. "People ain't supposed to hunt deer in the summer, but they do. Same way as they ain't supposed to get drunk and drive, but they do that too. Sometimes they go out at night and jacklight 'em." He slammed the screwdriver into the wall and chipped out a jagged piece of wood. "We arrest 'em when we catch 'em, but you can't always catch 'em. There's only me and Chief Truehart on the force full time, and a part-time deputy in the summer. Now one of the places these people know they can find deer is the woods around this lake, and sometimes we get calls from you people saying you hear shots at night. We run over here, but we know we ain't gonna find anybody, because all *they* have to do is turn off their lights." He slammed the screwdriver into the wall. "If they drive, we can get 'em when they come back to their cars, but plenty of times they walk—hide their deer until the next day, sneak it back into town under a tarp on the back of a pickup. Here we go." He twiddled the screwdriver in the enlarged hole, jerked it backwards, and a black lump of metal clattered to the floor. Spychalla buttoned it into one of his shirt pockets and stood up. His uniform shirt was so tight Tom could see his muscles move.

"So I could go out there and root through the woods, but I'd be wasting my time. There's a village ordinance stating that hunters are not permitted to discharge weapons within two hundred and fifty feet of a dwelling. Now let's think about where this came from." He grinned, and looked like a handsome robot. He walked to the far end of the desk and pointed to the broken glass. "It came in here, busted this lamp, and hit the wall—slanting downwards. So the rifle was probably fired from way up above one of those lodges on the other side of the lake. The man who fired the rifle didn't have no idea in *hell* where his bullet went. Every summer and fall, we get complaints from people whose lodges are hit by bullets—not a lot of 'em, but one or two. The funny thing is, this guy could have been a quarter mile away from you."

"What if it wasn't a hunter," Tom said, "but someone who was trying to shoot me?"

"Look, I can't blame you for getting excited," the policeman said. "But if a guy with a high-powered rifle was trying to kill you, he'd a done it. Even if it was dark in here, he'd a put a couple more bullets through that window. I'm telling you, this happens about once every summer. You're just the closest anybody came to getting hit."

And you're friendly Officer Spychalla, who doesn't really mind that the Mill Walk people get an accidental bullet coming their way once a summer or so, Tom thought. "Somebody pushed me off the sidewalk into traffic the other day," he said. "In town."

"Did you file a complaint?"

Tom shook his head.

"Did you see anybody?"

"No."

"Probably an accident, just like this. Some fat old tourist turned around and hit you with a hip the size of a front-loader."

"Probably if I was dead, you'd investigate a little harder," Tom said.

Spychalla gave him the robot smile. "What do you hunt down there on that island you live on, rum drinks?"

"It's not that kind of island," Tom said. "We mainly hunt policemen."

Spychalla slapped his pockets and marched toward the door, boots and Sam Browne belt creaking magnificently, his service revolver riding massively on his hip. He looked like a huge blond horse. "I'll file a report, sir. If you're worried about a recurrence of this incident, stay away from your windows at night."

He clumped down the steps to his patrol car.

A male voice came out of the dark. "Officer?" Sarah's father stepped into the ring of light on Tom's front steps, looking like someone used to being obeyed by policemen. He was wearing pajamas and a grey bathrobe. "Is this young man in any trouble?"

Spychalla said, "Go back to your lodge, sir. All the excitement is over."

Mr. Spence glared exasperatedly at Tom, then back at Spychalla, whose face made it clear that he had seen a lot of exasperation. He got in his car and slammed the door.

Mr. Spence put his hands on his hips and watched the headlights moving down the track. Then he turned around and tried to kill Tom with a look. "You are not to bother my daughter anymore. From now on there will be no communication between you and Sarah. Is that understood?" His big belly moved up and down under his shirt as he yelled.

Tom went inside and closed the door. He walked across the sitting room and went into the study. He realized that he was framed in the window, and his stomach froze and his blood stopped moving. Then he began sweeping broken glass off the desk into the wastebasket. After that he searched around the kitchen for a whisk broom and a dustpan, found them in a closet, and took them into the study to sweep the rest of the glass up from the floor.

He was returning the broom and the dustpan when he heard the telephone ringing, and he set them down on the table and returned to the study. He moved out of the line of the window and pulled back the chair. Then he sat down and answered the phone.

"This is Tom," he said.

"Are they still there?" his grandfather asked in a voice just below a bellow.

"He. There was one cop. He's gone."

"I told you to call me when they left!"

"Well, I had to do a few things," Tom said. "He just left a minute ago. He said what you said. It was a stray bullet."

"Of course it was. I told you that. Anyhow, thinking about it, I decided you were right to call the police. No question about it. Are you feeling better now?"

"Kind of."

"Go to bed early. Get some rest. In the morning, you'll see this in perspective. I won't tell your mother about this, and I forbid you to write anything to her that might upset her."

"Okay," Tom said. "Does that mean that you don't want me to come back right away?"

"Come back? Of course you shouldn't come back! You have some fence-mending to do, young man. I want you to stay up there until I tell you it's time to come back." Glendenning Upshaw went on to deliver a lengthy speech about respect and responsibility.

When he finished, Tom decided to see where one question would lead. "Grand-Dad, who was Anton Goetz? I've been hearing—"

"He was nothing. He did a bad thing once, and he was found out, and he killed himself. Committed a murder, if you want the specifics."

"On the plane up here, Mr. Spence wanted to tell me that you had done him some big favors—"

Upshaw grunted.

"—and he happened to mention this Anton Goetz, who he said was an accountant—"

"You want to know about him? I'll tell you about him, and then the subject is closed. You understand me?" Tom did not speak. "Anton Goetz was a little man with a bad leg who got in way over his head because he couldn't control his fantasies. He told everybody a lot of lies, me included, because he wanted social success. I tried to help him out because like a lot of con men, Anton Goetz had a lot of charm. I gave him a job, and I even helped him look more important than he was. It was the last time in my life I ever made a mistake like that. He got up to something with Arthur Thielman's first wife, and imagined it was much more than it was, and when she put him in his place he killed her. Then he killed himself, like the coward he really was. I held his properties for a long time because I wanted the stench of his memory to go away, and then I sold them to Bill Spence."

"So he really was an accountant," Tom said.

"Not a very good one. Come to think of it, Bill Spence wasn't brilliant either, which was why I let Ralph hire him away from me. And now Bill Spence is aiming for the same social success Anton Goetz wanted, but he's using his daughter to get it, not his prick. I hope my language doesn't shock you."

Tom said that he was grateful for his frankness.

"These men want what you had handed to you on a plate," said his grandfather. "Now get some sleep and tomorrow try to act like you know how to behave. Let's get everything sorted out by the end of summer."

Tom asked about his mother, and his grandfather said that she was doing better—almost off medication. He promised to give her Tom's love, and Tom promised to write to her.

The light in Neil Langenheim's bedroom went out, and a thin yellow trace disappeared from the lake. The big lodges across the lake had retreated into the overhanging trees, and uncanny light from the black and silver sky touched the ends of the docks, the tops of railings, and sifting leaves.

Through the broken window, the smells of pine and fresh water came to him wrapped in cool air, along with some other, deeper odor from the marshy end of the lake and the pilings beneath the docks, from the soft earth and the wet reeds and the fish that moved or slept deep in the water.

Tom felt a tremor deep within him that was like a tremor in the silvery, sleeping world beyond the window. He got up and walked through the ground floor of the lodge, turning off the lights. He undressed, went to bed, and lay awake most of the night.

41

Someone knocked on the door soon after Tom got up the next morning, and when he peered around it, hoping that Sarah Spence had managed to slip away from her parents, he saw a police car and another blue uniform. A man in his early thirties with straight shiny black hair that seemed too long for a policeman looked at him through the screen and said, "Mr. Pasmore? Tom Pasmore?" He looked both friendly and slightly familiar. Tom let him in, and realized that he looked a great deal like the Eagle Lake mailman. He was at least ten years older than he had looked at first—close up, Tom saw deep crow's feet, and a little grey swept back beneath the hair that fell past his temples.

"I'm Tim Truehart, the Chief of Police," he said, and shook Tom's hand. "I read the report about the shot that came in here last night, and I thought I'd better come out here and take a look for myself. Despite whatever impression you may have gotten from Officer Spychalla, we don't like it when people shoot at our summer residents."

"He was pretty casual about it," Tom said.

"My deputy has his good points, but investigations may not be one of them. He's very good at handling drunks and shoplifters, and he's hell on speeders." Truehart was looking around the sitting room as he spoke, smiling easily, taking everything in. "I'd have come myself, but I was out of town for most of the night. They don't pay the Chief much money up here, and I fly a little on the side."

Then Tom remembered. "I saw you at the airport when I came in—you were sitting against the wall in the customs shed, and you were wearing a brown leather jacket."

"You'd make a good witness," Truehart said, and smiled at him. "Were you alone in the lodge when the shot entered?"

Tom said he was.

"It's a good thing Barbara Deane wasn't here—Barbara had an unpleasant experience a couple of weeks ago, and getting shot at wouldn't help her recovery. How do you feel?"

"I'm okay."

"You had my deputy to reckon with, as well as everything else. You must be made of tough stuff." He laughed. "Would you show me where it happened?"

Tom took him into the study, and Truehart looked carefully at the broken window, the lamp, and the hole in the wall where his deputy had dug out the bullet. He went outside and looked across the lake at the wooded hill above the empty Harbinger lodge. Then he came back inside.

"Show me where you were sitting."

Tom sat behind the desk.

"Tell me about it," Truehart said. "Were you writing something, or reading, or looking out at the lake, or what?"

Tom said that he had been talking on the telephone to his grandfather, and that the shot had come just after he bent over to look out to see the lake, so that he could describe it.

"You didn't move anything?"

"Just swept up some broken glass."

"Was the lamp the only light showing in the room?"

"It was probably the only light showing on the whole lake."

Truehart nodded, and walked to the side of the desk and again looked carefully at the window, the lamp, and the place where the bullet struck the wall. "Show me how you bent to look out of the window." He walked backwards away from the desk as Tom showed him what he had done, and sat down on the couch against the wall. He joined his fingers and leaned forward on his elbows. "And you did that right when it happened?"

"The lamp exploded as soon as I bent over."

"It's a good thing you leaned down like that." Tom's stomach felt as if he had swallowed soap. "I don't like this much." Truehart was looking at him somberly, almost meditatively, as if he were listening to something Tom could not hear. "I don't suppose you've seen any high-powered rifles around here in the past few days."

Tom shook his head.

"And I don't suppose you know of anybody who'd have a reason to try to kill you."

Startled, Tom said, "I thought hunters shot stray bullets toward the lodges once or twice a year."

"Well, maybe not quite that often, but it happens. Last year, someone shot out a window in the club from up on that hillside. And two years before that, a bullet hit the back of the Jacobs lodge in the middle of a nice June night. People around here got excited, and I don't blame them, but nobody even came close to getting hit. And here you are, framed in this window like a target. I don't want to make you nervous, but I can't say I like it, not a bit."

"Buddy Redwing is pissed off at me because his girlfriend turns out to like me better," Tom said. "He was planning to get married to her. In fact, his family is pissed off at me too, and so is hers. But I don't think any of them would try to kill me. Buddy tried to beat me up yesterday, and I hit him in the stomach, and that was the end of that. I don't think he'd climb a hillside with a rifle and try to shoot me through a window."

"You have to be sober to do that," Truehart said. "Which more or less lets Buddy out." He pursed his lips and looked down at his hands. "Spychalla is up in the woods now, looking for anything he can find, shell casings, cigarette butts, anything that would be around where the shooter had to be. But realistically, the most we can hope for is some idea about what kind of rifle he had. You don't find footprints up there, not with that kind of ground cover."

"You don't think it was a stray shot from a hunter?" Tom asked.

"The odds are, that's what it was. But a lot of stuff has been happening on Eagle Lake lately." He let this sink in. "And you're not just an ordinary summer visitor."

These men wanted what you had handed to you on a plate, Tom remembered.

Truehart said, "I can't pretend to understand what's going on there, but *something* sure as hell is getting stirred up. And I have to consider that somebody might be getting at your grandfather through you."

"My grandfather and I aren't very close."

"That might not make any difference. I can't offer you any extra protection, but I think you ought to be careful about staying away from windows. In fact, you ought to be careful in general—Spychalla told me that you claim to have been pushed into the traffic on Main Street last Friday. Maybe you shouldn't go too many places alone for the next couple of weeks. And maybe Barbara Deane ought to spend more nights here with you. Do you want me to talk to her about it?"

"I could do it," Tom said.

"She likes her privacy, but right now she might want some company."

"There is one other thing," Tom said. "It's connected to her. I know there have been break-ins around this area in the past few years. I don't know if you've thought about this or not, but Ralph Redwing's bodyguards have a lot of nights and evenings free, and before they started working for Ralph, they called themselves the Cornerboys and did a lot of stealing. I think they did some burglaries on Mill Walk, and I think—" He decided not to mention Wendell Hasek, and instead said, "I think Jerry Hasek, the one who's sort of the leader, enjoys killing animals. I know he killed a dog when he was a teenager, and Barbara Deane's dog was killed, and the other day I saw him go nuts in the Lincoln when Robbie Wintergreen, one of the bodyguards, said the word dog in front of me."

"Well, well," Truehart said. "Do these people live in the compound?"

"In a house by themselves."

"I can't go in there, of course, unless I'm invited or can persuade a judge to give me a search warrant. But do you think they'd take the risk of storing stolen goods in the compound, where they'd have to carry them in and out right under Ralph Redwing's nose? Unless you think Ralph Redwing is getting a cut."

"No," Tom said. "I think I know where they put the stuff."

"This is getting better and better. Where is it?"

Tom told him about seeing the light moving around von Heilitz's lodge, following it up the path in the woods, getting lost, and finding the path the next day. Tim Truehart leaned forward on his elbows and listened to Tom's story with a bemused expression on his face. And when Tom described the house in the clearing and the skinny old woman who had come out carrying a rifle, he put his hands over his face and leaned back against the couch.

"What's wrong?" Tom asked.

Truehart lowered his hands. "Well, I'll have to ask my mother if she's storing stolen goods for a guy named Jerry Hasek." He was grinning. "But she'd probably hit me over the head with a frying pan if I did."

"Your mother," Tom said. "Mrs. Truehart. Who used to clean the houses around here during the summers. Oh, my God."

"That's her. She probably thought you were checking out her house for a robbery."

"Oh, my God," Tom said again. "I apologize."

"No need." Truehart laughed out loud—he seemed vastly amused. "If it was me, I'd probably have done the same thing. I'll tell you one thing, though, I'm glad you didn't say anything about this to Spychalla. He'd be talking about it until his jaw wore out." He stood up. "Well, I guess we're through for now." He was still grinning. "If we find anything up in the woods, I'll tell you about it. And I do want you to be careful. That's serious."

They left the study, and walked across the sitting room to the front door.

"Give me a call if you see this Hasek character do anything out of the ordinary. He might be a live one. And try to spend as much time as possible with other people."

Truehart held out his hand, and Tom shook it. The policeman

pulled a pair of wire-rimmed sunglasses from his shirt pocket and put them on as he trotted down the steps. He got into his car and backed down the track toward the club the way Spychalla had done. Tom stood on the steps and watched him drive away; he was grinning until his face was only a dark blob behind the windshield.

42

Roddy and Buzz unexpectedly decided to spend Buzz's last week of vacation with friends in the south of France, and the dinner Tom ate with them on the night before their departure seemed to him like the last friendly encounter he would be likely to have at Eagle Lake. The Redwings came late to the club and left early, and acknowledged no one but Marcello, who was a pet of Katinka's. The Spences occupied their table near the bar, and kept Sarah's back to Tom as they talked to each other in the loudest voices in the room, demonstrating that they were having a good time, the summer had just begun, and everything would turn out for the best. Neil and Bitsy Langenheim stared at Tom as he walked in with Roddy and Buzz, and whispered to each other like conspirators.

"Everybody knows that the police paid a couple of social calls to your lodge," Roddy said. "They're all hoping you've landed yourself in desperate trouble, so they will have something to talk about the rest of the summer."

"A hunter fired a stray shot through one of my windows,"

Tom said, and caught the sharp, questioning look that passed between his two new friends.

"Is your whole life like this?" Roddy asked him, and Tom said he was beginning to wonder.

So they talked for a time about other times hunters had come too near the lodges around the lake, and from there went on to the tension that had always existed between the village and the summer people from Mill Walk, and finally got to the subject most in their minds, their impulsive trip to France; but another, unspoken subject seemed to underlie everything they said.

"Marc and Brigitte have a wonderful villa right on the Mediterranean near Antibes, and Paulo and Yves live only a few kilometers away, and some friends of ours from London are coming down because their children have suddenly decided to become followers of a guru at an ashram in Poona, so even though it's a bit extravagant, we thought we should make a party of it for a week. Then I'll fly back to Mill Walk with Buzz and take care of some business for another couple of weeks before I go to London to see Monserrat Caballé and Bergonzi in *La Traviata* at Covent Garden. I don't think I'll be able to get back here until August."

Buzz would miss Caballé and Bergonzi at Covent Garden, but he would get to Paris in time for the *Carmelites*, and in October there was Hector and Will and Nina and Guy and Samantha in Cadaques, and in March there was a chance of Arthur and whoever it was now in Formentera, and after that . . .

After that there was, there would be, more. Roddy Deepdale and Buzz Laing (for that was Buzz's name, he was Dr. Laing at St. Mary Nieves and to his patients, who knew nothing of his peripatetic, well-furnished life) had friends all over the world, they were always welcome, they were always informed, they had favorite seats at their favorite opera house, La Scala, from which they had seen every Verdi opera except *Stiffelio* and *Aroldo*, favorite meals in favorite restaurants in a dozen cities, they cherished the Vermeers and the Rembrandt self-portrait at the Frick, they knew a psychiatrist in London who was the second most intelligent person in the world and a poet in New York who was the third most intelligent person in the world, they loved and needed their friends and their friends loved and needed them. Tom felt provincial, narrow, raw, beside them: the whisper of judgment in the glance he had seen pass between Roddy and Buzz separated him from them as finally as he had been separated from the Redwings, who were pushing back their chairs and preparing to leave, encased in the bubble of their insular importance.

But Kate Redwing came over to say hello and goodbye in the same breath: she, too, was leaving tomorrow; her allotted two weeks were up and she was going back to Atlanta and her grandchildren. All three at the table hugged her, and when she heard of their plans she said they ought to take Tom with them, and Roddy and Buzz smiled politely and said they wished they could, but they would make sure to see plenty of him on Mill Walk. Tom tried to imagine what these two men would say about Victor Pasmore, and what Victor Pasmore would say about them. Kate Redwing embraced him again, and whispered, *"Don't give up! Be strong!"* She turned away to follow her family down the stairs, moving away past the Spences' empty table with hesitant, old-lady steps in her print dress and flat black shoes. A few minutes later, Roddy signed for their meal, and they left too.

They dropped Tom off at his lodge and promised to invite him for dinner when they were back on the island—"as soon as things settle down."

Tom called Lamont von Heilitz later that night, but again was told that his party did not answer. He stayed up late reading, and went to bed feeling desolate.

The next morning curtains covered the big lakeside windows in the Deepdale lodge. A glazier came from the village to replace the broken pane in his grandfather's study and said, "A kid like you must have a lot of fun in a place like this by himself."

Tom swam in the mornings, walked around and around the lake, finished *The ABC Murders* and read Iris Murdoch's *Under The Net* and *Flight from the Enchanter*. He ate alone. Sarah's parents did not join the Redwings at the bar before dinners, and Sarah did no more than give him a regretful, chastened glance before her mother snapped her back with a sharp word. He swam for hours every afternoon, and twice Buddy Redwing took out his motorboat and wheeled back and forth in figure eights up at the north end while Tom breast-stroked and side-stroked between the docks on the south end. Kip Carson sat open-mouthed beside Buddy the first time, Kip and Sarah Spence together on one of the rear seats the second. Tom walked to the village and found a rack of paperbacks beside the *I Pine Fir Yew* ashtrays in the Indian Trading Post. He carried home a stack of books and called his mother, who said she wasn't getting out much, but Dr. Milton was taking care of her. Victor had been offered a job with the Redwings—she wasn't too sure what the job involved, but he would have to travel a lot, and he was very excited. She hoped Tom was meeting people and enjoying himself, and he said yes, he was.

Certain rules governed his conversations with his mother—he suddenly saw this. The truth could never be spoken: kindly, murderous hypocrisy was the law of life. It was a cage.

The days went by. Lamont von Heilitz never answered his telephone. Barbara Deane came and went, in too much of a hurry and too self-absorbed to talk to him. Tom could not get Sarah Spence out of his mind, and some of the things Buddy had said came back to torture him. He swam so much that night he dropped instantly into dreamless sleep, forgetting even the ache in his muscles.

On the fifth day after the bullet had exploded through the window, he was sitting on a rock at the edge of the woods where the private road to the lake came out to the highway and saw Kip Carson walking toward him, strapped into a backpack and dragging a duffel bag behind him. "Hey, man," Kip Carson said. "I'm on my way, man, it was really fun and everything, but I'm gone."

"Where?"

"Airport. I have to hitch. Ralph wouldn't let me get a ride, and Buddy didn't give a shit. Buddy's an asshole, man."

Tom asked him if he were going back to Tucson.

"Tucson? No way, no *fuckin'* way. Schenectady—my old lady mailed me a ticket. Do you think there's a barbershop at the airport? I gotta get a haircut before I get back home."

"I didn't see one," Tom said.

"Well, it's been grins." Kip flashed him a V with two fingers, hoisted his duffel, and went out to stand by the side of the highway. The second car that passed picked him up.

Tom walked back to the lodge.

On Saturday, the pain over Sarah Spence's absence still so constant as to feel like mourning, rejection, and humiliation joined together, he realized that he had been waiting for Tim Truehart to come back to tell him about whatever Spychalla had found in the woods. He had liked Truehart, and thought about calling him up as he swam back and forth between the empty docks. Of course Spychalla found nothing, and of course Truehart had other things to do. Then he realized that the reason he was thinking about Eagle Lake's police chief was that he missed Lamont von Heilitz. He climbed up on his dock, went inside the lodge, dressed, and sat down on the couch in the study to write out everything he knew about Jeanine Thielman's murder. He read what he had written, remembered more, and wrote it all over again in a different way.

His mind seemed to awaken.

And then the events of forty summers past became his occupation, his obsession, his salvation. He still swam in the mornings and afternoons, but while he swam he saw Jeanine Thielman standing in pale cold moonlight on her dock, and Anton Goetz in a white dinner jacket—looking like Humphrey Bogart in *Casablanca*—limping toward her, bowing in a parody of gallantry when he leaned on his cane and swung his useless leg. Tom still walked around and around the lake, but saw a cloud of Redwings in tennis sweaters and white dresses, chattering about the young woman from Atlanta Jonathan had decided to marry. He sat on his dock, seeing the bulllike figure of the young widower who was his grandfather walk slowly back and forth across the planks, his hand gripping the much smaller hand of a little girl in ringlets and a sailor dress.

Any event is altered by the perspective from which it is seen, and for days Tom replayed the events and circumstances of Jeanine Thielman's murder. He wrote about it in the third person and in the first, imagining that he were Arthur Thielman, Jeanine Thielman, Anton Goetz, his grandfather, even trying to see those events through the eyes on the anguished child who had been his mother. He played with dates and times; he decided to throw out everything he had been told about these people's motives and experiment with new ones. He saw gaps and holes in what he had been told, and prowled through them, following his instincts and his imagination as he had followed Hattie Bascombe through the courts and passages of Maxwell's Heaven. Here was his grandfather, just beginning to solidify his relationship with the Redwings and insure both his financial and social future; here was Anton Goetz, a "con man" who charmed women and men with stories about a romantic past and shielded Glendenning Upshaw's connection to the St. Alwyn hotel and the secret, unseen parts of Mill Walk; here was Lamont von Heilitz, seeing the world begin to come to life around him again.

He dreamed of bodies rising like smoke from the lake, raising their arms above their dripping heads and hovering in place with open eyes and mouths—he dreamed he walked through a forest to a clearing where a great hairy monster, of a size that made his own height a little child's, bit the head off a woman's white body and turned to him with a mouth full of bone and gore and said, *"I am your father, Thomas. See what I am?"*

One night he awoke knowing that his mother had picked up the gun on the deckside table and shot Jeanine Thielman—*that* was why her father had hidden her in Barbara Deane's house, *that* was why she screamed at night, *that* was why her father had sold her into marriage to a man paid to be her nursemaid. Another sleepless night: but in the morning, he could not believe this version, either.

Or could he?

If his mother had killed Jeanine Thielman, Glendenning Upshaw would not have hesitated to kill to protect her. *I am your father. See what I am?*

For most of another week, he was alone without being lonely: he imagined himself into the men and women who had come to Eagle Lake in 1925, and felt their shades and shadows around him, each with his own, her own, plots and desires and fantasies. He began sitting at the desk again during the day and at night, forgetting Tim Truehart's advice, and no bullets exploded through the glass; it had been a hunter's bullet after all, and he was not a potential victim. He was—it came to him at last—Lamont von Heilitz.

One night at dinner, he went up to the Spence table and ignored the glares to ask Mr. Spence how Jerry Hasek and the other two bodyguards were listed in the books. "Leave us alone," Mrs. Spence ordered, and Sarah gave him an urgent, irritated look he could not fathom.

"I don't know what business it is of yours, but I can't see any harm in telling you. They're listed as public relations assistants."

Tom thanked him, heard Mrs. Spence say, "Why did you tell him *anything*?" and went back to his book and his dinner.

On the Friday of the second week after Roddy and Buzz left the lake, Barbara Deane came in after her morning ride and found him lying on a sofa in the sitting room, holding a pen in his mouth like a cigar and squinting up at a sheet of paper covered with his own writing. "I hope you won't mind," she said, "but you'll have to eat lunch at the club today. I forgot to buy sandwich things, and we're all out."

"That's okay," he said.

She went upstairs. He heard her door close. The lock on the inside of the door slid into its catch. After a minute or two, water began drumming in her shower. Still later, her closet door creaked and something scraped along a shelf. Fifteen minutes later, she came downstairs changed into her black skirt and a dark red blouse he had not seen before. "Since I have to shop," she said, "I could pick up some extra things for dinner."

"That'd be nice," he said.

"What I mean is, you could come to my house for dinner tonight, Tom."

"Oh!" He swung his legs over the side of the sofa and sat up, sending dozens of yellow legal-sized papers sliding to the floor. "Thanks! I'd like that."

"You'll come?" He nodded, and she said, "I'm going to be busy today, so if you wouldn't mind walking to town, I'll drive you back after dinner."

"Great."

She smiled at him. "I don't know what you're doing, but you look like you could use a break. I'm on Oak Street, the first right off Main Street as you come in, and it's the fourth house down on the right—number fifteen. Come around six."

This reminder that other people met for dinner, had normal lives and saw their friends, made him impatient with his own loneliness. He swam for an hour in the morning, and saw Sarah's father and Ralph Redwing walking slowly back and forth on the sandy ground in front of the club. Ralph Redwing did most of the talking, and now and then Mr. Spence took off his cowboy hat and wiped sweat off his forehead. Tom breast-stroked silently in the water near his dock, watching them pace and talk. At the club that noon, the Spences joined the Redwings at the big table near the terrace. Sarah looked at him hard, twice, knitting her brows together as if trying to send him a thought, and Buddy Redwing grabbed her hand and pressed it to his mouth with loud growls and smacking sounds. Mrs. Spence pretended to find this hilarious. Tom left unobserved, and spent the rest of the afternoon trying to see something fresh in his notes.

He could *see* them, the tense, lean young Shadow standing on the edge of his dock, drawing on a cigarette—a Cubeb? a Murad?—and his grandfather in an open-necked white shirt leaning on his umbrella and Anton Goetz holding himself up on his cane, talking at the edge of the darkness outside the club. But he could hear their words no more than he could hear Ralph Redwing issuing orders to sweating Bill Spence.

Barbara Deane's house was a small four-room cottage with ugly, dark brown wooden siding, two small windows on either side of the front door, and a massive TV antenna on the top of the peaked roof. She had planted rows of flowers on the edge of her small lot, and a thick bracelet of flowers, pansies, bluets, and lupines grew all around the house.

"Come on in," she said. "This isn't much like the clubhouse, I suppose, but I'm going to try to give you a good dinner anyhow." She was wearing the black silk blouse, and the pearls were back in place. After a second he took in that she had put on lipstick and makeup. His loneliness recognized hers, and he saw also that Barbara Deane looked very good tonight—not as young as she had seemed in the first seconds of their initial meeting, but young in some internal way, like Kate Redwing, and naturally, instinctively elegant. Elegance had nothing to do with money, he thought, and then thought that she reminded him of the actress in *Hud*—Patricia Neal.

"I wish you could have seen this place before the burglars redesigned it," she said, showing him into her living room. "I used to have a lot of *things*, but I'm learning to live without them."

One of the things she was learning to live without was the television set that had occupied the empty stand beside the fireplace. Some high shelves stood empty too, for she had lost her mother's antique crystal, and her record player was gone, but a new one was on order in the village; and her family's silverware and china was gone too, so they would be using some cheap plates from the gas station—you got a free plate with every ten gallons of gas, wasn't that *odd*?—and stainless steel utensils she had picked up in the village that afternoon because she couldn't face making him use plastic knives and forks.

In spite of what she had lost, the little living room was bright and warm and comfortable, and he sat down on a worn sofa while she opened a bottle of wine, gave him a glass, and went in and out of the kitchen to check on dinner, asking him questions about school and his friends and life on the lake and Mill Walk.

He told her about the Friedrich Hasselgard scandal at the treasury, but did not mention any of his own conclusions and actions.

"And if that's what they tell you," she said, "then there's a lot more they aren't saying. Sometimes I think the only way to live on Mill Walk is to keep your eyes shut and go around like a blind person."

In a little while she announced that dinner was ready, and told him to sit at the table, which had been set for two at the end of the living room, near the kitchen. Tom sat down on a metal folding chair—her good chairs had been stolen too—as she carried a steaming tray out of the kitchen, set it on the table, then went back for serving bowls and containers.

She had made delicate, marinated veal rolled and tied around mysterious fillings, wild rice, potatoes, steamed carrots, a fresh green salad, food enough for four. "Young men like to eat, and it gives me a chance to cook," she said. The food was better than the club's, and Tom told her so: after a few more bites, he told her it was one of the best meals he had ever eaten, and that was true too.

"How did you meet my grandfather?" he asked her.

She smiled as if at an inevitability. "It was at the hospital. Shady Mount—they needed nurses, their first year, and I had a brand-new nursing degree. Your grandfather was on the board, and he was much more involved in the daily running of the hospital than most of the board members. You'd see him in the hallways and the doctors' offices—back then, he knew nearly everybody who worked at Shady Mount. It was a real project for him, his first big job after Elysian Courts, and it was on his own territory. He wanted it to be the best hospital in the Caribbean."

"In the car the other day, you said that he stuck up for you once when you were in trouble."

"Yes, he did. It was very brave of him. I suppose you want to know all about this, now."

"You don't have to tell me anything you don't want to," Tom said.

She looked down at her plate, and cut the string around one of the paupiettes. "It was a long time ago," she said. "A young man had been injured in a gun battle with the police. He was placed in isolation after his operation, and I was his nurse. I don't suppose there's any need to go into medical details." She looked up at him. "He died. Suddenly, and on my shift. I didn't even know it until I came into his room to check up on him—he had been showing signs of recovery, and I thought he might be able to speak in a day or two. Anyhow, he died, and I was blamed. They discovered that he had been given the wrong medication during the afternoon, and since I gave him his medications, I must have done it. For a while, they were going to take away my nursing license, and I was afraid I was going to be charged with a crime. My name was in the paper. My picture was in the paper."

She remembered her dinner, and cut off a small section of veal.

"And he helped you?"

"He took care of the charges somehow—he took over the hospital inquiry, and when the panel decided that there was no clear-cut case against me, the police could not charge me with anything. Plenty of other people could have come in and out of that room, and plenty of them did. Of course, I was ruined as a nurse. Glen suggested that I come up here for a time, and he found out about this little house, and I had enough money to buy it, so I came up here for six months. When I went back to Mill Walk, he got me into a midwifery course, and before long I was delivering babies. So I've always thought that your grandfather saved my life. He earned my loyalty, and I've given it to him."

"What did you mean when you said, in the car the other day, that you cleaned up his messes?"

"I suppose I meant that Glen was the kind of man who always turns to women when he needs help." She went back to her dinner, another minuscule section of veal, a sip of wine. Tom waited for her to say more. "But I was really thinking of that time he asked me to keep Gloria—he wanted me to go to his lodge and straighten it up for him. He said he'd left some of her things behind, toys and books and clothes, and she would want them. But he also wanted me to clean up—literally. The place was a mess. Glen always needed someone to pick up after him. So I cleaned out the ashtrays and straightened things up before I came back."

"Were you in love with him?" Tom asked.

"A lot of people assumed that your grandfather and I were lovers." She shook her head. "It was never like that. I wasn't his type, for one thing. And I wasn't going to pretend to be his type—I was grateful to him, and after a while I began to understand him. And then I understood what my duties were." She met his glance, and said, "Not to forget what I owed him."

"And you never did," he said.

"I never could," she said. "I have no complaints. None at all. I worked as a midwife up here for a long time—I registered with a service, and people got in touch with me by calling the service. I retired about five years ago, and I get a little money from your grandfather for looking after his place. I have more than enough to live on. My life is very peaceful, and I do what I want to do. Such as invite you for dinner."

"Are you lonely?"

"I wouldn't even know the answer to that anymore," she said. "Being lonely isn't so bad." She smiled at him. "But I imagine that you have all sorts of friends out at the lake."

"It hasn't turned out that way," he said, and gave her a general description of his difficulties with Sarah Spence and the Redwings. He told her about Buzz Laing and Roddy Deepdale and Kate Redwing, and then about the shot that had come through the window. "So after two police cars showed up at the lodge, my reputation is even worse than before, and I've been spending all my time by myself." He hesitated, then said, "The police chief, Tim Truehart, told me that I should ask you to stay in the lodge, kind of as protection. In case the shooting was somebody trying to get back at my grandfather for something."

"And you kept quiet about it for two weeks?"

"Well, nothing else has happened. And I got sort of busy."

"Would you like me to spend the nights there?"

He said no, it was not necessary, thinking that she would see it as another duty owed to his grandfather.

"Well, I've been thinking of coming back there anyhow in a couple of days. You tell me if you begin to feel uneasy, staying there by yourself."

"I will," he said.

Their earlier unease had left them, and they talked in the rambling, anecdotal way of people learning to know and like each other. She wanted to know about Brooks-Lowood, and the books and movies he enjoyed, and he asked her about horses and Eagle Lake, and eventually Tom felt that they had known each other a long time. "You don't have to answer this, of course, but you said you weren't my grandfather's type, and ever since you said that, I've been trying to figure out what that type was."

"I suppose that's an allowable subject," she said. "After all, we're talking about something back in the dark ages. I guess it's safe to say that he liked very girlish, submissive women. Magda, poor soul, was like that. I only knew one other woman Glen saw, a very poor choice, I thought, a girl who worked as a nurse's aide—that was how they met, back when Glen spent a lot of time getting the hospital to run the way he wanted it to. She was a pretty little thing, but underneath she was very hard. She came from a rough background, but she could make you believe that she was the soul of innocence."

Remembering his mother's judgment of Nancy Vetiver, he said, "Are you sure about her—that she was hard, I mean?"

"I'm sure she was calculating, if that's what you're asking. She and Glen got what they wanted or needed from each other, and I guess they finally became something like friends. In the end, I suppose he learned that he had to respect her. Carmen Bishop, that was her name—she was about seventeen or eighteen when she started at the hospital."

The name meant nothing to Tom.

"I think I heard that she got him to help her brother—she probably cared for Glen, but she was certainly using him, too."

"Seventeen or eighteen," he said.

"She might have been older—anyhow, I gather she was a match for him. The funny thing was, I don't think Glen ever did more than take her out to dinner a few times, so that he could be seen with her. That's all he ever did with me, which is how some people got the idea we were—you know. I think it was important to Glen to be seen with attractive young women, but I don't think it ever went any further than that, even with Carmen."

She gave him a slice of apple pie she had baked herself, and then wrapped the rest of the pie for him to take back with him.

It was just past ten when she dropped him off at the lodge, and she told him to call her if he wanted her to begin staying at the lodge. "I know I'll see Tim Truehart on the street one day," she said, "and he'll order me to start taking better care of you!"

"Oh, you do pretty well," he said, and she drove away.

The next day, Tom wrote another long letter to Lamont von Heilitz and carried it up the hill to wait for Joe Truehart. When the mailman appeared, he came out of the trees and gave the letter to him.

Truehart said, "I hear you think my mom's gone into the burglary business."

"I hear she's pretty good at it," Tom said, and Truehart laughed and turned his van around and drove off.

Tom realized that he had never opened his grandfather's mailbox—if Joe Truehart had anything for him, he would have given it to him when Tom gave him the thick envelopes for von Heilitz. He did not even know which aluminum box belonged to his grandfather, and had to go down the length of them, reading the names. Finally he came to Upshaw. He tugged at the catch and opened the box. It was jammed with folded pieces of white paper. There were dozens of messages inside the box. He scooped them out and unfolded the top sheet.

In large flowing black letters that virtually yelled with frustration, it read *DON'T YOU EVER LOOK IN YOUR MAILBOX?* The word *Friday* had been scrawled above this sentence, and the name *Sarah* had been written beneath, in such haste or irritation that it was only a straight line between the large S and the almost embryonic h.

Tom read through the stack of notes on the way back to his lodge. Then he read them all over again. He felt almost dizzy with joy.

43

Inside the lodge, he spread them all out on the desk and read them in order, from *My parents ordered me not to see you anymore, but I can't get you out of my mind,* to *DON'T YOU EVER LOOK IN YOUR MAILBOX?* There was one for every day since the day she had taken him into the compound. Some of them were love letters, outright and frank, the most passionate and personal statements that had ever been uttered to him; some of them burned with resentment against her parents and detailed the events of days filled with almost deathly boredom. One, written the day she had heard about the shooting, was filled with alarm and worry. One of them said only *I need you.*

One was a long extended metaphor comparing his penis to the Leaning Tower of Pisa, the Washington Monument, and the Eiffel Tower, all of which she had seen between the ages of eight and twelve.

Shall I compare thee to a summer's day? No, I hardly think so, since you're not very much like a summer's day, but you do remind me a bit of European travel. . . .

He called her lodge, and Mrs. Spence hung up as soon as he gave his name. He called back, and said, "Mrs. Spence, I'm sorry, but this is very important. Would you please let me speak to Sarah?"

"No one in this family has anything at all to say to you," she said, and hung up.

The third time he called, Mr. Spence answered, asked if he wanted a broken arm as bad as all that, and slammed down the phone.

He changed into his bathing suit and resolutely swam back and forth past their dock, but neither Sarah nor anyone else came through their back door.

For the rest of the afternoon, Tom tried to concentrate on the pages he had written about the murder, but his attention returned again and again to Sarah's wonderful letters—she had suggested meetings, made assignations, waited for him on the highway behind Lamont von Heilitz's lodge, tried to beam into his brain messages about looking at his mailbox.

He went to the club early that evening and waited at Roddy and Buzz's end of the bar. He ordered a club soda and ate a handful of goldfish crackers. He nervously downed a second glass of club soda, and ordered a Kir Royale. The first sip made him feel dizzy and light-headed. The Langenheims came up the stairs, nodded at him glumly, and went straight to their table.

Then Marcello's resonant voice came up the stairs, and Tom heard footsteps, and Ralph and Katinka Redwing appeared beside him—Ralph gave him a look of utter indifference, and Katinka did not see him at all. Behind them came the Spences. Mr. Spence looked happy and expansive, and Mrs. Spence was saying, "Oh, Ralph! Ralph!" Both Spences saw Tom at the same instant, and their faces went dead. Behind her parents came Sarah, walking upstairs with Buddy Redwing. Buddy said a sentence of which Tom heard only the word "toad," and Sarah's eyes flew to Tom's face, and locked with his own eyes. He felt all of his inner gravity alter, and he nodded three, four, five times, vehemently. Sarah rolled her eyes upward, closed them, opened them, and gave him a small, tucked-in smile of pure satisfaction.

"I don't think we'll go to the bar tonight," Ralph Redwing told Marcello, "it's a little crowded, just take us to our table."

Sarah was placed next to Buddy with her back to Tom.

In a loud voice from the head of the table, Ralph Redwing said, "Let's have two bottles of the Roederer Cristal to begin with tonight, Marcello, we have something to celebrate. These children have just become engaged to be engaged, and we're all tremendously happy with their decision."

Mrs. Spence looked at Tom with narrowed eyes and a gloating smile. He raised his glass to her in a mock toast, and her smile tightened.

When the old waiter came around to take his order, Tom asked if he could take his meal home and eat it there—despite his bravado, he could not ignore what was going on at the long table, and did not have the stomach to watch it.

He carried his meal home in a brown paper bag, set it out on the table, looked at it, then scraped it into the garbage and ate the pie that Barbara Deane had given him.

The next day, Tom heard voices coming from down the avenue of trees in front of the lodges, and went outside to see who it was. He walked down the track, and the voices got louder. Jerry Hasek was unloading trunks and suitcases from the back of the Cadillac, and shambling from side to side as he passed into the compound behind his parents, his white hair blazing in the sunlight. Behind him was the answer to Tom's problem, Fritz Redwing, come to Eagle Lake for another endless party with his cousin.

44

Tom paced around the sitting room, fidgeted with pens and papers at the desk, stared out of every window on the ground floor of the lodge, reread Sarah's letters, looked at his watch. Every minute that went by increased the likelihood that Fritz would not call him. Tom imagined Fritz in his family's lodge, his suitcases opened on the bed, jeans and chinos and shorts strewn across the floor, interrupting a conversation between his parents and his aunt and uncle about the jet and Ted Mornay with the comment that he sort of thought, you know, that he'd see what good old Tom Pasmore was up to. Uncle Ralph would make sure that he didn't see what good old Tom Pasmore was up to, and when Fritz saw Tom in the dining room he would shrug and shake his head and generally try to communicate that all conversation would have to wait until their senior year started, tough luck, and what did you *do* anyway, man?

When the telephone rang, Tom scrambled for it from the sitting room, and picked it up on the third ring.

Fritz's first words told him that all his worry had been pointless. "Tom! We're both here! Isn't that great?"

It sure was, Tom said, genuinely happy to hear Fritz's voice.

"Boy, I never thought this would really happen," Fritz said. "We're going to have such a great time. I guess Buddy had some real wild friends up here, I bet they got outrageous and outa sight, so tell me what you were doing—but please please don't tell me you just moped around reading books and acting like Mr. Handley. I'm fed up with Mr. Handley, he never makes any *sense*!"

Fritz had spent the past three weeks in a remedial reading tutorial with Dennis Handley.

"Come on over," Tom said. "Right away."

"Next year we're going to be *seniors*!" Fritz said. "This is going to be the best summer we ever had."

"Don't tell anybody where you're going, just get over here," Tom said.

In less than five minutes, Fritz was on the doorstep, wearing a polo shirt over bathing trunks and carrying a towel on his arm. "Good tan," he said when Tom opened the door. "I was afraid you'd be all white—I was afraid you'd have book scars all over your face.

"Book scars?"

"You know, those little lines you get under your eyes from reading too much. With Mr. Handley, I had to read a whole book out loud, and every time I read a sentence wrong, he read it *back* to me, it was like watching a guy *play* with himself, I got those lines all over under my eyes, I had to squint so I wouldn't have to see his face. So let's go swimming right away, okay, I want to catch up with your tan, I want some rays—"

They had walked into the living room, and Fritz suddenly stopped talking and gazed in horror at the heavily written-upon sheets of yellow paper lying in rows and stacks on the floor by the couch and fanned across its cushions.

"What is THIS?" He turned to look up at Tom with pale blue eyes like pinwheels. "You're doing next year's homework!"

"I'm thinking about something, it has nothing to do with homework."

"So?" Fritz said, meaning: so if it isn't homework, what is it?

"It's about a murder." Fritz looked at him with deep puzzlement. "I'll put on my swimsuit and be right down," Tom said.

"All *right,*" Fritz said when Tom came back downstairs. He had been holding a sheaf of Tom's notes in his hands, and he dropped them on the floor with evident relief. "Let's get in the water. I don't know what you're doing here, but you have got to get away from it, fast."

They walked through the study, and Fritz shook his head at the sight of yet more piles of paper. "It's a good thing I got here in time. I don't know how you got such a good tan, messing around with this crazy stuff. You even got Mrs. Thielman's name wrong, you dope."

"That was the first Mrs. Thielman," Tom said. "Just out of curiosity, what was the name of the book you had to read out loud to Mr. Handley?"

"Are you kidding? You think I remember?"

"What was it about?"

"This guy."

"What did he do?"

"We went after this fish. It didn't make any sense. Mr. Handley let me skip the hard parts."

"Mr. Handley made you read *Moby Dick*? Out loud?"

"It was terrible. It was lousy *and* terrible. What do you mean, the first Mrs. Thielman? There is only one Mrs. Thielman."

"The first Mrs. Thielman was killed right up here by a man named Anton Goetz, and Lamont von Heilitz solved it."

"The creep who owns that empty lodge?" They were now walking down Tom's pier, and Fritz pointed diagonally across the lake. "That guy everybody hates? I wish you owned that lodge."

"He's not a creep," Tom said. "He used to be incredibly famous, and he's old now, but he's an amazing man. I met him because he lives across the street from us, and he's solved hundreds of murders, and he really knows how our island works."

"Oh, everybody knows that," Fritz said. He whooped and jumped off the edge of the dock, drew in his knees and wrapped his arms around them, and hit the water in a noisy cannonball.

Everybody knows that?

Tom dove in after him.

"God, this is great," Fritz yelled, and for a time both he and Tom swam aimlessly and energetically in the wide part of the lake.

"Have you seen Buddy yet?" Tom asked.

"Buddy's still in bed. I guess they had some kind of celebration at the club last night. Weren't you there?"

"I left early. Buddy and I aren't exactly friendly, Fritz."

"Buddy's friendly with everybody," Fritz said. "Buddy's friendly with *Jerry*. He and Jerry are going out shooting this afternoon. Maybe we could go too. That'd be pretty cool."

"I don't think they'd want me along, unless . . ." *Unless they could use me as a target*, Tom thought. "There are some things you have to know," he said, and Fritz swam closer to him, his wide forehead wrinkled.

"Do you know what the celebration was about, last night?" Fritz shook his head. "Buddy is supposed to get married to Sarah Spence."

"Well, sure. What's the big deal?"

"He can't marry her," Tom said.

"How come?"

"She's too young. She's too smart. She doesn't even like him."

"Then how come she's going to marry him?"

"Because her parents want her to, because your Uncle Ralph picked her out for him, and because she hasn't been able to see me for a couple of weeks."

Fritz stopped paddling around and stared at him. His mouth was underwater.

"I've sort of been seeing her. We got close, Fritz."

Fritz lifted his mouth out of the water. "How close?"

"Pretty close," Tom said. "Buddy tried to tell me to stay away from her, and when I wouldn't agree, he tried to fight me, and I punched him in the gut. He went down."

"Oh, shit," Fritz said.

"Fritz, the truth is—"

Fritz clamped his eyes shut.

"Come on, Fritz. The truth is, Sarah was never going to marry him in the first place. She's going to college in the fall, and she'll write him a letter or something, and that'll be that.

They're not even engaged, it's just some kind of understanding."

"Did you screw her?" Fritz asked.

"None of your business."

"Oh, shit," Fritz said. "How many times?"

"I have to see her," Tom said, and Fritz dove underwater and began swimming back toward the dock. Tom swam after him. Fritz scrambled up on the dock and sat with his head on his knees. His hair glowed in the sun. When Tom pulled himself up on the dock, Fritz stood up and stepped away from him.

"Well?" Tom said.

Fritz glared at him. He looked almost ready to cry. He punched Tom in the shoulder. "Tell me you did," he said. "Tell me you did, shithead." He hit Tom in the chest, and knocked him backwards a step.

"I did," Tom said.

Fritz whirled around, so that he faced Roddy Deepdale's lodge. "I knew it," he said.

"If you knew it, why did you hit me?"

"I knew this was going to happen."

"What?"

Fritz turned around slowly. "I knew you were going to do something crazy like this." There was a gleam of pure naughtiness in his eyes. He jumped forward and shoved Tom's biceps with both of his hands. "Where'd you do it? In the woods? In your lodge? Inside or outside?"

Tom stepped backwards. "Never mind."

Fritz shoved him again. "If you don't tell me, I won't do anything for you." His eyes seemed to be all gleam now. "If you don't tell me *something*, I won't even ever talk to you again." He backed Tom down the deck, pushing at him like a little blond bear playing with its trainer. "Where was the first time?"

"On your uncle's airplane," Tom said.

Fritz's arms dropped. "On . . ." He blinked, three times, rapidly. He choked on a laugh, got the laugh out of his throat, and fell on his knees, bawling with laughter. "On . . . on . . . my uncle's . . ." He fell on his back, still laughing too hard to speak.

"Are you going to help me?" Tom said.

Fritz's laughter gradually subsided into a series of sighs. "Sure. You're my friend, aren't you?" He looked up, eyes gleaming again, from the deck. *"Moby Dick,"* he said, and sputtered with laughter again. Then his face turned serious, and he squinted into the sun. "Is there a real old guy in *Moby Dick*?"

"Sure," Tom said.

"And does the fish get all eaten up?"

"Eaten up?"

"You fart, you got the wrong book. Even I know Ernest whatzisname didn't write *Moby Dick*. Her parents were on that plane, right? They were right there, right?"

"There aren't any hard parts in *The Old Man and the Sea*," Tom said.

"Don't change the subject," Fritz said, and began giggling. "Oh, God. Oh, God. How can this be happening to me?"

"It isn't happening to you," Tom said. "It's happening to me."

"Well, what does Sarah Spence have to do with Lamont von Heilitz?"

"Nothing."

Fritz sat up and jiggled a finger in his ear. He cocked his head and looked at Tom. "But I heard my uncle and Jerry talking about him—right after I changed. They were on my uncle's porch. I told you."

"When was this?"

"When you said this old guy who used to be famous lived across the street from you, and I said, everybody knows that, that's when. Because I heard my Uncle Ralph on the porch with Jerry, and my uncle said, da *da* da *da* da dum, Lamont von Heilitz, or whatever his name is, and Jerry said, he lives across the street from the Pasmores."

"I wonder what that was about?"

"I'll ask him," Fritz said.

"No, don't ask him about it. Did your uncle say anything after that?"

"He said, have a nice time, Fritzie. Which is what I thought I was going to do." He picked himself up. "I suppose you want me to go get her and bring her here, and then go walk around the lake or something."

"Maybe you could call her up this afternoon, or talk to her at lunch," Tom said. "Say you'd like to go for a walk with her or something while Buddy's out shooting with Jerry, and go around the lake so her parents won't see you bringing her here. I just want to talk to her—I have to talk to her."

After a second Fritz boffed his chest again, and said, "Let's swim some more, huh? I'll take care of things. If you're in love with Sarah Spence, Buddy can always get married to Posy Tuttle. Buddy doesn't care who he gets married to."

They swam until Fritz's mother came outside the compound to the middle Redwing dock and began calling, "Fritzie! Fritzie!"

45

As soon as Fritz had run back to the compound, his wet bare feet leaving footprints behind him on the track, Tom dried himself off, changed into chinos and a polo shirt, and went to the club. It was just past eleven forty-five. Lunch did not normally begin until twelve-thirty, but he was hungry—he'd eaten nothing besides half of the pie for dinner the night before, and had skipped breakfast that morning. Besides, he was too tense to wait: he suspected that the real reason he wanted to eat early was that he could be out of the club dining room before the Redwings showed up, pleased with themselves for having negotiated their way through the obstacles to their son's engagement to be engaged. There would be one delicate hint to Fritz's parents about trouble with the Pasmore boy, and Fritz would be unable to keep himself from sneaking shining glances across the room.

"Book scars," Tom said to himself, and smiled.

The long table had been extended, and set for three more places. Fritz's parents would be formally introduced, in the lowest of low-key styles, with the formality that conceals itself, to the Redwing Holding Company's newest acquisition.

Oh, we've been expecting this for months.

Oh, I think the formal announcement can come whenever they're ready, but after a year I imagine our young lady here will transfer out to Arizona. She'll want to keep an eye on her boyfriend, won't she?

Laughter, knowing and tolerant.

It's so nice they didn't make us wait until the end of the summer—you know, I was actually afraid they'd do that!

Oh, Sarah is going to love her new life.

Tom knew the real reason he was eating early.

He sat in the empty dining room with an unread, unopened book next to his ketchup-smeared plate. Two younger waiters lounged against the bar, and sunlight blazed on the terrace and fell over the first three rows of the thick red floor tiles. Tom looked down at his hands folding a heavy pink napkin, and saw the hands of Lamont von Heilitz encased in light blue gloves. He dropped the napkin on the table and left the dining room.

Back at his grandfather's lodge, he leaned against the door. Then he began picking the papers up from the sitting room couch.

The telephone rang.

Tom hoped that Sarah had stayed behind in her lodge for a minute after her parents went to the club. "Oh, hello," he said. He put the stack of papers on the desk.

"Tom?" He did not recognize the voice, which was that of a woman in her twenties or thirties.

"It's Barbara Deane," the voice said. "I've been thinking—if Tim Trueheart wants me to stay at the lodge, I'd better stay there. Otherwise, I'm going to be afraid of running into him every time I go to the Red Owl."

"Okay," Tom said.

"I'll be along late tonight or tomorrow—don't wait up for me or anything, I'll just let myself in and go to my room." She paused. "There was something I didn't tell you the other night. Maybe you should know about it."

She wants to tell me she was his mistress after all, Tom thought, and said that he would see her the next day. He looked at Sarah's letters, a white stack of pages next to the much larger heap of yellow pages. He picked them up and folded them, then took all of his papers upstairs and slid them beneath his pillow.

A second later, he took them out and looked around the room. The drawer in the chessboard table seemed too obvious. At last he opened his closet and slid the papers on a shelf above his clothes.

Tom wandered out of the bedroom. He looked out the window at the end of the hallway into a tangle of rough green leaves and horizontal branches. Beyond them were more leaves and branches, and beyond these yet more, and then still more, until the clear empty air over the track. He turned around and walked to the staircase and looked down. If Fritz did manage to bring Sarah to him—if he could get her alone, if her parents allowed her out of their sight, and if she agreed to go—they would not arrive for hours. He walked down the hall to Barbara Deane's door, hesitated, and pushed it open.

She had something hidden on a shelf too, something she had examined on his first day at the lake and once after that. He had heard it sliding out of its hiding place, and the heavy thunk as she put it on her desk. If he found letters from Glendenning Upshaw, he told himself, he would put them back unread.

Tom went quickly into her bedroom, walked around the bed, and opened the closet door. A neat row of dresses, skirts, and blouses, mainly in dark colors, hung from a wooden pole. Above the clothes was a white wooden shelf, and down at the far end of the shelf, barely visible in the darkness of the closet, a wooden box with inlaid flags of a lighter shade. Tom stepped into the closet and reached for the box. Barbara Deane would have had to wedge herself behind the sliding door and strain up on tiptoe to touch it. Tom pulled it toward him, got it off the shelf, and backed out of the closet.

It was heavy, highly ornamented with inlay, but the heaviness was of the wood itself; nothing rattled when he shook the box. He set it down on the desk, took a breath, and opened the hinged top.

She was going to tell me anyhow, he thought.

He looked in and saw a small pile of newspaper clippings instead of the old letters he had expected. He reached in for the one on top and read the headline before he got it out of the box. NURSE SUSPECTED IN OFFICER'S DEATH. The article had been clipped from the front page of the *Eyewitness*. He took out the second: SHOULD THIS WOMAN BE CHARGED? Beneath the headline was a picture of twenty-year-old Barbara Deane, barely recognizable, in a white uniform and a starched cap. ONLY PERSON TO HAVE ACCESS WAS NURSE DEANE, said the next headline. Tom blushed—he felt as if he had walked into her room and found her naked. There were other articles below these, and all of them accused Barbara Deane of murder. He barely looked at them—maybe Lamont von Heilitz would have read them, but Tom felt that he had already gone far enough.

He leaned over to replace the articles and saw two sheets of yellowing notepaper folded at the bottom of the box, nearly the same shade as the wood. He touched them, afraid that they might crumble, and felt stiff creamy paper. He picked them up, put down the little heap of clippings, and unfolded the sheets of notepaper on top of them.

I KNOW WHAT YOU ARE, AND YOU HAVE TO BE STOPPED, read the first. The ink had turned the brown of dried blood, but the large printed capitals shouted louder than the headlines on the old copies of the *Eyewitness*. He set it down and opened the second. His throat was dry, and his heart pounded. *THIS HAS GONE ON TOO LONG YOU WILL PAY FOR YOUR SIN*.

Tom dropped the yellowing piece of paper into the box as if it had stung him. He swallowed. He reached back in and picked it up again. The T's had been crossed with a faintly curved line, and the S's slanted. A woman had written the notes, and he knew who she was.

He felt absolutely afraid for a second, as if Barbara Deane were about to rush through the door, screaming at him. *I know what you are*. He slid the two notes together with shaking hands and placed them carefully on the bottom of the box. Then he laid the clippings on top of them and closed the box. He picked up the box and realized that he did not know if it had faced forward or backward. Sweat broke out on his forehead. He carried the box to the closet and stepped inside. Tom put it on the shelf and slid it far down. He thought he remembered that it had been all the way against the closet wall: which way had it faced? He wiped his forehead on his arm and turned the box around, then around again. The house creaked, and his heart tried to jump out of his chest. He slid the box snugly against the wall, facing forward, stepped away, and closed the closet door. Then he wondered if it really had been closed all the way. He opened it and closed it again, then opened it an inch. He groaned, and shut it.

He turned around and saw his dusty footprints on the wooden floor, stamped as clearly as Fritz's on the track.

Tom yanked his handkerchief from his pocket and walked backward, erasing his tracks all the way to the door. Drops of sweat fell on the dull wood. They left shiny traces when he wiped them. He reached the threshold and backed out of the room and closed the door.

He went down the hall to his bathroom and splashed cold water on his face. He wanted to get out of the lodge—to run away. He looked up at his dripping face in the mirror and said, "Jeanine Thielman wrote those notes." He dried his face and remembered tense Barbara Deane opening the door to the lodge on his first day in Eagle Lake; and remembered the relaxed, friendly Barbara Deane who had lied and lied when she served him dinner.

I know what it is to be unjustly accused.

I wasn't his type, for one thing.

He walked slowly down the stairs, still afraid that she was going to walk in the front door. She would know in an instant what he had done, if she saw his face.

Tom collapsed on the couch. Barbara had not been unjustly accused, she had killed the policeman in the hospital by giving him the wrong medication; probably Maxwell Redwing had ordered her to kill him. Shady Mount Hospital was where the people who ran Mill Walk put its embarrassments when they wanted them to die. It was the most respectable hospital on the island, the safest place on Mill Walk for a discreet little murder: the Redwings went there themselves, didn't they?

Tom's grandfather believed in her innocence and saved her skin, got her out of Mill Walk, and parked her in the village of Eagle Lake. When Jeanine Thielman accused and threatened her, Barbara Deane had killed her.

Which meant that she had killed Anton Goetz too. Tom did not know how this had happened, but a strong young woman like Barbara Deane could have knocked down a cripple . . .

maybe, Tom thought, Goetz had been blackmailing Barbara Deane. Maybe he had even seen her shoot Jeanine Thielman, and helped her hide the body in the lake. His mother had seen him moving through the woods, sneaking back to his lodge for the old curtains. After von Heilitz accused him of the murder, he had gone back to confront her, and she had killed him too. And ever since, she had lived quietly in the village of Eagle Lake. She had even gone on delivering babies.

He told himself to calm down when it occurred to him that Barbara Deane might have shot at him through the window, imagining that he had seen the notes at the bottom of the box.

But he knew one more thing Lamont von Heilitz did not, and it was the crucial fact in Jeanine Thielman's murder: she had died because she had written those notes.

46

He was still trying to figure out what to do about the notes three hours later when someone began battering on his door. He jumped up from the couch and opened the door. Fritz Redwing nearly fell into the room. Sarah Spence gave him another push to move him out of the doorway. "Get inside, get out of the way," she said. "We walked all the way around the lake to avoid being seen, let's not blow it at the last minute." She closed the door behind her and leaned against it, smiling at Tom. "I make all these clever plans for meetings in out of the way places at night, and when Tom Pasmore, who writes a letter a day to Lamont von Heilitz but never—checks—his—mailbox—finally works things out, he has me come to his house in broad daylight."

"I'm sorry," Tom said.

"Don't you put those precious letters in the mailbox?"

"I just hand them to the mailman," Tom said. "How do you know I write to him?"

"He's your hero, isn't he? The one who started you off playing detective? I saw how you looked when Hattie Bascombe talked about him."

"Von Heilitz, von Heilitz," Fritz said. "Why is everybody talking about him all of a sudden?"

Neither Tom nor Sarah bothered to look at him.

"I read your letters a million times," Tom said.

"What letters?" Sarah asked. "I never wrote you any letters. I don't have to write letters to boys. I can't even imagine doing such a stupid thing."

"Oh, great," Fritz said.

"Didn't I used to know you once? A long time ago? So much has happened in the meantime, it's kind of vague."

" 'In the meantime'—is that the period when you wrote me every day, and arranged meetings in out of the way places?"

"No, it's the period in which I became *betrothed*," she said. "Or was it betrothed to be betrothed? Meeting people in out of the way places is far, far behind me."

"Should I just get out of here?" Fritz asked.

"Betrothed to be betrothed," Tom said. "That's kind of an interesting condition."

"I thought of it as a delaying action. Or do I mean withholding action?" She pushed herself away from the door. "Aren't you going to hug me, or something?"

"Me?" Tom put his hand on his chest. "I'm just someone you sort of used to know."

"I'll be the judge of that," she said. "I'm very particular about who I used to know."

"Your standards have slipped lately," Tom said, but before he could say any more, Sarah uttered a low growl and crossed the ground between them and wrapped her arms around him.

"You idiot," she said. "You moron. You think I'd write anything to you?"

"I should have known better," he said, hugging her for all he was worth. He lowered his head to her vibrant hair.

"Look," Fritz said, "is my part done now?"

Sarah raised her face to Tom's, asking to be kissed. Tom met her lips with his, and the shock of their softness echoed through his whole body.

"I'll see you guys later," Fritz said, and stood up.

"No," Tom and Sarah said, almost simultaneously, and

broke apart. "We're supposed to be having a nice long walk together," Sarah said. She twined her fingers through Tom's.

"We could all go someplace," Tom said.

"An excursion," Sarah said. "That's it. You've probably never gone on an excursion with Tom Pasmore. All sorts of brilliant things happen. Is there any way we could go out for a drive?"

"Sure," Fritz said. "I could get the keys to one of the cars."

"Better yet, you and I will get the keys, so everybody will see we're still enjoying ourselves, and Tom will walk around the lake and go up the hill to the mailboxes, and we'll meet him there."

"Wouldn't you rather be alone and stuff?"

"Oh, Tom has something else on his mind," Sarah said.

Tom's insides froze.

"You worked out a way to get me here, but . . ." Her forehead wrinkled. "You look terrible. You look like someone else took a shot at you about half an hour ago. What have you been doing for two weeks?"

"I don't know if I can talk about it now," he said. "I found something out, and I don't know what to do about it."

"Well, meet us up by the mailboxes in half an hour. That'll give you time to think about it."

She took Fritz by the hand and led him toward the door. "Someone *else* shot at you?" Fritz asked, trudging behind her. Tom shrugged. "He has a very exciting life," Sarah said, and pulled Fritz toward the door. They went outside, and Sarah leaned back toward the screen, shielding her eyes to see in. "Should I be worried about you?"

"I'll see you in half an hour," Tom said.

"If you don't, I'm calling Nancy Vetiver and asking for a consultation."

He waved, and she blew him a kiss before hurrying Fritz off the porch and down on the track. Tom heard them talking, Fritz asking baffled questions and Sarah returning elliptical responses like tennis smashes, as they moved away toward the compound. When they were out of earshot, he went upstairs to his bedroom and got his notes down from the closet shelf.

Tom sat at the chessboard table and read everything all over again. Now he saw Barbara Deane hiding behind the trees near the Thielman lodge, Barbara Deane throwing pebbles at a window and snatching up the gun careless Arthur Thielman had left lying on a table. . . . He had eaten at her table! Ridden in her car! Said she could sleep in the lodge!

When he had ten minutes to get up the hill to the mailboxes, Tom folded the wad of notes in half, and tried to jam them into a back pocket of his jeans. They would not fit. Some contradiction still clamored to be seen, and he pushed the notes back up on the closet shelf with the feeling that it would leap out at him if he scanned the papers one more time.

Tom walked the long way around the lake, chewing on his preoccupations, and reached the top of the hill panting but with no memory of having walked up the long winding track.

He sat on the bench and waited for Sarah and Fritz, who drove up in the Lincoln a few minutes later. Fritz was driving, and Sarah sat beside him in the front seat. "Come on in here," she said. "This is our reunion, and you're not allowed to look so gloomy."

He climbed in beside Sarah, who put an arm around him. "Now we are not going to do anything to embarrass or offend Fritz, but you need to be cheered up. So we are going to drive around and forget about this horrendous mess we're in. We will not once mention that I am supposed to marry Buddy Redwing."

"Okay," Tom said.

"Though someone ought to acknowledge that it was pretty good of me to come up with the idea of being engaged to be engaged."

"Why did you even do that?" Tom asked.

"Yeah, why?" said Fritz.

"Because it calmed everybody down right away. And Buddy stopped scheming about how he was going to manage to beat you to a pulp. Once you have the security of being engaged to be engaged, you forget all about your rivals and go back to your old pursuits. All I have to do is sit through lots of dinners, and listen to Buddy talk about how cool and far out everything is going to be when I transfer to Arizona. Our engagement is going to become official next summer, except that it isn't. When I come home at Christmas, I'll tell my mother I can't go through with it. Everybody will blame it on the influence of Mount Holyoke, and it'll be a lot easier to handle than it would be up here."

Nobody said anything, and Sarah said, "I think."

"Why do I feel so shitty?" Fritz said. "I should have stayed in summer school."

"Well, I'm happy you didn't," Sarah said.

"I know why, too," Fritz complained.

"*Is* it a horrendous mess?" Sarah asked. "Or is it maybe just a little one that we're blowing up out of proportion?"

"Does she always talk like this?" Fritz asked, leaning forward to look at Tom.

"I don't think so," Tom said.

"I really think it's just a little mess that looks like a big one," Sarah said.

"I don't think anyone ever decided not to get married to one of my relatives before," Fritz said. "Usually, it's the other way around."

"That's dandy, that's just dandy," Sarah said. She pulled her arm away from Tom, and was motionless and even silent for a moment. It took him a second to realize that she was crying.

Fritz leaned forward and looked at Tom again. His face had turned bright red. "Don't cry, Sarah," he said. "I know Buddy. I even *like* Buddy. But like I told Tom, I don't think he's gonna go crazy or anything."

"I like him too," Sarah said. "And believe me, I know what you're talking about."

She wiped her eyes, and Tom said, "You do?"

"How do you suppose I got into this in the first place? Of course I like him, at least when he isn't drunk or taking those stupid pills. I just don't like him as much as I like you." She put her arm around him again, and said, "This isn't much of an excursion."

"We might as well take a look at Eagle Lake, I mean the town," Fritz said, turning onto Main Street. "I've been coming up here all my life, and I never saw it before."

"Of course not," Sarah said. " 'Eagle Lake is a place apart from the family business. I had a thousand opportunities for investment up here, and I turned them all down.' "

" 'I never wanted to sully this place with money,' " Fritz said, speaking in an eerie imitation of his uncle's voice.

" 'We could turn this part of Wisconsin right around,' " Sarah said. " 'But we don't put a penny into Eagle Lake.' " She was smiling now. "The speech. Of course you've never seen the village. You might put a penny into it if you did, and Ralph Redwing would come awake like a vampire in his coffin, hearing someone creep up on him with a bottle of holy water and a wooden stake."

Fritz giggled at this blasphemy.

"Wait a second," Tom said. "I got it! I just got it!"

"Well, here we go," Sarah said. "Something's been bothering me too, but you didn't react that way about it."

"I know where they put the stuff. God, I really know where it is."

"What stuff?"

"This sounds like an excursion, all right."

"Oh, my God, I even knew this was going to happen—that's why I wanted to bring all those notes." He saw the expression of horror on Sarah's face, and said, "Different notes. All I have to do is remember the name of the street!"

"What's he talking about? All that crap he wrote?"

Tom began looking out of his window. The car was creeping up Main Street in heavy traffic, and sunburned people in T-shirts and visored caps filled the sidewalks. They passed Maple Street, which was wrong. Ahead he saw Tamarack Street, also wrong. "It started with an S. Think of street names that could start with the letter S."

"Suspicious Street."

"Shithole Street."

"That sounded just like Buddy."

"Street names!"

"Satyriasis Street. Scintillation Street. Sevens! Where I live!"

"I give up," Fritz said.

"Season Street."

"Ah," Tom said, and kissed her.

"I got it?"

"Yes," he said, and kissed her again. "You're brilliant."

"It was really Season Street?"

"It was Summers Street. Now all we have to do is find it."

Fritz protested that he could not find a street in a town he had never seen before, and Tom said that it was a small town, all they had to do was drive around for a while and they would run right into it.

"What's this about, anyhow?"

"I'll tell you after we find the place. If I'm right, that is."

"Don't you get the feeling that he's right?" Sarah said.

"No. I get the feeling I'm going to be sorry I'm doing this."

"You'll be a hero, Fritz," Tom said. "Wait. Slow down."

Tom had seen the newspaper editor walking up the sidewalk on his side of the street, and he put his head through the window. "Mr. Hamilton! Mr. Hamilton!"

Chet Hamilton looked over his shoulder, then looked across the street. Tom called his name again and waved, and the editor saw him and waved back. "How's the research going? You having a good summer?"

"Fine," Tom yelled. "Can you tell us how to find Summers Street?"

"Summers Street? Let's see. It's a little ways out of town. Just keep on going straight past town hall, take the first right, the second left, go over the railroad tracks, pass the Authentic Indian Settlement, and you'll run right into it. It's about four, five miles." He looked at Tom curiously, as did a number of other people on the sidewalk. "There's not much out there."

Tom thanked him and pulled himself back into the car. "You got that?" he asked Fritz.

"First right past the town hall, second left, railroad tracks, Indians," Sarah said. "What are we supposed to find, once we get there?"

"A whole lot of stolen property," Tom said.

"*What!*" Fritz screamed.

"That's my boy," Sarah said.

"What stolen property?" Fritz demanded to know.

Tom told him about the burglaries that had been taking place around Eagle Lake and other resort towns over the past few years. "If you walk away from people's houses with that much stuff, you need a place to store it until you get it to whoever you know who buys it from you. I think they must have to go a long way to get rid of it, and they can't get away all that often, so they need a big place."

They drove past the town hall and the police station, past

the signs at the edge of town, and Sarah said, "Here's the first right."

Fritz hauled on the wheel, and turned into a two-lane blacktop road. At first they drove past tarpaper shacks on lawns littered with bald tires and junked cars. FREE PUPPIES, read rain-streaked lettering on a crude sign. The shacks grew more widely spaced, and the land stayed empty. Narrow trees stood at the edge of a muddy field. Far off, a stooped figure moved toward a farmhouse.

"Fritz, your uncle would never buy or rent anything up here—in fact, he enjoys turning down deals, even when they might be good for him, because of the way the local newspaper treated his family."

"Well, here's the first left," Sarah said.

"I see it," Fritz grumbled, and turned into another two-lane blacktop road. Another sequence of muddy fields, these enclosed by collapsing wooden fences, rolled past them. They passed a large white sign reading 2 MILES TO AUTHENTIC INDIAN SETTLEMENT.

"So what?" Fritz asked.

"Two years ago, the Redwing Holding Company rented a machine shop on Summers Street. I saw it in a column in the *Eagle Lake Gazette* on my first day here."

"A machine shop?" Fritz said.

"It was an empty building—they probably rented it for a hundred dollars a month, or something like that."

"Oh," Sarah said.

Fritz groaned. He put his forehead against the top of the steering wheel. "What am I—what are you trying—"

"It's Jerry," Sarah said, once again arriving instantly at an insight.

"Jerry and his friends probably didn't know that the paper listed things like that, but they wouldn't have cared even if they did. They knew no Redwing would ever see it. And on the other side, the name protected them. The police would never suspect the Redwing company of being involved in a bunch of crummy burglaries."

A lonely set of train tracks crossed the road, coming from nowhere, going nowhere. The Lincoln bumped over them.

Five hundred yards farther on in an empty field, shabby

tepees circled a low windowless building of split logs with a sod roof. The hides of the tepees had split and fallen in, and tall yellow weeds grew in all the open places. No one said anything as they drove past.

After another hundred yards, a road intersected theirs. A green metal street sign, almost surreal in the emptiness, said SUMMERS STREET. The road past the abandoned tourist stop was not identified in any way.

"So where is it?" Fritz asked.

Sarah pointed—far down to the right, almost invisible against a thick wall of trees, a building of concrete blocks painted brown stood at the far end of an empty parking lot.

Fritz turned into Summers Street, and drove reluctantly toward the building. "But why would they do *burglaries*?"

"They're bored," Tom said. "They like the feeling of having a little edge."

The big car drove into the parking lot. Close up, the machine shop looked like the police station that clung to the side of Eagle Lake's town hall—it needed another building to complete it. Fritz said, "I'm not getting out of the car. In fact, I think we ought to leave right now and go swimming in the lake." He looked at Tom. "I don't like this at all. We shouldn't be doing this."

"*They* shouldn't be doing it," Tom said.

"Hurry up," Sarah said.

Tom patted her knee, got out of the car, and walked to the front of the machine shop. Above the door was a stenciled sign that said PRYZGODA BROS. TOOL & DIE CO. He leaned forward and peered into a window beside the door. A green chair with padded arms was pushed against one of the walls of an otherwise empty office. A few pieces of paper lay on the floor.

Tom turned around and shrugged. Fritz waved him back to the car, but Tom walked around to the side of the building, where a row of reinforced windows sat high in the wall. Some of the brown paint had separated cleanly from the concrete, and leaned out away from the wall, as stiff as a dried sail. The windows came down to the level of his chin. Tom looked in the first of them and saw only geometrical shadows. Most of the interior was filled with boxes and unidentifiable things stacked on top of the boxes.

Tom put his hands to the sides of his head and bent closer to the window. One of the objects stacked on top of the first row of boxes was faced with brown cloth framed by an inch of dark wood. On top of it, half lost in the darkness at the top of the room, sat another object like like it. Then he recognized them: stereo speakers. Tom turned his head and grinned at Fritz and Sarah, and Fritz swept his hand back toward himself again: *Come on!*

Tom moved down to the next window in line, blocked his face with his hands, and leaned forward. Propped against the row of boxes, the faces of Roddy Deepdale and Buzz Laing looked up at him from the chairs in which they had been painted by a man named Don Bachardy. Tom lowered his hands and stepped back from the window, and in that moment, an overweight figure in a grey suit too small to contain a watermelon belly walked around the back of the tall boxes, shaking something in an open cardboard box and peering down into it like a man panning for gold. Tom jumped back from the window, and a row of white rectangles reflected in Nappy's sunglasses as he looked up.

Tom bent beneath the windows and ran toward the car. He threw himself into the open door, and Fritz scattered dirt and stones with the back tires, yelling "They saw you! Dammit!" The car jolted forward. Tom reached for the open door and pulled it shut as they shot out on Summers Street. "Duck," Tom said to Sarah, and she bent forward beneath the dashboard. Tom slid down on the seat and looked out of the back window. Fritz stamped on the accelerator, and the Lincoln's tires squealed on the blacktop. Nappy LaBarre threw open the front door of the building and ran heavily into the parking lot on his short legs. He waved his short thick arms and yelled something. In a second the wall of trees cut him off.

"He saw us," Fritz wailed. "He saw the car! You think he doesn't know who we are? He knows who we are."

"He's alone," Tom said, helping Sarah sit up straight again. "There wasn't any phone in there, I don't think."

"You mean he can't call Jerry," Sarah said.

"I think he was putting some of the stuff in boxes for their next trip," Tom said. "Unless he walks back, he has to wait until Jerry comes by to pick him up."

Fritz turned left on another unmarked road, trying to find his way back to the village and the highway.

"The further adventures of Tom Pasmore," Sarah said.

"I want to say something," Fritz said. "I had nothing to do with this. All I wanted to do was go back to the lake, okay? I never looked in the windows, and I never saw any stolen stuff—I don't even think I saw Nappy."

"Oh, come on," Tom said.

"All I saw was a fat guy."

"Have it your way," Tom said.

"My Uncle Ralph is not just an ordinary guy," said Fritz. "Remember I said that, okay? He is not an ordinary guy."

Fritz drove along the bumpy road, gritting his teeth. He turned right on a three-lane road marked 41 and drove through a section of forest. Thick trees, neither oaks nor maples, but some gnarly black variety Tom did not know, stood at the border of the road, so close together their trunks nearly touched. Fritz ground his teeth, making a sound like a file grating across iron. They burst out into emptiness again.

"I didn't see Nappy," he said.

There was another long term of silence. Fritz came to a crossroads, looked both ways, and turned left again. On both sides muddy-looking fields stretched off to rotting wooden fences like match sticks against the dense forest.

The road went up over a rise and came down on a glossy black four-lane highway across from a sign that said LAKE DEEPDALE—DEEPDALE ESTATES. Fritz ground his teeth again, cramped the wheel, and turned in the direction of Eagle Lake.

"I don't know what you're so upset about," Tom said.

"You're right, you don't. You don't have the slightest idea." He turned into the narrow track between the trees that led to the lake, and when they reached the bench, he stopped the car. "This is where we picked you up, and this is where we're dropping you off."

"Are you going to call the police?" Sarah asked Tom.

"Get out of the car if you want to talk like that," Fritz said.

"Don't be a baby," Sarah snapped at him.

"You don't know either, Sarah."

Tom opened the door and got out. He did not close the door. "Of course I'm going to call them," he said to Sarah. "These people have been robbing houses for years." Fritz gunned the engine, and Tom leaned into the car. He looked at Fritz's furious profile. "Fritz, if you knew you had to see someone again, right after you learned something that made you pretty sure they'd committed murder, what would you do? Would you say anything?"

Fritz kept staring straight ahead. His teeth made the file-on-iron sound.

"Would you try to forget about it?"

Sarah gave him an anxious smile. "I'll come over tonight—I'll get out somehow."

Fritz pulled ahead, and Tom waved at Sarah. Fritz pushed the accelerator, and the car left Tom standing on the side of the road. After a couple of seconds, Sarah reached over to close the door. The car picked up speed as it went over the rise, and then it disappeared.

47

As soon as he got back to the lodge, Tom went into the study and found the number of the Eagle Lake Police Department in the telephone book.

A male voice answered, and Tom asked to speak to Chief Truehart.

"The Chief's out of the office until tonight," said the voice, and Tom saw Spychalla leaning back in his boss's chair, pumping his muscles to make his belt creak.

"Could you give me a time?"

"Who is this?" Spychalla asked.

"I want to give you some information," Tom said. "The stereo equipment and everything else stolen in the burglaries this year is being stored in an old tool and die shop on Summers Street. There's a Polish name over the door."

"Who are you?" Spychalla asked.

"One of the guys is still there, so if you go to Summers Street you can get him."

"I'm unable to respond to anything but emergencies, on

account of being alone here, but if you'll leave your name and tell me how you got this information. . . ."

Tom took the phone away from his ear and stared at it in frustration. He heard Spychalla's voice saying, "This is that kid out at Eagle Lake, isn't it? The one who thinks the Chief's mother is a burglar."

He put the phone to his mouth and said, "No, my name is Philip Marlowe."

"Where are you, Mr. Marlowe?"

Tom hung up. He wanted to go upstairs and hide under the bed.

He locked the front door, then walked across the length of the lodge and locked the door to the deck. Then he walked nervously around the sitting room for a time, and when the house made its noises, looked out the front windows to see if Jerry had come up on the porch. He went back into the sitting room and called Lamont von Heilitz, who was not at home.

The telephone rang when he had just reached the bottom of the first page of a letter to von Heilitz, and the pen skittered across the paper, leaving dashes. Tom set down the pen and looked at the phone. He put his hand on the receiver, but did not pick it up. It went dead, and then started ringing as soon as he took his hand off the receiver, and rang ten times before it stopped again.

The directory listed two Redwings: Ralph at Gladstone Lodge, Eagle Trail, and Chester, Palmerston Lodge, Eagle Trail. Chester was Fritz's father. Tom dialed the number and waited through three rings until a woman answered. He recognized the voice of Fritz's mother, Eleanor Redwing, and asked to speak to Fritz.

"Is that you, Tom? You must be enjoying yourself tremendously."

So Buddy's parents had not spoken about the difficulty with Sarah; and Fritz had kept quiet about the machine shop.

"Oh, sure," he said. "Tremendously."

"Well, I know that Fritz has been looking forward to seeing you up here ever since you left. Of course the big news around here is about Buddy and Sarah. We all think it's wonderful. She'll be so good for him."

"Wonderful," Tom said. "Tremendous."

"And of course she's had a crush on him since ninth grade. And they're so cute together, the way they keep sneaking off to be alone."

"I guess they have a lot to talk about."

"I don't think they spend a lot of time talking," she said. "Anyhow, here's Fritzie. Tom, I hope we'll be seeing you around the compound."

"That would be very nice."

A moment later Fritz took the phone. He did not say anything. Tom could hear him breathing into the receiver.

"What's going on over there?" he asked.

"Nothing."

"Nobody said anything about seeing us?"

"I told you, nothing."

"Where is everybody? Did you see Jerry or anybody after we got back?"

"About five minutes ago, my aunt and uncle went to Hurley in the Cadillac with Robbie. They're going to stay overnight with some friends."

"Did you see Nappy?"

"He's not around. Jerry's still out with Buddy, I guess. They took Sarah to look at a new boat."

Fritz breathed into the phone for a while and then said, "Maybe nothing's going to happen."

"Something has to happen, Fritz."

"So—you called, ah, you called who you said you were going to?"

"I didn't give any names," Tom said. "I just told them to look in that machine shop."

"You shouldn't of." Fritz breathed heavily into the phone for a few seconds. "What'd they say?"

"They didn't seem too excited."

"Okay," Fritz said. "Maybe they got everything out. I'm gonna say we were just driving around. Nobody saw anything."

"Did you try to call me a little while ago?"

"Are you kidding? Look, I can't talk anymore."

"You want to come over for a swim later?"

"I can't talk now," Fritz said, and hung up.

Tom paced around the lodge for another twenty minutes, then picked up a book, unlocked the back door, and went out on the deck.

He tilted the lounger back, stretched out, and tried to read. Sunlight bounced off the page, obliterating the print. Tom raised the book to block out the sun. Heat soaked through his clothes and warmed his skin, and bright golden light poured down to pool all about him. He could not keep his mind on the book: in a short time, his eyelids drooped, and the book tilted toward his chest and became a small white bird he held in his hands, and he was asleep.

A bell insistent as an alarm awakened him, and for a second he thought he was back in Brooks-Lowood—his body felt heavy and slow, but he had to change classes, he had to stand up and move. . . . He sat up. Sunburn tingled on his forehead, and his face was wet with perspiration. The telephone kept ringing, and Tom moved automatically toward the back door to answer it. He stopped when he put his hand on the doorknob. The phone rang twice more. Tom opened the door and went to the desk.

It's probably Grand-Dad, he thought.

He picked up the phone and said hello.

There was a brief moment of silence, and then a click and the dial tone.

Tom hung up, locked the back door, walked across the sitting room, went out and locked the front door with the key. He ran down the steps and crossed the track to drag the leafy branch away from the ruts made by Barbara Deane's car, went around it, and dragged the branch back. He stepped into the undergrowth between himself and the track, pushed aside vines and small stiff branches, and hunkered down at the base of an oak. Through chinks in the leaves, he could see his front steps, half of the porch, and a little of the way down the track to the compound.

Jerry Hasek came walking up the track thirty seconds later. He was wearing his grey suit and the chauffeur's cap, and his hands were balled into fists. He took the big steps two at a time, strode across the porch, and knocked on the screen door. Jerry spun on his heel and hit his fists together several times, rapidly. His face wore an expression of worried concentration that was familiar to Tom, and meant nothing: it was just the way Jerry looked. He spun back around and opened the screen door and pounded on the wooden door. Jerry's body told much more than his face—his movements were quick and agitated, and his shoulders looked stiff and bunched, as if he had developed extra layers of muscle and skin, like armor. "Pasmore!" he yelled. He banged on the door again.

Jerry stepped back and glared at the door. "Come on, I know you're there," he yelled. "Come on out, Pasmore." He put his hand on the knob and turned it, then rattled the door.

He moved to one of the windows and peered inside the way Tom had looked into the machine shop, with his hands cupping his face. He slapped the window with his palm, and the glass shivered. "Come on OUT!"

Jerry went backwards down the steps, looking upward as if he expected to see Tom climbing out of a window. He put his hands on his hips, and his shoulder muscles shifted underneath the fabric of the jacket. He looked from side to side, exhaled, and gazed back up at the lodge.

He bounded back up the steps, opened the screen door, and struck the door again several times. "You have to talk to me," he said, speaking in the voice he would use to a person who was hard of hearing. "I can't help you out if you don't talk to me."

He leaned his head against the door and said, "Come *on*." Then he pushed himself away from the door and trotted down the steps. His whole thick body looked energetic, electrified, as if you would get a shock if you touched him. Jerry went to the side of the lodge and went down between the trees to get to the back.

After a couple of minutes in which he must have banged on the back door and tried to get in, Jerry reappeared, heading toward the track with the cap in his hands and—for once—more concentration than worry in his broad face. He came out from beneath the oaks and turned to face the lodge. "You fucking dope," he said, and turned to walk back to the compound.

When he was out of sight, Tom came out of his hiding place and went up the steps. His feet resounded on the boards of the porch. He slid the key into the lock, and felt a hard, jittery presence in the air that was Jerry's ghost. Tom let himself in and locked the door behind him.

In the study, he dialed the operator and asked for his grandfather's number on Mill Walk.

The phone picked up on the first ring, and Kingsley's voice told him that he had reached the Glendenning Upshaw residence.

"Kingsley, this is Tom," he said. "Can I speak to my grandfather, please?"

"Master Tom, what a nice surprise! Are you enjoying yourself at the lake?"

"It's a great place. Could you get him, please?"

"Just a moment," Kingsley said, and put the phone down with a noisy clunk that suggested that he had dropped it.

He was gone much longer than a moment: Tom heard voices, footfalls, a door closing. Seconds ticked by, followed by more seconds. At last the butler returned. "I'm afraid your grandfather is not available."

"Not available? What does that mean?"

"Mr. Upshaw has gone out unexpectedly, Master Tom. I cannot tell you when he is expected to be back."

"Is his carriage gone?"

Kingsley paused a second, and said, "I believe it is, yes."

"Maybe he's visiting my mother," Tom said.

"He always informs us when he does not plan to dine at home," Kingsley said, and both his voice and his language sounded even stiffer than usual.

Neither Tom nor the old butler said anything for a moment.

"Is he really not there, Kingsley," Tom said, "or is he just unavailable?"

There was another brimming pause until the butler said, "It's as I told you, Master Tom."

"Okay, tell him I have to talk to him," Tom said, and they both hung up.

The endless afternoon passed into an endless evening. Tom realized that he was starving, and could not remember if he had eaten lunch—he could not remember eating anything all day. He went into the kitchen and opened the refrigerator—most of the food Barbara Deane had bought for him was still on the shelves, preserved in the supermarket wrappings. *I ate her food once before,* he thought, *and it didn't kill me.*

He scrambled two eggs in a bowl, buttered two slices of

whole wheat bread, cut slices off a garlic sausage and dropped them in the sizzling pan with the eggs. He turned the edges of the solidifying egg over the sausage, and after a few seconds, turned the whole thing out onto a plate. He ate in the kitchen and put the pan, bowl, plate, and his utensils into the sink and ran hot water over them.

Outside, sunlight still fell on the lake, but the shadow of the lodge darkened the deck nearly all the way to the pier. Tom pulled the living room curtains shut, and went to the desk and called the police department.

"Is Chief Truehart back in the office yet?" he asked.

"Is this Mr. Marlowe?" Spychalla asked. "Where are you calling from, Mr. Marlowe?"

Tom hung up and called his mother. No, her father had not been over that afternoon; no, she did not know where he might be. He was very busy with new plans for the Founders Club, and she had not seen him for days. Victor was out of town, doing something in Alabama for the Redwings. "Are you seeing all your friends?"

"I'm pretty busy," he told her.

Tom sat at the desk with the telephone before him, watching the shadow of the lodge slide across the deck and begin to darken the pier. Fish jumped silently in the lake. The air went grey. Inside, it looked like night.

When the sky began to darken, he put on a sweater and went out on the deck and locked the door behind him. Lights shone in the Langenheims' windows and reflected in narrow yellow lines on the water. Tom walked fast around the bottom end of the lake under a rising sliver of moon, passing the empty lodges—hurrying past the Langenheims'—until he came to Lamont von Heilitz's place, where he wound through trees and came out on the sandy shore of the lake. The old lodge looked like a haunted house in a movie—like Norman Bates' house, in *Psycho*. He jumped up on the stubby dock and walked out to the end and sat down on cool wood to look at the windows of the club.

The Redwings and their guests sat at the long table just inside the terrace. Tom could see the backs of the people on the window side of the table, Sarah Spence, Buddy, Fritz, and Eleanor Redwing. Across from them, Tom could see only the heads of Sarah's mother, Fritz's father, and Katinka Redwing. Ralph Redwing and Bill Spence sat at either end of the table. Marcello, his tuxedo shirt unbuttoned to his sternum, was passing out the giant leaves of the menus. When he came to Katinka Redwing, he bent down and whispered in her ear, and Katinka made a cat face. Buddy Redwing put his hand on Sarah's back and caressed her from the nape of the neck to her waist.

Marcello brought two champagne bottles in a silver bucket, and Ralph Redwing and Bill Spence each made toasts. Fritz's father made a toast, and Buddy's hand, fat as a starfish, slowly circled on Sarah's back. Fritz made a toast, which Tom wished he could hear. Buddy pushed back his chair, stood up, and made a speech. Marcello circled the table, filling glasses. Everybody was watching Buddy—they laughed, looked solemn, laughed again. Mrs. Spence waggled her glass in the air for more champagne. When Buddy sat down, Sarah kissed him and everyone applauded. She put her arms around his neck. Fritz's father said something, and everybody laughed again.

They ordered. Two more champagne bottles came. The fat brown starfish prowled across Sarah's back. Whenever Sarah turned to look at Buddy, her face glowed.

This was how it worked, Tom thought. The Redwings gobbled up food, drink, real estate, other people—they devoured morality, honesty, scruples, and everybody admired them. Sarah Spence could not resist them because nobody could.

Buddy was waving a fork, talking, and Fritz stared at him as adoringly as a little dog. A greedier, more adult version of the same expression came into Mrs. Spence's face whenever she turned to Ralph Redwing. Sarah's right hand, a slimmer, whiter starfish, rested between Buddy's shoulder blades.

Tom sat on the deck and watched them finish their dinner. There were two more bottles of champagne, coffee, desserts. At last they all stood up and drifted away from the window. A few minutes later, Tom saw them moving slowly on the track between the clubhouse and the compound, calling out good-byes loud enough to be heard across the water.

Lights came on in the upper windows of the lodges in the compound. A light switched on in the second floor of the Spence lodge. Birds called to each other, and a frog splashed in the reeds at the narrow end of the lake.

A car started up behind the compound, then another. The beams of headlights swept across the track between the compound and the club, and then shone upon the trees on the club's far side. A long black car came around the clubhouse, its headlights angled down the narrow road. It circled the top of the lake, and as it swung to go up the hill, Tom saw two heads side by side on the front seat, one dark, one blond. Another long car followed, this, too, with a dark and a blond head in the front seat.

The lights in the club dining room went out, and long blocks of yellow vanished from the surface of the lake. Tom walked the long way back to his lodge.

He cut across Roddy Deepdale's lawn and came up to his dock along the shoreline. He sat on the wood and swung his legs up, then took off his shoes. The shoes in his hand, he moved up to the deck, knelt in the darkness before the back door, found the lock with his fingertips, and slid in the key. He turned the knob and opened the door as softly as possible. Inside, he closed the door and turned the lock. Cold moonlight lay across the desk and washed the colors from the hooked rug.

Tom moved to the open door into the sitting room, and crouched over. Holding his breath, he slid into the big room, and stood, crouched and motionless, listening for any movement. The sitting room was dark as an underground cave. Tom waited until he was sure he was alone, and then he straightened up and took another step into the room.

The beam of a flashlight struck his eyes and blinded him.

"If I were you, I'd be careful too," a man said. "Just stay there."

The flashlight went off, and Tom instantly went into a crouch and began to rush into the office. A floor lamp snapped on. "Not too bad," the man said.

Tom slowly straightened up and turned around to face him. All the breath left his body at once. His hand still on the chain of the floor lamp, wearing a dark blue suit and gloves that matched his grey double-breasted vest, Lamont von Heilitz smiled at him from a couch.

"You're here!" Tom said.

The Shadow pulled the lamp chain, and the room went dark again. "It's time we had another talk," he said.

48

Tom groped forward. He bumped against the back of a chair, felt his way around it, and sat down. His own breathing sounded as loud as Fritz Redwing's on the telephone that afternoon. "When did you get here? How did you get in?" As Tom's eyes adjusted to the darkness, the long slender shape of von Heilitz's body took form against the paler couch. The detective's head stood out against the curtains behind him like a silhouette.

"I got in about an hour ago, by slipping the lock. You didn't go to dinner at the club, I suppose?"

"No. I went to your dock and looked through the windows into the dining room. I didn't want Jerry Hasek to find me here, and I wanted to know what was going on— I'm really glad you're here. If I could see you, I'd say that it was great to see you."

"I'm relieved to see you too, at least as well as I can. But I owe you an apology. I should have come for you long before this—I wanted you to find out whatever you could, but I underestimated the danger you'd be in. I never thought they'd shoot at you through windows."

"So you got my letters."

"Every one of them. They were excellent. You've done very good work, Tom, but it's time to get back to Mill Walk. We're flying back at four in the morning."

"Four in the morning!"

"Our pilot has to file his flight plan and get everything ready, or we'd leave earlier than that. We can't take the risk of staying another night."

"You don't think a hunter shot a stray bullet through the window."

"No," von Heilitz said. "That was a deliberate attempt on your life. And you upped the ante by looking into that machine shop. So I want to take you to a safe place now, and make sure you stay alive until we get on that plane."

"How do you know about the machine shop? I haven't even mailed that letter yet."

Von Heilitz said nothing.

"How long have you been here? You didn't just get to Eagle Lake an hour ago, did you?"

"Did you think I'd send you into this lion's den alone?"

"You've been here the whole time? How did you get my letters?"

"Sometimes I went to the post office and picked them up, sometimes Joe Truehart brought them to me."

Tom nearly jumped off his chair. "That was *you* I followed—that was you carrying the flashlight."

"You almost caught me too. I went to my lodge to pick up some things, and I don't see as well at night as I used to. Let's go, shall we? We ought to get back, and I do want to see more of you than that glimpse I had when you came creeping in. We have a lot to talk about."

"Where are we going?"

Von Heilitz stood up. "You'll see."

Tom watched the dark blur of the older man move toward him. His white hair shone in the moonlight. "That house in the clearing," Tom said. "Mrs. Truehart's cabin."

The tall shape before him tilted forward, and the white hair gleamed. Von Heilitz grasped his shoulders. "She probably wants to apologize to you too. She doesn't normally scare away visitors with a rifle, but I didn't want you to know I was there." He squeezed Tom's shoulders and straightened up.

Tom followed him into the study, and in the moonlight, von Heilitz turned and took him in, smiling. "I can't get over it," Tom said.

"You're what I can't get over," von Heilitz said. "You've done everything I hoped you would, and more. I didn't expect you to solve any burglaries while you were up here."

"I had a good teacher," Tom said, feeling his face get hot.

"More than that," the old man said. "Now open that door, will you?"

Tom unlocked the back door, and von Heilitz moved outside. Tom followed after him, and knelt to lock the door with the key again.

Von Heilitz placed his hand on Tom's shoulder, and left it there as Tom stood up. He did not remove it even when Tom turned to face him at last, and the two of them stood in the moonlight for a second, looking into each other's faces. Tom still felt the shock of pleasure and relief of seeing von Heilitz, and blurted, "I don't think Anton Goetz killed Jeanine Thielman."

Von Heilitz nodded, smiled, and patted Tom's shoulder before he lowered his hand. "I know."

"I thought—I guess I thought you might be angry or something. It was one of your most important cases—I know what it meant to you."

"It was my single biggest mistake. And *that's* what it means to me. Now you and I are going to put things right—after all this time. Let's go to Mrs. Truehart's, so we can talk about it."

Von Heilitz jumped neatly off the dock and began moving toward the shoreline. At Roddy Deepdale's, he led Tom across the grass toward the track. They cast identical long shadows in the moonlight. Neither of them spoke until they came to the opening of the path into the woods behind the Thielman lodge. Von Heilitz switched on his flashlight and said, "Tim Truehart arrested your friend Nappy, by the way," and plunged into the woods.

"He did?" Tom followed. "I didn't think Spychalla would give him the message."

"He might not have if Chet Hamilton hadn't been curious about why you were asking directions to Summers Street. He drove out there not long after you did, and got close enough to see Nappy stacking boxes outside the shop. He just turned his car around and went to the nearest phone. Spychalla couldn't ignore two calls."

"But what about Jerry?"

"Nappy is still claiming he did all the burglaries himself. He'll change his mind when it finally hits him that he'll serve a lot less jail time if he turns in his friends. Spychalla is looking for Jerry Hasek and Robbie Wintergreen, but so far he hasn't found them. This must be where you got lost the other night."

The flashlight shone upon smooth grey-brown tree trunks. He moved the beam slightly to the left, and the narrow path reappeared, wandering deeper into the woods. "It looks like it," Tom said.

"I was sorry to have to let that happen." Von Heilitz followed the bend in the path.

"So why did you?"

"I told you. Because I wanted you to do just what you have done."

"Find out that Barbara Deane killed Jeanine Thielman?"

The light stopped moving, and Tom nearly bumped into the old man. Von Heilitz let out a loud, explosive laugh that sounded like "WHA-HAH!" He whirled around and shone the light on the middle of Tom's chest. Even in the darkness and with his face hidden behind the glare of the light, he looked as if he were suppressing more explosive laughter. "Excuse me, but what makes you think that?"

As irritated now as he had been relieved before, Tom said, "I looked into a box I found in her closet, and along with some old articles that almost accused her of murder, I found two anonymous notes. Jeanine Thielman wrote them."

"My God," von Heilitz said. "What did they say?"

"One said 'I know what you are, and you have to be stopped.' The other one said something like, 'This has gone on too long—you will pay for your sins.' "

"Extraordinary."

"I guess you don't think she killed Jeanine Thielman."

"Barbara Deane never killed anybody in her life," von Heilitz said. "Did you think that Barbara Deane also killed Anton Goetz? Hanged him with his own fishing line?"

"She could have done it. He might have been blackmailing her."

"And she just happened to be waiting in his lodge to make a payment when he arrived with the news that I had accused him of murder."

"Well," Tom said. "I guess that part was always a little shaky." He did not feel angry anymore—he was relieved not to have to think of Barbara Deane as a murderer. "But if she didn't do it, and Anton Goetz didn't do it, then who did?"

"You told me who killed them both," von Heilitz said.

"But you just said—"

"In your letters. Didn't I say you accomplished just what I hoped you would?" Von Heilitz lowered the flashlight, and Tom saw him smiling at him.

Something else is going on here, Tom thought. *Something I don't get.*

The detective turned around and began moving quickly down the path through the woods.

"Aren't you going to tell me?"

"In time."

Tom felt like screaming.

"There's something else I have to tell you first," von Heilitz said, still moving rapidly down the path.

Tom hurried after him.

Von Heilitz did not say another word until they had reached the clearing. Moonlight fell on the Truehart cabin, and washed the flowers of all their color. The old man turned off his flashlight as soon as Tom stepped off the path to the grass, and their shadows lay stark and elongated over the silvery ground. The whole world was black and grey and silver. Tom stepped toward him. Von Heilitz crossed his arms over his chest. All the fine lines in his face were deepened by the moonlight, and his forehead looked corrugated. He looked like a person Tom had never seen before, and Tom stopped moving, suddenly uncertain.

"I want so much to do this right," von Heilitz said. "If I botch this, you'll never forgive me, and neither will I."

Tom opened his mouth, but could not speak—a sudden deep strangeness stopped his tongue.

Von Heilitz looked down, trying to begin, and his forehead contorted even more alarmingly. When he spoke, what he asked astonished Tom.

"How do you get on with Victor Pasmore?"

The boy almost laughed. "I don't," he said. "Not really."

"Why do you think that is?"

"I don't know. He sort of hates me, I guess. We're too different."

"What would he say if he knew that you and I know each other?"

"He'd carry on, I guess—he warned me away from you." Tom felt the old man's mixture of tension and earnestness. "What is this all about?"

Von Heilitz looked at him, looked at the silvery grass, back up at Tom. "This is the part I have to do right." He took a deep breath. "I met a young woman in 1945. I was much older than she was, but she appealed to me a great deal—enormously. Something happened to me that I had thought would never happen. I started by being touched by her, and as I got to know her better, I began to love her. I felt that she needed me. We had to meet secretly, because her father hated me—I was the most unsuitable man she could have chosen, but she *had* chosen me. In those days, I still traveled a great deal, but I started refusing cases so that I wouldn't have to leave her."

"Are you saying—"

He shook his head and walked a few steps away and looked at the forest. "She became pregnant, and didn't tell me. I heard about a very exciting case, one that really intrigued me, and I took it. We decided to get married after I came back from the case, and to—to lessen the shock, we went out in public for a week. We attended a concert together, we went to a restaurant, we went to a party held by people who were not in our own circle, but who lived on another part of the island. It was such a relief to do things like that. When I left for my trip, I asked her to come with me, but she felt she had to stay at home to face her father. I thought she could do that. She had become much stronger, or so I thought. She wouldn't let me deal with her father, you see—she said there would be time for that when I came back."

He turned to face Tom again. "When I called her, her father wouldn't let me speak to her. I gave up the case and flew back to Mill Walk the next day, but they were gone. She had told her father everything—even that she was pregnant. Her father kept her away from Mill Walk, and in effect bought her a fiancé on the mainland. She—she had collapsed. They came back to Mill Walk, and the marriage took place in days. Her father threatened to put her in a mental hospital if I ever saw her again. Two months after the marriage, she gave birth to a son. I suppose her father bribed the Registrar to issue a false marriage certificate. From that time on, Tom, I never accepted another job that would take me off the island. She belonged to her father again—probably she always belonged to her father. But I watched that boy. Nobody would let me see him, but I watched him. I loved him."

"That's why you visited me in the hospital," Tom said. Feelings too strong to be recognized froze him to the moonlit grass. He felt as if his body were being pulled in different directions, as though ice and fire had been poured into his head.

"I love you," the old man said. "I'm very proud of you, and I love you, but I know I don't deserve your love. I'm a rotten father."

Tom stepped toward him, and von Heilitz somehow crossed the ground between them without seeming to move. The old man tentatively put his arms around Tom, and Tom stood rigid for a second. Then something broke inside him—a layer like a shelf of rock he had lived with all his life without ever recognizing—and he began to sob. The sob seemed to come from beneath the shelf of rock, from a place that had been untouched all his life. He put his arms around von Heilitz, and felt an unbelievable lightness and vividness of being, as if the world had come streaming into him.

"Well, at least I told you," the old man said. "Did I botch it?"

"Yeah, you talked too much," Tom said.

"I had a lot to say!"

Tom laughed, and tears ran down his face and dampened the shoulder of von Heilitz's coat. "I guess you did."

"It's going to take both of us a while to adjust to this," von Heilitz said. "And I want you to know that I think Victor Pasmore probably did his best—he certainly didn't want you to grow up like me. He tried to give you what he thought was a normal boyhood."

Tom pulled back and looked at the old man's face. It no longer looked masklike, but utterly familiar.

"He did a pretty good job, actually, given the circumstances. It couldn't have been easy for him."

The world had changed completely while remaining the same: the difference was that now he could understand, or at least begin to understand, details of his life that had been inexplicable except as proof of his oddness and unsuitability.

"Oh, if you think *you* made a botch of it—" Tom said.

"Let's go inside," von Heilitz said.

49

Less than an hour later Tom was back in the lodge alone, waiting. When Lamont von Heilitz had learned that Tom wanted to return to the lodge to meet Sarah Spence, he had reluctantly let him go, with the promise that he would be waiting outside at one. Mrs. Truehart had gone to bed, and he and the old man had talked in soft voices about themselves, reliving their history. The conversation about Jeanine Thielman and Anton Goetz would have to wait, von Heilitz said, there were too many details to iron out, too many pieces of information to dovetail—there was a lot of it he still did not understand, and understanding would take more time than they had. "We have at least five hours in the air," he told Tom. "Tim Truehart is flying us to Minneapolis, where we get our plane to Mill Walk. There'll be time. When we land at David Redwing field, we should have everything worked out."

"Just tell me the name," Tom had pleaded.

Von Heilitz smiled and walked him to the door. "I want *you* to tell *me* the name."

So, too restless to sit down, too nervous about Jerry Hasek to turn on any lights, Tom waited for Sarah, hoping that she had not already tried to find him at the lodge. In the end, he slipped outside and waited behind an oak tree set back from the track between her lodge and his.

He heard the sound of her feet landing softly on the beaten earth, but did not come out from behind the tree until he saw her white shirt glimmer in the darkness. Her face and arms, already tanned, looked very dark against the shirt and the darker blond of her hair. She was walking quickly, and by the time he stepped out on the track she was nearly abreast of him.

"Oh!"

"It's me," he said softly.

"You scared me." She came nearer, seeming to sift through the darkness, and touched the front of his shirt.

"You scared me too. I wasn't sure you were coming."

"My double life takes up a lot of time—I had to go to the White Bear with Buddy and watch him get drunk."

Tom remembered Buddy rubbing her back, and her own hand resting on Buddy's. "I wish you didn't have to have this double life of yours."

She stepped closer to him. "You seem so jumpy. Is it about me, or this afternoon? You shouldn't be insecure about me, Tom, and I think Jerry and his friends ran off. Ralph couldn't find them after dinner."

"Nappy got arrested," Tom said. "Maybe they did take off. But it probably isn't that. I'm going back to Mill Walk tonight. A lot of stuff is happening, and I just found out—well, I just learned something very important about myself. I feel kind of overloaded."

"Tonight? How soon tonight?"

"In about an hour."

She looked at him steadily. "Then let's go inside."

She put her arm around his waist, and together they began walking toward the almost invisible lodge. "How are you getting back? There aren't any planes at night."

"We're going to Minneapolis," he said.

"We?"

"Me and someone else. The Chief of Police has a little plane, and he's taking us there."

She tilted her head and looked up at him as they walked along.

"It's Lamont von Heilitz, but Sarah, you can't tell anybody he was here. This is serious. Nobody can know."

"Do you think I talk about the things you tell me?"

"Sometimes I wonder," he said.

Her arms folded around him, and her face tilted toward his—made half of night and darkness. Her face filled his eyes. He kissed her, and it was like kissing the night. Sometimes she did talk about the things he told her, and sometimes he wondered, and to her these were the same, because they were both exciting. Like being engaged to be engaged; you got things both ways.

"Are we going to go into your lodge, or are we just going to stand out here?"

"Let's go in," he said.

He led her up the steps, let her in, and locked the door behind them.

He sensed more than saw her turning toward him. "Nobody ever locks their doors up north."

"Nobody but me."

"My father isn't going to come looking for us."

"It isn't your father I'm worried about."

She found his cheek with her hand. "Where are the lights? I can't even see you in here."

"We don't need lights," he said. "Just follow me."

"In the dark?"

"I like being in the dark." He was going to say something else, but saw her teeth flash in the darkness and reached for her. His hand fell on her hip. "I just found out that I'm not who I thought I was."

"You never were who you thought you were."

"Maybe nobody was who I thought they were."

"May*bee-ee*," she half-sang, half-whispered, and stepped closer into his grasp. "Am I following you somewhere?"

He took her hand and led her around the furniture toward the staircase in the dark. "Here," he said, and put her hand on the bottom of the banister. Then he clamped his arm around her waist, and slowly took the stairs with her. In the deep blackness, it felt like falling in reverse.

She stopped moving at the top of the stairs, and whispered, "The handrail disappeared."

Tom nudged her to the left, where faint light from the window showed the dark shape of a doorway. They moved together down the shadowy hallway. Tom leaned over the doorknob and noiselessly pulled the door toward him.

There was just enough dim light in the room to reveal the bed and the table. Black leaves flattened against the window. Sarah's arms were around his neck as soon as he closed the door. He smelled tobacco smoke in her hair.

50

Certain things she said:

Tom. *Oh*.
I love this, don't you love this?
Say you love me.
Yes, that. Do that some more.
I love the way—the way you fill me up.
Bite me. *Bite* me.
Oh, God.
Harder, yes, yes, yes . . .
Let's roll over—
Oh! Oh! Oh!
Sweet baby—
Oh, my God, look at you! Put it, put it . . . *yesss*.
Tell me you love me.

—I love you.

Sarah's head lay heavy on his chest. Whatever this was, it was good enough.

51

Jeanine Thielman in a dripping white dress rose up from the lake—her face dead and heavy—walking toward him through feathers of smoke—her mouth gaping open like a trap and her white tongue flapping as she struggled to speak. In his sleep Tom heard her scream, and his eyes swam open to an oily blackness. Jeanine Thielman's drowned body lay across his, and pain muffled his head. His chest was filled with oily rags, and something foul churned in his stomach. A scream? He tried to see his bedroom. The hairs in his nose crisped with heat. All he could see through the blackness was a fuzzy red rectangle—that was a window. A rushing, roaring sound came to him at last. He shook his head, and nearly threw up. He moaned, and slid out from under the body atop his own. The movement brought his hips over the side of the narrow bed, and he tumbled to the floor. He stared at a hand dripping off the bed before his eyes, and realized that the hand belonged to Sarah Spence. The floor warmed his knees.

Tom inhaled, and felt as though he had drawn fire into his

nose. “Sarah,” he said, “wake up! Wake up!” He yanked on her arm, and pulled her body toward him. Her eyes were slits. She said, “Whuzza?”

“The lodge is on fire,” he said, uttering something he had not known until it was spoken.

Her eyes rolled back into her head. Tom leaned over the bed and put his hands under her arms and pulled her toward him. She fell on top of him, and flailed out with one hand, hitting the side of his head. Tom fell back. The air was cooler and clearer on the floor. He noticed that he was wearing a shirt. Hadn't he taken his shirt off? He reached up and pulled a sheet off the bed. Then he slapped Sarah's face, hard.

“Shit,” she said, distinctly. Her eyes opened again, and she coughed as if she were trying to push her stomach out through her throat. “My head hurts. My chest hurts.”

Tom roughly put the sheet around her, then snatched off the blanket and put it over her like a hood. The bottom sheet lay loose and tangled on the bed, and he reached up and snapped it toward him and tugged it up over his body and began crawling toward the door. He heard Sarah crawling after him, coughing, through the furnace noise of the fire.

He bumped into the door and reached up. The brass knob felt warm, not hot, and he turned it. Voices and screams and the roaring noise came in on a rush of hot air. He flattened himself on the hot floor and snaked forward to look into the hallway.

A wall of boiling black smoke rolled toward him from the back end of the house. The door of the big bedroom and half of the staircase were invisible behind or within it. Dry wood snapped, sending streamers of glowing sparks through the blackness.

“Breathe through the sheet,” he yelled, and looked backward at Sarah. Her face peered out into the smoke from beneath the blanket, dazed and puffy, like that of a suddenly awakened child. She crawled forward another inch, tried to move the sheet up over her mouth, and collapsed under the blanket.

Tom wound his own sheet around his neck and went back and got his arms under Sarah. The blanket slithered off when he lifted her body, and he went back down on his knees and grabbed for it and pulled it over her. The blanket seemed important, essential. He got his right arm behind her shoulders, his left under her knees, and staggered upright. His eyes burned. He carried her out of the bedroom into the hall.

The force of the heat nearly knocked him down, and Sarah struggled in his arms, awkward in the blanket. His own sheet trailed like a shroud. Tom ran straight into the blast of heat—like a hand trying to hold him back. Burning air moved into his mouth and singed his throat and lungs, and he nearly fell again. Something banged into his hip, supporting him, and he realized it was the top of the banister. With sudden strength, he slung Sarah's body over his shoulder. A loose flap of the blanket curled against his face. He was already moving down the stairs. Voices drifted toward him through the noise of the fire, but they were not real voices.

Halfway down the stairs, he saw sparks and red lines of fire jumping across the sitting room. A beam thundered down from the back of the house, and a shower of sparks and individual flames flew out from the study, encased in dense smoke. Curls of smoke rose from the sofa and chairs. The rugs had begun to burn inward from the edges, and ovals of flame from the rugs were just now touching the legs of the chairs and tables and running up the walls. The curtains snapped into flame.

He ran off the stairs and turned in a circle, unable to see any way out. He had not taken a breath in minutes, and his chest fought for air that would kill him. The front door was locked, and flames coursed across its top. A runner of fire sped across the floor, and an old chair went up like a candle with an audible *poof*! A heavy piece of wood came crashing down into the study. Flames ran across the ceiling. He went across the floor, jumping over a low distinct line of flames, sobbing with frustration. Sarah was a limp heavy weight over his shoulder. His eyebrows and eyelashes sizzled away in the heat.

Tom reached the front door and reached for the lock with a sheet-entangled hand. The metal burned his fingers. He fumbled, then grasped it through the sheet, and turned it over, freeing the door. The sheet came away from his hand. He put his palm on the doorknob, and felt his skin adhering to the metal. He screamed, and turned the knob. A thunderous crash and an explosion happened at his back. Fire sprang across the wood directly in front of his eyes. Tom closed his eyes, ducked his head, and pushed at the door. Cold sweet air poured over him, and the fire directly behind him roared like a thousand beasts. He staggered forward into the screen door, heard it splinter and crash, and then moved across the porch on legs made of water, gulping in air. People he could not see screamed or yelled. His stomach turned itself inside out, and he vomited down the front of his body, soaking his sheet. He tasted smoke and ashes, as if he had thrown up a full ashtray. He could hear the top of the porch roaring away above him.

Tom walked off the porch on his wobbling legs and felt the weight of Sarah magically disappear from his shoulder, as if she had flown away. He opened his eyes without seeing, stepped into empty air, and sank into someone's arms.

Some time later he came to in the act of vomiting again. Hands held his shoulders. The air was unnaturally hot, but cooler than he expected: how could that be? He pushed himself back from the pink and brown puddle on the earth, and his feet snagged the bottom of the blanket that encased him. His vomit stank like charred wood, and so did the contradictory air. He tilted his head and saw flames jumping into the air on the other side of a row of people in robes and pajamas. A siren screamed. He remembered screams—a siren's? Bitsy Langenheim, in a yellow Japanese kimono with flapping sleeves and chrysanthemums the color of fire, looked over her shoulder and frowned at him. Leaves burst into flame on a tall oak tree ahead of them, and everybody backed a step toward him.

"Sarah?" he said—croaked. Razor blades and knives dug into his throat.

"She's okay. An ambulance is on the way, Tom. You saved her life."

He fell on his haunches. He was under the trees on the near side of the Spence lodge, and the great fire all the people were watching was his lodge. Wet wool filled his brain. Now Neil Langenheim had also turned to look at him, and there was nothing in his face but distaste.

"Was anybody else in the lodge?" Lamont von Heilitz asked him.

Tom shook his head. "You caught me."

"I was about to try to get inside when you came running

out—just in time too. I think the whole back half of the lodge collapsed about a second later."

"A second before," Tom said, remembering the explosion he had heard behind him. "Where's Sarah?"

"With her parents. You did the right thing by wrapping her in that blanket."

Tom tried to sit upright, and a heavy blackness swam in his head. "The plane—and people will know you're—"

"Our flight has been canceled, I'm afraid," von Heilitz said. "Anyhow, Tim will have to stick around here for a day, trying to work out how the fire was started."

"Want to see her," Tom said with his croaking voice, and the razor blades and knives moved another inch or two into the flesh of his throat.

An oak tree on the lake side of the burning lodge began to incinerate in a rattle of leaves.

"She told—she talked about—"

Von Heilitz stroked his arm through the rough blanket.

A black-haired man wearing a brilliant red silk robe over yellow silk pajamas and sucking on a long pipe stood at the end of the row of people watching the fire. He said something to a young man wearing only a tight pair of faded jeans, and the young man, who was Marcello, swept his arm from the fire to the trees between it and the Spence lodge. Somewhere distant, a horse whinnied in terror. Tom was going to ask von Heilitz what Hugh Hefner was doing here, when the irrelevant thought came to him that the publisher of *Playboy* would probably have the same kind of private jet as Ralph Redwing. Then he saw that the man in the robe was Ralph Redwing, and that Ralph's black little eye had just flicked toward him and von Heilitz before it flicked away again. On his smooth, firelit face sat an expression of worried concern as abstracted as Jerry Hasek's.

"Everybody saw you," he croaked to von Heilitz.

The Shadow patted his shoulder.

"No, they *saw* you," he croaked again, realizing that this was terrible, it must be undone.

The fire took another oak tree.

[illegible]

[illegible]

[illegible]

[illegible]

[illegible]

[illegible]

[illegible]

[illegible]

[illegible]

[illegible]

[illegible]

[illegible]

[illegible]

[illegible]

[illegible]

Part Eight

THE SECOND DEATH OF TOM PASMORE

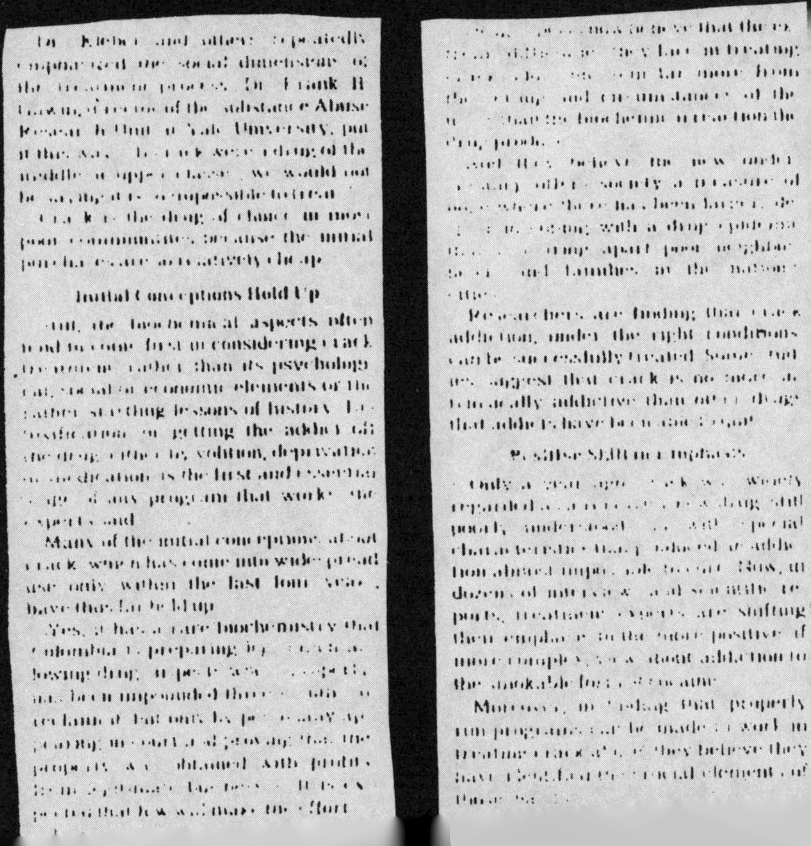

52

His room was not white, like his old room at Shady Mount, but painted in bright primary colors, lake water blue and sunlight yellow and maple leaf red. These colors were intended to induce cheerfulness and healthy high spirits. When Tom opened his eyes in the morning, he remembered sitting at a long table in Mrs. Whistler's kindergarten class, awkwardly trying to cut something supposed to resemble an elephant out of stiff blue construction paper with a pair of scissors too big for him. His stomach, his throat, and his head all hurt, and a thick white bandage swaddled his right hand. A twelve-inch television set on a moveable clamp angled toward the head of his bed—the first time he had switched this off with the remote control device on his bed, a nurse had switched it back on as soon as she came into the room, saying, "You want to watch something, don't you?" and the second time she had said, "I can't imagine what's wrong with this darn set." He just let it run now, moving by itself from game shows to soap operas to news flashes as he slept.

When Lamont von Heilitz came into the room, Tom turned off the set again. Every part of his body felt abnormally heavy, as if weights had been sewn into his skin, and most of them hurt in ways that seemed brand new. A transparent grease that smelled like room deodorizer shone on his arms and legs.

"You can get out of here in a couple of hours," von Heilitz said, even before he took the chair beside Tom's bed. "That's how hospitals do it now—no lollygagging. They just told me, so when we're done I'll pack and get some clothes for you, and then come back and pick you up. Tim will fly us to Minneapolis, and we'll get a ten o'clock flight and land in Mill Walk about seven in the morning."

"A nine-hour flight?"

"It's not exactly direct," von Heilitz said, smiling. "How do you like the Grand Forks hospital?"

"I won't mind leaving."

"What sort of treatment did you get?"

"In the morning, they gave me an oxygen mask for a little while. After that, I guess I got some antibiotics. Every couple of hours, a woman comes around and makes me drink orange juice. They rub this goo all over me."

"Do you feel ready to leave?"

"I'd do anything to get out of here," Tom said. "I feel like I'm living my whole life over again. I get pushed in front of a car, and a little while later, I wind up in the hospital. Pretty soon, I'm going to figure out a murder and a whole bunch of people will get killed."

"Have you seen any of the news broadcasts?" the old man asked, and the edge in his voice made Tom slide up straighter on his pillows. He shook his head.

"I have to tell you a couple of things." The old man leaned closer, and rested his arms on the bed. "Your grandfather's lodge burned down, of course. So did the Spence lodge. There's nobody left at the lake now—the Redwings flew everybody back on their jet this morning."

"Sarah?"

"She was released around seven this morning—she was in better shape than you were, thanks to that blanket you wrapped around her. Ralph and Katinka dropped the Spences and the Langenheims on Mill Walk, and flew straight to Venezuela."

"Venezuela?"

"They have a vacation house there too. They didn't want to stick around Eagle Lake, with all the mess and stink. Not to mention the crime investigation."

"Crime?" Tom said. "Oh, arson."

"Not just arson. Around two o'clock this afternoon, when the ashes finally got cool enough to sift through, Spychalla and a part-time deputy found a body in what was left of your lodge. It was much too badly burned to be identified."

"A body?" Tom said. "There couldn't be—" Then he felt a wave of nausea and horror as he realized what had happened.

"It was your body," von Heilitz said.

"No, it was—"

"Chet Hamilton was there when they found it, and all three men knew it had to be you. There wasn't anybody around to tell them different, and they even had a beautiful motive. Which was that Jerry Hasek—well, you know. Hamilton wrote his story as soon as he got back to his office, and it will run in tomorrow's paper. As far as anybody knows, you're dead."

"It was Barbara Deane!" Tom burst out. "I forgot—she told me she was going to come over late at night. . . . Oh, God. She died—she was killed." He closed his eyes, and a tremor of shock and sorrow nearly lifted him off the bed. His body seemed to grow hot, then cold, and he tasted smoke deep in his throat. "I heard her screaming," he said, and started to cry. "When I got out—when you were with me outside—I thought it was her horse. The horse heard the fire, and . . ." He panted, hearing the screams inside his head.

He put his hands over his ears; then he saw her, Barbara Deane opening the door to the lodge in her silk blouse and her pearls, worried about what he had heard about her; Barbara Deane saying, *I'm not sure any woman could have been what people think of as a good wife to your grandfather*; saying, *I've always thought that your grandfather saved my life.* He put his hands over his eyes.

"I agree with you," the old man said. "Murder is an obscenity."

He reached out and wrapped his fingers around the old man's linked hands.

"Let me tell you about Jerry Hasek and Robbie Wintergreen." Von Heilitz gripped Tom's fingers in his gloved hands: it was a gesture of reassurance, but somehow of reassurance in spite of everything, and Tom felt an unhappy wariness awaken in him. "They stole a car on Main Street, and drove it into an embankment outside Grand Forks. A witness said he saw them shouting at each other in the car, and the driver took his hands off the wheel to hit the other man. The car hit the embankment, and both of them almost went through the windshield. They're being held in the jail here in town."

"That's Jerry," Tom said.

"All this happened about eight o'clock yesterday night."

"No, it couldn't have. It must have been today," Tom said. "Otherwise, they couldn't have . . ."

"They didn't," von Heilitz said, and squeezed Tom's hand. "Jerry didn't set the fire. I don't think Jerry shot at you, either."

He let go of Tom's hand and stood up. "I'll be back in under an hour. Remember, you're posthumous now, for a day or two. Tim Truehart knows you're alive, but I was able to persuade him not to tell anyone until the time is right."

"But the hospital—"

"I gave your name as Thomas von Heilitz," the old man said.

He left the room, and for a time Tom did nothing but stare at the wall. *Remember, you're posthumous now.* The second shift nurse bustled into the room carrying a tray, smiled briskly at him, looked at his chart, and said, "I bet we're happy to be going home, aren't we?" She was a stout red-haired woman with orange eyebrows and two small protuberant growths on the right side of her face, and she gave him a comic frown when he did not respond. "Aren't you going to give me a smile, honey?"

He would have spoken to her, but he could not find a single thing to say.

"Well, maybe we like it here," she said. The nurse put down the chart and came up the side of the bed. A single long hypodermic needle, a cotton swab, and a brown bottle of alcohol lay on the tray. "Can you roll over for me? This is our last injection of antibiotics before we go home."

"The parting shot," Tom said. He rolled over, and the nurse separated the back of his robe. The alcohol chilled a stripe on his left buttock, as if a fresh layer of skin had been exposed to the air; the needle punched into him and lingered; another cold swipe of alcohol.

"Your grandfather looks so *distinguished*," the nurse said. "Is he in the theater?"

Tom said nothing. The nurse switched on the television set before she left the room, not with the remote but by reaching up and twisting the ON button, almost brutally, as if it were a duty he had neglected.

As soon as she was out of the room, Tom pointed the remote at the blaring set and zapped it.

53

"Up here, our victims aren't usually so well dressed," said Tim Truehart, standing in his leather jacket by the open door of an old blue Dodge as Tom and von Heilitz came out of the hospital's front entrance.

"*I'm* not usually so well dressed," Tom said, looking down at the suit the old man had brought for him. It was a grey and blue windowpane plaid, with the label of a London tailor, and except for being a little tight across the shoulders, fit him better than any of his own suits. Von Heilitz had also loaned him a white shirt, a dark blue figured tie, and a pair of well-shined black shoes, also his size, that felt stiff and resentful on his feet. Tom had expected the detective to show up with cheap new clothes, not his own, and when he had looked at himself in the mirror that hung in his room's tiny bathroom, he had seen a well-dressed stranger in his mid-twenties. The stranger had stubby eyelashes and only a few bristles for eyebrows. The stranger's face looked peeled. If he had seen himself in the dark, he would have thought he was Lamont von Heilitz.

Tom got in the back seat with the suitcases, and von Heilitz sat in the front with Truehart.

"I don't suppose you saw anybody around your lodge before the fire started," the policeman said.

"I didn't even know that Barbara Deane was there."

"The fire was started at both the front and the back of the lodge at roughly the same time—it wouldn't take more than a cup of gasoline and a match to get those old places going." Truehart sounded as if he were talking to himself. "So we know Tom didn't do it accidentally, and it didn't start in the kitchen, or anything like that. That fire was deliberately set."

For an instant Tom wished he were back in his bed in the kindergarten room, safe with his injections of antibiotics and the perpetual television.

Von Heilitz said, "Somewhere in Eagle Lake or Grand Forks, there's a man who is down on his luck. He probably has a prison record. He will do certain things for money. He lives off in the woods, and he doesn't have too many friends. Jerry Hasek learned this man's name by asking around in bars and making a few telephone calls. You ought to be able to do the same."

"There's probably fifty guys like that around here," Truehart said. "I'm not a famous private detective, Lamont, I'm a small-town Chief of Police. I don't usually play games like this, and Myron Spychalla is after my job. I'd hate to have to go to work."

Tom could not stop himself from yawning.

"You have Nappy LaBarre and Robbie Wintergreen in your jail," von Heilitz said. "That's all you really need. I think one of them will be happy to work out a little trade."

"If they know about it."

"Sure," von Heilitz said. "If they know about it. I'm not telling you anything new. I'm not a famous private detective, either. I'm a retired old man who has the leisure to sit back and watch things happen."

"And that's what you were doing up here, I guess." They passed the airport sign, and Truehart flicked on his turn signal.

"Semi-retired," von Heilitz said, and the two men grinned at each other.

"All right," said Truehart, "but this boy's mother is going

to go through hell when she hears that her son died in a fire. That's the part that bothers me."

"She won't."

"She won't *what*?"

"Won't hear. Her husband is off in Alabama for a couple of weeks, and she never watches television or reads the papers. She's an invalid. If her father finds out somehow, he won't tell her right away, and maybe he would never tell her. He has a history of protecting her from bad news."

That was right, Tom realized—if he had died in the fire, he would never have existed. His grandfather would never speak his name, and his mother would be forbidden to mention it. It would be the way his grandfather had wanted it all along. Her and her's Da.

Tim Truehart pulled up beside a long building with a grey metal skin, and Tom stepped out of the car after the men. The yellow light of a sodium lamp ate into everything like acid. Tom's hands were sickly yellow, and Lamont von Heilitz's hair turned a dead yellow-grey. Tom carried one of the old man's bags around the open front of the long metal building and saw a dismantled airplane on the yellow-grey concrete floor, a glass bubble rearing out of lifeless canvas, and an engine in parts like a diagrammed sentence, bolts like punctuation marks, the exclamation point of the propeller.

Von Heilitz asked him if he were all right.

"Pretty much," he said.

Truehart's plane had been pulled to the side of the hangar. The bags went through a narrow opening like an oven door. You climbed on the wing to get into the cockpit, and Tom slipped downwards before Truehart clutched his wrist and pulled him up. He sat in a single back seat, and von Heilitz sat beside the pilot.

The engine sputtered and roared, and the plane rolled forward into the emptiness before lifting into the greater emptiness of the air.

In Minneapolis he trudged down a long hallway lined with shops alongside von Heilitz. People moving the other way cast amused looks at them, an erect old man and a tottering boy without eyelashes dressed like actors on a stage, both of them a head taller than anyone else.

From Minneapolis they flew to Houston. Tom awakened once, choking on wood smoke, and saw the dark tubular shape of a jet cabin before him. For a second he thought he was flying toward Eagle Lake again, and fell instantly back into sleep.

Between Houston and Miami Tom came awake with his head on the Shadow's bony shoulder. He straightened up in his seat and looked across at his father, who slept on, his head tilted and his mouth open. He was breathing deeply and regularly, and his face, smoothed by the darkness of the cabin, was that of a young man.

A stewardess who looked like Sarah Spence's older sister walked past, looked down, saw that Tom was awake, and knelt beside him with an expectant, curious smile. "The other girls are wondering about something—well, I am too," she whispered. Her Texas voice put a slow, bottom-heavy spin on every vowel. "Is he somebody *famous*?"

"He used to be," Tom said.

In Miami they had to run to their gate, and minutes after they had strapped themselves into their seats, the plane rolled down the runway and picked itself into the air to fly south across hundreds of miles of water to Mill Walk. A group of nuns filled the seats in front of them, and whenever the pilot announced that they were flying over an island, they all crowded into the seats on that side of the plane, to see Puerto Rico and Vieques, and the specks named St. Thomas and Tortola and Virgin Gorda, and the little afterthoughts of Anguilla, St. Martin, Montserrat, and Antigua.

"Am I going to stay with you?" Tom asked.

Another stewardess placed trays with scrambled eggs, bacon, and fried potatoes before them. Von Heilitz made a face and waved his away, but Tom said, "Keep it, I'll eat that one too," and the stewardess replaced the tray and gave them the usual curious look. "I love the way you guys dress," she said.

Tom began devouring his eggs.

"No, I think you shouldn't," von Heilitz said. "I don't think you should go home, either."

"Then where should I go?"

"The St. Alwyn." Von Heilitz smiled. "Which Mr. Goetz claimed to own. I've already booked you a room, under the name Thomas Lamont. I thought you'd be able to remember that."

"Why don't you want me to stay at your place?"

"I thought you'd be safer somewhere else. Besides, the St. Alwyn is an interesting place. Do you know anything about it?"

"Wasn't there a murder there once?" Tom could remember some story from his childhood—lurid headlines in newspapers his mother had snatched away. Kate Redwing had mentioned it too.

"Two," von Heilitz said. "In fact, it was probably the most famous murder case in the history of Mill Walk, and I had nothing to do with it at all. A novelist named Timothy Underhill wrote a book called *The Divided Man* about it—you never read it?"

Tom shook his head.

"I'll loan it to you. Good book—good *fiction*—but misguided about the case, exactly in the way that most people were. A suicide was generally taken as a confession. We have about twenty minutes left up in this limbo, why don't I tell you the story?"

"I think you'd better!"

"The body of a young prostitute was discovered in the alley behind the hotel. Above her body, two words had been chalked on the wall. *Blue Rose*."

The nuns in the seats in front of them had ceased talking to each other, and now and then glanced over the top of their seats.

"A week later, a piano player who worked in some of the downtown clubs was found dead in a room at the St. Alwyn. His throat was slit. The murderer had printed the words *Blue Rose* on the wall above his bed. In the early days, he had played with Glenroy Breakstone and the Targets—the *Blue Rose* record is a kind of memorial to him."

Tom remembered his mother and von Heilitz playing the record—the soft, breathy saxophone making compelling music out of the songs mangled by Miss Gonsalves at dancing class.

"So far, the victims were marginal people, half-invisible. The police on Mill Walk couldn't get excited about a whore and a local jazz musician—it wasn't as though respectable citizens had been killed. They just went through the motions. It seemed pretty clear that the young man had been killed because he'd witnessed the girl's murder—even Fulton Bishop could work that one out, because the piano player's window in the St. Alwyn was on the second floor overlooking the brick alley. A short time after that, a young doctor was attacked, same thing, *Blue Rose*, but when it turned out that he was homosexual—"

The pilot asked all passengers to fasten their seat belts in preparation for landing on the island of Mill Walk, where the skies were cloudless and the temperatures in the low nineties. The nuns pulled the belts taut and craned their necks.

"Well, Fulton Bishop's patron, your grandfather, asked that he be assigned to a more salubrious case, and—"

"My grandfather?"

"Oh, Glen was very important to Captain Bishop, still is. Took an interest in his career from the beginning. Anyhow, Bishop was promoted, and a detective named Damrosch got the case. By now it looked like a curse. The *Eyewitness* was full of it, and the people were in the condition newspapers like to call 'up in arms.' What that really means is that they were titillated—they felt a kind of awful fascination. Now Damrosch was a talented detective, but an unstable man. Professionally, he was completely honest, and if he'd been a real straight arrow in every way, he could have gathered a nucleus of other honest policemen around him, the way David Natchez seems to have done. But he was a blackout drinker, he beat people up now and then, he'd had a very troubled youth, and he was a closet homosexual. None of this side of his life emerged until later. But even so, he had no friends in the department, and they gave him the case to make him the scapegoat."

"What happened?" Tom asked.

"There was another murder. A butcher who lived near the old slave quarter. And when that happened, the case virtually closed itself. No more Blue Rose murders."

The nuns were listening avidly now, their heads nearly touching in the gap between their seats.

"The butcher had been one of Damrosch's foster fathers—a violent, abusive man. Worked the boy nearly to death until young Damrosch finally got into the army. Damrosch hated him."

"But the others—the doctor, and the piano player, and the girl."

"Damrosch knew two of them. The girl was one of his informants, and he'd had a one-night stand with the piano player."

"What do you mean, the case virtually closed itself?"

"Damrosch shot himself. At least, it certainly looked that way."

The plane had been moving steeply down as von Heilitz talked, and now the palm trees and bright length of ocean alongside the runways whizzed and blurred past their windows: the wheels brushed against the ground, and all of the plane's weight seemed to strain backwards against itself.

A stewardess jumped up and announced over the loudspeaker that passengers were requested to remain in their seats, with seat belts fastened, until the vehicle had stopped moving.

"You could say that his suicide was a sort of wrongful arrest."

"Where were you during all this?"

"In Cleveland, proving that the Parking Lot Monster was a gentleman named Horace Fetherstone, the regional manager of the Happy Hearts Greeting Card Company."

The airplane stopped moving, and most of the passengers jumped into the aisle and opened overhead compartments. Tom and the Shadow stayed in their seats, and so did the nuns.

"By the way, was it clear that one of the victims survived? In Underhill's book they were all killed, but the real case was different. One of them made it. He'd been attacked from behind in the dark, and he didn't even get a glimpse of his attacker, so he was no use in the case, but he knew enough medicine to stop his bleeding."

"Medicine?"

"Well, he was a doctor, wasn't he? You met him this summer," said von Heilitz. "Nice fellow." He stood up, stooping, and moved out into the aisle. "Buzz Laing. Did you notice? He always wears something around his neck."

Tom looked straight ahead of him and saw the brown right eye of one nun and the blue left eye of another staring at him through the gap between their seats.

"Oh, one little thing." Von Heilitz leaned down beneath the overhead compartments. "Damrosch shot himself in the head at a desk in his apartment. There was a note saying *Blue Rose* in front of him on the desk. Case closed."

He smiled, and all the fine horsehair lines around his mouth cut deeper into his skin. He turned away and started moving up the aisle toward the front of the plane. Tom scrambled out of his seat.

"Occasionally," von Heilitz said, "what you have to do is go back to the beginning and see everything in a new way."

They passed through the open door of the airplane and entered the annihilating sunlight of the Caribbean, pouring down from a hazy sun in an almost colorless sky.

"Occasionally," von Heilitz said, "there are powerful reasons why you can't or don't want to do that."

The stewardess who had told them she liked the way they dressed stood at the bottom of the metal staircase, handing white printed cards to the passengers. A long way away, goats pushed their heads through a wire fence. The smell of salt water mingled with the airport smell of jet fuel.

"The handwriting on the note in front of Damrosch," Tom said.

"Printed in block letters." He accepted one of the cards from the stewardess.

Tom took one too, and realized that it was a landing card. The first line was for his name, and the second for his passport number.

He gaped at the stewardess, and she said, "Gee, what happened to your eyebrows?"

Von Heilitz tugged at his sleeve. "The boy was in a fire. He just realized that he doesn't have his passport."

"Gee," she said. "Will you have any trouble?

"None at all." He walked Tom across the tarmac toward the door.

"Why not?"

"Watch me," said von Heilitz.

At the baggage counter, the pool of yellow liquid seemed to have advanced another six or eight inches across the linoleum, and the American passengers gave it uneasy glances as they waited for their cases to ride toward them on the belt. Tom followed the old man toward the desk marked MILL WALK RESIDENTS, and saw him take a slim leather notecase from his pocket. He tore a sheet of perforated yellow paper from the case, bent over it for a second, and signaled for Tom to follow him to the desk.

He said, "Hello, Gonzalo," to the official, and gave him his passport and landing card. The sheet of notepaper was folded into the passport. "My friend has been in a fire. He lost everything, including his passport. He is the grandson of Glendenning Upshaw, and wishes to convey the best wishes of Mr. Upshaw and Mr. Ralph Redwing to you."

The official flicked bored black eyes at Tom's face, opened von Heilitz's passport, and pulled the note toward him. He shielded it behind his hand and opened the top half. Then he slid the folded note into his desk, stamped von Heilitz's passport, and reached back into the desk for a form marked *REPLACEMENT PASSPORT APPLICATION*. "Fill this out and mail it in as soon as possible," he said. "Nice to see you again, Mr. von Heilitz."

The first words on the form were: *No resident of Mill Walk shall be allowed to pass through Customs and Immigration until a replacement passport has been received.*

"What was in the note?" Tom asked.

"Two dollars."

They went outside into light and heat.

"How much would it have been without the best wishes of my grandfather and Ralph Redwing?"

"One dollar. Haven't you ever heard of noblesse oblige?"

Tom looked across the ramp and saw half a dozen carriages and gigs in the open parking lot. The odor of horse manure drifted toward him, along with the smells of fuel oil and salt water. They were home. Von Heilitz raised his hand, and an old red taxi with one dangling headlight pulled up before them.

A short, chunky black man with a wide handsome face climbed out and smiled at them, showing two front teeth edged in gold. He went around to open his trunk, and von Heilitz said, "Hello, Andres."

"Always good to see you again, Lamont," the driver said. The trunk smelled strongly of fish. He hoisted in the cases and slammed the trunk shut. "Where we going today?"

"The St. Alwyn." They all got in the car, and von Heilitz said, "Andres, Tom Pasmore here is a good friend of mine. I want you to treat him the same way you treat me. He might need your help someday."

Andres leaned over the back of the seat and stuck out an

enormous hand. "Any time, brother." Tom took the hand with his left, raising his bandaged right hand in explanation.

Andres pulled out toward the highway into town, and Tom said, "Do you know everybody?"

"Only the right people. Have you been thinking about what I said?"

Tom nodded.

"Kind of stares you right in the face, doesn't it?"

"Maybe," Tom said, and von Heilitz snorted.

"I don't know if we're thinking of the same thing."

"We are."

"Can I ask you a question before I say anything else?"

"Go ahead."

Tom felt a reluctant tremor move through his body like a slow electric shock. "When you were up at the lake, did you ever go swimming or fishing? Did you ever do anything that took you out into the lake?"

"Are you asking if I ever actually saw the front of your grandfather's lodge?"

Tom nodded.

"I never swam, I never fished, I never went out into the lake. I never set foot on his property either, of course. Congratulations."

But it was not like the time the Shadow had leaned beaming across a coffee table and shaken his hand. Tom fell against the back seat of Andres's taxi, seeing Barbara Deane wake up in a burning bed.

"He's so *bold*," von Heilitz said. "He told me one huge bold whopping lie, and I swallowed it whole. You know what really galls me? He knew it was the kind of lie—the kind of detail—that would really speak to me. He knew I would go right to town on it. He knew I would build an entire theory on that lie. It didn't take him an instant to figure all that out. From then on, everything fell into place."

"Everybody thought he left for Miami the day after Jeanine disappeared," Tom said.

"But he stayed long enough to kill Goetz."

Tom closed his eyes, and kept them closed until they pulled up in front of the old hotel. *There are things it might be better not to know*, Barbara Deane had told him.

Andres said, "Here we are, boss," and von Heilitz patted his shoulders. A door slammed. Tom opened his eyes to the lower end of Calle Drosselmayer. It was before eight in the morning on an island where nothing opened until ten, and the pawn shops and liquor stores were still locked behind their bars and shutters. A junk man's horse clopped past, pulling a rusted water heater, a broken carriage wheel, and the dozing junk man. Von Heilitz got out on one side, Tom on the other. The air seemed unnaturally warm and bright. Far up the street, in the fashionable section of Calle Drosselmayer, a few cars rolled east, taking office workers and store managers from the island's west end downtown to Calle Hoffmann.

Andres carried the old man's two bags to the sidewalk in front of the hotel, and von Heilitz gave him some bills.

"Aren't you going home?" Tom asked.

"Both of us ought to stay out of sight for a while," von Heilitz said. "I'll be in the room adjoining yours."

Andres said, "Big change from Eastern Shore Road," and pulled a little stack of business cards held together with a rubber band from a ripped pocket of his jacket. He pulled one out of the stack and presented it to Tom. The card was printed with the words *Andres Flanders Courteous Efficient Driver* and a telephone number in the old slave quarter. "You call me if you need me, hear?" Andres said. He watched Tom put the card into one of his pockets. When he was sure it was safe, he waved to both of them and drove off.

Tom turned around to look up at the tall façade of the hotel. Once it had been pale blue or even white, but the stone had darkened over time. An arch of carved letters over the entrance spelled out its name. Von Heilitz said, "I divided my clothes up between these bags, so why don't you just take that one and use what's in it as long as we're here?"

Tom lifted the heavy bag and followed him into the dark cavern of the St. Alwyn's lobby. Brass spittoons stood beside heavy furniture, and on the wall opposite the desk three small stained glass windows glowed dark red and blue, like the window on the staircase at Brooks-Lowood School. A pale man with thinning hair and rimless glasses watched them approach.

Von Heilitz checked in as James Cooper of New York City,

and Tom filled out a card for Thomas Lamont, also of New York. The clerk took in his bandaged hand and singed eyebrows, and slid two keys across the desk.

"Let's go upstairs and talk about your grandfather," von Heilitz said. The clerk's eyebrows twitched above the rims of his glasses.

Von Heilitz picked up both keys and bent to put his hand on the suitcase he carried in. "Oh," he said, having seen a stack of *Eyewitness*es in the gloom at the end of the counter. "We'll each have one of those." He straightened up and put his hand in his front pocket.

The clerk peeled two newspapers off the neat stack and pushed them forward in exchange for the two quarters von Heilitz slapped down on the counter, presenting them with the headline in the newspaper's lower right-hand corner.

The old man folded the papers under his arms, and they each picked up a suitcase and went to the elevator.

54

In Tom's room, they sat six feet from the bed in high-backed wooden chairs on opposite sides of a dark wooden table on the surface of which a traveling musician had once scratched PD 6/6/58. Tom reached the end of the article, and immediately began reading it again. The headline said: GLENDENNING UPSHAW'S GRANDSON DEAD IN RESORT FIRE.

A fire of unknown origin claimed the life of Thomas Upshaw Pasmore early yesterday morning. Seventeen years old and the son of Mr. and Mrs. Victor Pasmore of Eastern Shore Road, Pasmore had spent the first weeks of the summer at the lodge on exclusive Eagle Lake, Wisconsin, belonging to his grandfather, Glendenning Upshaw. . . .

The fourth-floor room stretched away from him, lighter than the lobby, but at seven in the morning filled with a twilight murk that obscured the painting above the bed. The other copy of the *Eyewitness* rattled, and Tom looked across the table to see Lamont von Heilitz folding the paper to read an article on the inside of the front page.

"When did you first begin to think that my grandfather murdered Jeanine Thielman?" he asked.

Von Heilitz snapped the paper into a neat rectangle, folded it in half, and set it down between them.

"When one of his employees bought the house on The Sevens. How do you feel, Tom? Must be unsettling, reading about your own death."

"I don't know. Confused. Tired. I don't see what we can do. We're back on Mill Walk, where even the police work for the people like my grandfather."

"Not all of them. David Natchez is going to help us, and we are going to help him. We have a rare opportunity. One of the men at the center of power on this island committed a murder with his own hands. Your grandfather is not a man to choose to suffer in silence, any more than the man who killed my parents. If he's charged with murder, he'll bring the whole house down with him."

"But how do we get him charged with murder?"

"We get him to confess. Preferably to David Natchez."

"He'll never confess."

"You forget that we have two weapons. One of them is you."

"What's the other one?"

"Those notes you saw in Barbara Deane's room. They weren't written to her, of course. She found them in the lodge when Glen sent her over to clean up. He probably left them on top of his desk—or maybe he even showed them to her. He knew that she'd sympathize with anyone falsely accused. He might even have said that the notes referred to his wife's death. I suppose Barbara got a few anonymous notes herself, back when the paper ran those stories about her."

"But maybe that's what they were—notes someone sent to her."

"I don't think she would have kept them, in that case. She would have burned them. She kept these because they troubled her. I also think she planned to show them to you."

"Why?"

"Because when you turned up, asking a lot of questions about Jeanine Thielman and Anton Goetz, you stirred up all the doubts she had about your grandfather. *She* didn't want to think he killed Jeanine, not after everything he'd done for her, but she was too smart not to wonder about it. He brought Gloria to her before the body was discovered—when nobody but the murderer knew that Jeanine was dead. I think Barbara was very relieved when I stumbled in and found Mr. Goetz hanged in his lodge."

Von Heilitz leaned back against his chair. A white stubble gleamed on his face, and his eyes were far back in his head. "Afterwards, people all over the mainland asked me to solve murders. I didn't want to admit I was wrong any more than Barbara Deane did. Anton Goetz had put me on my way."

"Could we reconstruct what really happened?" Tom asked. "There's a lot I still don't understand."

"I bet you do, though." Von Heilitz straightened up and rubbed a hand over his face. "Let's say that Glen knew immediately that Jeanine Thielman had written him those notes. She was threatening him with some kind of exposure. She knew something—something really damaging. Her husband was a business rival of Glen's, and Goetz might have told her more than he should have about your grandfather's business. Or, as I think, it might have been another kind of exposure. At any rate, she was telling Glen to stop whatever he was doing. He left a noisy party at the club—I think he had set up this meeting for the day before he was supposed to go to Florida, but I don't think he planned to kill her. He came to her lodge. She was waiting for him on her deck. He confronted her. Whatever she knew about was serious enough to ruin him. Jeanine refused to cooperate with him, or to believe his denials, and turned her back to go inside. He saw the gun her husband left on the table, picked it up, shot and missed, and then he shot again. Everybody else at the lake except Anton Goetz was at the club, having a good time dancing to a loud band—do you know how music carries, up there?"

Tom nodded. "But he was a bad shot. How did he hit her?"

"Because of the gun—he would have missed her both times, if the gun had been accurate. Anyhow, I don't think he was very far from her. After that, I think he pulled her off the deck so that she wouldn't bleed all over it. And then—"

He looked up at Tom, who said, "Then he ran across the little path and went through the woods to get Anton Goetz. My mother saw him through the window in her bedroom, but she wasn't sure who it was—she only had a glimpse of him. Goetz worked for him, but I bet he wasn't an accountant, any more than Jerry Hasek was a public relations assistant."

"He would have been a lot more useful than Jerry Hasek. Goetz could go everywhere, he could talk to people and hear things. Goetz did whatever Glen couldn't afford to be seen doing. Mainly, I suppose he carried money around for Glen and the Redwings. He was a criminal with a smooth façade. I misunderstood him completely, exactly in the way he wanted to be misunderstood." Von Heilitz gave Tom an angry, self-disgusted look. "Tell me what they did next."

"My grandfather and Goetz wrapped her body in the old curtains, weighted her down, and rowed her out into the lake after the party broke up at the club. Then they must have washed off the deck. My grandfather carried my mother over to Barbara Deane's house early the next morning, and then walked back to Goetz's lodge and spent the next four nights in the guest room, waiting to see what would happen. Goetz brought them meals back from the club. Everybody knew Grand-Dad was planning to go to Florida, and they just assumed that's where he was."

"And by the time I got to Miami, he was there waiting for me."

Tom looked down at the article about his death. "Oh, my God," he said. "Grand-Dad is going to know I didn't die in that fire. The Langenheims saw me, and the Spences know that I got out alive."

"When they read that a fire 'claimed your life' in the paper this morning, they'll think you died in the hospital. Smoke inhalation kills more people than actual fires. People generally believe what they read in the papers. You're dead, I'm afraid."

"I suppose that's a relief."

Von Heilitz smiled at him. "Tell me what happened to Goetz."

"After you talked to him at the club, he went back to the lodge to tell my grandfather that you'd accused him of the murder—he was an accessory, anyhow. As soon as Goetz told him that you thought he'd killed Mrs. Thielman, he knew—" Tom remembered Sarah's father saying, *"Your grandfather does everything by the seat of his pants, you know,"* and shuddered—"he knew how to solve all his problems."

"Glen strangled him, or knocked him down and suffocated him, or maybe just got the line around his neck and threw the spool over a beam and pulled him off the ground. It's no wonder the line nearly took Goetz's head off. Then he took a couple of shots at me just to slow me down, got his things together, and took off for Barbara Deane's house to pick up his daughter."

"Did you know all this when I went to your house, that first time?"

"I didn't really know any of it. When I began spending more time on Mill Walk, I did a little checking into the ownership of Goetz's house and lodge. One dummy company led to another dummy company, which was owned by Mill Walk Construction. Glen could have made it a lot more complicated, but he never thought anybody would bother to look even that closely. Once I knew that Goetz had worked for Glen, I began to think about Goetz bringing his meals home from the club, and telling Mrs. Truehart not to go into his guest room."

"But you didn't tell me about any doubts. You just told me about the case."

"That's right. I presented it to you exactly as it came to me."

For a moment they looked at each other across the table, and then Tom smiled at the old man. Von Heilitz smiled back, and Tom laughed out loud. Von Heilitz's smile broadened. "You handed it to me!"

"I did, I handed it to you. And you *took* it!"

"But you didn't think I'd actually go to Eagle Lake."

Von Heilitz shook his head. "I thought we'd have a few more peaceful conversations, and I'd let you know that Goetz worked for your grandfather, and things would go like that for a while."

"Peaceful conversations, nothing," Tom said. An astonishing bubble of hilarity broke free inside him; this laughter seemed to come from the same place as his tears, in the moonlit clearing when he had learned the answer to the puzzle of his childhood.

Von Heilitz kept smiling at him. "You turned out to be a

little more talkative and energetic than I bargained on. And it almost got you killed. I'm glad you're laughing."

Tom leaned forward in his chair. "It's hard to explain—but everything's *clear* now. We sit here talking for twenty minutes, and all of a sudden I can see exactly what happened—it's like points on a graph or something."

"That's right," von Heilitz said. "Clarity is exhilarating."

"The only thing we don't know is why it all happened." Tom leaned back in his chair and pushed his hands against his forehead, straining to capture some knowledge that seemed just out of sight—something else he knew without being able to see. "What were those notes about? What did Jeanine Thielman know he *was*?" He threw his arms out. "Maybe she knew that he killed his wife and faked her suicide. Maybe the newspaper editor was right."

"Would she say, *You have to be stopped—this has gone on too long*?"

"Sure, she could," Tom said.

"I saw Magda Upshaw's body at the same time Sam Hamilton did, and what he thought were stab wounds were the marks of the hooks on the drag."

"You think she killed herself."

The old man nodded. "But I don't know why she killed herself. Didn't one of those notes say *I know what you are*? Maybe Magda found out what he was, and it was too much for her."

"She found out he was a crook. Isn't that what we're saying? He was involved with dirty deals with Maxwell Redwing from the start—he was in Maxwell's pocket, and Fulton Bishop was in his?"

"That's what we're saying, all right, though we're talking about the days before Fulton Bishop."

Some other knowledge flickered in and out of Tom's sight. "Adultery? Younger women?" He groaned. "Actually, Barbara Deane told me that all he ever did with younger women was take them out, so that he could be seen with them."

"Even if he did sleep with them, I don't think that Jeanine would have gotten so excited about it. And is it a secret he'd kill to keep?"

"Not if he went out with them in public," Tom admitted.

The old man crossed his legs and yanked his tie down. "We can use this secret of his without knowing what it is."

"How?"

Von Heilitz stood up, and his knees cracked. He made a pained face. "We'll talk about that after I shower and have a nap. There's a little place to eat downstairs." He bent forward and pushed the folded newspaper across the table. "In the meantime, take a look at this article."

The Shadow stepped away from the table and stretched his long arms above his head. Tom scanned the short article, which was about the arrest of Jerome Hasek, Robert Wintergreen, and Nathan LaBarre, residents of Mill Walk, in Eagle Lake, Wisconsin on charges of housebreaking, burglary, and auto theft. Von Heilitz was looking at him with an overtone of concern that made him feel nervous.

"We already know this," Tom said.

"And now everybody else knows it too. But there's something else you have to know, though I hate to be the one to tell you. Read the last sentence."

" *'The three men are assisting the Eagle Lake police in their investigations of other crimes.'* " Tom looked up at von Heilitz.

"That little crime you solved is crucial to helping us with all the big ones."

"Does this have to do with what you and Tim Truehart were talking about after I left the hospital? About the man who lives by himself in the woods? Who's down on his luck?"

Von Heilitz unbuttoned his vest and leaned against the frame of the connecting door. "Why do you think your grandfather was in such a hurry to get you up north?"

"To get me off Mill Walk."

"Tell me what were you doing when someone took a shot at you."

"I was talking—" The physical sensations of the knowledge arrived before the knowledge itself. Tom's throat constricted. He felt as if he had been kicked in the stomach.

Von Heilitz nodded, bowing his whole body so that his clothes flapped over his chest. He looked like a sorrowful scarecrow. "So I don't have to tell you."

"No," Tom said. "That can't be true. I'm his *grandson.*"

"Did he tell you to come back home? Did he even tell you to call the police?"

"Yeah. He did." Tom shook his head. "No. He tried to talk me out of calling them. But after I called them, he told me it was a good idea."

Tell me, what do you see when you look out the window, this time of night? I always liked nights up at Eagle Lake.

"Grand-Dad knew where the phone was," Tom said. The boot was still in his stomach.

"He knew you'd have a light on. He wanted you framed in the window."

"He even made me face forward—he asked me what I saw out the window—but at the last minute I bent to see through my reflection . . ."

"He had it set up," von Heilitz said, in a voice that would have been consoling if he had been speaking different words. "The man Jerry hired knew when Glen was going to call."

"I knew he killed those two people," Tom said, unable to say their names, "but that was forty years ago. I guess I finally understood that he was mixed up in dirty stuff with Ralph Redwing. But I still thought of him as my grandfather."

"Glen is your grandfather, worse luck," von Heilitz said. "And he's your mother's father. But even when I knew him back in school, other people were never very real to him. They never have been."

Tom stared down at the newspaper without seeing it.

"Do you know what I mean, that other people aren't real to him?"

Tom nodded.

"It's a special kind of mind—it's a sickness. Nobody can change people like that, nobody can help them." He moved into the room. "Will you be all right for an hour or so?"

Tom nodded.

"We'll get him, you know. We'll rattle his cage. This time he went too far, and he'll know it as soon as he sees the paper."

"I guess I'd like to be by myself for a while."

Von Heilitz nodded slowly, and then went into his room and closed the connecting door.

A little while later, Tom heard the drumming of the shower in the next room.

55

His body felt light and insubstantial, and nothing around him seemed quite real. Everything looked real, but that was a trick. If he knew how, he could walk through the bed, pass his arm through the table, pierce the telephone with his fingers. He felt as if he could move through the wall—it would flatten itself against him and dissolve, like the smoke rising from Eagle Lake.

I always liked nights, up at Eagle Lake.

Tom stood up with dreamlike slowness and looked out of the window to see if Calle Drosselmayer was still real, or if everything out there was only painted shadows, like himself and the room. Bright automobiles streamed up and down on the street below. A man in a work shirt and wash pants, like Wendell Hasek years ago, cranked up the metal grille over a pawn shop window, uncovering guitars and saxophones and a row of old sewing machines with foot treadles. A woman in a yellow dress walked past a bar called The Home Plate, turned around, and pressed her face to the window as if she were licking the glass.

He turned around. He could disappear in this room. Disappearance was what rooms like this were for. They were places in which people had given up, stepped aside, quit—his mother's rooms on Eastern Shore Road and Eagle Lake were disappearance places akin to this hotel room. A green carpet flecked with stains, tired brown furniture, tired brown bed. A seam of pale yellow wallpaper stamped with some indistinct pattern lifted an inch off the wall beside the door.

He laid the suitcase flat on the carpet, opened it, and took out the Shadow's beautiful suits and lustrous neckties. After he put away the older man's clothes, he undressed, tossed the shirt and underwear back into the case, and hung up the suit he had been wearing—its wrinkles had been shaped by his own knees, shoulders, elbows. Solidity seemed to swim back into his body, and he went into his bathroom and saw another, older person in the mirror. He saw the Shadow's son, a kind of familiar stranger. Thomas Lamont. He would have to get used to this person, but he could get used to him.

He turned on the shower and stepped under the hot water. "We'll get him," he said out loud.

56

"Glen Upshaw and the island of Mill Walk came together at the moment when he could cause the most damage," von Heilitz said.

They were downstairs in a restaurant called Sinbad's Cavern, a dark hole with tall wooden booths and fishnets hung on the wall like spiderwebs. It had both a lobby and a street entrance, and a long bar ran along one wall. Above the bar hung an immense painting of a nude woman with unearthly flesh tones reclining on a sofa the color of the carpet in Tom's room. At the end of the bar nearest the street door two uniformed policeman with blotchy faces were drinking Pusser's Navy Rum out of shot glasses, neat. Their hats were placed upside down on the bar beside them.

"A generation earlier, he would have been tied in knots—David Redwing would have tossed him in jail or kept him straight. He wouldn't have let Glen start up a system of payoffs and kickbacks, he wouldn't have let him turn the police force into the mess it is."

He took another bite of the seafood omelette both he and Tom had ordered.

"If Glen had been born a generation earlier, he might have seen what would wash and what wouldn't, and imitated a respectable citizen all his life. He wouldn't have had any principles, of course, but he might have seen that he had to keep his vices private. If he'd been born a generation later, he would have been too young to have any influence over Maxwell Redwing. Maxwell was just an opportunistic crook who was lucky enough to be born into a helpful family. He wasn't as smart as Glen—by the time they were in their mid-twenties, Glen was operating almost like an independent wing of the Redwing family. And by the time Ralph came of age, Glen had so much power that he was sort of a permanent junior partner. He had the records and paperwork on every secret deal and illegal operation. If Ralph tried anything, all Glen had to do was leak some of those records to the press to make a stink big enough to drive the Redwings off Mill Walk. People here want to believe that David Redwing's legacy is intact, and they'll go on thinking that something like the Hasselgard scandal is an aberration and Fulton Bishop is a dedicated policeman until they're shown different."

"So what can we do?"

"I told you. We're going to rattle Glendenning Upshaw's cage. He's bothered already—Glen didn't know that Ralph's bodyguards were dumb enough to go around breaking into houses. He isn't going to want to face an extradition order, once Tim Truehart finds the man Jerry hired to kill you. There's already been too much trouble on Mill Walk. Ralph Redwing is waiting things out in Venezuela, and if I were Glen I'd think about going there too."

Von Heilitz dipped his chin in a nod like the period at the end of a sentence, and pushed his empty plate to the side of the table.

Tom shook his head. "I'd like to really *hurt* him."

"Hurting him is what we're talking about."

Tom looked down at the cold eggs on his plate and said, "You don't mean it the way I do."

"Oh, yes, I do. I want to take everything away from Glendenning Upshaw—his peace of mind, his reputation, his freedom—eventually, his life. I want to see him hang in Long Bay prison. I'd be happy to put the rope around his neck myself."

Tom looked up and met the old man's eyes with a shock of shared feeling.

"We have to get him out of the Founders Club," Tom said. "We have to scare him out."

Von Heilitz nodded vehemently, his eyes still locked with Tom's.

"Give me a pen," Tom said. "I'll show you what I'd do." The old man took a fountain pen from his inside pocket and pushed it across the table.

Tom took the paper napkin off his lap and smoothed it out on the table. He unscrewed the cap from the pen and in block letters printed I KNOW WHAT YOU ARE on the rough surface of the napkin. Then he turned the napkin around and showed it to von Heilitz.

"Exactly," the old man said. "He'll think he's being stung by a thousand bees at once."

"A thousand?" Tom grinned back, imagining his grandfather's living room overflowing with letters repeating the words Jeanine Thielman had written to him.

"Two thousand," von Heilitz said.

57

They went past the policemen drinking Pusser's at the end of the bar out to the Street of Widows. The rolled-up windows of a black and white police car in a no parking zone just outside the entrance reflected a red neon scimitar flashing on and off in the restaurant's window. To their left, cars, bicycles, and horse-drawn carriages rolled up and down Calle Drosselmayer. The St. Alwyn side of the street was in deep shadow; on the other, the shadow ended in a firm black line that touched the opposite sidewalk, and blazing sunlight fell on a shoeless native dozing on the pavement before a display of hats and baskets on a red blanket. On one side of the vendor was an open market with ranks of swollen vegetables and slabs of fish protected from the sun by a long awning. Melting ice and purple fish guts drizzled on the pavement. On the other side of the vendor, two wide young women in bathrobes sat smoking on the front steps of a tall narrow building called the Traveller's Hotel. They were watching the entrance of Sinbad's Cavern, and when Tom and von Heilitz came out, they looked at them for only seconds before focusing on the door again.

Von Heilitz strode diagonally across the street, came up on the curb just past the steps where the women sat, and turned beneath a gilt sign reading ELLINGTON'S ALLSORTS AND NOTIONS into the entrance of a dark little shop. Tom caught the door behind him, and a bell tinkled as he walked in.

Von Heilitz was already moving quickly down an aisle stocked with bottles of hot sauce, canned salmon, cat food, and boxes of cereal with names Tom had never seen in his life—Delilah's Own and Mother Sugar—to a shelf with ballpoint pens, pads of paper, and boxes of envelopes. Von Heilitz picked up a pad of yellow paper and six boxes of variously colored envelopes, swung around and passed them to Tom, and whirled away into another aisle.

"I thought you said two thousand," Tom said.

"I said it would feel like two thousand," von Heilitz called from the next aisle.

Tom rounded the top of the aisle and saw him swoop down on a loaf of bread, a bag of potato chips, a wrapped pound of cheddar cheese, a container of margarine, a long salami, a box of crackers, cans, bottles, bags—half of these things he tossed to Tom, and the rest he piled in his arms.

"What's all this food for?"

"Sustenance," the old man said. "What is food usually for?"

When both of them were carrying so much that the stacks of containers threatened to fall out of their arms, von Heilitz came around the last aisle and unceremoniously dumped everything he was carrying on a scarred wooden counter. A small bald man with toffee-colored skin beamed at him from the other side of the counter.

"Hobart, my dear old friend," von Heilitz said, "this is a close friend of mine, Tom Pasmore."

Tom put down his groceries, and the little man grabbed his hand. "Lamont, he looks like you! I declare it! I think he must be your nephew!"

"We use the same tailor." He gave a twinkling glance toward Tom. "Do you think I could use your back room tonight?"

"Tonight, tomorrow, any time." The shopkeeper snatched at von Heilitz's hand and pumped it.

Hobart added up the total on a scrap of paper and began putting their goods into bags while von Heilitz counted out bills on the counter. "Someone else will be joining you, Lamont?"

"One other man. Athletic-looking, with dark hair. In his late thirties."

"What time?" He gave a heavy bag to Tom with a conspirator's wink.

"Ten-thirty, eleven o'clock, around then."

Hobart filled the second bag and handed it to von Heilitz. "The lights will be off."

Von Heilitz marched off through the door, saying, "Thank you."

Hobart said, "He is a very great man," and Tom, following the detective, said, "I know!" He came out into the shower of blinding light. Von Heilitz had already carried his shopping bag halfway across the street. Tom stepped down from the curb into the shadow of the St. Alwyn Hotel. The two young women in bathrobes were sitting in the police car with the policemen who had been in the bar.

"Hurry along," von Heilitz said, holding open the door of Sinbad's Cavern. "We have notes to write, if we want to make today's delivery."

58

"Can you remember the exact words she used?" von Heilitz asked him. "For a second anyhow, we want him to see Jeanine Thielman standing right in front of him, pointing her finger at him."

On the other side of the table with its scratched-in initials, Tom sat with the old man's pen poised over a clean sheet of paper. I KNOW WHAT YOU ARE, he wrote. "That was on the first one, and then there was another phrase."

"Didn't the second note have two phrases too?"

Tom nodded.

"Then write down all four phrases, in any order, as well as you can remember them, and we'll put them together the right way."

"Okay," Tom said. Beneath the first, he wrote, THIS HAS GONE ON TOO LONG. Beneath that, he wrote, YOU MUST BE STOPPED; beneath that, YOU MUST PAY FOR YOUR SINS. He looked at the list of phrases. "That's pretty much right. Hold on." He crossed out the second MUST and wrote WILL above it. "That's better."

"The first one said 'I know what you are,' and . . . ?"

" '. . . and you have to be stopped.' That's right." Tom drew a line between the first and third phrases. "So the second note said, 'This has gone on too long' and 'You will pay for your sins.' " He connected these two with a line.

"Try it like that, and see how it looks," von Heilitz said.

On the same sheet of paper, Tom wrote:

I KNOW WHAT YOU ARE   YOU MUST BE STOPPED
THIS HAS GONE ON TOO LONG   YOU WILL PAY FOR YOUR SINS

"Does that look right?"

"I think so." Tom stared down at the page, trying to remember the words in rusty ink on the stiff yellow paper.

"I know what you are, and you have to be stopped," von Heilitz said.

" 'I know what you are, and . . .' " Tom looked up at von Heilitz's face, frowned, and added a comma and the word *and* to the first note. Then crossed out *must* and wrote *have to* above it.

I KNOW WHAT YOU ARE, AND YOU HAVE TO BE STOPPED.

"That's it," Tom said. "How did you know that?"

"You told me," von Heilitz said. "You said exactly those words, just now." He smiled. "Try to remember if there was anything special about the printing, and write out four or five separate copies. I have to make a couple of phone calls."

He stood up and left the room, closing the connecting door behind him. Tom tore another page off the pad and stared at it for a moment, then stood up and leaned on the window with his elbows, looking down at the curved necks of the saxophones and the intricate black shapes of the sewing machines in the pawnshop window. Tom closed his eyes and saw two yellow pieces of paper on the bottom of the inlaid wooden box.

He remembered taking them out, unfolding them, and putting them on top of the pile of clippings. He saw his hands holding the damning notes, the creamy yellow of the paper. The words leapt up at him. SIN.

Tom crossed a capital T with the curve in the neck of a tenor saxophone. SIN, with an angular, slanting S.

By the time Lamont von Heilitz came back Tom had written out four versions of each note on separate pieces of paper. The old man walked around the table to look down at what he had done. He laid a hand on Tom's shoulder. "You think you've done it?"

"They're as close as I can come."

"Then let's get the envelopes ready," von Heilitz said. He moved to the other chair, put the boxes of envelopes on the table, and took out eight envelopes in different colors. He dipped back into the bag for two ballpoint pens. "You address half, and I'll do the others. Print your grandfather's name and address on each, but vary the printing each time. We want him to open all these letters."

He took two versions of each note, and said, "The one about paying for his sin—it was sin, by the way, and not sins?"

"I'm sure it was."

"Good. I think that was the second one he got, don't you? We don't want to get them mixed up. He should get four of the first note today, and the other four tomorrow."

Tom addressed four envelopes to Mr. Glendenning Upshaw, Bobby Jones Trail, Founders Club, Mill Walk in varying styles of printing, inserted the notes, sealed them, and put them in separate piles. Von Heilitz added two envelopes to each pile, and looked at his watch. "Two minutes," he said.

"What happens in two minutes?"

"Our mailman arrives." Von Heilitz put his hands behind his head, stretched out his legs, and closed his eyes. Down on the street, a middle-aged man in sunglasses and a white short-sleeved shirt walked past the pawnshop and leaned against the façade of The Home Plate. He slapped a cigarette from a pack and dipped his head toward the flame of a lilghter. He breathed out a cloud of smoke the color of milk and raised his head. Tom backed away from the window.

"See anything?" The old man's eyes were still closed.

"Just a guy looking at the front of the hotel."

Von Heilitz nodded. An Ostend's Market truck crept down

Calle Drosselmayer behind half a dozen girls on bicycles. The back of the truck gradually moved past the shop window and The Home Plate. The woman in the yellow dress came out of the bar, dragging behind her a man in a plaid shirt. The man in the sunglasses was gone.

Von Heilitz said, "Enter Andres," and a soft double knock came from the door.

Tom laughed.

"You doubt?" Von Heilitz drew in his legs, and stood up and went to the door. A second later, he ushered the driver into Tom's room.

Andres tossed him a roll of stamps in a cellophane wrapper. "So—want me to mail some letters for you?" He wandered over to the table, where the old man was removing the stamps from their container and sticking them on the letters.

Von Heilitz gave him a stack containing a red, a grey, and two white envelopes. "Here's what I need, Andres—these letters all have to be mailed today before ten, from different points around the island. Drop one in the Elm Cove post office, another one downtown here, one at the substation in Turtle Bay, and the last one out at Mill Key." Andres sketched a map in the air with his forefinger, nodded, and put the letters in the right-hand pocket of his ripped coat. Von Heilitz gave him the second batch of envelopes, and said, "Mail these in the same places after ten o'clock tonight. Is that all right?"

"Isn't everything always all right?" Andres said. He put the second batch of envelopes in his left pocket. Then he slapped his right pocket, and said, "These you want to arrive this afternoon." He slapped the left pocket. "These you want to arrive tomorrow. From all over the island. Easy."

He leaned over and peered into the shopping bags. "You want me to call you when I'm done? It doesn't look like you're going anywhere."

"Call me around one," von Heilitz said. "We'll want to take a little trip in the afternoon." He stood up and walked Andres back to the door. His hand went into his pocket, and a folded bill passed into the driver's hand. Andres slapped his forehead, mumbled something to the old man, and took a paperback from his left pocket and passed it to von Heilitz, who thrust it into a jacket pocket. He came back into the room, bent over the shopping bags, reached down, and pulled out a shiny gold and blue bag.

"What do we do now?" Tom asked.

Von Heilitz tore open the bag along its seam, pointed the open end at him, and said, "Have a potato chip."

Tom took a chip out of the bag. The old man set the bag on the table and walked around to the window.

"Was the man you saw looking at the front of the hotel an ordinary-looking fellow in his fifties with thinning black hair, a little portly around the middle, and wearing black boots, tan slacks, a white shirt, and sunglasses?"

"That's him," Tom said, and nearly knocked over his chair to get to the window.

An immensely fat woman carrying a load of washing on her head passed the pawnshop.

"Well, he's not there now," von Heilitz said.

Tom squinted at him. This close, von Heilitz smelled of soap and some more personal odor that was faintly like the scent of a freshly opened apple. The wrinkles at the side of his eyes were as deep as furrows.

"I saw him outside the hotel this morning." Von Heilitz pushed himself back from the window. "Doesn't have to mean anything. There are two hundred people in the St. Alwyn, and nearly all of them deserve to be followed." He went back around the table, holding his sharp chin in his hand the way a child holds an ice cream cone. "Still, in the next couple of days we'd better go in and out through Sinbad's Cavern."

He fell into the other chair and placed his hand on the telephone, still clutching his chin. He looked up, said, "*Hmm,*" and let go of his chin to dial a number. "Hello, I'd like to speak to Mr. Thomas, please. . . . Hello, Mr. Thomas? This is Mr. Cooper at the central post office, I'm the sub-manager for your region? . . . I'd like to inquire if you and your members at the Founders Club feel that the service you've been getting from us is satisfactory . . . I'm happy to hear that. As you know, our delivery hours are varied from time to time, and I wondered, as you are certainly one of our priority districts, whether you felt the members had a preference . . . Well, Mr. Thomas, everybody on the island would prefer that, but morning delivery would compromise the same-day service we're so proud of . . . I see. Well, I'll speak to the route manager, see if we can shuffle things around a bit, and get your members' mail to you closer to noon than four o'clock . . . Of course, Mr. Thomas. Good-bye."

He hung up and looked across at Tom. "We really do have an extraordinary postal system, you know. It's one of the best things about this island." He uncoiled from the chair, went to the window and looked down at the sidewalk, and walked to the connecting door, rubbing his hands together. "I think we might get Andres to take a spin out to the Founders Club around three-thirty. Wouldn't you like to see what happens when your grandfather reads his mail?"

Tom nodded cautiously.

"How do we get on the grounds without going past the guardhouse?

Von Heilitz pushed himself off the door frame and looked up in mock amazement. "Is it possible that you've never climbed a fence?"

Tom smiled at him, and said that he probably had, once or twice, in his childhood.

"Well, that's a relief. Oh, I got something for you to read. Here." He pulled the paperback out of his pocket and tossed it to Tom.

The cover illustration of *The Divided Man*, by Timothy Underhill, was a close-up of the face of a man who resembled a younger Victor Pasmore. He wore a grey hat and a trench coat with a turned-up collar, and deep shadow obliterated half his face.

"It's the book I told you about—a way of seeing those Blue Rose murders. We're going to be here for a long time, and I thought you'd like something to read, knowing you."

Tom turned the book over to read the blurb, and von Heilitz stretched out on the sofa against the wall. His feet protruded far over the sofa's armrest.

"I met Tim Underhill when he came to Mill Walk for a little while to do research for the book. He stayed here, in fact—a lot of that book is set in the St. Alwyn."

Von Heilitz closed his eyes and crossed his hands over his chest. "When we get hungry, we'll make some sandwiches."

59

Tom moved to the bed, and began reading Timothy Underhill's book. After thirty pages, he unlaced the sleek black shoes and dropped them on the floor; after seventy, he sat up and removed his jacket and vest and yanked down his necktie. Von Heilitz fell asleep on the sofa.

Tom had expected *The Divided Man* to be set on Mill Walk, but Underhill had located the murders in a gritty Midwestern industrial city of chain-link fences, inhuman winters, foundries, and a thousand bars. Its only real resemblance to Mill Walk was that the city's wealthiest citizens lived on the far east side, in great houses built on a bluff above the shore of an enormous lake.

At the start of the fifth chapter, the novel's main character, a homicide detective named Esterhaz, woke up in an unfamiliar apartment. The television set was on, and the air smelled like whiskey. So hung over that he felt on the verge of disappearance, Esterhaz wandered through the empty apartment, trying to figure out who lived in it and how he had come to wake up there.

Men's and women's clothes hung in the closet, dirty dishes and milk bottles filled with green webs of mold covered the kitchen counters. He had a dim memory of fighting, of beating someone senseless, hitting already unconscious flesh again and again, of blood spattering on a wall . . . but there was no blood in the apartment, no blood on his clothes, and his hands ached with only a faint, tender ache, as if a demon had kissed them. A nearly empty whiskey bottle stood beside a bedroom door, and Esterhaz drank what was left in long swallows and went into the room. On the floor beside a mattress covered by a rumpled blanket, he found a note that said, *One anguish—in a crowd—A minor thing—it sounds—Come back tonight.—G.* Who was G.? He stuffed the note into his jacket pocket. Esterhaz found his coat balled up in a corner of the room, and buttoned himself into it. He shuddered with nausea, and the thought came to him full-blown, as if he had just read and memorized it, that invisibility was more than a fantasy: invisibility was so real that most of the world had already slipped into a great invisible realm that accompanied and mocked the visible.

Esterhaz walked down a dark, clanging staircase and went outside into a bitter cold and a tearing wind. He saw that he was next door to a bar called The House of Correction and recognized where he was. Four blocks away stood the St. Alwyn Hotel, where two people he knew had been murdered. Esterhaz walked through a snowdrift to get to his car, took a pint bottle from the glove compartment, and let a little more reality into his system. It was some unearthly hour like six-thirty in the morning. *A little anguish in a crowd*, he thought, *that bitch knew what she was talking about*. He put the pint bottle between his knees, started his car, and drove to a deserted parking lot on the lakefront. Absolutely still curls and feathers of smoke clung to the grey surface of the lake, frozen into place.

"Pretty good, wouldn't you say?"

Tom looked up through the memory of smoke feathers tethered to the surface of Eagle Lake, and saw von Heilitz bending over the table, making sandwiches with chunks of cheddar cheese and slices of salami.

"The book," von Heilitz said.

60

Andres drove them past the tall white walls of the Redwing compound and through the old cane fields where rows of willows, the only trees that would grow in the tired soil, nearly hid all that was left on Mill Walk of the original island. Far ahead, a smooth cement riser took shape on the right side of the coastal highway, and swung to the right as it followed the curve of a blacktopped side road. This was the access road to the Founders Club, and the riser became the cement wall that ran down the southern end of the club property to the beach south of Bobby Jones Trail and Glendenning Upshaw's bungalow. An identical cement wall bordered the northern end of the club. The guardhouse was located just past the point where the two walls were closest. Past the guardhouse, the access road divided into Ben Hogan Way and Babe Ruth Way, each of which led past the clubhouse to the members' bungalows.

"Pull into the cane field and hide the car," von Heilitz said.

Andres said, "You bet, Lamont," and swerved across the road into the field. The old taxi jounced over the rough ground, snapping off dry bamboolike bristles, and pitched and rolled past the first row of willows. Andres patted the steering wheel.

"We should be back in two hours, maybe less," von Heilitz said.

"Take your time," Andres said. "Don't get hurt."

Tom and von Heilitz got out of the car and walked through the dry stubs of cane. They crossed the road. Ahead, the white cement wall curved toward them, then curved away to cut across an empty swath of sandy ground covered with broom grass, palms, and low bushes all the way down to the low flat plane of the water. Von Heilitz moved quickly through the long grass toward the fence, which was no more than an inch taller than the top of his head. "Tell me when you think we're about level with Glen's bungalow," he said.

"It's way down, on the first road off the beach."

"The last bungalow on its road?" He looked back over his shoulder at Tom without slackening his pace.

Tom nodded.

"That's good luck."

"Why?"

"We can just walk around the far end of the wall—down on the beach, where it comes to an end. This wall is more decorative than functional." He smiled back at Tom, who was hurrying to catch up.

"That's lucky for you, then," Tom said. "I think you'd have a hard time getting over this fence, anyhow."

Von Heilitz stopped moving. "Do you? Do you really?"

"Well, it's as tall as you are."

"Dear boy," von Heilitz said. He put his hands on the top of the wall, hopped, and effortlessly pulled himself up until his waist met the smooth top of the wall; then he swung one leg up. In a second, he had disappeared over the top. Tom heard him say, "Nobody's looking. Your turn."

Tom reached up and grunted his upper body over the top of the wall. He felt his face turn red. The pad of the bandage slipped on the cement. Von Heilitz looked at him from beside a tall palm. Tom lowered his chest to the top of the wall and tried to swing his legs up. The tips of the glossy shoes struck the side of the wall. He leaned forward to get his hips over the top, lost his balance, and fell to the sandy ground like a downed bird.

"Not bad," von Heilitz said. "Any pain?"

Tom rubbed his shoulder. "You're not supposed to wear suits when you do things like that."

"Shoulder all right?"

"Fine." He grinned at the old man. "At least I got over the thing."

Von Heilitz looked down through the palm trees and sand dunes on this side of the wall to three rows of bungalows about a hundreds yards away. The last bungalow in the row closest to the beach protruded far beyond the others. They could see straight across the terrace into a high-windowed room with leather furniture and an ornate desk. "I suppose that's the one?"

"That's it," Tom said.

"Let's wait for the mailman's appearance behind the bunch of palms in front of the last set of bungalows." Von Heilitz pulled back his sleeve and looked at his watch. "It's about a quarter to four. He'll be along soon."

They worked their way through the sand, moving from one clump of palms to another, until they reached a group of four palms leaning and arching up out of a sturdy patch of long grass. Hairy coconuts lay around them like cannonballs. Tom sat on the grass beside the old man. He could see the table where he and his mother had eaten lunch; through the high windows, he saw the dim books behind glass-fronted cases, and the lamps burning in the study. It was something like the view seen by the person who had shot at him.

A few minutes later, a red Mill Walk mail van pulled into the parking lot, and a mailman opened the door and stepped out into the sunlight. Blue water sparkled behind him. He dragged a heavy brown bag from the side of the van, and moved out of sight, going toward the bungalows.

"He'll go to Glen's first," von Heilitz said. "It's closest." His voice sounded different, and Tom turned to look at his profile. A pink line covered the top of his cheek, and his eyes had both narrowed and brightened. "Now—now we *see.*"

Maybe he won't do anything at all, Tom thought. Maybe he'll shake his head and scratch his fingers in his hair. Maybe he'll shrug and toss the notes in the wastebasket.

Maybe we made it all up.

The mailman had to trudge across the parking lot, and then

carry his bag across Bobby Jones Trail. Walk up the stairs and pass into the inner courtyard. Knock on the door, and wait for Kingsley to shuffle to the door. Kingsley had to go back to the sitting room and present the mail to his master. The master had to stroll toward the study, examining each letter as he went.

Finally the door at the back of the study opened. Glendenning Upshaw, a great white head atop a massive blackness, appeared moving toward his desk. He was frowning down at a stack of letters in his hand—frowning simply from habit, not with anger or displeasure. As he came nearer the windows, Tom caught the red and grey of two of their envelopes.

"He got them," von Heilitz breathed.

Tom's grandfather stood behind his desk chair in his black suit, shuffling through eight or nine letters. Three of these he tossed immediately into the wastebasket beside the desk.

"Junk mail," von Heilitz said.

He pulled his chair out from behind the desk and sat. He took up one letter, slit the long white envelope with an opener, and pondered it for a moment. He set it down at the far end of the desk, took a pen from his pocket, and leaned over to make a note at the bottom of the page.

Next he took up the red envelope. He looked at the handwriting and examined the postmark. Then he slit the envelope open and pulled out the sheet of yellow paper. He unfolded it and read.

Tom held his breath.

His grandfather was motionless for a second: and then, though he did not move, gesture, or change in any way, his body seemed to alter its dimensions, as if beneath the black suit it had suddenly deflated and expanded like a bullfrog's air sac. He seemed to have drawn all the air in the room into himself. His arms and his back were as rigid as posts.

"And there we are," von Heilitz said.

Tom's grandfather whirled sideways in his chair and looked through the window and out across the terrace. Tom's heart slid up into his throat and stayed there until Upshaw slowly revolved back to the note. He stared at it for another second. Then he pushed the yellow paper to a corner of his desk and picked up the envelope to look at the handwriting and the postmark. He turned his head to make sure the door was closed, and then looked back out the window. He pulled all the rest of the letters toward him and shuffled through them, setting before him on the desk a grey envelope and two white envelopes, set down the others, and held each of the three up to examine the printed address and the postmark. One by one, he slit them open and read the notes. He leaned back in his chair and stared up at the ceiling for a moment before reading the notes again. He pushed his chair away from the desk, and then stood and moved to the window and looked both right and left with an unconscious furtiveness Tom had never before seen in him.

The pink line across the top of von Heilitz's cheeks had heated up like an iron bar. "Not going to get much sleep tonight, is he?"

"He really did kill her," Tom said. "I don't know if—"

Von Heilitz put a finger to his lips.

Tom's grandfather was walking around his study, describing an oval that took him to the glass-fronted bookcases and back to his desk. Every time he returned to his desk, he looked down at the notes. The third time he had done this, he grabbed the notes, and went around the back of his chair to throw them into the wastebasket. Then he leaned heavily on the back of the chair, pulled it out and sat down, and leaned over to retrieve the notes. He shoved them into the top drawer of the desk along with the envelopes. He opened another drawer, removed a cigar, bit off the end, and spat it into the wastebasket.

"Saint Nicotine," von Heilitz said. "Concentrates the mind, soothes the nerves, eases the bowels."

Tom realized that they had been watching his grandfather for only something like fifteen minutes. It felt as if they had been there for hours. The misery that had been gathering in him ever since Glendenning Upshaw read the first note swam up out of his own bowels like a physical substance. He stretched out in the tall grass and the sand and rested his head on his hands. Von Heilitz gently patted his back.

"He's figuring out what to do—trying to work out what he risks by telling somebody."

Tom raised his head and saw his grandfather exhaling a cloud of white smoke. He plugged the cigar back in his mouth, and began turning it around and around with his fingers, as if trying to screw it into place. Tom lowered his head again.

"Okay, he's reaching for the phone," von Heilitz said. "He's still not too sure about this, but he's going to do it."

Tom looked up. His grandfather sat with the receiver in his left hand and his right barely touching the dial. The cigar sent up a column of white smoke from an ashtray. He began dialing. He pressed the receiver to his ear. After a moment, he spoke a few words into the phone, waited, snatched at his cigar, and leaned back in his chair to say a few more words. He held the cigar in toward his chest like a poker hand. Then he hung up.

"Now what?" Tom asked.

"That depends on what he does. If it looks like he's expecting someone right away, we stay here. If not, we'll go to the hotel and come back here when it gets dark."

His grandfather opened the desk drawer and peered down at the notes. He lifted out the envelopes and considered the postmarks before putting them back and closing the drawer.

"It's what he does now that tells us," von Heilitz said.

Tom's grandfather looked at his watch, stood up, and began pacing back and forth. He sat down at the far end of the room and worked at the cigar; in a moment, he got to his feet again.

"It won't be long," von Heilitz said.

A slender brown lizard with a stubby tail and a Pleistocene head padded toward them across the sand, its splayed feet lifting and falling like hammers. When it saw them, it raised its snout—one forefoot poised in the air. A vein beat visibly in its neck. The lizard skittered around and darted toward the next clump of palms. The mailman worked his way between the bungalows on the street in back of Bobby Jones way. Tom sweated into his suit. Sand leaked into his shoes. He rubbed his shoulder, which was still sore. A white-haired man and woman in golfing clothes came out on a terrace behind the farthest bungalow in the third row and stretched out on loungers to read magazines.

"Have you ever tasted lizard?" von Heilitz asked.

"No." Tom propped his head on his cupped hand and looked up at the old man. He was leaning sideways against a palm with his knees drawn up, his whole body contracted into the spider-shaped shadow of the palm's crown, his face youthful and alight. "How does it taste?"

"The flesh of a raw lizard tastes like dirt—soft dirt. A cooked lizard is another matter. If you don't dry it out too much, it tastes exactly the way a bird would taste, if birds had fins and could swim. Everybody always says they taste like chicken, but lizard isn't nearly that delicate. The meat has a pungent, almost tarry smell, and the flavor's *gamy*. Lot of nutrition in a lizard. A good lizard'll keep you alive for a week."

"Where did you eat lizards?"

"Mexico. During the war, the American OSS asked me to investigate a group of German businessmen who spent a great deal of time traveling between Mexico and various South American countries. Mill Walk was technically neutral, of course, and so was Mexico. Well, these men turned out to be setting up escape routes for important Nazis, establishing identities, buying land—but the point is, one of them was nutty about certain foods, and ate lizard once a week."

"Raw or cooked?"

"Grilled over mesquite."

This story, which may or may not have been the strict truth, went on for twenty minutes.

A black car swung into the parking lot. Two men in dark blue uniforms slammed the doors. One of them was the officer Tom had seen ordering David Natchez upstairs in the hospital lobby, and the other was Fulton Bishop. The two men moved quickly across the parking lot and disappeared from view.

"Glen isn't going to say anything in front of the other man," von Heilitz said. "He'll make Bishop send him out of the room. Watch."

Tom's grandfather circled around the right side of the room, landed in the chair, and almost immediately bounced up again. He ground out the stub of the cigar in the ashtray. Then he straightened up and faced the door.

"Heard the bell," von Heilitz said.

Kingsley entered the study a moment later, and Bishop and the other man came in after him. Kingsley left, closing the door behind him. Glendenning Upshaw spoke a few words, and Fulton Bishop turned to the other man and gestured toward the door. The second policeman walked out of the room.

"Bishop is Glen's man," von Heilitz said. "He wouldn't have a career at all if Glen hadn't smoothed his way, and without Glen's protection, I don't think he could keep his hold on things. But Glen can't possibly trust him enough to tell him the truth about Jeanine Thielman. He has to tell him a story. I wish we could hear it."

Tom's grandfather sat behind his desk, and Fulton Bishop stayed on his feet. Upshaw talked, raised his hands, gestured; the other man remained motionless. Upshaw pointed at the upper part of his right arm.

"Now what is that about?" von Heilitz said. "I bet . . ."

Tom's grandfather opened his desk drawer and took out the four letters and their envelopes. Fulton Bishop crossed to the desk and leaned over the notes. He asked a question, and Upshaw answered. Bishop picked up the envelopes to examine the postmarks and the handwriting. He set them back down and stepped to the window, as if he, too, feared being overheard. Bishop turned around to speak to Upshaw, and Upshaw shook his head.

"He wants to take the letters with him. Glen doesn't want to give them up, but he will."

The mailman came walking back to his van through the parking lot.

Bishop looked through all four of the notes and said something that made Upshaw nod his head. Bishop passed one note and the red envelope back to Tom's grandfather, unbuttoned his uniform pocket, folded the notes together, and put the remaining notes and envelopes into the pocket. Glendenning Upshaw came close enough to Bishop to grip his arm. Bishop pulled away from him. Upshaw jabbed his finger into the policeman's chest. It looked like a loud conversation. Finally he walked Bishop to the door and let him out of the study.

"Bishop's got his marching orders, and he won't be very happy about it," von Heilitz said. "If Glen comes back to the window, look at his right sleeve and see if you can see anything there."

Tom's grandfather moved heavily back to his desk and took out another cigar. He bit, spat, and sat down to light it. After a few minutes, Fulton Bishop and the other policeman appeared in the parking lot. They opened the doors of their car and got in without speaking. Glendenning Upshaw turned his desk chair to the window and blew out smoke. Tom could not see anything distinctive about his right sleeve. Upshaw put the cigar in his mouth, turned back to the desk, leaned over to open a drawer on the right side, and took out a pistol. He laid the pistol on the top of the desk beside the note and the red envelope and looked at it for a moment, then picked it up and checked to see that it was loaded. He put it in the top drawer, and slowly closed the drawer with both hands. Then he shoved back the chair and stood up. He took a step toward the window and stood there, smoking. Kingsley opened the study door and said something, and Upshaw waved him away without turning around.

Tom leaned forward and peered at his right arm. He saw nothing except the black sleeve.

"I guess it's impossible to see it," von Heilitz said, "even with excellent eyes. But it's there."

"What?"

"A mourning band," von Heilitz said. "He told Bishop that those letters were about you."

Tom looked back at the heavy white-headed man smoking a long cigar at the window overlooking the terrace, and even though he could not see it, he did: he saw it because he knew von Heilitz was right, it was there, a black band Mrs. Kingsley had cut from an old fabric and sewn on his sleeve.

His grandfather turned away from the window and picked up the yellow paper and the red envelope. He carried them to the wall behind the desk, swung out a section of paneling, and then reached in to unlatch some other, interior door. The note and the envelope disappeared into the wall, and Upshaw latched the interior door and swung the paneling shut. He took one tigerish glance through the window and left the study.

"Well, that's what we came for," von Heilitz said. "You don't have any more doubts, do you?"

"No," Tom said. He got to his knees. "I'm not sure what I do have."

Von Heilitz helped him to his feet. The couple reading magazines on their terrace had fallen asleep. Tom followed the detective to the white concrete wall, and von Heilitz stooped and held out interlaced fingers for him. Tom put his right foot into von Heilitz's hands, and felt himself being propelled upward. He landed on the other side of the wall with a thud that jarred his spine. Von Heilitz went over the wall like an acrobat. He dusted off his hands, and brushed rimes of sand from the front of his suit. "Let's go back to the hotel and call Tim Truehart," he said.

61

Tom trudged after the detective on legs that seemed to weigh a hundred pounds each. His shoulder still hurt, and his burned hand ached, and sand in his shoes abraded his toes. The old man's suit hung on him like lead. Von Heilitz looked at him over his shoulder. Tom yanked at his lapels, trying to wrestle the suit into a more comfortable accommodation with his body.

When they got into the cane field, von Heilitz turned around. Tom stopped walking. "Are you all right?" von Heilitz asked.

"Sure," Tom said.

"You don't like me very much right now, do you?"

"I wouldn't say that," Tom said, and that was true too: he wouldn't. He wouldn't say anything at all.

Von Heilitz nodded. "Well, let's get back to town." He started walking toward the row of willows, and Tom followed, unable to make himself shorten the distance between them.

The old man was waiting beside the battered red car when Tom came around the first of the trees, and as soon as he saw Tom he opened his door and got in. Tom got in the other door and sat squeezed against it, as if there were two other people in the back seat.

"Everything go all right, Lamont?" Andres asked.

"We saw what we had to see."

Tom closed his eyes and slumped down in the seat. He saw his grandfather inhaling all the air in the study as he read a little yellow note; he saw him turn instinctively toward the window, like a lion that has felt the first arrow in his side.

Tom did not speak during the drive back to the middle of town, and when von Heilitz held open the door of Sinbad's Cavern for him, he hurried past as if fearing that the old man would touch him.

They rode up in the elevator in black silence.

Von Heilitz opened the door to his room, and Tom walked around him to unlock his own door. A maid had straightened the bed and organized the things on the table. The papers and envelopes were stacked on a chair, and the cheese and sausage had been put back in their bags. He picked up the novel about the Blue Rose murders, and threw himself on the bed. From the adjoining room came the sounds of von Heilitz speaking into the telephone. Tom opened the book and began to read.

A few minutes later von Heilitz came into his room. Tom barely glanced up from his book. The old man spun a chair around and straddled it backwards. "Do you want to know what Truehart's been doing?"

"Okay," Tom said, reluctantly closing the book.

"He knows of a man that Jerry could have hired—a guy named Schilling who makes a shaky living brokering used rifles, old cars, even a few motorboats, whatever he can get his hands on. He did a two-year stretch in the Wisconsin state prison for receiving stolen goods a few years ago, and ever since he's been living in a little place near a run-down tourist attraction outside Eagle Lake. Near that machine shop where they kept the stolen goods, too. Two people saw this Schilling talking with Jerry Hasek in a bar. The night of the fire, he disappeared."

"That doesn't prove anything," Tom said.

"No, not exactly, but Tim went to the local bank. Schilling has a little account there, and after Tim had a long talk with the manager, he had a look at the account records. Every summer for the past four years, Schilling has been putting something between eight and ten thousand in his account." Von Heilitz grinned at him.

Tom didn't get it.

"Schilling was Jerry's fence. He went back to his old business when Jerry and his friends started breaking into lodges."

"What does that have to do with the fire? Or with someone shooting at me?"

"The day before you arrived in Eagle Lake, our hero deposited five thousand dollars in his account."

"Five thousand dollars," Tom said.

"It was a half payment, most likely. He would have collected the other half when your body was discovered, but by then Jerry and his friends were in jail, thanks to you."

"He hired his fence to kill me?"

"Probably Schilling volunteered, once he learned there was ten thousand dollars in it for him. Now, Schilling's sister lives in Marinette, Wisconsin. She's married to another con, a friend of her brother's, who's in jail on an armed robbery charge. Tim thinks our man might have gone to stay with her for a week or so, and he called the Marinette police to watch her house."

"So they'll probably get him," Tom said. "They should. They should get the person who killed Barbara Deane." He looked down at *The Divided Man*, and opened it again.

"Tim thinks that your old friend Nappy LaBarre is getting close to telling him what he already knows. If they arrest Schilling, Nappy's information isn't going to do him any good. Nappy's going to have to sell out Schilling in a hurry, if he wants to turn state's evidence and have his charges dropped."

"Okay."

"Is that all you have to say? Okay? The noose is tightening around your grandfather's neck, and it's all because of you."

"I know."

"Is part of you sorry about that?"

"I wish I knew," Tom said. He saw his grandfather again, turning toward the window like a wounded lion.

Von Heilitz stood up and turned the chair around. He sat down facing Tom, put his elbow on his knee, and cupped his chin in his hand.

"It's just that he's my grandfather, I guess. I was brought up to think he was really special—a kind of hero. He kept everything safe. Everything *depended* on him. And now I feel—I feel cut off from everybody."

"Come with me to talk to David Natchez," von Heilitz said. "For one thing, you might be able to help us work out where Glen would be likely to go, if he wants to hide somewhere while he gets ready to leave the island. It would help you get over the shock."

Tom shook his head.

"I'm serious—you have had a shock, a serious one. I know you're angry at me, and that you don't want to be. In the past two days, everything you thought you knew turned inside-out, and—"

"Stop," Tom said. "Maybe I am angry with you, but you don't know everything I'm feeling." Saying this made him feel like a sulky child.

"No," von Heilitz said. "But after all this is over, we'll be able to get to know each other a lot better."

"Couldn't you have gone after my mother, seventeen years ago?" Tom asked. "When you came back to Mill Walk and found that her father had taken her to Miami? You just let him take her away—you just gave up. You might have lived across the street from us, but I never saw you, except for those two times you came to the hospital."

Von Heilitz had straightened up in the chair. He looked uncomfortable, and said, "Glen would never have let me see her. Even if he had, she wouldn't have left with me."

"You don't know that," Tom said. "She was over eighteen. She could have married anyone she wanted. You just let her slip back into—into helplessness. You let her be sold to Victor Pasmore. Or you let Victor be bought for her, or however it worked." Then it seemed to him that he was talking about Sarah Spence and Buddy Redwing, and another degree of misery entered him. "You didn't do *anything*," he said, and then could not say any more.

"You think I haven't thought about that?" the old man said. "I was in my forties. I was used to living by myself, and going wherever I liked. I didn't think I'd make a very good husband. I never pretended not to be selfish, if selfishness means giving yourself permission to concentrate on a few things at the expense of everything else."

"You liked being alone," Tom said.

"Of course I did, but that wasn't the most important reason. I think I was just another kind of father to Gloria. You can't have a real marriage on that basis. Not only that, what I wanted to do would have half-killed her. I couldn't marry Glen Upshaw's daughter. Can't you see that? Just after you were born, I began to realize that he had killed Jeanine Thielman. I wanted to destroy him. Things turned out the way they did because we were all the people we were—Gloria and Glen and me. The only good thing that came out of it was you."

"You only came to see me twice," Tom said again.

"What do you think it would have done to your mother if I had insisted on seeing you?"

"That's not why," Tom said. "You were too busy being shot at and eating lizards and looking through windows and solving murders."

"You can see it that way, if you like."

"The only time you wanted to really spend time with me was when you saw that you could use me. You wanted me to get interested in what happened to Jeanine Thielman. You wound me up like a clock and turned me loose. And you're pleased because I did just what you wanted me to."

"And you did it because of who you are," von Heilitz said. "If you'd been another sort of kid, I . . ."

"You wouldn't have done anything at all."

"But you're not another sort of kid."

"I wonder what I am," Tom said. "I wonder who I am."

"You're enough like me to have met me next to Hasselgard's car," von Heilitz said. "And to have turned up at the hospital on the day Michael Mendenhall died."

"I'm not sure I really want to be like you," Tom said.

"But you don't want to be like your grandfather, either." Von Heilitz stood up and looked down at Tom, sprawled on the St. Alwyn's double bed with a paperback book beside him. Tom felt strong and conflicting currents of emotion—the old man wanted to come near him, put his hand on his cheek, hug him, and what he had said made it impossible.

"What I told you in that clearing was the truth, Tom. I do

love you. And we're going to accomplish something great. It's been a long time coming, but we're going to do it—together." He put his hand on the bottom of the bed, and hesitated.

Tom thought, *I don't want any speeches*, and what von Heilitz saw in his face made him back away from the bed. "You don't have to come over to Hobart's with me. I'll check in with you before I go."

Tom nodded, scarcely knowing what he wanted anymore and too unhappy to think about it clearly. He did not see von Heilitz walk out of the room. The connecting door closed. He picked up his book and began reading. He could hear von Heilitz pacing around his room. In the book, Esterhaz drove along the shore of a steaming lake. It seemed to Esterhaz that another person, a barely visible person of terrifying strength, lived inside him, and that this other person was someone he had once been. Von Heilitz began speaking into his telephone. *Why did I talk to him like that*? Tom wondered; *it's like I expect him to be an ordinary father*. Victor Pasmore was an ordinary father, and one of those was enough. Tom nearly got off the bed and went into the other room, but his enduring unhappiness, an unhappiness that tasted like anger, kept him nailed to the bed and the book.

There was a lot of invisibility in the world, Esterhaz thought. He took another pull from the pint bottle between his thighs. A lot of people disappeared into it, and other people barely noticed they were gone. Sorrow played a role, humiliation played a role. It was a foretaste of death, death in advance of death. Being left behind by the world was a big part of it. Drunks, wastrels, and murderers, combat soldiers after a war, musicians, detectives, drug addicts, poets, barbers, and hairdressers . . . as the visible world grew more and more crowded, so did its invisible counterpart. Esterhaz pulled up at a stoplight, and for a moment willed himself to see the invisible world he had just imagined, and a mob of shuffling, indifferent Invisibles, dressed in rags and old clothes, pulling on bottles like his own or leaning against lampposts, lying down on the snowy sidewalks, slid effortlessly into view.

Tom looked up from the book, awakened by a memory that seemed to come from some version of himself hidden within him—a memory of having seen himself here in this shabby room, alone and reading the book he was reading now. He had *looked at* the self he was now, the almost grown Tom. A nearly abstract violence surrounded this memory—an explosion of smoke and fire—as it surrounded Esterhaz.

Exhaustion that seemed to come from every cell in his body pulled him downward, and Tom thought, *I have to get up*, but the book slipped from his hand, and he saw the caged animal that was his grandfather snapping his heavy body sideways toward a window as the arrow pierced his haunch. He reached for the book. His fingers touched the dark half of the face on the cover, and his grandfather looked up from the yellow note into his eyes, and he was asleep.

Or not. He looked at the window once, and saw darkening air. Some time after that he heard Lamont von Heilitz come through the connecting door and walk up to the side of the bed. I'll come with you, he said, but the words stayed inside him. The old man untied Tom's shoes and slipped them off his feet. He turned off the light. "Dear Tom," von Heilitz said. "It's okay. Don't worry about anything you said."

"No," Tom said, meaning, no, don't go, I have to come with you, and von Heilitz stroked his shoulder and leaned over in the darkness and kissed his head. He moved backwards, moving away, and a line of light came into the room from the door, and he was gone.

Tom was moving down a hazy corridor toward a small blond boy in a wheelchair. When he touched the boy's shoulder, the boy looked up at him from a book in his lap with a face darkened by rage and humiliation. "Don't worry," Tom said.

62

Dimly aware of the presence of a crowd of hovering figures, Tom leaned closer to the boy and saw that he was looking into his own, now barely recognizable, boyhood face. His heart banged, and he opened his eyes to a dark room in the St. Alwyn Hotel. The yellow glow of a street lamp lay on the window, and a filmy trace of light touched the ceiling. He reached for the bedside lamp, still seeing in his mind the face of the child in the wheelchair. Sudden light brought the room into focus. Tom rubbed his face and moaned. "Are you back?" he called. "Lamont?" It was the first time he had used the old man's first name, and it felt uncomfortable as a stone in his mouth. No response came from the other room.

Tom looked at his watch and saw that it was ten-fifteen. He thought he must have been asleep for three or four hours. He swung his legs off the bed and walked on stiff legs to the connecting door. "Hello," he called, thinking that von Heilitz might have come back from the meeting at Hobart's and gone to bed. There was no answer. Tom opened the door. Here was another dark room, identical to his own—two chairs at a round table by the window, a double bed, a couch, a closet, and a bathroom. The bed was made, and a depression in the pillow and wrinkles in the coverlet showed where von Heilitz had lain.

Feeling as if he were trespassing, Tom walked through the dark room to the window. One carriage rolled up Calle Drosselmayer, the headlights of the cars behind shining on the muscular flanks of a pair of black horses. A few people paraded down the sidewalk in the warm night air, and a flock of sailors ran across the street. The grille had been pulled down over the pawnshop window. An overweight man in a white shirt and tan trousers leaned against the wall beside the entrance to The Home Plate, smoking and looking across the street to the steps of the hotel. The man looked up, and Tom stepped back from the window. The man yawned, crossed his arms over his chest, flipped his cigarette into the street.

Tom went back to his own room to wait until the Shadow came back from his meeting with David Natchez. He ate bread and cheese and slices of salami, and read twenty pages of *The Divided Man.* When had von Heilitz left for the meeting at Hobart's? Two hours ago? Nervous, Tom laid the book open on the table and paced the room, listening for noises in the hall. He opened the door and leaned out, but saw only the empty corridor and a long row of brown doors with painted-over metal numbers. Someone down at the end of the hallway played scales on a tenor saxophone, someone else listened to a radio. Footsteps came toward him from around the corner leading to the stairs, and Tom ducked back behind his door. The footsteps rounded the corner, came nearer, went past his door. He peeked out and saw a small, dark-haired man with a ponytail carrying a trumpet case and a brown paper bag moving toward a door at the end of the hall. He knocked, and the saxophone abruptly inserted two honks into the E-minor scale. "Hey, Glenroy," said the man at the door. Tom leaned his head out into the hall, but saw no more than the door opening wide enough for the trumpet player to slide into the room.

He sat down at the table and ate another wedge of cheese. He took his key from his pocket and scratched TP into the wood near the PD. Then he tried to rub it out, but managed only to darken the thin white lines. When he looked out the window, the man in the white shirt was staring at a group of women who had just left The Home Plate and were walking up Calle Drosselmayer, talking and laughing. Tom pulled the telephone nearer to him and dialed Sarah Spence's number.

She answered in the middle of the first ring, and he imagined her watching television in Anton Goetz's dream palace, reaching out her hand with her eyes still on the screen, absently saying, "Hello?"

He could not speak.

"Hello?"

What did you tell people? Tom said silently. *Who did you tell?*

"Isn't anybody there?"

For longer than he had expected, she held the phone, waiting for a response.

Then: "Tom?"

He drew in a breath.

"Is that you, Tom?" she asked. Very faintly, he could hear the singsong of a television behind her voice. From farther away than the television, her mother yelled, "Are you *crazy?*"

Tom hung up, then dialed his own house, without any idea of what he could say to his mother, or if he would say anything at all. The telephone rang twice, three times, and when it was picked up Dr. Milton's voice said, "This is the Pasmore residence." Tom slammed down the phone.

He looked at his watch and watched the minute hand jerk from ten-fifty to ten fifty-one.

Then he lifted the receiver again and dialed von Heilitz's telephone number. The phone rang and rang: Tom counted ten rings, then eleven, then fifteen, and gave up.

Unable to stay in the room any longer, he went to the bed and put on the shoes von Heilitz had taken off him, splashed water on his face in the bathroom, glanced at a taut face in the mirror, dried himself off and straightened his tie, and let himself out into the hallway. Through the last door came the sounds of a trumpet and tenor saxophone softly, slowly playing "Someone to Watch Over Me" in unison. Voices drifted toward him. He walked to the stairs and went down to the lobby.

A few sailors had spilled out from Sinbad's Cavern, and stood in a tight knot around the door, holding glasses and beer bottles. The night clerk leaned over the desk in a pool of light, slowly turning the pages of an *Eyewitness*. Tom came down the last steps, and the clerk and a few of the sailors glanced up at him, then looked away. Steel drum music from a jukebox came faintly from the bar and grill. Lamp light fell on worn leather chairs and couches, and illuminated red and blue details in a patchy Oriental carpet. On the other side of the St. Alwyn's glass doors, cars streamed up and down the street. Tom began moving through the sailors, who parted to let him open the door of the bar.

The steel drum music instantly sizzled into his head. Women and sailors and men in loud shirts filled the room with shouts and laughter and cigarette smoke. A couple of sailors were dancing in front of the crowded bar, flinging out their arms, snapping their fingers, drunkenly trying to keep in time to the music. Tom slowly worked his way down the bar, squeezing through the sailors and their girls, cigarette smoke making his eyes water. At last he reached the door, and went outside to the Street of Widows.

The market was closed, but the vendor still sat on his rug beside his hats and baskets, talking to himself or to imaginary customers. Across the street men went up the steps to the Traveller's Hotel. A CLOSED sign hung in the door of Ellington's Allsorts and Notions. When the light changed, the cars and buggies began to move toward Calle Drosselmayer. The ping-ping-ping of the steel drums sounded through the window with the flashing neon scimitar. At a break in the traffic, Tom ran across the street.

"Hats for your lady, hats for yourself, baskets for the market," sang the barefoot vendor.

Tom knocked on Hobart's door. No lights burned in the shop.

"Nothing in there, the cupboard be bare," the vendor called to him.

Tom beat on the door again. He searched the frame and found a brass button and held it down until he saw a small dark figure moving toward him through the interior of the shop. "Closed!" Hobart shouted. Tom stepped back so the shopowner could see his face, and Hobart darted to the door, opened it, and pulled Tom inside.

"What do you want? What you looking for?"

"My friend isn't still here?"

Hobart stepped backward and said, "What friend? Do I know what friend you're talking about?" He was wearing a long cream-colored nightshirt that made him look like an angry doll.

"Lamont von Heilitz. I came here with him this morning. We bought a lot of things—you said I looked like his nephew."

"Maybe I did, maybe I didn't," Hobart said. "Maybe a man says he's gonna be somewhere, maybe he never means to come. Nobody tells Hobart—no *reason* for anybody to tell Hobart, don't you know that?" Hobart stared at him stonily, then took a step toward the door.

"You mean he didn't come?"

"If you don't know, maybe you're not supposed to," Hobart said. "How do I know what you are? You're no nephew of that man's."

"Did the policeman show up?"

"There was someone here," Hobart admitted. "Might have been him."

"And my friend never came for the meeting," Tom said, for a second almost too stunned to worry.

"If you're his friend, how come you don't know that?"

"He left the hotel hours ago to come here."

"Could be that's what he told *you*. Man came here and waited, could be that's what he *wanted* him to do," Hobart said. "I see you're worried, but I tell you, I worried about Lamont twenty, thirty years, it never did a bit of good. He put on a stringy old wig and a bunch a rags, and he stood on a street corner somewheres, watching for something he knew was gonna happen. I'm talking straight to you now, nephew." Hobart put his hand on the doorknob.

"How long did the other man wait for him?"

"He was here a good hour, and when he left he was steaming. Don't look for any favors from that man." Hobart's teeth gleamed in the dark shop. "Nearly tore off my bell, way he went through the door." He patted Tom's arm. "You just go back and wait for him. This is the way your friend *works*, don't you know that yet?"

"I guess not," Tom said.

"Don't worry." Hobart reached up to hold the bell with one hand as he cracked the door open with the other.

"That's what *he* told me," Tom said, and went outside. The door closed silently behind him.

"You got in, but did you buy?" the vendor chanted.

Tom glanced at the shoeless figure leaning against the wall. He nearly laughed out loud—relief made him feel lighter than air. He walked past the entrance of the Traveller's Hotel toward the vendor and knelt on the sidewalk beside him. "You had me worried," he whispered. "Why didn't you—?"

The vendor was a foot shorter than von Heilitz. Two doglike teeth jutted from his upper jaw, and ragged brown scars sewed shut both of his eyes. "A basket, or a hat?"

"A hat," Tom said.

"Three dollars, pick your size, pick your size."

Tom gave the man bills and picked up a hat at random.

"Did you hear a fight, or a scuffle, or anything like that, a couple of hours ago? It would have been outside the bar across the street."

"I heard the Angel of the Lord," the vendor said. "And I heard the Lord of Darkness, walking up and down in the world. You'll look handsome, in that hat."

Tom gave the hat to a sailor as he passed through the bar to go back to his room, and the sailor placed it on the head of a pretty whore.

63

Laughter, soft conversation, and music filtered into the fourth-floor hallway. Tom let himself into his room and went to the window without turning on any of the lights. The man in the white shirt was picking his teeth with a fingernail, and a young woman in skin-tight shorts, high heels, and a halter top whispered in his ear. The man shook his head. She leaned against him, and rubbed her breasts against his arm. The man stopped picking his teeth. He turned his head and uttered two or three words, and the girl jumped away from him as if she had been touched with a cattle prod.

Tom pulled a chair up to the window and sat down, his chin on his forearms. After three or four minutes, he pushed up the window. Warm, moist air flowed over him. Steady traffic passed before the hotel on Calle Drosselmayer, and now and then a taxi pulled up and let out couples and single men who walked across the sidewalk and up the steps to the hotel.

At one o'clock, the man in the white shirt went into The Home Plate. He came out ten minutes later and went back to the wall.

Tom had been at least partially reassured by his talk with Hobart Ellington, and for a long time as he watched the street beneath him, he waited for the sound of Lamont von Heilitz coming into the adjoining room. Tom had never seen what went on at night in downtown Mill Walk, and while he waited, expecting the old man to come in at any minute, he watched the street life, fascinated. The number of cars and other sorts of vehicles on the street had actually increased, and more and more people packed the sidewalks: in couples, their arms around each others' waists; in groups of five or six, carrying bottles and glasses, having an ambulatory party. Men and women on the sidewalk now and then recognized people in the cars and open carriages, and shouted greetings, and sometimes ran through the traffic to join their friends. Neil Langenheim rolled by in an open carriage, too drunk to sit up straight, as a wild-haired girl nuzzled his red face and moved to kneel on top of him. Moonie Firestone went past in the front seat of a white Cadillac convertible, her arm slung comfortably around the neck of a white-haired man. At one-thirty, when the traffic was at its height, he heard footsteps in the hall, and jumped up to go to the connecting door; when the footsteps continued down the hall toward the party in Glenroy Breakstone's room, he went back to the window and saw the head of a girl with shoulder-length blond hair nestled on the shoulder of a black-haired man driving another long convertible. It was Sarah Spence, he thought, and then thought it could not be; the girl moved, and he saw the flash of her profile, and thought again that she was Sarah. The car moved out of sight, leaving him with his uncertainty.

By two-thirty the crowds had gone, leaving only a few wandering groups of young people, most of them men, moving up and down the sidewalk. The man in the white shirt had vanished. At three, a tide of men and women poured out of The Home Plate and stood uncertainly outside as the lights went off behind them, then drifted off. The noises from down the hall ceased, and loud voices and footsteps went past the door. One car went up Calle Drosselmayer. Traffic lights flashed red and green. Tom's eyelids closed.

Noises from the street—a junk man tossing cases of empty bottles onto his cart—brought him half of the way into wakefulness hours later. It was still dark outside. He staggered to his bed and fell across the covers.

64

Hunger awakened him at ten. He left the bed and looked into the next room. Von Heilitz had not returned. Tom showered and put on clean underclothes and socks from the suitcase. He dressed in a pale pink shirt and blue linen suit he remembered from his first visit to von Heilitz's house. Before he buttoned the double-breasted vest, he knotted a dark blue tie around his neck. In von Heilitz's clothes, he walked back into the other room, thinking that the detective might have come in and gone out again while he was asleep, but there was no explanatory note on the table or the bed.

The owner of the pawnshop was pushing up the metal grille, and the man in the white shirt, like von Heilitz, had not returned.

Tom sat on the end of his bed, almost dizzy with worry. It seemed to him that he would have to stay in this little room forever. His stomach growled. He took out his wallet and counted his money—fifty-three dollars. How long could he stay at the St. Alwyn on fifty-three dollars? Five days? A week? *If*

I go downstairs and eat, he'll be here when I come back, Tom thought, and let himself out into the hall.

The day clerk rolled his eyes when Tom asked if any messages had been left for him, and laboriously looked over his shoulder at a rank of empty boxes. "Does it look to you like there are any messages?" Tom bought a thick copy of the *Eyewitness*.

Tom went into Sinbad's Cavern and ate scrambled eggs and bacon while a hunchback mopped spilled beer off the wooden floor. The paper said nothing about the fire at Eagle Lake or Jerry Hasek and his partners. A paragraph on the society page told Mill Walk that Mr. and Mrs. Ralph Redwing had decided to spend the rest of the summer at Tranquility, their beautiful estate in Venezuela, where they expected to be entertaining many of their friends during the coming months. Tranquility had its own eighteen-hole golf course, both an indoor and an outdoor pool, a tennis court, a thirteenth-century stained glass window Katinka Redwing had purchased in France, and a private library of eighteen thousand rare books. It also housed the famous Redwing collection of South American religious art. The street door opened, and Tom looked over his shoulder to see the same two policemen who had been there the day before easing their bellies up to the bar. "Usual," one of them said, and the barman put a dark bottle of Pusser's rum and two shot glasses in front of them. "Here's to another perfect day," one of the cops said, and Tom turned back to his eggs, hearing the clink of the shot glasses meeting.

He went back to the lobby and climbed the stairs, praying that he would find the old man in his room, pacing impatiently between the bed and the window, demanding to know where he had gone. Tom came down the hall and put his key in the lock. *Please.* He turned the key and swung the door open. *Please.* He was looking into an empty room. The food in his stomach turned into hair and brick dust. He walked inside and leaned against the door. Then he moved to the connecting door—this room, too, was empty. Fighting off the demon of panic, Tom went to the closet and put his hand in the pocket of the suit he had worn the day before. He found the card, and went to the table and dialed Andres's number.

A woman answered, and when Tom asked to speak to Andres, said that he was still asleep.

"This is an emergency," Tom said. "Would you please wake him up?"

"He worked all night long, Mister, it'll be an emergency if he don't get his rest." She hung up.

Tom dialed the number again, and the woman said, "Look, I *told* you—"

"It's about Mr. von Heilitz," Tom said.

"Oh, I see," she said, and put down the telephone. A few minutes later, a thick voice said, "Start talking, and you better make it good."

"This is Tom Pasmore, Andres."

"Who? Oh. Lamont's friend."

"Andres, I'm very worried about Lamont. He went out to a meeting with a policeman early last night, and he never showed up for the meeting, and he's still not back."

"You got me up for that? Don't you know Lamont disappears all the time? Why do you think they call him the Shadow, man? Just wait for him, he'll turn up."

"I waited up all night," Tom said. "Andres, he told me he'd be back."

"Maybe that's what he wanted you to think." It was like talking to Hobart Ellington.

Tom did not say anything, and finally Andres yawned and said, "Okay, what do you want me to do about it?"

"I want to go to his house," Tom said.

Andres sighed. "All right. But give me an hour. I have to make a pot of coffee before I do anything else."

"An hour?"

"Read a book," Andres said.

Tom asked him to pick him up outside the entrance of Sinbad's Cavern at eleven-thirty.

Beside the sewing machines and the row of tenor saxophones with necks curved like the top of Jeanine Thielman's capital T's, a fiftyish man in a white shirt with rolled sleeves leaned against the wall and drew on a cigarette while looking at the entrance to the St. Alwyn through his sunglasses. Tom backed away from the window and paced around the room. He understood why people tore their hair out, why they bit their nails, why they banged their heads against walls. These activities weren't brilliant, but they kept your mind off your anxieties.

Then an idea struck him—maybe it was not brilliant either, but it would help fill the time until Andres came. And it would answer the question he had failed to ask Kate Redwing, back when he had thought his most serious problem was getting through lonely meals at the Eagle Lake clubhouse. He sat down and picked up the telephone—and nearly did start chewing on his fingernails, from sheer doubt of the rightness of what he intended to do. He thought of Esterhaz pulling on his bottle, seeing phantoms all around him, and of a real detective named Damrosch, who had killed himself, and dialed information and asked for a telephone number.

Without giving himself time to reconsider, he dialed the number.

"Hello," said a voice that brought back an avenue of trees and the touch of cool water against his skin.

"Buzz, this is Tom Pasmore," he said.

There was a moment of startled silence before Buzz said, "I don't suppose you've seen the papers. Or is this a *very* long distance call?"

"Someone else died in the fire, and I came back to the island with Lamont von Heilitz. But nobody else knows I'm alive, Buzz, and I want to ask you not to tell anybody. It's important. Everybody will know in a couple of days, but until then—"

"I won't tell anybody, if you want to stay dead. Well, I might tell Roddy—he felt as bad as I did. In fact, I can hardly believe I'm talking to you! I called your house to speak to your mother, but Bonaventure Milton answered, and I knew he wouldn't let me say anything to her. . . ." Buzz inhaled and exhaled a couple of times. "Frankly, I'm reeling. I'm so glad you're alive! Roddy and I saw the article in the paper, and it reminded us of those times you were nearly injured, and we wondered—you know—"

"Yes," Tom said.

"My God. Whose body did they find, if it wasn't yours?"

"It was Barbara Deane."

"Oh, heavens. Of course. And you came back with Lamont? I didn't even know that you knew him."

"He knows everybody," Tom said.

"Tom," Buzz said. "You got our portrait back! I don't know how you did it, but you were brilliant, and Roddy and I are forever in your debt. The Eagle Lake police called last night to say that it's safe. Is there anything in the world I can do for you?"

"There is one thing. This is going to sound funny, and maybe you'll think it isn't any of my business."

"Try me."

"Kate Redwing mentioned something to me about your first job."

"Ah." Buzz was silent for a moment. "And you were curious about it—about what happened."

"Yes," Tom said.

"Did she say I was working with Boney Milton?"

"She just said it was an important doctor, and something reminded me of it a few minutes ago."

Buzz hesitated again. "Well, I—" He laughed. "This is a little awkward for me. But I could tell you sort of the bare bones of the thing, I suppose, without violating anybody's confidentiality. I used to take home Boney's files at night, in order to catch up with the patient histories. I was a pediatrician, of course, so at first I just read the files of the kids I was seeing, but then later I started reading the files on their parents too, so I could have the whole family history in mind when I saw the kid. I had the idea that what happened to the parents played some kind of role in their kids' lives—Boney didn't think much of this idea, which is typical of him, by the way, but he didn't mind much, and I was always tactful when I noticed that he had missed something, or goofed something up. Anyhow, one time I made a mistake, and brought home the file of one of the patients Boney kept for himself, and I thought I saw some classic indications of real trouble, if you see what I mean. Vaginal warts, vaginal bleeding, and a couple of other things that at the time should at least have called for further investigation and were probably an indicator for psychiatric counseling. Do you see what I'm talking about? This was in the woman's childhood. Really it could only mean one thing. I can't be more specific, Tom. Anyhow, I said something about it to Boney, and he hit the ceiling. I was out on my ear, and that's why I don't have any patients at Shady Mount."

"Did you know a policeman named Damrosch?"

"You are digging into things, aren't you? No, not really. I knew *of* him, and I would have recognized him if I'd seen him on the street. The period I'm talking about was around the time of those Blue Rose murders, though."

"After the first one?"

"After the first two, I think. I was supposed to be the third, as I guess you know by now. Scarcely my favorite memory. Lamont must have told you about my connection to all that."

Tom said that he had.

"Of course there's no connection between my encounter with a maniac and Boney's throwing me out of his practice—I'm still not convinced that Damrosch was the person who attacked me, but I can tell you one thing—I'm damn sure it wasn't Boney!"

"No," Tom said, though at this moment almost anything would have seemed possible to him.

They said good-bye a few seconds later. Tom jittered around the room, thinking about what Buzz had told him, and then could no longer stand the tension of being alone, and let himself out into the hallway and walked downstairs to the bar and grill. He drank two Cokes and stared out the window past the flashing neon scimitar. A battered red taxi slid up to the curb.

65

Tom ducked down in the back seat when Andres turned east on Calle Drosselmayer. "Now what?" Andres said. "You think some fellow is *watching* you?" He chugged coffee from a plastic cup with an opening in its lid and chuckled. "How do you come to think this fellow is watching?"

Tom slowly straightened up. They were a block east of the hotel. Two hundred yards ahead lay the glossy shops which had seemed a paradise of earthly things from Sarah Spence's little car. "Did you see a man in sunglasses and a white shirt across the street from the hotel?"

"I might have seen that man," Andres said. "I won't say I didn't."

"Lamont saw him when we first came to the St. Alwyn. He's been there ever since, just watching the front of the hotel."

"Well, careful does no harm," Andres admitted. "But there's no sense in what we are doing now. Get me out of my bed, look for Lamont. When Lamont does not want to be seen, nobody on earth can find him. I know Lamont forty years, and I know that man can drive you crazy. He does not explain himself. This is true! He say, I will be here, and is he? *Sometimes*. He say, I will see you in two hours, and when does he come? Maybe two days. Does Lamont care, I get out of bed after sleeping two hours? He does not. Does Lamont care, you worry when he stays out? I assure you, my friend, he does not. This is Lamont. Lamont is always working, he goes here, he goes there, he stands in the rain twelve hours, and when he is done he says, 'Very few men on Mill Walk are wearing purple socks.' He has a different music in his head."

"I know, but—"

Andres was not through yet.

"And now we are going to his house! Do you have a key? Do you think he left the door open? You cannot think a circle around Lamont, you know."

"I'm not trying to out-think him, I just want to find him," Tom said. "If you want to go back to bed, I'll walk."

"You'll walk. You think just like he does. You're so worried about Lamont you stay awake a whole night, and you want me to go back to bed. What do you think happens, if I go home? My wife asks me, did you find Lamont? I say, no, I need my sleep. She says, you sleep after you find Lamont!" He shook his head. "It's not so easy, being his friend. Who do you think found him when he was nearly killed in back of Armory Place? Who do you think took him to the hospital? You think he did that himself?"

"You're worried too," Tom said, having just understood this.

"You have not been listening to me," Andres said. "That is my lot, worrying about Lamont von Heilitz. So let us go to his house, and you will walk in and find him making a cup of tea and he will say, 'Your grandfather's horse has thrown its right front shoe,' and you will go back to the hotel and think about it, and I will go back to bed and not think about it. Because I know better than to think about the kind of things he says."

Andres turned off Calle Berlinstrasse into Edgewater Trail. Waterloo Parade, Balaclava Lane, Omdurman Road. The houses spread apart and grew larger. Victoria Terrace, Stonehenge Circle, Ely Place, Salisbury Road. Now he was back in the peaceful landscape of his childhood, where sprinklers whirred over long lawns and bright sunlight fell on bougainvillaea and hibiscus trees with lolling red blossoms. Here every child attended Brooks-Lowood School, and a traffic jam was one servant riding a bicycle into another servant's bicycle, spilling clean laundry into the clean street. Yorkminster Place. Some of the houses had red-tiled roofs and curving white walls, some were of smooth white marble that ate the sunlight, some of grey stone piled into turrets and towers, others of shining white wood, with broad porches and columns and verandas the size of fields. Sprays of water played on the broad green lawns.

Andres turned into The Sevens and pulled up to the curb. He turned around and laid an arm along the top of his seat. "Now I sit here, the way I always did for Lamont, and you go to his place, okay? And see what you see. Then you come back and tell me about it, and we'll decide what to do after that."

Tom patted his thick arm and got out of the car. Delicately scented air drifted toward him from Eastern Shore Road and the ocean. Tom walked away from the car and turned toward Eastern Shore Road on Edgewater Trail. His scalp and the back of his neck prickled with the sensation that he was being watched, and he moved quickly up the block. The flat blue line of the sea hung between the great houses.

Dr. Milton's buggy stood in front of his house, and two men carried a wrapped couch down the Langenheims' walk toward a long yellow van marked Mill Walk Intercoastal Movers. The feeling that someone was watching him grew stronger. Tom hurried past the Jacobs house and walked up onto Lamont von Heilitz's concrete drive. On the lawn, fresh cuttings lay amongst the blades of grass. From down near An Die Blumen, no louder than a bee, came the dim whirring of the big mower used by the lawn service. The curtains hung in the windows as always, blocking the secret life of the house's owner from the eyes of the neighborhood children. *He's okay*, Tom thought, *I don't have to go any farther*. Von Heilitz would be back in the St. Alwyn, fuming at Tom for disappearing when he needed him to look for purple socks or thrown right front horseshoes. He glanced over his shoulder at his house and went reluctantly up von Heilitz's drive. At the point where the drive curved around to the back of the house and the empty garage, a flattened cigarette butt lay between a black line of tar and the edge of the concrete.

Tom came around the back of the house and saw an oil stain on the concrete halfway between the garage and the back door.

He stopped moving. All old driveways had oil stains. Wherever you had cars, you had oil stains. Even people who didn't own cars had oil stains on the driveways. The back door would be locked, and he would ring the bell a couple of times, and then go back around the block to reassure Andres. Tom walked around the glistening stain toward the step up to the back door, following faint scuff marks on the concrete.

The small pane of glass nearest the doorknob was smashed in, as if a fist had punched through it to reach inside and open the door. Tom put his hand on the knob, too disturbed now to bother with ringing the bell, turned it, and heard the bolt slide out of the striker plate. He pulled the door toward him. "Hello?" he said, but his voice was only a whisper. He stepped into a coatroom where a lifetime's worth of raincoats hung on brass hooks. Two or three coats lay puddled on the floor. Tom walked through into the kitchen. A smear of blood lay like a tiny red feather on the counter beside the sink. Water dripped slowly from the tap, one drop hitting the bottom of the sink as another formed and lengthened on the lip of the faucet. A nearly empty pint bottle of Pusser's Navy Rum stood on the counter back in the shadows beneath the cabinets.

"No," Tom said, in the same strangled voice.

Here's to another perfect day.

He came out of the kitchen and stopped short as whatever was in his stomach slammed into his throat. Toppled file cabinets and scattered papers lay all across the floor. Horsehair and curd-colored stuffing foamed from the leather furniture where he and the old man had sat talking. Torn books ruffled like hair on top of the wreckage. Tom took a blind, dazed step into the enormous room. "LAMONT!" he yelled, and this time his voice was as loud as a bugle. "LAMONT!" He stepped forward again, and his foot came down on a thick fan of papers leaking from a yellow file. He bent to pick them up, and more papers streamed from the file, papers marked *Cleveland, June 1940*, and *Crossed Keys Motel, Bakersfield*, and covered with a dense, obsessive handwriting he realized he had never seen before. He moved to set them down on the coffee table where he and von Heilitz had put their feet and saw that the table had been broken in half, its filigreed leather surface sagging over the broken wood and stamped with dusty boot prints. There were no paths through the maze now, it was all chaos and obstruction, and he stepped over a file cabinet vomiting old issues of the *Eyewitness* and sent the wheel of a bicycle ticking around against its frame. Paintings floated atop shoals of papers and books; records torn from their sleeves leaned against paper mountains. Tom wandered through the chaos and saw an empty file marked *Glendenning Upshaw, 1938–39*. Beside it was another, *Blue Rose Affair*. The desks had been rifled and overturned, their drawers tossed aside—scissors and bottles of glue surfaced here and there in the litter—the tops of library lamps shattered into green fragments across ripped couches. The sharp, dog-pound smell of urine came from the ruined couches. Beneath the globe that had stood on a filing cabinet he saw the words *Blue Rose* again and pulled out the sleeve of the Glenroy Breakstone record. "Oh, God," he said. A red smear in the shape of a hand jumped toward him from the dark paneling on the staircase. Another strong, fetid odor announced itself, and he looked down and saw a massive human turd on a bare patch of carpet. A little scatter of coins lay beside it. He scrambled over a series of files and reached the bottom of the staircase. On the tread beneath the handprint was a dark sprinkle of dots.

Tom ran up the staircase and threw open a bedroom door. The stench of blood and gunpowder hung in the room, along with some other, more domestic stink. The mattress had been pulled off the bed, and both bed and mattress had been slashed again and again.

In the middle of the floor, a pool of blood sent out rays and streamers extending beneath the mattress and toward the closet doors. Red footprints and red dots and splashes covered the carpet. Another impatient handprint blared from a white closet door. Tom felt the shimmer of violence all about him, and moved across the slippery floor to the closet. He pulled it open, and his father's body fell out into his arms.

Too shocked to scream, he pulled the limp body from the enclosure of the closet and sagged to the floor. Tom hugged the body and kissed the matted hair. It seemed to him that he left his body: part of him separated cleanly out of himself and floated and saw the whole room, the ripped bed and the bloody footprints like a dance pattern leading toward and away from the closet, the clear round dots made by some round thing dipped in his father's blood. He saw himself shaking and crying over the body of Lamont von Heilitz. He said to himself, "The point of an umbrella," but these words were as pointless and absent of meaning as "purple socks" or "thrown horseshoe."

After a long time, the back door slammed shut. Someone called his name, and his name brought his floating mind back into his body. He gently laid his father's head on the bedroom carpet, and moved backwards until he struck the frame of the bed. Footsteps came up the stairs. Tom gathered his legs beneath him and listened to the footsteps coming toward the door. A man appeared in the door, and Tom sprang forward and caught the man around the waist and brought him down and wrestled himself on top of him and raised his fist.

"It's me," Andres yelled. "Tom, it's me."

Tom rolled off Andres, panting. "He's in there," he said, but Andres was already on his feet and moving into the bedroom. He knelt beside the body and stroked the old man's face and closed his eyes. Tom got up on watery legs. Von Heilitz's face had changed in some unalterable fashion that had nothing to do with the disordered hair or the suddenly smooth cheeks—it had become another face altogether, a face with nothing in it.

"This is hard," Andres said. "Hard for you and me both, but we have to get out of here. They come back and find us here, they'll gun us both down and claim we killed Lamont."

He stood up and looked at Tom. "I don't know where you plan on going now, but you'd better change your clothes. Be arrested in a second, go out looking like that."

Tom looked down and saw red blotches and smears covering the pale blue linen. His knees were red circles.

Andres took a suit on a hanger out of the closet and came toward the door.

"What do you smell in here?" Tom asked.

Puzzled, Andres stopped and sniffed the air. "You know what I smell. Did you go crazy?"

"I'm not crazy now. Tell me what you smell."

"You're like *him*." Andres glanced down at the body. "I smell what you smell when someone is shot to death."

"Isn't there something else?"

Andres's face contracted into a knot of worry and despair. "What?"

"Cigars," Tom said.

"A lot of cops smoke cigars," Andres said, and took Tom's arm and began marching him down the hall to the stairs.

"Take off your shoes," Andres said in the kitchen. He peeled the jacket off the hanger and hung the trousers over his arm.

"Here?"

"Take off the shoes," Andres said. "You're too big to change clothes in a car."

Tom unlaced the shoes and slipped them off. He handed the bloodied pants, vest, and jacket to Andres, and Andres balled them up under his arm. He handed the fresh trousers to Tom like a tailor, and then snatched them back. "Wait. Rinse your hands at the sink."

Tom obediently went to the sink and for the first time noticed that his hands were smeared with blood. He looked at Andres, and saw red stains on his shirt. "Go ahead," Andres said, and Tom washed the blood from his hands. After he put on the clean trousers and tied his shoes, Andres handed him a belt, and watched with patient concentration as he worked it through the loops. Another vest, another jacket. "Your card," Tom said, and Andres smacked his forehead and rooted through the pockets of the blood-soaked jacket until he found the card. He put it in his shirt pocket, and then deliberated and handed it back to Tom.

They went past the side of the garage and came out into the backyard of a long white manor two houses down from the Spences. In what seemed another life, a family named Harbinger had lived in this house. Now it was as empty as their lodge at Eagle Lake, while the Harbingers took their twenty-year-old daughter to Europe to make her forget the mechanic she had rashly married.

"If I had an idea, I'd give it to you," Andres said.

"There's a policeman I have to talk to," Tom said.

"The police! The police did this!"

"Not this one," Tom said.

66

Down at the lower end of Calle Hoffmann, a concrete plaza called Armory Place, with benches, rows of palms, and big oval planters of bougainvillaea, sat between the pair of symmetrical stone steps leading up to police headquarters and the Mill Walk courthouse. Both of these buildings were cubes of a stark, dazzling white that stood out against the washed-out sky. On the far side of Armory Place, crowded into a row of pastel Georgian buildings with fanlights and three ranks of windows, were the Treasury, Parliament House, the old Governor's Residence, and the Government Printing Office. A network of narrow streets lined with restaurants, coffee shops, bars, drugstores, stationers, law offices, and secondhand bookstores radiated out from Armory Place, and it was to one of these, a passageway called Sugarcane Alley, that Andres reluctantly drove Tom.

"Do you know what you're doing?" he asked.

"No, but Lamont was going to meet with this man before the other policemen picked him up. I don't know who else I can trust."

“Maybe you can’t trust *him*,” Andres said.

Tom remembered Hobart Ellington telling him that Natchez had waited an hour in his back room, and said, “I have to start somewhere.”

Andres said he would wait around the corner, and Tom walked into a small Greek café and ordered a cup of coffee and took it to a booth along the wall. He sat down and sipped the hot coffee. For a moment the shock and misery of Lamont von Heilitz’s death caught up with him, and he bent over the steaming cup to hide his tears from the counterman.

I am an amateur of crime. An absurd phrase, of course.

He wiped off his tears and went to the pay telephone at the back of the café. A ragged Mill Walk directory with a photograph of Armory Place on its cover hung beside the phone on a fraying cord. The photograph seemed to be of a beautiful tropical square—white buildings and palm trees against a pale blue sky. Tom dialed the police department number listed on the inside of the front cover.

It took a long time to get David Natchez, and he was abrupt and unfriendly when he finally came to the phone. “This is Detective Natchez, and what do *you* want?”

“I want to talk to you. I’m in a Greek coffee shop just behind Armory Place.”

“You want to talk to me. You couldn’t be a little more specific, could you?”

“Last night you were supposed to meet a man named Lamont von Heilitz in the back room of a shop across the street from the St. Alwyn Hotel. I want to talk about what he was going to tell you.”

“He never showed up,” Natchez said. “And frankly, I have my doubts about you.”

“He’s dead,” Tom said. “Two policemen must have picked him up as soon as he left the hotel. He was taken to his house and murdered. Then the policemen ransacked his house. Are you interested in this kind of thing, Detective Natchez? I hope you are, because I don’t have anyone else to talk to.”

“Who are you?”

Tom said, “I’m the person who wrote to Captain Bishop about Hasselgard.”

There was a long silence.

"I guess I owe it to myself to get a look at you," Natchez said.

"I'm at the little—"

"I know the place," Natchez said, and hung up.

Tom returned to his booth and sat facing the door. Something was going to happen now; it almost did not matter what. One man would come through the door, or a dozen. Someone would listen to him, or someone would take him out and kill him. There would be an interesting problem when they discovered that he was already dead, but it would not be interesting for long. A day later they would be sitting in another bar, drinking Pusser's Navy Rum and talking about perfect days. All of his life to this moment slammed shut behind him, separated, and floated off, self-sufficient and uninhabitable, as his conscious self had taken leave of him in his father's bloody bedroom. What was left was the part of him that had held Lamont von Heilitz's body, for now he had to do Lamont von Heilitz's job. He swallowed cooling coffee and waited to see what would happen.

In about six minutes, the amount of time it would take a man to hang up a telephone and walk down from an upper floor of police headquarters, then down the broad stone steps to Armory Place and through narrow lanes with the old names of colonial Mill Walk—an island that no longer existed—to Sugarcane Alley, a sturdy-looking man in a dark blue suit came past the window of the café and turned to come in the door.

He saw Tom instantly, and Tom saw that he took in everything else too, and at the same moment: the unshaven counterman, the mummy-sized slab of pork revolving on a skewer in the window, the telephone and the doors to the toilets, the enlarged black and white photographs of Poros above the booths, and the old woman and child seated together past the curve of the counter at the front of the café—everything Tom himself had not really observed until this second. All of this information swam into the focus of his attention, because it was his attentiveness that kept him alive.

He strode down the row of booths with the crisp athletic muscularity Tom had seen once before, an ordinary-looking man with short dark hair and large features. A fatalistic electricity crackled about him, a sort of self-referring reflexive command that denied ambiguities and shades of grey. An absolute gulf separated someone like him from Lamont von Heilitz: Tom understood that there were two ways of being a detective, and that men like David Natchez would always find people like von Heilitz too whimsical, intuitive, and theatrical to be taken seriously.

Natchez ordered a cup of coffee with a gesture and slid into the booth opposite Tom. In the next ninety seconds, he destroyed most of the preconceptions Tom had just formed.

"You're sure that von Heilitz is dead?"

"I just saw his body. My name is Tom Pasmore, by the way."

"I know that," Natchez said, and smiled. "You were at the hospital the day Mike Mendenhall died. You had some kind of conversation with Dr. Milton and Captain Bishop."

"I didn't know you noticed me."

"I don't know why not—you saw me notice everything when I came in here." The counterman brought his coffee to the booth, and Natchez acknowledged it without ever taking his eyes off Tom's face. "The prevailing opinion is that you died of smoke inhalation in a hospital up north. I guess you came back here with the old man." He sipped the coffee, still keeping his eyes on Tom. "For what it's worth, I envy you your relationship with him. I didn't know anything about Lamont von Heilitz until Captain Bishop sent me to his house to roust out the typewriter used for that note, but after I'd met him I checked back into his history. He was a great man, and I don't use that term loosely. I respect him more than I can say. The man was a natural resource. I wish that I'd had the chance to get to know him."

Tom's own emotions embarrassed him in the midst of these astonishing words, and he turned his head away to hide the fresh tears that had come to his eyes. His chin trembled like a baby's. A very firm hand gripped the wrist of the hand he was using to hide his face.

"Look, Tom, a lot of what happens on this island is well-nigh intolerable to me, but when Fulton Bishop's goons kill the greatest detective in maybe a century five minutes before I have a meeting with him, I take it as a *personal affront*. You and I are going to sit here until you tell me everything you know. I don't have Lamont von Heilitz to work with anymore, and you don't either, but I think we can do each other a lot of good."

He released Tom's wrist. "Tell me about the letter you wrote."

"I have to go back to the time when Wendell Hasek showed up drunk in front of our house carrying a bag of rocks," Tom said, and Natchez propped his elbows on the table and hunched forward to rest his chin on his interlaced fingers.

Half an hour later, Tom said, "And on the floor of the bedroom where I found him I saw these little round stamped-out red stains from where my grandfather's umbrella must have touched the blood. And I smelled his cigars. So I thought he must have stood there watching while they killed him and pushed him into the closet, and I sort of went crazy for a couple of minutes, thinking about how I got mad at him just because he'd shown me the truth. Anyhow, after Andres dragged me out and dressed me in clothes that weren't all covered with his blood, all I could think to do was to call you."

"So you really did it all," Natchez said. "I'll be damned."

"No, I just stumbled along," Tom said. "I never even wanted to admit that it must have been my grandfather who killed Jeanine Thielman and Anton Goetz."

"But you knew it anyway. And you figured out who shot Marita Hasselgard. And it was your idea to send the notes that spooked Glen Upshaw—"

"Into killing my father."

"Upshaw would have killed you too, if you had gone with von Heilitz. And anyhow, from the way you describe it, he had the same idea."

But he would never have known about the notes if I hadn't found them, Tom thought, and the names of all the people who would still be alive if he had gone to Dennis Handley's apartment and looked at a typescript of *The Spoils of Poynton* marched through his mind: Foxhall Edwardes, Friedrich Hasselgard, Michael Mendenhall and Roman Klink, Barbara Deane, Lamont von Heilitz.

"The only mistake you made was to send your letter to the wrong cop," Natchez said. "Let's go out to the Founders Club and break some bad news to Glendenning Upshaw." He stood up and put three dollars on the table.

Tom stood up and saw a worried-looking figure peering at them through the window.

"Your friend Andres?"

Tom said yes.

"Real watchdog, isn't he?" Natchez went through the door of the café, and Andres glanced at Tom and backed away. "Hold on," Natchez said, and Tom said, "Andres, it's all right."

Andres took another step backwards.

"This is the man Lamont was going to talk to. We're going to go out and pick up my grandfather. Go home and I'll call you when it's over."

The driver turned around and began moving to the corner, with many doubtful glances back.

Tom and Natchez went back through the narrow lanes to the rear of the row of Georgian buildings. The policeman told him to wait at the top end of Armory Place until he came around with a car, and trotted off toward the police parking garage. Tom walked around the side of the Printing Office and down the long plaza, feeling conspicuous in his father's suit. Policemen in blue uniforms sunned themselves on the benches beneath the potted palms. He heard church bells ringing, and realized that it was Sunday.

"One thing I don't understand," Natchez said, braking in front of the guardhouse at the Founders Club. "How did your grandfather and Fulton Bishop get together? It turned out to be a partnership like Gilbert and Sullivan, but Glen Upshaw couldn't have known that at the beginning. Fulton Bishop was just a young cop from the near west end of the island. I don't think he ever showed any signs of exceptional promise, but someone was always watching out for him, getting him promoted, making sure he got taken off assignments he couldn't handle." A guard sauntered toward them, looking disdainfully at the dented black Studebaker Natchez had drawn from the motor pool. "Take that Blue Rose case. Bishop was in so far over his head he had to dog paddle, and instead of being sent off to a sleepy little precinct like Elm Grove, he's promoted into an office at headquarters and Damrosch—"

The guard had circled all around the car, and came up to

Natchez and leaned on the window. "Did you have some business here, sir?"

Natchez flipped open his shield case and shoved his badge to within an inch of the man's nose. "Step away from the car, or I'll run over your foot," he said.

The guard snatched his hands off the window and moved back. "Yes, sir."

Natchez drove past him into the grounds of the club. "And Damrosch, as I was saying, gets handed the case and winds up losing his mind. I'm not exactly familiar with this place. Where do I go?"

"Right," Tom said. "Don't you think Damrosch was the Blue Rose murderer?"

"Well, I guess Damrosch thought he was. Why didn't von Heilitz ever work on it?"

"He was fascinated by it, I know that much. But he told me he was always busy with other cases in those years, and by the time he was free to think about it, it was all over. . . . We go down here now."

Natchez turned from Suzanne Lenglen Lane into Bobby Jones Trail and said, "Jesus, who named these streets? Joe Ruddler?"

Tom pointed to the last bungalow on Bobby Jones Trail, and Natchez swung in next to the curb below Glendenning Upshaw's house. "I mean, I like sports as much as the next guy, but that yelling degrades public taste." He left the car, and Tom got out on the other side.

"What are you going to say to him?"

"It'll come to me."

Natchez jogged up the steps. They crossed the terrace and passed beneath the white arch into the bungalow's central courtyard. Natchez pushed the bell. "He has servants?"

"Mr. and Mrs. Kingsley. They're both in their eighties."

Natchez pressed the bell again. After a long time, the sound of Kingsley's shuffling footsteps came to them.

Natchez did not take his finger off the bell until the door opened and Kingsley's skeletal face appeared. "I am sorry, sir, but Mr. Upshaw is—" Kingsley saw Tom standing a pace behind the policeman, and his already white face turned the color of paper. All the bones beneath his skin seemed to push forward.

"Hello, Kingsley," Tom said.

The old man tottered backward, literally gasping for breath, and Natchez gently urged the door open. If he had pushed any harder, Kingsley would have fallen down.

"Master Tom," the butler said. "We thought—" He stopped to draw in breath, and his lips disappeared, exposing the pink false gum of his dentures. He was not wearing the frock coat, and his sleeves were rolled up.

"I know," Tom said. "The newspaper made a mistake. Where's my grandfather?"

Natchez walked into the entry, and passed without hesitating into the wide hallway that led to the sitting room at the front of the bungalow and the study, dining room, and terrace at the rear. He turned toward the study. Kingsley shot him an agonized glance. "Mr. Upshaw isn't here, Master Tom. He left in a great hurry about an hour ago, and gave us instructions to pack his clothes—he said he'd be spending the rest of the summer at Tranquility—" Kingsley sat down on a dark wooden bench beside the suit of armor.

"Did he say where he was going when he left?"

"He said I should not speak to any reporters or let anyone in the bungalow—but of course we didn't know that you—" He gaped at Tom for a moment. "I am sorry about that time when you called from the lake. He seemed so *distressed* ever since, and I've been waiting for news of your burial, and so when a call came this afternoon—"

Natchez came storming down the hall. He gave Tom a wild look. Mrs. Kingsley was moving behind him, reaching out as if to grab his coat. "He's gone," Natchez said. He turned to Kingsley and said, "What call?"

"It was from a police officer up north," Mrs. Kingsley said. "My husband was packing clothes in Mr. Upshaw's bedroom, and I answered."

"Truehart?" Tom asked.

"I don't think so, no, Master Tom. It was some *funny* name."

Tom groaned. "Spychalla."

"That's the name. After Mr. Upshaw hung up, he handed me the phone and asked me to arrange a ticket to Venezuela for him as soon as possible. I tried to get him a flight today, but there are no international flights on Sundays, so he said he'd do it himself later."

"Nappy talked," Tom said. "Or they arrested the man who actually set the fire, and Jerry turned around and pointed the finger at my grandfather."

"Your grandfather was a fine man," said Mrs. Kingsley. "You ought to remember that."

"Who's this Spychalla?"

"The chief's idiot deputy, up in Eagle Lake."

"He *called*?" Natchez bellowed. "Follow me." He set off up the hallway toward the study.

When Tom came in, Natchez was already behind the desk, holding the telephone with one hand, demanding to be put through to the Chief of Police in Eagle Lake, Wisconsin, and opening the drawers of the desk with the other. He turned to Tom and said, "Where's that safe?"

Tom went to the wall at the side of the room and began feeling the panels. "Give me Chief Truehart," Natchez said. "Chief, this is Detective David Natchez on Mill Walk, and I'm in Glendenning Upshaw's house with Tom Pasmore. Upshaw got a call from one of your men, and took off. What the hell is going on up there?"

Tom pushed a panel that yielded under his hand. He ran his fingers down the seam of the panel until they slid into an indentation. He pulled, and a square door opened in the wall. Six inches inside the wall was another door. A simple hook held it shut. Tom lifted the hook out of its catch, and opened the second door. He was looking into a deep empty recess.

"Well, your friend is dead," Natchez said. "The boy found his body this morning."

Tom walked to the couch that faced the terrace and fell into it.

"Spychalla thought what? . . . Well, if you were waiting for this urgent call from Marinette, why weren't you present to take it?"

"He was on a flying job," Tom said.

"A flying job?" Natchez shouted into the phone. He listened a moment, then said, "Yes, I am blaming you . . . Well, I'm glad you're blaming yourself too, but that doesn't do me much good,

Chief Truehart . . . Okay, take care of whatever you can, and I'll get back in touch with you."

He slammed down the phone. His face was blazing. "Your grandfather called the Eagle Lake police twice yesterday, concerned to know how the investigation into the fire was coming along, and today when this clown Spychalla learned that the police in Marinette had arrested the guy who actually set the fire, he thought he'd be the first to let him know the good news." He swiveled the chair around to look at the wall. "Tell me all those papers are still in there."

"It's empty," Tom said.

Natchez lowered his gaze to Tom. "Do you realize how bad this situation actually is?"

Tom nodded. "I think so."

Natchez just looked at him for a moment. He opened his mouth, then closed it.

"He still thinks I'm dead, doesn't he?"

"That won't do us any good if he gets on a plane."

"He needs a place to wait. He needs a place to store those records."

Mrs. Kingsley came a single step into the room. "Get out," Natchez said.

She ignored him. "You should be defending your grandfather," she said. "Shouldn't be helping this man—you're only doing it because you're weak, like he always said." Tom looked up in astonishment, and saw that she was furious. "He was going to give you a college education and a career, and how do you repay him? You come here with this renegade policeman. He was a great man, and you're helping his enemies destroy him."

Kingsley fussed in the entrance of the study, trying to shut her up.

"You should be ashamed to draw breath," she said. "I heard you, I heard you defending that nurse against Dr. Milton, when you came here for lunch."

"Do you know where he went?" Tom asked her.

"No," Kingsley said.

"Raised on Eastern Shore Road," said Mrs. Kingsley. "What you deserved was—" Her eyes skidded off him, and she turned the full force of her rage and disdain toward Natchez.

"Eastern Shore Road," Tom said. "I see. You think I deserve something else. What do I deserve, Mrs. Kingsley?"

"I don't know where Mr. Upshaw went," she said quickly. "But you'll never find him."

"You're lying," Tom said. Barbara Deane and Nancy Vetiver spoke within him, and a sweet conviction caused him to smile at her.

Mrs. Kingsley stopped trying to murder Natchez with a look, and pushed past her husband. All three men heard her stamping down the hall. A bedroom door slammed.

"He never told us where he was going," Kingsley said. "She's very upset—afraid of what could happen. Master Tom, she didn't really mean—" He shook his head.

Tom said, "I know he didn't tell you anything. But I know where he went."

Natchez was already on his feet, and Tom stood up. "Don't bother packing any more of his clothes, Kingsley."

The old man wobbled out into the hall, and Tom and the detective followed him. "We'll let ourselves out," Tom said.

Kingsley turned away as if he had already forgotten they were in the bungalow.

Tom and Natchez went down the hallway and walked outside into the heat and light on the other side of the courtyard.

"All right," Natchez said. "Where did the old bastard go?"

"Eastern Shore Road," Tom said. They went quickly down the steps to the black car. Natchez looked questioningly at Tom as he walked around the front of the car, and Tom grinned at him as he got into the baking interior. Natchez let himself in behind the wheel. "The other Eastern Shore Road," Tom said.

67

"His sister?" Natchez said. "I didn't even know he had a sister."

Past the St. Alwyn Hotel they drove, past the pawnshop and The Home Plate.

"Carmen Bishop is the reason my grandfather singled out Fulton Bishop—Barbara Deane told me about her one night when we were having dinner at her house. She used to be a nurse's aide, back when Shady Mount first opened. She was about seventeen or eighteen, and my grandfather used to take her out. He did the same thing with Barbara Deane. Both of them must have been very pretty, but they didn't have anything else in common."

"Your grandfather was in his thirties—his *late* thirties—and he had affairs with teenage girls?"

"No, that's the point. He didn't have affairs with them. He just took them out. He wanted to be seen with them. I don't think he had any interest in affairs. He was using them in another way."

"Which was?" On the detective's face was a look both interested and skeptical, as if he were asking just to hear what Tom would come up with by way of an answer: as if the whole thing were now no more than a story in which he need take no more than a spectator's share. It doesn't come down to only *this*, his expression said, Fulton Bishop's sister. And Tom knew without saying it that it did not: it came down to something else—something Buzz Laing had discovered in Boney Milton's records.

"To make him look normal," he said, remembering his mother's dull, thudding screams in the middle of the night. "Better than normal. He did favors for them, and they made him look like a stud. He was around the hospital a lot in those days, and he met a lot of young girls. When he came across Carmen Bishop, he found a perfect match. Barbara Deane said that in the end, he had to learn to respect her. She did what he wanted in the hospital, and went out with him in public, and in return he helped her brother."

" 'She did what he wanted in the hospital,' " Natchez said. "Does that mean what I think it does?"

"Barbara Deane's reputation got ruined when it looked like she caused the death of a patient who was injured in a gun battle with the police."

"At Shady Mount," Natchez said. "With Bonaventure Milton running the show."

"I don't suppose they built it to be a way of getting rid of inconvenient people, but once it was there—"

"—once it was the most respectable hospital on the island—"

"—someone like Carmen Bishop could be a kind of court of last resort," Tom said. "I bet Buzz Laing survived the attack on him because he went to St. Mary Nieves."

"I thought you said von Heilitz never had the time to work on the Blue Rose case."

"He didn't—I'm just thinking about something Dr. Laing told me this morning."

They drove between the can factory and the refinery and dipped down into Weasel Hollow. Tom said, "Have you ever been to the Third Court?"

Natchez shook his head, and in the way he did not look at Tom but idly out at the weedy lots where people lived inside houses that were only blankets wrapped around leaning poles, the boy saw that he had never been inside Elysian Courts at all.

They went through an intersection, and Tom looked up a garbage-strewn street at the rusted, burnt-out hull of a sports car that now rested flat on a sheet of plywood. A sheet of canvas had been rigged to slant over its top, and the back of a chair stuck up where the passenger seat had been. Friedrich Hasselgard's Corvette had been recycled into a one-bedroom apartment. Natchez turned up the hill toward the island's near west end.

The street numbers advanced from the twenties into the thirties. They drove past a big peaceful church in a swarm of bicycles, and turned into 35th Street to go past the zoo, then past the perpetual cricket match ticking away in the field at the south end of the park, past the twisted cypresses, and downhill into Maxwell's Heaven.

The buildings blocked out the sun. OLD CLOATHES CHEAP. HUMIN HAIR BOUGHT AND SOLD. Far down past the leaning tenements lay the dump in coruscating light, and Mr. Rembrandt hung in a gilded frame on Hattie Bascombe's wall. Tom pointed to a nearly invisible cobblestone path between a dark archway, and said, "Go in there."

Natchez drove down past peeling walls and windows hung with dirty net until he came to the bottom of the well, a cobbled court surrounded by crossbarred doors and iron bars. "What happens to the car down here?" Natchez said.

"Percy takes care of it," Tom said, and a door creaked open, and a bearded mountain in a leather apron lumbered out, squinting into the dirty light.

68

Tom led David Natchez through the arched passageway into the First Court, saying, "I came here to see a nurse named Nancy Vetiver, who got suspended for taking care of Mike Mendenhall too well to please Dr. Milton. He was afraid of what Mendenhall would say, and he said a lot—that's how I really learned about you."

"Don't go so fast," Natchez said in the musty darkness.

They came out into the visual chaos of bars and lodging houses around the First Court. Cold moisture and a faint smell of sewage tainted the air, and a hum of voices came from the passages that led deeper into Maxwell's Heaven. FREDO'S sign flickered on and off. "Fulton Bishop and his sister grew up in the Third Court. My grandfather built this place—it was his first big project. He'd know it was a perfect place to hide."

"Do you remember how to get to the Second Court?" Natchez wandered out into the center of the court and looked down at the brass plaque that named Glendenning Upshaw and Maxwell Redwing.

"I think so." Tom looked doubtfully around the square. Half a dozen crooked lanes led away into a sprawl of half-visible streets. The same laundry seemed to droop on lines between windows above them, and the same ragged men passed a different bottle back and forth in front of a lighted doorway. Flies clustered over a muddy stain a few feet from the plaque. Tom turned toward a narrow brick opening beneath an overhanging wooden room, and walked toward it until he saw the white lettering in the brick: Edgewater Trail. "This is it."

They came out into a cobbled lane between black wooden walls that he remembered. A woman huddled against the wall when she saw them, and a child ran past screaming. The stench of excrement grew stronger. Tom pointed to a wooden flight of steps on the other side of the sluggish stream that ran down the middle of the lane. He went up to the edge of the stream and jumped across. Natchez followed him up the stairs and through echoing darkness until they emerged at the top of the matching steps that led down into the Second Court.

Wooden balconies lay across the front of the buildings on all sides, and at every corner steps went downward into arcades and intersecting narrow streets. "When I was here," Tom said, the atmosphere of the place making him whisper, "I saw Bishop pass through. He came down these steps and went straight across the Court to that corner."

Natchez and Tom descended the stairs and walked across the court. A few men eased out of the shadows on the walkways and watched them go. Tom paused at the top of the steps at the corner of the building where Nancy Vetiver had grown up, and went down.

He came out on a flat concrete bridge over a muddy stream. To his left, the bridge ended in steps leading down to a row of hunched brick buildings built along the low banks of the stream. An enormous black rat darted up out of a hole in the concrete and slithered over the top of the bank to disappear between two of the buildings. At the right end of the bridge, the concrete flooring became the beginning of a lane that twisted past a wooden tenement. Footsteps sounded behind them. Tom turned right.

The buildings huddled closer together. The lane divided, and Tom took the left-hand fork because the right sloped downward into a dead end where murky lodging houses loomed over an empty yard.

They walked past a barred and empty shop on the ground floor of a tenement. Women leaned out of windows and watched them pass beneath. Tom had the feeling they were circling around beneath the Second Court, and only the occasional glimpse of sky above the leaning buildings let him know that they were instead following the slope of the hill down toward the old slave quarter.

Abruptly the lane widened, and the concrete turned to brick cobbles. A broken cart leaned against a wall, which leaned against a leaning building. Two men who had been talking beside the cart vanished into a doorway. "That's what happens when they see a cop in a place like this," Natchez said. "I guess this must be the Third Court."

It was a combination of the first two: wooden walkways and exterior staircases clung to the sides of the four-story tenements. Straw and broken bottles lay across the concrete before them. A peaked wooden roof covered the entire court, intensifying the gloom and the thudding of rock and roll from a basement bar with a hand-painted sign in a window at ground level that read BEER-WHISKEY. Footsteps coming toward them from the concrete lane slowed, then stopped. Natchez backed under a walkway, stood against the wall of the rear tenement, took out a pistol with a long barrel, and peered around the side of the building. Then he shook his head and shoved the pistol back into his holster. "I just want to point out," he said in a quiet voice, "that we could have saved ourselves a lot of trouble by walking around to the other side of this place."

"How?" Tom asked.

"Because that's where we are." He nodded at an arched passageway like a tunnel that ran down the side of the building across from them. On the other end of the tunnel, diminished as if by a telescope looked through backwards, a car rolled downhill in bright unreal daylight. Tom sagged against the tenement wall.

They were standing far back in the shadow of one of the walkways. Both of them looked up at the bleak dark walls on the opposite side of the court. The smells of sewage and stale beer, of unwashed skin and blocked toilets, mingled with the low sounds of voices and clashing radios. In one room a girl cried out; from another Joe Ruddler bawled baseball scores. Tom felt the blood beating in his temples. His eyes stung.

"Well, you have any brilliant ideas?" Tom asked.

"I don't exactly feel like knocking on a hundred doors," Natchez said. "We want something that will get him out of her rooms, if that's where he is."

"Oh, he's here. He's up there somewhere, hating every second he has to be in this place." And this, he felt with an overwhelming certainty, was true: a kind of inspiration had caused Tom to make David Natchez bring him to this place, but now that he was here, he knew that there was no other place on the island where Glendenning Upshaw would have gone. He flew by the seat of his pants, and he relied on women to solve his leftover problems. He had no friends, only people who owed him services. Tom thought that maybe Carmen Bishop was the only person in all of his grandfather's life who had understood him.

"So let's get him out," Natchez said.

"Right," Tom said. "If we just stand here shouting his name, he'll never move. What we want is something that only my grandfather will respond to—something that wouldn't mean anything special to everybody else up there, but that'll make him feel like he's being stung by a thousand bees."

Natchez frowned and turned to Tom in the darkness beneath the walkway.

Tom smiled, though it was almost too dark for Natchez to see it. "Two thousand bees," he said.

"Well?"

"He had von Heilitz killed because he thought nobody else could have sent him copies of Jeanine Thielman's notes. They meant that von Heilitz had finally worked out what really happened to her."

He felt more than saw Natchez nodding.

"So let's convince him that someone else knew about those notes. He might recognize my voice, but he wouldn't know yours. How do you feel about stepping out there and shouting 'This has gone on too long'?"

Natchez said, "I'll try anything once." He moved out from beneath the dark shadow on the walkway, cupped his hands around his mouth and bellowed, "THIS HAS GONE ON TOO LONG!" He moved back—the radios still bleated and chattered, but all other voices had fallen silent. "Well, they heard me," Natchez whispered.

Tom told him what to say next, and Natchez came out from under the walkway and yelled, "YOU WILL PAY FOR YOUR SIN!"

Someone pushed up a window, but the only other sounds were of radios, suddenly louder in the quiet. Jeanine Thielman's words bounced off the wooden roof and echoed on the tenement walls. Tom imagined the words rolling through all of Maxwell's Heaven, freezing the rats in their holes and waking babies, stopping the bottles in their passage from hand to hand.

"I know what you are," Tom whispered, so softly he might have been talking to himself.

Natchez ducked out again. "I KNOW WHAT YOU ARE!"

Someone above them threw down an empty bottle of Pforzheimer beer, and it exploded against the brick cobbles. "Go away!" yelled a fuzzy male voice, and another suggested that they fuck themselves.

"You must be stopped," Tom whispered.

"YOU MUST BE STOPPED!"

Another bottle smashed against the bricks, sending glass shrapnel across the court. More windows went up. A door slammed, and heavy footsteps came out on a wooden walkway two or three floors up in the tenement to their right. The wood creaked beneath his grandfather's weight. Tom's heart caught in his throat as his grandfather took another step forward: he imagined him leaning on the railing and scowling down into the grimy court, twilit in the middle of the day. His grandfather's voice floated down: "I can't see you. Walk out into the court, whoever you are."

"Well, well," Natchez whispered.

"I'm curious," came Tom's grandfather's voice. "Did you come here to make a deal?"

With the random irrelevance of an orchestra tuning itself, all the other voices started speaking again. Glendenning Upshaw stepped back from the railing and began walking toward the staircase at the opposite end of the tenement. The wood creaked with every step he took. When he reached the stairs, he thumped down toward the next level. Tom counted each step, and at ten Upshaw reached the next walkway and moved to the railing again. "You won't disappoint me, will you? After going to the trouble of finding out so much about me?" He waited. "Say something. Speak!" His voice was that of an enraged man almost succeeding in concealing his rage.

Natchez pulled Tom into the concrete passage by which they had entered the Third Court.

"Then wait for me," Upshaw said, and began to work his way down the next flight of steps. Tom counted to six, and heard his grandfather's slightly bowed black legs carrying his massive body down to the fifth tread of the near staircase, one flight up, of the tenement to the right of the passage where he and David Natchez stood waiting. "Still there?"

Natchez rapped his knuckles against one of the supports for the walkway above their heads.

"There was once a ridiculous man on this island." Upshaw came down another step.

"He came into the possession of certain papers of sentimental interest to me." Down another step.

"I have no quarrel with you, whoever you are." Upshaw stepped on another creaking tread.

"I'm sure that we can come to an arrangement." He came down the last two steps, and reached the walkway immediately above them. The wood groaned as he stepped forward on the walkway and looked down. "The original papers were written in 1925. The matter they referred to is no longer of any importance." Tom heard him panting from exertion—it had been a long time since his grandfather had had to cope with stairs. He chuckled. "In fact, it was not of much importance at the time. Are you going to come out and let me see your face?"

Natchez tapped Tom's shoulder and pointed to the topmost walkway of the tenement on the other side of the court. Deep in the shadow, a pale shape that might have been a man in a white shirt and a pair of tan trousers moved with foglike slowness toward the nearest staircase.

"You're being foolish," Upshaw said. "You cannot frighten me—you just came here to sell what you have."

Tom and Natchez waited in the passage. The man in the white shirt reached the staircase and began noiselessly to move down.

"All right, I'll do it your way," Upshaw said. He turned away from them and stumped along the walkway to the staircase at the opposite end. "How much do you think those notes are worth? A thousand dollars apiece?" He chuckled, and reached the stairs on the other side of the next tenement and began coming down. Tom saw his white hand sliding along the railing. The vague shape of his shoulder, his white hair, came into view. He reached the bottom of the stairs and turned around. "If so, you're sadly mistaken. They aren't worth a hundred each to me."

He stepped forward, and moved under the walkway. His body lost definition in the darkness and became only a black shape coming down the front of the tenement toward the passage. Tom glanced across the court and saw that the man in the white shirt had stopped on the next walkway down.

"Send the other man away," Natchez said.

"If you like." Upshaw stopped moving and called across the court, "Go out and wait on the street."

The man said, "Sir?"

"Do it," Upshaw called to him.

The man came out of the shadows and trotted down all the flights of steps and slipped into the long tunnel that led to the street.

"All right?" asked Tom's grandfather.

"I'm going out," Natchez whispered.

"No, he has to see me," Tom whispered back, and moved out of the passage and stepped backward in the shadow of the walkway.

"Who is that?" Upshaw shifted forward, now letting more of his anger show itself. "Who are you?"

Tom moved an inch nearer the lighter darkness of the court. His grandfather would be able to see his body, but not his face.

Glendenning Upshaw stopped moving. Tom felt the air around him tighten, like the pressure inside his head. The black cloud of his grandfather's body sent out a wave of shock like a flash of lightning. Two loud breaths came from him. Tom's own chest heaved.

"To hell with you," his grandfather said. "Von Heilitz is dead."

Tom moved backwards away from the passage.

"What the hell is this, a charade? Some babyish *trick*?"

Tom moved backwards in the darkness, and saw the black cloud of his grandfather's heavy body surge forward toward the passage where Natchez stood concealed. Another arrow had flown into his haunch, but for Tom there was none of the confusion and depression of yesterday, only a bleak satisfaction. A slanting black line of absolute shadow obliterated the top half of the old man's body from shoulder to hip, and what was visible was only half-visible, but pain and outrage boomed toward him as his grandfather shouted, "Stand still!" and moved closer to the passage.

"I know what you are," Tom said. He stepped backwards again, and heard doors opening in the tenements above him.

His grandfather moved past the open passage, and his head came free of the shadows of the walkway. Shadowy light fell on his white hair. His face was savage. Almost instantly, the shadow of the next walkway obliterated all but the impression of relentless moving force.

"You murdered Jeanine Thielman," Tom said. A door slammed above him, but neither he nor the man coming toward him noticed.

"That's very interesting," his grandfather said.

Tom saw David Natchez slide out of the passage with his pistol upraised.

"The way I saw it," his grandfather said, "she chose to commit suicide. Weak people do that with a terrible frequency. I've been surrounded by them all my life."

"Blue Rose," Tom said.

His grandfather sighed heavily.

"All you were was a flunky for the Redwings," Tom said.

His grandfather stopped moving. He was a foot or two short of the point where he and Tom would see enough of each other's faces to be recognized. "I know you, by God," Upshaw said, and again Tom felt the moment of shock that was like an arrow piercing his grandfather's hide.

"No, you don't," Tom said. "You never knew anybody at

all." He stepped out from under the walkway into the murky courtyard.

"By God," his grandfather said. "Tom. You were hard enough to get rid of, boy, but I imagine—" His hand went into his pocket and came out with the gun Tom had seen him take from his desk drawer.

Tom's gut went cold. He looked over his shoulder at David Natchez, who shouted, "Upshaw, put down—"

His grandfather pointed the gun at him and pulled the trigger. Fire and smoke came out of the end of the gun, and the explosion struck Tom like a blow. Mortality whizzed past his head, heating the air, and before the bullet splatted against the wall, another explosion banged into his ear drums. His grandfather had vanished into the gloom beside him, and Tom looked toward the passage and saw only empty space. He sensed a crowd of people staring down from the walkways. He turned sideways and saw what looked like the barrel of a cannon pointed at his head. His grandfather held it with arms extended, almost cross-eyed with concentration. Tom saw an index finger fat as a trout pulling on the trigger, and Natchez yelled, and the barrel jerked away from his face. It exploded again. Tom jumped backwards with the explosion in his head and saw a black hole appear in his grandfather's head, just above the bridge of his nose. Flags of red and grey stuff flew out of the back of his head. The gun sank, and his grandfather twitched backwards and righted himself and went down on his knees, still trying to pull the trigger. A ringing clamor filled Tom's ears like a physical substance. He was dimly aware of David Natchez walking toward him from beneath a walkway. Natchez said something that did not penetrate the molten lead filling his ears. His grandfather settled down into himself and fell foward. A muffle of sound came from Natchez, and all the heads hanging over the railings jerked back, except for that of a woman with a rag-doll face. Carmen Bishop lingered at the railing, looking as if she wanted to fly down at him, and then slowly backed away. Tom wobbled sideways and sat down.

Another muffled pillow of sound came from Natchez. Beneath the fullness in his ears, the words reached him at last. *I don't know how he missed you.*

The gun didn't pull to the left, Tom said, and felt his own words as individual, cottony wads striking his ears from the inside of his head.

Natchez looked puzzled, and Tom felt himself say, *It's an old story*. He reached out and touched his grandfather's back.

He looked back up at the walkways and Carmen Bishop screamed something down at him that disappeared entirely into the noise in his ears. "We're going to do something with him," he said, and this time dimly heard his own voice—tinny as an old record heard through a wall, but real words, not bubbles of pressure inside his head.

"I'll call the station," Natchez said in a nearly identical voice. "And I'll send someone out to pick up von Heilitz's body."

Tom shook his head. "We're going to take him with us."

"Take him where?"

"Back to the bungalow," Tom said. He leaned forward and picked up his grandfather's pistol. It seemed surpassingly ugly, and heavy as an iron weight. He put it in his jacket pocket. Two men came through the long tunnel from the street, and Tom and Natchez turned to look at them as they walked into the court. One of them was the man in the white shirt, and the other, a few paces behind him, was Andres. The man in the white shirt looked down at Glendenning Upshaw's body, glanced at Natchez, and shoved his hands in his pockets. Andres reached down, and Tom took his hand and stood up.

"You could make this a perfect day," Natchez said, "by telling me you know where this pile of shit hid his papers and records."

"I do know," Tom said. "You do too."

Natchez looked at his own pistol as if it had just been magicked into his hand, and pulled back his jacket to slip it into his holster. "Holman, go up to the third level on this side," he said to the man in the white shirt. "Captain Bishop's sister lives up there. I want a box of papers and journals, anything like that. Bishop's finished."

"I can see that," the man said, and began moving toward the stairs. The woman with the rag-doll face was peering down at them again.

"No," Tom said. "That's not where they are. My grandfather stopped somewhere on the way here. He gave them to somebody for safekeeping."

"Who was that?" Natchez asked.

Tom managed to smile at him, and saw understanding gradually cross Natchez's face.

"You want me to go up?" the other policeman asked.

"No," Natchez said. "If you want to stay out of jail, go home and keep your mouth shut. I have some business to take care of with this boy here, and then I'll call you. I'll pick up the papers, and then you and I are going to take two drunken shitheads to the Elm Cove station and arrest them for the murder of Lamont von Heilitz."

The other man swallowed.

"We were never here," Natchez said. "Is that right?" he asked Tom.

"That's right," Tom said.

The other policeman faded away toward the long passage out to the street, and Natchez leaned down to try to pick up Glendenning Upshaw's body. After a second, Andres bent to help him.

69

The red taxi with the dangling headlight was parked across the sidewalk from the back end of Maxwell's Heaven. The two men carried Glendenning Upshaw's limp body to the rear of the taxi, and Tom opened the trunk. When he slammed it down on the curled-up body, the noise came to him soft and diminished, like the closing of a bank vault.

Andres got behind the wheel. "Maybe I shouldn't have followed," he said. "I went out to the Founders Club behind you, five or six cars back, all the way, and I parked where I did yesterday. After you came out, I followed you back here and saw you go into the Courts. I went in behind you, and then I got lost, so I walked around until I found my way back out, and then I drove around to the other side. When I heard the shots, I came in."

"You did the right thing," Natchez said. "What I wonder about is whether we're doing the right thing."

"Drive," Tom said, and Andres pulled away from the curb.

Natchez flashed his badge at the guardhouse, and the red taxi wound through the palms and sand dunes to Bobby Jones Trail and pulled up in front of the long white bungalow. When the three of them got out of the cab, Kingsley came out through the arch and began making his way down the steps. Tom held up a hand and stopped him. "Get your wife and take her into your quarters. Leave the front door open."

"But—"

"Stay in your rooms until I tell you to come out. Something is going to happen that you can't see."

"What?" Kingsley said, too disturbed to remember his usual formality.

"We're going to find my grandfather," Tom said.

"But Master Tom, he—"

"Make sure your wife stays in the room with you," Tom said.

Kingsley nodded sadly and turned himself around and began tottering back up the steps.

"Kingsley," Tom said.

The butler sagged aginst the railing and looked back at him.

"Has the mail come yet?"

"It just arrived, Master Tom. I put Mr. Upshaw's letters on his desk."

"Fine," Tom said.

Kingsley gazed at Tom like an old dog that fears a beating, and said, "He was at home that night, Master Tom. You remember—the night you called him from Eagle Lake?"

"I don't blame you for anything," Tom said.

The butler nodded again and began toiling up the steps like a marionette with a couple of broken strings. Tom went back to the car and stood beside the two men, who had opened the trunk and were staring down at the swollen black thing inside it. At the back of the trunk, a little fringe of white hair showed above the rucked-up jacket and a bent arm.

"I guess I know what you want to do," Natchez said. "But why do you want to do it?"

"Poetic justice," Tom said.

"Does this have anything to do with Damrosch?"

"I don't know. It might. I think he tried to kill Buzz Laing, and he could have gotten rid of Damrosch to end the investigation. I think Lamont von— I think my father was trying to get me to think about that before he was killed."

"Are we going to take him out of the car?" Andres asked.

"I'll help Natchez do it," Tom said. "Would you wait for us out here, Andres? It'd be better if you didn't see this."

"I didn't see nothing all day except Lamont," Andres said. He stepped back, and Tom and Natchez leaned into the trunk and pulled out Glendenning Upshaw's heavy legs. One of his trousers had ridden up on his leg, and a long expanse of white flesh glared from the top of his sock. One of his feet swung from side to side over the black road. They leaned back in and pulled his waist and hips farther out of the trunk, and the stiff foot thumped the asphalt. The front of the suit was wet with urine, and Tom's hand instantly felt slimy. He wiped his hand on the hem of the soft black jacket. A bubble of gas farted out of the body. Tom and Natchez got their hands on his shoulders and pulled him upright. His head lolled back, and his mouth fell open.

"Get his right arm over your shoulders," Natchez said, "and put your left arm around his back. I'll get on his other side, and we'll try to walk him in."

Tom propped one thick, heavy arm around the back of his neck and positioned himself. When Natchez was ready, they lifted up with their legs. Glendenning Upshaw hung between them like a fat scarecrow filled with wet cement. Something in his stomach sloshed and gurgled. His head fell forward, and Tom smelled cigars, blood, aftershave, and gunpowder. It felt like his grandfather was trying to push him down through the asphalt. Natchez stepped forward, and Tom moved with him. They moved up on the sidewalk and began dragging the body toward the steps.

"He must weigh three hundred pounds," Natchez said.

Tom had to stoop so that the dead arm would not slip off his shoulders, and his back ached by the time they got up the steps. Blood from the back of the black suit soaked through to his arm.

Natchez said, "Do you want to put him down for a second?"

"If I put him down, I'll never want to pick him up again," Tom said.

They carried him beneath the white arch and through the

open door. Upshaw's feet hooked the rug and dragged it along until it caught in the study door and fell back as his feet slipped over the top of the fabric. Through the ringing in his ears Tom could hear Mrs. Kingsley ranting in a room somewhere far back in the house. Her husband gave tired monosyllabic answers.

"I suppose you want to put him in the desk chair."

"Right," Tom said.

"Don't let him fall until I brace the chair, or we'll have to clean a lot of blood up off the floor."

They dragged the body toward the desk. A dozen envelopes of various sizes and colors had been neatly stacked on the shiny surface. Natchez leaned forward to twirl the chair around, and Tom hastily dipped under the body when it began to slide away from him. "Okay," Natchez said. "We have to turn around and try to get his ass over the seat of the chair."

They revolved, and Natchez went up on his toes to try to get Upshaw's legs in the right position. "Let's go down slow," Natchez said. As they bent their knees, both Natchez and Tom reached back for the seat to hold it steady. They pulled it forward and bent another six inches. Glendenning Upshaw landed in the chair with a soft wet sound. Tom straightened up, and Natchez bent over to get the body to sit more naturally. Then he grunted and pushed the chair toward the desk. He wiped the back of the chair with his handkerchief.

Tom fanned the letters out on the desk and picked up the four with hand-printed addresses. He ripped open the envelopes and took out the four pieces of yellow paper and put them down before the body. The other letters he gathered into an untidy pile beside the ripped envelopes and the notes. Finally he took the heavy black pistol from his pocket and put it on the desk. He looked over his grandfather's body at Natchez.

"You think he dropped off all his records at Wendell Hasek's place," Natchez said.

"I'm sure he did." Tom stepped back from the desk.

"I hope to hell you're right."

"He wouldn't give them to Carmen Bishop. She'd burn them as soon as he left the island. He'd trust Hasek with them, because Hasek's a crook. When my grandfather had his own company robbed, Hasek stored the stolen money for him. He distributed payoff money for him for years. My grandfather was used to trusting him."

Natchez nodded slowly. He slid the gun toward him on the desk, moving it around the notes with their stark block letters. "Poetic justice, hell," he said.

"That's part of it," Tom said. "My mother's another part of it. She'll have to learn a lot of things about her father, but I don't want her to know that he was shot while he was trying to kill me face to face."

"But what you really want to do is make him look even worse than he was." Natchez picked up the gun and began wiping it down with his handkerchief. "You want to make it look like he broke—like he crumbled."

"He can't look any worse than he was," Tom said. "But you're wrong. I want poetic justice."

"You think life is like a book," Natchez said. Holding the barrel of the gun in the handkerchief, he came around behind the back of the chair to Upshaw's right side and bent down to fit the grip in his open palm. He closed the thick fingers around the grip and wedged the index finger into the trigger guard. Then he straightened up and pushed Upshaw's body back against the chair while he held the hand with the gun upright. Glendenning Upshaw sat upright at his desk in a bloodstained suit, his head tilted forward and his eyes and mouth open. His tongue protruded a little bit between his teeth. Natchez took a handful of white hair in his left hand and yanked the staring head upright. He bent the hand with the gun around so that the barrel faced toward Upshaw and lined it up with the wound. Natchez laid his own index finger on top of Upshaw's, and grimaced while he brought the barrel right up to the black hole above the bridge of his nose.

"Well, here goes nothing," he said. "Literally."

Natchez pressed the dead man's finger into the trigger. The gun went off with a roar, and the head jerked in his hand. Blood-soaked brains, hair, and bone splattered on the wall behind Upshaw's corpse. Natchez dropped the head, and bent down to let the hand fall open and release the pistol.

"Sometimes life is like a book," Tom said.

70

On the Saturday of the second week in September, two months after the second death of Glendenning Upshaw, Tom Pasmore sat on an iron bench fifty feet inside the entrance of the Goethe Park zoo. Men and women, most of them herding tribes of small children, streamed through the open gates and past him, going toward the balloon vendor and the ice cream cart stationed at the point where the cobbled entrance widened out to meet the concrete that led to the first row of cages and the paths into the zoo. The people pushing baby carriages or strollers, Tom noticed, always relaxed when they got off the cobbles and hit the smooth concrete. They stood up straighter, and you could see the tension leave their spines and back muscles. Some of the people who passed Tom's bench took a second to look at him: he wore a chalk-striped grey suit with a vest with lapels, a dark blue shirt and a tie of a deep red, and on his feet were a pair of scuffed brown loafers. It was three o'clock in the afternoon, and in the dusty gaps between the cobbles lay crushed cigarette packets, the tan specks of shattered potato chips, and one right-angled bread crust fought over by a cluster of chirping sparrows.

Other benches were closer to the zoo's gates, and some of them were empty, but Tom had chosen this one so that he would be able to watch Sarah Spence come in without her seeing him. He wanted one objective, unmuddled look at her before they had to reckon with each other again: he wanted the reckoning, but he also wanted the moment of pure *looking*, to see her for the space of a few seconds as anyone else would. Since the night of the fire, Tom had glimpsed her once in a courtroom, while her father had testified about what the government prosecutor had described as the more acceptable face of the Redwing businesses—he himself had been waiting, as he was to wait for two more weeks, to speak about finding his grandfather's body in the study. There were trials inside trials, trials intersecting trials, and Tom was only peripheral to them, but he had been required to spend three more weeks on the witness benches, and during that time the Spences had left the island. The trials and investigations would go on for another year, it seemed, but Tom's part in them was done: he spent what seemed like half of every day with lawyers and accountants, but these meetings were about other matters, surprising to Tom, but of no relevance to what filled the headlines of the *Eyewitness*.

Sarah came in through the gates with a knot of people, distinct from them as a cardinal is distinct in a throng of pigeons, and began floating across the cobbles toward the cages. She wore tight faded jeans—jeans that looked nothing like a boy's—tucked into high cowboy boots, an oversized white shirt that reminded Tom of Kip Carson and was fastened to her hips by a wide belt, and her thick hair had grown long enough to be gathered at the back of her head into a great loose braid, from which honey-colored wisps and streaks escaped about her face. Fifteen minutes late, she swung along over the cobblestones with long strides, scanning the benches. Her eyes moved past him, and she took another long effortless floating stride before her gaze snapped back to him and she stopped moving. She turned to come toward him with a wondering, slightly bemused smile, and he stood up to greet her.

"Well, look at *you*," she said. "You're a vision of something or other."

"So are you."

"I mean those *clothes*."

"I don't," he said. "I just mean you."

They stood looking at each other for a moment, not knowing what to say. "I feel kind of embarrassed," she said, "but I don't really know why. Do you, too?"

"No," he said.

"I bet you do, though. I bet if we danced together, I'd feel you trembling."

He shook his head. "I'm glad your mother let you come."

"Oh, after everything that happened she got over being so mad at you." She took a step nearer, and hesitantly put her arms around his waist. "I saw you in the courtroom."

"I saw you too."

"Did you call me, once? Right after that article about the fire was in the paper?"

He nodded.

"I knew it. Well, I thought it was you. I didn't think you could have died, especially since you carried me out. . . ."

"It was just a mistake," he said.

"Were you burned at all?"

"Not really."

She looked up at his face as if trying to read it, and took her arms from around him. "Why did you want to come here?"

"Because I've never been here," he said, and hooked his own arm around her waist. They began to walk along with the crowd toward the cages. "We drove past it once, remember? I thought it would be nice to see the animals. They've been here all the time, sitting in these cages, and I guess I thought they deserved a visit."

"A social call," she said.

They drifted past the first set of cages, still adjusting to the fact of each other, weighing what they had to say. A black panther paced around and around in relentless circles, and a male lion lay like a tawny sack on the floor of its cage, peering at or through the bars with rheumy eyes while a female lion lay on a dead branch above its head, asleep with her back to the spectators. Tom and Sarah turned into the path leading toward the elephants and Monkey Island. From far off they heard the barking of sea lions.

"Everything's so different now," Sarah said. She took her

arm from around his waist, and he put his hands in his pockets. "The Redwings are all in Switzerland. I heard Fritz is going to a school there. Can you imagine Fritzie Redwing in a Swiss school?"

"Not very well. I guess Fulton Bishop is in Switzerland too—he got out in time, and Ralph Redwing gave him some kind of job."

"Well, they're *all* in Switzerland," Sarah said. "My father says they still have plenty of money."

"They would." The elephants moved slowly around their big cage, nosing the heaps of straw with their trunks. A man leaned forward over the bar and held out a peanut, and one elephant shuffled forward and extended his grey, wrinkled trunk to pick it off his palm with a quick, delicate gesture. "They'll always have plenty of money," Tom said. "They'll always have enormous houses and lots of paintings and cars and people who work for them, and they'll never think it's enough. They just won't have their own island anymore."

"Are we still friends?" Sarah asked.

"Sure," Tom said.

"I didn't tell other people everything you told me," she said.

"I know that."

"I just said a few things to my father, and he didn't know what they really meant any more than I did. Or he didn't really believe them."

"No, he didn't believe them," Tom said. "Did he get another job?"

"Yeah, he got another job. We don't have to sell our house, or anything. Everything worked out kind of okay, didn't it?"

"In most ways," Tom said.

They drifted along to Monkey Island, where a tribe of anarchic miniature people with tails and body hair scrambled over a rocky hill separated from the real people by a moat. Children screamed with pleasure as the monkeys surged from one end of the island to another, squabbled over food, masturbated, hopped on each other's backs, berated each other in squeaks and howls, hit each other with tiny balled-up monkey fists, turned and addressed their spectators with oratorical flourishes, wild gestures of pleading or outrage.

"You must be sorry about your grandfather," Sarah said.

"I'm sorry he was the kind of person he was. I'm sorry he did so much damage." *Her and her's Da,* came his mother's voice. "I guess I was depressed for a while when I finally had to admit . . ." Sarah smiled at the antics of the monkeys, and he smiled at her. "You know. When I really had to admit to myself what kind of man he was."

"After he killed himself."

"No, before that," Tom said. "A day or two before that."

Her and her's Da. Because there were just the two of us in this house.

She turned away from the monkeys. "Well, that was terrible, what happened to your friend. Mr. von Heilitz, I mean." She looked at him with both sympathy and a kind of impersonal curiosity, and he knew what was coming.

"Yes. That was terrible."

"Did you know he was going to leave you everything?"

"No. I didn't know anything about it until his lawyers called me, and I went down to see them."

"And you live in his house now?"

"Now that I have it cleaned up."

They were walking down a path past brown bears and polar bears penned in small separate cages. The bears lay flat on their sides in the heat, smeared with their own excrement.

"I guess you don't really ever have to work, do you?" Sarah asked.

"Not at a job. I'm going to have plenty to do, though. I have to finish up Brooks-Lowood, and I'll go to college, and then I'll come back and see what I can do."

"Those are his clothes, aren't they?"

"I like his clothes," Tom said.

"But are you going to dress like that at school?"

"Are you going to dress like that at Mount Holyoke?"

"I don't know."

"I don't know, either."

"Tom," she said.

"What?"

"Are you mad at me?"

"No. Maybe this zoo is a little depressing."

She turned toward the bears, frustrated with him. "There were millions, weren't there? My father said there were millions.

Isn't that *something*? Isn't it really *something* to know that you can do anything you want? Isn't it exciting?"

"I didn't want his money," Tom said. "I wanted him—to keep on knowing him."

"Well, why did he give everything to you?"

"I used to go over and talk to him." Tom smiled at her. "Maybe he wanted to give me the right start in life."

"What did your parents say?"

They moved away down the path toward a high dark building at the farthest end of the zoo. A sign at the entrance announced that it was the REPTILE HOUSE. "I don't feel like going to the Reptile House, do you?"

She shook her head. "Well, what did they say?"

"When I told my mother, she was too sort of stunned to say much, but she was pleased. She liked him too."

"Pleased," Sarah said. "She should have been pleased."

"She had to sign a lot of papers, but she didn't really know what they were. What concerned her most was that I wanted to move out, but it was just across the street. I go home for meals, and to talk to her. She's getting better. And my father didn't say anything, because he wasn't around to hear about it. He just kind of disappeared. He took off. I don't think we'll ever see him again."

Sarah's face had expressed shock, concern, and dismay as he spoke, and when he was done, she said, "But you don't act like you care if he comes back!"

"I do care—I hope he never does come back. We're all a lot happier this way."

"Your mother's happier?"

"She misses him, but yes, I think she's a lot happier. He didn't actually like either one of us very much."

"Everything's so *different* now!" Sarah cried.

"Everything was different before, only nobody could see it."

"But what about you and me?" Sarah asked.

"We know each other better."

"That isn't all," she said. "Oh, we missed the sea lions. We're back at the start again. I heard the sea lions, but we never saw them."

"There was a path we didn't take," Tom said.

They had come out at the other side of the panther's cage, and the pacing creature looked through the bars and met Tom's eyes with a quick, questioning look that stopped him cold. The panther was crazy, but it was beautiful in a way that even the craziness of imprisonment could not diminish. The animal possessed a native, unconscious splendor—it was helpless before this splendor, it could only helplessly express it, like the tired lions in the next cage. "Do you want to go back?" he asked Sarah, but he was looking at the panther.

"It's only a sad little zoo, isn't it?" she said. "No. Tom, let's get out of here and go somewhere else."

The panther's eyes flicked away from his, and the panther prowled once more around its cage and turned back and met his eyes again. The panther's eyes were huge and inhumanly yellow, filled with their urgent question, which might have been *Who are you?* or *What are you going to do?*

"Tom!" Sarah said. "That panther's looking at you!"

Who he was and what he was going to do were the same thing, Tom realized.

"Are you laughing at me?" Sarah asked. "Tom?"

The panther made another circuit of its cage.